Three Complete Jacqueline Kirby Mysteries

Elizabeth Peters

Three Complete Jacqueline Kirby Mysteries

The Seventh Sinner
The Murders of Richard III
Die for Love

DORSET PRESS • NEW YORK

This edition published by Dorset Press,
a division of Marboro Books Corp.,
by arrangement with Elizabeth Peters
c/o Dominick Abel Literary Agency
1992 Dorset Press

ISBN 0-88029-726-3

Printed and bound in the United States of America

M 9 8 7 6 5 4 3 2 1

CONTENTS

The Seventh Sinner   1

The Murders of Richard III   169

Die for Love   361

The
Seventh
Sinner

To Theron

with thanks for all these years of help and advice,
and especially for being godfather to this book

CHAPTER ONE

Jean would never forget her first encounter with Jacqueline Kirby. It was years before she could think about it without blushing all over. An acquaintance which begins with assault and battery, however inadvertent, can hardly be termed auspicious.

There was some slight excuse for Jean's behavior. All morning she had been working, or trying to work, in the Institute library. There were distractions. First and omnipresent was the siren call of the city outside the dusty library stacks. April in Paris is famous, but May in Rome has an allure that can distract the soberest student. The city of Michelangelo and the *dolce vita*, the capital of the papacy and the Caesars—whatever it is you may be seeking, you can find it somewhere in Rome. Jean's prized fellowship at one of the world's most famous institutions of art and archaeology was a poor substitute for Rome on a spring morning; and the call of duty was not as effective as Ulysses' waxen earplugs against the siren's song.

Michael was a second distraction, and if he was not as overwhelming as an entire city, he was closer at hand. Michael should have been working too; but his sense of duty was as neglected as his shaggy, shoulder-length brown hair. He dithered aimlessly about the stacks, peering at Jean through gaps in the shelved books and edging up to her whenever she got into a dark corner.

Emerging, breathless and disheveled, from one of these encounters, Jean had to admit she wasn't avoiding them as wholeheartedly as she might have done. Michael would leave her in peace if she retired into her office and closed the door. The small windowless cubicles assigned to the student fellows were spartan affairs, with only a desk and chair and a couple of bookcases. The doors had glass panels on the upper halves, but they served the same purpose as the sported oak of Oxford. When the door was closed, the occupant did not wish to be disturbed. Nothing less than a fire or general insurrection justified so much as a knock.

As she stood contemplating her own office door, Michael caught up with her again. His arm went around her and Jean came back to her senses with a start to find that her undisciplined body was responding. She pulled away. All she needed was to be caught in dalliance by one of the members of the fellowship committee, two weeks before that committee met to decide on the renewal of student grants for a second year.

"All right," she hissed irritably. "I give up. . . . No, damn it, I don't mean that! I mean, let's get out of here."

Jean was never quite sure which of them was responsible for the disaster. The Institute's halls were magnificent expanses of polished marble. As Jean emerged from the library she saw that the corridor was deserted—a long, snowy stretch of emptiness, shining like ice and just as slippery. She couldn't resist. She broke into a run, with Michael in enthusiastic pursuit.

They turned the corner together. Jean had one flashing glimpse of a face, open-mouthed in consternation, and then there was a melee of flailing arms and legs, a stifled shriek, and a dull thud. She and Michael, who had somehow kept their feet, stood staring down at a prostrate, motionless form.

"Holy Christ," said Michael sincerely. "Is she dead?"

The fallen woman didn't look very lively. Jean had seen her in the library during the past few weeks and had classified her, disinterestedly, as a summer visitor—a teacher or scholar. She usually wore neat tailored dresses and horn-rimmed glasses, and her hair was pulled back into a severe knot at the back of her neck.

In her present state of collapse she looked quite different. A huge purse had gone flying at the impact, and its contents littered the floor for yards around, like the debris left by a miniature tornado. The demure knee-length skirt had been disarranged, displaying legs that drew an admiring whistle from Michael. A shaft of sunlight fell across the woman's head and shoulders, spotlighting a face whose features looked pallid and austere—high cheekbones, a firm chin, long, curved lips like the mouth of an archaic Greek statue. The hair was spectacular. It had been loosened by the fall, and lay about the peaceful face like a pool of molten bronze, gleaming with amber highlights.

"Did we kill her?" Michael demanded.

"Don't be ridiculous. . . . I hope not!"

Suddenly, without preliminary fluttering or blinking, the closed eyes opened. They were a true, clear green, an unusual color for human eyes. They looked translucent, like seawater, and they focused on Jean with an expression of concentrated malevolence made all the more alarming by contrast with the placidity of the face in which they were set.

The woman's compressed lips parted.

"Here, too, O Lord?" a plaintive voice inquired.

Jean, who had been thinking in terms of concussion, revised her diagnosis. Clearly there was some kind of brain damage. She dropped to her knees.

"Don't try to talk," she said agitatedly. "Just don't move. Did you break anything? Did you—"

"Did I break anything?" The implacable green eyes moved on to examine Michael, who stirred uneasily. "I have no intention of moving. I may stay here for the rest of the day. It seems to be the safest place. Unless you trample on helpless bodies around here."

Jean sat back on her heels.

"I think you're all right."

"I am all right. Not good, but all right. No worse than usual . . . I talk like this all the time. Who are you?"

"Jean Suttman, Michael Casey," said Michael. "Do you want me to help you up?"

"No," said his victim distinctly.

Michael sat down on the floor.

"Who are you?" he asked conversationally.

"Jacqueline Kirby."

"Hello."

"Hello."

Jean looked from Michael, cross-legged on the floor like an Indian mystic, to Jacqueline, still prone and looking as if she had every intention of remaining in that position indefinitely. She began to laugh. The others contemplated her with disfavor, and their sour expressions only made her laugh harder. When she had calmed herself, Jacqueline said severely, "If you have *quite* finished, you might start collecting my belongings."

"Sure," Jean said. She added meekly, "Would you mind getting up, Miss—Mrs.—Doctor—"

"Considering the informality of this meeting, you may call me Jacqueline. Why do you want me to get up? I'm perfectly comfortable."

"She doesn't care how you feel," Michael explained calmly. "She just wants to get the evidence of her crime up off the floor before one of the senior fellows comes along. They're meeting pretty soon to decide which of us gets a second year here."

"Oh, really," Jacqueline said thoughtfully.

Jean stopped in her crawling pursuit of compacts, pens, postcards, and a small bottle of what appeared to be crème de menthe.

"That 'really' has a blackmailing sound to it," she said. "You wouldn't, would you?"

"I guess not," Jacqueline said with regret. "Ah, well. You may help me up, Michael."

Michael obliged, with a last appreciative look at Jacqueline's knees. Jacqueline saw the look; stepping gently away from Michael, who was brushing haphazardly at her back, she remarked,

"Thank you. For everything. . . . Show's over. I now revert to my real self."

She gathered in the fiery hair rippling down her back and began to knot it up.

"What are you doing that for?" Michael demanded. "Let it

hang out and down and all like that. You have beautiful hair, lady.''

"I know," Jacqueline said coolly. "It's my sole vanity, however, and it doesn't suit my present image. Jean, did you find any hairpins?''

"Here.''

Jacqueline jammed them into her chignon, seemingly at random, but the heavy coil remained miraculously in place. Jean rose to her feet, holding the purse.

"You missed the box of Band-Aids," Jacqueline said. "Behind the potted palm. And that's my rock, under the bust of Aristotle.''

"Your rock," Jean repeated stupidly. She gathered up that item, and the Band-Aids, and an eyebrow pencil which had previously eluded her, and resisted the temptation to inquire whether Jacqueline didn't want Aristotle too. The cold green eyes fixed on her discouraged levity. But as she handed over the purse she couldn't resist saying,

"I used to think men were unfair when they made jokes about women's purses.''

"I like to have things available." Jacqueline peered myopically into the purse. "I don't think you got everything, Jean. I don't see the flashlight, or that bottle of—"

"Maybe if you put your glasses on," Jean said, offering them.

"Don't I have them on? Oh. No, I don't. Thank you.''

Jacqueline put the spectacles on, and Jean stared. The transformation was complete. Glasses, demure coiffure, modest dress—a well-bred middle-aged lady rooted through her overflowing handbag, muttering ladylike middle-aged epithets like "drat" and "blast.''

"Hey," Michael said, grinning. "I think we've found a friend, Jean. Come on, Jacqueline. We'll buy you a drink, to settle your nerves.''

"Why don't you have a slug of that?" Jean suggested, as Jacqueline, with a murmur of satisfaction, produced the miniature green bottle from the depths of the purse.

Jacqueline stared at her.

"Drink this? It's for my cat.''

"Naturally," Michael said. "A feline aphrodisiac, no doubt. Or does it turn the cat into a woman, in the dark of the moon?"

"A little old lady in Trastevere makes it," Jacqueline said. "But it isn't really my cat. It—"

"It owns you. We know." Michael took her firmly by the elbow. "Come along, Jacqueline. You need something. I'm not sure what, but you'll have to settle for an espresso."

"Gino's?" Jean said uncertainly. "Michael, do you think the others will—"

"Don't let me intrude," Jacqueline said primly.

Tidy and bespectacled, she had the reserved dignity Jean associated with visiting maiden aunts and high-school Latin teachers. Jean found her formidable, quite a different person from the green-eyed witch sprawled across the Institute's marble floor. Michael was not intimidated. He took a firmer grip on Jacqueline's arm and said,

"The others will be fascinated."

II

As always, Jean was fascinated by the contrast between the grounds of the Institute and the street beyond the high enclosing wall. The Institute was housed in one of the stately old trans-Tiber villas, and its gardens were famous. The somber pointed cypresses and the famous umbrella pines formed a dark background for colorful masses of azaleas, bougainvillea, and oleander, and gave shade to the white marble benches scattered about.

The aristocratic villa withdrew, fastidiously, from the plebeian buildings which had sprung up around it, and from the crowded, noisy street. The shop fronts bore garish advertisements of the products to be found within, and the crumbling brown plaster of the walls carried copies of those proclamations to the citizenry in which the city government rejoiced. They were unsightly notices, flapping long tatters of dirty paper in the air, but Jean had never gotten over her thrill at the sight of the black initial letters which had two thousand years of dignity behind them. S.P.Q.R.— Senatus Populusque Romanus. The Senate and the People of

Rome. Corrupt and crippled as the symbol had become, it still recalled the first great republic.

Gino's café was small and open-fronted, with a few rickety tables and chairs set out on the sidewalk. It had only one advantage over others in the area—the view. Located on top of a hill, it permitted its patrons to look out across a vista of trees and rooftops to where the dome of St. Peter's hovered among the clouds. In the opposite direction it was possible, on a clear day, to get a vision of the old city. Such days were rare; a gray fog of automobile exhaust shrouded the city of the Caesars most of the time.

As they plodded up the hill, Jean saw that three of her friends had already arrived at the café. Their faces were so familiar to her now that she never really looked at them. But today the presence of a stranger gave her a renewed and not wholly welcome insight. It was as if she had borrowed Jacqueline's glasses and acquired the owner's viewpoint with them.

One member of the group was conventional enough; Rome abounds in priests, of all sizes, nations, and degrees. Padre Ximenez wore the long black cassock which was *de rigueur* for his order while in the capital. Seeing him as a newcomer might, Jean was struck afresh by something she had unconsciously forced herself to ignore since the beginning of their friendship: José's dark Spanish features were strikingly handsome.

The Scovilles were brother and sister, although from a distance it was hard to tell which Scoville was which. The resemblance was superficial; a good deal of it resulted from the current fashions, or lack thereof. Anne wore the same faded jeans and tailored shirts as her brother. The red-gold Scoville hair resembled the coiffure affected by a number of well-known characters, among them Little Orphan Annie, Struwwelpeter, and Art Garfunkel. The coiffures were identical, except that Andy's hair was a little longer than his sister's. It framed Andy's face like a nimbus. There was nothing saintly about Andy's other features; it is difficult to imagine a saint with freckles, and Andy's blue eyes had the sparkle one associates with supernatural characters of the opposite persuasion. Beside him his sister looked drained and faded, as if she had contributed half the vitality which should have been hers to increase Andy's charm.

Michael had relapsed into one of his silent moods. He

dropped into the nearest chair and took out the sketch pad that went everywhere with him, leaving Jean to make the introductions and explain Jacqueline's presence. Andy found the story highly amusing. He broke into a loud guffaw, which ended abruptly as Jacqueline's basilisk stare fell upon him.

"I'm sorry," he muttered, with less than his usual aplomb. "It wasn't funny."

"Oh, it was," Jacqueline said gently. "If the custard-pie, pratfall school of comedy turns you on. . . . I'm not here by choice, you know. I was dragged. I'm not even sure I want to be here. What is this group of yours? A cell of an international conspiracy? A society for the prevention of something?"

The reactions of the three who were encountering Jacqueline's tongue for the first time were as varied as their personalities. Anne looked distressed. She was silent and shy at best, and controversy bothered her. José smiled. Andy, who had recognized a gift of restrained invective equal to his own, relaxed.

"If anything, we are a society for the encouragement of, not the prevention of, anything. We are part of the group, but not the whole. Our motto—"

"Shut up, Andy," Jean said equably. She looked at Jacqueline. "We just got into the habit of meeting here every morning for coffee. Four of us are student fellows. The Institute awards these fellowships, for a year's study in Rome—"

"I am well aware of that function of the Institute."

"Well, we four are this year's fellows. José is studying stained-glass design with one of the artists at the Institute, and the other two members of the crowd are also foreign students, who use the Institute library part of the time."

"Seven of you," Jacqueline said.

"It just happened that way. We really aren't a secret society."

"She thinks that's true," Andy said solemnly, "but she misses the point of numerology—the deeper meaning of it. We were Drawn Together. There is a Purpose in our coming here, from all over the world, to a meeting in the Center of it all."

"Hmmph," Jacqueline said. She edged her chair back in order to examine Andy more closely. Without looking up from his sketch, Michael grabbed her chair. Jacqueline gave him a startled glance and Jean said soothingly,

"Don't mind him. If he could talk he would tell you he's sketching you, and doesn't want you to move."

"Oh, he can talk; I've heard him. Why—"

"He's an artist," Andy said. There was a low growl from Michael, who continued to sketch, and Andy went on, "Painter, I should have said. They are real weirdos, these arty types. . . . All right, Michelangelo, but I have to call you something; would you prefer 'artistic?' No, I didn't think you would. . . . Anyhow, my own sister here happens to be one of them. She's a sculptor. And don't call her a sculptress, if you value your life. You wouldn't think people who work with their hands could get so hung up on words, would you?"

"Everybody is hung up on words," Jacqueline said. She smiled at Anne, who gave her a faint smile in return, but said nothing. "So Michael and Anne represent the 'art' half of the Institute for Art and Archaeology. You and Jean are the archaeologists, Andy?"

"The Institute discriminates against archaeologists," Andy said. "Jean is a compromise. An art historian."

"It averages out, over the years," Jean said earnestly. "They try to keep a balance."

"She is a compromise in several senses," José said, smiling at Jean. "She tries to keep the peace among us. It is not always easy."

"I believe you." Jacqueline's emerald eyes inspected him, an appraisal he met with smiling calm. The eyes moved on to examine Michael. Jacqueline's expression did not change, but Jean couldn't help wondering what she made of that young eccentric. He was about as aesthetic-looking as a wrestler. His features were heavy and blunt, with one exception, and only a keen observer would have noticed it—his mouth, thin-lipped and almost delicate in configuration. His hands were big, with thick, blunt-tipped fingers—the fingers of an artisan rather than an artist, according to the principles of palmistry. His heavy shoulders and habitual slouch made him look shorter than his actual height of nearly six feet. His shirt resembled the tie-dyed medleys so popular with young Americans, but Michael's rainbow version was not planned, it simply reflected the colors of his palettes over the past year. The shirt was open, not to the waist, but to a lower region where the band of Michael's faded jeans happened to have settled.

Jacqueline glanced over her shoulder at the entrance to the café. It gaped dark and forbidding as a cave mouth. There was no sign of life within.

"Where's our genial host?" she asked. "I could use some coffee at that."

The concerted burst of laughter from the others made her eyebrows lift.

"Genial is such an appropriate word," said Andy, the self-appointed spokesman for the group. "Gino hates us all. I'd like to chalk it up to xenophobia, but I think he just doesn't like us personally."

"So he makes you wait," Jacqueline said musingly. She turned suddenly, and in a voice which could have been heard a block away, bellowed, *"Senta!"*

Everyone jumped except Michael, who was too far out in his own world to hear anything. Like a genie called by an incantation, Gino appeared in the doorway. His heavy black brows were drawn down in a formidable scowl; his unshaven jowls shone. The white apron draped across his paunch was stained with coffee, wine, and other unidentifiable marks. Jean suspected that he had been drawn out by outraged curiosity rather than zeal, but no one stopped to inquire into his motives.

"Un capuccino, per favore," Jacqueline said in a soft contralto. The others took advantage of Gino's speechless rage to give their orders, and after a comprehensive glower Gino vanished.

"Magnifico," José said admiringly. "Where did you learn to do that?"

"For ten years I was known as the loudest mom on the block," Jacqueline said complacently. "My children used to come home half an hour early to prevent me from letting out my famous voice."

"How many children do you have?" Jean asked.

"Two."

"Well? Aren't you going to show us their pictures?" Andy asked, glancing at the loaded purse squatting at Jacqueline's feet. A shapeless white lump, it looked alarmingly like the hideously animated leather bag that haunts one of M. R. James's most effective ghost stories; Jean kept expecting it to shoot out tiny withered arms and grab at someone's ankles.

"No. I'm not going to talk about them, either."

"Why not?"

"Because," said Jacqueline, glaring, "I have been talking about them and to them and with them and at them for twenty years. This is the first summer they've been on their own. I think they've survived my tutelage in fairly good shape, but I don't want to talk about them. Change the subject. Where are the other members of your secret society?"

Andy pointed dramatically.

"Peace, break thee off, look where they come," he misquoted.

Jean thought she would never again walk up that hill so unself-consciously. The café provided a fine vantage point for a critical observer.

Small and slight and serious, Ted looked like a sixteen-year-old, with his heavy glasses and short, "square" haircut. But the long white scar on his forearm was the result of a bayonet cut acquired during the Six Days' War, and Ted was already re-spected in academic circles for his research on rock-cut tombs. He was a true sabra, a native-born Israeli; his father, a high-rank-ing government official and a hero of the 1948 war, lived in Tel Aviv. That was about all they knew of Ted's family history; he talked a blue streak about everything else, but not about himself.

Dana talked of very little else. In the first weeks after she joined the group the others heard so many references to hunting, and servants, and lawn tennis that they began to get suspicious. Fi-nally Andy made a sarcastic comment about the upper classes, and Dana took the hint. When she forgot herself, her accent was strongly reminiscent of the Beatles' dulcet tones—straight Liverpudlian—and Jean imagined that betrayed Dana's real back-ground.

Someone had told Jean once that she and Dana looked enough alike to be sisters. Her first reaction had been pleasure. A literal physical description could fit both girls—straight brown hair, dark eyes, round face, turned-up nose. They were approxi-mately the same height, five feet five inches, but Dana weighed ten pounds more than Jean's one hundred and nine. This should have been a plus for Jean; she gained weight easily, and fought a constant battle with the pasta which is Italy's contribution to a limited student budget. But she had to admit Dana's extra poundage was distributed in the best possible way. The rest of Dana's features weren't particularly attractive; her complexion was rather muddy and her mouse-brown hair had none of the beauty of Ann's red-gold halo. Yet Dana exuded sex appeal, and Ann. . . .

Social life requires a certain degree of hypocrisy. While these thoughts occupied her mind Jean greeted the newcomers and watched with a tight social smile as Dana wedged herself into a chair between Michael and Andy. Gino appeared with a tray and distributed cups. He was visibly sulking, and slammed most of the cups down with his usual heavy hand; but Jacqueline's *capuccino* was placed before her with delicate care.

José lifted his cup from the swimming saucer.

"Always my cup is the most mistreated," he announced gloomily. "Clearly Gino is anticlerical. Possibly a Communist."

"One need not be a Communist to be anticlerical," Ted said. "One must only be logical."

"My favorite adversary," the priest explained to Jacqueline. "You have perhaps noticed what a catholic group we are?"

"Catholic with a small *c,*" Dana explained patronizingly.

"But of course. Catholic, with a capital *C,* Protestant, Jew, pagan—"

Andy bowed mockingly.

"And apostate," José concluded, with a nod at Michael, who went on sketching.

"You need a Moslem," Jacqueline said.

Andy let out a shout of laughter.

"I don't know who and what you are, lady, but you make a great straight man. You keep feeding me cues. Only I've already used the best line. All I can say is—brace yourselves. Here he comes."

Jean turned her head. Midway up the hill she saw the figure to which Andy pointed.

"It's only Albert," she said resignedly. "What a ham you are, Andy."

"Who is Albert?" Jacqueline asked. "Another of the group?"

"No, I told you it was a mystic number. The Seven Sinners."

"Why sinners?"

"The name is Andy's invention," Ted explained. "He thinks it is funny. He has a primitive sense of humor."

"But we're all sinners," Andy declared. "All miserable sinners, in a sinful world. Right, José?"

The priest raised his eyes heavenward and sighed loudly. Andy went on,

"Albert is one of our crosses. We bear him patiently because we are trying to improve ourselves. Albert was sent to us so we could practice on him. If we ever learn to love Albert, we can love anything."

Jacqueline adjusted her glasses, which had a tendency to slip, and stared at the plodding figure.

"What's wrong with him? Or are you just anti-Moslem?"

"He is not a Moslem," Ted said coolly. "As usual, Andy is inaccurate. He is a Maronite—a Lebanese Christian. And we have Andy to thank for his charming presence among us—another sin on Andy's extensive list. They were boyhood friends in Beirut."

"Friends, hell," Andy protested. "His old man and my old man taught at the American University years ago, and we went to the same school. Don't hassle me, Ted; Albert would have forced himself on us even if he'd never seen any of us before. That's the kind of creep he is."

No one replied. The newcomer was now upon them.

Jean had to admit that Albert was not only ugly, he was unprepossessing. The two qualities are not necessarily synonymous. Physical ugliness can be appealing, even attractive. She had seen homelier men than Albert—though not many. He had not a single redeeming feature.

His scanty forehead was half hidden by greasy locks of black hair. His face was deeply pitted with the scars of acne. In order to accommodate his protruding front teeth his upper lip had stretched to an unbelievable degree; in profile his face looked anthropoid, chinless and loose-lipped. He was also fat—not chubby or plump, but flabbily obese. Like Michael he wore his belt around his hips instead of his waist, but while gravity pulled Michael's belt down his lean body, Albert's immense paunch eliminated his waistline altogether. He had small, squinting eyes, which were buried, when he smiled, between his fat cheeks and his overhanging brows. The worn leather briefcase he carried wherever he went seemed to drag one shoulder down, so that he walked with an odd lurch.

Yet it was not Albert's looks that made him repulsive; it was his manner. He exuded spiritual malaise like a bad smell. Consciously Jean felt sorry for him, but when he dragged a chair next to hers and patted her on the knee with a pudgy paw, she had to force herself to smile back at him instead of pulling away as from a leper.

One of Albert's maddening, yet pathetic, qualities was his unawareness of how he affected people. His face shone greasily as he greeted them. Tenderly he stowed his briefcase under his chair. The squinting eyes inspected them, lingering longest on Jean and on Dana—who responded with a curl of her lip—and then discovered Jacqueline.

"Albert Gébara," he announced, giving the first name the French pronunciation.

"How do you do. I'm Jacqueline Kirby."

"Not a student," said Albert, eyeing her. "Too old, eh? *Madame ou mademoiselle Kirby? Docteur, peut-être?*"

"Just Jacqueline."

"*Mais non, ce n'est pas bien de parler à une dame d'un certain âge—*"
Andy groaned.

"Our tactful Albert. Look, you *crétin*, don't you know it isn't polite to refer to a lady's age? And for God's sake speak English. You can if you want to. Sort of. . . . It's rude to use a language the people you're with don't understand."

Albert's beady eyes remained fixed on Jacqueline.

"*Mais vous comprenez français, vous comprenez fort bien ce que je vous dis—*"

"*Un peu,*" Jacqueline admitted cautiously.

"*Alors. Madame Kirby? Madame la professeur? Madame la—*"

"No," Jacqueline said. "I'm not a teacher. I'm a librarian."

"*Une bibliothécaire.*" Albert nodded with satisfaction. He got up, taking his chair and his briefcase with him, and moved around the table to sit next to Jacqueline. Under cover of the ensuing conversation Andy muttered,

"Thank God, somebody else who speaks French. I was getting tired of being the sole recipient of Albert's confidences. His conversational style has its points, though; he gets the information. A librarian! I wouldn't have figured it."

"You wouldn't?" Dana didn't bother to lower her voice. "Men are so unobservant. I spotted her at once. Dull, dreary, and middle-class."

"Unlike you," said Andy. "A model of courtesy; that's our Dana."

Dana subsided. Andy was the only one who could squelch her effectively.

Albert was now in full spate. He was speaking English; apparently Jacqueline's "little" French had failed her. Conversation died in Albert's presence; his loud tones overwhelmed other voices, and his remarks were so outrageous that they held his auditors in a spell of unwilling fascination.

"I am Christian, you understand," he explained to an incredulous Jacqueline. "You think me dirty Moslem, perhaps. But I am—"

"No," Jacqueline said. "Not exactly."

The sarcasm was lost on Albert.

"Not a dirty Moslem," he repeated, lingering pleasurably on the word. "Good Christian, true Christian. I love Holy Mother of God, all the saints. I come here, I work, I study, for the blessed saints. The Church not good Christian. No good now. Need good Christian like me to make better."

Jacqueline glanced at José, but got no support from that source; the priest's eyes looked glazed.

"You are going to improve the Church?" Jacqueline repeated. "In what way?"

Albert patted her approvingly on the knee. He clearly had a fetish about that part of the female anatomy.

"Save saints," Albert explained. "The Church say not—she say —à renoncer les saints. Mais les histoires des saints sont incontestables. Les saints—"

"It is the bee in his bonnet," said José, no longer able to restrain himself. He spoke directly to Jacqueline, as if he were trying to deny Albert's existence. "He refers to the revision of the calendar of saints several years ago; and I cannot seem to make him understand that there is no rejection of those saints who were removed. They may still be venerated, still receive devotions. But the legends—"

"No, no, you are wrong," said Albert, with his usual tact—and with a command of English which increased miraculously whenever he wished to voice a direct insult or contradiction. "You are stupid. The Church deny—that is right word, deny—older saints. Saint Christopher, Saint Barbara, *les autres*. All true. All real. I prove. The Pope is wrong, stupid, like you."

"I hate to agree, but I never did forgive the Holy Father for dumping Christopher." Michael looked up from his drawing. He had a disconcerting habit of reentering a conversation after a long silence, with a remark that proved he had been paying attention after all. "The week after he was kicked out, I ran my cycle into a tree."

The comment struck the right note. José grinned unwillingly and relaxed.

"I grant that you on a motorcycle need all the help you can get, Michael. But the legends of such saints were long overdue for reappraisal. It is not heretical to question such stories, the Church itself does so. Early theologians were untrained in historical method; they misinterpreted—"

"No, no, no," said Albert. "No misinterpret. All true. Truth comes from God, only God. We know truth already. But heretics need proof. I find."

"Albert," said Andy, "why don't you shut up?"

Albert beamed at him.

"I find proof. Seven virgin saints—"

José put both hands on the table, as if he were trying to keep them in sight so they wouldn't get away from him and commit violence.

"There are not seven virgin saints," he said, between his beautiful white teeth. "There are hundreds of virgin saints. Or forty-two, or nine, or none at all. But not seven. It is a magic number, a relic of paganism—"

"Seven," said Albert obdurately. "I prove."

He dragged the bulging briefcase out from under his chair and began fumbling with the catch.

Andy stood up.

"I'm copping out," he announced. "I have had it. So long, troops."

"Me too," Dana said. "I'm not in the mood to discuss virginity today. Going back to the library, José?"

One by one they got to their feet, collecting their belongings, settling their destinations. Albert continued to talk. Jean knew he would trail them, talking, all the way back to the Institute. Clutching his briefcase to his ample chest, he started to rise.

Jacqueline turned.

"You cannot come," she announced, in the same voice that had electrified Gino. "I don't want to talk to you any more today. Stay here. We will talk another day. Good-bye."

She put her hand on Albert's shoulder and shoved him down into his chair. He was sitting there, his mouth ajar, as the others fled.

Jean found herself walking with Jacqueline. After a moment she realized that someone was singing softly. It took several more moments to decide that the sound was in fact coming from the bland, dignified person at her side; it was that ditty beloved of the young radical, "The Times They Are a-Changing."

" 'The battle outside rages,' " crooned Jacqueline. Catching Jean's look, she broke off and inquired suavely, "Am I embarrassing you?"

"Why should I be embarrassed?"

"My daughter always was. Between the ages of twelve and seventeen she never walked beside me in public."

"You didn't sing all the time, did you?" asked Jean, willing, by now, to believe it.

"No, but she never knew when I was going to burst out. It was worst at Christmas. I love Christmas carols."

"And Bob Dylan?"

"And Salvation Army hymns, German lieder, and song hits of the nineteen forties. I know all the words. I know," said Jacqueline proudly, "more totally useless things than anyone you'll ever meet."

"Not everything you know is useless. You disposed of Albert beautifully." Jean glanced at her companion's rather bony profile, saw an encouraging gleam of humor in the one visible green eye, and said, without premeditation, "I can't figure you out. How many people are you?"

"You can't be that young," said Jacqueline contemptuously. "Don't you know that every human being is at least a dozen different people? I'm indulging myself this summer, and letting them all hang out, as Michael would say. When I'm working I'm not so visibly schizophrenic."

Having reached the gates of the Institute, the group stopped to reorganize itself. Turning, Jean realized that José, walking behind them, had been listening to the conversation. His dark eyes were intent on Jacqueline.

"You have just voiced a great truth," he said.

"About schizophrenia?" Jacqueline didn't smile.

"About the complexity of personality. Half the trouble in human relations arises from expecting human beings to conform to a single one-dimensional image. We are all hydra-headed monsters. But most people never learn that."

With an abrupt nod he strode off, his long black skirts flapping. Ted ran to join him, tossing a casual word of farewell over his shoulder. The others lingered.

"Stick around, Jake," Andy invited. "We may need you, if Albert materializes again."

"I," said Jacqueline, ignoring the nickname, "am lunching with your hereditary enemy, the distinguished librarian of the Institute. She hates to be kept waiting, and I am already late."

"She's a friend of yours?" Andy demanded incredulously.

Jacqueline's lips quivered.

"She sees only one of my numerous images. It matches hers—dignified, prim, and passionately interested in the deficiencies of the Dewey Decimal System."

"Andy is supposed to be passionately interested in the archaeology of Rome," Ann said firmly. "Come on, boy. Dad is arriving next week, and your report to the fellowship committee had better be finished by then."

"Damnably true," Andy admitted, with a groan. "And if the résumé isn't turned in I won't get my fellowship renewed, and then dear old Dad will murder me."

"Your father is coming?" Dana's eyes widened. "Wow! I've got to meet him, Andy. He's the most glamorous figure in our field."

"And glamorous archaeologists are rare," Jean said drily. "He's a brilliant scholar—"

"Brilliant, hell. He's got dash—panache. That photo of him dangling over the cliff in Iran, at the end of a rope—"

"Panache is right," Andy muttered. "The Behistun inscription has been copied a hundred times. Sam only did it to show off."

"And the workman he rescued from the rockfall at Tiryns?" Jean demanded. "That was showing off?"

"And the book on pre-Attic pottery," Dana said.

"All right, so you're all members of the fan club. I'll arrange a soirée. . . . Hey, that's a good idea. We'll have a party and some of you fans can pitch in and keep him entertained. He needs an audience the way some people need insulin. He goes into a coma without it."

"Don't mind him," Ann said, with a nervous smile. "He thinks Sam is great, really. Come *on,* brother. Work. W-O-R-K. Remember?"

They went off, arm in arm, and Michael, watching them, said lazily, "There's something allegorical about those two."

"Beauty and the Beast," suggested Dana, with a giggle. "Or how about Orestes and Electra? There's a nice normal brother-sister team for you."

Michael gave her a smack on the bottom that echoed like a pistol shot. She yelped. Jean, hoping to prevent further horseplay under Jacqueline's cynical eye, said at random, "How about the Bobbsey twins? I never can remember their names—"

"Nan and Bert," said Jacqueline. "That's enough of that. What a nasty-tongued bunch you are. . . . Michael, let me see that sketch you made of me."

"Huh?" Michael retreated, clutching his sketch pad. "Be damned if I will."

"Undoubtedly. Hand it over."

With a shrug, Michael obeyed. Jacqueline studied the page in grim silence. Jean couldn't resist. Craning, she looked over Jacqueline's shoulder.

Michael hadn't done one sketch; the page was covered with small figures. Jacqueline sprawled on the floor of the Institute, like a marble figure on a somewhat risqué tomb; Jacqueline telling someone off, mouth wide open, finger raised; Jacqueline peering over the top of her glasses, looking quite feeble-minded; Jacqueline wearing the helmet and breastplate of Minerva, and her own horn-rimmed glasses; Jacqueline wearing nothing at all, in the classic pose of the Venus of Cyrene.

Dana was making strangled sounds of stifled amusement, but Jean didn't find the sketch funny, even though the individual portraits were wonderful caricatures. Michael could have overheard Jacqueline's remarks about multiple personality; but the sketch had been finished before the conversation took place. At times Michael's insights verged frighteningly on clairvoyance. He had sketched all his friends at one time or another. Dana was a favorite victim, which explained her delight in another victim's unveiling.

Finally Jacqueline returned the sketch. She gave Michael a long, steady look. There was no amusement in her face, nor was there resentment. When she spoke, Jean knew she wasn't joking.

"You're lucky to be living in this century, Michael. Five hundred years ago they'd have burned you at the stake. And I'd have been in the audience, poking the fire."

CHAPTER TWO

The next day Jean was seized by one of those productive fits which strike only too rarely. She worked in a grim fog, resisting the blandishments of her friends. Since the library of the Institute was one of the few places in Rome that kept American hours, she could work straight through from early morning till eight at night. It was at that hour, a week later, that the attack passed, leaving her blinking blearily at a page covered with words which suddenly looked as meaningless as hieroglyphs. Her stomach was a cavernous complaint, and her head felt as if it were floating several inches away from her neck.

Jean gathered her papers together in an untidy pile and left her office. She was starving, and not only for food; she wanted company, laughter and conversation, a glass of wine, an enormous plate of spaghetti alla bolognese, twelve hours' sleep, and a bath—not necessarily in that order. None of these reasonable desires seemed to be immediately available. The nearest trattoria was half a mile away, and all her erstwhile friends seemed to have vanished.

As she approached the stairs, one of the office doors opened. Jean stopped. The hall was dimly lit, but she recognized the smooth helmet of bronze hair and the bulky lump of the purse. It seemed to have gained in weight and girth since she had seen it last, and she wondered what incongruous objects it now contained.

"Good evening," Jacqueline Kirby said. "You look like an underdone biscuit. How are you?"

"Fine." The word came out as an unconvincing croak, and Jean cleared her throat. "I'm just hungry. I've been working for . . . what day is it?"

"Friday. I know you've been working; I've been watching you." There was more envy than commiseration in Jacqueline's voice. "I could do it too, when I was your age. That and a lot of other things that are no longer within my capabilities. . . . Want a ride home? Or are you going directly to Andy's?"

"I feel fine," Jean repeated vaguely. She was thinking about the last paragraph she had written. Then, belatedly, a fact penetrated the lingering fog of scholarship.

"Andy's? Andy's party! For his father . . . has he gone?"

"Who? Where?"

"Andy. He was in his office all afternoon."

"He left at five, to get ready for the party."

"Yes, the party." Jean shook herself. "Lord, I am shot! I've got to hurry. Gosh. I look like . . . what time is it?"

"Calm down. The party doesn't start till nine, which means it won't get interesting until about ten. You have plenty of time to repair the ravages of hard labor."

"What about you?" Jean shook her head. "I seem to be saying the most stupid things tonight. I mean, you look fine the way you are. You don't need—"

"At my age there isn't much I can do anyway," Jacqueline said sadly. "Still, I suppose I should make an effort. . . . Do you want a ride or don't you?"

Jean looked at her, saw the twinkle in her eye, and relaxed.

"Thank you. I would, if it isn't out of your way. I didn't know you had a car."

"You've missed a lot the last few days. While you were in your fog, my friend Frau Hilman went off on vacation, leaving me her car and her apartment."

"It's nice to have friends."

"She also left me her Persian cat, her pink poodle, and a tank of assorted and delicate tropical fish. By the time I dredge the cat out of the fish tank and chop the poodle's daily gourmet dinner, I begin to wonder whether I made such a good deal."

They emerged from the building into the balmy dusk of a Roman night, and Jean took a deep, restorative breath.

"The car's down this way," Jacqueline said. She hesitated, and then said, almost reluctantly, "Would you like to come back with me and have scrambled eggs or something? There's also a shower. I'm not trying to sound like a TV commercial for soap, but I've lived in student lodgings myself, and I know about those little washbasins in the corner of the room, the kind with two cold water taps."

"That's very nice of you," Jean said.

"Oh, nice is the word for me," Jacqueline agreed sarcastically. She turned the key in the ignition and was rewarded by a peculiar grinding noise. Looking flustered, she made movements with her feet; the noise subsided into a dull roar. "I hate this car," she muttered. "I hate driving in Rome."

"Why do you do it?"

"Masochism. In New England we call it self-discipline, but it's the same thing." The car jerked out into traffic, and Jacqueline relaxed a trifle. "Luckily, the Institute and the apartment are both on this side of the river. If I had to fight my way through that maze of streets in the old city, I'd chicken out."

"Are you sure you want me to come?" Jean asked.

"Why not?"

It was not a particularly gracious reply, but the tone reassured Jean.

"Could we stop by my place and let me get a clean outfit? I live just off the Via di San Pancrazio."

"Sure."

It took Jean approximately three minutes to go up to her room and come back. Her chauffeur regarded her with respect.

"That was fast."

"I've only got one clean dress."

They retraced their route, getting lost only once. At this point Jacqueline commented pungently, and it was Jean's turn to look at her with respect.

"You don't sound like a librarian," she said.

"I'm on vacation." Jacqueline laughed. "Well, I suppose there is an image, isn't there? But stereotypes are awfully misleading. There are typical librarians, but not all librarians are typical. Any more than any other profession."

"Such as archaeology," Jean agreed. "From what I've heard about him, Dr. Scoville isn't typical."

"Oh, yeah? The swinging anthropologist is a subcategory of the general stereotype. The ivory-tower image irks some scholars; they have to prove they are just as much with it as the next man, just as brilliant about contemporary issues as they are in their specialty."

"I don't think Dr. Scoville is trying to prove anything."

"Oh, dear, I'm attacking one of your heroes," Jacqueline said sweetly. "On the surface he appears to have everything—sex appeal, virility, scholarly prestige, popular charm. But maybe the really basic thing about the man is that he gets bilious when he eats onions, and has to pull in his stomach when he looks at himself in the mirror. This would explain his deeds of derring-do, which, you must admit, verge occasionally on exhibitionism."

Jean studied her companion's calm profile in amazement.

"I don't think I've ever heard anything more cynical in my life."

"You're young yet."

Jacqueline turned the car into a dark, narrow street, lined on both sides with high walls. She switched on the headlights; in the modern, well-lit streets she had used only the driving lights prescribed by Roman law. Jean said, "I don't think I've been this way."

"This is the old Via Aurelia," Jacqueline said. They both winced as a car roared toward them and passed without, to their mutual surprise, any scraping of fenders. "It's hard for me to drive it; I always want to climb the right-hand wall when I meet another car. But the very name thrills me."

"I'm glad to see you're not a hardened cynic."

"I'm only cynical about people. Places and things still make me go all soft like a jelly doughnut. That's a sign of middle age, if you like."

The walls disappeared, to be replaced by new apartment

buildings; the street widened, and the romance died. Jacqueline made several more turns, following a maze of side streets, and finally drove through a narrow entranceway which was marked "private." There was a small lodge; a *portiere* came out, recognized the car, and returned to his dinner.

"Wow," Jean said. "I didn't know library work paid this well."

The drive led into one of the private apartment complexes which were becoming common in the new subdivisions of the city. The only car entrance was the one through which they had come, with its guard on duty to question tradesmen and uninvited guests. Unlike the big blocklike apartments for lower-cost living, this complex had only four apartments to a building, and these were scattered at random through a handsomely landscaped park. Even the poorest Roman apartment has one balcony; these had five or six. As they followed the private drive, past bushes of evergreens and azaleas, Jean saw that the soft shaded lights in the center of the compound illumined a large swimming pool, its waters glowing soft blue-green.

"Wow," she said again.

"Wow indeed." Jacqueline slid the car into a slot between a low-slung European sports car and a Cadillac limousine. "Don't get any wild ideas. Lise has a private income in addition to her salary. Come along; you ain't seen nothing yet."

The building had an elevator, which did not open until Jacqueline inserted a key into the door lock. Above, it opened directly into the foyer of the apartment. This room, which was larger than Jean's bedroom, was marble-floored. The marble extended into the *salone*, or living-dining area, which occupied the entire front of the building. One curving wall was all windows, with two French doors opening onto the long front balcony. Through the glass Jean could see masses of flowers, geraniums and plumbago and roses, in boxes along the balcony rail. Beyond, the shimmering aquamarine shape of the pool looked like a magnified jewel.

Feeling particularly grubby, Jean followed her hostess into the room, which was furnished with oriental rugs and heavily carved and gilded rococo furniture. The ambulatory part of the menagerie was waiting for them. The cat, a big ball of silver fur, blinked green eyes at them and remained on the brocade-covered couch.

The poodle was really pink. It bounced across the floor, yelping shrilly, and made a dive at Jean's ankles.

"*Nein,* Prinz," Jacqueline said firmly.

The dog rolled over, with its miniature paws dangling. A ribbon, of a rosy shade slightly darker than its curls, was tied around its topknot.

"Poor little thing," Jean said, bending over to scratch the exposed stomach. "Why do poodles always strike me as pathetic?"

"He's really a nice little guy," Jacqueline said; the poodle responded by wriggling and licking Jean's bare toes. "People tend to treat them like toys instead of dogs, that's why they're pathetic. Nothing pathetic about Nefertiti over there; she rules the roost, and she knows it."

The cat blinked again. Its expression was one of concentrated contempt.

When Jean had finished her shower she found Jacqueline in the kitchen. The poodle was lying at her feet making suggestive whining noises. Nefertiti sat on the table. The cat's eyes were on a level with Jacqueline's as she sat beside the table, and the expressions on the two faces, feline and human, were so much alike that Jean couldn't repress a burst of laughter.

"Quiet," Jacqueline said, without turning her head. "I'm trying to outstare her."

Then Jean saw the bottle. It was the same small green bottle she had seen once before. There was a medicine dropper beside it.

"It really is for the cat," she exclaimed.

"I said it was, didn't I? It's a tonic. Lise swears by it. Personally I think this animal needs tranquilizers instead of vitamins, but . . . look, would you mind holding her back legs?"

The struggle would have been funny if it hadn't been so painful. Jean had two bleeding scratches on her forearms before it was over, and Jacqueline was liberally spattered with green liquid. It smelled like mint and was very sticky. The cat retired, spitting and drooling greenly, and Jacqueline directed a few well-chosen words at its furry rear. She fed the dog and sprinkled a handful of food in the fish tank in the *salone*. Then, with a martyred sigh, she began to scramble eggs.

They ate scrambled eggs with chopped prosciutto, salad, and

fresh rolls with a soft cream cheese that came in little cardboard pots. The shower had increased Jean's appetite. Only when her plate was scraped clean did she take a deep breath and apologize for gluttony.

"Want coffee?" Jacqueline asked.

Jean looked at her watch.

"Hadn't we better go?"

"There's no hurry." Jacqueline got up and filled two coffee cups, which she brought to the table. "You really haven't been with it the last few days, have you?"

"Why? Has something happened?"

"Yes and no. Maybe it's just my imagination getting out of hand." Jacqueline sighed. "I've always been very square about things such as grades, and doing well in school. But lately I'm beginning to wonder whether your contemporaries who complain about academic pressure haven't got a point. Does the renewal of your fellowships really mean that much to you? I mean 'you' plural."

"I wouldn't say so," Jean said slowly. "In fact, I think I'm the only one who's uptight about it. Michael really doesn't care; he's so far out, nothing bothers him. He'd live in a cave if it had a northern light. Have you seen his room?"

"No."

"Well, it's the most incredible mess. . . . He picked it because it has a skylight. Ice forms on things in the winter, and in summer it's like walking into a Turkish bath. He has to keep the skylight open to get some air; the roof is a playground for little kids, and a place where the teen-agers go to make out, and a breeding ground for a tribe of wild Roman cats. If the kids aren't howling obscenities through the skylight, the cats are making messes through it, or some ardent Casanova is falling through it. Literally. One dazed kid crashed right through one night, and landed on top of Michael's latest painting, which wasn't dry. . . . All right, it sounds funny, I know, but the funniest thing is that Michael doesn't even *notice*. Oh, he noticed the boy who fell on his painting, but only because he smeared it. How he could tell the difference I don't know."

"He's a nonrepresentational painter?" Jacqueline asked, through her laughter.

"You might call it that. I haven't seen much of his work; he's very secretive about letting people see it. He says he hates criticism. He does, too. He's supposed to be studying with Professor Lugetti, but he won't let the man in to look at his paintings. Michael has a studio at the Institute. Every few weeks Lugetti gets mad and forces his way into the studio, and you can hear the argument all over the building. They stand there and scream at each other for about an hour and then Lugetti stamps out, cursing in Italian, and Michael jumps up and down cursing in English."

"Lugetti's temper is a byword," Jacqueline said. "I'm surprised he doesn't throw Michael out of the place."

"That's what's so funny. He swears Michael is the hottest talent since Monet."

"I admit Michael doesn't sound like the worrying type. What about the others?"

"José and Ted and Dana aren't Fellows. I suppose they have their private worries—who doesn't?—but the renewal problem isn't bugging them."

"Aren't they here on some kind of scholarship aid?"

"Dana is pretty vague about her means of support; I think her family is staking her."

"José is being sponsored by his college?"

"College?"

"He's a Jesuit, isn't he?"

"Right. He doesn't need to worry about money then, does he?"

"No, I suppose not. Not money. . . . And Ted?"

"It's funny," Jean said, frowning, "but we never talk about things like that. . . . I guess he's got a grant from the government or something. I do get the feeling he's been having personal worries. He hardly ever talks about himself, but he's engaged, to a girl back home. When he first came, he talked about her quite a bit. Showed us her picture, and all that. Lately he hasn't mentioned her. Let's see, who else is there? Oh, the Gold Dust twins."

"Do you call them that? I didn't think any of you remembered that old advertising gimmick."

"Ann mentioned the phrase. I think she's self-conscious about their closeness. They look enough alike to be twins, but she's a year older than Andy."

"Isn't it unusual to have a brother and sister both Fellows of the Institute, in the same year?"

"Well . . ." Jean scraped crumbs into a neat pile with her forefinger. "I think they're both talented. But—it's a practical world, isn't it? And Dr. Scoville has a lot of friends in the archaeology business."

"I'm glad to see you aren't as naïve as you look. How good are the Scovilles, really? Be honest—if you can."

"I can't judge Ann's work, it's not my field," Jean said defensively. "But I happen to know Andy's doctoral dissertation was a really brilliant piece of work. The university wanted to publish it, and they don't do that with many dissertations."

"Andy has his doctorate?"

"Yes, he got it at some incredible age—twenty-one or twenty-two. But he doesn't like to be called Doctor. He's very modest."

"No academic worries for Andy, then."

"Oh, no. If anyone gets his fellowship renewed, it will be Andy. Look, Jacqueline, I don't want to rush you, but—"

"Don't be polite," Jacqueline said, in the deceptively gentle voice Jean was beginning to know, and dread. "Just tell me outright you think I'm a nosy old gossip."

"No," Jean admitted. "You aren't a gossip. Something's bugging you. What is it?"

"I definitely do not believe in premonitions," Jacqueline said, half to herself. "But there's an atmosphere. . . . You get so you can feel it in your bones. Like earthquake weather."

"Premonitions, intuition—I believe in them, but they're always based on some real fact your conscious mind hasn't recognized. Something must have happened to set you off."

The kitchen light gleamed off Jacqueline's bronze hair and drained her face of much of its color.

"Your friend Albert, for one thing. It seems he's disappeared."

II

Ann and Andy had an apartment in Trastevere. Their father, who had had considerable success as a writer of popular nonfiction, was contributing to their income; the stipend awarded to Fellows barely covered the cost of a room in a cheap boardinghouse. Formerly a working-class district of questionable repute, Trastevere was now considered picturesque. A trip to its night spots was on the agenda of many tourists. Luckily the wide-eyed tourists, in their drip-dry nylon dresses and lightweight business suits, couldn't understand the comments hurled at them by barefoot students and harassed waiters.

With his linguistic gifts and ready sympathy, Andy had made himself part of the local scene almost from the first. Andy's friends reaped the rewards of his popularity. Parking is a problem anywhere in Rome. In Trastevere it is a joke. When Jean and Jacqueline arrived, they found the street completely filled; there were cars parked in every available space, including those marked by the slashed red circle signs which indicate that parking is forbidden, and even the sidewalks were littered with Vespas, motorbikes, and ordinary bicycles. Jacqueline was looking around in dismay when a young man sauntered up and put his head in the window.

"Friends of Andy's? Leave the car, signora, I will take care of it."

"It's all right," Jean said. "This is Alberto Sordi; he's an engineering student. Alberto, this is Signora Kirby."

Alberto managed to bow without taking his head out of the window—a feat which only an Italian can accomplish. Jacqueline gave her companion a dubious look, but she got out, leaving the keys in the car.

"It isn't my car," she said apprehensively. "You will be careful . . . ?"

Alberto, hand on his heart, made a more sweeping bow.

"Signora, if there is a scratch, anywhere, tomorrow, you may inflict a corresponding wound on my body."

Jacqueline looked startled at this effusion, and Jean, who knew they were being royally kidded, took the older woman's arm.

"Andy probably will do just that," she told Alberto, and

grinned unwillingly as a look of exaggerated terror replaced that worthy's broad smile. "Thanks, Alberto. See you later."

She pulled Jacqueline into the doorway of the building as Alberto leaped eagerly into the driver's seat. Jean knew he would live up to his promise; the car wouldn't have a mark on it when he returned it. But it would be well for Jacqueline's nerves if she didn't see how he drove.

The Scovilles had the top floor, the most desirable part of the building because of the wide terrace that surrounded it on three sides. But the top floor was the sixth, and there was no elevator. As they climbed, the sounds of the party became louder and clearer.

"I wonder the neighbors don't complain," Jacqueline said, panting.

"Nobody in Trastevere complains about parties. They all come out on the landing and enjoy the noise. . . . *Buona sera, signora* . . . *signori.* . . ."

The last remark was addressed to the inhabitants of one of the fifth-floor apartments, who were standing in their open doorway, nodding and tapping their feet in time to the music.

They were the last of the crowd to arrive. Ximenez caught Jean's eye first; his severe black was conspicuous among the gay costumes of the others, both male and female. There was another priest present; his cassock was the bright scarlet worn by German clerics while in Rome.

In honor of the occasion Ann was wearing a dress—or perhaps it was one of her brother's shirts. Severely tailored, a solid green in color, it reached only to the tops of her thighs and displayed legs which, as Jean had noticed before, were attractively shaped. Ann made no further concessions to femininity; she stood with her usual slouch as she faced Ted, with whom she was carrying on an animated conversation.

Jean's eyes swept the room. There was Michael, sitting on the floor in the corner. His knees were drawn up and his bare feet had charcoal-gray soles. He held a glass of wine in both hands, and he looked sulky, withdrawn, rather like an autistic patient squatting in a hospital corridor.

For once Dana wasn't with him, and Jean located the other girl where she had expected her to be—hovering at the elbow of a tall, gray-haired man whom Jean recognized from his pictures and from his resemblance to his son.

Dana was dressed to catch the eye. Wide gold hoops glittered against the masses of her dark hair, and an off-the-shoulder white blouse carried out the gypsy look which was now fashionable. Blazing scarlet, electric blue, wide stripes of chartreuse and orange contributed to her layers of skirts; a sash of purple encircled her waist, and she jangled with bracelets and necklaces.

She was not the only acolyte worshiping at the famous scholar's shrine. He was surrounded by people, Andy's student friends and two of the older Fellows from the Institute. He towered above them physically. His gray hair was cut short. Burned brown by the eastern suns of successive winter digs, he looked twenty years younger than his real age, and his broad shoulders were those of a man who has done his share of the punishing physical work required on an archaeological excavation.

The contrast between his casual but conventional white shirt and dark slacks and Andy's peacock-colored clothing was as extreme as the difference in their complexions, but the resemblance was there—not only in the features of the long, clean-cut faces but in the crackling vitality that animated those faces. Andy was on the fringe of the group near his father, but he was not part of it. Lounging against the wall, he held a half-filled glass, and the expression on his face as he watched his father was one of patronizing amusement. He turned his head, saw the newcomers, and bounded toward them, emitting cries of welcome.

"I gave you up," he said to Jean.

The blue eyes met hers with an intensity that cut the two of them off from the rest of the room. Then Andy remembered his manners. He turned to Jacqueline. "You look beautiful. Come on and meet the great man."

Jacqueline gave Jean a look of half-comic appeal as she was drawn away, but Jean refused to respond; the great man had too many panting females in his entourage as it was.

She wandered over to the refreshment table and helped herself to a glass of wine. She was joined at once by Ximenez, who greeted her with pleasure.

"You have been working too hard," he said. "We missed you at our daily meetings; you are our peacemaker, you know."

"From what Jacqueline tells me, you haven't needed much arbitration," Jean said; and then, at José's look of bewilderment, she elaborated. "Albert. Jacqueline says he's disappeared."

"Disappeared? What a word." Ann's cool voice broke in.

"He was strange that last day we saw him," José said thoughtfully. "Outside of himself."

The odd phrase struck Jean disagreeably.

"What do you mean?"

José's black eyes narrowed thoughtfully.

"It is hard to describe. Excited? That is not quite the word. There is an English word—'fey.' Perhaps I do not understand its correct meaning. . . ."

"I hope not. It has something to do with a premonition of approaching doom."

"It also means crazy," Ann said irritably. "For God's sake, you all talk as if he'd vanished in a cloud of smoke, in front of sixty witnesses. Why make such a big thing of it?"

"Right on. Let's not talk about awful Albert." Michael had joined the group. "Hey, José, have you seen the watercolors at that new gallery on the Via Margutta?"

José had. The conversation became too technical for Jean, who was not in the mood for shoptalk after her days of strenuous study. Turning, she caught Andy's eye. She had the feeling he had been watching her for some time, and she felt herself flushing absurdly, like a schoolgirl. Andy was the only male in the group who could affect her so. Ted and José were good friends. Michael? There was a potential spark in that relationship, but Michael was too emotionally unstable for Jean. He was definitely the flitting type—from flower to flower to flower. Andy was something else. When he summoned her, with a smile and a slight movement of his head, Jean obeyed.

"Having fun?" he asked softly. The words were trivial, but the tone, and the look that accompanied it, invested the commonplace phrase with special meaning.

"It's a good party, Andy. Everyone is having fun."

"Including our Jacqueline," Andy said, grinning. "Dig that technique, will you?"

Jean turned her head and saw Jacqueline and Scoville Senior walking toward the doors that opened onto the terrace.

Jacqueline's dignified librarian friend would have had difficulty recognizing her in her present costume; the jade-green of her fashionable pants suit darkened her eyes to emerald, and set off her slim figure. Her hair was coiled around her head like a metallic wreath. As she smiled at her tall companion, whose head was bent attentively, Jean saw with amusement that Jacqueline's glasses were no longer in evidence. Only one item detracted from an otherwise perfect vision of sophisticated elegance: the Purse. Jean found that she was thinking of it in capital letters.

The couple vanished into the darkness of the terrace, and Andy laughed aloud.

"She lifted him right out from under Dana's nose," he said admiringly. "Our Dana is losing her touch."

Jean started to answer; but the words caught in her throat as she saw the change in Andy's face. He was staring past her at the doorway. Jean whirled around, expecting some cataclysmic vision. Her eyes fell upon an object which, if unsightly, did not at first glance seem horrifying enough to explain Andy's consternation. It was only Albert, returned from his temporary absence.

Albert's presence never produced ecstasies of joyful welcome; but now the silence that gradually spread through the room, freezing the guests in mid-sentence and mid-gesture, had a special quality. As Jean stared, she began to understand the silence, and the alarm on Andy's face.

Though his person was ugly, Albert was normally fastidious about cleanliness; his cheap clothing was neatly if clumsily patched, and he was always clean shaven. On this occasion he sported a straggling growth of black beard, and his shirt and trousers looked as if he had slept in them, not once but several times. As he stood blinking into the brightly lit room, his heavy shoulders hunched and his hands dangling, there was menace in his stance and in his squinting eyes.

If his appearance was alarming, his initial speech was even more so. Although Jean's French was poor, she knew the word he hurled at them like a missile.

"Voleur!"

A ripple of reaction ran through the staring crowd. Jean had time to wonder how personally some of the Trasteverites might

take that accusation of "thief." The reputation of the district
. . . Albert's voice rose to a shriek as he warmed to his subject.
"Il a disparu. On l'a volé! Mon tresor, ma seule chose précieuse!
Aujourd'hui, today, when I go to eat the lunch—you steal—"

To Jean's horror, he began to cry. Though he continued to
speak, the words were lost in his mammoth grief; the tears trickled down his face and collected in greasy puddles amid the folds
of his vast brown cheeks. The crowd reacted as people usually do
to an outburst of honest emotion; they turned their backs and
resumed their conversations, a little more loudly than before.

Andy started toward the doorway. He reached his sobbing uninvited guest and slapped him on the back. It was a good hard
slap, prompted by fury rather than camaraderie, but it stopped
Albert's cries. He turned toward Andy, who began to speak, softly
but urgently; and after a few moments Albert nodded and
swabbed at his face with his sleeve. Andy took his arm and pulled
him toward the table where the food was spread out. Jean relaxed. Andy had the situation well in hand. Albert could always
be distracted by food. As she backed daintily away, she saw Ann
making her way toward the table. The girl's face was set in an
expression of controlled distaste, but she was obviously prepared
to do her share in the dirty work.

Jean retreated, without shame. Albert in his normal state was
bad enough; she had no desire to socialize with him while he was
in his present state of mind. She joined a group of Italian students who were singing; one of them was strumming Andy's guitar. Over the melodious chords she could still hear the booming
gutturals of Albert's voice. The sound of the syllables was unfamiliar; apparently he had relapsed into his native tongue. Andy
admitted that he had forgotten most of the language which he
had learned as a child, but the inattention of his audience never
stopped Albert from talking.

For a while Jean forgot about the intruder. Then another
flurry around the refreshment table caught her attention. Andy
was no longer there, but José and Ted had joined Albert. After a
moment Ann broke away and came hurrying toward Jean. She
was flushed and distressed.

"What's the matter?" Jean asked.

"Oh, just Albert being Albert."

"What did he do, pinch you?"

"After a year in Rome I'm used to being pinched," Ann said. "That nasty little . . . if I were sure he's only ignorant and uncouth I wouldn't mind so much."

"I know what you mean. Can't the boys sort of edge him out of here?"

"The minute Andy left . . ." Ann was still preoccupied with her grievance.

"He's back," Jean said. "He's offering Albert more wine. I think he's trying to get him drunk."

Reluctantly, Ann turned.

"That won't work. Most people get more repulsive when they're drunk. Can you picture Albert?"

Ann was honestly distressed. She seemed close to tears, despite her caustic comments. Jean put her arm around the other girl.

"Let the boys handle him. Why should we be noble?"

Ann produced a faint smile.

"They really are great—Ted and José, I mean. They both came rushing up when they saw I was having a hard time. If they hadn't—"

She broke off with a gasp as someone screamed.

It was only an overexcitable young lady who had misinterpreted the scene now transpiring. Whether Andy had planned it or not, Albert had definitely taken too much of something. He began to fold up, with Andy holding one arm and José the other. Carefully the two lowered him until he lay on his back on the floor. Even in unconsciousness Albert was not silent. He snored hideously.

"Out cold," Andy said, in the midst of a fascinated silence. "Somebody help me with him. Mike, Carlo—"

Michael put his sketch pad away.

"What did you do, slip him a Mickey?"

"I was thinking of it," Andy admitted. "He must have had a few drinks before he got here. He couldn't pass out on a couple of glasses of wine."

"Get him out of here, Andy," Ann said. She stared down at the prostrate form, her face a mask of disgust. "What a mess!"

Michael reached out to help, but Andy needed none. Stooping, he hoisted the limp body to his shoulder. The boy named

Carlo followed him out. Jean gathered that Carlo had been elected to return Albert to the shabby room he called home.

"That young man is getting to be a problem," said José.

"A well-developed persecution complex," Ted agreed.

"But if someone robbed him . . ." Jean began.

"A delusion," José said. "The poor wretch has nothing worth stealing. Even his clothing is cheap, worn—"

"Perhaps he has lost his priceless collection of holy pictures," Ted said callously. "I thought I caught a reference to Saint Petronella. Whoever she was."

Jacqueline and Scoville joined the group in time to hear the last comment.

Scoville shook his head.

"I must say, this lad is an unprepossessing specimen. I remember his father, vaguely. Never amounted to much. . . . Why did you take up with him, after all these years, Ann?"

Andy, dusting his hands ostentatiously, came back into the room. His grin faded as he heard his father's question.

"He picked us up," he said, scowling. "And he's no weirder than some of your pals."

Scoville laughed and slapped his son on the back. Andy looked stoical, and the others, slightly embarrassed by this display of parental regard, pretended not to notice.

"That's the truth. Right on. I guess it runs in the family. Andy has a weakness for lame ducks. I remember that poor kid—"

"Why Petronella?" Ann said. "I never heard of a saint by that name."

"Rome is full of churches dedicated to saints nobody ever heard of," Andy said irritably.

"But the legends are interesting," Dana drawled. She leaned gracefully against the wall, and the neckline of her blouse slipped down another inch. One deep breath, Jean thought, and that blouse is going to go; and if she's wearing anything under it, I'll be a—

"You may sneer," José said. "But you must admit that many of these so-called legends have been substantiated by archaeology."

Dana shrugged. Four pairs of masculine eyes shifted hopefully, but were disappointed; she had calculated the shrug to a hair's breadth.

"José, darling, don't bring up the Vatican excavations again."

"But they prove my point." José turned to Scoville, who nodded knowledgeably. "Even to a skeptic, the ruins found under the basilica of St. Peter must be impressive. Legend said that Saint Peter was buried beneath the high altar; and behold, a cemetery was found. There are Christian tombs among them; they date from the period of Nero, when Peter was supposed to have been martyred. At the base of the altar, human bones were found—the bones of a man of strong physique and advanced age. But the skull was missing. And, since the sixteenth century, there has been in the church of St. John Lateran a reliquary containing the head of Saint Peter."

The argument wasn't new to Jean; they had fought it out, animatedly but good-naturedly, after their joint expedition to the excavations. It was evidently new to Jacqueline, though, and her reaction amused Jean; she was so intrigued she caught José by the arm.

"Is that true? I read something about the excavations, but I didn't know they had actually found the remains of Saint Peter!"

"Uh-uh," Andy warned. "Don't flip, my love. Not even the Vatican has come out with a definite statement on that. The bones were there, but there were a lot of bones—tombs and graves all over the place."

"But the bones of an elderly man . . . the missing skull. . . ."

With her face animated and her green eyes shining, she looked almost as young as the students around her. Scoville beamed approvingly at Jacqueline, and his son said tolerantly,

"Look, Marian, this happens to be a particularly complicated problem in excavation. It would take me two days to give you a summary of the details. But José is cheating a little. For one thing, there's not a single inscription mentioning the name of Saint Peter. When the early pilgrims visited the tombs of the martyrs they scribbled prayers on the walls. There are such prayers at Bethlehem and Jerusalem, at St. Peter's shrine on the Via Ostia—but not on the walls under the basilica."

"The name is there, in the cryptic alphabet," said José.

Andy took himself by the hair and appeared to be trying to lift himself up off the ground.

"I knew you were going to say that! Don't say that! There is no cryptic alphabet! It's just another one of those nutty theories—"

"Andy," said his sister firmly.

Jacqueline, her eyes still fixed on Andy, plunged one hand into her purse and began to rummage. The others watched, fascinated, until the hand finally emerged with a pen and notebook.

"Give me some references," she ordered.

Grinning, Andy obliged.

"Talk about a busman's holiday," he remarked. "Don't take us too seriously, Marian. Basically, Ignatius and I agree."

"These nicknames of Andy's!" José complained. "They drive me insane. I do not mind being addressed by the name of the founder of my order, but I do not comprehend, Jacqueline, why he calls you 'Marian.' "

"I was afraid someone was going to remember that," Jacqueline said resignedly. "There is a charming musical comedy whose heroine has that name. She is a librarian. Now—" she said quickly as Andy showed signs of being about to break into song, "tell me on what you both agree."

"On the basic factuality of legends," José said.

"The thing is," Andy explained, "when we talk about legends being confirmed by archaeology, we mean that the basic fact is confirmed. The details always turn out to be quite different from those in the story. And, sadly enough, the romantic, magical elements are the ones that vanish under close examination. There probably was a British chieftain named Arthur, or Artos, who lived in the sixth century; but the Round Table and the chivalry and the shining towers of Camelot are pure fiction. The bull-man called the Minotaur never roamed the passages of the palace of Knossos; and the Great Flood of Genesis was a petty local affair. That," said Andy, "is what historians do. They are killers of the dream, murderers of legend."

José laughed.

"You don't kill dreams so easily, my egotistical friend. Legends have a kind of truth which is independent of reason. A belief is a fact in itself; that is what you skeptics never admit."

Absently, Andy made an extremely rude Italian gesture toward his friend, who responded in kind before resuming.

"In fact, when the legends of the saints can be checked, a

surprising number can be confirmed. The underground excavations Andy has been showing us are a case in point. Under the
most ancient churches there are Roman houses. . . ."

"There are ancient Roman remains under every damn building in the city," Michael said. "What would you expect to find?
Egyptian pyramids?"

"Wait a minute, wait a minute," Jacqueline interrupted. "You
keep talking about excavating under churches. How can they do
that without destroying the church?"

"But this is Andy's specialty," Ted said. "Have you escaped his
lectures? How did you manage to do that?"

Andy gave him a friendly shove.

"You dragged us through miles of your ancestral catacombs,"
he said. "And Jean showed us mosaics till the sight of a pile of
gravel made me break out in hives. The Vatican picture galleries
echoed to Michael's critical sneers, and Dana got her innings
when we went through the classical collections." He turned to
Jacqueline. "We're showing each other Rome," he explained.
"Early Christian Rome is part of my specialty, so I'm taking the
crowd through subterranean excavations. It is possible to dig
without destroying the overlying structure, but it isn't easy."

"Interesting," Jacqueline admitted.

"Oh, we're all very earnest and hard-working," Michael said
sarcastically. "And trying to get cultured. Personally, I find it
uphill work. I don't dig this archaeology bit. Ann's tour was kind
of interesting; I really go for Egyptian sculpture."

He smiled at Ann; and Ann, surprised and pleased, gave him a
shy smile in return. Jean was so intrigued by this exchange that
she lost track of the conversation momentarily. She returned to it
in time to hear Andy inviting Jacqueline to join them on their
tour next morning.

"We're going to San Clemente," he explained. "It's a prize
specimen; not just one subterranean level, but two. Three layers
of construction. The present church was built in the twelfth century, on top of a fourth-century basilica which, in turn, stands on
the walls of some Roman houses and a temple to Mithra."

"A Mithraeum?" said Scoville, his eyes narrowing.

"Oh, no, you don't," said his son.

"Don't what?"

"Horn in on my lecture tour. You're leaving for Sicily tomorrow."

"I see why you want me out of the way," Scoville said. "All that talk about finishing your report to the Fellowship Committee was a blind; you probably did it long ago. You just want to lecture without my critical eyes on you."

"I don't want you butting in," Andy said. "You can't keep quiet while somebody else talks about archaeology."

"Not when they make mistakes I can't keep quiet."

"I," said Andy, "never make mistakes. Tell you what. If you keep your mouth shut you can come along when we go to San Sebastiano. I made an appointment for the twenty-ninth."

"That's a deal."

"That gives you time to read up on the subject," Andy said, grinning.

"If I'm to be at the church at ten, I'd better get home," Jacqueline said. "Andy, it's been a lovely party."

Scoville left with her, claiming he had to hit the sack early if he wanted to catch his 6 A.M. train. Watching them leave side by side, Jean wondered. In the doorway Jacqueline turned, and Jean's pleasant speculations died. Jacqueline's face was not that of a woman who is headed toward a romantic tête-à-tête. She looked worried. Jean recalled her odd comments earlier that evening, and all at once, with an illogical certainty as strong as Jacqueline's, she knew the older woman was right. There was something wrong, some false note in the once harmonious relations of the group. It had been present all evening, under the seeming hilarity of the party. She had no more idea than Jacqueline what its source might be, but one thing was sure: Albert's grotesque behavior was part of the problem.

CHAPTER THREE

*T*he small sunken courtyard was paved with brick. The same warm reddish-brown material composed the facade of the church, with its unpretentious entrance portico supported on four small columns. The sun beat down onto the bricks; it was going to be a hot day.

They were there, all seven of them, plus Jacqueline Kirby. Most of them looked as if they wished they had stayed in bed. Michael was a study in sagging muscles and wrinkled cloth; he had propped himself up against one of the columns of the portico. Ann was wearing sunglasses, but when she took them off for a moment Jean saw stark purple circles under her eyes. A blue bandanna, tied in back of her head, confined her hair. Her dark jeans and shirt made her face look paler; her lipstick, carelessly applied, suggested a streak of orange paint.

Andy never looked tired; lack of sleep only stimulated him. The casual dark clothing that made his sister look sexless and boyish only increased Andy's good looks.

Of all the group, the one who was most obviously hung over was Ted. He had all the symptoms: his eyes were bloodshot, his hands shook, and he winced visibly whenever a car out in the street blasted its horn. The sight of him made Jean's jaw drop. Ted seldom drank anything more potent than wine, and not much of that. She had never seen him drunk, and even with the obvious stigmata, which are considered so amusing by people who have never experienced them, Jean could hardly believe it if Dana had not confirmed her suspicion.

"You missed all the excitement, leaving so early," the English girl said in a gleeful whisper. "Ted was a panic. I mean, he was the life of the party. He was singing and reciting limericks in Hebrew and making passes at every girl in the room—"

"All of them?"

"Well, primarily me," Dana admitted, with a smirk that made Jean want to smack her face. "I've underestimated that lad. He's really something after he's loosened up a little."

Jean looked up and saw Ted watching them. He gave her a sickly smile and she glanced away.

"Do shut up," she said nastily. "I'd rather hear Andy lecture on his specialty than you on yours."

As Andy was the first to admit, he loved to talk, and he had inherited his father's gift for smooth, popular description. But this morning he was cutting the lecture short. The restlessness of his audience seemed to affect him. Even José, who was usually a courteous listener, finally called out,

"Andy, let's get inside, shall we? This quaint costume of mine is weighing me down."

"Right," Andy said. "I just wanted to say—ah, hell, look it up in the guidebook. And listen—anybody who wants to come back to our place and finish up the leftovers from last night is welcome. Just be back here at twelve. I'm not going to search that maze below for lost Sinners."

The group broke up and Jean, feeling somewhat fed up with her unkempt friends, crossed the courtyard to where Jacqueline stood demurely in a corner like a prim little wren in a crowd of starlings. Her feet, in neat white pumps, were placed at an angle of forty-five degrees; her auburn hair shone like a cap, with not a strand out of place; her ladylike silk print dress came down to the center of her knees. She was even wearing white gloves. The purse, of course, was prominent.

"Who are you trying to impress?" Jean asked.

"The elderly Italian lady with whom I am lunching. She happens to be a dear friend of the head of the university library where I am currently employed."

"You're a hypocrite," Jean said, remembering the sleek pants suit of the previous night and the general air of relaxation that had accompanied the change in costume.

"I merely adjust to my surroundings."

"Camouflage?"

"Protective coloring." Jacqueline's voice was unexpectedly hard. "Survival is a lot more difficult than you think, my friend." And then, as if she regretted her momentary lapse into cynicism, she added in a lighter tone, "The head librarian of the Classics Collection is retiring next year, and I may be in line for the job if I can prove I spent the summer studying the subject. I trust I need not remind you that the Institute library is one of the best in the world in that field."

"That must be why you're cultivating us," Jean said, with a grin. "Are you picking our brains?"

"Naturally," Jacqueline said, with an answering smile.

"You may regret that admission. We're all indefatigable lecturers."

They entered the church, and Jacqueline glanced appreciatively around its columned nave, with the brilliant mosaic of the apse at the far end.

"I'd rather hear you lecture about this than discuss classification with Lise. Go ahead, educate me. . . . What's the matter with Andy? He looks as if he's about to have a fit."

"He wants us to come. That must be the entrance to the underground area, over there."

"But I want to see this," Jacqueline complained.

Jean beamed.

"On behalf of my century, let me thank you. Mosaics are my thing, you know, and this is a particularly good one."

Instinctively they spoke in subdued voices. Though there was no service in progress, worshipers knelt at the various altars. Jacqueline lagged, deliberately.

"It's beautiful. And look at the frescoes in that chapel! Aren't they by Masaccio?"

"The attribution is disputed," Jean said, in mild surprise. "You have been doing your homework, haven't you?"

"I read my *Guida di Roma* last night," Jacqueline admitted. "The one put out by the Italian Automobile Association is first-rate. I can't help it anymore, it's habit, after all these years, to look everything up. . . . Blast and curse Andy; what does he want now?"

"He wants us to come and see his pet ruins," Jean said, laughing. "This basilica is twelfth-century; Andy won't even look at anything later than the fourth. We'd better go; we can come back here later."

Andy was waiting for them at the entrance to a room which had been fitted up as an office. There were books and souvenirs for sale; Dana leaned over the ticket counter chatting with a very young, very handsome boy in the white robe of a Dominican. Jean went to the counter to buy her ticket, and overheard a snatch of conversation which explained some of Dana's fascination.

". . . it'll be the oldest of thim in the city," said the soft Irish voice; then the priest looked up, smiled, and offered Jean her ticket.

As she stood waiting for Jacqueline to pay her hundred lire, Jean caught a glimpse of someone walking down the nave of the church. It was only a fleeting glimpse, but the shambling form was unpleasantly familiar. It wouldn't be unusual for Albert to track them down and add himself, uninvited, to the group. Hastily Jean trotted down the stairs to the first landing, where she was out of sight from the nave, and after a moment Jacqueline joined her. If she had seen Albert she didn't mention it, and Jean decided not to bring up the subject.

At the bottom of the long flight of stairs the modern world vanished. They stood in a vast dark place smelling of damp, and Jean had to look back at the well-lit staircase to assure herself that she had not been suddenly transported into another era.

A shadowy form materialized beside them.

"Boo," it said, in sepulchral tones.

Jean started.

"Damn it, Andy, that isn't funny."

"It's not funny, but it's appropriate," Jacqueline said. They still spoke in low tones; the atmosphere of the place was more suggestive of cemeteries than churches, but the inhibition was similar; there was a feeling that a loud voice might raise something better left undisturbed. Jacqueline added,

"I'm completely confused. Where are we?"

"We're standing in what was once the narthex—the porch—of a basilica built in the fourth century A.D.; one of the first churches ever built. It wasn't until after Constantine legalized Christianity in the early fourth century that the Christians dared construct public places of worship. It's hard to picture how this place looked in its original state. There are walls now where columns stood originally; when they excavated this place, in the last century, they had to leave a lot of the fill in place, to keep the church up above from collapsing. The basilica above this is almost exactly on top of the fourth-century church, wall for wall."

Involuntarily both women glanced up at the dark ceiling, which now seemed to be pressing down on their heads.

"I hope they left plenty of nice solid dirt in place," Jean muttered. "You know, Andy, a person could get claustrophobia down here."

"There isn't much to see in this area," Andy admitted. "Just a few moldy fragments of frescoes. When you're finished here, take those iron stairs down, and you'll drop back another three hundred years—back to the first century A.D. The walls you'll see down below were built to replace houses that burned in the great fire of Nero."

At some point in the next half hour Jean lost Jacqueline. That was one of Jacqueline's better qualities: you didn't have to talk to her, or be polite. Not only did she expect you to do your own thing, she was quite capable of going off and doing hers, without comment or explanation. The spell of the dark ruins was a melancholy, morbid charm, but it was hypnotic. Occasionally she encountered other shadowy wanderers; once she caught a glimpse of Ann's flaming hair. There were few other tourists; San Clemente was not on the regular route, and only specialists and people who had many weeks to spend in Rome found time for it.

Confusing as the fourth-century church was, it was a marvel of simplicity compared with the lowest level. Jean knew approximately what she was going to see there. As Andy had explained, there were essentially two buildings—or rather, parts of two buildings, for both had been only partially excavated. One of them was a private house, or palazzo, with rooms surrounding a large courtyard. The other structure was an apartment building, in the courtyard of which, eighteen hundred years earlier, a small temple of Mithra had been built.

The low vaulted ceiling suggested the roughly rounded roof of a cave, an impression which was reinforced by the damp atmosphere. The lighting was artfully dim, but it was enough to illumine the benches built along both the long walls, and the stone altar in the center of the floor.

Jean was examining the relief on the side of the altar when José joined her.

"A friendly face," he said, with relief. "I think I have been lost. This area is truly a maze."

"The level above is almost as bad." Jean indicated the relief, which showed a vigorous, youthful male figure in the act of stabbing an animal which it held by the horns. "I take it this is Mithra?"

"No doubt." José peered at the stone. "The youthful hero who slew the bull and, by the outpouring of its blood, gave immortality to mankind. An eastern cult . . . but you would know more about that than I."

"I don't know much either. Except that it was popular in the early centuries of the Christian era, and had some elements in common with Christianity."

"What elements?"

"Mithraism had a high ethical code, if I recall correctly. And the concept of sacrifice . . . Immortality through the shedding of blood. . . ."

"The Blood is the Life," said José. His voice echoed oddly in the low-ceilinged chamber, and Jean glanced at him in surprise. His dark, chiseled face had an abstracted expression. "It is an old idea, is it not? It must go back beyond civilization, into the prehistoric time, when the ape-people died red the bones of their dead to restore to them the hue of life. . . . Brrr." He smiled; the flash of white teeth lightened the somber planes of his face. "I make myself morbid. This place is too dark; I am going up into the sunshine."

"I'll see you later."

Jean watched the tall black-robed figure move out through the narrow doorway; and she thought that his archaic costume suited the place. She was the one who was out of place here; the very walls seemed to reject her short skirt and bright flowered blouse, her sandaled feet and long, unbound hair.

She went out into the corridor, passing a fat lady and her balding husband, in order to investigate some of the rooms on that side. If the area had a plan, it eluded her completely. Rooms and corridors succeeded one another in a mazelike muddle. And all of it was empty. The neat tiled floors were dusty, and the walls had been stripped down to the naked brick. The emptiness was not just the absence of any accouterment of living, it was a positive force that pressed down on any creature daring enough to penetrate those chambers. Now and again Jean met other visitors, and passed them without speech; they all had the same blank, awed stare she felt on her own face.

Eventually she passed through a narrow doorway and found herself treading a path through a corridor walled in by rough, unexcavated heaps of rubble. She heard approaching footsteps long before she could identify the person who made them. Then she recognized Michael.

"Hey," Michael said. "It's you. . . . A few more minutes and I'd have started seeing ancient Roman ghosts. What a place!"

"What is it about the place? I've been in ruined buildings before. . . . Pompeii, the Acropolis, various digs. . . . The only other place that oppressed me in this way was the catacombs."

"It's a dead place," Michael said. His eyes were so wide she fancied she could see a rim of white all the way around the iris. "It's inimical to life."

"Getting psychic?" Jean asked jokingly.

Michael shrugged—or shivered, she wasn't sure which.

"Oh, crap," he said, in a more normal voice. "It's all calculated effect. The light, just dim enough to make your vision uncertain; the chilly dampness; the . . . listen."

In the silence Jean heard the sound to which he referred—a distant, rippling murmur that rose and fell like the voices of a far-off crowd.

"It's water," she ventured.

"An underground spring or stream. They had to dig a tunnel out to the main sewer to keep these rooms from being flooded. There's one room, back over on the other side of the palazzo, where water rushes through the wall and the overflow trickles out through holes into a channel. It's a small trickle. But if you stare at it too long, the sound of the water gets louder and louder, and you start thinking maybe it will burst out, through the wall, and you wonder whether you'd have time to make your way through all these corridors and get to the stairs before the flood caught you. . . ."

"My God, you're in a morbid mood." Jean peered at him through the gloom, and saw, with a stir of alarm, that he was perspiring, even in the chill air. "Michael, are you sick?"

"Sick in the head," said Michael, with an odd choked laugh. "They call it claustrophobia. Such a nice sterile name for a feeling that turns your guts inside out and makes your brain clang around in your skull like a bell in a belltower. . . ."

Jean reached out and caught his hands, which were groping for something to hang on to. He fell back against the wall, his eyes closed, breathing heavily. Jean didn't know what to do, except maintain the clasp that was numbing her fingers. After a few seconds Michael opened his eyes.

"That's better," he mumbled. "Company helps. But I think I'd better get out of here."

There was barely room for them to walk side by side. Jean kept pace with him; she sensed that he was exerting all his self-control to keep from breaking into a head long panicky run.

"Is this new?" she asked.

"No. I spent two years in analysis, sometime back."

"But we do this underground bit all the time! I remember now, when we went to the Callixtus catacomb you didn't say a word the whole time; we were kidding you about it. . . . And when Ted showed us the Jewish catacombs you acted funny, and you said you had the emperor of all hangovers. . . . Why didn't you tell us about your phobia?"

"It sounds so stupid," Michael said. His voice had a childish petulance that made Jean want to laugh, but she knew better than to do so. There might be a degree of masochism in

Michael's behavior, but there was also a considerable amount of courage.

"It does not sound stupid," she said firmly. "A lot of people have a slight touch of claustrophobia; I have myself, but it's just enough to add a certain spice to these expeditions for me—the way you enjoy hearing a ghost story even more when the room is dark. But in its severe form the feeling must be awful. I don't think a doctor would approve of you pushing yourself this way."

"The only way I'll ever beat it is by pushing myself," said Michael. He sounded almost normal; only the painful grip of his hand betrayed his feelings. "Here we are. The stairs—freedom! Are you going to escort the baby up and out?"

"No," Jean said, stopping short. "You don't need an escort, and I—oh! Oh, my Lord—what's this? It's a grave, right on the wall—"

Michael laughed, more easily; her inadvertent alarm had been, by chance, the most tactful emotion she could have expressed.

"There are several graves. Enjoy yourself with the ghosts; I'll see you later."

He went up the steep modern iron staircase with more speed than caution, his long legs eating up the steps. When the echo of his steps had died away, the place seemed very quiet.

Jean turned to examine the graves. Cut into the perpendicular face of the wall, they were of the same type as those found in the catacombs. She knew she was reacting to Michael's nervousness, and with deliberate intent she made herself linger, trying to decide whether the scratches on the wall were only scratches, or a half-obliterated inscription. Illogically, the sound of footsteps approaching did not reassure her; she started nervously, and stared down the gloomy corridor as if she might see something. . . .

The something turned out to be Dana; which, Jean told herself, was not much better than nothing.

However, the other girl also seemed to be affected by the atmosphere. She greeted Jean with moderate enthusiasm.

"Thank God. I was beginning to feel as if I ought to be lying flat on my back, with my hands folded on my chest. Where does Andy find these jolly little places he takes us to?"

"It's funny you should feel that way."

"Why? Don't you find the place a bit uncanny?"

"Yes," Jean admitted. "But I should think this would be right up your alley. Aren't you used to digging up the dead past?"

"I've done some excavating. But on a normal dig you aren't working underground. Not unless you find tombs, and they're rare. . . . What's become of Andy? I haven't seen him since I came down to this level."

"I haven't either."

"I'm bored to tears and dying for a drink," Dana said petulantly. "This place is tedious. I don't know why Andy dragged us here. There's only one halfway decent thing, the ceiling stuccos on the pronaos of the temple. I rather liked them."

"I didn't see any stuccos. Just the benches and the altar."

"That room isn't the pronaos, it's the triclinium. The dining area," Dana added patronizingly. "Where they held the ritual meal. The pronaos is across the hall. You didn't see it? You must not have been looking at much."

"You must have paid more attention to Andy's lecture than I did."

"I cheated." Dana's sulky face relaxed. "I bought a guidebook. Look here, it has plans of all three of the levels on transparent paper, so you can see exactly where each section lies in respect to the one above and below."

"Hey, that's neat. I wish I'd had it before. I don't know where I've been."

"You can borrow it," Dana said. She yawned, brushing her mouth with the back of her hand. "You haven't run into Mike, have you? I promised I'd meet him here; but I guess he got tired of waiting."

"He went upstairs a few minutes before you came."

"Thanks."

She went up the stairs, undulating. With a comment that would have been represented in the old days of publishing by a dash and an exclamation point, Jean swung on her heel and marched back along the passage. It was injured dignity, not interest in the stuccos Dana had praised, that made her go that way, but when she reached the end of the passage she decided she might as well have a look at the stuccos. She realized then that Dana had not given her the guidebook, and she swore again, more emphatically. Surely, though, she could find her way back the way she had come.

The assumption turned out to be incorrect. After several turns, which seemed to her to be the reverse of the course she had originally followed, she found herself in a room she didn't remember having seen before. It was a fairly large room, approximately twenty feet square. Its floor was formed of buff-colored tiles, laid in a neat herringbone pattern. There were small blocked-up openings which might have been windows once upon a time, but it was difficult to imagine that any normal human activity had ever been carried on here. The room was not only deserted, it looked as if it had never been occupied.

For several minutes she had been increasingly conscious of a sound. It was not a frightening noise, being, in fact, the murmur of water Michael had mentioned earlier. As she proceeded, through a narrow curved corridor, the sound increased in volume. There was a single door at the end of the corridor. Beyond, in the odd dusty light, she could see part of a brick wall. She went on, hoping to find a passage through.

In the doorway she stopped short. There was no other door. The passage by which she had come was the only entrance into the room. But it was not the finality of the fact that caused her to stop and drove the breath out of her lungs in an explosive cry of horror.

Unlike the other, this room was occupied—but not, she thought, by any living thing. The man who lay face down on the floor, in a sickening puddle of red, was not alive. Nothing could bleed that much and still be alive.

When the sprawled body moved, she tried to scream, and failed; she had forgotten to breathe in, after the first shocked exhalation. Then she forgot about screaming. The eyes in the ashen face were glazed, but they caught her own eyes with a concentrated intensity of demand that made her forget her feelings. Jean knelt down on the dreadful floor and reached out to support the man's hanging head.

She had recognized Albert even before she saw his face, from the patched clothing and plump body. She was never sure afterward whether he knew her or not; but he sensed another presence, and his desire to communicate was so strong it drove his fading will to an effort she would have believed impossible.

He tried to speak. She saw his mouth move and concentrated on its shape because she could not, would not, look at the gaping gash below. He had nothing left to speak with, not even breath. The fading eyes closed. Then they opened again on a new blaze of will, and one stained finger moved.

Later, trying desperately to find some small redeeming feature in the situation, Jean was glad that Albert's failing mind missed the obvious source of writing material. His finger left no bloody trail; it merely scratched a darker pattern through the dust of the floor, and if she had not seen the shapes forming, she would never have recognized them. Caught in the hypnotic pull of the dying man's concentration, she followed the slow, painful strokes with pent breath.

Then the hand clenched in a sudden spasm. The head dropped heavily onto Jean's supporting hands. Gently she lowered it to the floor and stared with dilating eyes at her reddened hands, and the ugly streaks on her knees and skirt. She rose jerkily to her feet. Softly in the background, like a musical accompaniment, she could still hear the rippling murmur of running water.

CHAPTER FOUR

Jean was under the mistaken impression that she was thinking quite rationally. She began to scream—not in panic, she assured herself, but simply as a means of procuring help. She couldn't run away, because that would mean leaving . . . him. It? The living entity has gender; the dead are neuter. She wondered whether she had chanced on some deep philosophic truth, or whether the difference only mirrored a meaningless distinction taken over from a language in which all nouns have gender. The designations made no sense; why should a French pen be feminine, and a pencil masculine?

Her breath gave out, and she stopped screaming. In the silence she heard footsteps. They were approaching rapidly, almost at a run. Someone had heard her. Her knees went weak with relief and she knew, then, how close she had come to hysterics. With a long, childish wail of distress and welcome, she stumbled forward and threw herself into Jacqueline Kirby's arms.

"What is the matter with—" The voice, sharp with concern, broke off in a gasp as Jacqueline saw. There was a moment of absolute silence; Jacqueline's store of expletives was evidently inadequate for the occasion.

"All right," she said, after a moment. "Stop that bawling, Jean. Stop it right now, do you hear me?"

Without waiting for a response she pulled herself away from Jean and began fumbling in her purse. Her voice, deliberately harsh and unsympathetic, had quieted Jean somewhat, but she was still too distressed to see what Jacqueline was doing until an exquisite agony invaded her nostrils and turned the interior of her head to fire.

"Oh, God, that hurt!" she moaned, wiping streaming eyes. "Smelling salts! You sadistic, mean—"

"That's better." Jacqueline restored the bottle to her purse. "Someone has to go for help, Jean. I don't think anyone else heard you."

Pushing the tangled hair back from her eyes, Jean looked at her companion and saw another facet of Jacqueline's complex personality. Her face was ashen and as hard as her voice. Its strength was reassuring, and a little frightening.

"I didn't do it," Jean said, gulping.

"For God's sake, don't say that to anyone else!" Jacqueline's hard-won control broke momentarily. The green eyes turned glassy with a new fear. "Don't volunteer anything. Oh, God—you aren't in any state to be left alone, are you?"

"I think," said Jean, swallowing strenuously, "I think I'm going to be sick."

"Get it over with, then," Jacqueline said brutally. She fumbled in the purse and eventually produced an object that made Jean's eyes widen, even in her queasy state. It looked like—it was—a policeman's whistle.

The succeeding interval was unpleasant enough to occupy Jean's entire attention. She was vaguely aware of piercing blasts from the whistle, and of firm hands that held her shoulders while she suffered. When she had recovered sufficiently to notice what was going on, the room seemed to be filled with people. The first one she saw was Andy; his fiery mop of hair stood out in the dusty room, and it looked even brighter against the greenish pallor of his face. Someone was kneeling by the body, hiding all of it except the outstretched legs. No—there were two people kneeling, both wearing the long ecclesiastical robe. One white and one black; José, and one of the Dominican fathers. They rose, and as they stood side by side they resembled symbolic representations of good and evil, hieratic, in their medieval robes. The young Dominican was as unmistakably Irish as José was Latin; but the two faces had a peculiar identity of expression. They exchanged glances, and José nodded slightly.

II

"I'll have to be calling the police, then," said the soft, inflexible Irish voice.

As she gazed around the room, Jean thought that surely no criminal investigation had been carried on in more outré surroundings. The triclinium of the temple of Mithra had seen strange rites in its time, but nothing quite like this.

José had suggested the temple room, with its rows of built-in benches, as the least uncomfortable place in which the witnesses might wait. There was really no other suitable room in either of the two lower levels, and the upper church, with its crowd of local worshipers, was obviously unsuitable. So they were herded one by one into the ancient sacred place as the priests located them— the seven, and Jacqueline, and half a dozen miscellaneous and distracted tourists. Dana and Michael were the last to be found, in a remote corner of the fourth-century church. Nobody asked them what they had been doing there, but as they came into the room Andy laughed, suddenly and sardonically.

"Number six and number seven," he said. "Fellow Sinners, it appears that the name was a meaningful inspiration after all."

"If you mean what I think you mean, you are jumping to conclusions," Ted said. He was sitting beside Ann, who looked terrible. Her freckles stood out like dots made with the blunted end of a lipstick. Ted went on, "You don't know how he was killed. It might have been an accident."

"His throat was cut," Jean said. The sound of her own voice made her jump.

"Jesus, Mary, and Joseph," muttered Michael. "Did you—" He looked at Jean, who was sitting between Jacqueline and an elderly American lady.

"Yes, I found him. And if you don't mind, I'd rather not describe it. I'll have to tell the police when they arrive. . . ."

"Yes, and where are your precious fuzz?" Dana demanded. "I've been sitting on this damned stone slab so long. . . ."

She completed the sentence with a picturesque if unoriginal metaphor that made the gray-haired lady gasp. One of the other strangers, a bearded youth with bare feet and a knapsack on his back, beamed admiringly. Two other women looked like schoolteachers. One of them said drily,

"I agree with the sentiment, if not the exact words. Have the police been summoned? There were two of them lounging about outside when we came in—the ones who wear those gaudy uniforms, with the cocked hats and the swords."

"*Caribinieri,*" Andy said. He was looking sick and strained, but he could never resist explaining things. "A case of—a case like this wouldn't come under their jurisdiction. There are three different kinds of cops here. The *caribinieri* are a military force, though they can pursue and apprehend civilian-type crooks. The city police—the *polizia municipale*—are the ones you see directing traffic and giving tickets. I think we'll be questioned by the third group, the *agenti* of the Commissario di Pubblico Sicurezza. Each district of Rome has its own local subdivision—"

"I do not see why we should be questioned." The speaker was a stout, balding man who was accompanied by his stout wife. Jean couldn't place his accent; he wasn't American or British. "I intend to complain. I fail to see why we have been detained."

"I agree," snapped one of the teachers. "I don't even know what has happened."

"A man is dead," Jacqueline said. It was the first time she had spoken, and all of them turned to look at her. "He died violently. We must expect to be detained. That is normal procedure in any civilized country."

She had reverted to her prim librarian role, with her glasses firmly in place and her gloved hands folded over the pregnant bulge of the purse. For Jean, the purse had assumed a magical aura; from its depths, only today, had come the smelling salts, the whistle, a huge man's (man's?) handkerchief with which to mop her wet face, and a mysterious little white pill. Jean suspected the pill was only aspirin. Jacqueline was not the type to carry tranquilizers. But its psychological effect had been excellent. She felt numb, but calm.

"But I don't know the man!" one of the other tourists protested. "Why drag us into this?"

"That's up to the police, not us," Jacqueline said. "If you don't know the victim you probably won't be detained for long. So what are you worrying about?"

"Very true."

Occupied with their bickering, they had not observed the unobtrusive approach of the newcomer. As they saw him, a silence of awesome proportions fell on the group. It was broken by Dana.

"Well, she said softly. "I have to admit it was worth waiting for."

The man standing in the doorway was obviously the police official they had been expecting. He was, just as obviously, the kind of Roman gentleman female visitors dream of meeting but seldom do.

His dark hair shone, thick and soft, in the dim light. The two wings of silver lifting from his temples were almost too perfect; they looked as if they had been sprayed on. Jean who was sitting near the door, saw his face in profile, and the sharp, delicate features reminded her of an antique portrait head from ancient Rome. The modeling of nose and chin and cheekbone was so precise they might have been cut from marble; except for his superbly tailored modern clothing, the man could have stepped out of the procession carved on Augustus' Altar of Peace.

After making a leisurely survey of the group seated on the right-hand benches, he turned his head to the left, and Jean's glance met his wide-set dark eyes. A little shock ran through her. The young Octavian, planning his rise to imperial power, might have had eyes like those—cool, appraising, frighteningly intelligent.

The eyes moved over them, one by one.

"I am di Cavallo. A humble *agente* of the Questura."

Andy, who had been slumped wearily against the wall, sat up with a start.

"Aren't you Lieutenant di Cavallo?"

"That is my official title. I do not recall having had the honor of your acquaintance. . . ."

Andy smiled faintly. There was a curious gleam in his eyes as he measured the other man.

"You have a certain reputation, Lieutenant." He turned to the others. "We're honored, ladies and gentlemen. Normally a simple *agente*, or maybe a noncom, is in charge of criminal investigations. I didn't expect an officer of the lieutenant's distinction."

Di Cavallo was unmoved by the flattery.

"Your knowledge of our governmental procedures is admirable, young man. Now, if you have finished displaying that knowledge, perhaps I may proceed? Thank you. . . ." He turned to Jacqueline, clearly approving her poised look and respectable appearance. "I am told, signora, by Father Finnegan, that you appear to be acquainted with the dead man, and also with several of these witnesses. Can you tell me what happened?"

In a few sentences Jacqueline identified Albert and explained his relationship to the other members of the group, whom she introduced. When she had finished her brief account the lieutenant nodded.

"The papers in the wallet of the dead man identify him as you have said. You, you, you two—" Unerringly he selected the casual tourists. "You have never met this Albert Gébara? Then you may leave. Please give your names and your local addresses to the police officer in the vestibule. Thank you."

When the outsiders were gone there was a noticeable change in the atmosphere. Di Cavallo sat down in one of the vacated places and reached into the breast pocket of his jacket. Taking out a gold cigarette case which looked too flat to hold anything thicker than a toothpick, he offered it to the group at large before taking one himself. Jean felt fairly certain that detecting was not di Cavallo's sole source of income. Surely, if he were a dishonest cop, he wouldn't display his opulence so openly. He must come from a wealthy family.

"Lieutenant," Ted began, "are you not being rather casual about those others? Just because they say they do not know the murdered man—"

"Murdered?" Di Cavallo raised his eyes from the tip of his

cigarette and exhaled a cloud of fragrant smoke. "Why do you think this is a case of murder?"

The silence vibrated. Finally José said drily,

"The man's throat was cut, Lieutenant. That could hardly be an accident."

The lieutenant's eyes settled on the priest, and met their match. For a moment the two pairs of dark eyes locked. Then di Cavallo grinned.

"Padre Ximenez? I would have recognized the Jesuit even without the cassock. You are quite right, Father. It is not often that a man slips so badly while shaving, and a man does not shave without water, soap, and a mirror, does he? No, we can certainly dismiss the idea of accident. But there is another category of violent death."

"Suicide!" Dana was never ingenuous; the exclamation was designed to catch the lieutenant's eye. It succeeded. The eye lingered.

"That is correct, signorina. What do you know of this matter?"

Dana shrugged prettily.

"Fortunately, I wasn't the one to find the body."

"Fortunately indeed. It was not a nice sight."

"That wasn't what I meant," said Dana. Her eyes flickered. "In England . . . but you said this wasn't a case of murder."

"I have not yet said what it is a case of," said di Cavallo, handling the complicated English sentence with complete aplomb. "In England, you were about to say. . . ."

"Oh, well." Dana shrugged again, bringing all kinds of useful muscles into play. "In English detective stories the one who finds the body is always a prime suspect. But as you said—"

Outrage overcame Jean's exhaustion, and she sat upright, glaring.

"Of all the—"

Her voice clashed with, and was overruled by, di Cavallo's voice.

"As I said, it does not seem to be a case of murder." He shrugged; the exquisite gesture made Dana's shrug seem crude. "I am violating regulations by saying this much; we have not yet completed our investigations. But this is an unusual case. We like to extend courtesy to our foreign visitors; we realize that our system of law is alien to the Anglo-Saxon, and that includes, I believe, most of you. So I will tell you, in confidence, that we have found the weapon under the body of the dead man. It is a common sort of knife, a kitchen knife, which may be purchased in any store here. And the nature of the wound bears out the assumption of suicide. It only remains, then, to find a reason why this unfortunate young man may have wished to end his life.''

"He was crazy," Mike said.

All eyes focused on him where he sat huddled in a corner. His knees were drawn up and his elbows rested on his knees; the pose was almost the classic embryonic position of withdrawal. Remembering his confession, Jean felt sorry for him—until she remembered where he and Dana had been found.

"He really was crazy," Michael repeated. "Everybody knows how he's been acting lately."

"Mike is right," Andy said. "Look, Lieutenant, it isn't as if the poor devil was a good friend of ours. We didn't know anything about his private life. He more or less butted into our group—I mean, he invited himself—"

"I know the English idiom," di Cavallo said stiffly.

"What? Oh . . . sure. What I was going to say was, even a casual acquaintance could tell he was mentally disturbed. And there was a change for the worse in the last few days. Wasn't there?"

His appeal to the group produced a murmur of agreement.

"Andy is correct," José said. "Albert was always peculiar, and lately he had become even more peculiar. You may not consider us good judges of normal behavior, Lieutenant; but perhaps you will accept Mrs. Kirby's opinion."

"Ah." Di Cavallo settled back, crossing his legs. "Mrs. Kirby, yes. Signora, you are an official of the Institute of Art and Archaeology?"

"No, I'm only a visiting librarian—a friend of Frau Hilman, who is librarian at the Institute. I'm not an expert on psychiatry, either, but I agree with my friends here that Albert was decidedly odd."

Clearly di Cavallo approved of Jacqueline; his eagle eye softened whenever he looked at her. He nodded agreeably.

"In what specific way was he odd, signora?"

"Lieutenant," Ann said softly. "I'm sorry to interrupt, but Jean —she's the one who found him—it was a terrible experience for her, and she doesn't look at all well. Can't we take her home?"

For the second time that day Jean felt the full focus of di Cavallo's unnerving stare. She knew she must look as pale and pathetic as she felt, and the lieutenant's expression was properly sympathetic. But it didn't deceive Jean for a moment. Neither her youthful pathos nor Dana's sultry looks would have the slightest effect on this man.

"But of course," di Cavallo said. "If the young lady will first tell me—"

Ann got to her feet.

"She's in no condition to tell you anything. You know where to find us, we aren't going anywhere. Can't you question her later?"

"But there isn't anything to tell," Jean said. "I just walked into the room and there he was. I went to him, and knelt down; I thought perhaps I could help him. I didn't see the—the wound, then, not until he raised his head—"

Di Cavallo sucked his breath in sharply through his teeth.

"You are telling me, signorina, that the man was not dead when you found him?"

The suave manner was gone; voice and face were sharp with newly aroused suspicion. Jean realized that the others were staring at her with the same startled incredulity.

"He was dying, but not . . ." Jean turned to Jacqueline. "You saw him. . . . No, you didn't come till after. . . . But he was alive! Just barely. I know it sounds incredible, but—"

"Not impossible," José's cool voice broke in. "There have been cases of fatally injured men who lived for—"

"Very well, Father, very well," di Cavallo interrupted. "Until I speak with the police surgeon, such speculation is irrelevant. Now, signorina. He raised his head. Did he speak, then?"

"No." Jean remembered that horrible voiceless whistle of breath, and a shudder ran through her. "He tried to, but he . . . he wrote something, though. On the floor, with his finger."

The general incredulity was so thick Jean could almost feel it. Di Cavallo continued to stare, but there was now more impatience than suspicion in his face. Apparently he took her for one of those suggestible witnesses who invent dramatic details after the fact.

"I saw the room, signorina. There was, I assure you, no last message scrawled in the dying man's blood."

"It wasn't scrawled in blood," Jean snapped. "He just scratched it in the dust. It was probably obliterated when he fell forward."

"Very well." Di Cavallo sighed. "And what were the man's dying words?"

"Not words. Not even one word." Jean looked wildly at the faces of her friends, and found them pitying, amused, protesting—and all unbelieving. "I tell you, he wrote it! The number seven!"

III

The room was almost dark when Jean woke up from a nap she had had no intention of taking. Sitting up too suddenly, she clutched her spinning head and tried to orient herself. Slowly, memory returned. She was in Jacqueline's apartment, and apparently Jacqueline had slipped her a Mickey in that ritual cup of tea. She might have known that even Jacqueline wasn't old enough to really believe in the restorative properties of a nice hot cup of tea. . . .

Something was in the room with her. She could hear it breathing. After a long, horrible moment, she identified the lump at the foot of the bed as the sleeping poodle. Jean crept out of bed without rousing the animal; it looked so comfortable she couldn't bring herself to disturb it.

She located her hostess on the balcony off the *salone*. The railings were screened by thick masses of blue-flowered plumbago and the trailing greenery of ivy geraniums, pink and white and salmon-colored. Wearing shorts and a sleeveless blouse, Jacqueline was seated at a small table reading a book. She put the book down and greeted Jean coolly.

"How do you feel?"

"Groggy." Yawning, Jean dropped into a chair and propped her chin on her hands. "What did you give me?"

"A mild sedative."

"Mild!"

It was still daylight, but the sky to the east was beginning to darken. The evening breeze felt good after the airless bedroom; it lifted Jean's hair from her forehead, and she turned her face to it gratefully. Through the flowered greenery she could see the blue sparkle of the pool below.

"Corruption," she said dreamily.

"What?"

"Money corrupts. I wish somebody would try to corrupt me. I could learn to like living this way."

"So enjoy it while you're here. Would you like something to eat?"

With an effort Jean roused herself from the pleasant lethargy induced by the seductive air and the setting.

"You've done enough. Not that I don't appreciate it, but I can't let you coddle me any longer. I'm going home."

"I'm not offering to serve you pheasant under glass on a tray in bed," Jacqueline said drily. "Prosciutto and rolls are what I had in mind. Your stomach is completely empty, and if you leave now you'll just pass out on the street somewhere. That doesn't make much sense, does it?"

She sounded as grouchy as an arthritic old lady, and Jean stared at her in surprise.

"You don't have to do this for me," she said stiffly.

"What else could I have done? You were in no state to be alone."

"Ann wanted me to come home with her and Andy."

"Yes, and your whole blasted club would have gone along, and sat there yelling and talking and rehashing the whole business. Seven Sinners, indeed! You're a bunch of irresponsible kids, every one of you."

"You really didn't want me to come here, did you?"

"No."

"Then why—"

Jacqueline sighed. She turned slightly in her chair and stretched her legs out. They were, Jean noticed, very good legs.

"I'm sorry, Jean, I shouldn't have said that. Don't take my meanness personally; I really like all of you mutts, even if you do exasperate me. It's just a personal foible. . . . Let's have a sand-wich, and then you can go home. I'll wash my hands of the lot of you, with pleasure."

Her voice was light, and Jean knew her mood had improved. They brought their impromptu meal out onto the balcony; it was almost too beautiful to be real, with the sky slowly darkening to the precise, gleaming blue that appears in the starry vaults of the medieval church mosaics, and the perfumed breeze blowing through the heavy flower clusters. Jean found she was ravenous. Unashamedly she polished off every scrap of food on the table, and accepted a second helping.

"Every time I come here I eat like a glutton," she said apolo-getically. "You've been awfully nice. I really do appreciate it."

Jacqueline made a face.

"For God's sake don't use that word. Damning with faint praise. . . . Nice, indeed."

"No, really," Jean persisted. "You're nice to put up with us. I suppose we seem pretty juvenile to you. What do you really think of us?"

Jacqueline considered the question.

"The Seven Sinners," she said, with a faint smile. "I guess the thing that strikes me is your mixture of erudition and naiveté. You're a bright lot, you know—collectively and individually. But you are very . . . young. I have to say that," she added, her smile widening. "If I praised your wisdom, the inner council of the over-thirty crowd might hear about it and I might mysteri-ously disappear some dark night. No remains would ever be found; only a terrified peasant would babble of flaring torches in a remote grove, where white-robed figures met in judgment over a traitor."

Jean laughed.

"Not bad. You ought to write thrillers."

"I've read too many of them," Jacqueline admitted. "When I started out, I worked in a small-town library where business was slow. Detective stories are among the few types of literature you can pick up and put down a dozen times per day." She took a sip of her wine—a beverage that, in Rome, accompanies the smallest snack. "And, in the last few hours, this has become a thriller. This life of yours."

"How true. Jacqueline . . . do you honestly think Albert was the suicidal type?"

Silence followed the question. It was dark now; Jean saw her companion only as a featureless outline in the shadows. Finally Jacqueline said,

"Is there a suicidal type?"

"Don't quibble," Jean said. "Of course there isn't; I've had some experience along those lines myself; who hasn't? But I've never known any suicide, successful or unsuccessful, who acted like Albert."

"I keep forgetting what it was like to be twenty," Jacqueline said musingly. "And I gather it's worse these days. . . . How many suicides have you known?"

"Only one. And it turned out she was on acid. But I've heard a lot of people talk."

"God, yes. Of course you have. . . . All right, Jean, if you really want to go into this. Do you think Albert was taking any kind of drug?"

"No. No, I don't. You can tell."

"I know. Do I know. . . . You find me a parent who can't recite the symptoms of everything from hash to speed and I'll show you a stupid parent. . . . The autopsy will answer that question finally, but I think you're correct. Albert wasn't on anything. So?"

Jean made a despairing gesture.

"So. . . . It's hard to express it. Albert was crazy, sure. But one thing he had, he had a very high opinion of Albert. Whether he was crazy or not . . . whether his theories were weird or not . . . he didn't know they were weird. He thought he was God's gift to the heathen world. All right, maybe I don't know enough about mental illness. Maybe he flipped. Maybe he went from a manic state to a depressive state, and realized that his pretensions were all lies, that he was an ugly, repulsive—"

Her voice broke. For a few seconds the silence was complete. Then Jacqueline's disembodied voice said,

"Epitaph for Albert. . . . You have a rather nice mind yourself, child. Also you have had too much wine after a hard day. Make yourself another sandwich and listen while I agree with you. This business bothers me. It has bothered me all day. But, like yourself, I don't have any logical reason for being bothered.''

The sound cut through her voice like a buzz saw; both of them jumped.

"Blast that doorbell," Jacqueline muttered. "It has the ugliest sound. . . . Stay here. I'll answer it."

By the time Jacqueline had reached the elevator door, switching on lights as she went, Jean had recovered herself. In the glow from the *salone* she calmly made herself another sandwich. She was chewing on it—the hard Italian rolls made mastication a real exercise—when Jacqueline returned with the man who had rung the doorbell. The sight of him was not cheering to Jean, but she couldn't help being amused at Jacqueline's expression. It was, as the old romances used to say, a study.

"Signorina." Di Cavallo made a bow so punctilious it looked like a joke. "You are feeling better now?"

Jean nodded and smiled. She couldn't speak; her mouth was full.

At Jacqueline's invitation the lieutenant sat down and accepted a glass of wine. He sighed loudly.

"How lovely it is, here in the darkness. And how lovely it would be to forget all unpleasant things. Alas, I must not allow myself, or you, that indulgence."

"What have you found out?" Jacqueline asked.

Di Cavallo sipped his wine.

"The case seems obvious. I now tie up the loose ends."

"Suicide?"

Di Cavallo nodded. He reached for the briefcase which all proper European businessmen, of all professions, habitually carry.

"Be so good to look at this," he said, taking out a sheaf of papers and handing them to Jacqueline.

Jacqueline shifted her chair so that she was sitting in the shaft of light from the *salone*. She peered nearsightedly at the papers.

"I can't see a thing," she muttered. "What did I do with my glasses?"

"They're on top of your head," Jean said, watching her curiously. When Jacqueline acted disorganized and incoherent she was usually up to something.

"How ridiculous. What would they be—" Her groping hand
found the glasses. Giving Jean a hard stare, she perched them on
the end of her nose and began to read.

She read for some time, in silence. Her face was a studied
blank, giving nothing away. After a time she glanced inquiringly
at the lieutenant and then handed the papers to Jean.

The papers were Albert's notes. They were covered with writing in French, Arabic—and, surprisingly, in Latin. Not so surprising, though, Jean thought, as she leafed through the sheets. Albert's sources dated from the early Christian era, so naturally
most of them would be written in Latin. But. . . .

"But," she said slowly, "this is gibberish. None of it makes any
sense."

"You understand the languages, signorina?"

"Yes, I read Latin and French, though I don't speak them. But
it would be obvious, even with a slight command of the languages. All of it seems to be either prayers or . . . well . . .
blasphemies. The names of saints, over and over . . . 'Santa
Cecilia, *ora pro me*—Saint Cecilia, pray for me. Saint Christopher,
pray for me. . . .' And this part seems to be a series of epithets,
directed at the Pope."

"Yes, yes," di Cavallo said impatiently. "The work is that of a
person whose religious views are eccentric, to say the least. What
I wish to know is—are these papers as worthless as they seem to
be?"

"They're not only mad, they're meaningless," Jean said, handing the papers back to di Cavallo. "Have you shown them to
Andy Scoville? He knows more about the subject than I do."

"I have talked with him. He agrees."

"Is this all?" Jacqueline asked. "All you found in his room?"

"All, yes. A few shabby clothes, books . . . letters from his
mother. . . ."

"His mother," Jean repeated stupidly.

"He had a mother, yes; it is not unusual." Di Cavallo studied
her without sympathy or prejudice. "Signorina, it is all very sad,
no doubt; but the world is full of tragedies, they occur every
thirty seconds and many of them are sadder far than this loss
of a very disturbed young man who might have injured some

innocent person eventually if he had not had the kindness to remove himself first."

"You are sure?" Jacqueline's voice sounded odd, and di Cavallo peered at her through the shrouding darkness.

"Very little in this world is sure, Signora Kirby—as I think you, like myself, have learned through painful experience. But I am as sure as I am ever sure. . . . There are only a few loose ends. For example, this story of a theft."

"Who told you about that?"

"Padre Ximenez. He disapproves of me, as I do of him, but we respect one another. He pointed out to me that the accusation of theft must have been directed at one of your small group of friends, since Gébara knew none of the other guests."

"Yes, but that didn't mean anything. Nobody stole anything from Albert. He didn't have anything worth stealing."

"So one might conclude from the poverty of his belongings. Your friends agree that he never mentioned any particular treasure before last night. . . . The Seven Sinners," di Cavallo said musingly. "Very quaint. . . . You did say, signorina, that the symbol written by the dying man was the number seven?"

For a second, Jean's breath stopped. Then she recovered herself.

"Would it be contempt of court or something if I said 'damn you,' Lieutenant?"

"It would only be very rude," said di Cavallo calmly.

"Yes, I did see him write that, and I stick to my story. But if this is suicide, the Seven Sinners can't have anything to do with Albert's dying message."

"I cannot see how," di Cavallo agreed. "If this were not so obvious a case—if there were any suspicion of foul play . . . even then, I cannot see that there is a clue in that number. Because in a group of seven, any one might be number seven. You did not have numbers, did you, like the secret gangs in the old romances?"

"Of course not. We didn't even have an official name, it was just Andy's fooling."

"Well, then, we will never know. And it does not greatly matter. . . . Ladies, I think that is all. You are staying here tonight, Miss Suttman?"

"No, I'm going home. I've imposed on Mrs. Kirby long enough."

"Ah? Then I will be happy to take you home, if you are ready to go now."

"Well . . . thanks."

Jacqueline said nothing. She preceded them to the door, and Jean was gratified to note that di Cavallo shared the weaknesses of lesser men. His appraisal of Jacqueline's legs was leisurely, expert, and approving.

The lieutenant's car was an official vehicle, complete with driver. After asking directions, di Cavallo was silent until they reached Jean's apartment building. To her surprise and unexpressed alarm, he got out with her. He saw the alarm; there was amusement in his face as he condescended to explain.

"The other young woman—Miss Dana—also lives in this building, I believe. I wish to speak to her."

"She may not be in," Jean said, as they entered the building. "Dana leads an active social life."

"Yes, I would think she might," said the lieutenant gravely. "I wonder why, since your friend lives here with you, it was left to Mrs. Kirby to take you home today, after your bad experience."

"Dana doesn't live with me, she just has a room in the same building. We aren't exactly . . . I mean, we are friends, but not—"

"I think I understand."

"I wish I thought you did," muttered Jean. "What do you want to see her about?"

"Only to tie up the—"

"Loose ends. All right, ask a stupid question and you get a stupid . . . sorry, I didn't mean that," she added quickly.

When they reached the third floor di Cavallo knocked on Dana's door. Jean hovered, unashamedly curious. She expected di Cavallo to order her away, but he did not, and when it became apparent that Dana was not at home, she suggested, "Maybe I could help you. What was it you were going to ask Dana?"

"I only wish to ascertain where each person was at the time of the tragedy. It is part of the routine."

"An alibi." Jean considered this. "You didn't ask me."

"But signorina," said di Cavallo silkily, "I know where you were when the man died. You were kneeling by his side. Is that not correct?"

CHAPTER FIVE

As it goes from the Piazza Barberini to the Porta Pinciana, the Via Veneto curves and climbs. Jean was trying to hurry because she was late, but she found it hard going. By the time she reached Doney's, at the far end of the street, she was limping perceptibly.

Jacqueline was already there, at one of the sidewalk tables under the blue-and-white awning. Her blue linen suit matched the blue of the awning and turned her eyes aquamarine. She was knitting busily. The wool was a lovely shade of blue, a bit darker than her suit, but it had a slightly battered look and Jacqueline scowled at it over the tops of her glasses, which rested precariously on the end of her nose. She looked up as Jean approached, and the scowl deepened into a look of concern.

"What happened to you?"

"Have you been waiting long?" Jean dropped into a chair.

"No, I was late myself. But what—"

"If I'd known you were going to be late I wouldn't have hurled myself under a taxi. Some less drastic excuse would have done just as well."

"You're kidding."

"Well, I didn't actually jump," Jean said. She stretched out her legs and inspected her scraped knees. "I was pushed."

Jacqueline bundled up her knitting with a carelessness that explained its dilapidated condition, and put it into the purse. She took out the box of Band-Aids and a small bottle.

"Oh, no." Apprehensively, Jean recognized the red liquid in the bottle. "Jacqueline, you are too much. Don't tell me you always carry . . . you can't do that here!"

Ignoring Jean's wails and the fascinated stare of the waiter, Jacqueline administered first aid as calmly as if she had been alone with her patient. The damage was extensive. When Jacqueline had slapped a series of bandages across each knee she put her materials back in the purse, glared at the waiter, who tried to look as if he were somewhere else, and inquired, "Are you all right?"

"Oh, sure. It isn't the first time some idiot has pushed me off the curb. Only this time . . . well, I was lucky the taxi driver had good reflexes."

She spoke lightly, but the memory would not leave her in a hurry—the sick knowledge of her own helplessness as she looked up and saw the shining chrome of the grill bearing down on her.

"Anyway," she added, "I'd have gotten here if I had to crawl. It isn't every day I'm invited to lunch on the glamorous Via Veneto. We don't hang out here, it's too expensive."

"It's a tourist trap and an affront to the laboring masses," Jacqueline agreed placidly. She took the knitting out of her purse, studied it dubiously, shrugged, and began to knit.

"What is it?" Jean asked. "I don't want to sound nosy, but I can't see you as a doting grandmother, somehow."

"It's supposed to be a sweater," Jacqueline said doubtfully. "For an unfortunate baby of my acquaintance. Not a grandchild, no. I don't *think* I'm about to acquire one in the near future. The real function of this mess is to keep my hands occupied so I won't smoke."

"I think you just dropped a stitch."

"The baby won't know the difference," Jacqueline said callously. "And if you keep up those smart remarks, I'll let you do it. How is your work progressing?"

"I'm through, more or less. The reports aren't due till the end of the week, but I'm wrung dry."

With an air of guilt, Jacqueline shoved the knitting back into the purse and took out a pack of cigarettes.

"I gather the others aren't as far along as you are. I haven't seen them for the last few days."

"They've been working. But most of them were at Gino's, yesterday."

"The same as always?"

"The same . . . I promised myself I wasn't going to talk about it."

"It's supposed to be cathartic to talk it out. Whatever it is."

"Oh, you know what it is. It will be a long, long time," said Jean softly, "before I can close my eyes at night without seeing him the way he looked, just before—"

"Forget it. I mean it literally, even if it does sound cruel. The time will come when you won't think of it. And much sooner than you believe."

"But that bothers me too. Death is such a final thing, it ought to . . . well, affect the world more than it does. It doesn't seem right that a man can die and leave so small a mark behind. Even someone like Albert. He was a human being, after all, and now the gap just closes up, and it's as if no one was ever there."

The waiter returned, and Jacqueline ordered food. As soon as the waiter had left, she leaned forward.

"What's bothering you, Jean?"

"Just nerves, I guess. . . . Except—do you think the police really believe it was suicide?"

"Why not?"

"Well, yesterday Dana mentioned, oh so casually, that she had had a drink or two with Lieutenant di Cavallo." Jean made a grimace of disgust. "She calls him Giovanni."

Jacqueline lit another cigarette.

"My dear infant, there are reasons why a man might drink with Dana."

"Oh, sure. . . . I didn't know you smoked."

"I didn't." Jacqueline regarded her cigarette with hatred. "I quit six months ago."

"Have we driven you to smoking?"

"You aren't the most restful companions a middle-aged lady could have. Look what you've gotten me into since I arrived in Rome."

"You don't know the half of it. I think we're all cracking up."

"Why, what else has happened?"

"What hasn't?" Jean bit into her sandwich and looked at it with pleased surprise. "Hey, this place does have a slight edge over Gino's. . . . Well, for one thing, Dr. Scoville is back in town. Ahead of schedule."

"I know."

"You do?" Jean looked at the other woman, who smiled demurely. "Aha."

"Aha yourself. I'm having dinner with him tonight, but only because his revolting offspring have told him to leave them alone till Friday. The way Andy treats that poor man—"

"Yes, but he adores Andy. I feel sorry for Ann."

"He loves her too. But Andy is a rarity. It isn't often that a man has a child—and a son, at that—who is a conspicuous success in his own field. And on his own merit; there is a certain amount of nepotism in the academic world, but it doesn't carry a person far by itself."

"Ann is talented too," Jean said. "It would be ironic, wouldn't it, if she turned out to be the real genius in that family?"

"She would never let it show. She's been overshadowed by those two peacocks for too long. You must admit that Dr. Scoville is a very attractive man."

"Too old for me."

"I'm glad you think so. Dana doesn't. She was practically chasing him up the wall the other night."

"Mee-ow," Jean said, grinning. "What a pleasure it is to meet another feline female. Dana chases everything male. Even. . . ."

"Even who?"

"I do get mad at her," Jean burst out. "Poor José; I guess he knows how to handle it, but after all, he's made his choice, and it doesn't seem fair to make it harder for him."

"I doubt that Dana makes it harder," Jacqueline said drily. "She doesn't strike me as his type. Women who see men as a challenge to be overcome are usually pretty insecure."

"Sure, sure, I know all the patter. I guess Dana is upset. She

won't be back next year. Mama and Papa have cut off the funds.
She'll have to go to work."

"What a catastrophe."

"I'm crying."

They grinned nastily at each other, and then Jacqueline said,
"What's Ted's problem?"

"I think that girl he's engaged to is giving him a hard time.
When I asked him when she was coming, he said she couldn't
make it this year."

"Oh, dear."

"It may not be so bad at that. I think Ted and Ann could have
a thing going, if they'd let themselves."

"What a pair of gossips we are. . . . Would you like some
dessert?"

"No, thanks. What shall we do now?"

"Not much we can do. Everything is closed for the afternoon."

"We can walk down the Veneto and look in the windows."

"Good idea."

They strolled down the street, stopping at one of the newspaper kiosks, where Jacqueline bought several paperback books.
Jean viewed her choice of reading matter with amusement.

"Still reading murder mysteries? What low taste."

"That's one of the advantages of middle age. You don't have to
pretend you're cultured. But I'm willing to be cultivated, if you
can think of any intellectual sites that are open at this hour."

"There's a church not far from here that I'd love to show you.
It's my favorite baroque church."

"The Gesú?"

"You do read something besides murder mysteries. . . . No, it
isn't one of the big famous churches. It's a small place, a little
jewel box of a church, all rose and ivory and gold, like the inside
of a seashell by Fabergé. San Andrea al Quirinale. It's . . . well,
it's my place. The place where I go when I want to be reassured
about the world."

"I suppose many people have at least one place like that."

"Look at that gorgeous sweater," Jean exclaimed, stopping in
front of a window. "I'll bet it costs thirty thousand lire. . . . Yes,
it's funny, but we all have our own places here in Rome. Even
Dana has admitted that when she's depressed she goes and sits

on a rock in the Forum. That's not very original, but then neither is Dana.''

"What about Michael?''

Jean laughed sharply.

"Michael. Would you like to see his place? We're practically on top of it. And five will get you ten Michael is there right now.''

Jacqueline murmured agreement, and Jean led the way down the street. Her scraped knees were killing her by this time. They had almost reached the scene of her recent near-demise when she stopped under the grateful shade of a tall tree, and gestured.

"There it is.''

Jacqueline studied the stairs that led up to an undistinguished church facade.

"Michael in a church?''

"Just wait,'' Jean said. "Just wait.''

Jacqueline had read her guidebook; before they reached their final destination Jean saw comprehension begin to dawn on her face. But no amount of reading could prepare a viewer for the actuality.

It was an unpretentious place, only half a dozen small chapels opening off of a long, drab-painted corridor. The decorations were the source of the attraction. They were composed of human bones.

The long bones of arms and legs were piled in neat stacks, and human skulls formed the altars. Walls and ceilings were festooned with swags and scallops of vertebrae; a series of hip bones made a particularly ornamental pattern. Only the humbler members of the group had served as decorative sources; the more distinguished had been allowed to remain intact. They were present—some hanging from hooks, some lying flat in niches, all garbed in the drab-brown Capuchin habit. Their bony faces wore the same expression of fleshless laughter.

"Argh,'' Jacqueline said, and then smiled weakly at the single living member of the order, who was standing guard in the corridor. "I've read about this place. I had decided that under no circumstances would I visit it.''

"I'm sorry,'' Jean said. "It was a dirty trick, sneaking you in here. I loathe the place myself. I'll never forget the first time Michael brought me here. I had *not* read about it.''

"You should read Mark Twain's description," Jacqueline said. She glanced into the next chapel, which contained more of the same, and glanced quickly away. *The Innocents Abroad* is still one of the greatest travel books ever written. . . . I'd love to meet the man who thought this up."

"You can meet someone with the same type of mind," Jean said grimly. She gestured. "Look. What did I tell you?"

Michael was propped against the wall by the farthest chapel. He looked completely plastic and incapable of standing alone; the curve of his shoulders, back, and legs made a perfect arc. He was barefoot, and the shirt and flapping trousers he wore were of the same muddy hue as his tanned skin. He seemed to be unaware of them, and of the tourists who passed him, giggling or squealing according to their moods. His brooding profile, framed by the locks of his long dark hair, was bleached out by the artificial light.

"He looks frighteningly appropriate, standing there," Jacqueline said after a moment.

"Christ contemplating the damned in hell," Jean said. "Don't think Michael doesn't cultivate the resemblance. With a beard, he'd look like one of the paintings of Jesus."

"In the earliest representations of Christ, he is shown as young and beardless," Jacqueline said.

"Where do you learn these things?"

"My mind is a hopeless jumble of useless information," Jacqueline admitted. "Shall we steal quietly away?"

"He's seen us."

Michael's head turned. No other part of his body moved, but a smile spread slowly over his face.

"*Ciao,*" he said amiably. "What are you two doing here?"

"*Sssh,*" Jean said. "This is a chapel, isn't it?"

"It's okay; they know me here. Hey, Jake. How do you like it? This last chapel is the best. The three small skeletons are children of the nephew of some Pope or other."

After one incredulous glance Jacqueline turned her back on the arrangement Michael had been admiring.

"I hate it, if you really want to know. In fact, I'm leaving. If you two want to stay—"

"Not me," said Jean.

"I'll come with you, then," Michael said. "I guess I've been here long enough."

"How long have you been here?"

"Geez, I dunno. An hour, maybe."

They emerged into the sunlight and air of the street, and Jean took a deep breath. Michael shook himself, like a dog coming out of the water; even his expression had changed. He looked at Jean as if seeing her for the first time that day.

"What happened to you?"

"I fell."

"In the middle of the Piazza Barberini," Jacqueline added.

"Old accident-prone," Michael said. "That's the second time in two days you've fallen on your face, love. Maybe you need a keeper."

Jacqueline made an odd sound, halfway between a cough and a groan. Clearing her throat, she asked,

"The second time? What happened the first time?"

"She took a tumble down the stairs at her place. Some fool kid left a toy on the step."

"Trust me to step on it," Jean said. "If the light bulb on the landing hadn't burned out, I'd have been all right."

"The light was burned out," Jacqueline repeated.

"It happens all the time."

Michael had lost interest in the subject.

"What about a cup of coffee? If you have any bread, that is," he added disarmingly. "I'm flat broke."

"How were you planning to get home?" Jean inquired.

"Hitchhike. Walk. Who knows?"

"But we're supposed to meet the others at four," Jean said in exasperation. "Or weren't you planning to go to Ostia with us?"

They sat down at a table; outdoor cafés run three to a block on the Via Veneto. Michael ordered an espresso.

"Sure, I'm going," he said. "I can be back by . . . what time is it now? Two-thirty. Plenty of time."

"Oh, you're all going swimming," Jacqueline said.

"Yes. Want to come along?"

"You do not know to whom you speak," Jean said. "She has a pool in her apartment compound. She doesn't have to mingle with the hoi polloi on a public beach."

Jacqueline did not respond to this provocative comment, which was unlike her. Jean realized that she was looking peculiar too. Her cheeks were damp with perspiration, and her glasses had slipped clear down to the tip of her nose. Jean had come to regard the glasses as indicative; like the formal props of a *noh* play, they showed which of Jacqueline's multiple personalities was uppermost. When the glasses were seated firmly on the bridge of her nose, the efficient librarian was in command; when they perched farther down and Jacqueline peered hazily over them, she was confused, or pretending to be. Occasionally the glasses rode high on the top of Jacqueline's head, held in place by her thick hair. Then she was feeling giddy and eccentric. The absence of the glasses usually meant that Jacqueline was in a feminine mood and following Dorothy Parker's famous advice.

Meeting Jean's curious eyes, Jacqueline took a deep breath and pushed her glasses firmly back into place.

"You might as well use my pool, if you want to swim. Most of the neighbors are away for the summer. There won't be anyone else in the pool."

"Great," Michael said happily.

"And you a revolutionary," Jacqueline said.

"But that's what the revolution is all about," Michael explained. "Making the effete luxuries of the Establishment available to everybody."

Again Jacqueline was uncharacteristically silent. Watching her, Jean saw the spectacles sliding slowly down her patrician nose.

II

As the afternoon passed, Jean decided she had become too fanciful about Jacqueline's glasses. Her mood improved rapidly, and after they had collected the other Sinners, who were assembled at Andy's apartment, she became her usual cheerfully caustic self.

When Jacqueline remembered that she was supposed to have a dinner date, she called the hotel and insisted that Scoville join them. The archaeologist agreed at once; when Jean saw him in his swimming trunks she could understand why he didn't mind parading around in a crowd of younger males. He made Ted look like an adolescent and Michael like a hairy white ape. Andy was the only male in the group whose shoulders were as broad as his father's.

The water felt so heavenly that Jean soon forgot the sting of her scraped legs; floating serenely she watched the sky darken and the shapes of the pines turn to black silhouettes. She felt more relaxed than she had for days. The pool had a night-lighting system, and the water shone like liquid sapphire.

The others seemed to be enjoying themselves. Ted swam solemnly with his nose just above water like an anxious dog. Scoville, in hilarious spirits, strutted like a rooster under Dana's admiring eyes. Dana was doing more admiring than swimming; her bikini was obviously designed for a minimum of physical activity.

Jacqueline was not swimming. Jean assumed she was being nice to José, for whom mixed bathing was on the forbidden list. For some reason she couldn't pin down, she found Jacqueline's claim that she was a poor swimmer unconvincing. It couldn't be shyness that made Jacqueline refrain; the shorts and halter she wore displayed as much of Jacqueline as a regulation bathing suit would have done, and Jean knew by now that Jacqueline would have walked down the Via Veneto in the same costume, with perfect self-possession, if she had a good and sufficient reason for doing so.

Later in the evening Jean pulled herself out of the water to rest for a while, and sat down on the wet tiles near Jacqueline and José. Lazily studying the two familiar faces, she was struck by the fact that they were equally familiar. She had not known Jacqueline long; yet she felt she knew her well, although Jacqueline was not verbose about her personal history. She came from a small New England town, and was now employed at one of the big Eastern universities. Her children—boy and girl—were both of college age. The girl was in graduate school, working for a doctorate. Jacqueline's father, a retired contractor, lived in California with one of Jacqueline's brothers. A prosaic, unvarnished history, so far as it went—and to Jean it did not go far in explaining the enigma that was Jacqueline. But then, she wondered dreamily, how many people can be adequately accounted for by a factual biographical paragraph or two? Perhaps some of Jacqueline's personality traits had been produced by the omissions in her biography. The most conspicuous omission was the absence of any reference to a husband. Jean assumed such a person had existed, but whether Jacqueline's silence was the result of grief for a beloved spouse prematurely deceased, or of contempt for a resented spouse belatedly divorced, she couldn't even guess.

As she watched, there was a howl of laughter from the far end of the pool and Andy surfaced, holding aloft a small dripping scrap of cloth. Shouting threats, Dana struck out toward him. Andy vanished, still holding his trophy.

"I knew the top of that bathing suit was going to come off sooner or later," Jean said sourly.

"There goes *il professore dottore* Scoville," murmured José, as the lean brown body cut the water in a spectacular dive from the small island in the deep end of the pool.

Jacqueline laughed.

"You two are a pair of prudes," she said.

"But Jean is a prude by nature," José said, smiling. "I, as your English adage says, have only acquired prudery. And it was not easy, I can tell you."

"I am not a prude," Jean said, without heat. "I just—Look at that, will you! Like father, like son. . . ."

"The father wins," said José. "Andy has only the lady's bathing suit. *Il professore* has the lady. . . . Ah, yes; and what has happened to the lights at that end of the pool, I wonder? It is very dark there. . . ."

"The *portiere,*" Jacqueline said resignedly. "Someone has bribed him, I suppose. It always happens when there's a party. Look at that old wretch ogling Dana."

Jean had already noticed the *portiere,* an elderly man with a gray moustache. Dana wasn't the only one he ogled. After he had switched on the lights, there was no reason for him to linger; but he did, his mouth hanging open appreciatively as he watched the girls.

Jacqueline started to say something, but Jean didn't wait to hear what it was. She plunged into the pool, sending a spray of water high into the air. She swam in steady strokes toward the island and clung to it, her arm hooked over the edge of the stone coping. Dana had recovered the top of her suit and was making a big production of getting it back on. Someone—Michael—was behind her, tying the strings . . . or not tying them, as the case might be. There was a lot of splashing and yelling, as Dana tried to preserve her modesty by staying underwater—or tried not to stay underwater. . . .

A head popped up, right under her nose, and Jean let out a squeal. In her dark bathing cap and suit Ann was almost invisible, except for her face. How different people's faces look without hair framing and softening them, Jean thought.

"Having fun?" she asked.

"Wonderful. This is nice of Jacqueline."

"What does your father think of her?"

"Oh, Sam is quite captivated," Ann said coolly. "She's handling him very well; nothing fascinates him like indifference."

Jean had heard equally cynical appraisals from other offspring, but coming from demure Ann, this remark did surprise her.

"Hey!" Standing up in the water like a seal, Andy called them. "We're playing hide and seek. Get moving, you two. I'm 'it,' and I'm after Jean. . . ."

He disappeared under the water and Jean, who knew his talent for breath holding, got moving as requested. The game was a success; it gave scope for every variety of acrobatics, practical jokes, and ingenuity. Finally everyone had been "it" but Jean. Ted was the poorest swimmer of the group, and had gotten caught most often, but he didn't seem to mind. Since they had all made it safely back to base, represented by Jacqueline and José, the last time, Ted was "it" again.

Diving down, Jean struck out for the dark end of the pool. The shadowy area behind the island made a good hiding place. When she came up for air the pool looked uncanny; there wasn't a person, or part of one, in sight, only the rippling blue water. Then a head popped up—sleek, dark. It was Michael. He took a deep breath and disappeared again. Ted was the next to come to the surface. He was wheezing and blowing; Jacqueline leaned out and shouted something. Jean caught a few words—something about "too tired."

Ted shook his head and resubmerged. His feet flopped agitatedly for a few seconds before they disappeared. Jean decided she had better go under and keep an eye out for him; with the lights reflecting off the water she couldn't see what was going on under the surface.

She had no warning, except the smallest whisper of sound, and that might have had any number of causes—a lizard scuttling across the pine-needle-covered ground, or the drop of an acorn. Then the darkness solidified and fell in on her. She had a moment of intense pain, but it was soon over; she never felt the water closing in over her head, filling her mouth and lungs.

III

The room was almost dark when she awoke from a nap she had had no intention of taking. Sitting up too suddenly, she clutched her spinning head and tried to orient herself. Slowly memory returned. She was in Jacqueline's apartment, and apparently Jacqueline had slipped her a Mickey in—

"No," Jean said aloud.

The word came out as a croak. Jean collapsed back onto the pillow. Her throat hurt, but that pain was minor compared to the throbbing headache that clamped over her skull. What had happened? This wasn't the first time she had awakened in Jacqueline's apartment; it was not the day Albert . . . or was it? Had all the rest been a vivid, lifelike dream?

A light went on. It was a small, dim light, but it made Jean's head pound. She closed her eyes with a wordless mutter of protest.

"I was beginning to think that fool doctor was wrong," said a familiar voice. "Apparently you don't have concussion. Your head must be as hard as a rock."

"It feels cracked," said Jean thickly. She opened her eyes cautiously. It wasn't as bad this time. Jacqueline's head and shoulders cast a shadow over her face. "What happened?"

Jacqueline sat down on the edge of the bed. She was wearing a thin blue negligee, sleeveless and long, belted in around her waist, and her hair was loose, flowing down her back. She looked rather lovely—except for her face. It was colorless and hard, with lines in it Jean had never noticed before. The green eyes were slitted, like a cat's, and dull, without the gleam of humor that normally brightened them.

"What happened?" Jean repeated.

Jacqueline lit a cigarette.

"Do you remember anything?"

"We were playing hide and seek; Ted was 'it.' I remember, yes —I was in the dark part, watching Ted, and then . . . that's all." She looked helplessly at Jacqueline. "I don't remember anything else. What hit me?"

Jacqueline blew out a neat smoke ring and contemplated it critically.

"Apparently a chunk of that stone coping came loose and landed square on your head."

"But how—"

"You weren't hanging on to it—trying to pull yourself out of the pool?"

"I don't think so. I can't remember. I feel so awful. . . ."

"I imagine you do. José pumped a couple of gallons of water out of you."

"José?"

"Mmmm. I gather the rest of you kid him when he tells you what a good swimmer he is. I couldn't swear to that, but he's an expert at resuscitation. And fast. If he hadn't been. . . ."

She sat half turned away, smoking with quick, nervous puffs. Jean stared at her, conscious of an odd sensation in her stomach which had nothing to do with the water she had swallowed.

"I almost died," she said in a small voice. "Didn't I?"

Jacqueline swung around to face her, and Jean saw that the hand holding the cigarette was shaking.

"Yes, and you had a lot of nerve almost doing it in my pool. I'm too old for that sort of thing. It takes too much out of me."

"I'm sorry," Jean said meekly.

Jacqueline made a wild gesture of disgust, and then they both laughed—not hilariously, but they laughed. Jacqueline stood up and said, in a calmer voice,

"I'd better reassure the death watch. They've worn a hole in the rug pacing, and they're getting on my nerves."

"Is everybody still here?"

"No, just Ted and José. The two," Jacqueline mused, "with the greatest degree of social conscience? Anyhow, they insisted on staying, and I was glad to have the moral support. Ann wanted to stay, but she was a shaking wreck, so Andy took her home. And somehow or other Dana convinced Sam Scoville that her hand needed holding, so they went off together."

"I might have known."

"Sam was very touched at her affectionate nature," Jacqueline said drily.

"And Michael?"

"He just . . . left. As soon as we were sure you were going to be all right."

She went out, leaving the door open. Jean heard the murmur of voices, and the sound of the elevator coming up. When it had descended again, with her friends, Jacqueline came back.

"Could you eat anything, or does the idea repel you?"

"I could drink something. My throat hurts."

"I'll see what I can find."

She went out, and Jean dragged her pillows together and sat up. She felt fairly good, except for the headache. Experimentally she wriggled one toe, and watched it move with a new interest. How beautiful it was to be able to wriggle a toe—to move all the muscles of her body and feel them respond—to sense her breath moving in and out, and the pumping of her heart.

The sound of the elevator distracted her from these pensive thoughts, and instinctively she stiffened. She made herself relax; it was ridiculous to be so nervous. There were other apartments in the building, after all.

But the elevator stopped at their floor and the door buzzer sounded. Jacqueline's footsteps approached the door. Instead of opening it, she called out, "Who is it?"

Jean didn't hear the reply, but evidently Jacqueline was satisfied; the door opened and a murmured colloquy followed. Footsteps tapped down the uncarpeted hall.

"Michael," Jean said.

He stood in the doorway staring at her vacantly.

"You *are* all right," he said. "You're not dead."

"I told you she was all right." Jacqueline glided up behind him and came into the room, carrying a glass. "Why don't you go home and go to bed? You can't squat in the shrubbery all night; the *portiere* may understand, but the other tenants won't.''

"All right, I'll go home," Michael said meekly. "I just wanted to make sure she was all right."

"I think we've established that fact."

"Hey, Jean. What happened?"

"Why ask me? I seem to have missed all the fun."

"Something hit you on the head?"

"So they tell me."

"You really don't remember anything?"

"For God's sake!" Jean yelled, and then clutched her head. "Get out of here," she mumbled. "That's all I need, you hanging around asking stupid questions."

"She really doesn't remember a thing, Michael," Jacqueline said.

"Amnesia?"

Standing straight and slim by the bed, Jacqueline looked him up and down with dispassionate interest. He was a pathetic sight, unkept and haggard; apparently Jacqueline's description of his whereabouts had been literal, for he was covered with twigs and dried leaves and dust.

"No," Jacqueline said, after a moment. "This is not a case of temporary amnesia, Michael. Something came down out of the dark and knocked her cold. That's all that happened, and that's all she'll ever remember."

"Uh-huh," Michael said. "I get it. You both ought to go to bed, get some sleep," he added, looking at them disapprovingly.

"As soon as you get out of here," Jean began, her voice rising dangerously.

Jacqueline took Michael by the arm and led him out.

The elevator door had barely closed before the phone rang. There was an extension in the bedroom. Jacqueline took the call there, with a muttered exclamation in good gutter Italian.

"Pronto!" she yelled into the mouthpiece, and then her frown smoothed out. "Oh, Andy. Yes, yes, she's fine. No. Really; she's awake now. Want to talk to her?"

She handed Jean the phone.

"Hello," Jean croaked. "Andy, I don't want to talk, my throat hurts."

"I know, honey, and I'm sorry to call at this ungodly hour; but Ann's staggering around here like Medea—or do I mean Medusa?—accusing herself of failing you in the breach and chickening out, and various other crimes. If I could tell her you'll live—"

"You can't get rid of me that easily."

"I didn't realize your head was so hard," Andy said. Then his voice changed. The next words were so soft she could barely hear them, but they made a shiver go down her back. "I'm going to kill that cretinous *portiere.*"

"It wasn't his fault."

"He's supposed to keep the place in repair. It was criminal negligence, to say the least."

"Was that really what it was, a piece of the coping? I didn't see a thing."

"Michael found the chunk on the bottom of the pool."

"Oh. Well, all's well that ends well," Jean said inanely.

"Right. I won't talk anymore. Good night, darling."

He hung up, leaving Jean staring at the telephone.

"Darling?" she repeated.

"Your near-demise has brought out all sorts of tender feelings," Jacqueline said. She took the telephone and put it back on the stand, but she kept her hand on it. "I wonder how long. . . ." As Jean stared, she began to count. "Forty-one, forty-two . . . not bad."

The phone rang.

"Hello," Jacqueline said. "Oh, yes, Sam, is it really you? It was good of Andy to call you; naturally you were concerned. Oh? Oh, she is . . . of course she's upset. I do think it's terribly sweet of you to be so kind to her. . . . Well, you just tell the poor little thing that Jean is fine, and that I am going to blow Giorgio up, personally, tomorrow morning. . . . Yes, evidently that was what did the damage. Jean didn't see a thing, just felt the blow. . . . All right, Sam. Yes, you too."

She hung up and turned to face Jean, who was having trouble stifling her rising laughter.

"Talk about women being catty," she chuckled. "Dana wouldn't care if I were dead and buried. The professor just wanted you to know they had spent the night together."

"You think so?"

Jacqueline wasn't laughing. Absently she reached for another cigarette, lit it, and blew out a cloud of smoke. It wreathed her face like fog; and from the fog Jacqueline's voice said,

"That was the last. All of your friends have been heard from. Now which of them was it, do you think, who tried to kill you tonight?"

CHAPTER SIX

*U*nemotionally Jean considered the question. It should have aroused a cry of disbelief or denial, or, at the least, of horror. Instead it seemed to crystallize a fact she had known, without admitting it, for a long time.

"I don't know," she said.

Abruptly Jacqueline sat down.

"Well, thank God for that."

"For what? That I don't know?"

"No, no. For accepting the idea. I was afraid you would think me hysterical. I keep forgetting how intelligent you are, under that Alice in Wonderland exterior. You look so blasted young. . . ."

"And I thought I was the one who was imagining things. Jacqueline, I'm not that clumsy, really I'm not. One accident, even two . . . but three in a row. . . ."

"You honestly don't remember anything about tonight?" Jacqueline lit another cigarette. The incessant chain-smoking was the only sign of nerves she displayed; her hands were steady and her face showed only alert concentration. "I backed up your claim of ignorance as a matter of policy; obviously you didn't want anyone to get the idea that you suspect the identity of your attacker. But do you?"

"No, honestly. It could have been anybody. It was a madhouse; I don't suppose anyone kept track of anyone else. . . . Oh! You said José—"

Jacqueline shook her head reluctantly.

"Even José. He had left, to go up to the apartment for a minute. I didn't notice him after that, till he grabbed you away from me and tossed you down and started pushing your ribs around."

"Away from. . . . Now it all comes out. Were you the one who dragged me out of the pool?"

"Why do you think I was sitting on the sidelines like a dainty old chaperone?" Jacqueline snapped. "I was watching you; and a heck of a job it was, too, the way everyone was milling around. But in my hastily formed opinion you were safer in a small pool than you would have been in the ocean at Ostia."

"That is a point," Jean said slowly. "Jacqueline, you aren't a dainty old anything, you're a witch. How long have you had this suspicion?"

"Since Michael mentioned your first 'accident,' right after I had seen the scars of the second. I wasn't sure, of course; how could I be? But I started to get a nasty cold feeling in the pit of my stomach, and when you mentioned going swimming, it occurred to me what a perfect setup that would be for another accident. I couldn't warn you, I was afraid you would think I had flipped. All I could do was transfer your activities to a place where I thought I could keep an eye on you. When I think how nearly I failed, even then. . . ."

"You saved my life," Jean said snuffily.

"Yes, well, let's both sit and cry about it, shall we? Anyhow," Jacqueline said grimly, "you'd better save your thanks. You aren't in the clear yet. And you won't be until we figure out who is doing this, and why."

"The 'why' is pretty obvious, isn't it?"

"Yes, in a way. In another way—no, curse it! You're thinking of Albert's death. So am I; it more or less rises up and hits you in the face. But don't you see that that assumption only raises another, stickier problem? You were the one to find Albert. Not only was he capable of communication when you found him, but he actually did communicate. That's such a classic situation it's almost corny. But in every thriller I've ever read, the witness is only in danger while he remains silent. The murderer has to shut him up before he can spill the essential clue. But you have already spilled it! Just to keep the record straight—Albert did not say anything, or write anything other than what you have already described to me—and to all your friends, and the entire police department?"

"No."

"And there was no object in that room which might have provided a clue to a hypothetical murderer? No item—no discrepancy, or inconsistency—that the police could have missed, but that might have significance to someone else?"

"No." Jean shook her head. It still hurt, but she was far too preoccupied to notice a minor thing like physical pain. The relief of being able to talk about the subject that had harassed her subconscious was enormous. She also had a lively interest in the topic; it involved no less a matter than her life or death. "Don't you think I've been over it and over it in my mind? I can still see that room vividly when I close my eyes; it was absolutely bare, except for—him. He said nothing, he wrote nothing, except what I've already described—as you say, to half the city of Rome. They didn't even believe me," she added glumly.

"Another good point. In attempting to silence you, the murderer runs the risk of drawing attention to the very thing he wants to hide. He's obviously a capable person; Albert's death was neatly planned. Why would he take such a risk unless you present a very real and immediate danger to him?"

"You keep saying 'him.' "

"The standard male chauvinist pronoun of indefinite reference," Jacqueline said, with a smile that was not very convincing.

"I'd love it to be Dana," Jean said wistfully.

Jacqueline burst out laughing.

"Well, thank goodness you've got some gumption," she said approvingly. "If you collapsed into a quivering jelly of terror it would present a problem."

"I'm really scared," Jean said in a low voice. "I realized tonight how much—how much I want to go on being alive."

"Then it's up to us to keep you that way," Jacqueline said

briskly. "And we're really starting from scratch, Jean. It must be one of the six. But I have no idea which one; not even a suspicion."

"You're sure it's one of them?"

"Well, let's be logical. Conceivably Albert might have been killed by an outsider—some private grudge. The exits at the church weren't closed until sometime after the attack took place and the killer could have escaped into the anonymity of the street before the alarm was sounded. He would have no reason to linger—unless he was one of the Seven Sinners, who were following a schedule. On that basis I eliminate the other tourists who were caught in the net that day. The lieutenant isn't as casual as he sounds. He will have checked them all."

"That's reasonable. But the killer didn't plan on my finding Albert. He might have lain there for hours before anyone found him. We'd have all cleared out by then."

"True, but irrelevant. Albert would have been identified eventually; his connection with all of you would have been traced, and the police would have discovered that you were there, on the spot, at the time of his death. The murderer's plan was to make his death look like suicide, and it succeeded admirably."

"Right."

"None of this knocks out the possibility of an outsider having committed the crime. But the attempts on you are something else again. I'll grant that an unknown party could be following you around, shoving you under cars, and turning out lights in strategic places. But tonight there was no one in the pool except your friends."

"And Dr. Scoville."

"And," Jacqueline repeated, "Dr. Scoville. . . . Oh, no, that really is farfetched."

"Still, so far as opportunity is concerned, we have to include him. It wouldn't be hard to set up an alibi. . . . Look here, Jake, he said something about taking a train the next day, but how do we know he did? Suppose he took a plane instead, later in the day? It would be almost impossible to prove, one way or the other; he wouldn't need his passport for travel within Italy."

"What about motive?"

"Oh, motive be damned. We haven't even started on that yet."

"Okay, let's include him," Jacqueline said callously. "That brings our suspect list back to the original seven. I'm assuming you wouldn't half drown yourself just to add verisimilitude to an otherwise unconvincing narrative."

"Bald and unconvincing narrative."

"I'm glad to see your generation reads something besides Leonard Cohen and *Steppenwolf*. . . . Have we now limited our suspects to seven?"

"I know it's unlikely that an outsider could have sneaked in," Jean said stubbornly. "But that pool area was dark. It isn't impossible, Jake."

"You are missing the point," said Jacqueline, reaching for another cigarette. "An outsider might pursue you. But how does he know he should? No one except your friends—and the police—know that Albert was alive when you found him."

Jean was silent. Jacqueline went on, in a more kindly tone,

"I know you don't want to admit it. You're fond of all your friends—even Dana, in a fashion. But the facts are inescapable."

"I know. And I appreciate your effort to make this seem like an intellectual game. But it isn't a game."

"It's a dangerous game. As soon as it's morning I'm going to call our friend the lieutenant."

"You can't do that."

"Why not, for heaven's sake?"

"They won't believe you. The lieutenant has already decided Albert's death was suicide, and that suits him fine. He isn't going to reopen the case on the basis of what has happened to me. We may be sure that these accidents weren't accidents, but he'll just laugh. Anyhow, what could he do about it?"

"The police could check alibis," Jacqueline said stubbornly. "There have been three separate attacks on you; surely they could weed out some of our suspects by finding out where they were at the time—"

"At what time? You were on the spot tonight; can you eliminate anyone? The stair incident is the vaguest of all; it might even have been coincidence. We don't know when the light was turned off, and when the toy was left on the stair. The car incident—we already know that Michael was in the neighborhood at the right time. Dana and Ted were both downtown that day; she planned to do some shopping, and Ted was having lunch with a man who lives near the Spanish Steps. That's only a couple of blocks from the Piazza Barberini. I'll bet the others will be just as hard to pin down.''

"It's interesting," Jacqueline said. "My generation automatically turns to the police when anything goes wrong; yours has an instinctive mistrust. Still, you have a point."

"They can't do anything we can't do," Jean argued. She pulled herself up in bed, fired with new energy. "Jake, this must go back to Albert's death. If we could prove that wasn't suicide—"

"How?"

"Let's think! There must be something."

Jacqueline settled herself more comfortably.

"There is nothing in the physical circumstances of his death," she said thoughtfully. "The weapon was found nearby, where it could have fallen from his hand. The nature of the wound was such that it could have been self-inflicted. Di Cavallo asked whether he was right- or left-handed, and nodded in that smug way of his; so clearly that part of it made sense."

"He was right-handed," Jean said. "Which means that he could have been killed by a right-handed person standing behind him. If you were planning to cut someone's throat, that's where you would stand. To avoid being covered with blood."

Jacqueline gave a look of mingled admiration and surprise.

"You're a cold-blooded little creature, aren't you?"

"I can be girlish and squeamish when I want to be," Jean said grimly. "But, as we agreed, this isn't a game. . . . Obviously the murderer stood behind him. You don't advance on a victim waving a knife; you come up behind his back. You gain the element of surprise, you avoid incriminating bloodstains, and you produce the kind of wound that looks like suicide. If I can think of these things, a clever murderer surely would."

"There would have to be some blood. On the killer's hands and arms."

"It was a hot day, everyone wore short sleeves, or none. And there is a stream of running water in that room. The overflow from the conduit in the wall."

"Good Lord," Jacqueline muttered. "I'd forgotten that. . . . I thought perhaps the murderer had chosen that room because of its remote location, but maybe there was another reason. What about fingerprints?"

"I don't think much of the fuzz, but I'm sure they would have looked for fingerprints."

"And found only Albert's. But the murderer couldn't have worn gloves without being rather conspicuous."

"He could have stuffed them in his pocket and gotten rid of them later. Nobody searched us."

"We don't seem to be making much progress," Jacqueline said. "What about alibis for Albert's death?"

"Hopeless. We were all more or less lost. Besides, do they know when the attack took place? Albert didn't die until later."

"Yet that avenue needs exploring. I can ask, in a casually nosy fashion. It seems to me that Ann and Ted were together much of the time."

"Yes, but alibis like that aren't any good. Michael and Dana were together part of the time too; but they might lie for each other. Actually, both of them were on the lowest level only minutes before I found Albert."

"I," said Jacqueline, "have sort of an alibi. Don't look so surprised; if you haven't suspected me, you're pretty dim. I got tired of your bloody ruins and went up to look at those lovely frescoes in the chapel of St. Catherine. The priest selling tickets must have seen me go up, and anyone going down would have to pass him. When I went back down to look for you, Ann and Ted were talking to the priest on duty. If they had been there for any length of time. . . ."

Jean shook her head.

"We're on the wrong track. The police could do this sort of thing much more effectively than we can, and I'm sure we can't narrow it down to a single suspect. It's motive we ought to explore. Why would anybody want to kill Albert? That is the one aspect of the case we can investigate better than the police. We know the people involved."

"It's also the weakest part of the case. If you know anything about murders, real or fictional, you know that people have killed for reasons which would strike you and me as ludicrously inadequate. That's why motive is, quite rightly, a secondary consideration in police investigations."

They stared at one another in despairing silence. Then Jacqueline got up and went to the French doors onto the balcony. She threw back the heavy wooden shutters. The sun had just lifted above the horizon. A pearly hush lay upon the drowsy world, and through the still cool air a burst of bird song rippled.

For several seconds Jacqueline stayed at the window, her arms raised. With an art critic's eye for line and color, Jean commended the pose. The pale sunlight on Jacqueline's unbound hair was like a wash of gold.

Then the poised statue turned and said in a flat, weary voice, "We're both shot. Maybe we can think better after we get some sleep. There are twin beds in this room; do you mind if I—"

"Why should I mind?"

"I hope you don't. Because, whether you mind or not, from now on I'm sticking to you like the proverbial limpet. You are moving into this apartment, and you are not going out of it without me."

"We may be all wrong," Jean said. "About everything."

"Maybe. But I'm not taking any chances. Tomorrow we'll start detecting."

"If we only knew what to detect!"

"Don't worry about that," Jacqueline said coolly. "I'll think of something."

II

"Seven saints?" José said. "Where did you get that notion? Oh. . . ." There was the slightest possible check in his voice. "From Albert, of course."

They were standing in front of the altar of Santa Cecilia, looking at Maderno's famous statue of the saint. In the past forty-eight hours Jacqueline had carried on a mad rush of sightseeing, dragging with her every available member of the Seven. Only four of them were with her that day; Dana had flatly refused to come, and Andy was barricaded in his room with coffee pots and ice bags, and Ann in devoted attendance. The résumés were due in two more days.

Jean knew why Jacqueline was doing this; at least she knew

what the motive was, even if she couldn't understand the underlying logic. Santa Cecilia was an old church, and it contained
some lovely things, but it was not one of the major attractions in
the city.

"I guess it does sound silly," Jacqueline admitted ingenuously.
"But you know, I got to counting, and I did find seven of them."

"Santa Cecilia being one?" Ted regarded the statue with interest. "Do you know that after they cut her head off, she lay for
three days on the floor of her bath, fully sensible, and joyfully
awaiting her crown of martyrdom?"

Jean snickered, and José smiled even as he shook his head.

"Ted, you do not play fair. You quote from a popular account
of the saint's life. Books written for children always sound foolish
when they are quoted to intelligent adults."

"Anyhow, you're misquoting," Jacqueline said severely. Taking
a small book from her purse, she brandished it. "This is the
Penguin *Dictionary of Saints,* and the writer is quite skeptical of
such legends."

"May I?" José held out his hand, and Jacqueline gave him the
book. He leafed through it. "Yes, here we are. 'Sentenced to be
stifled to death in the bathroom of her own house, the heat and
steam failed to suffocate her, so a soldier was sent to behead her.
He struck three ineffective blows, and she was left to linger three
days before she died.' Improbable, but not as ridiculous as your
version, Ted."

Jean glanced at Michael, who stood a little to one side. He was
staring steadily at the statue, which lay in a glass-fronted case
under the altar.

"Oh, I don't mind these stories," Ted said tolerantly. "They
are pretty stories—if you discount the basic Freudian hangup
about virginity. . . ." He dodged the fist José raised, and went
on, "The part I like best is the description of finding the saint's
body."

"That isn't in my book," Jacqueline said.

"Good, then I can tell you. In 1599, the tomb of the saint, in
the catacomb, was opened. I do not know why. They were a morbid lot, your ancestors. . . . A great party of dignitaries was present, including the artist Stefano Maderno. And behold, there lay
the body of the saint, uncorrupted, unchanged; her garments

still modestly arranged, as you see them in the statue, her averted face veiled. The body was brought here and reintombed; and Maderno ran home and made his statue—a literal copy, according to his own account, of the actual body of the saint as she looked fifteen centuries after her death."

They all turned to contemplate the life-sized marble. The figure was that of a young woman lying on her side, with her knees bent and her limp hands gracefully disposed. The features were indistinct, but around the neck the line made by the executioner's sword was clearly visible.

"Pathetic," Michael said, breaking his own prolonged silence. "Bathetic. Schmaltz. Kitsch. Let's go, it's cold in here."

The others followed him. Blinking in the sunlight of the portico, Ted turned to Jacqueline.

"What are you doing now, collecting virgin saints? We have seen—yes, six churches." He turned his wide, innocent stare on Jacqueline. "What is the seventh?"

"Santa Prisca," said Jacqueline coolly.

Michael let out a howl.

"Good God, that's clear out on the Aventine. You don't want to see that one, Jake. It's a drag. And it's probably closed. And besides—"

"It's a beautiful day," Jacqueline said, settling her glasses firmly on the bridge of her nose. "And the Aventine is beautiful on a beautiful day. And besides—"

"Well?"

"If you're broke again, which I suspect you are, you'll have to stick with me or you won't get any lunch."

"Thanks be to God, I have no such problem," said Ted piously. "I will see you all tomorrow, at Gino's?"

"Maybe not," Jacqueline said. "I'm going sightseeing again."

"Not more churches?" Michael said pathetically.

"Oh, yes. Tomorrow we start on the seven pilgrimage churches. There were," Jacqueline said sweetly, "seven, weren't there?"

III

"You're flipping," Andy said. "Or else you're going in for numerology. Why the passionate interest in septets?"

He looked, that evening, as close to collapse as a robust, tanned young specimen can look. There were circles, not only under his eyes, but all around them.

"Stop talking and eat," his father ordered.

Obediently Andy shoved a huge forkful of spaghetti into his mouth. The others watched as he tucked in the dangling ends, *alla italiano*. As soon as Andy became vocal again, he said mildly,

"Not that I'm not proud of my skill in eating spaghetti, but do you all have to stare at me? I have eaten before, I am eating now, and I will eat again. It's no big deal."

"You may have eaten, but not recently," Ann said, looking at him anxiously. "We ought to thank Jacqueline for insisting on taking us out to supper. You can't go on working without food or sleep. I'm going to slip a couple of those sleeping pills in your coffee tonight."

"I do thank Jacqueline," said Scoville, with a smile at that lady, who dimpled and batted her eyelashes. She was not wearing her glasses. "But you should have called me earlier, Ginger. I'd rather have this young idiot lose every fellowship under the sun than get sick."

"Like hell you would," said Andy, through another mouthful. "Better dead than dishonored, that's the motto in this family. . . . Okay, that takes care of the appetizer. While we wait for the next course, may I change the subject to something more interesting than my personal habits? I repeat: why the passionate interest in sevens, Jake?"

Fumbling in her purse in search of cigarettes, Jacqueline didn't answer at first. They were eating at a trattoria in Trastevere, one of the few that had escaped the tourism craze. Twilight had fallen, the soft blue dusk of a Roman summer; and they sat outside, with a thick hedge separating them from the bustle of the pedestrian traffic, and an awning protecting them overhead. Between the pots in which the bushes of the hedge were planted, a lean, suspicious cat wove in and out, casing the diners for potential handouts.

"Mystic number," Jacqueline said finally. Triumphantly she produced a battered pack of cigarettes; Scoville flung himself across the table to light one for her, and she went on, "It keeps cropping up, doesn't it? Saints, churches, hills—"

"And sinners," Andy interrupted. "Don't beat around the bush. You're trying to figure out Albert's last words, aren't you? There's another seven for you, by the way—the Seven Last Words of Christ."

He looked at Jean. Everyone else looked at Jean—the three Scovilles, Jacqueline and Michael. Michael hadn't been invited, but he was there anyway. It was hard to get rid of Michael. He was too big to evict physically, and too obtuse to notice hints. If his ubiquity had increased, his loquacity had not. Tonight he sat in silence, his eyes moving from one speaker to the next; he had slid down as far as the straight chair would permit him to do, with his legs stretched out. He was feeding long strings of spaghetti to the cat, a lean black-and-white tom, which absorbed the pasta like a true Roman.

"I thought you didn't believe me," Jean said.

"Of course we do," Ann said, a little too quickly.

"So maybe I imagined it," Jean said defiantly. "No one else saw anything. There wasn't a sign of any mark left when the police got there."

"A lot of heavy flat feet scuffled through the room," Andy said. "According to you, the marks were indistinct to begin with."

Jean looked at him gratefully.

"You believe me."

"We all believe you," Ann said. "But perhaps you misinterpreted what you saw. The last reflex contraction of muscles—"

"All right, Ginger," Scoville said. "What difference does it make? If the gesture had meaning, it is lost forever now. The vagaries of a dying man—"

The waiter brought the next course, and for a few moments they were all quiet, sampling the entrees. Then Andy said,

"Maybe so. But it's bound to haunt you, isn't it? What did he want to say all that badly? Why can't we see it?"

"It's been driving me crazy," Jacqueline admitted. "I have that type of inconsequential mind. . . . But I'll be darned if I can think of anything."

"You can't? I can think of only too many things. This city is swamped with sevens. Albert's saints, the pilgrimage churches, and the hills. . . . There's a good quiz question for you. Name the seven hills."

The others looked blank, but Jacqueline appeared to be enjoying the game. She began counting on her fingers.

Scoville cleared his throat.

"I fail to see—"

"There are lots more," Andy grinned. "How about the Seven Churches of Asia? Ephesus, Smyrna, Pergamus—"

Michael assumed an upright position with such abruptness that the cat, who had learned to suspect any violent movements, vanished behind a shrub.

"Of all the crap . . . you might as well try to find some application in Beethoven's *Seventh Symphony*. Or in seven-card stud."

"Seven Wonders of the World," Jacqueline contributed. "None of them in Rome, though. . . ."

"Seven Sages," Jean said wildly. "The Seven Sleepers of Ephesus. Seven Against Thebes. The Seven Deadly—"

She stopped speaking abruptly, and Andy, who had been watching her, said mildly,

"Your acquaintance with sin is purely nominal, my lamb. But it makes a suggestive list, doesn't it? Seven sins and seven sinners. They're such unusual sins, not at all the kind of thing you might expect. My favorite is Languid Indifference—the original Greek *acidia* sounds better. . . . Anger is Michael, of course, and Pride —spiritual pride—must be José's sin. Gluttony doesn't seem appropriate to any one of us, offhand."

"Me," Jean said. She could not have said why, but she didn't like the turn the conversation had taken. "I adore food. I'd be a little fat girl if Vanity weren't stronger than Gluttony."

"Sorry, but Vanity is not one of the Seven," Andy said. "Vainglory, yes; but it isn't the same thing. Now Unchastity—"

"Stop it," Ann said. "It isn't nice to talk about someone who isn't here to defend herself."

There was a general explosion of laughter, and Andy said fondly,

"Very good. That's one of the few catty remarks I've ever heard you make. Now, as the antithesis of the Seven Sins there are also Seven Virtues—"

"I think we've had enough sevens," Scoville interrupted. "Not only are your ideas getting farfetched, but you are ignoring one vital fact."

"What's that?" Jacqueline asked meekly.

"None of your categories is ordered. The number seven can only refer to one member of a septet. How do you know which, if the lists aren't numbered?"

"Good gracious," Jacqueline murmured. "I declare, that is true, isn't it? How clever you are, Sam."

Scoville expanded visibly; and Jean, after one look at Jacqueline's studiously sweet expression, bent over and pretended she was calling the cat.

IV

"Dana can't make it," Michael reported. "She says she has to get some work done."

"You sound as if you don't believe her," Jean said.

"I think she's working on dear old Dad Scoville. And vice versa."

"I thought he had better taste."

Michael kicked a stone. It rattled along the sidewalk and smacked into a tree.

"Your girl friend turned him down. He's on the rebound—or trying to show her he doesn't give a damn."

"Oh," Jean said disinterestedly. She turned her back on the splendid tree-lined boulevard and stared out across the space beyond. It was sunk below the modern street level, and its expanse was filled with a clutter that would have struck a modern city planner as extremely unsightly. Fragments of brick walls, covered with ivy and half veiled by weeds, rose up in unconnected sections. Columns of all sizes and shapes and conditions stood randomly about: columns of white marble and dark-red granite, half columns and lonely column bases, columns in rows and circles and colonnades. The Roman Forum, enclosed on the far side by the tree-darkened slope of the Palatine, was almost as crowded that day as it had been in its glory, when merchants and senators and slaves thronged its shops.

"Who are we waiting for?" Michael asked.

"Nobody asked you to wait. In fact, nobody asked you to come in the first place."

"Dana told me to tell you—"

"And how did you happen to know Dana was meeting us here?"

Jean turned, leaning against the iron fence that kept impetuous and impecunious tourists from leaping down among the ruins. "I keep thinking somebody's following me, Michael. It can't be paranoia; it must be you."

"You never used to object to my following you."

"You didn't—oh, forget it. Why don't you go away? You've seen the Forum a dozen times, and you don't care anything about the seven Caesars."

"What do you mean, seven? Who says there were seven?"

Jean gave him a long, appraising look. Considering the subject, it was inevitable that the pertinent quotation should come to her mind. The lean and hungry look was quite pronounced these days. Even Michael's eyes looked strained; they were constantly moving, darting quick glances from side to side. She had never noticed the habit before. The word "hunted" came into her mind.

"You think too much," she said flippantly. "Such men are dangerous."

"I've been thinking about sevens. We all have; we're hung up on numbers. What is that woman up to, Jean?"

"What do you mean?"

"Two weeks ago you'd never heard of her. Now she's practically adopted you. What does she want? Are you sure she isn't queer?"

Jean didn't know whether to laugh or be angry. Anger won; her nerves weren't at their best. And in her anger she broke the rule she and Jacqueline had been observing from the first—never to express their suspicions openly.

"Yes, she's queer! It's queer, these days, to put yourself out for another human being. Just because she's trying to keep me from getting killed—''

Michael's eyes shifted, and Jean turned. Jacqueline had arrived. She was wearing sunglasses: with the inquisitive green eyes hidden, she looked remote and unfamiliar. Her short, sleeveless dress was golden yellow. The purse was held tightly in the curve of her arm.

"Sorry I'm late," she began. "I couldn't get—what's wrong with you two?"

"So that's it," Michael said softly. "They weren't accidents. You believe that too."

"I didn't mean to say that," Jean babbled. "I wasn't thinking. I mean—"

"Wait a minute." Jacqueline put a hand on her arm. "Did you say 'too,' Michael?"

"What do you think I've been following her around for?" Michael made a violent gesture. "I don't stick around where I'm not wanted unless I've got a reason. Why do you think I've been prowling around your apartment half the night?"

"You've been what?"

"Be quiet, Jean," Jacqueline interrupted. "I knew he was there. Giorgio told me."

"Why, that fat pirate!" Michael exploded. "After all the glasses of *bianco* I've bought him, and the sad stories I told him about unrequited love and a rival—"

"He thinks you are a very *simpatico* young romantic," Jacqueline said. "But I paid him. Grow up, Michael. . . . Are you trying to tell us that you've been watching Jean in order to protect her? That you are also suspicious of her so-called accidents?"

"Right on."

"Why?"

"Why was I suspicious? Why were you?"

"All right," Jacqueline said, with a sigh. "What else strikes you about the situation?"

"That it's tied in with Albert's death," Michael said promptly. "Hell, it's obvious, isn't it? You think it was murder, not suicide."

"What do you think?"

"No reason why not. If I ever met a cat who was asking to be murdered, it was Albert."

Jean was still speechless. Jacqueline said calmly,

"That's an interesting contribution. Our problem has been that we couldn't figure out why anybody would want to kill him."

"Good Lord, there are fifty reasons."

"Such as?"

"Ah, hell," Michael said. "You're probably being too logical. There never is a good reason for murder, is there? According to your ethos, anyhow. Except maybe to save a crippled child from an ax murderer, and like that. But murders are committed every second of the day, for all kinds of lousy reasons. Albert was a born victim. He was nosy, rude, and insensitive; sooner or later he was bound to stick his nose into something that was none of his business."

"You're suggesting that he was killed because he had stumbled on someone's secret? You know who the suspects are, don't you?"

Michael's eyes flickered.

"Sure. That's obvious. The Seven—your mystic number."

"Which implies," said Jacqueline patiently, "that one of you nice young intelligent kids has a guilty secret. It's hard to believe, Michael."

"Nice young intelligent kids," Michael repeated, with a note of wry amusement. "Lady, you are really out of it. We are all cruddy with guilty secrets."

He looked from one of them to the other, and suddenly anger seized him.

"You think I'm kidding? All right, I'll show you. What time is it? If we hurry, maybe we can catch him."

"Who? What are you talking about?"

Michael was already moving, pulling Jean by the hand. She held back, but he was too strong for her. Jacqueline followed, demanding explanations. Michael paid no attention to either.

"Taxi," he said. "There may be time if we take a taxi."

He caught one by the simple expedient of stepping out in front of it, and shoved the women in.

"Piazza Colonna," he told the driver. "*Subito, pronto,* fast—okay?"

The traffic was heavy, and the drive took longer than Michael liked; he kept up a stream of muttered complaints, and absolutely refused to answer questions. When they reached the piazza, marked by the tall circular column of Marcus Aurelius, he pushed them out of the taxi as ruthlessly as he had pushed them in. Jacqueline tossed the driver some money; she didn't get to collect her change.

Michael dragged them into the famous pastry-shop café that occupied one corner of the piazza. As usual, it was crowded with people.

"They're still there," Michael said. "I can see them. Move up to the door, but don't go out. Third table on the right, in the outside row."

Through the doorway Jean could see the expanse of the Galleria, a favorite meeting place for opulent tourists. It was a long glass-covered shopping arcade, and the café had tables occupying a considerable stretch of the paving. It was one of the more expensive cafés in the city; a musical ensemble played, and the prices, like the pastry, were rich.

"I don't even know who I'm looking for," Jean said irritably. "What—"

Then she saw the pair Michael indicated.

Ted was sitting with his back to them, but by that time Jean knew her friends well enough to recognize them from any angle. The girl across the table from him was facing the doorway. Jean could see her features plainly. It was someone she had never seen before.

She wasn't a pretty girl. Her features were too sharp and too strongly marked for beauty. But it was a striking face, the sort of face some people might turn to stare at. The girl was as dark-skinned as a Sicilian, but the high cheekbones and fierce, slightly hooked nose had never come out of an Italian village. Her black hair, swept back from a high forehead, was held in place by a band of brightly embroidered fabric, but that was her only concession to feminine vanity. She wore no jewelry and no makeup; the open-necked tan shirt showed a slim throat whose tendons stood out with the vigor of her conversation. She was angry or distressed, or both; the black eyes flashed and the wide mouth shaped vehement words.

"She came after all," Jean said, bewildered. "Ted's girl friend. Why don't we go and—"

Michael's hand clamped tightly over her shoulder.

"No, you idiot! That isn't Ted's fiancée."

"How do you know?"

"He showed us her picture."

"Yes, but—"

"But you don't remember it. Faces are my thing," said Michael. "That girl is not Ted's girl. My God, how could you forget a face like that?"

"She looks like a young hawk," Jacqueline said softly. "A beautiful, predatory falcon."

"Oh, she's beautiful," Michael said, as if it didn't matter. "And Ted has been meeting her here every day at about this time. This place is way out of our usual beat. I guess that's why he thought it was safe. I happened to come through this way last week, and spotted them then."

"Once? How did you know they would be here today?"

"They were here yesterday and the day before," Michael said. "I checked."

"Why?"

The dark girl looked up, and Michael pulled Jean back out of the doorway. She smacked at his hand.

"Stop pushing me around. I don't understand all this, Michael. Why the secrecy?"

"I didn't initiate the secrecy," Michael pointed out. "Ted did. We know each other's friends; why hasn't he introduced her to any of us? Why do they meet here, in this tourist trap, unless it's to avoid attention?"

"But it's Ted's business whom he meets," Jean exclaimed. "If he has a thing going with some girl, and a fiancée back home—"

"Look at them," Jacqueline interrupted. "Does that look like romance to you?"

The two had risen. Ted still had his back to them, but even his back radiated anger. He stood stiff as a judge, his slender body drawn up to its full height and his hands clenched into fists. The girl, leaning slightly forward, continued to speak; she looked as if she were spitting the words out. Her body was as slim as a boy's and the tanned forearms, braced on the table, were corded with muscle.

Suddenly she turned on her heel and marched away. The

waiter came hurrying up, and Ted, who stood staring after her, relaxed. He started to turn. The three conspirators hastily withdrew. Scuttling like the eavesdroppers they were, led by Michael, they made their escape into the street and didn't stop moving until they had ducked into an alleyway a block down the Via del Corso.

"I still don't understand." Jean was the first to speak.

"God, you're dumb," Michael said disgustedly.

"Maybe we're the ones who are jumping to conclusions," Jacqueline said. "At least I'm pretty sure I jumped to the same one you are now perching uncomfortably upon. . . . Jean, what would you guess that girl's nationality to be?"

"Could be a lot of things."

"True. I said guess."

"Well—Israeli, I suppose. She could be Italian or Spanish, but the bone structure isn't right. Though I've seen a few Spaniards with cheekbones like that."

"The Moors were in Spain for a long time," said Jacqueline.

Michael gave her a meaningful look and nodded.

"Yeah. It's the same conclusion. . . . That face comes out of the Near East, Jean. She could be an Israeli, a sabra—native-born. Or she could be an Arab."

"Like—Albert."

"Like Albert. And before you start babbling about coincidence, let me remind you who's at war with whom."

"I can't believe it."

"That the girl is an Arab? If she's Israeli, why doesn't Ted bring her around and introduce her? We're not a bunch of scandal-mongering old ladies; nobody is going to write anonymous letters to his girl."

Jean continued to shake her head.

"We must be wrong. Wrong about everything. A person could have three accidents in a row; wilder things have happened."

"We can't assume that," Jacqueline said. "We can't afford to take chances. But I don't like this new development you've tossed at us, Michael. If we're getting into the hairy underworld of espionage. . . ."

"Oh, no," Jean groaned. "That I won't believe!"

"It does open vistas," Jacqueline argued. "And it provides a possible motive for murder. That's all we're looking for at this stage—possibilities."

"Oh, you're looking for motives, are you." Michael's flat voice turned the question into a statement. "How many have you come up with?"

"Several," Jacqueline said calmly. She saw Jean's look of surprise, and said nastily, "Oh, come on, Jean, don't be so naïve. I told you—every human being is at least a dozen different people. How much do you really know about your friends? Albert was an inquisitive man. If he had stumbled on a secret that threatened someone's security—"

"Such as?"

"This is all theoretical. But take José. He loves his work and knows he's lucky to be allowed to do it; the Church considers other matters more important than a man's talent. If Albert had caught him in some peccadillo, it would threaten his work. The order would certainly discipline him, and without its support he couldn't go on with his studies."

"Go on," Jean said.

"Ann. I've seen her look sick when Albert made a pass at her. What may appear to be only fastidiousness might be a well-developed neurosis, and Albert was not the man to take a hint. If he cornered her down there, and got nasty about it. . . ."

"My God," Michael said. "You ought to be locked up. Well?"

"Dana," said Jacqueline coolly. "I refer now to an incident everyone else seems to have forgotten—Albert's accusation that someone had robbed him. You all scoffed at this because of Albert's poverty; but that doesn't prove he might not have had some object of value with him. A family heirloom, perhaps. Dana's need of money is notorious."

"No more notorious than mine," Michael muttered.

"You have a source of income adequate for your needs. I'm inclined to accept your claim that you don't care about money. I could be wrong, though."

Michael looked dazed. He shook his head, muttering. Jean felt dazed too. Unwillingly, she remembered the look on Michael's face that day, when he had confessed his carefully hidden phobia. Could such a need be strong enough to drive a sufferer to murder? If Albert had found Michael in that closed-in room and, as a malicious joke, barred his way out. . . .

"No," she said in a strangled voice. "It's weird. All of it."

"*She's* weird," said Michael, jerking a thumb toward Jacqueline. "What a mind. . . . All right, now that I've given you a motive for Ted, what about Andy?"

"I'm still working on him," Jacqueline said. "And on you."

"All this is the wildest speculation," Jean insisted. "You haven't proved a thing."

"One thing," said Jacqueline. "The futility of this kind of theorizing. I was just trying to convince you, and myself, that motives could be found. But we're going at this the wrong way around. All these motives are conceivable, but unless we have some other kind of evidence they are unprovable. No. We'll have to go at it another way."

"Count me in," Michael said firmly.

"Naturally," Jacqueline said. She avoided Jean's eye; and Jean knew what she was thinking. Michael's touching concern for her safety, his exposure of Ted—none of these absolved him from suspicion. Quite the contrary. They were moves a clever man might make in order to win the confidence of his next victim.

CHAPTER SEVEN

When the phone rang next morning, Jean answered it. Jacqueline was still asleep; Jean had the impression that she had been up most of the night, walking and muttering, or simply sitting and staring at the wall while she smoked one cigarette after another.

It was Andy. His greeting made Jean groan.

"Oh, no, Andy. I'd forgotten all about it. I can't. I'm not in the mood for any more subterranean rambles."

"That's silly. Look, Angel, I set this appointment up a month ago. You have to have connections to see this place."

"I don't think I can stand anyone as cheerful as you are this morning," Jean grumbled. "I take it you finished your résumé?"

"Yes. Dropped it off this morning. Come on, babe, I'm celebrating. Jake is coming, isn't she?"

"I don't know. She's still—"

Jean glanced up. Jacqueline stood weaving in the doorway, her face puffed with sleep and her eyes peering blearily through a fine cloud of copper hair. She made violent gestures, and Jean said,

"Wait a second, Andy," and covered the mouthpiece with her hand.

"What's he want?"

"We're supposed to go out to San Sebastiano today, to see some more damned catacombs."

"Oh." Jacqueline's eyes narrowed still further. "Is that where some scholars say Saints Peter and Paul were buried?"

"Yes. How did you know that?"

"Once a librarian, always a librarian. I read." Jacqueline gestured at the telephone, which was emitting frustrated squawks. "Okay, tell him we'll come."

After Jean had hung up, she looked reproachfully at her friend.

"What is this, detective fever or just general curiosity? I don't particularly want to go."

"A little of both," Jacqueline said, ignoring her complaint. "I'm an inveterate sightseer, and this business of saints is obsessing me. It keeps cropping up. . . ."

"You don't think you're going to solve Albert's murder by locating the relics of Saint Peter, do you?"

"There is something," Jacqueline muttered. "Something . . . I've been trying to think."

"So I see." Jean fanned the air ostentatiously. It was still thick with stale smoke; they had taken to locking the place up tightly at night. "I feel like Watson. Remember Holmes's habit of sitting up all night smoking his awful pipes?"

"You'd better let me be Watson, I don't seem to be doing very well as Holmes. Maybe I'm more the Miss Marple type."

"With a figure like yours?"

"My figure is sagging, and so are my brains. After a few more days of this, they'll be running like butter. . . . Where are we meeting the others?"

"At the Colosseum. The Via Appia bus leaves from there."

They took a taxi, since Jacqueline refused to drive in the old city. By the time they reached their destination Jean was beginning to sympathize with Jacqueline's daughter; Jacqueline sang most of the way. Her voice was pleasant and not too loud, and the taxi driver didn't seem to mind; like most taxi drivers, he had already seen everything. But Jean found her friend's repertoire unnerving. It ranged from "Work, for the Night is Coming," to "Smoke Gets in Your Eyes," to a lugubrious German song Jean didn't know.

The bus was crowded; this was a popular, cheap tourist excursion as well as a regular bus route. Pummeled and shoved, Jean collapsed onto the nearest seat. When she had caught her breath and brushed her hair back from her face she was edified to note that Jacqueline had neatly snagged Professor Scoville. He was sitting beside her, his head turned, and a smile on his face as she chatted. Experience counts, Jean thought. She had seen Dana clinging to Scoville's arm as the taxi drove up. Three seats back, across the aisle, Dana was scowling like a thundercloud. Wearing a thin knit sleeveless shirt which displayed her adherence to one of the basic principles of Women's Liberation, and a skirt so short it looked like an apron, she was the center of a circle of admiring eyes.

The others were scattered. Michael and Ann had found seats together; Jean noticed that unlikely combination with interest. The two of them got along amiably enough, but Michael's rampant masculinity clearly made Ann nervous. "She acts like a Christian virgin cornered by Attila the Hun," Michael had complained once. He had been careful not to push her, and now she seemed to be enjoying their conversation. There was a faint flush on her cheeks as she talked.

Andy and José were also sitting together; they were apparently absorbed in one of their interminable arguments. Jean saw José roll his eyes in mock despair as Andy, laughing, made some inaudible point.

Ted was sitting directly across the aisle.

Seeing his familiar face, with its thick glasses and broad smile, Jean was seized by a sensation of unreality. It was impossible, the idea Michael had suggested. . . . Then, juxtaposed to Ted's face, her imagination shaped that other—the face of the falcon girl, as Jacqueline had called her. Michael was right; that face, once seen, could not easily be forgotten.

"Hey." Ted nudged her. "What are you thinking about? Your face has gone blank, like a statue's."

"Oh, nothing much. . . ."

"You're not worrying about your report, are you? Forget it for a time. That's over; the die is cast, one way or another."

"That doesn't make me stop worrying," Jean said wryly.

"But it should. Once the deadline is past, or the decision has been made, the worry is useless. To wait for the deadline . . . to make the decision—that's the agonizing part."

"Now you're blanking out," Jean said, forcing her voice to sound casual. She had never seen Ted look quite like that. His face was older, harder.

"Are you American?" The girl sitting next to Jean spoke, and Jean turned to talk to her. No matter how much you might love Rome, it was a pleasure to hear your native language spoken, and a common tongue was introduction enough. She talked to the other girl—a student from an Eastern college, on a summer tour —until Ted nudged her again. It was time to leave the bus.

They were almost the only ones to get off the bus at that stop; most of the travelers were going on, to the better-known catacombs or to a spot farther out in the country from which they could hike back to town, visiting "sights" as they went. The nine of them clustered together, and Andy indicated the building across the narrow road.

"There it is. The basilica of San Sebastiano. One of the seven pilgrimage churches," he added, with a quick glance at Jacqueline. "But we aren't here to visit the church, which, for you ignorant laymen, has little of interest. We have an appointment with Padre Montini, one of the archaeologists in charge of the excavations."

"I am disoriented," José said, looking around. "Ah, no, I see one landmark. That is the tomb of Cecilia Metella, is it not?"

He indicated a gray structure farther down the road.

"Right." Andy nodded. "This is, of course, the Via Appia Antica, the ancient road famed in song and story. It was lined with tombs and cemeteries in ancient times. Almost all of them have been vandalized and carried away now. This is the road Saint Peter took when he copped out during the Neronian persecution, and back that way a piece he met the Saviour and asked the well-known question. There's a church on the spot now—the church of Quo Vadis, Domine. But the best relic of the occasion is here, in San Sebastiano—the footprints of Christ, in the actual rock where he stood."

"Oh," said Ted innocently. "I would very much like to see that. Can we go into the church?"

"You know very well," said José, "that no one believes—"

Grinning, Andy glanced at his watch.

"We're a little early. I guess we can run quickly around the interior of the basilica. I'd hate to have Moshe miss any relics."

"Moshe?" Jacqueline asked. "I know you all have a passion for nicknames, but—"

"I developed an eye infection the first week I was here," Ted explained soberly.

"Silly joke," Dana muttered. She was still sulking, but at least she was condescending to talk. Jean fell into step with the other girl as they crossed the road and, in an effort to improve her humor, asked,

"Aren't those catacombs we visited out this way somewhere?"

"There are catacombs all over the place," Andy answered, before Dana could speak. "We'll see one set this morning. Possibly the originals. This area was called *catacumbas* in ancient times, so the name came to be applied to the underground cemeteries in the region. That's what catacombs are—burial places. They weren't limited to the Christians, either. There are pagan catacombs and Jewish catacombs—at least four of those have been located, and Ted thinks he may be on the track of another."

"Is that right?" Scoville asked, turning toward Ted with considerable interest. "What material are you using?"

Ted looked as sly as a round-faced, amiable youth could look, and Dana said, with a laugh,

"You ought to know better than to ask another archaeologist a question like that, Sam."

"He's safe from me," Scoville said, smiling. "If it were an Etruscan cemetery, now. . . ."

Glancing over her shoulder, Jean caught a peculiar expression on Jacqueline's face and wondered what, if anything, in the conversation had prompted that look of sudden surmise. She had no opportunity to ask; Andy marshaled them into a group and led the way into the church.

Ted enjoyed the relics thoroughly. The footprints, twice

normal size, were such crude fakes that even José was unable to keep a straight face. Chuckling with quiet malice, Ted pointed out an arrow in a glass case. He said nothing, merely raised an eyebrow inquiringly. Glumly, José nodded.

"You know too much about the legends of the saints," he said. "I think you read them only to annoy me. . . . Yes, Sebastian was the saint who was martyred by being shot full of arrows."

"All right, all right, break it up," Andy interposed. "Let's go. We're supposed to meet our guide next door, in the museum."

Padre Montini, wearing a coarse cowled robe and rope belt, was a lean man of middle height with a rugged peasant face. He greeted the girls with broad appreciative smiles, and José with reserve. Scoville got a deep bow and a handclasp that lasted longer than he wanted it to last. The padre knew him by reputation, it seemed.

Montini began by showing them a cleverly constructed model that showed the existing basilica in relationship to its fourth-century predecessor and to the ancient cemetery which had preceded both churches. Andy had already explained that the basilica had not always been named after Saint Sebastian. In the early Christian centuries it had been known as the Church of the Apostles; and the ruins of a Christian cult center, under the church, confirmed the fact that the two great saints were connected in some fashion with the place.

Andy interrupted at this point to ask a question. Jean didn't follow his Italian, which was considerably more fluent than hers; but the effect on Montini was amazing. His face turned bright red and he burst into speech. Scoville Senior backed up his offspring, and the argument raged. Bewildered, Jean turned to José, who stood beside her.

"What's the fight about?"

José grinned.

"Andy asked Montini about the old problem of Saint Peter's daughter. The church holds that the relationship was a purely spiritual one, but Andy is insisting that Petronella was the Apostle's physical child."

Jacqueline joined them in time to hear the question and José's answer.

"Doesn't the Bible mention Peter's wife?"

"I believe so," José said indifferently. "It is not a question of great importance."

Jacqueline shook her head, muttering. Jean caught a few words; they sounded like "another virgin saint."

Finally the disputants calmed down, and Montini announced, "And now, *andiamo! Discendiamo nel sotterraneo!*"

Jean looked at Michael, and met a cold glare. Apparently he was still climbing back on the horse that had thrown him. After seeing the condition he had been in once before *"nel sotterraneo,"* she wasn't sure this trip was a good idea.

Fifteen minutes later she was sure that it wasn't a good idea. They had visited catacombs before, and she had not liked them much; for an atmosphere of pure concentrated gloom there is no place worse than the corridor of a catacomb. These were even more depressing than the others she had visited. Some of the more popular catacombs, often visited by tourists, had a feeble lighting system. Here the group walked in single file, holding candles as the sole source of illumination. The corridors were so narrow that the bigger men—Scoville, Andy, and José—had to turn sideways in some places. The low ceiling was only inches over their heads. And on either side, yard after yard and block after block, the grave niches filled the walls from floor to ceiling —tiers of graves, row on row on row, stretching out into the darkness eternally.

Jean wondered how on earth Michael could stand it. Had he been joking about his claustrophobia—inventing it, to explain a distress which might have had another cause? Jean wondered. She couldn't imagine how anyone who had found San Clemente disturbing could endure this place.

Half the candles had gone out, as the result of incautious movements on the part of the bearers. From the head of the procession Montini called out a cheery reassurance. They were not to worry, he could find his way through this maze blind-folded.

Jean found the statement unconvincing. People had been lost in the catacombs; the corridors had no regular plan, they branched and intersected at random. There were no landmarks, only the same grimly monotonous walls and their blocked-up niches. A few of the graves had been opened; the gaping

blackness within held shadowy suggestions of what had once inhabited the space. Occasionally there was an inscription or a
sketchy drawing on the plaster that sealed the grave. Montini's
voice echoed hollowly as he pointed out some of the symbols—
the dove, the fish, the olive branch, other emblems of the Faith—
and the rare epitaphs. "Be of good cheer; no man is immortal,"
one read, with a Spartan fortitude that struck Jean as more pagan
than Christian. The most common epitaph was the simple phrase
"in peace."

They might have been a funeral procession from the time
when the catacombs were still in use. The roughness of the floor
necessitated a funereal shuffle; the dim light illumined faces that
seemed drawn and anxiously shadowed, leaving the rest of the
figures in darkness. Gradually an unholy fascination replaced
Jean's nervousness. She kept stopping to stare at the mute shapes
of the graves, morbidly picturing what lay within them. She was at
the end of the line, and there was a tendency on the part of the
others to crowd forward, close to the comforting figure of their
guide. They were silent. Even Montini had stopped talking. The
atmosphere discouraged speech. All at once Jean looked up from
her contemplation of a very small niche, whose miniature dimensions had struck her poignantly, and found that she was alone.

She strained her eyes through the enclosing darkness and tried
to deny the fact. It was impossible. They had to be here, they
couldn't simply disappear. . . . From somewhere seemingly an
immense distance away there was a hollow echo of a voice, or a
laugh.

Jean took three quick running steps and stubbed her toe on a
protruding stone. The small yellow candle flame flickered wildly.
Gasping with terror, Jean sheltered it with her hand. If that light
went out she was done for. "The horror of the darkness. . . ." It
was Saint Jerome who had said that. He must have known it
himself—not the ordinary lightlessness of night, but the darkness
of death and the grave.

Jean knew it would be folly to move. She was completely disoriented, and there were branching corridors every few yards.
Sooner or later they would miss her, and Montini, who presumably knew where he had been, as well as where he was going,

would retrace the path to look for her. If she stayed where she was, she was safe. . . .

The word suddenly struck her with a new and terrible meaning. Safe from abandonment she certainly would be, unless she panicked; but if her theories were correct, another danger had been haunting her footsteps for many days. Was this episode to be a fourth, and final, "accident?"

When she heard a sound, she started violently. Magnified and distorted, it sounded more like a howl than a name, but as soon as she steadied herself, and her precious candle, she realized that it was a name—hers. The sound demolished what few wits she had remaining. She began to run—whether toward a rescuer or away from a faceless killer she did not know—and plunged headlong into an approaching figure. Her candle went out, which was fortunate, since otherwise it would have ignited the man's shirt. He saved his own candle by a complicated last-minute stretch, and caught her in his free arm.

"Michael," Jean whispered.

"Undeniably. What's with you? Why all the panic?"

"You're a fine one to ask that." Jean stepped back, and he let her go at once. "Are you—are you all right?"

"Who, me? Fine." He smiled. "I'm cured. I'm even getting to like this."

"I'm not." There was something else she didn't like; the look on Michael's face and the way his eyes shone in the candlelight. They looked solid, the pupils greatly dilated. With his faint, enigmatic smile, it was an unnerving expression.

"Now that you've been good enough to rescue me, let's join the others," she said.

"Why? It's nice and quiet here. This is the way it was supposed to be. No wisecracking sightseers, gaping and pretending to be frightened. . . ."

"Michael—"

"I haven't been to mass since I was thirteen," Michael went on, in a dreamy voice. "I was so turned off I couldn't pass by a church without spitting. And the Jesus movement never got to me, I don't dig that kind of exhibitionism. But in a place like this you begin to see what they were driving at. The meaning behind the symbols; the fact that two opposites don't clash, but resolve into a synthesis. Death and resurrection; the body back to the dust it came from, and the soul to God."

"Michael," Jean repeated. She had to fight an insane instinct to shout, as if she were calling him back from a great distance. "Please. You're frightening me."

"What are you frightened of? They'll find us soon. Unless we move—back that way. . . ."

Jean decided she was going to scream. She didn't want to; surely she must be imagining the pressure of Michael's body against hers, forcing her back into one of those dark side corridors. Even so, she was going to scream.

She opened her mouth—and Andy came plunging around a turn in the passage. He was holding his candle high, and the light made his mop of hair glow like a nimbus.

"All right, sorry to break it up," he said coolly. "But Montini is having fits. He's been telling us gruesome stories of people who got lost down here and weren't found for years and years and . . . so suppose you find a more appropriate place, hmm?"

"Anytime I pick a place like this to make out you can have my head examined," Michael said, in his normal voice. "We were merely exchanging philosophical comments. Lead on, you louse."

The others were waiting for them in a tiny rough-walled chapel. Montini burst into agitated speech when they came in. When he had finished his scolding and the procession moved on, Jean managed to slip in next to Jacqueline.

"Sorry," she said, under her breath. "I don't know how that happened. Do you think. . . ."

"I don't think so. But—for God's sake, stick close."

Almost immediately they came out of the dismal corridors into an open underground space. It was roofed by a complex system of ancient beams and modern girders, and Jean realized, before their guide spoke, that they were now under the church. Two different ages of history were represented by the structures in that open area. There was a row of Roman mausolea in front of them, neat little brick houses whose pointed facades looked as if they had been built within the past decade. Off to one side were the remaining walls of the Christian cult center, which had been constructed over the street of tombs two or three centuries later.

Montini began explaining the layout, and Jean stopped listening. She really didn't care whether Peter and Paul had been buried at all, much less where. Michael had had a point, even though she didn't think he had chosen a good time or place for his theological musings. The body went back to the dust; physical relics were only trinkets, like the pebbles or shells collected by a child as mementos of a trip. Wasn't it Paul himself who had said, "But when I became a man, I put away childish things"?

Yet she could understand the appeal made by those worthless remnants of mortality. The soul was so barricaded by flesh that it needed concrete objects to cling to. Squatting down under the low eaves of the church floor above, Jean felt a sympathetic quiver run through her as she viewed the graffiti scratched onto the wall by the men and women who had come to pray near the bones of the Apostles.

"Paule ed Petre, petite pro Victore," she read aloud; and Jacqueline, squatting beside her, translated.

"Peter and Paul, pray for Victor. How do you like that? I do remember a little Latin from twenty years ago."

"Very good," said Andy, behind them. "Ignore Jean's accent, though, she's a medieval Latinist, and the way she pronounces the language sets my teeth on edge."

"I'd better keep my mouth shut, then," Jacqueline said, pushing her glasses back into place. "I keep forgetting that most of you know Latin as well as you do English."

"It's a working language for us," Andy agreed. "All right, girls, tear yourselves away. Time for some pagan tombs."

The others were on the lower level, in front of the mausolea. Over one brick facade a marble plaque still remained in place, recording the name of the man to whom the tomb had belonged. With the others egging her on, Jacqueline tried to translate the inscription. She was having a fine time; her hair was coming loose, and her glasses kept sliding down her nose.

"I can't even get the first word," she complained. "MCL—is that a date?"

"M for Marcus," Andy said. "Marcus Clodius Hermes—that was the guy's name."

"Oh. I see. 'Marcus Clodius Hermes, who'—I've got it! 'Who lived . . . years. . . .' Now that is a number. Wait a minute, I always have to count Roman numerals on my fingers. 'Who lived seventy-five years. . . .' "

Her voice died away. Dana laughed and prompted her; but Andy, more perceptive, reached out and caught her arm.

"Jake, what's the matter?"

Jacqueline turned. The sight of her face made Jean recoil. It was white as paper, with two bright spots of color burning on her cheeks. Coils of loosened bronze hair curled around her ears like copper ornaments. She paid no attention to Andy, or to the others, but broke through them, brushing them aside as if she were brushing at flies.

She caught Jean by the shoulders and shook her. Jean was too astonished to resist. Her head bobbed back and forth.

"You overeducated brats and your damned erudition," Jacqueline said, literally between clenched teeth. "Here. Paper. Pen. I've got one here someplace. . . ." She rummaged frantically in the purse, like a puppy in pursuit of a gopher. "Hell, take my eyebrow pencil." She shoved it into Jean's limp hand. "Write. Write down what you saw Albert write. Go on! Exactly what he wrote."

Even then Jean couldn't understand what she was getting at. But she did as she was told; and as the strokes emerged, smudged and dark, they had an unnerving resemblance to the uneven strokes Albert's finger had made. Jacqueline snatched the pad and waved it in the air.

"I thought so," she exclaimed. "How we could have been so stupid. . . . Not the number—the numeral! The Roman numeral seven."

CHAPTER EIGHT

A chastened Jacqueline was led, gently but firmly, across the street to the bus stop. She was still muttering to herself. Padre Montini, who had been vexed by Jean's adventure, found Jacqueline's outburst the final straw. He was glad to bid them all farewell and retire to his pasta.

The others knew what Jacqueline was talking about, but Dana voiced their mutual feelings when she said she couldn't understand what the flap was all about.

"What difference does it make? A seven is a seven whether it's a Roman or an Arabic numeral."

There was a soft-drink stand in the shady parking lot across from the church, and after their tramp through the dusty centuries they were all glad for a drink. They stood around sucking soda pop through straws like a party of Scouts on an outing. Andy said thoughtfully, "It does make a difference. It provides a context."

Jacqueline, drinking Coke with such concentration that her cheeks were concave and her eyes practically crossed, looked at him.

"You're a bright lad, Andy. Jean, why didn't you—"

"I'm stupid," Jean admitted. "But as Andy said, we all think in Latin half the time. Every contemporary document I refer to is written in Latin—manuscripts, inscriptions, everything. Even graffiti. I'm so used to seeing it. . . ."

"I know. I'm sorry I yelled at you. Was I awfully rude?"

"As invective," Andy said meditatively, "it was pretty feeble. But it had a familiar ring."

"Stop it, Junior," said his father, affectionately but firmly. "Haven't I taught you to be polite to a lady?"

"Jacqueline is not a lady," said Ted. He smiled at her. "She is one of us."

Jean felt a chill run up her spine. Before Ted's smiling regard, Jacqueline changed color and looked away.

They split up after that, the majority of them returning to the Institute. José had a sketch he wanted to finish, and Andy admitted that he could spend a few hours working without actually hurting himself. Ted said nothing about his plans. When the bus disgorged them beside the Colosseum he simply removed himself, smiling affably, and strolled away down the Via dei Fori Imperiali.

Turning, Jean met Michael's eye, and knew what he was thinking. Ted had taken the shortest way to the Piazza Colonna.

II

Jean went to the library with the others, but she was unable to concentrate. Instead she sat and doodled idly on a piece of paper. There were a few people in the reading room at that time, the drowsy, warm, post-lunch hour. The three art students had gone to their studios and Andy had retired to his private cubicle in the stacks. The sunlight pouring in the big windows made Jean sleepy. She drew stiff Byzantine figures across the pages of her notebook, and brooded.

After all the excitement of Jacqueline's discovery, she couldn't see that they had progressed. What difference did it make whether Albert's last message was in Latin or Arabic numerals? Andy had said something about the context. Jean understood; like the others who worked with Latin, Albert would be more inclined to use that numbering system if the subject uppermost in his mind related to things Roman. Which meant precisely nothing. Saints, hills, churches, many of the other exotic ideas they had considered were "Roman" subjects. None of these subjects had offered any fruitful ideas to begin with, and they still didn't.

Jean groaned, and regarded her drawing with disfavor. Unconsciously she had been sketching a mosaic from one of the Ravenna churches—a long line of lady saints, more or less identical except for the symbols that distinguished one from the other. Saint Agnes and her lamp, Saint Catherine and her wheel, Saint Barbara and her tower. . . .

Could there be some meaning in Albert's raving about his virgin saints? Iconography was one of the fields she had to know, since the saints and their symbols were a favorite theme in medieval mosaics. There weren't seven virgin saints, there were thousands of those unfortunate females, counting Saint Ursula of Cologne and her thousand fellow-sufferers. But suppose Albert hadn't been thinking about German saints or Armenian saints or French saints. The Roman saints and their churches; could anything be made of that?

A fly buzzed by and settled on her paper. Jean swatted at it, and missed; she hadn't meant to hit it anyway. She was getting sleepy, the droning fly and the hot sun acted like sedatives. Virgin saints and Roman churches. It would make a good title for a book, a popular book on early Christian archaeology.

That was all the sense it made, though. Jacqueline wasn't too communicative these days, but she had already considered this equation, and Jean assumed she had derived nothing meaningful from it. Their expeditions to Santa Cecilia and the other churches dedicated to virgin saints had produced no comment from Jacqueline; in fact, Jean had wondered at the time if the sightseeing was only an excuse for conversation with various Sinners.

There was one consoling feature in their discovery of that morning. It was unlikely that Albert would think of his seven acquaintances in terms of Roman numerals. The Seven Sinners . . . She cursed Andy for inventing that unoriginal name. . . .

"Hey," Andy said in her ear. "If you're going to sleep you might as well do it in a bed."

"I wasn't asleep." Jean rubbed her eyes. "Not very asleep. . . . This place is getting hotter by the minute."

"It's even hotter back in the stacks. How about a swim?"

"All the way to Ostia? I haven't got the strength."

"Maybe Jake would let us use her pool. We wouldn't need to bother her. Oh, cripes," Andy said. "I forgot. Maybe you don't feel like swimming."

"Sure I do," Jean said, with more bravado than truth. "I don't think Jacqueline would mind. Let's go ask the others."

The others were only too glad to leave their sweltering studios. José was the only holdout; barely glancing up from his easel, he informed them that he almost had it, and if they would get their worthless carcasses out of there he just might get it. All right, all right—he would meet them later for dinner, he would do anything they wanted—later. But now, would they please get out?

They left, unoffended; all of them had been through that stage themselves.

The quickest way to their goal was along the old Via Aurelia, which Jean had traveled once at night, by car. It was a hot, dusty walk, and by the time they reached the back entrance to the compound where Jacqueline lived, they were all panting. Jean had shared the apartment for a week now and had her own key; she led the way upstairs without a second thought. She did caution the others to be quiet. Jacqueline might be taking a nap, since she had expected to be alone all afternoon.

But when they stepped out of the elevator, Jean realized that Jacqueline was not asleep. Nor was she alone. A few breathless words and an odd scuffling sound from the *salone* alarmed her; she darted forward, followed by the others. Then she stopped, staring.

On the couch that faced the foyer, Jacqueline was disentangling herself from her visitor. She was flushed and disheveled. Her companion looked familiar to Jean. Tall, suave, distinguished, elegantly dressed in a pale tan suit and dark shirt. . . .

"Lieutenant," said Jean, her voice rising to a squeak.

"Signorina," said di Cavallo resignedly. "And"—his voice

became a snarl—"signori, signorina. . . . Are there more of you? I see, Signora Kirby, that you are *molto occupato.*"

"Too busy for that," Jacqueline said, closing her mouth with the snap of a trapdoor shutting. "I must say, Lieutenant, that your behavior—"

"Enough," said di Cavallo, bounding to his feet. "We have no more to say to one another. It is finished. *Buona sera, signora. Arrivederla.*"

Regrettably, Jean found this amusing. *Arrivederla* is the formal version of the Italian word for "good-bye," which Americans use so casually and inaccurately. *Arrivederci* is properly applied only to intimates, children, dogs, and the Almighty—should one ever have occasion to say "Good-bye, God"—and di Cavallo was quite correct in using the formal word to address a lady who had resolutely indicated her intention of avoiding informal relations. It sounded funny, all the same, when Jean remembered her first sight of the couple. To complete her demoralization, she caught sight of a small fuzzy pink head poking out from under the brocaded flounce of the couch. Prinz looked apologetic, as well he might; as a watchdog he wasn't very courageous.

Di Cavallo saw Jean's grin, and his handsome face froze into a mask of fury. Looking six inches taller than his actual height, he stalked toward the elevator. There was an unseemly melee in the foyer; the other invaders had retreated precipitately as soon as they realized what was going on, and they were milling in an uncertain group near the door. Finally di Cavallo managed to reach the elevator. He entered it, and stood with his back to them until the door closed.

Meeting Jean's eye, Andy twisted his features into a grimace of amused chagrin. She made a reassuring gesture and advanced tentatively into the *salone.*

Jacqueline, smoothing down her ruffled hair, said coolly, "You may as well come in. All of you."

"I'm sorry," Jean began.

"You'd be within your rights to blast us," Andy added. "We had no business barging in here."

"Dear boy, don't apologize. Who knows," Jacqueline said dreamily, "what you may have saved me from? A fate—"

"I'd prefer that to death any day," said Ann. "What did he come here for, Jake?"

"Hey, babe," Andy said, staring at his sister in surprise. "Watch it."

"That's all right," Jacqueline said. "He dropped by to give me the latest results of the investigation. The police seem to assume I'm the adult responsible for this group of nuts. Sorry about that."

"We're sorry you were dragged into it," Andy said, still glaring at his sister. "You've been damned nice, and the only reward we seem to offer you is involvement in our messy private affairs. Am I right in supposing the lieutenant was only using that as an excuse to—er—call on you?"

"I refuse to answer on the usual grounds. Anyhow, the suicide theory stands. I imagine that's something of a relief."

She looked at them inquiringly. It was Andy who answered.

"Not really. I don't know about the rest of you guys, but I haven't thought much about it. That sounds calloused, I suppose, but—well, there wasn't much doubt, was there?"

"At any rate, it's over and done with," Jacqueline said. "And," she added casually, "so is my visit to Rome almost over. Lise is returning on Sunday, and my work here is done. So I'll be leaving."

"Oh, no," Andy said. "You can't leave us like this. What are we going to do without our mother image? And her swimming pool?"

"You'll have to return to your slummy, poverty-stricken existence," Jacqueline said nastily. "That's the trouble with giving you long-haired degenerates a few comforts; you get so you expect them. When you're my age, you'll appreciate the value of hard work and a set of decent moral values. I don't know what this generation is coming to. Immoral, shiftless, pot-smoking . . . . Ann, darling, don't look like that. I'm joking."

Ann's sober face lightened. She glanced uncertainly from one grinning face to the next; and Andy said cheerfully, "Jake's just getting back into practice. That's the way she talks to students when she's on duty."

Jean managed to produce a smile, but she felt as if someone had kicked her in the pit of the stomach. Fond as she was of

Jacqueline, it wasn't the loss of the mother image, as Andy had called her, that bothered Jean; it was Jacqueline's change of attitude. No one with any sense of compassion or responsibility could walk out on an unsolved murder and a very vulnerable witness; and Jacqueline was not lacking in either trait. What had di Cavallo told her, before his hormones got the better of him? Jean tried to be rational. If Jacqueline had become convinced that their murder theory was baseless—and no other theory could explain her readiness to withdraw—then there was nothing for Jean to worry about. Her mind believed it, but every nerve in her body howled in protest.

"I'll move out today," she said. "I never meant to stay so long."

"Jean," Ann said hesitantly. "You did have a bad shock. If you're still nervous about being alone, Andy and I would love to have you."

"Especially Andy," said that gentleman, with a hideous leer. "No, seriously, honey—Ann is right. You don't realize how long the effects of shock can last. I know. It happened to Ann once. Suicide—a friend of ours. She went along cool as a cucumber for a couple of months, and then, whammo; it hit her. She was out of this world for a long time."

Jean didn't dare look at Ann. The other girl had never referred to this incident, and Jean couldn't help resenting Andy's mention of it now, even though his motive for doing so was kind. Ann rallied quickly. She had made one sharp, uncontrolled motion of protest; now she said quietly,

"He's right, Jean. Though maybe you don't feel like moving in now, with a—a crazy woman."

"Don't put on airs," Michael said, before Andy could protest. "You aren't the only one."

"To have a friend kill himself?"

"Oh, that. Look, honey, they fall like flies in my profession. Unstable artists, you know. No, I mean you aren't the only one who's spent time on some shrink's couch. It's the in thing nowadays. We're all a little crazy, one way or the other. Hadn't you noticed?"

"There's no need for Jean to make up her mind right this minute," Jacqueline said. "You might as well wait till Sunday,

Jean, and move out when I do. Anyway, you can't leave before tomorrow. I'm having a party. A farewell party, for me."

"Great," Andy said heartily. "When, tomorrow night? Are we all invited?"

"Naturally. Spread the word to the others, will you?"

"Can I bring my daddy?" Andy asked, in a plaintive squawk.

"I hope you will. It's a costume party. Will Dr. Scoville mind?"

"He's the biggest ham in Europe. Where do you think I get it? He'll probably want to come as a Pharaoh; that's his favorite disguise. Gives him a chance to show off his muscles."

"But I don't think we have—" Ann began.

"I'll think of something," her brother waved her objections aside. "It'll be a surprise."

"Surprise," Jacqueline repeated. She bent over and began to rummage in the purse, which squatted on the floor at her feet. But Jean had seen her face before she moved to hide it, and its sudden pallor told the younger woman all she needed to know. The conversation, the party, di Cavallo's visit—all were part of a larger plan. And the consummation of that plan appalled even the woman who had arranged it.

Jacqueline didn't join them at the pool, but she sat on the balcony watching every move they made. Jean hadn't been aware of apprehension; but when the actual moment of entering the water came, it took all her willpower to make her body comply. She paddled sedately around the edge, in full view of the balcony, and everyone carefully refrained from commenting on her caution.

They left Jacqueline preparing to go out. Jean wondered with whom she was dining, but of course did not ask. They had been selfish, assuming she had no other friends in Rome.

Their own dinner was a quiet affair. Everyone seemed subdued, and when José joined them, to be informed of Jacqueline's plans, he received the news with a silent shrug. Somewhat to Jean's surprise, the idea of a costume party seemed to please him.

"I am thinking," he said, pressing his fingertips to his temples. "I will invent something."

"Why don't you come as Torquemada?" Andy asked. "That would be in character."

Under cover of the ensuing argument, Jean turned to Michael.

He was back to his sketching again. She tried to see what he was doing, but he shook his head and moved the book away.

"Wait till it's finished."

"What costume are you going to wear?" Jean asked.

"Dunno."

"Don't shave tomorrow," Andy advised. "Then you can come as a Skid Row bum. In your usual clothes, of course."

"You're even more vicious than usual tonight," Jean said admiringly.

"Mike's sartorial tastes have always offended me," was the reply.

Michael glanced up from his sketch to survey his friend with contempt.

"Anybody who would wear a pink flowered shirt and a string of blue love beads has got no business criticizing my clothes."

"What about me?" Jean asked, to avert another uproar. "You haven't made any suggestions for me."

Andy's face softened as he looked at her.

"Come as a saint," he said. "Almost any saint would do."

Michael made an odd choking sound.

They broke up early, by mutual consent. José had some complex scheme for a costume, which demanded immediate action, and the others planned to track down Ted and Dana, to tell them about the party. Jean had been hoping they would go their respective ways before she made her move; but they lingered, and finally she was forced to action. She hailed a taxi.

Andy greeted this gesture with rude comments about the rich and the rich by association. Jean's retorts were weak, but this was one promise, made to Jacqueline, that she intended to keep.

Michael closed the taxi door for her. As he withdrew, Jean felt something flutter down into her lap. The sheet of paper had been folded several times, but she knew it must be one of Michael's sketches. The light was poor, so she didn't try to look at it.

It was still early; Jacqueline would not be back from a conventional dinner for some time yet. But as Jean nerved herself for the entrance into a darkened hall, she realized that the apartment was not deserted. The foyer was lit, and there were sounds from the kitchen. She hesitated, holding the elevator door open. Then footsteps shuffled down the hall. Jacqueline's appearance matched her dispirited shuffle. She was wearing a faded cotton robe and her face had sagged into weary lines.

Jean stepped out and let the door close.

"What are you doing back so early?"

"It was a business dinner," Jacqueline said, with an odd twist of her mouth. "You took a cab?"

"Yes. Are you going to tell me what's going on?"

Jacqueline dropped into a chair.

"I don't think I'd better," she said.

Jean sat down, and the poodle came trotting across the floor and flung himself down on her feet. The French doors to the balcony were open; a breeze drifted in, bringing with it the scent of pines and the soft sea sound which was the rustle of branches in the wind. The sounds and smells and sensations blended into a unique whole which would always recall these Italian nights, just as the sun on a hot street lined with old houses would always summon up the nostalgia of Rome on a summer day. I don't want to lose this, Jean thought. And I will; it will be lost in nightmares unless. . . .

"Then you haven't changed your mind," she said. "About Albert's death."

"No. Did you think I was running out on you? I ought to be insulted."

"I didn't really think that. In fact, I wondered whether the lieutenant's visit might not be more than coincidental."

"Look," Jacqueline said wearily. "I'm not being mysterious for the fun of it. There are reasons. Just don't worry. You'll be all right. . . . What's this?"

"One of Michael's sketches, I think. He gave it to me tonight."

Jacqueline raised an inquiring eyebrow and Jean nodded. Jacqueline spread the paper out on the coffee table. The sudden tension of her shoulders roused Jean's curiosity. She leaned over to see the sketch.

It was brilliant, one of the best things Michael had ever done— and one of the most terrifying. It was done in a manner quite different from his usual broad, quick technique; the figures were small, the detail precise. And it stopped Jean's breath for a moment, because the subject was so similar to the one she had been sketching that day.

Like hers, Michael's drawing showed a row of stiff Byzantine saints. Or—Sinners? There were seven of them. The faces were exquisite little portraits, but it was the detail of costume and symbol that made Jean start to wonder.

As people will, she looked first at herself. Her initial reaction was pleasure; Michael had flattered her, it was a lovely little face, heart-shaped, smiling her own triangular smile. He had shown her as Saint Agnes, with a lamb at her feet. . . . Jean straightened up, with a snort of mingled amusement and fury. The lamb had her face too. Even when she studied it closely she couldn't see how Michael had managed it; the face was that of a juvenile sheep, muzzle, ears and all, and yet it was immediately recognizable as her own.

Dana was Mary Magdalene. The subject was more popular in Renaissance art, with its fondness for the naked body, but Michael had produced a wonderful satire of the stiff Byzantine style, with long, stylized waves of hair that exposed more than they concealed, and the false modesty of the fat little hands.

Ann was another virgin saint. Michael had dealt kindly with her—or at least Jean thought he had until she examined the face more closely. It was a face suited to a saint who died a martyr; there were lines of torment under its seeming placidity. Jean had to find the symbol before she could identify the lady. It was Saint Barbara, carrying the tower in which her wicked father had imprisoned her before turning her over to the torturers as a recalcitrant Christian.

The armor and the lance with its dripping dragon's head identified Andy as the handsome Saint George. Did Michael really see him as a dragon slayer? Ted made a charming Saint Stephen; he had caught the first rock in his upraised hand, and his look of supercilious superiority would have driven any mob to stone him.

José was harder to identify. He wore a bishop's robes and miter, but the higher ecclesiastical ranks have produced a good many saints. However, his expression of studious concentration and the book he carried enabled Jean to recognize Saint Augustine—who had once remarked, "Lord, give me chastity—but not yet." That was really too bad of Michael. The eyes under José's studious brow held a gleam that belonged to the pre-conversion part of Augustine's career.

Bringing up the tail of the procession came Michael's drawing of himself, and after her first chuckle of laughter Jean's mouth curved down, and she forgave him his casual digs at the others. Emaciated, hideous, wild-eyed, it was the ugliest representation of John the Baptist Jean had ever seen. The ribs stood out and the ragged hair framed a face only one step removed from madness.

The Seven Sinners made up the procession, but there were two other figures hovering in the background. Jean glanced at Jacqueline. To date, her hostess had demonstrated no particular religous sensitivities, but the figure with Jacqueline's face might have been considered slightly blasphemous. The flowing hair framed a face which was neither virginal nor motherly—at least not in the sense of that Ideal Motherhood the figure was supposed to exemplify. Jean had seen such a look on her own mother's face, however, under circumstances she did not care to dwell upon. The figure wore a crown; it was tipped over one ear, and the halo was distinctly ragged.

With trepidation, Jean looked to see what Michael had done with Scoville. Some lingering remnant of piety had kept him from casting that gentleman in either of the obvious roles—or else he did not see Scoville as exemplifying divinity. At first Jean couldn't decide what the professor was supposed to be, other than a Roman gentleman in a neatly draped toga. Then she saw what was poking out from under the skirt of the toga, and examined the shape of the curls on the figure's forehead more closely, and again she gasped. That was going too far. Scoville might be a sinner, like all the rest, but to make him the Prince of sinners was an exaggeration.

"The boy is fantastic," Jacqueline muttered. "I've never seen his serious work, but he could win a lot of prizes with this sort of thing."

"It's cruel," Jean said.

"So was Hogarth. So was Daumier."

"You think he's that good?"

"Good Lord, yes. It needs more than technical skill. The great caricaturists have a touch of extrasensory perception. They see through people."

"He does that. Though I don't understand some of these. Yours—you don't mind—"

"It makes me writhe," Jacqueline said. "I didn't think I was that transparent. What about yours?"

"I think it's funny," Jean admitted. "But I don't get it. Or, if I do get it, I'm mad."

"There are worse things than being thought of as a woolly lamb. Hang on to this, Jean. Or—let me keep it for you. May I?"

"You can have it," Jean said. "As a souvenir."

Jacqueline shivered.

"I think I'd prefer a bright brass paperweight in the shape of St. Peter's. Or a cerise satin pillow with *'Arrivederci Roma'* embroidered on it. Something bland and meaningless."

"I know," Jean said wearily. "It hasn't been pleasant for—" Her voice broke off, and she looked at the drawing with aroused interest. "Are you saying that this sketch means—"

"I'm not saying anything else. I'm too incoherent." Jacqueline rose; and Jean noticed that she held the drawing by its edge, as if it were hot to the touch. "Let's get some sleep. Believe me, we're going to need it."

CHAPTER NINE

*T*he day of the party dawned bright and clear and hot. The close air woke Jean at sunrise; she kicked off the sheet that had covered her and moved her sweating body to a cooler spot, dislodging Nefertiti, whose affectionate position under her knees had not reduced the temperature. The cat arose, cursing, and removed itself. Jean looked at the other bed. The covers were thrown back, but Jacqueline was not there.

She fell asleep again, too tired to do more than wonder briefly; and when she finally woke again the sun was high and the room was even hotter. The shutters were closed; bright parallel streaks of light crossed the gloom.

Jean staggered out into the *salone,* which was brighter and not quite so hot. She found Jacqueline fully dressed, drinking coffee. The efficient professional was in command again; Jacqueline's eyes were sunken, as if she hadn't slept well, but her mouth was tightly set and her glasses rode high on the bridge of her nose.

"You have a somewhat haggard aspect," said Jacqueline critically. "Didn't you sleep well?"

"I had a bad dream," Jean said. She shuddered. "Really bad. I'm still shaking."

"Here, have some coffee. What was it about?"

"I dreamed I met Saint Agnes," Jean said, accepting the proffered cup. "Walking down the Via Nomentana."

"The Via—"

"Nomentana. That's the street her church is on, the one outside the walls. I knew it was the Nomentana, even though it looked completely different from the way it looks now. It was like a country road instead of a street, and it was paved with those big dark stone blocks, like the ones you can still see in sections of the Via Appia Antica. There were trees lining the way—dark, pointed cypresses, and pines, and mimosa. Trees and tombs. Some of them were brick mausolea and some were big, elaborate white marble buildings. And then she—she came up out of a stairway that went down into the ground. Like the entrance to the catacombs." Jean sipped her coffee. She said in a small voice, "She was carrying her head under her arm."

"You have an accurate imagination," Jacqueline said. "She was beheaded, wasn't she? You know where you received the stimulus for this—"

"Sure, I know. Damn Michael and his sketches. . . . But you know how nightmares are, this was much worse than it sounds when I describe it; when I was dreaming it I was absolutely paralyzed with terror. She wasn't horrible-looking, I mean, there wasn't even any blood. In a way, that would have been better. She —the head—smiled at me. And winked one eye."

"That's enough," Jacqueline said hastily.

"I know it doesn't sound—"

"It sounds ghastly. Forget it. We've got a lot to do. Grocery shopping, cooking, cleaning—and somehow we've got to invent a couple of costumes."

From then on Jean didn't have time to brood—or ask questions. The entire apartment had to be cleaned, and that meant floor scrubbing, waxing, and so on. Jacqueline admitted blandly that she hadn't done much cleaning, and since her friend's *tuttofare* was also on vacation, the apartment had gotten into a state which a persnickety Swiss lady would rightfully resent. It must be spotless before Lise returned, and though some of the work would have to be done over again, after the party, the hard-core cleaning might as well be done at once.

By midafternoon they had finished most of the work, including the manufacture of what seemed to Jean's weary fingers to be thousands of dainty little hors d'oeuvres. She was preparing to collapse when Jacqueline reminded her that they had done nothing about costumes.

Jean's response was profane.

"I have to have one," Jacqueline pointed out. "It was my idea, after all."

"I can't imagine what made you think of such a thing," Jean groaned. "Can't we do something with a bed sheet? A nice toga, maybe."

"Not with Lise's sheets we can't. Have you ever tried to turn a bed sheet into anything resembling human garb of any period? I have been concocting Hallowe'en costumes for longer than you've been alive, and believe me, the easiest thing to do is go to the nearest five-and-ten and buy one. Come along."

Still protesting, Jean was carried off. In a local branch of CIM, the most popular Roman department store, they found a section devoted to folk art and souvenirs. Jean looked dubiously at a shelf of pillows which said *"Arrivederci Roma."*

"What did you have in mind?" she asked.

"You can be a gondolier," Jacqueline said, picking up a straw hat with a bright crimson streamer down the back. "You've got blue slacks; all you need is the hat and one of those red-and-white striped jerseys."

"Okay, I'll take anything. What about you? You could be the Virgin." Jean indicated a counter where cloth was sold. "Ten yards of that blue. . . ."

"I've done that. In fourth grade, in the Christmas play. I'm afraid the part doesn't suit me any longer."

"How about Lady Godiva? It's a shame to waste that hair. Or Rapunzel."

"It's a pity," Jacqueline said regretfully, "that only saints, fairy-tale heroines, and the cast of *Hair* wear their tresses long and flowing. Oh, the hell with it. Let's get some cheesecloth and I'll drape a toga, or the female equivalent. Lise must have some books that show how to do it."

There were books, but they showed only the finished product, and by the time the two had Jacqueline's *palla*—the female equivalent—draped to their satisfaction, they were both helpless with laughter. The effect was good, though, and Jacqueline's red-gold coronet made her look quite imperial. They were trying to decide which empress she ought to be when the buzzer sounded. The first guests had arrived.

There were three of them; the Scovilles had come *en famille.* Professor Scoville, wearing a raincoat and a sheepish expression, demanded a room in which to change. When he reappeared, Andy caught Jean's eye and gave her a broad wink. Scoville, as predicted, had come as an Egyptian Pharaoh. The wide jeweled collar showed off his broad chest and shoulders, and the short tunic bared legs which, if rather hairy, were neither spindly nor shapeless.

Ann and Andy had come as their namesakes, the famous Raggedy twins. Jean fancied that even in Rome, which is accustomed to fantastic garb, they must have aroused considerable attention on the way over. That wouldn't bother Andy, but Jean wondered how he had persuaded his sister to appear in public with Raggedy Ann's bright-painted face.

"With our hair it was inevitable," Andy explained, rumpling his sister's bright mop. "We don't even need wigs."

The others came before long, and it was amusing to see what costumes they had chosen. Michael had taken Andy's cheerful insult literally; his beard was heavy anyway and by letting it go he had achieved a desperately unkempt look. He carried a half-empty jug of wine and seemed to feel that that was all he needed for a complete disguise.

José was Montezuma, complete with (imitation) feathered cape. He refused to explain where he had procured the costume, but it was magnificent. Ted, who had dug out a doublet and tights from a friend's amateur theatrical collection, promptly decided that he was Cortes. With a borrowed eyebrow pencil he drew himself a black Spanish moustache, and went off arm in arm with the Aztec ruler.

Jean expected that Dana would be the last to arrive, and she had anticipated that Dana's costume would be sexy and insubstantial. What she had not expected was that Dana would bring a date.

"I knew you wouldn't mind," she cooed, giving Jacqueline a triumphant glance. "You all remember Giovanni, don't you?"

She was, of course, Cleopatra. And her Mark Antony was Lieutenant di Cavallo.

His appearance cast a momentary pall on the company. Then Jacqueline rose to the occasion, greeting her guest with cool charm. In a short time the lieutenant had become what is commonly known as the life of the party. He sang, he strummed Andy's guitar, he made jokes with José, and he discussed the smuggling of antiquities with Scoville. By midnight the party was in full swing, and everyone seemed to be having a fine time.

Jean was not. She had been suspicious of the party from the first, and di Cavallo's appearance confirmed her suspicions. He looked magnificent in his sweeping white toga, but Jean knew he was miscast. Mark Antony, the rough, tough soldier who had let passion for a woman override ambition, was not the right role for this man. Again Jean was reminded of the cold, handsome face which appears on so many statues in Rome: Augustus, the most enigmatic of all the Julians, a man ruled throughout his life by calculating intelligence.

It was exactly midnight when di Cavallo pounded on the table and proposed a toast. The hilarity was at its height and it took him several minutes to get them all together, with their glasses of wine. José's headdress was tipped onto the back of his head and Ted's moustache had run into a shapeless smudge. Scoville was sulking; he had been trying all evening without success to get Jacqueline out onto the balcony. Now they all gathered around the big table in the dining area of the *salone,* and di Cavallo opened a fresh bottle.

"A toast to a lovely and charming lady," he said, lifting his glass. "Our hostess."

They drank. Di Cavallo filled the glasses again.

"We thank her," he said oratorically, "for a memorable evening. For this masquerade. And now, my friends, the masquerade is almost over."

The change in his voice struck them, even Scoville, who had consumed more wine than anyone else. One by one the relaxed figures straightened and turned, until they sat like a circle of frozen images, staring at the man who stood at the head of the table.

"The masquerade is over," di Cavallo repeated. The resemblance Jean had noticed was pronounced; the face was cold and beautiful and quite merciless. "Some of you, perhaps, have been deceived as to the purpose of this evening's entertainment. Yet I think that in your hearts none of you has ever been wholly deceived. You have known the truth, and tried for a number of different reasons to conceal it even from yourselves. But the truth cannot be concealed. It is time for it to emerge. It is time now."

Di Cavallo was enjoying himself. His expression had not lost any of its cool calm, but Jean sensed the streak of sadism underneath. His voice rolled.

"To come here under false pretenses was not the act of a gentleman. I feel no shame; because in my humble fashion I serve justice, and justice, my friends, sometimes demands the sacrifice of honor. Yet I cannot claim the credit for discovering the truth. That distinction rests with another, and it is for her to explain it to you."

His outstretched hand indicated Jacqueline. Gathering up the folds of his skirt in a royal gesture, he sat down.

Jacqueline's hands were loosely clasped around the stem of her glass and her eyes were fixed on the glowing burgundy liquid. She was as white as her robe, but her voice was perfectly steady when she began to speak.

"The lieutenant gives me too much credit—if that is the word. But I won't talk about blame or credit, honor or justice. This had to be done. Whether I like it or not is beside the point. In every human society, every culture of which we have record, one crime is the ultimate crime, punishable by the extreme penalty. On that, human ethics are unanimous. Murder is wrong."

She looked up. She was still pale, but her face had a shadow of the same ruthlessness Jean had seen in di Cavallo's. There was a stir around the silent table, a shift of bodies; but no sound.

"Albert's death was murder," Jacqueline went on. "I wonder how many of you were really deluded into thinking it anything else? The police were not. The scene was skillfully set, and at first the pattern seemed plain. But Lieutenant di Cavallo is far too good a policeman to be fooled. His intuition told him the truth, but there seemed no way of proving it, nor any way of finding the killer. It could be any one of a number of people. Yet the lieutenant was convinced that it was indeed one of that number. He supported the theory of suicide only because it seemed advantageous to let the killer think he had succeeded in that aspect of his crime."

She looked at Jean, and now there was a hint of apology in her voice.

"I went to the police, Jean, as soon as I realized you were in danger. It would have been inexcusable to do anything else. I expected to be laughed at, but that didn't bother me; ridicule, as a weapon, is only effective against the young. I was astounded to find the lieutenant was ready to believe me. Since then we have been working together. It has been a genuine collaboration; without the facts I was able to supply he could not have proceeded, but without him I would have been helpless to act."

She transferred her glance back to the tabletop, and her voice became impersonal again.

"We speculated about motive. The police were able to investigate the backgrounds of the suspects much more efficiently than I could, and they came up with some surprising facts." There was another uncomfortable stir around the table; Jacqueline disregarded it and went on. "Though several of your case histories provided possible motives, no single suspicious fact emerged. It became clear to us that an inquiry into motive was a dead end. We had to go at the problem from another angle.

"Let us look, then, at the simple physical facts. Albert's death was carefully planned. Nothing contradicted an assumption of suicide. Even if one assumed it was a case of murder, no clue indicated one suspect over another. It might be argued that a woman could not commit such a crime. By its very nature it would seem to demand physical strength and a certain degree of ruthlessness. But the modern female is not the fragile vessel her ancestress was. For all his bulk, Albert was not particularly muscular. And it wasn't difficult to imagine circumstances in which a woman might have found it easier than a man to get Albert into a vulnerable position. On his knees, perhaps, her hand twining in his hair as she bent over him. . . . It isn't a pleasant picture, I agree; but very little about this case was pleasant.

"The question of alibis is inconclusive. At least three of you were in the lowest level, not far from the scene of the crime, within minutes of its discovery. I include Jean, of course. To the police she was as prominent a suspect as anyone else. And she mentioned having spoken to Michael and to Dana just before she found Albert. None of the others has verifiable alibis, except for Ted and Ann. According to the priest on duty, they were talking to him at the time the murder was discovered. The only flaw in this alibi is that we are not sure how long Albert lay there before being found. I thought, then, that it was unlikely he could have lingered for very long, but I am told by the police surgeon that there are some amazing examples of survival. So, although I was inclined to eliminate Ted and Ann, I could not do so completely."

So far none of this was new to Jean; but she was sickly amused to note that the tactful first person plural with which Jacqueline had begun had now become an unequivocal "I."

"Thanks to your restless habits," Jacqueline continued, "I couldn't give anyone an alibi for the other suspicious events. Jean had two so-called "accidents" before the incident in the pool, when she nearly drowned. All three attacks were carefully planned; any one of them might have been accepted as the accident it appeared to be. The first one, caused by a toy left on the darkened stairs of her apartment building, was a most oblique type of attack; there was absolutely no way of tracing it back to its perpetrator. By that very fact, it was also inherently unsuccessful. I regard it as a wild stroke; something that might or might not work, but which was worth a try because it involved so little risk to the killer.

"The second attempt was more direct—pushing Jean into the path of a car. Here, one would think, the murderer took a greater risk. And yet again it was impossible to alibi any of you. The time of day was well chosen; it was the lunch-siesta period, when the streets are crowded. It is true that you are all rather distinctive-looking, easily recognized. But wigs are cheap here; a change of clothing, or simple disguise, could make any of you safe from a casual glance. And that incident had its own built-in safeguards. If Jean had recognized a friend she would have hailed him—or her—and then the attempt would not have been made.

After she had fallen into the street, the chance of her being able to recognize anyone was, to say the least, unlikely.

"The third attempt took place here, in the pool; and I find it hard to forgive myself for that, because I was expecting it. Expecting—and praying that it wouldn't happen. It did happen, right under my nose, and only luck got her out alive that time. And again I found it impossible to clear any of the suspects. But the incident confirmed what had been until then only a nasty hunch.

"The attempt in the pool also demonstrated the killer was getting desperate. The more 'accidents' Jean had, the less plausible they became; and in the third case the killer had to take an extraordinary risk of being recognized. I could only conclude that his need to silence Jean was great. She must pose a threat so potentially dangerous that he had to risk drawing official attention back to this little circle of people—the Seven Sinners, as Andy calls them."

"One moment," Scoville said. "May I point out one flaw in your masterful exposition? You claim the murderer had to silence Jean because of her knowledge. What if he is that strange but not uncommon type, a killer who enjoys killing? Could not these crimes have been committed by an outsider who hates students, or foreigners, or something of the sort?"

Jacqueline nodded. Jean noticed that she would not meet Scoville's eyes.

"I considered the possibility, of course. However, the police eliminated the tourists who were in the church when Albert died. On that occasion, and again in the third attempt on Jean's life, the only people present were the students. Add the fact that Jean was the one to find Albert, the one to whom he tried to speak, and I think you will admit the conclusion is hard to avoid."

She waited, courteously. Scoville shrugged, and leaned back in his chair.

"Therefore," Jacqueline resumed, "I returned to the one fact that set Jean apart. Albert could not speak to her, but he did communicate. He scratched a symbol in the dust before he died. No one else saw it. It may have been purposely obliterated. More likely, it was wiped out when Albert fell forward in his death agony. But Jean was the only one to see it."

"So she says," Dana interrupted. Her voice was openly hostile.

"So she says," Jacqueline repeated. "Naturally one has to consider the possibility that Jean lied. But why should she? There have been murderers who thrust themselves into public view, either from arrogance or from an anxious desire to be on the scene and know what's happening. It is a stupid thing to do; the sensible killer lets someone else find the body and stays as quiet as he can. But let us assume Jean is this psychological type. Surely it would be foolish of her, though, to insist on facts that raised further suspicion and obscured the very impression she was trying to create. For the murderer obviously tried to suggest a case of suicide. If Jean was the killer and wished to invent a last message from her victim, wouldn't she invent one that strengthened the assumption of suicide?

"I was forced, then, to the conclusion that Jean's story was true. But what a confusing story it was! Not only did Albert's message make no sense, but Jean had told it to everyone in the group, including the police. I kept coming up against that, like a brick wall; there seemed to be no point in trying to silence her after she had spoken.

"But was that single symbol the full extent of Albert's message? Perhaps Jean had not told all she knew."

"I did," Jean interrupted. "I keep telling you—"

"So you did. And I believed it. Let us suppose, however, that he wrote something other than what you say he wrote. The only possible reason you might have for concealing the truth was if Albert had written something which betrayed the identity of the killer. You might lie if he had accused you—or someone you cared for deeply enough to lie for him.

"That was feasible—before I started examining it. For, then, all you had to do was keep silent. Albert was dead when I arrived; you had time to obliterate his scrawl and claim you had found him dead. No one would have questioned such a statement; the police surgeon was astounded that he had lived so long. Every hypothesis seemed to lead me back to the same conclusion: that you had told the literal truth. The very meaninglessness of the statement made it more believable. For why should you invent a message that made no sense?

"I thought," said Jacqueline wryly, "I was going to burst a blood vessel in my brain over that crazy seven. I went through every wild theory I could think of. I pursued saints, because I was haunted by Albert's *idée fixe*. He had been obsessed by his saints, and I became obsessed too. Nothing came of it; not, at least, in the way I expected.

"The revelation finally came that day in the catacombs. Looking at the numbers over the lintel of the tomb, it hit me like a thunderbolt. Jean had never written the number, she had only named it. I scared her to death, and made the rest of you think I was losing my wits, by demanding she write it out. And, as I had come to expect, it was the Roman numeral instead of our familiar, Arabic seven.

"Up to that point, my confusion had been open, and openly expressed. After that . . ." Jacqueline's voice changed, and Jean felt her muscles tighten. This was it. They were getting to it now.

"I acted," Jacqueline admitted. Her pallor was more pronounced. "I still didn't have any proof, and I was afraid of what the killer might do next. I was no longer concerned for Jean, for I felt sure she had now expressed the knowledge the killer had tried to keep her from telling. It must have been a hideous shock to him when he learned Albert had lived long enough to leave an abortive but damning message. He saw its signifcance at once; but he was clever enough to realize that the significance might be obscured forever if he could keep Jean from repairing her inadvertent blunder."

Jacqueline took a sip of wine, and put the glass down. The wine, or some more subtle intoxicant, had stiffened her resolve. There were bright spots of color in her cheeks, and her eyes were angry.

"Sevens," she said. "Sevens all over the scene—scattered, like chaff, to confuse the picture. I said once, remember, that you were all overeducated. Didn't any of you see the truth, even after reading the inscription on the tomb? Was it too obvious for the subtle academic brain, or was the killer too successful in obscuring the issue? Yet he wasn't the only one; we all did it. I did it myself. And all the while the simple, obvious explanation was staring us in the face."

She looked around the circle, and the others looked back, unspeaking, almost unbreathing. Jacqueline banged her hand down on the table, and they all jumped; the wine glass tipped, spilling a small puddle of red onto the smooth mahogany.

"What would a dying man choose for his last message?" Jacqueline demanded. "Forget the subtleties and the ingenious theories. I've read the classic thrillers myself, and I know all the variations. I've admired the ingenuity of the author even while I questioned his basic premise. Because a dying man is not at his keenest intellectually, I question whether he could go through the tortuous deductions that mystery writers attribute to him, in order to produce a cleverly confusing message. And don't bring up that brilliant but equally unconvincing variant—that a dying man might produce a deliberately ambiguous message because his murderer is still present. Obviously the murderer would destroy anything he wrote. What does a dying man want to tell the world?"

Again her eyes went around the circle. Di Cavallo, who presumably knew the answer, was silent. He was smiling very slightly, but the upward curve of his lips did not warm his expression. Finally—of all people—Michael answered.

"The name of the person who killed him," he said.

"Yes," Jacqueline said. "And that is what Albert tried to write."

"Seven?" Ted said. "I still don't—"

"You're still bemused by the number. Hypnotized, as we all were. Forget the number. It has nothing to do with it. Albert didn't write a number. Look," Jacqueline said, with a terrible weariness. "This is what he wrote."

She used the puddle of wine for ink, so the word came out crudely scrawled with the tip of a reddened finger, as the dying man might have written it.

VII.

Someone got it. There was an intake of breath, so sharp it must have hurt the throat that made it. Jean didn't look up to see who had reacted. Her eyes were glued to the red letters.

"And this," said Jacqueline, "is what he was trying to write."

Her finger dipped again into the crimson puddle.

VIRGINIA.

Scoville pushed his chair back. It screamed like a living creature across the marble floor.

"Prove it," he said. "There are so many possible variations—"

"Not all that many," Jacqueline said. "The third letter, which Albert never completed, might be any one of a number of letters —*E, L, P, B*—others. But starting from this, the rest of the case can be, and has been, built up. The motive only made sense after we knew who the murderer was. And there is only one person in this group whose name begins with those three—or two and a half—letters."

Jean knew then. But she still didn't believe it.

"You're all accustomed to nicknames," Jacqueline said. "Albert wasn't, though. The first day I met him he insisted on knowing my correct name and title. He had no sense of humor; the joke behind some of your epithets must have eluded him completely. All this is irrelevant, really. What matters is that even before I checked the official records I was able to deduce which of you had a given name that matched Albert's scrawl."

For the first time since the talk had begun she looked directly at the two people sitting across the table from her. They always looked a great deal alike; now, in their common horror, the resemblance of their features was uncanny.

"Raggedy Ann and Andy," she said. "I'm an old-fashioned librarian, you know. As soon as I saw the hair and heard the names I remembered the stories. They were charming characters, those two rag dolls; but I wondered whether parents would really christen their children with those names—particularly when the son and daughter were born a year apart. I noticed that sometimes people called one of you Ginger. That's a logical nickname for a redhead; it becomes even more logical when the given name is Virginia—Ginnie—you see? I noted also that the other was sometimes called Junior. This can be a term of affection, but it is often a literal designation. Those are your real names, aren't they? Samuel Junior and Virginia. Albert knew both of you when you were children. He would think of you by the names he used then—not by family nicknames, which would not have been employed by your teachers."

"No," Andy said suddenly. "I'm not going to let you get away with this. Of course you're right about the names; when have we ever made a mystery of them? They're on all the records, passports. . . . We've used the nicknames for years. All you've done is cook up a crazy theory on the basis of a wild coincidence. You try it in court! Go ahead! That alibi of Annie's is better than you think."

"I agree," Jacqueline said.

Scoville sat up in his chair. Andy, stopped in mid-peroration, stared stupidly. Jacqueline said wearily,

"Of course all this is worthless legally. But the motive isn't."

"What motive? What reason could anyone have—"

"We go back," said Jacqueline, "to the saints. They kept cropping up, didn't they? There was one fact, at the very beginning, that would have made me wonder about the theory of suicide even if Jean hadn't started having accidents. When the police searched Albert's room, they found only a pitiable scrawl which presumably represented his total output after a year or more of work. It was incoherent and rambling—the product of a sick mind.

"We've all agreed that Albert was peculiar. But mental illness is not a discrete disease with a single set of symptoms, like chicken pox. I questioned—as did Jean—whether Albert's eccentricities were those of a man who might develop suicidal tendencies. Never once did he indicate any doubt of the value of his work. Fanatics of that type don't kill themselves. They cannot be convinced of the worthlessness of their life's work, because their belief in it is not based on rational premises. Up till the end Albert was enthusiastic, cocksure, contemptuous of critics.

"These attributes characterize the screwballs who hang around the lunatic fringes of scholarship. But they are also characteristic of scholars who are regarded as fanatics by their contemporaries. Classical scholars jeered at Schliemann and his dreams of Troy. Galileo and Semmelweis fought all their lives for recognition. I needn't go on; there are many examples.

"The fact that Albert had an *idée fixe* did not prove his idea was wrong. If he wasn't mad, if he didn't commit suicide—then what of his behavior on the night of the party? Was it possible that his wild accusation was not a sign of paranoia, but a statement of fact? Was this, in short, a crime for gain?

"We theorized about a family heirloom, a genuine treasure, which could have been possessed by a man who was grindingly poor in every other way. And all the while the answer was staring

us in the face. Albert did own one thing of supreme value to him
—his treasure. His work, in other words.

"To my surprise, I found a single assumption answered all my
questions. It explained Albert's accusation and the discrepancy
between the scanty sheaf of papers found in his room and the
bulging briefcase he carried—a briefcase so heavy it made him
walk lopsided. It also provided a motive for murder. If Albert had
stumbled on something important, a discovery worth stealing, it
could not be stolen with impunity. Albert was not stupid; if another scholar had published his discovery he would have recognized it. And while he might not have been able to prove it was
originally his, he could raise enough fuss to seriously discredit
the thief. Scholarly reputations are fragile."

"But," Jean said, "I thought you said it was murder for gain.
Doesn't that mean—"

"Killing to gain possession of something which is not rightfully
yours. Our trouble is that we think in material terms. Yet you of
all people—scholars and artists—should realize that there are
desires much more compulsive than the desire for mere money.
Someone needed an idea, a piece of original work. Good God, a
man can earn money, or steal it in comparative safety these days;
it is much less logical to kill for monetary gain than for an intan-
gible which cannot be procured by such simple means. You've
got it or you haven't got it, as the saying goes. The one thing a
man cannot produce on demand is a genuine creative idea. And
if he needs it badly enough. . . ."

"You speak in riddles now," said José. "I admit your point; you
are right, we can surely comprehend the hunger for scholarly
fame. But you do not speak of Ann. She is a sculptor. She could
not use the work of a man like Albert."

"That is true. Yet Albert thought his attacker was Ann."

"A disguise," Andy said sharply. "You spoke of that earlier—
how easy it would be—"

Jacqueline broke in. "Yes, a disguise. Who? Most of you are
automatically eliminated, if my theory of motive is correct. Michael is like Ann, he couldn't use Albert's discovery. Neither
could José. Jean? Again, no. As a librarian, I know how narrow
your scholarly fields are. Jean has been working in medieval art
history. She couldn't produce a book on Paleo-Christian

hagiology without raising eyebrows. That only leaves three possibilities. The three people who deal, in one form or another, with Roman archaeology and history. Because we can't be sure, even now, precisely what form Albert's work took."

Slowly, inevitably, all eyes focused on a single figure.

"No!" Dana exclaimed. Clumsily she got to her feet. The appeal of Cleopatra had fled; there was only a sallow, rather chubby girl in a funny costume, fumbling at the table to keep from falling. "No, I didn't! I couldn't! I—"

"Someone catch her," Jacqueline said. "She's going to fall. She didn't do it."

"She's a girl," Andy said. "The only one who could disguise herself as Ann. A wig—"

"Don't you see," Jacqueline interrupted, "that it's no use, Andy? You can't use Albert's material now. It would be a dead giveaway, after this. You've failed; it was all for nothing. Won't you speak, and end this? It's too hard on—on everyone."

Andy shook his head.

"You're crazy," he said in a low voice. "A crazy old—"

Jacqueline glanced at Scoville. She spoke quickly, as if she wanted to get it over as quickly as possible.

"The light in the murder room was poor, but it was not that poor. Dana couldn't by any conceivable trick have made Albert think she was Ann. Their figures, for one thing . . . and clothing; the killer didn't have time for elaborate changes of costume, nor could he walk into the church carrying a suitcase. Even a wig would require a box. Ted is the only other person who might have had a motive, and I needn't point out the absurdity of his trying to disguise himself. But the resemblance between Ann and her brother is striking. Ann is tall for a girl and Albert was short; he wouldn't have noticed the height differential unless brother and sister were together. Hair, clothing—they were both wearing dark slacks and shirt that day—all Andy needed was a smear of lipstick, a scarf over his head, and a pair of sunglasses. It would serve, for long enough to do the job.

"Once I knew the truth, everything pointed to Andy. He fits both criteria—motive and means—and he is the only one who does. It would be natural for Albert to talk to Andy about his work; Albert thought of him as a boyhood friend and a fellow enthusiast. Albert's English was poor, and his conversation was hard to follow; but Andy knows French and, I suspect, more Arabic than he admits. He's an excellent linguist. He is the one among you most likely to understand what Albert was doing, and to recognize a meaningful discovery. He is also the one who could most easily profit from Albert's work. It is, essentially, his own field. And he needs an idea. Shortly the trustees will be deciding on the renewal of the fellowships. Andy must have his. Everyone expects him to get it. And he is . . . Sam, I'm sorry; I'm not blaming you, no one could; but he is haunted by the fear of failing, failing himself and you. A different kind of child might have reacted differently to the magnificent image you project. Andy felt impelled to equal and surpass it."

"My thesis," Andy said in a strange, high voice. "I don't need to steal ideas from anybody. He's brilliant, Andy is. He's brighter than anybody in the whole—"

"Oh, God," Dana muttered.

"The thesis," Jacqueline said. "And the boy, the friend, who committed suicide. Who had the nervous breakdown, Andy? How often has Ann lied to protect you? Did she know, in that other case, or did she only suspect?"

Andy fought visibly for control. The wild light in his eyes faded, and his quivering features grew hard.

"Now stop it," he said. His voice was so calm, so reasonable that they all stirred uneasily. "I'll end this business right now. You're saying the murderer is the one who stole Albert's work, right? Albert claimed his precious whatever-it-was was stolen the day of the party—when he went out to eat. All right. I was in the library that afternoon, the whole bloody time. Some of you must have seen me there."

"He is right," Ted said. "I was in the stacks at noon, and saw him in his office. For several hours thereafter I sat in the reading room. I would have seen him if he had left."

"I saw him too," Jean said.

"All right," Jacqueline said. "To the last painful word, is that it? Ann."

Ann had been sitting with her grotesquely painted face hidden in her hands. She looked up. Tears had streaked the makeup, but her face did not look at all comic.

"One or the other of you is going to be accused of murder," Jacqueline said. "The logic can't be faulted. The motive can be applied to either; your devotion to your brother is well known, you might steal for him. You would probably prefer suffering yourself to seeing him suffer. You've done it all your life. But can you let him go free, knowing him for what he is? He's sick; he may not be incurable. Whether he is or not, whether or not you are ready to sacrifice yourself for him, you have no moral right to sacrifice his potential victims. This will happen again."

For a long moment the whole room waited, without breathing. Then Ann's head drooped.

"It was me," she said, so softly they had to strain to hear. "In the library that day. You said—how easy it is for us to look like each other. . . . He said it was part of a practical joke. Then, after Albert died . . . nobody ever asked! And I didn't want to believe. . . ."

Di Cavallo had been poised and ready, but Andy's supple quickness caught him off guard. It was Michael who pulled the clawed fingers from Ann's throat, and it took both of them to hold him until he finally collapsed into a sobbing heap. But bad as it was, Jean knew this was not the sight that would haunt her. It was Scoville's face, as he cursed his daughter for betraying his son.

CHAPTER TEN

*T*oward morning a thunderstorm moved in over the city, in a spectacular display of Jovian thunder and lightning. Next day the air over Rome was sparklingly clear. The mighty dome of Michelangelo floated on a sea of green branches. The suburban streets looked as if they had been newly painted in the warm earth colors Jean would always remember when she thought of Rome—umber and orange, gold and brick-red. The sky had the heavenly blue shade Fra Angelico used in the cloaks of his Madonnas, and wild poppies glowed like rubies in an empty lot beside the café.

Jean was the only customer at Gino's. She had left the apartment early that morning, before Jacqueline awoke, and she didn't expect any of the others to join her in their old haunt. The Seven Sinners would never meet again; and the commonplace neighborhood café held memories she would not be able to face comfortably for a time.

Yet when she recognized the two figures coming up the hill she was, somehow, not surprised. At the sight of them something shifted and fell back into focus. The past could not be obliterated; it had to be endured. And among its memories were some that were too good to be discarded.

José was back in his customary suits of solemn black, but the ghost of Montezuma still haunted his aquiline face. Ted looked the same, outwardly, but there was something different about his expression, and a new swing to his step. They greeted her rather diffidently.

"We hoped you would come," Ted said. "But we wondered—"

"About many things," José interrupted. "We could hardly linger, last night, to ask questions."

"Don't expect any answers from me," Jean said. "I'm just as baffled as you are. The whole thing—"

Her voice broke. José said calmly,

"Was unendurable. That is why we must ask the questions, talk like little gossips. It is the only way—to extract the commonplace and the rational from disaster. It could have been worse." Meeting Jean's eyes, he added, "You might have loved him. That would have been worse."

"I did love him. The same way I love all of you."

Ted nodded.

"Our feelings for one another run deeper than I had realized. But you must admit there is a difference between those feelings and the one José is talking about."

"Yes. For a while I thought . . . hey, look! Isn't that Jacqueline?"

"Jacqueline and Michael," José corroborated.

Michael was looking almost spruce this morning; not only had he shaved, he had combed his hair and he wore his "good" shirt —the one without holes. Jacqueline was faultlessly attired in a blue linen suit. Her purse and gloves were of the same pale ivory as her shoes, and her hair was coiled into a knot at the back of her neck.

The two men rose to honor this sartorial elegance, and José pulled out a chair.

"I expected you," he said.

"I had to come." Pulling off her gloves, Jacqueline looked at each of them in turn. "I'm leaving Rome today, and I may not see you again.

"But I knew you'd all be bursting with questions. I owe you that much, to know the truth before it comes out in the newspapers."

Now that the invitation had been given, none of them could think of anything to say. After a moment Jacqueline said, with a faint smile,

"I wasn't sure any of you would be speaking to me."

"Why not?" Ted asked in astonishment. "Oh! Oh, I see. You are thinking of the stool-pigeon syndrome, perhaps. We are not a street gang, to place loyalty to the mob above all other virtues."

"You yourself said it," José added. "In all cultures there is one ultimate crime."

"Not to mention the minor detail of Jean's skin being kept intact," Michael contributed. "We like it in the shape it's in."

"Sorry," Jacqueline said ruefully. "I guess I've been dealing with the less logical segment of your age group for too long."

"Before we start asking questions," Ted said, "maybe we should wait to see if Dana is coming."

"She's coming," Jacqueline said. An odd little smile curved her mouth. "But we needn't wait. . . . Ah, here she is."

A car came down the street. It was not until it pulled over to the curb and parked, in bland disregard of the sign forbidding such activity, that they recognized the occupants. The vehicle was an open sports car, silver in color, and di Cavallo was at the wheel. Beside him, Dana looked as smug as a Persian cat.

The two got out of the car and joined the others. After greetings had been exchanged, di Cavallo said briskly,

"Have you finished your lecture, then?"

"I haven't even begun. Really, I think we covered most everything last night, didn't we?"

"One thing I did not understand," José said. "The reference to an earlier suicide—a friend of Andy's. Was that really as it sounded to me?"

"It was one of the facts that turned up in the police investigation of your backgrounds," Jacqueline said, after waiting for a moment to see whether di Cavallo would answer. "However, there had been references to it more than once. Nothing can be proved now; there is no need, it would only cause needless pain for the boy's parents. But I think—I am almost sure—it was

Andy's first venture into murder. His much-admired thesis was written after his friend died."

"I don't see how Andy could get away with it," Jean said. "What about the boy's adviser, his other friends? Wasn't anyone suspicious?"

"How much do you know of the details of anyone else's work? It's amazing how seldom people really listen to one another. The boy's adviser? Well, believe it or not, I wrote a thesis once myself in the prehistoric past. I met my adviser once a month, and he told me the latest cute stories about his dog. Maybe that's an exaggeration, but the amount of genuine communication between us was very limited. At least he was willing to meet with me. Not all advisers are."

"Master's or doctor's dissertation?" José asked.

"What's your field?" Ted demanded.

"That's beside the point," Jacqueline said demurely. "I am merely trying to demonstrate that Andy was fairly safe in stealing someone else's ideas. Assume the unlikely did occur and someone noted a resemblance between his work and the tentative theories of another man. The conclusion would be that the other man had copied Andy. No, there was very little risk for Andy. If he hadn't panicked and attacked Jean, he might have gotten away with Albert's murder."

"Except for the detective talents of Mrs. Kirby," said Ted. "To what do you attribute your success?"

"To a unique combination of circumstances that could never possibly recur," Jacqueline said, rather too forcefully. "A librarian is a hanger-on around the fringes of the scholarly world. I knew enough about that world to comprehend the motive, but not enough to get bogged down in the irrelevant details that confused the rest of you. And if there's one thing we learn in my job, it's research. We deal with many fields; we don't know much about any one of them, but we do know where to go to get the facts. I know, there are some librarians who regard books as little boxes to be arranged and classified and rebound from time to time; but you'd be surprised how many of us actually read the darned things! I started out in a small town library, where I covered a little of everything from children's books to archaeology and mystery stories. I've read hundreds of thrillers, and I've always been skeptical of those complicated dying messages."

"Me, too," Michael said. He was doodling again; he didn't even look up from his sketch pad.

Jacqueline stared at him.

"Are you trying to tell me—"

"Oh, sure, I saw that part of it right away." Michael looked up and smiled angelically. "I don't think in Roman numerals either."

"After all my pompous remarks . . . why didn't you say something?"

"What, for instance? People think I'm crazy anyhow, especially the fuzz—er, police. I didn't know about Albert's work, or any of that jazz, remember. I just thought maybe he cornered Annie and she flipped. I always liked Annie."

There was a baffled silence. Then di Cavallo said, in a muted roar, "Young man. Am I to understand—"

"I couldn't fit Jean's accidents into it, though," Michael went on calmly. "I didn't think Annie would hurt Jean, but . . . I didn't know what to think."

"You thought about Andy," Jacqueline said.

"Yeah, sure. After Albert accused him of stealing his precious. Shades of Tolkien . . . Albert was definitely a Gollum type, you know." The silence got to him after a while. He looked up, saw the circle of fascinated faces, and blushed slightly. "Well, why else would Albert come straight to the Scovilles' apartment after he found his treasure was missing? Nobody told him about the party; we didn't want him horning in. It had to be Ann or Andy he was looking for. I don't know much French, but that was a masculine noun he used—"

" '*Voleur!*' " Jean exclaimed. "How could we have been so dumb?"

"And," Michael went on, "the way Andy moved in on him, to shut him up before he could say too much, was very cool. Andy can—could—talk the leg off a table; I suppose he told Albert some story, promised to help him track down the thief, or said he'd borrowed the material, or something. . . . Andy ducked out, then, into the john, and not long afterwards Albert passed out. It was too quick and neat to be coincidental. Ann mentioned once they had sleeping pills. Even so, I couldn't be sure about Andy. I thought of Albert's treasure as some family jewel or other, couldn't dig why Andy would want a thing like that."

Jacqueline opened her purse and took out a sheet of paper.

"Michael says I can keep this, Jean. Is that okay with you?"

"Sure," Jean said, recognizing the line of saints. The sketch of Andy, debonair as Saint George, made her feel a little sick.

"This," said Jacqueline, spreading it out, "was a graphic statement of the truth. It hit me with quite a shock when I saw it."

They studied it in absorbed silence; most of them had not seen it before.

"Who the hell . . . oh," Dana said. "Mary Magdalene. Michael, I don't think I like that look. . . ."

"Nor do I," José said. "One of these days, Michael, someone is going to send you a bomb through the mail."

"It may be me," Ted said. "Saint Stephen indeed. I admit that it may have a certain appropriateness—perhaps more than you realize."

"Oh, I realize," Michael said. "I know who your new girl friend is. Talk about martyr complexes. . . . If your old man doesn't kill you, she will."

"So everyone knows," Ted said resignedly. "Except my father . . . he soon will. I wrote to him this morning."

"I don't know," Dana said. "Have you jilted your fiancée? Men are all finks."

"That other was a family affair," Ted said defensively. "She will not be hurt; she didn't care."

"Yeah," Michael said, "but to get involved with an Arab girl. . . ."

"Not only an Arab," Ted said. "She is a member of a Palestinian guerrilla group."

There was a short, respectful silence. Remembering the handsome hawk face of the girl in the café, Jean understood. Apparently Michael had gone through some of his student contacts to discover the girl's identity.

"But surely," said di Cavallo, as intrigued as the others, "isn't that a trifle . . . ?"

"Not a trifle. My father will disown me," Ted said. His voice was resigned, but there was a light in his eyes that made him look even more like Michael's sketch. "But feelings do not follow politics, do they? And not all of us, in my generation, are so free of guilt as our fathers, with their one obsession. To repossess Eretz Israel, we dispossessed half a million people. Do the sufferings of millions of Jews, through thousands of years, justify the infliction of more suffering, on others? Since I fought in the war my feelings have changed. I have argued with my father; now I argue with Salwa, because I do not believe that her kind of violence will right this new wrong any more than our violence against her people righted our ancient wrong. I hope to convert her—not to change her principles, but her methods. Someday, out of all this, there must be a way to peace."

"Ishmael and Isaac were both sons of Abraham," Jacqueline murmured. "I admire your principles, Ted. I hope you succeed. But the moderate usually gets stoned by both sides."

"I have methods of persuasion with Salwa which are quite effective," Ted said modestly. "If I go down under the stones I will go down fighting. And," he added with a sudden grin, "I shall have one hell of a good time before I fall."

"And we thought you were a spy," Jean said. The look on Ted's face made her laugh. "You wouldn't believe some of the things we thought. I didn't suspect Andy any more than I did the rest of you."

"Michael did," Jacqueline said. She pointed to the sketch. "His identifications were—forgive me, Dana—alarmingly accurate. All his saints were pacifists except one. Saint George was the heroic murderer, the only one of the lot who committed violence. And he was the patron of the Crusaders. They did a lot of damage among the Arabs, if you recall."

"I wasn't thinking of that," Michael muttered.

"That's what makes you so terrifying," Jacqueline said severely. "You don't think; you just reach in and drag out people's souls. Why did you make Ann into Saint Barbara?"

"Needed some virgin saint or other."

"Yet her legend is very suggestive. It was her father, if you recall, who locked her in the tower, and later betrayed her."

"Which stood out like a billboard." Michael's voice was savage. "Damn that bastard Scoville; he's the one who caused all this."

"Don't dump on my generation," Jacqueline said. "We're the

victims of our genes and our surroundings and our parents, just as you are."

"Blame is useless," José said heavily. "We are all victims. . . . And I feel myself particularly a victim. I should rather be Beelzebub than Saint Augustine, as you show him."

"I don't get it," Dana said, staring blankly at the sketch. "None of them make any sense, except maybe Jean as a little lamb. . . . And this one of Jake is downright blasphemous."

"Not blasphemous, just plain insulting," Jacqueline said. "I may be a reluctant mother, Michael, but my halo is not a bit ragged. It's big and shiny and neat, and I earned it over twenty-one hard-working years."

Michael smiled.

"Talk about hangups," he said. "You didn't want to get involved with us, did you? It was a case of the triumph of instinct over common sense."

"Not instinct—habit. In both my professional capacities I've been laying down the law to the young for twenty years." Jacqueline rose, picking up her purse. "So now I think I'm entitled to a weekend off. If I don't see you again, I'll be following your varied careers with considerable interest. In my reluctant way, I've become rather fond of all of you."

Di Cavallo was on his feet; the others followed suit, even the girls. The occasion seemed to demand something, but no one knew exactly what to say. It was José who found the words.

"Be of good cheer," he said, his dark eyes intent on the older woman's face. "No man is immortal."

The ancient pagan epitaph should have sounded strange from him, as he stood straight and tall in the dark robe of the militant Christian order, but it seemed to strike the right note. Jacqueline's sober face relaxed into a smile.

"Good-bye," she said.

Di Cavallo followed her as she walked swiftly to the car. He opened the door for her, and closed it; then, with one sweep of his long legs, he got into the driver's seat and started the engine. It was not until the car had pulled away, with a triumphant roar of the exhaust, that the abandoned watchers fully grasped what had happened. Jean looked from one blank face to the next.

Dana's expression put the final touch on the situation. Jean burst into shouts of laughter.

"Outfought and outmaneuvered," she gasped. "Sorry, Dana; I can't help it."

"I wonder where they are going," Ted said.

"None of our business. Do you realize how little we know about that lady? Did she ever a mention a husband?"

"If she did, this is not the time to bring it up," José said.

Dana's face was still a study. Finally her mouth relaxed into a grudging smile.

"That son of a gun," she said, using a more explicit term. "He's been rushing me like crazy the last few days. And all he wanted was an excuse to be on the spot at the right moment."

"Maybe he was protecting you," Michael said coolly. "Didn't you ever think you might be in danger?"

Dana paled.

"You're trying to scare me."

"I've been thinking some more," Michael said pensively. "Everybody, including Andy, thought Jean was his big danger. I'm not so sure. The fuzz aren't Latinists, and they have those nice simple minds like Jake keeps bragging about; so they would have been on the track, probably, if they had ever seen the seven written out. Di Cavallo must have known the official names, since he checked us out with the Embassy and all that. But I don't see how he could have proved anything. That's why they had to stage that sticky little drama last night. Without a confession—"

"All right, all right," Dana said impatiently. "What about me?"

"The seven clue was useless without the motive," Michael went on, maddeningly deliberate. "So long as Albert was considered a crackpot there was no way of nailing Andy for the murder. Which reminds me—there's a question nobody asked. At some point Andy substituted his crazy composition for Albert's real notes. But the big question is—how could he steal the material and risk leaving Albert on the loose? He must have known the guy would complain."

Dana, still morosely wrestling with the unpalatable possibility Michael had presented, was silent. It was Ted who asked meekly,

"All right, Holmes. How?"

"I'm not even Watson," Michael said. "But Jake and I were talking about it on the way up here. We'll never know for sure, unless Andy . . . But Jake thinks Andy tried to knock Albert out earlier—left him a drink loaded with dope or something. Obviously it didn't work. But the technique is typical of Andy; he tried the indirect method at first, with Jean, before he closed in on her."

Dana took a deep breath.

"What about me?" she cried. "You said—"

"I'm getting to that. Now, as I said, it was unlikely that di Cavallo would ever figure out the motive. He isn't a scholar, and he accepted our evaluation of Albert. But there were two people who knew enough about Albert's subject to be able to spot the value of his work—you, Dana, and Ted. Ted is an Israeli, and a male—on both counts not the kind of audience Albert would seek out. You, on the other hand. . . ."

Dana's face was green.

"But I did know. I mean—didn't any of you—"

"Ah, no," José muttered. He smote himself heavily on the brow. "I do not believe this. You knew?"

"Well, yes. I mean—"

"You knew," José shouted, "that that miserable young fool was not a fool, that those pitiful notes were not his, that he had found a valuable and important thing—and you did not contradict the police when they talked of suicide?"

"Yes—no!" Dana was close to tears. "I never thought of it like that. . . . I mean, people kill themselves for weird reasons! How was I to know the notes weren't his? And that weird idea of his— it was just weird, I didn't know! He kept following me around, you know how he was, and he talked all the time, and I didn't pay much attention—"

"Now, now," Ted said soothingly. "We understand. No imagination," he explained sadly to the others. "Combined with a greatly inflated ego . . . what do you expect? As Jacqueline said, no one ever listens."

"He might have killed me," Dana sniffed.

"I doubt that you were in danger." José looked a little sheepish. "Dana, I apologize for shouting. You understand, it was prompted by frustrated curiosity. For days we have been talking about Albert's work, and his great discovery, and his treasure; and none of us knows what it is! Relieve our curiosity, since you are the only one who can."

"Well, I didn't really listen," Dana repeated. She blew her nose into the handkerchief José handed her; Gino's café did not boast such amenities as napkins. "It was something about a saint's tomb, under one of the churches."

The others exchanged glances. Ted said delicately,

"Do you happen to remember which church?"

"No. Oh—Saint Petra, something like that."

"Could it have been Santa Petronilla?" José asked.

"Right, that was it. He'd been reading old manuscripts. You know, the *Notitia ecclesiarum* and ancient pilgrims' books—that stuff."

"Yes, I know that stuff," José said in an odd voice. "Pilgrims began coming to Rome even before the fourth century. They wrote travel books . . . an incurable habit. . . . Do you mean Albert stumbled upon a reference no one else ever noticed?"

"Not just one—it was, like, putting together a lot of clues from different sources. Like with St. Peter's. Wasn't there someone, back in the third century, who wrote that he saw Saint Peter's memorial on the Vatican? Nobody paid much attention to it until they dug and found the memorial. It was like that. Somebody saw the tomb, way back when, and said it had a long inscription on it. Something about the daughter of Saint Peter. I remember that because it struck me as weird. I didn't even know he was married."

"Married," José repeated, like a machine. "Inscription. . . . But no. If such a thing once existed, it must have been destroyed. Albert was a crazy fanatic."

"Andy wasn't," Jean reminded them. "He valued Albert's work enough to steal it. You know—it isn't impossible. I bet Albert knew more about the virgin saints than anybody. Even his obsession gave him an advantage; he would take literally facts that other students might dismiss as legend."

"Like Schliemann and the *Iliad*," José agreed.

"He kept comparing himself with Schliemann," Dana said. "He had it all worked out. He even got down into the crypt of the church and found a fragment of stonework that matched someone's description back in 1143—oh, I don't know how he did it, but he was convinced the tomb was still there."

José kept shaking his head.

"It is more than possible," Ted said, his eyes glittering as the idea grew on him. "It has happened before. Several of the catacombs were lost during the Middle Ages and only rediscovered in modern times. What a fantastic thing!"

Dana was sniffling pathetically into José's handkerchief.

"Now stop it, all of you," Jean said. She leaned across the table and patted the other girl's hand. "Don't mind them, Dana. Michael was putting you on. Where's that darned Gino? We all need some coffee."

Gino stood in the doorway, wiping his hands on his apron. His eyes moved over the group and then, for the first time, he spoke to them as fellow human beings.

"Where are the others? The young boy and the girl with the red hair. You are only five today, not seven."

"They won't be coming again," Michael said, in the painful silence. "But we'll be here, Gino. We'll all be here. For a little while longer."

The
Murders
of
Richard III

To Marge

A dear friend and a fellow-traveler along
the thorny by-ways of Ricardian research

CHAPTER ONE

*T*he portrait was that of a man. Recent cleaning had brought out the richness of the colors: a background of smoldering scarlet, the crimson of rubies in the jeweled collar and hat brooch, the gold threads in the undertunic displayed by open collar and slashed sleeves. Yet the overall impression was sober to the point of grimness. Shoulder-length brown hair framed the man's spare face. It was not the face of a young man, although the subject had been barely thirty years of age when it was painted. Lines bracketed the tight-set mouth and made deep vertical indentations between the narrowed eyes, which were focused, not on the beholder, but on some inner vision. Whatever his thoughts, they had not been pleasant ones.

The portrait had an odd effect on some people. Thomas Carter was one of them. He had seen it innumerable times; indeed, he could summon up those features in memory more clearly than he could those of his own father, who was enjoying an acrimonious eighth decade in Peoria, Illinois. Thomas could not explain the near-hypnotic spell cast by the painted features, but he sincerely hoped they were having the same effect on his companion. He had private reasons for wanting Jacqueline Kirby to develop an interest in Richard III, quondam king of England, who had met a messy death on the field of battle almost five hundred years earlier.

Thomas had not changed a great deal since the day he and Jacqueline had first met, at the eastern university where Jacqueline was employed at one of the libraries. He had acquired a few more silver threads, but they blended with his fair hair. His baggy blue sweater tactfully concealed a slight tendency toward embonpoint. Thomas was a fair golfer and a good tennis player; but he was also an amateur chef, and this latter hobby left its marks on his figure. The blue sweater and the shabby tweeds were British made, but Thomas was not, although he was presently lecturing at one of England's oldest universities.

His prolonged bachelordom had given rise to predictable rumors. Thomas knew of the rumors and did not resent them; indeed, he encouraged them by his abnormal reticence about his personal affairs. Although he would have denied the charge indignantly, he was a rather old-fashioned man who believed that gentlemen do not boast of their conquests. He also found his reputation a useful tactical weapon. It reassured the ladies and put them off guard.

Neither this device nor any other had aided Thomas's campaign with Jacqueline. He had begun his pursuit the first day he saw her ensconced behind the desk in the library, glowering impartially on all comers from behind her heavy glasses. Thomas noted the emerald-green eyes behind the glasses, and the rich coppery bronze of the hair pinned back in a severe knot. He even judged, with fair accuracy, the figure under the tailored wool suit. The job offer from England ended the campaign before it had fairly begun. However, he and Jacqueline had become friends, and Thomas appreciated Jacqueline's quick unorthodox mind and weird sense of humor as much as he did her other attributes. When Jacqueline wrote him that she was spending part of the summer in England, he had replied enthusiastically, offering his services as guide to the glories of London. He had not, at that time, had ulterior motives. The motives had arisen in the interim, and had directed them to the place where they presently stood. The National Portrait Gallery, though one of London's accepted tourist "sights," was not high on Jacqueline's list of things to see. Thomas glanced at her uneasily. If she resented his arbitrary choice she would say so, in no mellow tones.

Jacqueline was regarding the portrait with a fixed stare. Her horn-rimmed glasses rode high on her nose, but she had left the rest of her tailored working costume at home. She wore a short, clinging dress of her favorite green; the short sleeves and plunging neckline displayed an admirable tan. Tendrils of bronze hair curled over her ears and temples. Without turning her head, she spoke. The voice could not by any stretch of the imagination be called mellow.

"The Tower of London," she said. "Westminster Abbey. Buckingham Palace. I'm just a little country girl who has never been abroad. What am I doing here? I want to see the Changing of the Guard. I want to have tea, a real English tea, in a real London tea shop. I want—"

"You just had lunch," Thomas said indignantly. "At Simpson's on the Strand. You had an enormous lunch. Don't you gain weight?"

Instead of replying, Jacqueline let her eyes drift sideways. They focused on Thomas's midriff. Reflexively Thomas sucked in his breath, and Jacqueline went on with her mournful monologue.

"I don't even mind looking at portraits. Elizabeth the First, Charles the Second . . . I adore Charles the Second. He was a very sexy man. I could contemplate Keats and Byron and Shelley without resentment. And what do I get? A bad portrait—if it is a portrait, and not a seventeenth-century painter's imaginative guess—of a famous villain. Old Crouchback himself."

"Old Crouchback!" Thomas was indignant. "Look at him. See anything wrong with his back?"

Jacqueline studied the portrait again and Thomas let out a little sigh of relief as the glasses began to slip slowly down her narrow, high-bridged nose. The glasses were a barometer of Jacqueline's moods. When she was interested in, or worried about something, she forgot to push them back into place. In moments of extreme emotion they perched precariously on the tip of her nose.

"No," Jacqueline said finally.

"There is a slight hint of deformity in the set of the shoulders; one looks higher than the other. But that could be due to bad painting. He certainly was not a hunchback. He's even good-looking, in a gloomy sort of way. It is a contemporary portrait, of course?''

Thomas glanced at her suspiciously. She continued to contemplate the portrait of Richard III with candid interest, but Thomas was not deceived. Art history was one of Jacqueline's specialties.

"No. It's been dated to about 1580. Like most of the other portraits of Richard, it was probably copied from a lost original. The only one that might be a contemporary portrait is in the Royal Collection. When it was X-rayed recently, the experts found that parts of it had been painted over. Originally the right shoulder was lower, even with the left, and the eyes were not so narrow and slitlike.''

Jacqueline's eyebrows lifted. She would never admit it, but Thomas knew that he had caught her interest.

"Retouched, to suggest the hunchbacked, squinting villain? That does suggest that the original was a contemporary portrait, too flattering to suit Richard's enemies. Let's see; if I remember my history lessons, Richard's successor was Henry the Seventh, the first of the Tudor kings and the last heir of the house of Lancaster. Richard was the house of York. Henry got the crown by killing Richard at the Battle of Bosworth—''

"Henry Tudor never killed anyone in a fair fight," Thomas said contemptuously. "At Bosworth he was running for the rear when Richard was cut down by a dozen men. It was Richard's good name Henry tried to destroy. Henry had no real claim to the throne and no popular support. He'd have lost the Battle of Bosworth if his widowed mother hadn't been smart enough to marry one of the most powerful nobles in the kingdom. Lord Stanley and his brother marched to Bosworth field as Richard's vassals and then treacherously attacked him. The only way Henry could justify his seizure of the throne was to show Richard as a usurper and a tyrant. Otherwise Henry was the usurper, and a rebel against the rightful king. Henry began the Tudor legend about wicked King Richard. He literally rewrote history. He—''

"He wasn't sexy," said Jacqueline regretfully. She had moved on; Thomas joined her in front of the portrait of Henry VII. "Grasping hands, and a mouth like a steel trap. And a shifty, suspicious expression.'' She turned to the neighboring portrait. "Who's the simpering doll-faced blond lady?"

"Henry's queen, Elizabeth of York. His marriage with her united the houses of Lancaster and York, and ended the Wars of the Roses. She was Richard's niece, the daughter of his elder brother, Edward the Fourth. Whom you see before you, in this portrait. He was supposed to have been one of the handsomest kings England ever had—a big blond six-footer, with an eye for the ladies."

"He doesn't look very sexy," said Jacqueline, eyeing the flat, doughy features of Edward IV critically.

"Sexy, hell. If I had realized you suffered from historical necrophilia, I'd never have brought you here. Ready to leave?"

"Oh, no. You brought me here, and I'm not leaving till I've seen all my heroes. Keats, Shelley—and of course King Charles. Where is he? 'Here's a health unto his Majesty—' "

"I had forgotten your regrettable habit of bursting into song at odd moments. Jacqueline. . . ."

It took Thomas over an hour to extract Jacqueline from the gallery. The portrait of Charles II had to be admired and the long line of his official mistresses subjected to a scathing commentary. Jacqueline said they were all too fat. When Thomas finally got her out the door, Trafalgar Square was raucous with late-afternoon traffic, and Jacqueline said she was faint from hunger.

"No wonder I love England," she remarked some time later, after devouring most of a plate of cream-filled buns. "People eat so often here. Morning tea, breakfast, elevenses, lunch, afternoon tea—"

"I don't think I can afford you," said Thomas.

"I know you can't." Jacqueline gave him a look that left him momentarily speechless. She pushed her glasses firmly back onto the bridge of her nose and regarded him severely. "All right, Thomas. I know you're up to something. First you invite me to a country weekend with a lot of people I've never met; then you deluge me with information about one of the most mixed-up periods in English history. There must be a connection, but I can't figure out what it is. Go on; I can see you're dying to lecture about something. I recognize your classroom scowl."

"I'm not going to lecture," Thomas said self-consciously. "How much do you know about—"

He stopped, staring at Jacqueline. She had slipped sideways in her chair. One arm dangled; the hand at its end was out of sight under the tea table, but it seemed to be making violent motions.

"For God's sake," Thomas snapped. "What are you looking for? If it's cigarettes, I'll buy you some. You'll never find anything in that purse. Or is it a briefcase? Anyhow, I thought you had kicked the habit."

Jacqueline resumed an upright position. In one hand she held a ball of white thread; in the other, a metal shuttle. Thomas watched, open-mouthed, as she wound the thread around her fingers in a pattern that resembled a one-handed form of cat's cradle.

"I have kicked the habit nine times since you last saw me. I have taken up tatting in order to help me kick it once again. I tried knitting, but that didn't work; every time I reached in my purse I stabbed myself on a knitting needle."

"I suspect this isn't going to work either," said Thomas. "Forgive me for mentioning it, but your fingers are turning blue. I think the thread is too tight."

Jacqueline put the shuttle down and began unwinding the thread.

"Thomas, you are too easily distracted. If I should choose to chin myself on the chandelier, it should not interrupt your discourse. I am listening. How much do I know about what?"

With an effort Thomas wrenched his eyes away from the struggle between Jacqueline and her fancywork.

"It wouldn't surprise me if you did. Chin yourself, I mean. . . . How much do you know about Richard the Third?"

For answer, Jacqueline arranged her features in a hideous scowl. Out of the corner of her mouth, in the accents of a movie gangster, she said,

" 'I am determined to prove a villain, And hate the idle pleasure of these days!' "

"Oh, forget about Shakespeare," Thomas said. "He based his *Richard the Third* on the Tudor historians, and they maligned Richard to please Henry the Seventh. Shakespeare's version is great theater, but it isn't history. Let's try another question. How much do you know about the Wars of the Roses?''

"I know a little bit, but not enough, about everything," said Jacqueline. "I'm a librarian, remember? Oh. . . ."

The last word was a low moan. Tenderly she freed her swelling fingers from entwined thread, wadded the whole mass up, and thrust it back into her purse. The second failure had soured her temper. She went on disagreeably,

"I never did understand the Wars of the Roses. I don't think anybody understands the Wars of the Roses. I don't want to understand them . . . it . . . the Wars of the Roses. The houses of Lancaster and York—the red rose and the white—were fighting for the throne. That's what the Wars of the Roses were about. That's all I know and all I need to know."

"Okay, okay," Thomas said soothingly. "The last of the Lancastrian kings was Henry the Sixth—not to be confused with Henry the Seventh, the first of the Tudors. Henry the Sixth was a nice ineffectual old idiot—part saint, part mental defective. His successful Yorkist rival was Edward the Fourth, the big handsome blond, whose contemporaries considered him sexy, even if you don't. Edward got rid of Henry the Sixth, and Henry's son, and a few miscellaneous malcontents, and settled down to enjoy himself. His biggest mistake was to marry a widow lady, Elizabeth Woodville by name. Everyone was shocked at this marriage with a commoner; they resented Edward's failure to strengthen England with an alliance with a foreign princess. Elizabeth had a couple of sons by her first marriage and a crowd of brothers and sisters. They were a predatory crew, and Elizabeth helped them advance. The noblest families in England were forced to marry the queen's sisters; the marriage of her twenty-year-old with the Dowager Duchess of Norfolk, aged eighty, scandalized the country. Edward begat a clutch of children on his beautiful wife—two sons and a number of daughters. The eldest daughter was also named Elizabeth."

"These people all have the same names," Jacqueline grumbled. "Edward, Elizabeth, Henry. Can't you call them Ethelbert or Francisco or something?"

"I could," said Thomas coldly. "But those weren't their names. Stop griping and concentrate."

Jacqueline reached for a cucumber sandwich. They were having the genuine English tea she had demanded, in the lounge of one of London's dignified old hotels. The chink of silverware and the subdued rattle of china were no louder than the genteel murmuring voices of the other patrons.

"Edward the Fourth," Thomas went on. "The Yorkist king—Richard's brother. Got that? Okay. Edward died at the early age of forty, worn out by riotous living. He left two sons. The eldest, on his father's death, became Edward the Fifth. . . ." He ignored Jacqueline's grimace and went on relentlessly. "Yes, another Edward. He was only a kid—twelve years old, too young to rule alone. A protectorate was necessary; and the obvious candidate for the role of Protector was the kid's only paternal uncle, Edward the Fourth's younger brother—a brilliant soldier, a first-rate administrator, devoted to his wife and little son, loyal, honest, popular—Richard, Duke of Gloucester."

"Three cheers and a roll of drums," said Jacqueline. "Gee whiz, Thomas, to think that all these years I've had the wrong idea about Richard the Third. He was a swell guy. I'm surprised they haven't canonized him. Beloved husband, fond father, admirable brother. . . . Loving uncle?"

"You have a tongue like a viper."

"Thanks. Look here, Thomas, what is the one thing people do know about Richard the Third—if they know anything? He was the wicked uncle par excellence. He murdered his nephews—the two little princes in the tower—and usurped the throne that was rightfully theirs."

"He did not!" Thomas shouted.

Heads turned. A waiter dropped a fork.

Thomas subsided, flushing.

"Damn it, Jacqueline, that is the most fascinating, frustrating unsolved murder in history. There is no evidence. Do you know that? Absolutely no proof whatsoever that Richard had those kids killed. Only rumor and slander on one side—"

"And on the other?"

"Richard's character. The otherwise inexplicable behavior of other people who were involved. Simple common sense."

"I wouldn't say his character was exactly—"

"I mean his real character, not the one the Tudor historians invented. Everything that is known about Richard's actions supports the picture of a man of rare integrity, kindness, and courage. At the age of eighteen he commanded armies, and led them well. He administered the northern provinces for his brother the king, and won lasting loyalty for the house of York by his scrupulous fairness and concern for the rights of the ordinary citizen against rapacious nobles. He supported the arts. He was deeply religious. As for his personal life—oh, he sired a few bastards, everybody did in those days, but after he was married, to a girl he had known since they were children together, he remained faithful to her while she lived and mourned her sincerely when she died. The death of his little son threw him into a frenzy of grief. In a time of turncoating and treachery, he never once failed in his loyalty to his brother, Edward the Fourth. There was a third brother, the Duke of Clarence, who tried to push his own claim to the throne and even took up arms against Edward. Richard persuaded Clarence to come back into the fold, and when Edward finally got exasperated with Clarence's plotting and ordered his execution, Richard was the only one who spoke up for Clarence.''

''That ain't the way I heard it,'' said Jacqueline, eating the last sandwich.

''No, you heard the Tudor legend—the myth of the monster. By the time Sir Thomas More wrote his biography of Richard, in the reign of Henry the Eighth, Richard was being accused of everything but barratry and arson. According to More, Richard murdered Henry the Sixth and Henry's son; his own wife; and his brother, the Duke of Clarence. He had his nephews smothered, usurped the throne, and decapitated a group of noblemen who objected to his activities.

''Modern historians admit that Richard was innocent of most of these charges. He did execute a few nobles, including some of the queen's Woodville relatives. He said they had plotted against his life, and there is no reason to doubt that they had. When Richard killed people he did it in broad daylight, with plenty of witnesses, and made no bones about it. But the little princes just . . . disappeared.''

''Very interesting. But what does all this have to do with the mysterious house party? You've been very cryptic about it, and I don't see—"

"I'll get to that. Stop looking wistfully at the waiter; I'm not going to order any more food, you've had enough for two people already. Pay attention. I'm not just trying to improve your knowledge of English history; all this has bearing on a very contemporary problem.

"We return, then, to the time right after Edward the Fourth died. Richard was in the north when it happened, at his favorite castle of Middleham. The new young king had his own household in Wales. At the news of his father's death he started for London, with his Woodville uncles—the queen had made sure her brothers had control of the heir to the throne—and an escort of two thousand men. Richard, on his way south for the funeral, had only six hundred. He obviously didn't anticipate trouble.

"But somewhere along the way, he got word that the Woodvilles were planning to seize power and cut him out of the job of Protector. They may have planned to kill him. They virtually had to; he had the popular support and the legal rights they lacked, and he was not the sort of man to turn the other cheek.

"Two men warned Richard of what was happening. One was Lord Hastings, his brother's old friend and drinking companion. The other was the Duke of Buckingham, of royal descent himself, who had been forced to marry one of the queen's upstart sisters.

"Richard moved like lightning. He caught up with the young king's entourage, arrested the boy's Woodville relatives, and escorted young Edward to London. The queen rushed into church sanctuary, taking the other children with her. Later she was persuaded to let the younger boy join his royal brother. The two kids were lodged in the royal apartments in the Tower, which was the conventional place for kings to reside in before their coronations. Up to this time, Richard's behavior had been perfectly reasonable and forthright."

"Richard the Forthright," murmured Jacqueline.

Thomas pretended he had not heard.

"Then, around the middle of June 1483, all hell broke loose. England was astounded to learn that Edward the Fourth had never been married to Elizabeth Woodville. He had entered into a precontract with another lady, and in those days a precontract was as binding as a marriage ceremony. That meant that all Edward the Fourth's children were bastards, and that young Edward the Fifth had no right to the throne.

"The Tudor historians claim Richard invented this story, but all the evidence indicates that it was true. The man who broke the news was no fly-by-night flunky of Richard's; he was one of the great prelates of England, the Bishop of Bath and Wells. The story was accepted by Parliament and embodied in a formal decree, *Titulus Regius,* that proclaimed Richard's right to the throne. Both his brothers were dead; Clarence's children were barred from the succession because their father had been executed as a traitor; and if Edward's children were illegitimate, the rightful heir was Richard himself."

"Oh, that's all right, then," said Jacqueline. "If the boys were bastards, Richard had every right to smother them."

"Damn it, he didn't smother them!" Thomas felt his face reddening. He got control of himself with an effort. "The boys were seen, playing in the Tower, in the summer of 1483. Except for a few doubtful references in the official royal account books, that is the last anyone ever heard of them.

"In 1485, two years later, Henry Tudor landed in England. Thanks to the treachery of the Stanleys, Richard was killed at Bosworth and Henry became King Henry the Seventh.

"Now, what would you have done if you had been Henry? Here you are, occupying a shaky throne in a country seething with potential rebellion. Your claim to the throne comes via your mother, who is descended from an illegitimate child of a king's younger son. There are a dozen people still alive who have stronger claims than that. The man you succeeded is dead, but he is by no means forgotten, especially in the north of England. You propose to strengthen your claim by marrying young Elizabeth, Richard's niece, but a lot of people think she is illegitimate; and if she is not, then her brothers, if they are still alive, are the real heirs to the throne. There have been rumors that the boys were killed, but nobody knows for sure what happened to them.

"If you had been Henry, surely one of your first moves would have been to find out the truth about the princes. The Tower of London is in your hands. You would look for those pathetic little bodies, and question the attendants who were on duty when they were killed. The Tower is a huge fortress, full of people—servants and warders and scrubwomen and cooks and officials. There are dozens of people still alive who must know what happened. You can't eliminate two state prisoners without someone noticing that they have vanished between sunset and sunrise.

"Henry did nothing of the sort. I don't think he could—because the boys were still alive when Henry entered London in 1485. But they wouldn't stay alive, not for long."

Jacqueline nibbled a piece of bread and butter.

"Someone confessed to the murder, didn't he?" she asked tentatively.

"Yes—a man named Sir James Tyrrell. *Twenty years later,* after the supposed murderer had been arrested on another charge. The confession was never published. It was not made public until after Tyrrell's execution on another charge. The version given in Sir Thomas More's biography of Richard bristles with contradictions, misstatements, and downright lies. It is such a palpable tissue of—"

He broke off, eyeing Jacqueline with a sudden wild surmise. She stared owlishly back at him over the rims of her glasses; and Thomas, who seldom did so, swore imaginatively.

"You know all this! You, who claim to have read every detective story ever printed. . . . Of course you know it. You've read *The Daughter of Time.*"

"Sure."

"Then why didn't you say so?"

"I lo-o-ove to hear you talk," said Jacqueline silkily.

"There are times when I could kill you."

"I read all Josephine Tey's mysteries," Jacqueline said. *"The Daughter of Time* is absolutely brilliant. But it's a novel, not a work of serious history. It is far from unbiased."

"What else have you read?" Thomas asked with resignation.

Jacqueline reached for the last bun.

"Once a librarian, always a librarian," she said, nibbling. "When I read historical fiction I always check to see what's real and what's made up. Tey got her material from one of Richard's apologists, and she is just as biased as the Tudor historians, only on the other side—Saint Richard the Third, full of love and

peace and flowers. I read some historical novels about Richard,"
she added, finishing the bun with a snap of her white teeth.
"Most of them portrayed him as a sensitive martyr, wringing his
slender hands and sobbing. I doubt that he cried much."

"You are really—"

"So now we come to the house party," said Jacqueline. She
eyed the crumbs on the empty plate regretfully, and went on, "I
assume the party has to do with your hero. What is it, a meeting
of some organization? There is a group that is concerned with
Richard's rehabilitation. They call themselves Ricardians, and are
not to be confused with the followers of the economist, David
Ricardo. They put *In Memoriam* notices in the *Times* on the anniversary of the Battle of Bosworth."

Jacqueline's tone gave this otherwise innocuous statement
implications that made Thomas's eyes narrow with exasperation.
His sense of humor triumphed, however, and he smiled
sheepishly.

"There are several groups interested in Richard the Third. I
suspect ours is the freakiest of them all."

"That's nice."

"You needn't be sarcastic."

"I'm not being sarcastic. There is no happier outlet for our
inherent aggressive instincts than the belligerent support of an
unorthodox cause. I myself," said Jacqueline proudly, "am a
member of the friends of Jerome." She watched Thomas sort
through his capacious memory for potential historic Jeromes,
and added, "Jerome is a place, not a person. It's an absolutely
marvelous ghost town in Arizona. It sits on top of an abandoned
mine, and if we don't get busy, it is going to slide right down the
hill into—"

"That's even crazier than our organization."

"One attribute of eccentric groups is their lack of sympathy for
other eccentrics. Tell me about Richard's friends."

"Don't call us that. It's one of the names of the older organization from which we reneged when they denied Sir Richard's ille-
gitimacy."

Jacqueline had again produced her tatting. She studied it fixedly for several seconds before she looked at Thomas.

"Just say that again, Thomas. Slowly."

"Our founder and president is Sir Richard Weldon," Thomas explained. "He claims to be descended from one of Richard the Third's illegitimate children. The Richard the Third Society wouldn't accept his claim, in spite of well-documented—"

"Thomas!"

"Well, it could be true. Richard had several bastards; everybody did in those days."

"That resolves all my doubts. You tempt me, Thomas," Jacqueline said pensively. "I'd like to meet Sir Richard . . . Weldon. That isn't the department store?"

"Stores, not store. They're all over England. But you'll like Sir Richard," Thomas added with seeming irrelevance. "He's a nice guy, even if he does have an *idée fixe*. The house party is to be at his home in Yorkshire. It is a special meeting of the executive board of the society. Usually we forgather on the anniversary of Richard's birthday—October second."

"He was a Libra," said Jacqueline, interested. "That's a point for your side. Libras are well-balanced individuals, not liable to bursts of passion or ungoverned rage. They are sensitive to beauty, fond of justice—"

"Now stop that!"

Jacqueline grinned. Then she sobered and shook her head.

"Thomas, I'd adore coming to the meeting, but I don't think I can manage it. I had planned to go home early next week."

"Why must you? College doesn't open till the middle of September. You're not worried about the offspring, are you? Surely they're old enough to manage for another fortnight."

"Oh, they'd be delighted to have me stay away permanently. They have my car, my TV set, my refrigerator, and my bank account—such as it is—at their mercy. They are probably having nightly orgies."

"They can't be doing anything too bad. . . ."

"Oh, yes, they can. However," Jacqueline said, brightening, "they manage to keep me unwitting. So far they seem to have buried the bodies and settled out of court."

"You're a damned unnatural mum. I don't know how they put up with you. Jacqueline, you've got to come. I'm counting on you."

"It's not polite to visit people without an invitation. I was brought up to be a lady."

"I've already told Sir Richard you're coming. He's delighted."

"Oh, you have, have you?"

"Don't be so hostile. You haven't asked me why the meeting is extraordinary."

"Why," said Jacqueline in the same steely voice, "is the meeting extraordinary?"

"We've found the letter. The one from Elizabeth of York, Richard's niece."

The bald statement had the desired effect. Jacqueline's hard stare softened.

"You're kidding."

"No."

"The letter in which the girl says she's in love with her uncle and wants to marry him? That she wishes the queen would hurry up and die? That Richard is her—"

" 'Only joy and maker in this world,' " said Thomas, thoroughly pleased with himself. "That's the letter."

"The girl was at court," Jacqueline said thoughtfully. "Her mother let her and the other princesses leave sanctuary after Richard was crowned. He agreed to provide for them, and not to force them into unsuitable marriages. But the letter is apocryphal, Thomas. I remember; it was quoted by one of Richard's earliest defenders, back in the seventeenth century—"

"Buck."

"Yes, Buck. He said he had seen the original, in Elizabeth's own handwriting. But then it disappeared. Most authorities doubt it ever existed. Because, if it did—"

"Uh-huh," said Thomas. "If it exists, it absolves Richard of one of the Tudor slanders—that he tried to force his unwilling niece into an incestuous marriage in order to improve his claim to the throne."

"Yes, I remember. I was particularly struck by one part of that story—the Christmas party at court, where Queen Anne and young Elizabeth appeared in identical dresses."

"Everyone at court was struck by it. The gesture was in singularly bad taste. The queen was dying of tuberculosis; she must have looked like a haggard ghost next to a handsome, healthy young girl. Richard was accused of thinking that one up, of course.''

"A man would never think of a thing like that. It's a woman's trick. Not the queen's; she wouldn't give another woman a gown like hers, especially if the other woman was younger and prettier. I thought, when I read about it, that Elizabeth must have planned the trick herself—had the dress copied.''

"Excellent,'' Thomas said approvingly. "I hadn't thought of that, but it bears out my own theory. There certainly was a rumor going around that Richard planned to marry the girl. When Richard heard it, he denied the story, publicly and emphatically. It would have been an extremely stupid move from his point of view. The girl was illegitimate, a commoner, his own niece, one of the hated Woodvilles. He had everything to lose and nothing to gain by such a marriage.

"No, I'm sure young Elizabeth started the rumor herself. Wishful thinking. Richard was only about ten years older than she was, and the queen was dying. . . .''

Jacqueline shook her head violently. "No, Thomas, it's too much. Granted that the girl was ambitious—granted that she was in love with her uncle. Even so. . . .''

Thomas finished the sentence. ". . . it is inconceivable that she should want to marry the murderer of her brothers. I couldn't agree more. It's hard enough to explain how the queen mother could have entrusted her daughters to Richard's protection after he had ruthlessly slaughtered her sons. She accepted a pension from him, even wrote to her son by her first marriage, who had fled abroad, urging him to return because Richard would treat him well.''

Jacqueline was still shaking her head. "Maybe the two Elizabeths didn't know the boys were dead. The date, Thomas. What was the date of the letter?''

"That won't wash. The letter was probably written in January or February of 1485—a year and a half after the boys were supposed to have been killed. All England prayed for saintly Henry Tudor to come over and rescue them from the monster. You can't have it both ways. Either the truth was known—and in that case the boys' family couldn't help knowing it—or the boys were still alive and the accusations were malicious lies spread by Henry's agents. Agitprop is not a modern invention, you know.''

"Hmm." Jacqueline acknowledged his logic by abandoning the argument. "The letter would support your second alternative. It isn't absolute proof, but. . . . Good Heavens, Thomas, it's an important document! And your little society is sitting on it like a broody hen. Who found it? Where was it found? Has the provenance been checked? Have any reputable authorities seen it?''

"An authority is about to see it."

He had rarely seen Jacqueline taken aback. Now she gaped at him, unable to believe her ears.

"Me? Is that how you got me invited? Thomas, I'm not—"

"You took a course in authenticating manuscripts, didn't you?''

"Oh, for God's sake—just the usual survey sort of thing. I'm no—"

"And you studied handwriting analysis, didn't you?''

"I can read your fortune in the Tarot, too, if you like. That has nothing to do with—''

"Could you spot an out-and-out fake?''

Jacqueline studied him thoughtfully. Her indignation faded as she realized his concern was genuine.

"A crude one—of course. Errors in vocabulary, spelling, and the like. . . . So could you. For anything more complex I'd need a laboratory. They can test the paper, the ink. . . . And I'm no expert on fifteenth-century orthography. What's wrong, Thomas? Do you think one of your fellow enthusiasts forged this letter?''

"I don't know! I'm sure the letter did exist. Buck couldn't have invented it out of whole cloth. But it's too damned fortuitous to have it turn up now, after all these years. The scholarly world and the press think we're a bunch of crackpots now. If we make a big public spectacle of this—as we are planning to do—and then some goateed expert strolls in and says, 'You've been had, ladies and gents; this is Woolworth's best stationery. . . .' You can see how idiotic we would look. And . . . maybe you won't understand this. But we honestly are concerned with a little matter of justice, even if it's five hundred years late. A fiasco like this . . .''

". . . could hurt Richard's cause," said Jacqueline, as he hesitated. She spoke tentatively, as if the words were too bizarre to be uttered; but as she studied the flushed face of the man across the table, her own face changed. "My God. You really feel . . ."

"I guess it sounds silly," Thomas said, with no sign of anger. "I can't explain it. In part, it's the fun of an unsolved puzzle; in part, the famous Anglo-Saxon weakness for the underdog. But it's more than that. Do you remember what they wrote about Richard in the official records of the city of York, after they heard the news of Bosworth? 'King Richard, late mercifully reigning upon us, was . . . piteously slain and murdered, to the great heaviness of this City.' The men of Yorkshire knew him well; he had lived among them for many years. It took guts to write that epitaph with Henry Tudor on the throne and Richard's cause buried in a felon's grave at Leicester. . . . If there is such a thing as charisma, maybe some people have an extra-large dose. Enough to carry through five hundred years."

Jacqueline's eyebrows went up. "That's a scary idea, Thomas. I refuse to pursue it. . . . Okay. If you feel that strongly, I'm your woman. In a limited sense," she added. "What is going on this weekend? Do you reenact the Battle of Bosworth, or what?"

"It's like a regular professional meeting," Thomas explained. He didn't thank her; they knew each other too well for that. "We start on Friday with a dinner at Dick's place; after dinner we'll hear papers, have discussions, the way they do at the scholarly society meetings. More lectures, et cetera, on Saturday. Saturday night we're having our big banquet and ball. The Sunday afternoon meeting is when Dick is producing the letter. God, they've invited the BBC, and I understand half the papers in England are sending reporters. Not because the find is important, you understand; they just want to see a bunch of nuts making a spectacle of themselves."

"It sounds rather dull."

"Well. . . ."

"Ah! Come clean, Thomas. You *are* going to reenact the Battle of Bosworth. Only this time Richard wins?"

"That's an idea," said Thomas interestedly. "History as it should have been. I'll have to propose that some time."

"Thomas."

Thomas came as near to squirming as a dignified adult male can come. "We—er—dress up," he said reluctantly. "In costume of the period."

"Indeed."

"You don't have to, it's optional. And then we—well, we take parts. Various historical characters."

He looked at Jacqueline and saw with regret, but without surprise, that her green eyes were sparkling. Her mouth was fixed in a line of exaggerated composure.

"Really, Thomas? What fun! And who are you, darling?"

"Clarence."

"Richard's brother, the Duke of Clarence? The one who was drowned. . . ."

"Yes, that one. Really, Jacqueline, for a woman of your age and supposed refinement, you have the most raucous laugh."

"I'm sorry." Jacqueline wiped tears of mirth from her eyes. "I had a sudden mental picture of you, head down in—"

"That story about the butt of malmsey is ridiculous! Can you imagine anyone drowning an enemy in a barrel of wine? It would ruin the wine, for one thing." Thomas grinned unwillingly. "Sorry to disappoint you, but I'm not going to dive into a barrel with my feet kicking in the air just to entertain you."

He was to remember this statement later as a particularly dazzling example of "famous last words."

CHAPTER TWO

*T*homas had tomato on his tie.

"I'm getting tomato on my tie," he said.

"Lean forward and drip on the floor," Jacqueline advised.

She was also eating an egg-tomato-and-cucumber sandwich. Thomas was irked to see that there wasn't a spot on her snowy-white pants suit.

He followed her advice and her example. At least there was no one to see the ridiculous picture he made. They were sitting side by side in the front row of seats on the top of the double-decker bus. There were only two other passengers on this level; both were local people, far at the back, and superbly disinterested in the foreigners up front. An occasional bird or squirrel in the leafy branches that brushed past the windows might be observing his graceless posture, but they were probably equally disinterested.

Thomas dabbed at the spot on his maroon tie. It bothered him more than it ought to have done, and this fact made him wonder, in his introspective fashion, whether he was as indifferent to worldly concerns as a scholar ought to be. He had been only mildly vexed when Jacqueline insisted on traveling into Yorkshire by local bus; he was undisturbed at the idea of disembarking from one of the lumbering green monsters, along with a crowd of yokels, at the gates of his titled host's country residence. At least his conscious mind was undisturbed. Then why, he asked himself, had he been relieved when Sir Richard suggested that they disembark in the next village but one, where they would be met by Sir Richard's chauffeur? Why did he hope the bus would be early and Jenkins would be late with the car? He had encountered Jenkins before, and the thought of the supercilious chauffeur watching him descend from this plebeian form of transport induced a definite qualm. Jenkins, who doubled as Sir Richard's valet, would certainly notice the spot on his tie.

Jacqueline, who had been staring at the panorama of English countryside unrolling before them at a genteel speed of ten miles an hour, delved into her purse and eventually produced a small tube.

"Spot remover," she said, proffering the tube without looking at Thomas.

"I don't see why we couldn't have a decent lunch instead of munching sandwiches on top of a bus," he grumbled.

"We'd have missed the bus," Jacqueline said patiently. "And there isn't another one till tomorrow."

"Ridiculous idea, anyhow." The spot remover worked beautifully. Thomas went on, in a more affable tone, "We have had to transfer three times already."

"You've lived in England for years. Have you ever taken local buses before?"

Memory gripped Thomas, so unexpectedly and so strongly that he felt an actual physical pain.

"Thirty-five years ago," he said. "Before the war. I was sixteen. It was my first trip abroad."

Jacqueline was silent, which was just as well; Thomas would not have heard her. What was the name of that girl? He had written to her for almost a year. . . . He had forgotten her name, but he could see her as vividly as if he had parted from her, in the bluebell-carpeted woods, only yesterday. Hair like pale-yellow silk and eyes as blue as the flowers. . . .

With a nostalgic sigh he turned to Jacqueline.

"You're a witch. Are those rumors about your purse true?"

"What rumors?"

"The students claim it's magic. That you can produce anything you want out of it."

"Such nonsense."

"You mean you always carry spot remover?"

"When I'm wearing a white suit and taking buses to visit a noble peer of the realm I do. Be sensible, Thomas."

II

In the year 1466 Sir John Crosby, alderman of London, built a town house in the city district called Bishopsgate. The Great Hall of this handsome residence still survives in a new location on the Embankment. Since Richard III, for whom Jacqueline was developing a distinctly ambivalent attitude, had once rented Sir John's house, Jacqueline had been taken to Chelsea to see Crosby Hall. Ricardians liked to visit the place and gaze sentimentally at the walls that had once enclosed their hero. They are perhaps among the few who appreciate the irony of the Hall's present location. The adjacent building was the home of the saint and martyr and questionable historian, Sir Thomas More, whose biography of Richard infuriates that king's modern admirers.

The Yorkshire copy of Crosby Hall looked just as out of place as its London original. It was an exact replica, but instead of building a house to go with it, Herman Weldon, the father of the present owner, had attached the Hall onto an existing country residence. This mansion, Georgian in date, seemed to turn its back on the addition. The mellow red brick did not clash with the pale stone of the Hall; it ignored it.

Jacqueline didn't comment directly on the unfortunate juxtaposition. She merely remarked that bastardized combinations of architectural styles sometimes succeeded, but only, in her opinion, when they grew naturally through the centuries. Thomas said nothing. He agreed with the aesthetic judgment, but the romantic appeal of a fifteenth-century Hall superseded taste; he would have like it if it had been built onto a high-rise apartment building.

He could tell by Jacqueline's face that the architectural

monstrosity had confirmed her prejudice against its owner. He had given her a brief biography of their host. Sir Richard had inherited his title, his house, and his Ricardian enthusiasm from his father, who had been a highly successful merchant. It was inevitable that the merchant's son should be named Richard, but far less likely that Old Crouchback's namesake should have reacted so positively to his father's obsession. Instead of rejecting it, as a healthily antagonistic offspring is supposed to do, the boy had embraced it with even greater fervor. The Weldon fortune having survived war, post war inflation, and death duties, Sir Richard was a member of that increasingly rare breed, a gentleman of wealth. He lived with, for, and among his collection of Ricardiana.

Jacqueline and Thomas were received at the door by a member of that equally rare breed, a genuine butler. As he took their suitcases, a door at the far end of the hall opened, and from the shadow of the arch the original of the portrait at the National Gallery came walking out of time to greet them.

Weldon wore his brown hair at shoulder length. His head was covered with a black velvet hat pinned with a jeweled brooch— copied from the portrait, as was his long fur-trimmed gown. The pleated garment was belted in at the waist. The neck was open, showing the high-necked undertunic, or paltock.

Thomas heard Jacqueline's breath catch at the first sight of this fantastic figure; as it moved out into the light he heard another sound, which was one of courteously suppressed amusement. He smiled to himself. Whatever Jacqueline's prejudices, they would soon be dispelled. No one could dislike a man as cheerful and gentle as Richard Weldon.

The resemblance to Richard of Gloucester was cultivated and not really very close. Weldon's short, slight figure suited the image, but his snub-nosed face had no resemblance to Gloucester's somber countenance. It was pathetic to watch Weldon struggle with his facial muscles; he tried to keep his face as sober as that of its painted prototype, but his features were not designed for melancholy.

He was beaming as he marched forward, both hands extended. After greeting Jacqueline warmly, he turned to Thomas.

"Brother!" he exclaimed, and flung both arms around Thomas. "Noble Clarence! God wit ye well!"

"Now, now," said Thomas, disentangling himself from yards of loose velvet sleeve. "Hadn't we better stick to our own names? It's confusing enough as it is."

"Oh, dear," said Weldon, looking chagrined. "Of course you're right. Do come into the drawing room and meet the others."

The drawing room was a lovely Georgian chamber, but its fine lines and discreet ornament were obscured by an outré collection of bric-a-brac and furniture, an overflow from the famous Weldon collection of Ricardiana. A mammoth carved chest, black with age, loomed threateningly over a little ormolu table. An ivory sofa was disfigured by a plush cushion with the legend "Souvenir of Middleham Castle." Clearly Weldon could not bear to throw anything away if it had the slightest connection with Richard of Gloucester.

All the people present were wearing medieval costume. Some were sweating inelegantly under the muffling folds of velvet and the heavy fur trim. The feminine garb of the period, romantic and graceful as it was, only suited the slim. The woman who strode forward to meet them, with the air of one who knows her rights of precedence, was far too massive for the dress. The full skirts were supposed to be belted in just under the breasts, but in this case it was hard to tell where that area was located. Her massive bosom went out and out and further out; from its extremity the crimson cloth of gold billowed instead of falling in graceful folds. The neckline and skirt of the dress were trimmed with bands of ermine. Against the white fur the woman's neck was scarlet, streaked with runnels of perspiration. She had a visible moustache, and her iron-gray hair was almost concealed under a velvet-banded hennin—the tall pointed hat popular with assorted fairy princesses. From its peak a long gauzy veil stood straight out every time the wearer moved. It was an impractical appendage, as the tears and snags in the fragile fabric indicated.

"Mrs. Ponsonby-Jones," said Weldon in a subdued voice. "My late cousin's wife."

"And your queen," said Mrs. Ponsonby-Jones, in a voice that made her gauze veil flutter. She gave Weldon a coy glance and a

dig with her elbow. "Richard's wife, Queen Anne. Good day,
Thomas—dear brother Clarence, I should say, though you were
not very kind to poor little Anne, were you? You must get into
costume at once, we are having such a jolly time pretending."
Thomas, who had been opening and closing his mouth, had no
chance to reply. Mrs. Ponsonby-Jones turned her attention to
Jacqueline, not liking what she saw and making no effort to conceal it. "Hem. Yes, as Richard's hostess, let me welcome you, Miss
—er—hem. Of course you will want to join our little game of
make-believe. I fear that all the major parts are taken; but you will
no doubt enjoy portraying one of the ladies of the court, or
perchance a serving wench. I am sure I can find some costume
for you in the old-clothes basket, Miss—er—Mrs—hem."

"How nice of you, Mrs. Ponsonby-Jones," said Jacqueline. She
turned to the other older woman in the group, and Richard
Weldon said quickly,

"Lady Isobel Crawford."

The only word for Lady Isobel was "skinny." "Thin" would
have been an understatement. She was barely five feet tall, and
thirty years earlier she might have been a petite, dainty little
woman. Her robe was a copy of one worn by Edward IV's queen,
Elizabeth Woodville, in a National Gallery portrait. The trun-
cated hennin of gold brocade matched the metallic sheen of her
bleached hair and was adorned with a butterfly veil, supported by
three fine wires that gave it its shape. Her gown of black velvet
was trimmed at cuffs and neckline with matching gold brocade.
The neckline was cut low, showing an embroidered undertunic
and a pair of bony shoulders. Chains and pendants jangled when
she moved.

"How do you do, Dr. Kirby," said Lady Isobel. She went on,
with an amused glance at Mrs. Ponsonby-Jones, "I fear our little
charades must strike you as foolish. I assure you, they are not—to
those of us who share a touch of the divine spark of creativ-
ity. . . ."

Modestly she examined her fingernails, and Weldon said,

"I'm sure you have read Lady Isobel's novels, Dr. Kirby. Her
book about Richard is particularly admired."

"The Gallant Young King," said Jacqueline. "Oh, yes. I read it."

"How sweet," murmured Lady Isobel. She examined

Jacqueline. Suddenly she gave a little squeal and clapped her hands. "Oh, my dear, you must participate. You've no idea of the mystical insight of identification—the understanding one derives of the person one is representing—the passions, the suffering, the—I've always thought . . . the aura, in short. One feels it— here." She clasped her hands over her flat bosom, and smiled at Jacqueline. "Unfortunately, all the major parts do seem to be taken. I would offer you my own part of Elizabeth Woodville, but I'm afraid you would simply pop out of my costume!"

"So sweet of you," said Jacqueline enthusiastically. "But I couldn't take such an important part—a visitor like myself. Oh!" It was a diabolical imitation of Lady Isobel's squeal. Jacqueline clapped her hands girlishly. "I know! I shall be Richard's mistress. That is, if Sir Richard doesn't mind?"

She beamed at Sir Richard, who was looking a little bewildered.

"Not at all," he said heartily. "Jolly good."

"Mistress!" Lady Ponsonby-Jones exclaimed. "Richard, I really do not think it is suitable—"

"Get on with the introductions, Dick," said Thomas.

Weldon presented the third woman in the party. She was young and slim. Her pale-pink robes were trimmed with brown fur and belted high under shapely breasts; the lifted skirt showed an embroidered underskirt of deeper rose. Brown curls escaped from under her tall cap with its dependent veil. Her features would have been unusually pretty if they had not been marred by a sulky pout and by the latest in mod makeup. To Thomas's conservative eyes her face looked like a mask; but the over-all effect was not unpleasing.

Certainly Weldon did not find it so. His eyes shone with fond affection as he made the introductions.

"Here is our young Elizabeth of York. Her real name is Elizabeth Ponsonby-Jones, so that's one less for you to remember, Jacqueline. I may call you that, I hope? We are all friends here."

"Well, don't call me Elizabeth," drawled the girl. "Liz or Bessy or Hey-you, but not Elizabeth. I'm an unwilling sacrifice on the altar of family feeling. I think I ought to be Dickon's mistress instead of ghastly Elizabeth of York. She's the sickest character of the lot."

"You are Elizabeth of York?" Jacqueline asked. "The writer of the famous letter?"

Liz laughed. "Yes, that's me. I'm Dickon's niece and I'm supposed to show a hopeless incestuous passion for him."

She leered at Sir Richard, who smiled fondly.

Mrs. Ponsonby-Jones moved in. She was so much larger than Sir Richard that she seemed about to engulf him like a giant amoeba, and the look she gave her daughter held no maternal warmth.

"Don't be offensive, Elizabeth. You are distracting your cousin Richard from his duties as host."

"Elizabeth distracts all of us." A man sauntered toward them. "My name's Kent, Dr. Kirby. I'm glad you could join us. As the only heretic in this group, I welcome support. Hello, Thomas."

Kent's short, stocky body appeared almost cylindrical in his long black-and-gold robe. He wore his gray hair clipped short. All his hirsute efforts had been concentrated on his moustache, which curled out and up like the horns of a buffalo. The sleeves of his robe were slit to the shoulders, and the heavy hanging folds were fur-trimmed, as was the hem of the garment. On Kent's head was perched an absurd tall hat with a rounded top and a yellow padded edge.

"Major General Sir Archibald Kent?" Jacqueline asked, shaking hands.

"Thomas has briefed you?"

"He had no need to do so. Even in the wilds of America the newspapers follow your career with interest. Don't you find Ricardian research a little dull after your—er—activities in the Middle East?"

"Not at all." Kent displayed long, yellowing teeth in a wolfish smile. "The Arabs and Israelis are easy to deal with compared with my colleagues."

"Why do you regard yourself as a heretic?" Jacqueline asked. "I thought membership in this society was contingent upon belief in Richard's innocence."

"You make us sound rather like a peculiar religious sect," Weldon said with a smile.

Kent gave a brusque, barking laugh. "That's what we are, Dick. You see, Doctor, the others admire Richard because they believe he was innocent of the vital crime—the murder of his nephews. I admire him because I think he was guilty. They want to make him a medieval liberal left-winger; I see him as a practical politician and a damn good soldier. It was sound policy in those days to rid yourself of disinherited princes; they were a focus for rebellion."

"Fascinating," said Jacqueline.

"Disgusting," said Mrs. Ponsonby-Jones.

"He doesn't mean it," said Lady Isobel, with a high-pitched giggle. "He loves to tease us."

Jacqueline hadn't taken her eyes from Kent. "What part are you playing?" she asked.

"Buckingham." Kent barked again. "Very appropriate, eh? I insisted on the role. The duke is one of the strong suspects for the murder, you know. His behavior was damn peculiar; first his solid support of Richard against the Woodvilles—he was one of the first to urge that Richard take the crown. Then suddenly he is leading a rebellion against his former ally."

"It was peculiar behavior."

"Not at all," Kent said promptly. "Buckingham wanted to be the power behind the throne. Richard wouldn't stand for it. So Buckingham decided to play Kingmaker with Henry Tudor, who might prove more malleable. Perhaps he planned to claim the throne himself, after he had made use of the Tudor. Perfectly sensible plan."

"It makes more sense than you do," Thomas said, scowling. "Ignore him, Jacqueline; he'll argue on either side of a question just for the fun of it. No more debate, colleagues, until the formalities are over."

There were only three others to be introduced. Donald Ellis, a chubby man with eyes of luminous innocence, wore gorgeous purple velvet and a crown. A pastor of the Church of England, he had chosen to portray the lusty, virile Edward IV. Thomas's eyes, meeting Jacqueline's, saw the amusement in them and knew she had not missed the implications. The roles played by these people had meaning on a number of levels.

John Rawdon looked alarmingly like Abraham Lincoln, even to the wart on his cheek. He was a Harley Street specialist who was prominently featured in the newspapers because of his advocacy of natural foods. His reputation as an internist made it difficult for his exasperated colleagues in the medical profession to deni-grate his recent enthusiasm. Certainly the doctor was a living testimonial to his eating habits; his tall, thin body moved with the vigor of a young man's, and his coarse black hair had not a touch of gray. His head was uncovered; the chaperon, a cap with a formal version of the medieval hood, was flung back over his shoulder and attached to his belt by a long liripipe. His velvet skirts did not suit his vigorous stride; he kept kicking them out of the way as he walked. He represented the last Lancastrian King. Saintly, feeble Henry VI.

Then the last member of the group rose from behind the grand piano, which had hitherto concealed all but his head and shoulders.

Alone of the men, Philip Rohan had chosen to wear the short tunic. And short meant very short. It was belted in at the waist like the long robe, but its skirts were only six inches long. The rest of Rohan was covered by tights as revealing as those of a dancer. Thomas couldn't even suspect him of padding the tights. The ripple of muscle fore and aft indicated that the shape was all Rohan. And Jacqueline was taking it in with fascinated interest.

Finally her eyes moved up from the pale-gray tights to the green-and-silver tunic, with its padded sleeves and fur-trimmed neck. Rohan's chest was broad enough without the extra width of the sleeves; he looked almost wasp-waisted. The chaperon, which he wore on his head, was very becoming. The fall of cloth along one side of the face softened features that were too hard for conventional handsomeness, but which had a rakish appeal. He too wore his hair long. It was fair, so pale a gold that it looked like silver, and as fine as a girl's. But there was nothing girlish about the rest of him.

"Well, well," he said softly, surveying Jacqueline as candidly as she had observed him. "What a pleasant surprise. I expected any expert Thomas collected would be hawk-nosed and hideous."

"You are an actor, of course," said Jacqueline.

"How did you know?" The deep, controlled voice quivered with amusement. "I am also Hastings, Richard's best friend, whom he beheaded one morning between elevenses and lunch."

"After he had treacherously plotted against Richard," squeaked Lady Isobel indignantly.

"And conspired with the Woodvilles," added Weldon. "It is difficult to explain Hastings' change of loyalty. No doubt he was seduced by—"

"You sound like one of your own articles," Liz interrupted. "Do be quiet, darling Uncle Dickon, and let Jacqueline have some tea."

"She'd much rather have a drink," said Philip. "Wouldn't you, darling?"

"No," said Jacqueline. With Philip's assistance she removed her jacket, displaying a sleeveless green jersey top. Looking cool and relaxed, she settled on one of the sofas and smiled at Weldon. "Tea would be splendid."

For a time no one spoke. The silence was unusual and, to Thomas, slightly disturbing. It was as if they were all wary in the presence of a stranger—afraid of giving something away.

"Why all the cops and robbers about our arrival, Dick?" he asked, to break the silence.

"I meant to ask if you had had any difficulty," Weldon said.

"Difficulty? Why should we?"

"The wolves are gathering," said Mrs. Ponsonby-Jones melo-dramatically. "We are virtually besieged, Thomas."

"I did notice the village was unusually crowded. You mean those people are—"

"Newspaper persons," said Lady Isobel, as one might say "bur-glars." "Frightful people! One of them actually tried to creep into the house."

"But you're going to admit the press on Sunday," Thomas objected. "What's all the fuss about?"

It was Kent who answered, with his barking laugh.

"They want to catch us—what's your popular phrase?—with our pants down. Attired in ludicrous costumes, playing childish games—drunken and lecherous, hopefully. Fleet Street is quiet this week; no crises, only the same boring old wars."

"The silly season," Jacqueline said. "You must admit you make good copy. Many of you are famous in your own fields."

"And some of us simply adore being good copy," said Liz. Her eyes moved from Lady Isobel, who pretended not to notice, to Philip, who laughed aloud.

"I've no objection to being photographed," he said, striking a pose.

"Well, the rest of us do object," said Mrs. Ponsonby-Jones vigorously. "I cannot imagine why people are so ill-bred!"

"Piltdown man," said Jacqueline unexpectedly. They all stared at her; most of them looked blank, but a few got the point. The vicar chuckled, and Philip's mouth widened in a cynical smile.

"The disclosure of the Piltdown hoax made headlines," Jacqueline went on. "People love to see the experts deflated. You have publicized your find extensively. If, after the publicity, it should turn out to be another hoax. . . ."

"Impossible," cried Lady Isobel.

"I only wish we could be certain."

It was the rector who spoke. Ruffled white hair framed his rosy face like a halo, but the cherubic features were worried.

"But you were the one who found the letter," Weldon said.

"I did not find it," said Mr. Ellis irritably. Thomas sensed that he had tried to make this point before, without convincing his fanatical audience of its importance. "It was sent to me anonymously, and if that is not significant. . . ." He glanced at Jacqueline, who was watching him steadily, and smiled. "Yes. Mrs. Kirby sees my point, if the rest of you do not. Now, Mrs. Kirby, I have stated the fact somewhat baldly. The letter enclosed with the manuscript gives adequate reasons for the sender's wishing to remain unknown at present. It also provides a plausible history for the manuscript, which was last seen by Buck, in the seventeenth century. We are not so naive as we appear; all of us are familiar with manuscripts and letters of this period, and there are no egregious errors in this letter which would suggest forgery. All the same. . . ."

"Yes," Jacqueline said. "All the same . . . frankly, Mr. Ellis, I wouldn't touch it with a ten-foot pole. What prompted you to go ahead with this unnecessary publicity?"

"I deplore it!" Ellis looked like a vexed baby. "I have always argued against that aspect. After I had shown Sir Richard the letter, we agreed that the executive committee should examine it. Sir Richard very kindly suggested a weekend here, so that we could discuss the problem at leisure. I don't understand quite how these arrangements evolved. . . ."

"All sorts of strange things evolve when this committee meets," said Kent sarcastically. "However, Ellis, you are too timid. What do we risk? There can be no question of legal fraud, since our anonymous donor has not asked for money; he is willing to wait until the manuscript has been officially authenticated before he is paid, and even then he throws himself on our generosity. How can we object to that?"

"But the embarrassment. . . ."

"Bah," said Kent. He was the only man Thomas had ever met who actually said "bah," and he said it with emphasis. "There will be controversy in any case. Have you ever known two experts who can agree on a technical point? Every important scientific or cultural discovery has been greeted with mingled cheers and hisses. The Piltdown skull was accepted by experts for years; the authentic cave paintings of Altamira were considered fakes by most of the historians of the day. If our letter is a forgery, it's a damned good one. Some experts will accept it and some will reject it, and the same thing will happen if it is genuine. I'm not keen on the publicity either, but it can't do any harm—unless we manage to make asses of ourselves in some other way."

Silence followed this pronouncement, which was, Thomas had to admit, a perfectly reasonable summary of the situation. Kent was no fool, for all his outspoken belligerence and his deplorable tendency to punch reporters in the nose.

Jacqueline looked at Weldon.

"Why not call in an expert?" she asked.

"But we have." Weldon smiled engagingly at her.

"Have we, though?" Lady Isobel giggled maliciously. "As an *expert,* Mrs. Kirby, you surely are familiar with Sir Richard's reputation. He is one of the foremost authorities in the world on fifteenth-century manuscripts."

"Yes, I surely must be familiar with that, mustn't I," said Jacqueline. She glanced at Thomas in a way that boded no good.

"Well," said that gentleman hastily, "I think I'll just run upstairs and change. All that bus travel—"

"I'm being a bad host again," Weldon said sadly. "Dr. Kirby, you must be tired too. I'll ring. . . ."

Before he could do so, the door opened.

"They have arrived, Sir Richard," said the butler.

"They?" Thomas repeated. "Who is missing?"

"Why, Thomas," said Liz, in an affected drawl. "Don't tell me you haven't noticed that my fiancé is not here? Frank is so conspicuous."

"Frank is a nice young fellow," Thomas said. "I like him. It's just that the rest of us are rather obtrusive."

Liz smiled mockingly. Mildly embarrassed, Thomas went on, "Who else is coming?"

"A most distinguished guest," said Mrs. Ponsonby-Jones. "The new president of the American branch of our society is flying over in order to be present at this great moment. His name is O'Hagan."

"Frank is the only one of us coming by automobile," Weldon explained. "That is why I asked him to meet Mr. O'Hagan at Heathrow. O'Hagan has never been out of the States before, and I gather from his letters that he is somewhat apprehensive about traveling alone. This is a difficult place to find. . . ."

Two men appeared in the doorway. After his *faux pas* Thomas made a point of greeting Frank Acton with particular warmth.

All the same, he had to admit that Frank did not stand out in a crowd. He was of medium height and build, with one of those pleasantly nondescript faces that blur in one's memory. His dark hair was long but neatly barbered and his clothes were conservative. Thomas remembered that the young man was a budding solicitor, a very lowly member of the firm that handled Sir Richard's affairs. It was through this connection that he had met Liz. Thomas had wondered, when their engagement was announced, what the girl saw in him.

The American Ricardian was a tall, stooped man of about Thomas's age. His square-jawed, hawk-nosed face might have been attractive if it had not been set in an expression of timid terror. Projecting front teeth increased his resemblance to a nervous rabbit, and a bushy white moustache vibrated like whiskers when he was agitated. There was no doubt as to his identity; fastened to his left lapel with a large safety pin was a name tag. Thomas had an insane vision of the American society affixing the label as they pushed their president onto his plane like a bundle. Or had O'Hagan labeled himself? It was an equally insane idea. Weldon had said the American sounded apprehensive. That was an understatement. What was wrong with the man? Maybe he couldn't talk.

He could. The voice was a high-pitched whine and the moustache vibrated like a hummingbird's wings.

"Frightful, frightful," he exclaimed. "Those people at the gate —like a howling mob, ladies and gentlemen! I felt quite hunted, I assure you!"

"Not very bright of you, Frank, old boy," Philip said. "You ought to have driven in the stable gate instead of coming to the front of the grounds."

"No one bothered to warn me." Frank's voice was low and well modulated, with impeccable vowels, but he sounded irritated. He glanced betrayingly at Liz, who raised a languid hand in greeting, before he went on. "I hadn't realized you were turning this meeting into a circus. It's been a rotten day. I had difficulty finding Mr. O'Hagan; he wasn't where he was supposed to be—"

"It is such a confusing place," said Mr. O'Hagan pathetically. "All those *large* buildings—and people running around, bumping into you and pushing you—"

"The worst is over, Mr. O'Hagan," Weldon said soothingly. "You are perfectly safe with us. Do you . . . do you feel up to meeting the others?"

Mr. O'Hagan was able to nerve himself to the ordeal, but the introductions were marred by Liz's tendency to giggle. As soon as they were completed, Thomas excused himself. Jacqueline followed suit, and a neat parlormaid showed them to their rooms.

They needed a guide. Weldon House was like a maze. The copy of Crosby Hall was not the only accretion; wings and annexes proliferated. As they paced along behind the maid, Thomas heard Jacqueline mutter something about rabbits. He didn't know whether she was referring to the warren of corridors and rooms, or to Mr. O'Hagan, and he didn't inquire. He was not looking forward to his next conversation with Jacqueline.

Their rooms were adjoining. Thomas wondered whether this was accidental or not. The maid was certainly well trained. She didn't even blink when Jacqueline reached out a long arm and dragged Thomas into her room.

"I've got to unpack," he said, retreating.

"I expect you have been unpacked. I see I have. Doesn't the maid unpack for guests at these high-class affairs?"

"They do here, at any rate, and I hate it," said Thomas, still backing toward the door. "I always feel as if I have holes in my underwear even when I know I don't. Maybe I can get there before—"

"Close the door," said Jacqueline ominously.

There was no use putting it off. Thomas obeyed. When he had done so, Jacqueline dropped into a chair and beamed at him.

"Thomas, you are the love of my life. How can I ever thank you for bringing me here?"

"You aren't mad? I didn't warn you about Sir Richard—"

"Being an expert on the fifteenth century? Oh, that's all right. His appraisal is meaningless anyhow. He wants to believe in the letter. That's fatal to objectivity."

Masochistically Thomas continued, "And those frightful old women! I'm sorry you had to put up with their insults. Of course both of them are after poor Dick, and they regard every other woman as a rival. He's years younger than either of them, but he is quite a matrimonial catch."

"He's a catch, all right. He's sweet. Oh, Thomas, I am enjoying this! Let me see if I've got everybody straight in my mind. Sir Richard is Richard the Third, of course; no one else could possibly play Richard. And that enormous Ponsonby-Jones women copped the role of Richard's queen—pale, frail consumptive Queen Anne. How did she get away with that?"

"The Ponsonby-Joneses are Sir Richard's only relatives. They are distant relatives, but he feels responsible for them. He's particularly fond of young Elizabeth Ponsonby-Jones."

"Who is Elizabeth of York," Jacqueline resumed her summary, "Richard's niece, and later the queen of Henry the Seventh. The nice little rector is Edward the Fourth, Richard's brother—does he see himself in his secret day-dreams as a lusty lecher? Dr. Rawdon is poor, weak Henry the Sixth, which is equally inappropriate—he's so healthy-looking, it hurts to look at him. General Kent isn't suited to the role of Buckingham, either; Buckingham must have been a vacillating character; he changed his mind so often. Kent is certainly not indecisive. Lady Isobel—oh, Lord, Thomas, have you read any of her ghastly books?—is Edward the

Fourth's queen, Elizabeth Woodville. She probably would have preferred to be Richard's queen, but she wouldn't object to playing Elizabeth Woodville, the fabulous beauty with the silver-gilt hair who seduced a king into marriage. Philip Rohan as Lord Hastings—yes, but he could play any part. He's a gifted actor. He has a beautiful voice."

"It wasn't his voice you were admiring," said Thomas.

"Now, Thomas. Whom have I forgotten?"

"Well, you know I'm playing Clarence, the brother of Richard and Edward. You've forgotten Frank, Liz's fiancé. Everybody forgets the poor guy."

"I know one reason why I forgot him; I don't know what part he's playing. Did you tell me?"

"I guess not. He's Edward of Lancaster, the son of Henry the Sixth. He was the first husband of Anne, whom Richard later married. Edward was killed in battle, but the Tudor historians accused Richard of murdering him."

"I know that. Okay, I guess I've got them sorted out. Thomas, do you realize what this is? It's an English house party, darling, straight out of all those British detective stories I revel in. These people are classic characters. They couldn't be better if you had invented them. The doctor, the vicar, the village squire; the catty middle-aged hags and the sulky, beautiful young heroine, and the two juveniles—homely and nice, handsome and rakish. There is one missing. But I suppose it would be too much—"

The door burst open.

"Ah," said a voice. "You must be thinking of me—the missing character! The offensive, precocious small boy!"

The final adjective could only have referred to the apparition's relative age. His cheeks were still soft and downy, his voice high tenor. Otherwise he was more than large; he was elephantine. His puffy pink face was perfectly spherical. His features were regular and well shaped, but they were drowned in fat. His costume was unfortunate. The tights, stretched to bursting point, enclosed legs like Karnakian pillars, and his tunic was dragged up in front by a pot belly that would have disgraced a middle-aged beer drinker. The front of this garment was streaked with food and drink stains.

"Offensive is right," said Thomas distastefully. "Jacqueline, this is Percival Ponsonby-Jones, the son and heir of the lady you met downstairs. I needn't introduce you to him; he knows who you are. He knows everything. How long have you been eavesdropping, Percy?''

"Long enough to hear my mother referred to as a middle-aged hag." Percy came into the room and dropped heavily onto the bed. From a pouch at his belt he took a handful of cookies and began to eat them, scattering crumbs deliberately.

"Hag was an ill-chosen word," admitted Jacqueline. "It suggests someone who is haggard and undernourished. . . . What part are you taking in this charade, child? The court jester? Or perhaps Clarence's son, the one who was mentally retarded?"

Thomas blinked. Jacqueline was not usually so brutal. The attack disconcerted the boy. He hesitated, trying to decide which insult to answer first.

"I'm Edward the Fifth," he said. "The one who was murdered by Henry Tudor."

"Not smothered in the Tower by Richard?" Jacqueline asked.

Percy finished the cookies and extracted an apple from the same place.

"Everyone knows Richard didn't kill the princes," he said scornfully. "That's a Tudor slander. I expect you don't know who the Tudors were."

"But I thought the bones of the boys had been found in the Tower," said Jacqueline gently.

Percy expanded. Thomas felt a faint twinge of pity for the boy; he ought to have been warned by Jacqueline's earlier comments, but he was too young and too conceited to know better.

"The bones were found in 1674, when some workmen were demolishing a staircase outside the White Tower. It wasn't till 1933 that the bones were examined by a doctor and a dentist. *They* said the skeletons were of two children, aged about ten and twelve.

"Now . . ." Percy took another bite of apple and continued in a muffled voice, "you wouldn't know this, of course, but the very precision of the ages given is suspect. In order to blame Richard for the crime, you have to prove that the boys were exactly ten, and between twelve and thirteen, when they died, and you can't prove that because it's impossible to determine the ages of bones of young people that accurately. You can't even tell whether they were boys or girls before puberty. The description of where the bones were found doesn't agree with Sir Thomas More's story, either, but I won't go into that, because it's too complicated for you to understand.''

He smirked at Jacqueline and took another huge bite.

"More says they were buried 'at the stair foot, meetly deep in the ground under a great heap of stones,' '' Jacqueline murmured. "The accounts of the seventeenth-century workmen who found the bones imply that they were under the foundations of the stairs. Not only would that have been a much more laborious operation than the one More describes, but it doesn't agree with his statement that the bones were later removed and reburied elsewhere by a certain priest. There is also the evidence of one anthropologist consulted by Kendall, who believed that the older child could not have been more than nine years of age. In the absence of a dating process, which cannot at present be used effectively on human bone, we do not know how long the remains were in the Tower. They could have been buried at any time after 1100 A.D. I must admit I share your doubts as to the identification of these skeletal remains with the two princes.''

Percy's mouth hung open, giving the viewers an unattractive vista of masticated apple.

"Think you're clever, don't you,'' he said feebly.

"I don't think, I know,'' said Jacqueline. She added parenthetically to Thomas, "There is no point in being subtle with him, Thomas. Now, Percy, go away. Don't ever come in here again without knocking and waiting for permission. If you do, I will belt you one—as we crude Americans are wont to say.''

"You wouldn't dare. . . .'' Percy stood up.

"But you can't be sure. Taking chances lends variety and interest to life.''

Percy began to look trapped. "I'll tell them you've got Thomas in here. I saw you drag him in. My mother would like to hear *that.*''

Jacqueline laughed.

"What a little horror you are,'' Thomas said. "If young Edward was anything like you, it's no wonder he was smothered.''

"You're wasting words," Jacqueline said. "Never tell them more than once. Never bluff. Act."

She rose and advanced purposefully on Percy, who proved her point by retreating, at full speed, and without further comment. In the doorway he collided with Sir Richard, who was passing along the corridor.

"So there you are," Weldon said. "Your mother is looking for you, Percy. Run along now."

Percy left, with an eloquent look at Jacqueline, and Weldon shook his head.

"I do hope he hasn't been bothering you. He's a rather difficult child. Extremely intelligent; but it's not easy for his mother, lacking a man's authority. . . ."

He looked wistfully at Jacqueline, who smiled brightly.

"Don't apologize, Sir Richard. I enjoyed my chat with Percy very much."

III

At the hour appointed, Thomas made his way back to the drawing room. He was wearing slacks and a sport shirt; Weldon had decreed that the evening meeting and meal were to be informal. Thomas was relieved that he did not have to wear his medieval robes. It was an unseasonably warm evening, and he was shy of displaying himself before Jacqueline's ironical eyes.

He found the drawing room deserted except for Wilkes the butler, who was sourly studying the drinks tray. Thomas rather liked Wilkes; he was as well trained and as formal as Jenkins, but his manner was not so supercilious as that of the tall chauffeur. A stout, balding little man, he looked up as Thomas came in.

"Am I the first one down?" Thomas asked, accepting a whiskey and soda. He didn't really like whiskey and soda, but it seemed the proper thing to have.

"They have retired to the library," Wilkes said. "I proposed to Sir Richard that I should follow with the tray, but he assured me they would return immediately."

Thomas understood the butler's air of pique. Soothingly he

said, "I'll go after them. Maybe I can casually mention the passage of time."

Wilkes's melancholy expression did not change. Thomas had
to agree that his errand was probably vain. When Sir Richard got
into the library it was hard to get him out, especially when he had
a new audience.

The door of the room stood open; from the corridor Thomas
could hear Weldon's voice rising and falling in gentle, uninter-
rupted cadence. He paused in the doorway for a moment, enjoying the chance of watching the others before they realized
they were being observed.

Most of them had abandoned medieval garb, but Percy still
wore his messy costume. Either he didn't know how terrible he
looked, or he didn't care. Philip, leaning gracefully against the
carved stone mantel, was also in costume. Unconsciously Thomas
pulled in his stomach.

He was next struck by the unnatural alliance between Mrs.
Ponsonby-Jones and Lady Isobel, who were seated side by side.
They looked comical together, the ample girth of the one em-
phasizing the scrawniness of the other. They were united by a
common emotion; two pairs of narrowed eyes stared intently at
the enemy. Jacqueline was wearing her favorite green, a misty
shade that set off her tanned arms and shoulders. It clung to her
tall body, and the ladies weren't the only ones who were staring.

Weldon had taken Jacqueline's arm in order to lead her
around. He was still talking.

There was plenty for him to talk about. High-ceilinged, with
French doors opening onto the terrace, the room contained two
tiers of bookshelves with an open gallery running around three
sides and stairs leading up to it. Another flight of narrow circular
steps went up from the gallery. It opened, as Thomas knew, into
the private sitting room of Sir Richard's suite, so that the scholarly gentleman could reach his beloved books without a long
walk through the house.

A big library table and an equally mammoth desk were dwarfed
by the dimensions of the room. Fat leather chairs and sofas were
scattered about. Thick wall-to-wall carpeting muffled voices and
footsteps. Glass cases, spaced at intervals, contained some of the
rarer items of Weldon's collection, and there were other exhibits

on the wall over the fireplace—an impressive array of medieval weapons. Prominent among these was an enormous two-handed sword. It was this object Weldon was discussing as Thomas entered.

"I am convinced it was Richard's. It comes from Leicester, near Bosworth, and the tradition—"

Kent interrupted with a snort.

"Nonsense. The weapon is certainly sixteenth century. You may be the handwriting expert, but I'm the authority on armament, and I assure you—"

Weldon turned. He looked almost grim enough for Richard III.

"I beg your pardon. The historical tradition—"

Kent gave another volcanic snort and Frank said tactfully,

"I can't understand how any soldier could wield a weapon so heavy. How long is it precisely, sir?"

Instead of answering, Weldon climbed nimbly onto a chair and lifted the sword down. Jacqueline stepped back as the mammoth blade left its support, but Weldon handled it easily.

"It only weighs fourteen pounds and a bit," he said.

"Overall length, eighty-nine inches," Kent added. "The blade is well over six feet."

The startling dimensions of the sword became clearer when Weldon held it upright. He was several inches under six feet; the hilt topped his head by a foot and a half.

"You are thinking in terms of modern dueling," Kent said to Frank. "That didn't begin until the seventeenth century. In Richard's time the idea was to whack your enemy as hard and as often as you could. The sword was used for cutting, not thrusting."

He demonstrated, taking the weapon from Weldon. The blade cut the air with a deadly and surprising precision; even Thomas, in the distant doorway, stepped back a pace.

"There's a knack to it," Kent warned, as the others crowded forward, wanting to try their hands. "Don't swing it as I did, you'll lop an ear off someone."

Frank was the first to try; he was properly cautious, remarking on the poor balance of the weapon. Lady Isobel made a show of trying in vain to lift the weight. Jacqueline gave her a thoughtful look and hoisted the sword without difficulty, remarking, "My purse weighs more than that." But when Percy swaggered forward and reached for the sword, Thomas decided it was time to intervene.

"Hey," he said. "You're all supposed to be back in the drawing room. Wilkes is sulking. . . ."

It was too late.

"Dinner is served," said Wilkes, and gave Thomas a reproachful look.

IV

They were dining early so that the business meeting could start at a reasonable hour. It was still light outside; from his seat Thomas could see out across the wide lawns toward the maze and the rose garden. The softening light made the fabulous turf look like smooth green velvet. It was a lovely view, a scene out of the England of glamorized history and legend.

Then two figures appeared, one human, the other four-legged. A watchman, with a large mastiff on a leash.

It was ridiculous, Thomas thought sourly. All this fuss and furor over a few reporters. You'd think the place were under siege by howling Lancastrians waving pikes and thirsting for Weldon's head.

Thomas was sulking, although he would not have chosen that word. Rohan and Kent, the most aggressive males in the group, had grabbed the chairs next to Jacqueline. Weldon had disposed of the two older women with the skill a hunted man develops. Mrs. Ponsonby-Jones sat triumphantly at the foot of the table as hostess, but Lady Isobel had won the seat at her host's right. Thomas was stuck between Mrs. Ponsonby-Jones and Liz, and was getting no attention from either. Liz was preempted by Frank, on her other side, and Mrs. Ponsonby-Jones was preoccupied with her son. Percy was directly across from Thomas, and the latter watched Percy eat with fascinated disgust. Eat was hardly the word; the wretched boy swallowed food like a python, and his besotted mother kept urging him to eat more. Thomas averted his eyes and let fragments of conversation drift through his ears into his brain. The discussion, as might have been expected, was predominantly Ricardian.

". . . Richard blamed the Woodvilles for Clarence's death. They had a pressing motive for wanting him out of the way if, as seems probable, he knew about the precontract."

". . . try to eat another teeny bit of beef, darling. A growing boy must keep up his strength."

". . . wore German armor. It was the best available."

". . . might have won if Northumberland had not remained aloof from the battle. Richard ought to have known he was treacherous. . . ."

"Why? He had loaded the rascal with favors."

The rector's voice rose over those of the other speakers. He and the American visitor were refighting the Battle of Bosworth, and Thomas smiled to himself as he saw others turn toward the debaters. He was reminded of Southern friends talking about a more recent war. "If Stonewall Jackson hadn't been killed. . . . If England had come in on our side. . . ." The lost causes, the romantic failures . . . the flight to Varennes, the Forty-Five, Bonnie Dundee and the Lost Dauphin. "If only. . . ." Futile speculations, impractical and thoroughly irresistible.

The American answered.

"Richard's popularity in the North threatened Northumberland's position in that region. If Henry Tudor won, Northumberland could expect to be supreme—"

"He didn't have to risk supporting the wrong side," Kent interrupted. "All he had to do was sit tight and refuse to move. Shrewd—very shrewd."

"Despicable, you mean," squeaked Lady Isobel.

"Ah, the gentle illogic of women," Kent said, with a vicious smile. "I regret Richard's betrayal as much as you, dear lady, but I must admit he did not act with his usual good sense. If he had anticipated the treachery of the Stanleys—"

A chorus of voices drowned him out.

"Yes, the Stanleys were the decisive factor."

". . . incredibly naive of Richard. Stanley was the husband of Henry Tudor's mother."

"What do you mean, naive? Richard had Stanley's own son as hostage. . . ."

"Stanley knew Richard wouldn't kill the boy. He was too damned soft-headed."

"Too sensitive and kind! No, poor dear Richard's greatest error was in attacking Henry Tudor personally. He ought to have remained safely in the rear!"

"Balderdash. That was a brilliant move, and it came damned close to winning the day. Richard was a bonny fighter and Henry was a coward. Five more minutes and Richard would have smashed the rascal's skull—"

"Five minutes? Two minutes! Richard struck down the biggest brutes in Henry's bodyguard. . . ."

Thomas was shaken by a vertiginous shock of confusion. Had it happened five hundred years ago, or only yesterday? Turning, he met the eyes of the girl beside him and saw his own incredulity mirrored in her face.

"We're all mad," she muttered.

"It's a harmless madness," Thomas answered slowly. "And you at least seem impervious. . . ."

Liz shook her head. Her fine brown hair shifted silkily.

"I'm as bad as they are. 'King Richard, alone, was killed fighting manfully in the thickest press of his enemies. . . .' It was his enemies who said that about him; even though they hated him and murdered him, they couldn't deny him that tribute. And I. . . ." She laughed softly, but there was a note in her voice Thomas didn't like. "I've got a schoolgirl crush on him. I'm too sophisticated to fall for the pop musicians and the nude centerfold types. I dream about a man who's been dead and rotten for five hundred years."

"Liz. . . ."

The girl shook her head again. The cloud cleared from her face, which regained its habitual expression of sulky boredom.

"Thomas, you are too much," she said lightly. "One can't resist teasing you, you're so trusting."

Without giving Thomas time to reply, she raised her voice in a shout.

"Mother! Isn't it time for the ladies to retire? We'll never start the meeting at this rate."

Mrs. Ponsonby-Jones glared. She was not quick at repartee. It was Weldon who replied amiably.

"What conventional circles you move in, Liz. I thought your generation lingered over the port along with the men."

"Port is not what we linger over," said Liz. "You're close, though."

"None of us is going to linger tonight," Weldon said, as Philip laughed and Mrs. Ponsonby-Jones pondered Liz's comment. "We'll have coffee later, at the meeting, if that is agreeable. In the Great Hall at eight, then. Frank, you're giving the first paper."

"Right, sir. I'd better go up and get my notes together."

Weldon gave the younger man a friendly pat on the back.

"Not nervous, are you?"

"Oh, no, sir."

"Nothing to be nervous about. We're all friends."

Frank glanced from Philip's wide white grin to Kent's anticipatory smile. His affable face took on a look of deep gloom.

V

The reverberations of a gong summoned the members to the meeting. Thomas had been refreshing his memory with Kendall's *Richard III*; when he reached the Hall, most of the others were already present. He stopped in the entrance to enjoy a moment of sentimentality; the reconstruction of Richard's former home delighted him. Jacqueline, also late, came up behind him, and Thomas moved aside so she could see.

It was a vast room, its floor of unpolished Purbeck marble stretching away like a skating rink. The fireplace was a simple rounded arch of carved stone, without mantel or hood. At the far end a minstrel's gallery, balustraded in dark oak, was reached by a winding stair. Windows filled the upper half of the Hall; each light rose to a pointed arch framed in stone trefoils. Panes of stained glass replaced some of the diamond-shaped panes, and Weldon had made sure Richard's coat of arms was included along with those of other characters in the Ricardian drama. The lower half of the walls was covered with priceless old tapestries from Weldon's collection.

The real glory of the room was its ceiling. Sculptured, painted beams intersected in complex patterns, with bosses and hanging ornaments at the points of intersection. Enough of the natural wood had been left to provide a mellow brown background for the designs in crimson and green and shining gold. Thomas had never asked, but he felt quite sure that the gilt was genuine gold leaf.

On the dais at the far end Weldon had placed a table, as long as a fallen oak, surrounded by chairs that were copies of fifteenth-century furniture, with high, carved backs and seats of crimson velvet. Weldon was already seated at the head of the table. His mammoth chair dwarfed his slight body, and Thomas's mouth pursed in a silent whistle as he observed the chair. It was new since his last visit, and from the crown on the back to the shape of the arms it rather suggested a throne.

Perhaps it was the throne that had cast a hush over the assembled group. The silence continued as Thomas escorted Jacqueline down the length of the room. He felt like the victim of some formal ceremony, marriage or investiture or coronation, and he wondered if the floor was as slippery as it looked. Jacqueline paced solemnly at his side, looking neither to right nor to left. Thomas knew she was enjoying herself immensely.

Liz winked at him as he took his seat. Philip was sitting next to the girl; he nudged her and said something in a whisper, so close to her ear that his breath stirred the curls on her cheek. Liz giggled. Her mother glared.

Frank was the only one who had not arrived. Thomas wondered if the boy really was nervous. Surely a lawyer ought not to suffer from stage fright. It was a hard audience for a novice to face, though. Frank was new to Ricardian controversy, having joined the society after he became engaged to Liz. Now he had to perform before a group of critical experts, and in the presence of his fiancée's equally critical family—including the wealthy, expert head of that family.

Thomas glanced at the program. Weldon didn't do things by halves; the document was printed on expensive paper and bound in calf. Frank's was the first paper of the evening, and Thomas sighed inwardly as he read the title.

"Who Murdered the Princes?"

That was the trouble with amateur societies, they kept

rehashing the same old material. The "murder" of the princes had been written about so often; there was nothing to be said that hadn't been said a thousand times. But it fretted Ricardians like a bad tooth. They couldn't leave it alone. And some of the poor innocents couldn't tell the difference between logic and wishful thinking, between the relevant and the extraneous. They threw everything in together and served it up, assuming that the warmed-over mixture of fact and fancy would appeal to an audience.

However, Thomas had to admit that amateur historians were not the only ones who suffered from this particular weakness. The scholarly journals were full of trivia and faulty argument.

Absorbed in his own mildly pompous thoughts, he was unaware of the rising murmur of impatience until Philip called out,

"Sir Richard, what's happened to Frank? It's nearly half past eight."

"Probably he's hiding under the bed," said Percy, with a hoarse chuckle. He was eating jelly beans, or some form of confectionery that resembled them, brightly colored and very slippery. There was a constant rattle of fallen candies from his direction.

"Can he have fallen asleep?" Lady Isobel wondered. She looked groggy herself, and if there was the odor of jelly beans from Percy's direction, a scent of another kind wafted from Lady Isobel. Seeing her flushed face, Thomas felt sure she had taken a nip or two in the privacy of her room before coming to the meeting.

Jacqueline glanced at her watch.

"Is he often absentminded?"

"Quite the reverse; most methodical young fellow I know." Weldon looked worried. "It's foolish—a healthy specimen like that, nothing could have happened, but perhaps we had better. . . ."

"Quite right," Kent said briskly. "Let's hunt him out. You ladies stay here, we'll soon find him."

Lady Isobel didn't look capable of movement, and Mrs. Ponsonby-Jones inclined her head in majestic acquiescence, but Jacqueline was already on her feet, and Liz followed suit. In a disorganized group they trailed one another up the stairs.

The most logical assumption was that Frank had fallen asleep. In fact, Thomas thought with a small shock, there was no other logical assumption. If an emergency had kept the young lawyer from the meeting, he would have sent a message.

Percy was the first to reach Frank's room, not because he was more nimble, but because the others tended to hang back. The fat boy flung the door open, and as Weldon came forward, he announced with the relish some people feel at proclaiming bad news, "He's not here. Unless he's under the bed."

He was not under the bed. Feeling like a fool, but driven by an inexplicable compulsion, Thomas looked.

For a few moments they stood staring at one another. Then Kent said brusquely, "Ridiculous. Organization, that's what we need. Ring for Wilkes, Dick. Perhaps one of the servants has seen the lad."

None of the servants had, not since the whole group had gone upstairs after dinner. This was not surprising, since the staff had been at its own dinner in the servants' hall; but the news cast a pall over the group. Percy's was the only cheerful face.

"All right," Kent said, after the butler had gone back to his duties. "Let's keep the servants out of this; it's bound to be a tempest in a teapot. I'm going out to inquire of the outdoor staff. Perhaps Frank went for a walk and dozed off. Dick, look in the library, lounge, drawing room. Philip. . . ."

"We'll investigate the bedrooms," said Philip, taking Liz's hand.

"But what would he—" Liz stopped. The enameled facade of her face was beginning to crack.

"He might have fainted," Thomas said. "He looks healthy enough, but I suppose he might have a heart condition, or epilepsy, or something. . . ."

"No," Liz said positively.

Weldon gave her an odd look and then said firmly, "We are becoming fanatical. I feel sure there is some unalarming explanation."

They separated. Kent, moving briskly, was soon out of sight. The doctor and the rector followed. Weldon gave the others a hesitant smile before heading for the stairs. O'Hagan trailed after him. Percy followed Philip and Liz along the corridor; he had, Thomas thought, a propensity for bedrooms. That left Thomas and Jacqueline, and when they were alone Thomas turned toward her.

"You've been very quiet. What are you thinking?"

Jacqueline didn't answer immediately. She reached into her bag and took out her glasses. The purse was a good deal larger than it looked, as was characteristic of Jacqueline's purses. Settling the glasses firmly on her nose, Jacqueline said,

"I think something is wrong. I've thought so ever since we arrived. If I were psychic, I'd roll my eyes and mumble about auras. Thomas, it is almost nine o'clock. Can you think of any reason why that young man should not be where he is supposed to be?"

"None that convinces me."

"Nor I. Let's go look for him."

"Where?"

"We'll check the Hall first; he may have appeared in the meantime. If not—I suppose this place has a cellar?"

"It has a cellar the size of Mammoth Cave. Why do you suppose—"

"I don't suppose anything. But all the other parts of the house are being searched."

Frank had not gone to the Hall. The two older women were still alone there. Lady Isobel had fallen into a tipsy doze, her head at an uncomfortable angle and her mouth wide open. Mrs. Ponsonby-Jones was watching her with a malicious smile. She did not see the pair in the doorway, who beat a hasty retreat.

The cellars had, of course, been electrified. They were almost as large as Thomas claimed, stretching the full length and width of the house. Thomas saw Jacqueline shiver as they descended into clammy, dust-shrouded silence.

The house was well staffed, but not even Weldon's fortune could pay enough servants to keep the lower regions dust-free. There was a light coating on the floor, and almost at once they saw signs that someone had been there. There were no footprints, but rather a scuffed, faintly visible path.

"It needn't have been Frank," Jacqueline said, as Thomas squatted to peer at the marks. "The servants must come down here, at least to the wine cellar."

"There are no other marks," Thomas said. "If he was down here, he went this way."

It took some time to carry out the search. The lighting was poor and the switches were located in obscure corners. The scuffed trail branched off from time to time, toward storerooms and the furnace room. The heating plant was a vast monstrosity, antique but still capable of functioning. Weldon had enough food stored to withstand a siege. Thomas got lost twice.

"Yes, I've been here," he said irritably, as Jacqueline made a sarcastic comment. "Weldon showed us over the house the first time we came. But that was a couple of years ago, you can't expect me to . . . that must be the wine cellar, over there. It's about the only place we haven't looked."

"Then we'll look there."

"This is silly," Thomas grumbled, trailing Jacqueline. She had lifted her skirts, and her silver sandals twinkled in the dim light. "I'll bet they found him snoring in the garden."

Jacqueline opened the door of the wine cellar. She stood quite still; only her fingers moved, a bare fraction of an inch. The shadowy green skirts came whispering down to the floor.

Thomas ran forward.

Frank lay face down in the center of a gleaming dark puddle. Red stained the back of his white shirt and shone wetly in his hair. The only light was the feeble glow from the bulb outside the small room; monstrous shapes loomed in the shadows beyond the fallen body, and sparks of light winked like a thousand squinting eyes.

CHAPTER THREE

*I*t was several seconds before Thomas identified the shapes as barrels and realized that the light was reflected from the rows of bottles neatly racked along the back wall. There were winking sparks on the floor as well. Broken glass.

He groped for a light switch and found a hanging cord instead. He pulled it. The overhead light came on, giving the scene a distinctness that made it even more unbelievable.

Jacqueline lifted her skirts. Thomas held her back.

"Stay there," he said, relieved to find his voice even. "No point in ruining your dress."

"He's alive," Jacqueline said.

"Of course he is," Thomas said soothingly. "That's wine, not blood. Must have broken a bottle."

He picked a careful path through the shattered glass and spilled Burgundy, and ran his hand over Frank's hair. When he took it away, his fingers were red and sticky, but not with blood.

"Just a bump," he announced with relief.

Frank groaned and stirred. Thomas put his hand on the young man's shoulder.

"Take it easy, Frank. You have quite a lump on the head. You must have fallen, knocking down a bottle as you collapsed."

Frank muttered something unintelligible.

"How did he get wine on the back of his shirt?" Jacqueline inquired softly.

Thomas looked at her in surprise. Then Frank rolled over and sat up. Jacqueline gasped, and Thomas saw his comfortable theory go glimmering away down a dark corridor of improbability.

There was only one way of accounting for the marks that disfigured the young man's face. He had been in a fight—and if Frank hadn't lost it, Thomas thought, he would hate to see the other guy. Dark bruises marked jaw, cheekbone, and temple. Cuts ran like jigsaw pieces over the whole of his face, and the crusted stains above his mouth were certainly not wine.

"Good Lord," Thomas said. "Jacqueline, go for help. We'll have to carry—"

"No, no, I'm all right," Frank said unconvincingly. "Oh, Lord —what happened?"

"We hoped you could tell us."

"I don't remember a thing after I followed that fellow in a trench coat down the stairs."

Thomas glanced at Jacqueline.

"Get him upstairs," she said. "This is not the time nor the place for a debate."

II

It was ten o'clock before the meeting finally began, and the topic of conversation was not the murder of the princes. Frank was present. After vigorous ablutions he had convinced them that the damage wasn't as bad as it looked, and Rawdon had confirmed the diagnosis. Most of the blood on Frank's face came from his nose. Sheepishly he had explained that he was very susceptible to nosebleed. The cuts were mere scratches. The chief damage was to his self-esteem, and on this subject he discoursed with vigor and fluency.

"He must have hit me with a bottle," he finished bitterly. "I don't remember a thing—not even a fight—but I couldn't have dislodged one of those bottles accidentally. If I could only re-member!''

"Temporary amnesia is not uncommon after a blow on the head," the doctor said reassuringly. "It will probably come back to you."

"What he does remember is bad enough," said Kent. "Some intruder made his way into the house. How?"

"It doesn't seem possible," Weldon said. "I've men patrolling the grounds. . . ."

"Nevertheless, someone did get in. Frank, you haven't given us a very good description. A trench coat and a wide-brimmed hat, you say?"

"I never saw his face," Frank said. "Just caught a glimpse of the fellow ducking under the stairs as I came down them. I was early—wanted to get my thoughts organized before the meeting began. I followed him—saw the door of the cellar wide open—and that's all I remember."

"Obviously one of those horrid reporters," said Lady Isobel, whose nap had revived her. She shuddered fastidiously. "Isn't that the costume they habitually wear?"

"You ought to know, dear," said Lady Ponsonby-Jones. "You claim the creatures are always pursuing you."

"We'd never be able to identify him," Kent said. "Not from that description."

Mrs. Ponsonby-Jones gave a little scream. They all jumped.

"Perhaps he is still here!" she cried. "Still in the house!"

"No, no," Weldon said. "That would be foolish of him, to remain after committing an assault."

"I'm not sure," Philip said thoughtfully. "He might assume we would reason along those lines and feel it safe to remain. We'd better all look under our beds tonight."

His handsome rakish face was sober, but he glanced at Mrs. Ponsonby-Jones, who cried out again.

"Richard, I'll not be able to sleep a wink!"

"I'll have the servants search the house," Weldon said reassuringly. "Just to be on the safe side."

He rang and gave orders to the butler. Percy followed Wilkes out.

"Philip might think it safe to stay," Liz said. "He's that sort of fool. But I'm sure most reporters have better sense."

Philip smiled at her, and the rector said,

"Quite right, quite right. After all, dear lady, these chaps are not criminals; you would be in no danger if you did find one under . . . that is. . . ."

Liz burst out laughing.

"You certainly wouldn't need to worry, Mother."

Kent brought his fist down on the table with a crash.

"Of all the irresponsible fools I've ever seen, this lot is the worst. We're wasting valuable time. If this chap was a reporter, there's no harm done. I can deal with reporters." A reminiscent red gleam shone in his eyes. "But what if it wasn't a reporter?"

The others stared at him.

"I've heard a rumor," Kent went on. "They say that there is a stranger at the village inn. A stranger to them, but not to us. . . . Ladies and gentlemen, I suspect that the man is no other than—James Strangways!"

An unenlightened outsider would have thought Kent had told them there was a bomb in the room. Faces turned pale; eyes glazed; Lady Isobel sank back in her chair with a gasp; and Mrs. Ponsonby-Jones tried to faint.

Thomas glanced at Jacqueline. He suspected she recognized the name. She gave no indication of it. Clasping her hands in a gesture of exaggerated horror, she gave Sir Richard his cue.

"Good heavens! Sir Richard! Who is—James Strangways?"

Weldon's round face was grim.

"He is the worst enemy I have in the world."

Mrs. Ponsonby-Jones changed the scene from melodrama to farce.

"Your enemy? What about me? Don't you remember that dreadful insulting letter he wrote about my little article on Richard's religious beliefs?"

"Oh," said Jacqueline. "That Strangways."

Weldon nodded solemnly.

"Perhaps I should call him Richard's worst enemy. The man is a menace. One might call him a renegade, because he was once a strong supporter of Richard's."

"He wrote a biography of Edward the Fourth," Jacqueline said. "The authoritative biography."

"That is correct. In an appendix he asserted his belief in Richard's innocence of the murder in very strong terms."

There was no need for Weldon to explain which murder he meant; in Ricardian circles the young princes were the only victims worth mentioning.

"But that was ten years ago," Weldon went on, "when Strangways was a rising young scholar at one of your American universities. Since then he has changed his attitude. Not only has he written derogatory articles about Richard, but he attacks pro-Ricardians on every possible occasion. Until recently he was a member of the American branch of the society, but our colleagues in the States finally had to expel him."

"For treason?" Jacqueline inquired seriously.

Sir Richard looked at her reproachfully.

"Indeed, Jacqueline—"

"Forgive me; I didn't mean to poke fun at the society."

"Of course not." Sir Richard smiled at her. "I suppose we do sound a bit foolish to outsiders; but Strangways is really a most unpleasant chap. We consider him our most pernicious opponent, for the man has prestige and a certain literary style—"

"A most disgusting, cynical style," Lady Isobel said. Her sallow cheeks were flushed. "It has no literary merit. Pure invective, that is all it is."

"Strangways was extremely rude about *The Gallant Young King*," the rector chirped sympathetically. "The review was rather widely read; it appeared in one of your local American newspapers."

"*The New York Times*," Thomas said, straight-faced. "It does have a moderate circulation."

Philip gave Thomas an appreciative look.

"Your little local papers," he said grinning. "Well, we know about Americans, don't we, Lady Isobel? No taste. Barbarians."

"I resent the implication," O'Hagan said suddenly. "You denigrate the valiant efforts of the American branch, under whose auspices I am proud to appear here."

He was an indignant rabbit. His face was flushed and his white moustache twitched vigorously. The group hastened to make apologies, which were interrupted by another bang on the table from Kent.

"Good Gad, are we going to sit here babbling all night? Dick, I move we adjourn normal business until tomorrow morning; we can have an extra session at ten A.M. to hear the papers that were to have been read tonight. At the moment—"

"This is not proper procedure," said the rector, looking shocked. "You must entertain a motion—"

"To hell with procedure," Frank said. "Sorry, Mr. Ellis, but I agree with the general, and so do all my scrapes and bruises. This affair may have more serious implications than you realize. If the intruder was not a newspaperman, he may have been after something more important than scandal."

Surprisingly, few of them had considered this possibility. Weldon was the exception.

"The letter is locked in my safe," he said. "No one but myself has the combination."

"Strangways may not know that," mumbled the doctor.

"But how do we know—"

"Just a minute," Thomas interrupted in exasperation. "We're beginning to babble again. First of all we ought to find out whether this business about Strangways is anything more than an idle rumor. One of us must go to the village in the morning and investigate. Is the stranger really Strangways? If so, can he provide an alibi for tonight?"

"I'm sure he'll be delighted to describe his movements to you," Liz said sarcastically.

"We needn't ask him. Discreet questioning of the personnel of the inn—"

"Good thinking," Kent said approvingly. "I'll go 'round in the morning."

"Not you," Weldon objected. "Every reporter in England knows your face."

"Humph," said Kent.

"I'll go," Thomas offered. "Jacqueline and I are of no interest to the press."

"Your faces may not be known," Philip said, with a cynical smile, "but do you know the face you hope to see? Do any of us know the notorious Strangways by sight?"

A damp silence fell. Finally Jacqueline said mildly, "Would there perhaps be a photograph on the jacket of his book?"

Weldon went trotting out to get the book. When he returned, the others crowded around the head of the table and stared at the small photo on the inside back flap of the jacket.

"No good," Frank said. "Just a head and shoulders."

"I like his nose," Jacqueline said pensively. "Big and bold and Napoleonic. And a good square jaw."

"This is not a male beauty contest," Thomas said in exasperation. "The point is that the photo isn't much use as a means of identification. I'll bet it's ten years old. That square jaw you admire may be buried in double chins, and the hair—pardon me, Jacqueline, the thick black hair—may be gone altogether."

The door burst open. Percy appeared, coated with a blend of cobwebs and crumbs, and followed by the butler. Before Wilkes could speak, Percy announced shrilly, "No one. But we found a window open."

"That is correct, Sir Richard," said Wilkes, icily proper. He shot Percy a glance of burning hatred.

"Thank you, Wilkes."

The butler left. Percy dropped heavily into one of the chairs and his mother exclaimed, "Darling boy, you are absolutely filthy. You must pop straight into a hot tub."

"No," Percy said insolently. "I might miss something. What happened while I was gone?"

"Isn't he amusing?" asked Lady Ponsonby-Jones fondly. "To summarize, darling boy—"

"Do you mind summarizing on your own time?" Jacqueline inquired. "I'm rather tired, and Frank ought to be in bed. His injuries may be superficial, but he suffered quite a shock."

"Of course." Weldon got to his feet, running his hand distractedly through his mane of brown hair. "This has been a confusing evening. I'm sure you are all tired and distressed."

But they weren't, Thomas realized. They were having the time of their lives. Even Frank's abused face showed more anger and excitement than worry. As he had often done before with this group of engaging monomaniacs, he felt as if he were the only adult in charge of a nursery class. He looked at Jacqueline, and thought he saw a similar sentiment on her face. She had once mentioned that she didn't much care for children.

III

Thomas was up early next morning. Weldon had implied that it would be nice if they all made it to the meeting scheduled for ten o'clock. The society was touchy about its rituals. And after Frank's nonappearance and its melodramatic sequel, a missing member would arouse general hysteria. Before the meeting Thomas and Jacqueline had to undertake their espionage operation in the village, seeking the nefarious James Strangways.

On a sunny summer morning the breakfast room at Weldon House looked particularly charming. It suggested a photograph out of *Country Life*—a prewar *Country Life,* when such items as Georgian silver and Chippendale tables were commonplace. Silver chafing dishes sparkled along the mahogany sideboard, and Thomas's nostrils sorted out a variety of tempting odors. It was not power that corrupted, he thought—it was soft living. Any invading barbarian would succumb to this fare. Bacon—solid English bacon, like slabs of ham marbled with fat; scrambled eggs, boiled eggs, coddled eggs; oatmeal, and a variety of cold breakfast cereals—removed from their plebeian cardboard containers and elegantly encased in crystal; rows of toast in silver toast racks; cut-glass pots of jam; black cherries glowing like dark rubies in crystalline syrup; thick orange marmalade, solid with rind; amber honey from Weldon's own hives; hot biscuits, and . . . Thomas's eyes widened as he identified a platter of jelly doughnuts. He had mentioned his passion for jelly doughnuts the last time he stayed at Weldon House. Damn it, he thought affectionately, you couldn't help liking a man who remembered a trivial remark like that. He wondered if the tastes of the others had been catered to also, and decided in the affirmative as he saw the rector piling his plate with what appeared to be deviled kidneys. He waved his fork, adorned with kidney, at Thomas as the latter joined him at the sideboard.

"Good morrow, brother Clarence, good morrow! How is it with you?"

Thomas rolled an eye toward the table, where Jacqueline sat in more than oriental splendor. The sunlight streaming through the bay windows made her hair glow like fire; she was wearing white slacks and a silky garment printed in shades of green, peacock blue, and gold. She looked up from the austere cup of tea and piece of toast on which she was breakfasting, and winked. Reassured, Thomas turned back to the rector, who was, he recalled, his Ricardian brother, Edward IV.

"Hail, my liege," he said valiantly. "How is it with you?"

The doctor, who had just entered, clucked disapprovingly.

"No, no Thomas; 'your Grace' would be more suitable." He put a heaping spoonful of a pale-gray substance on his plate and studied the rector's pile of kidneys disparagingly. "As for my fellow king here, he isn't going to be at all well if he eats that frightful mess. I shudder, friend Edward, to think of the lining of your stomach."

"Then don't think about it," said Mr. Ellis cheerfully. "Really, Rawdon—forgive me, King Henry—we ought to exchange roles. Not that I claim to be a saint, and there are those who believe poor mad Henry qualified for that position—"

"As a man of the cloth you are closer to the role of saint than I," Rawdon admitted. "Actually, I believe Henry was a mental case, not a saint, but that may be a professional prejudice."

"You may both be right," said Thomas, helping himself to bacon. "Henry was a gentle, kindly man who was also considerably confused. I suspect your diet would appeal to him at that, Rawdon. What is that stuff?"

The doctor's long face brightened.

"Barley cereal, honey, malt, and a few other of nature's gifts to man. It's my own invention. Weldon is good enough to have it prepared for me when I come. Really, Thomas, you ought to try it. It would do wonders for your—"

"No, thanks," Thomas said. He didn't want to hear what organs the revolting mess would do wonders for, much less eat it.

The rector chuckled.

"It's better than malmsey wine—eh, brother Clarence?"

Thomas acknowledged the witticism with a sour smile. He was getting tired of references to the famous butt of malmsey.

He retreated to the table and sat down beside Jacqueline, who turned emerald-green eyes upon him.

"Hail, brother George. I may call you brother, I hope? As the mother of Richard's bastard children—"

"Cut it out," growled Thomas.

"Certainly not. I have decided to fling myself wholeheartedly into the spirit of the thing. Have I told you my name is Katherine? Nobody seems to know who Richard's mistresses were; I have formed a theory that one of them was Hastings' wife Katherine. That would explain why Richard was so hasty—" a flicker of long dark lashes emphasized the pun, and Thomas made a wordless grimace of disgust—"so hasty in executing Hastings. We know that Richard's illegitimate daughter was named Katherine; what would be more natural than for her to be named after her mother? Richard dedicated a chapel to Saint Katherine—"

She broke off as Kent came to join them. In the bright light of day the general's face looked like that of a well-preserved mummy, but his eyes were snapping with energy and appreciation as he surveyed Jacqueline's cool elegance. He put his plate down, and Jacqueline eyed it with consternation. Two white-eyed fish looked back at her.

"Very interesting idea," Kent said, beginning to debone the nasty-looking specimens. "Don't believe I have ever heard it before. Would you give us a lecture, Jacqueline?"

"I was just joking," Jacqueline said meekly. She seemed subdued by the fishy stare.

"Mustn't joke about serious matters." Kent chuckled. "Do you know, the more I think about it, the more it attracts me. Lady Hastings as Richard's mistress. . . ."

"Now wait a minute," Thomas said. "That's a ridiculous idea. She was too old in the first place, and in the second place—"

Kent paid no attention. Turning to the rector, who had taken the chair beside him, he began to recapitulate Jacqueline's theory. Rawdon, eating with slow, well chewed bites, also listened attentively. Jacqueline caught Thomas's eye and lifted her own eyes in pious resignation.

"Fascinating," the rector said. "Indeed, Jacqueline, you must write an article for our little journal. Or—no! May I call you Katherine?"

"Oh, do," said Jacqueline wildly. "Do."

"Where are the others?" inquired Thomas, in an attempt to change the subject before Jacqueline waxed violent and profane.

"Let me see." Ellis considered the question, as if it were an exercise in historical research, which it did rather resemble. "Our good host and his lady have come and gone, as has my excellent spouse. Young Edward—your son, my dear doctor—has also breakfasted, as has the other young Edward, my son and heir. I do not know about the others."

It took Thomas a few moments to sort out the aliases.

"Sir Richard, the two older ladies, Frank, and Percy," he translated, for the benefit of Jacqueline, whose eyes were glazed. "I'll bet Percy was the first to come and the last to leave."

"No doubt." The idea seemed to distress the doctor. He put his fork down and considered his half-empty plate doubtfully. "The boy has an excellent appetite. . . ."

"The boy is a menace," Thomas said. "He won't live to grow up."

"Being overweight is unhealthy," the rector agreed innocently.

"I didn't mean that. I mean someone will kill him before he grows up. It might be me. Rawdon—what's the matter?"

The doctor was bent over his plate, his hands covering his mouth. Suddenly he leaped up, overturning his chair. Thomas caught a glimpse of his face as he bolted from the room. It was pale pea-green.

The remaining breakfasters stared at one another.

"Sick," said Kent succinctly. "No wonder, that ghastly mess he's been eating—"

"He eats it every morning," Thomas said. "I hope he isn't coming down with something—a virus—"

"I had better see if I can be of help," said the rector. He popped the last kidney into his mouth. Thomas couldn't blame him for the smug look on his round face.

The rector trotted out. Jacqueline was staring at the doctor's plate.

"I wonder. . . ."

"No time to wonder," said Thomas briskly. "Come on, Jacqueline. If we're to be back by ten, we'd better get moving."

Jacqueline went upstairs to get her gloves—"I can't possibly go to the village without *gloves,* Thomas!" Thomas took the statement in the spirit in which it was offered. He knew what Jacqueline was going to get. The Purse, in one of its giant manifestations.

As she started up, the butler approached Thomas. He proffered a note on a silver salver.

"This was found in your room, sir, by the maid."

The envelope had Thomas's name on it in a hurried scrawl. Thomas opened it.

Jacqueline, on the landing, leaned over the banister. Her hair gleamed like an infernal aureole.

"What is it, Thomas?"

Thomas read the note again. It didn't take long; the message was brief.

"Come down to the wine cellar after breakfast. I think I've found something. Frank. P.S. Don't tell anyone. This could be dangerous."

The word *anyone* was heavily underscored.

"Thomas, what does it say?"

Thomas looked up.

"Nothing much. I'll meet you here in five minutes."

The cellar lights were on. This might have alerted Thomas or reassured him, depending on his state of mind; but in fact he didn't even notice. He was sure Frank had nothing of importance to show him, but he wanted to check it out before he went haring off to the village on what was probably a wild-goose chase. He was also moved by a less noble motive. Jacqueline was lovely and charming and witty, but she was also irritating, with her amused contempt and her air of omniscience. If he could find out something she didn't know. . . .

Absorbed by these ignoble but satisfying thoughts, Thomas was taken unawares by the blow that struck him down. He saw stars, but that was all he saw, except for the blackness that swallowed him as he felt himself falling.

He came to his senses after an indeterminate period of time, and it took more time, equally impossible to calculate, before he figured out where he was. His position seemed to be the product of delirium or delusion; it couldn't be real. The growing congestion in his aching head finally convinced him. He was standing on that very head—upside down, to put it plainly. His arms were tightly bound to his sides and his legs were tied together. A gag covered his mouth. He was blind. Literally blind; his eyes were uncovered and open, but he could see nothing. He could smell, however. The smell filled his nostrils and increased the nausea which his position and his injury had instigated. One other sense, normally unused except by the genuinely blind, came feebly to his assistance—the generalized sense of location centered in the nerve cells of his face. Thomas's brief state of consciousness was fading again, but he was a man of considerable intelligence; his reeling brain put the data together and came up with an incredible answer. The smell of stale wine, the sense of enclosure in something narrow and confining, the absurd, humiliating position. Thomas tried to swear, choked, and fainted again.

When he regained consciousness the second time he opened one eye to check the stimuli before deciding whether to retain his senses. The result was reassuring. He was prone and horizontal; his limbs ached, but they were free; light greeted his eyes, and there had been a fleeting suggestion of a face, haloed in flame and pale with what Thomas hoped was anguish on his behalf. He opened his mouth and croaked like a frog.

"What did you say?" The voice was Jacqueline's. It was cool and controlled and mildly querulous.

Hurt, Thomas opened both eyes and blinked them till they got used to the light. It seemed blinding after the darkness that had surrounded him earlier, but it was only the dim bulb in the ceiling of the wine cellar. He was lying flat on the dusty floor, and beside him, turned over on its side, was an empty barrel—a large barrel, fully five feet high when erect.

Someone put a glass to his dry lips. Thomas drank. The liquid tasted like vintage champagne to his dusty throat. He realized that it was champagne. Jacqueline had opened a bottle. Thomas swallowed, and repeated his question.

"I'm afraid so," Jacqueline said regretfully.

"I was in a barrel?"

"That's the third time you've asked that."

"I still can't believe it. I won't believe it. Oh, God—" Thomas sat up and glared wildly. "Who else saw me?"

"This is no time to be worrying about your male ego," Jacqueline said. She spread her knees and received Thomas's head neatly in her lap as he fell back. "Thomas, darling, you aren't hurt, you know. Only the classic bump on the head. But—you really did scare me for a minute!"

The wobble in her voice restored some of Thomas's battered vanity. Her lap felt comfortable—soft, cool, silky. He wriggled his head into an easier position and relaxed.

"It took you long enough," he said grumpily. "It's a wonder I didn't die of congestion of the brain or something."

"You were only in—in that thing for a couple of minutes."

"How do you know? It felt like days."

"I waited for ten minutes before I started to look for you. Considering the time it took to knock you out, truss you up, and —er—insert you. . . ."

Jacqueline's voice was still unsteady, but Thomas suspected another emotion than concern. He squinted up at her, saw the corners of her mouth quiver, and suddenly smiled with the good humor that was one of his most endearing characteristics.

"I must have looked like an absolute fool," he said. "My feet sticking up out of that thing . . . I don't blame you for laughing."

"I'm not laughing," said Jacqueline.

Thomas sat up. He gathered Jacqueline into his arms and for a time they sat in silence while she made gulping noises into his shirt front. Finally she detached herself and sat up on her heels. Her face was smudged with dust and her eyes were still damp; two tendrils of hair had come loose and curled wickedly over her ears.

"No," she said, fending Thomas off as he reached for her again. "That's enough of that."

"Is that all I get for being knocked on the head and stuck into a barrel upside down?" Thomas inquired plaintively. "If I lost an arm and a leg, I suppose you might—"

"You're drunk," Jacqueline said coldly. "Thomas, be serious. I got something of a shock, that's why I acted so silly; but this is no joke. And I'm afraid your male ego is going to suffer, although I was the only one to see you *in situ*. We'll have to tell the others.''

Jacqueline's therapy had been amazingly successful. Except for a slight headache, Thomas felt fine. He reached for the champagne bottle, which was sitting on the floor beside him. After a long drink, he nodded.

"Yes, I see what you've got in mind. Oh, well. At least I won't have to hear Lady Isobel recite her poem about gallant King Richard.''

IV

The emergency meeting was in full swing, and it was getting absolutely nowhere. Thomas's head was aching. He no longer felt like a kindly adult watching the antics of cute children; he felt like a lion tamer with a cageful of feline schizophrenics. People were pacing around the room shouting questions at each other. At the head of the table Weldon pounded his gavel. No one paid the slightest attention. The pounding only increased Thomas's headache.

As he had feared, the first reaction to the news of his misadventure had been hilarity. Outrage soon replaced the laughter, but this emotion was just as noisy and just as ineffectual. Frank was the most indignant; he kept insisting that he had not written the note that had lured Thomas to his doom. Thomas kept reassuring him, but Frank demanded paper and pencil and produced a specimen that was certainly quite unlike the handwriting Thomas remembered. He had to depend on his memory, for the note was no longer in his pocket.

Jacqueline was curled up in one of the big chairs. She was wearing her glasses. Her green eyes flickered as she glanced from one gesticulating speaker to the next.

Finally she rose. Conversation gradually died as she walked slowly to the head of the table. She smiled at Weldon, who stepped back and, with a wordless gesture, invited her to take his place. When she faced the group, the silence was almost complete.

"I'd like to say a few words," she began in a soft voice. "May I please have your attention? No comments, no questions—and no bloody interruptions!''

A mouse's squeak would have been distinctly audible.

"Very well,'' Jacqueline went on, glaring at them over her glasses. "I'll begin at the beginning. Last night Frank was attacked by a figure that was in essence that of a masked man. Or perhaps I should say masked person. . . .

"In your Ricardian charades, Frank is taking the part of the Lancastrian Prince Edward, the son of Henry the Sixth. The Tudor propaganda accuses your hero, Richard, of being responsible for the death of this young prince. Edward was killed in battle, and the earliest commentators simply state that fact. Later historians imply that he was killed after he had surrendered, by the attendants of the victorious Edward the Fourth. One of the Tudor propagandists says Richard stabbed him as he knelt and begged for mercy.

"I apologize for repeating what you all know. I do so in order to set the record straight and clarify my thoughts as well as your own.''

It was admirably done, Thomas thought. A professor of English history couldn't have sounded more pompous.

"The death of this prince,'' Jacqueline continued, "may be considered the first of Richard's murders, if one follows the Tudor line. Edward's injuries are not specified, but we might suppose that a man killed in battle would suffer wounds from sharp-bladed instruments such as swords and daggers, plus blows from maces, battle-axes, and the like. His body would have been bruised and cut.''

She went on without waiting for a reaction. The reaction had begun; the sharper-witted listeners showed signs of horror and disbelief.

"The second of the murders of which Richard has been accused was that of Henry the Sixth, who was a prisoner in the Tower of London. The Tudors added this death to Richard's account, saying that he had personally stabbed the poor old man. I don't know whether anyone suggested that Henry was poisoned, but the body, when publicly displayed, as was the custom, showed no marks of violence, and poison was often suspected in cases of sudden death.

"This morning Dr. Rawdon, who represents Henry the Sixth, was taken ill after eating a dish specially prepared for him.

"Up to this point no one could have seen the connection between the seeming accidents. Thomas's adventure makes the connection explicit. The comedian among us is getting more direct. Thomas, who represents the Duke of Clarence, was knocked on the head and placed in a barrel of wine. Fortunately the barrel was empty, but the joker went to considerable lengths to make the position ignominious. Thomas was held erect—if I may use that word—by rope attached to his ankles and then looped around the top of the barrel.

"No reputable historian believes that Richard was really responsible for the death of his exasperating brother, but the Tudor legend blamed him nevertheless. Now," said Jacqueline, in the same mild, pleasant voice, "do you really want us to go to the village looking for imaginary villains, or shall we start collating our alibis?"

The amazed Ricardians stared dumbly, too thunderstruck to speak at first. Thomas leaned back in his chair and folded his hands across his stomach. By finding a common denominator, Jacqueline had reduced his ludicrous adventure to part of a puzzle. One does not mind being made a fool of quite so much if one has plenty of company.

"I cannot believe it," the rector said finally. His ruddy face had paled. "Dear lady, are you certain—"

"Let's not waste time denying the obvious," Kent interrupted. "The connection is there. But I question your conclusion, Jacqueline. Alibis?"

"It seems equally obvious to me," Jacqueline said. She looked so smug that Thomas wanted to throw something at her. "We cannot completely eliminate the possibility of an outsider. But in order to act, such a person would have to have access to the house as well as knowledge of the roles you are playing. The first is not impossible. Despite Sir Richard's precautions, this place is not really secure. It is not a medieval castle with a moat and a drawbridge, but an open, modern house surrounded by a wall that I can guarantee to climb in ten seconds flat. As for the special knowledge required, that, too, might have been accessible to an outsider. The servants could have been bribed; none of them would feel they were betraying a trust by divulging such trivial information. Some of you may have talked to your friends. However—''

"But you've just contradicted your own suggestion," Frank said, frowning. "You've proved that an outsider could have the necessary opportunity. As for the motive—obviously someone wants to make us look foolish. None of us would do such a thing."

The rector made noises of enthusiastic agreement. Mrs. Ponsonby-Jones, whose slow-moving brain had finally grasped the situation, nodded her massive head. The others were silent; and gradually all eyes focused on a single object.

Percy giggled.

"I wish I had thought of it. I'd love to have seen Thomas in the butt of malmsey."

"Now, young man," Sir Richard began angrily.

He was interrupted by Mrs. Ponsonby-Jones, whose wits moved more rapidly in the face of a threat to her son and heir. With a piercing cry of indignation she gathered Percy to the maternal bosom.

"How dare you accuse Percy? Why, the poor boy hasn't the strength, even if he were capable of imagining such nasty things."

Thomas had to admit that the woman had a point. Most of Percy was fat, and he doubted that the boy had the muscle to overpower and move a grown man. Otherwise Percy was a perfect candidate. Childish, precocious, malicious . . . malice. As he considered the word, Thomas understood why Jacqueline looked so grave.

A squeaky cough from the end of the table drew everyone's attention. The American visitor cleared his throat.

"Must be an outsider," he said, breathing agitatedly. "And I know who. Strangways! The man is capable of anything. Must be here. Look for him!"

"Do you know him, Mr. O'Hagan?" Jacqueline asked.

"Good gracious, no." The suggestion seemed to infuriate O'Hagan. His moustache quivered. "Would I associate with such a scoundrel? Know of him, though. Capable of anything."

"You said that before," Philip remarked. "I've another idea.

Some particularly enterprising newsman could have engineered these tricks. It would make a marvelous article—the mad Ricardians carrying their roles to insane extremes. If the chap carried a camera and took pictures of the victims. . . ."

A low groan of horror issued from Thomas's unguarded lips. Frank didn't actually groan, but he looked as if he wanted to.

"My God, I'll have to emigrate," he muttered.

"Me, too," Thomas said. "If my students ever saw a photo—"

"Nonsense," Jacqueline exploded. "What's wrong with all of you? Theoretically an outsider might have played these tricks, but he'd have to have had the luck of the Irish and the cloak of invisibility to play them without being caught. If this is not an inside job, I'll—"

Liz said something under her breath. She seemed more shocked than any of the others; under the mask of makeup her face was pale.

"What?" Jacqueline asked.

"I think everyone is mad," Liz muttered. "I'm tempted to pack up the whole business and clear out of here."

"There's no need for you to worry, darling," Philip said. He was no longer smiling, and his handsome face looked hard and dangerous. "Elizabeth of York survived Richard for a good many years. I'm the one who ought to pack it up. Hastings was Richard's next victim—if our comedian continues to follow the Tudor chronology."

"Think about that for a while." Jacqueline dropped the words like stones into the stricken silence. "Come on, Thomas, let's go to the village. If we can eliminate the possibility of an outsider, maybe your friends will face the facts."

She walked out of the room.

Thomas had to run to catch up with her. They were outside the house, walking along the terrace, before Jacqueline was calm enough to speak rationally.

"It's not the logic of the situation," she muttered. "It's the atmosphere. Can't they see it? The malice, the nasty sense of humor—it's a domestic crime, that's what it is. People don't play vicious practical jokes on total strangers. And if they aren't practical jokes. . . ."

Thomas took her arm as they descended the shallow steps that led from the terrace into the rose garden.

"That's precisely why they won't face the facts. The facts aren't very pleasant. Stop seething, love, and smell a rose. It's too nice a day to stay mad."

"I'll bet it will rain before night," Jacqueline said.

But the beauty of the morning would have moved a stone; her face cleared as she took a deep breath. She stopped on the path and cupped a full-blown rose gently in her hand. It had a heart of pure pink that shaded off into ice-white petals.

"I've never cared much for roses," Thomas said placidly.

"What are your favorite flowers?"

"What red-blooded American male will admit to having a favorite flower? I don't think much about 'em. Deadly nightshade? It reminds me of you."

He put his arm around her, and Jacqueline burst out laughing.

"Thank you, Thomas, I'm touched. Was I too awful just now?"

"No, they had it coming." They strolled on, their arms around one another, and Thomas felt a wave of sheer felicity sweep over him. "An English garden in the sunshine, and the woman I love," he said poetically. "What could be better?"

"A loaf of bread and a jug of wine. I'm getting hungry. Do you suppose we could get beer and cheese at the pub?"

Jacqueline's face was alight with a radiance the roses had not inspired. Thomas hugged her.

"You can have a barrel of beer if you want it."

"Let's not talk about barrels."

"If I can talk about them, you have no reason to object. Do you really think we'll find out anything in the village?"

"To tell you the truth, the thought of beer predominated when I agreed to go," Jacqueline said pensively. "But I suppose we have to check."

"You think Strangways is there?"

"I would be, if I were he. He is as obsessed by Richard as your friends; more obsessed, in a way, because his feelings are a sort of love-hate combination. He's been so abusive that his scholarly reputation hangs on Richard's villainy. Any discovery that supports Richard threatens Strangways. Yes, I would certainly be on hand if I had heard of a startling new document."

They had entered a belt of trees that protected the back of the gardens. The shade felt cool and refreshing. Thomas took his arm away so they could proceed single file.

"How do you know so much about Strangways?"

"Naturally I've read his articles. I don't walk into situations like this one without doing my homework."

"Ah. Wednesday afternoon, when you said you had to go to the hairdresser—"

"I merely implied that was my goal. I spent the afternoon at the British Museum."

"Where, to be sure, you have professional connections in the Reading Room. You are really the most. . . . If I may say so, your Freudian analysis of the unfortunate Strangways is a bit far-fetched."

"Not at all," Jacqueline said coldly. "My professional duties necessitate contact with the weird world of historical scholarship. I know one man who is besotted with Mary, Queen of Scots. In his study at home there is a little shrine with a portrait of that appalling female draped in crimson velvet, with an eternal light and a white lily in a vase. Owing to the difficulty of procuring a constant supply of lilies on a professor's meager salary, the flower is plastic; but the sentiment is no less sickening."

"Anybody I know?" Thomas inquired, fascinated.

"You know him." Jacqueline grinned at him over her shoulder. "But my lips are sealed. I've never told anybody about your crush on Nefertiti, have I?"

"Everybody had a crush on Nefertiti at some point in his life," Thomas said. He could feel himself blushing, and changed the subject.

"Here's the fence. Ten seconds, did you say? One thousand, two thousand. . . ."

He should have known better. Jacqueline was over the fence by the time he got to eight thousand. Thomas followed. Before Jacqueline could announce his time, he said quickly,

"You've torn your slacks."

"Cripes." Jacqueline tried to look over her shoulder, with a notable lack of success.

Thomas brushed at the seat of her pants and then announced mendaciously, "No, it's okay, just a streak of rust. Where did you acquire your stock of expletives? I haven't heard anyone say 'cripes' since I was eight years old."

"I'm trying to reform my vocabulary. The students have a bad effect on me. The words sound foul enough coming from them, but from a lady of my years and dignity . . . which way do we go?"

The path led along the fence and then wandered off into a hilly meadow decorated, as if deliberately, by black-and-white cows. Jacqueline began to sing. It was a maddening sound. Thomas wouldn't have minded if she had sung aloud, for she had a pleasant voice and the pastoral surroundings were appropriate for gentle harmony; but Jacqueline's singing was a kind of musical soliloquy, not an expression of well-being, and it issued as a low drone. Nor did Thomas find her choice of melodies soothing. She started with a snatch of the Mad Scene from *Lucia*, edited for untrained contralto, and went on to "Elinor Rigby" and that grisly memorial of old English murder, "Edward." Thomas was relieved when they finally reached the village and Jacqueline stopped muttering about drops of gore.

From his earlier visits Thomas remembered the Weldon Arms with pleasure, even if it had changed its name to flatter the current lord of the manor. It was an authentic fourteenth-century inn, and its former name, The Blue Boar, reminded Ricardians of their hero. Richard's badge of the white boar had furnished the inspiration for a number of inn signs during his brief reign; when the Tudors took over, sensible innkeepers hastily painted the boar azure in order to avoid offense.

Now he let out a hiss of exasperation as they turned the corner and saw the inn ahead. The narrow street was lined with cars and motor skooters. A thin blue veil of exhaust smoke dulled the brilliance of sunlight and flower gardens. Gaping tourists filled the gaps between vehicles, such as they were, and Thomas found himself trying to decide which nation could claim the least-attractive tourists.

Jacqueline jabbed him in the ribs as he studied a long-legged blonde damsel—Swedish, perhaps?—wearing a sleeveless low-cut open knit top.

"Don't become a dirty old man, Thomas, it's so boring. How are we going to get to the inn? The place is teeming."

"Let's go around to the private entrance," Thomas said. "I was introduced to Mr. Doakes last time I was here; maybe he'll remember me."

The harassed Doakes did not remember Thomas, but when the latter mentioned his name and Sir Richard's, the man's broad red face lost its worried frown.

"I'm sorry, sir, I truly am. I ought to 'ave known you. But you can see. . . ." He gestured toward the crowded street. "Not that I'm complaining, mind. It's good for trade. Come into the parlor, I keep that clear for my regulars. And this lady is . . . ? A pleasure, Mrs. Kirby, I'm sure."

The inn parlor was a haven of peace and a gem of English architecture. The massive beams were genuine, though Thomas was a little suspicious of the copper pots strewn about. The small leaded windows muted the sunlight, so that the room was pleasantly shadowed. It smelled of ale and sausage and brass polish.

One of the regular customers was asleep in a corner. He was so old, so brownly withered, and so silent that Thomas wondered for a moment whether he was real. Jacqueline shared his qualms; when their host left to get them food and drink, she nudged Thomas and whispered, "Thomas, I think he's stuffed. Mr. Doakes keeps him around to add atmosphere."

"Maybe he died just recently, and nobody noticed the difference."

Doakes returned with ale and home-baked bread and some of the excellent Wensleydale cheese. He seemed glad to get away from the uproar in the public bar; when Thomas asked him to join them, he accepted with alacrity.

"Forty years I've been 'ere, and every day I've missed old London," he said. "But now, when I see what the town is breeding up. . . ." He shook his head and applied himself to his modest pint. It did not cheer him. He continued gloomily, "With all respect to Sir Richard, it's 'is fault we've this crowd on our 'ands. All that nonsense up at the manor. . . ."

A grinding noise, like that of rusty gears, turned Thomas's head toward the shadowy corner where the elderly apparition sat. He started. A pair of evil blue eyes had opened in the mummified face, and a toothless mouth was emitting sounds. The lack of dentures and an incredible Yorkshire accent made the resultant

speech unintelligible. Thomas turned to Doakes for enlightenment.

"Will says Sir Richard is the best master in the West Riding and
'e won't 'ear a word against 'im," Doakes translated. "All right,
Will, all right, I'm of your opinion. Didn't Sir Richard send my
own little grandchild to that 'ospital in London when she was
ailing last year? But I still say it's no way for grown men and
women to carry on. Fancy dress and playacting, that's bad
enough, that is; but when it comes to pretending you're a dead
man—well, all I can say is, it isn't 'olesome."

Apparently the aged Will agreed; the blue eyes had closed and
the rusty jaws remained shut. Thomas exchanged a glance with
Jacqueline and saw that she was thinking the same thing he was.
The proceedings at Weldon house were not secret. No doubt the
whole village knew what was going on.

Jacqueline finished her ale and stared pointedly at her empty
glass. Thomas ordered another round. Under the influence of
his own excellent brew, Doakes began to brighten.

"Ah, well," he said philosophically. "Sir Richard is a fine little
man, for all his foolishness, and I wish 'im well. Here's to 'im,
and the lady of 'is choice."

"Mrs. Ponsonby-Jones?" Thomas asked dubiously.

Old Will's mouth opened again. The sight was horribly reminiscent of Boris Karloff on the Late Late Show; from the black
cavity came a series of sounds like a prolonged death rattle.
Thomas would not have identified them as laughter if Doakes
had not chuckled.

"The gentleman will 'ave 'is joke, Will. Not that the old—er—
woman wouldn't like to be Lady Weldon, and the skinny old one
too. Sir Richard's not that foolish. All of us will be glad to see
Miss Liz as lady of the manor. She's a fine lass, for all 'er modern
ideas."

"But . . ." Thomas began. He subsided as Jacqueline trod
heavily on his foot. She was right; they were wasting time.

"Sir Richard sent me to ask for your help, Mr. Doakes," he
said. "Someone broke into the house last night."

Doakes's grinning face sobered as Thomas explained. He
shook his head.

"Now we can't 'ave that. Breaking and entering—that's against the law, that is."

He made no objection to fetching the hotel register and going over it with Thomas. There were only six strangers resident in the inn, and Doakes's descriptions made it clear that none of them could be James Strangways. Further questioning elicited the information that no man of that description was renting a room in any of the cottages that accepted boarders. They thanked Doakes and rose to leave.

"Tell Sir Richard not to worry," said the host. "There'll be no more breaking in. We'll see to that."

Thomas glanced at Old Will and was not surprised to see that the blue eyes were open and alert. He believed Doakes's promise. The village would close ranks when one of its own was threatened, and Thomas pitied the unwary reporter who ran afoul of any of them—even old Will. The very sight of him limping out of a dark doorway with his toothless mouth agape would set a nervous man screaming.

They were about to go out the door when old Will made his final pronouncement. The rolling "ooms" and "oops" filled the room like thunder. Doakes hesitated a moment before translating.

"He says the playacting is all to the good if it clears King Richard," he said finally. "He says King Richard never done it. And he says they'll all be watching, on Sunday, to see it proved that he never done it."

Old Will was mumbling furiously, and Thomas knew the old man was off in some imaginary world of his own. He wondered if that world was the same one in which Weldon spent part of his time. How could anyone believe for a moment that the dead past was really dead? It animated this semiliterate octogenarian as well as a group of supposedly sophisticated worldings. The thought was a little frightening.

Doakes ushered them out the back door into the street. He seemed embarrassed at Will's outburst; before closing the door he said under his breath, "You'll excuse old Will, sir and madam. He wanders a bit. . . . But then they're all strange on the subject of King Richard in these parts. I tell you, it isn't 'olesome!"

CHAPTER FOUR

*J*acqueline was preoccupied and silent on the way back. When they reached the house, she went to change. The return trip over the fence proved that while her physical condition was excellent, white slacks were impractical for climbing rusty iron fences.

Thomas wandered into the gardens. He was full of bread and cheese and disinclined to face a horde of contentious Ricardians. Passing through the rose garden, he headed for an area he remembered from an earlier visit—a secluded paved courtyard whose mellow brick walls supported swags of ivy and trellised vines. There were stone benches, if he remembered correctly, and a fountain.

His memory was accurate, and the glory of late-summer flowers rewarded the effort it took to find the place. Seated on one of the benches were Liz and Frank.

Thomas hesitated in the gateway. It was an appropriate spot for a pair of lovers, but he had the impression that his arrival had interrupted a spat rather than a fond tête-à-tête. The warmth of Liz's greeting and Frank's brusque "hello" confirmed the impression. Thomas sat down between them—they were at opposite ends of the bench—and tried to think of something to say. He was remembering the innkeeper's gossip about Weldon and the girl. It made him self-conscious.

"Any luck?" Liz asked.

"No Strangways." Thomas told them what he had found out.

"Hell and damnation," Frank said gloomily. "I didn't really expect you'd come up with anything, but I hoped. . . ."

"There's nothing to worry about," Thomas said, with an optimism he did not feel. "No one has been hurt. In fact, the comedian, as Jacqueline calls him, has been rather considerate."

"Hah," said Frank, fingering his scratches.

"Superficial," Liz said, looking at him contemptuously. "You're right, Thomas. Rawdon is on his feet again."

"What was in his food?"

Liz giggled. She looked absolutely delightful.

"An emetic of some kind, apparently. Rawdon won't say which one. The names that come to mind create amusement rather than sympathy."

"So he, too, was more humiliated than hurt," Thomas said. "As for me—"

"I think that was frightfully dangerous," Liz said. Thomas thought what a charming, sympathetic girl she was. "Surely you'd have been in bad shape if you hadn't been found right away."

"But I was found right away. Everyone knew we were going to the village, and Jacqueline is not the patient type. When I didn't appear on schedule, the joker could assume she would go looking for me."

"And how did she know where to look?" Liz inquired.

"Wilkes saw me heading for the nether regions," Thomas said, remembering the explanation Jacqueline had given as they returned from the cellars. "But it was partly intuition, I suppose. After Frank's encounter. . . ." He broke off with a gasp. "Oh, now, you can't suspect Jacqueline. She's a stranger—"

"Precisely. She's the only newcomer in our midst and the only one who isn't dedicated to the cause. And I imagine she has a rather weird sense of humor."

Thomas sputtered. Frank burst out laughing.

"Come off it, Liz. You're accustomed to having every damned

male in the crowd flap his wings and crow as you walk past. Now you have a bit of competition."

Liz glared at him. Frank evidently felt he had gone too far. He added quickly, "Jacqueline isn't the only stranger."

"O'Hagan," Thomas said thoughtfully. "Hadn't any of you met him before?"

"No," Liz said. "I must admit he's odd. Maybe he has a few screws loose."

"It seems to me," Frank said, "that the most important thing is to forestall any further accidents. If we can't identify the comedian, perhaps we can anticipate his next move."

"Good," Thomas said approvingly. "So far he seems to be following the Tudor legend. So the next victim should be—"

"Lord Hastings," said Frank. "Who is, of course, our popular idol of stage and screen."

Liz had been inspecting the foxgloves with what seemed to Thomas sinister interest. Now she turned. "And you are looking forward to that, aren't you?"

"Why not?" Frank looked defiant. "I've been made a fool of; allow me to enjoy watching someone else deflated. If anybody asked for deflation—"

They glowered at one another, and Thomas felt a sentimental amusement. It had been many years since he had engaged in a battle of words with a pretty girl. . . . His debates with Jacqueline were hardly in the same category.

"The point is not to enjoy Philip's humiliation but to catch the miscreant," he said mildly. "If you are right, then all we have to do is guard Philip."

"Right," Frank said reluctantly. "Don't worry, Thomas; I'm not foolish enough to neglect my obvious duty simply because—"

"You're jealous," Liz said. "You accuse me of jealousy; why, you're livid with it! Phil is handsome and famous and talented and confident—"

"And I'm not." Frank stood up. His face was red but there was dignity in his anger, and in his control of it. "All right, Liz, that's all I'm going to take today. Find yourself another whipping boy." He stalked out of the garden.

When he had gone, Liz seemed to droop. She gave Thomas a

glance in which defiance and misery were equally mixed, and turned back to the foxgloves. "You think I'm frightful, don't you?"

"Of course not. I think you're worried. But you ladies don't have any cause for concern. Not even his enemies accused Richard of murdering women."

"Except his wife." Liz turned. She was smiling faintly. "And that is my darling mum. How do you suppose your comedian plans to counterfeit consumption?"

"It will be poison, if our boy is following the Tudor myth," Thomas said uneasily. "Your mother is not a young woman, my dear. I don't like the idea of someone playing tricks on her."

Liz smiled. She rose and held out her hand to pull Thomas to his feet.

"You really are a darling. Come along, Thomas, the afternoon meeting will be starting shortly. We mustn't miss it. Dickon has strictly forbidden discussion of our mystery; he says we've wasted enough time already."

"So we're to hear Frank rehashing the murder of the princes," Thomas said, falling in step beside her.

"And Lady Isobel reading her new poem—if time permits."

"Time probably won't permit," Thomas said, cheered by the thought. "We're two meetings behind schedule now. All the same, Liz, are you certain about Hastings being the next victim? Haven't the Tudor slanderers implied Richard murdered Edward the Fourth?"

"Not even Sir Thomas More would be that absurd." Liz frowned thoughtfully. She looked very pretty when she frowned. Thomas was tempted to put his arm around her, but thought better of it.

"Unless," Liz went on, "one might claim that Richard was indirectly guilty of Edward's death because he made no attempt to dissuade him from the debauchery that hastened his end."

"Beautiful," Thomas said, laughing. "I'm surprised More didn't think of that one. Remember his statement that Richard was responsible for Clarence's execution, although he protested publicly against it, but that he didn't really protest as loudly as he might have done, and so probably didn't mean it?"

"This isn't getting us anywhere, Thomas."

"No. But we will have to watch Philip closely."

"That," said Liz, "I can do."

II

Earlier, Thomas had found the Ricardians exasperatingly emotional. He now found himself in the inconsistent position of deploring a demonstration of British phlegm. The afternoon meeting was proceeding according to schedule, and so far no one had referred to the unfortunate tricks.

However, as he glanced around the room, Thomas saw that the mystery had left its marks. The effect showed in flushed faces and glittering eyes, in the rector's troubled frown and in Rawdon's sickly pallor. It showed most plainly in Philip. The hard, handsome face was calm as he followed Weldon's introductory remarks. The actor's long, flexible hands were relaxed. But one foot tapped in a restless rhythm on the carpeted floor.

They were meeting in the library, since the Great Hall was being decorated for the evening's festivities. Nervously Thomas rehearsed in his mind the steps of the dance he had been practicing. Then he forced himself to pay attention to the proceedings.

Weldon looked more like his hero than ever. There was only one sign of nervousness, and that was a gesture he might have borrowed from Richard III, whose portrait showed him fingering a ring on one hand—a habit mentioned by historians. In the portrait Richard wore three rings on his right hand—a modest collection for a man of his clothes-conscious era. Weldon wore only one; he kept twisting it and pushing it up and down as he talked.

His remarks included a welcome to the distinguished American visitor, who squeaked an acknowledgment, and a hint of the joys in store for the evening. Weldon ended by introducing the first speaker, and Frank walked up to the temporary rostrum.

Thomas had not expected to do so, but he found Frank's talk fairly interesting. The young man had a logical mind, in spite of his legal training. Even the bruises on his unhandsome face did not detract from his poise, and his low voice, with its beautifully modulated vowels, was a pleasure to hear.

Thomas glanced at Jacqueline. He suspected she was more sympathetic to Richard than she admitted; but it would be like her to take the negative side out of sheer perversity. And she knew quite a bit about the subject. That was another of her irritating qualities, Thomas thought, trying to harden his heart against the effect of the elegant profile framed in ruddy hair. If she would just admit she knew, instead of pretending girlish ignorance and then walloping the unwitting victim with a cartload of specialized data. . . .

Frank took the conventional—among Ricardians—view that the real murderer of the princes was Henry VII. He recalled Henry's inexplicable failure to discover the fate of the boys after he entered London, and summarized the inconsistencies in More's story of the confession. He pointed out that Richard's behavior was equally illogical if he was guilty of the crime. As England's grim history proved, a deposed monarch was often as good as dead; but the bodies of the other murdered kings had been publicly displayed so that there could be no doubt of their deaths. If Richard wanted to prevent rebellions in favor of his nephews, he had to make sure they were known to be dead.

As Frank went on, Thomas found his attention straying from the speaker to Sir Richard. Weldon's hands were not still for a moment, the ring moved up and down, around and around. There was a queer little smile on his face as he listened to the lecture.

With a sudden thrill Thomas remembered the letter. The fantastic events of the past twenty-four hours had put it out of his mind, and yet it was the raison d'être of the whole weekend. What was in that letter? Was it the cause of Weldon's secretive smile?

If so, the rector did not share Weldon's feelings; he was sober and preoccupied, nodding absently from time to time as Frank made a point. So far as Thomas knew, Ellis was the only other member of the group who had seen the letter. That wasn't right. The committee should have its chance before the public fanfare began. Wasn't that why they were here? Thomas wondered if the others, like himself, had been so worried about the unpleasant jokes that they had forgotten the purpose of the meeting. He promised himself that he would corner Weldon as soon as the session ended.

He had to contain himself while the doctor spoke on medieval medicine and Percy read a pompous long-winded paper on the education of a boy of noble rank in the fifteenth century. As the afternoon wore on, the room began to darken. The sun had vanished behind the rain clouds Jacqueline had predicted earlier. A cool wind came through the open window, and Thomas fidgeted impatiently. A burst of applause brought him out of his brown study. Percy had finished and his fond mama was clapping. Thunder rolled in ominous echo as Sir Richard brought his gavel down, ending the meeting.

Thomas caught up with his host at the library door and drew him aside. The others were heading for their rooms to prepare for the banquet. Jacqueline lingered, but Thomas scowled at her and made shooing motions with his hand. He wanted to tackle Sir Richard alone. For a wonder, Jacqueline obeyed.

The interview was not satisfactory. Weldon was vague. Of course he meant to show the letter to his colleagues. There had been so many distractions. . . . Tonight? Possibly. . . . They would discuss it later. Would Thomas excuse him? He had to consult with Wilkes about the arrangements for the banquet. . . .

Weldon slid away, smiling sweetly. Thomas swore. He felt the need of something to calm his nerves, so he rang and ordered a drink. It was brought by one of the footmen; Wilkes was evidently busy. Carrying his glass, Thomas went upstairs.

He took off his coat, tie, and shoes, and settled himself comfortably on the bed with a copy of Sir Thomas More. Rain hissed softly against the window; drawn draperies and an excellent reading light gave a warm, enclosed feeling to the room. The slanders of Sir Thomas exacerbate the feelings of Ricardians, but his prose is not particularly stimulating. Thomas's eyelids drooped. . . .

He was awakened by a tap on the door. He fumbled for the book, with the unreasonable sense of guilt people feel when they are caught sleeping during the day.

Jacqueline slipped into the room. She was wearing a dark-green housecoat that matched her eyes. Thomas sat up. He was no longer sleepy, but one look at Jacqueline's face told him that his hope was in vain.

"I came for a chat," she said, sitting down in an armchair. "What are you reading? Oh, Sir Thomas More. Or do you follow the school that claims Morton wrote the book?"

Thomas sighed. Really, Jacqueline's expertise was very exasperating.

"Bishop Morton was one of Richard's bitterest enemies. More undoubtedly got some of his information from the old wretch, but . . . no, I think More wrote it. What does that prove? More may be a saint but he's not canonically infallible. Damn it, it's a terrible book! Full of lies, innuendos, dirty—"

"You people are such masochists," Jacqueline said. "Why do you read it if it infuriates you so much?"

"I don't know. Maybe it's incredulity; I can't believe an intellectual like More could produce such stuff. He's a master of doublethink. Listen to this:

'He slew with his own hands king Henry the sixth, being prisoner in the Tower, *as men constantly say,* and that without commandment or knowledge of the king, which would undoubtedly if he had intended that thing, *have appointed that butcherly office to some other* than his own brother.' "

Thomas's tone italicized the phrases. He added, with mounting indignation, "Pure rumor, in other words. 'Men say!' And did you get that incredible piece of logic in the last part? If the king had ordered Henry to be killed, he wouldn't have sent his own brother to do the deed; but men say Richard did it, so therefore it must have been done without Edward's knowledge! The book is full of that sort of thing. Here. . . ."

"You don't have to convince me. I agree with you."

"Here, where he says . . ." Thomas put the book down. "If you agree, why are you being so obnoxious about Richard? Want to join the society?"

Jacqueline smiled. She stretched lazily; the long, wide sleeves fell away from her arms. Clasping her hands behind her head, she wriggled down into the chair.

"I'm not being obnoxious, just logical. You can't clear Richard of the boys' death any more than you can convict him. There is no proof. It is incomprehensible to me that any historian can take More's *Richard* seriously; or rather, it would be incomprehensible if I didn't know historians as I—Thomas, you aren't listening."

"Why don't you come over here and get comfortable?" Thomas suggested.

"I'm very comfortable right here."

"I'm not."

Jacqueline lowered her arms and folded her hands primly in her lap. "Finish your drink," she said in a kindly voice. "No, Thomas, stay right where you are. I refuse to engage in dalliance —if that is the phrase—during an English country weekend. How conventional! And Percy is probably listening at the door."

Thomas glanced nervously at the door. He didn't take the suggestion seriously enough to get up and look, but it dampened his ardor. Reaching for his glass, he said in resigned tones, "Well, at least you have an open mind. I still think there is serious doubt about Richard's guilt."

"You don't really believe Henry the Seventh—"

"Yes, I do. I think that during the summer of 1483 the boys were removed from the Tower to a remote northern castle. That's why we don't hear any more of them in the contemporary annals, which were written by Londoners."

Enthusiasm made Thomas's eyes shine and his face glow. Jacqueline's eagle eye softened as she watched him, but Thomas was oblivious. He went on,

"All the anomalies are resolved by the assumption that Richard was innocent. Sir James Tyrrell did murder the boys—in 1485, at the command of Henry the Seventh, not Richard the Third. Twenty years later, after Tyrrell was safely dead, Henry put out the 'confession,' altering the facts to fit the assumption of Richard's guilt. He didn't do it very skillfully; the story, as it has come down to us, is inconsistent throughout. But by that time there was no one alive who could or would challenge Henry's version. Elizabeth Woodville, the boys' mother, was dead—"

"The boys' sister was still alive," Jacqueline interrupted. "Henry's queen, Elizabeth of York."

"Henry's queen, and the mother of the heir. What could she do, even if she knew the truth? I've always suspected Elizabeth of

York was not the paragon of virtue the Tudor historians described. There is an old story that she took an active part in the conspiracy against Richard, and wrote personally to Henry Tudor promising to marry him if he was successful. She didn't love Henry; she'd never even met him, and by all accounts he was a particularly unlovable character. She wanted revenge—revenge against Richard, who had cast her family down from its high place, and publicly humiliated her by announcing he had no intention of marrying her. I think she was in love with Richard, before he rejected her. *He* was capable of inspiring love; one old woman, who had known him personally, described him as the handsomest man in the room, after his brother Edward—"

Jacqueline stood up.

"You talk about them as if they only died last week," she said sharply. "It's unnerving, Thomas."

The room was very still. Only the rustle of rain against the window broke the silence.

"It's only a game, Jacqueline," Thomas said, after a moment. "An intellectual game, slightly absurd, perhaps, but harmless."

"Not so harmless. You people are maddening. You sit around debating five-hundred-year-old murders while a mad comedian is in your midst. Have you forgotten what happened to you this morning?"

"No, and I haven't forgotten the letter, either." Thomas told her of his talk with Weldon. "He's acting damned peculiarly," he concluded. "I can't figure out what's bugging him."

"Can't you?"

"Oh, well, he's worried about his precious letter. Nothing else seems to matter to him. I'm more concerned about the jokes. You know Philip is next on the list?"

Jacqueline nodded.

"I just stopped by to visit him."

"You went to his room?" Thomas sat up. "Really, Jacqueline. . . ."

"You didn't object to my coming here." A glint of some indefinable emotion warmed Jacqueline's green eyes. "He's on the alert. I hadn't finished knocking before he had the door open and both hands wrapped around my throat. They didn't stay there," she added thoughtfully.

Thomas decided not to pursue the subject. "Well, I'm glad he's expecting trouble. Maybe he'll catch the joker."

"Or vice versa."

"Stop giving out mysterious hints," Thomas snapped. "Is there something you want me to do? What can we do? Shall we tackle Sir Richard once more again about the letter?"

"No. I don't think the letter is important now." Jacqueline drifted toward the door. "I've got to get dressed."

"What in?" Thomas asked curiously.

"Just a little thing I whipped up." Jacqueline turned her head and smiled at him over her shoulder. "If I do join the society, Thomas, I'll join the American branch."

Whereupon she departed, leaving Thomas to ponder this most mysterious hint of all. After some minutes of fruitless cogitation he rang for another whiskey and soda.

Suitably refreshed, he turned to the matter of his costume. He had tried it on before, so he knew its intricacies, which were not many. There were no points to be tied—how the Hades did one tie a point, anyway?—no elaborate ruffs to be adjusted or tights to be smoothed over the legs. The outfit was surprisingly comfortable. Giving his fur-trimmed skirts a tentative kick, Thomas wondered why women were so determined to get into trousers. Skirts gave a feeling of freedom, a lack of constriction. . . . He tripped, caught hold of a chair, and untangled his shoe from the hem of the garment. Of course it was rather difficult to *do* anything in skirts. They were suitable only for a leisured progress, a lounging, deliberate pace. The men of the fifteenth century didn't go to war in their elaborate robes. Romans wore the toga only on state occasions.

Meditating on costume, a subject he knew very little about, Thomas draped a heavy gold chain across his shoulders and studied the effect. Very nice. Too bad that men of his generation couldn't wear jewelry; it was a human impulse to like glitter and bright jewels. Only in the last century had men been deprived of their peacock habits and forced into somber blacks and grays. Pepys had gloated over his gold-trimmed cloak; the cavaliers had swaggered in plumes and velvet, in lace collars and crimson satin breeches.

Thomas added another chain, studied his reflection

complacently, and went on reassuring himself. Tutankhamen's jewel boxes had bulged. Roman generals wore golden armor. D'Artagnan flaunted the queen's diamond ring and Porthos his embroidered cloak; male dress uniform, even now, sparkled and shone and dazzled the eye with primary colors. Maybe, Thomas thought musingly, that was what was wrong with the older generation today. Repressing their natural tendencies in order to conform to some neurotic notion of propriety. . . . Thomas put rings on six of his ten fingers and viewed the posturing image in the mirror with complete satisfaction.

From the shadowy depths the Duke of Clarence looked back at him. Long fair hair flowed from under a gilt coronet. Jewels winked in miniature bursts of color. Velvet smoldered richly; ermined bands stood out like streaks of snow. One ringed hand rested lightly on the hilt of a jeweled dagger.

Thomas felt a small shock. He had not been aware of reaching for the dagger. Odd, how atavistic memories lingered. The hilt had felt right, somehow.

The dagger was a compromise between the sword Thomas secretly yearned to wear and his knowledge that such a weapon would have been inappropriate with court costume. He didn't think the dagger was out of character. The Duke of Clarence had been a sneaky devil, who suffered—with justification—from feelings of persecution.

The first warning bell echoed down the corridor. Thomas adjusted his coronet and smoothed the long flaxen locks that fell to his shoulders. The wig was the only part of the costume that made him self-conscious, but it would have spoiled the effect to omit it. He turned from the mirror. He had ten more minutes before the next bell, which would summon the committee to cocktails in the drawing room, but he did not linger. This period of time was potentially dangerous, for the guests had to pass along the mazelike corridors. Perhaps Jacqueline had been hinting, in her oblique fashion, that Philip could do with an escort.

Thomas peeked out into the corridor. It was deserted. Picking up his skirts, he went to Philip's room and knocked on the door.

It was not until he felt the prick of a sword point at the base of his throat that he realized Philip might misinterpret his motives.

"Hey," he croaked, looking down the shining blade at Philip's grim face. "It's only me."

"Oddly enough, that doesn't reassure me." Philip stepped back a pace, but the sword remained in position. "Come in, if you like. Sit down over there."

Walking very lightly, Thomas crossed the room and took the indicated chair. He smiled. "It's only me," he repeated.

Philip lowered his point. He was wearing a costume similar to the one he had worn the day before, but even more striking. His doublet of black velvet was trimmed with ermine and had enormous padded sleeves. Across his broad chest hung a heavy chain of silver suns and roses—the Yorkist collar. Black and silver made a somber dress, Hamletian rather than Ricardian; Frank had probably borrowed it from a colleague's theatrical wardrobe. The actor's coloring echoed the cold shades. His silver-gilt hair shone pallidly, and his gray eyes were as hard as the steel of the sword blade.

"I didn't recognize you at first," he admitted. "Where the hell did you get that wig?"

"Costumer's in London." Thomas adjusted his coronet, which had slipped sideways. "Don't you like it?"

"Absolutely love it, dear boy," Philip said viciously.

Thomas leaned back in the chair, but he was not feeling happy. The other man was not merely tense; he was a mass of jangled nerves.

"What are you worried about?" Thomas asked. "The jokes are probably finished. They were easy to arrange when no one was suspicious, but now that we've been alerted to the danger, the unknown can't hope to catch you off guard. You can handle yourself pretty well, even without that sword. And there's no cause for alarm. At worst, just a joke; a little embarrassing, maybe, but. . . ."

His voice died as he saw the other man's eyes.

He could not entirely blame himself. It had been a long time since he had been that young. Maybe he had never been that young; an average bumpkin, with no particular vanities, he had taken the inevitable jokes of his contemporaries with equanimity. But the prickly years of adolescence are always painful. It is a period of mental imbalance; every glance silently criticizes you, every whisper concerns your secret weaknesses.

But, Thomas reminded himself, you grow out of it. You learn, with mingled relief and chagrin, that people are too absorbed in themselves to care much about you; you discover that you are no more and no less comical than any other man. Your doings are just as trivial in the vast web of the universe, and the only way to endure your own insignificance is to laugh at it before the last great joke is played upon you.

This boy had never learned any of these things. He was still a boy, whatever his actual age, and his acquired facade was as smooth and as brittle as an eggshell. He could suffer pain, but he could not endure humiliation.

The moment of communication had been mutual. Philip looked away. He straightened up, lowering his blade. He knew his trade; even when he was intensely preoccupied his movements were graceful and economical.

"Let's have a drink."

"I've already had one."

"So have I. I'm about to have another."

Sheathing his sword, he crossed to the bureau, took out a bottle, and splashed liquid lavishly into a glass.

"I know it's ill-bred to carry one's own booze," he said sarcastically, handing the glass to Thomas. "But I'm not an aristocrat by birth, and it unnerves me to have servants popping in and out. Cheers."

He raised the bottle to his lips and kept it there so long that Thomas was moved to remonstrate. "Take it easy. If our mystery man is gunning for you, you'll need all your wits about you."

Philip lowered the bottle—but only, Thomas thought, because he needed to breathe. The theatrical profession was not noted for sobriety, but surely, in this case, getting drunk was contraindicated. Philip was no fool. . . .

And maybe he wasn't worried, for the best of all possible reasons. The man was an actor, Thomas reminded himself. The display of nerves could be pretense. If Philip was the joker, he could drink himself insensible, knowing himself to be safe.

Thomas drank. He had been born with a constitutionally weak

head and ordinarily was careful about imbibing, but now he felt
the need to steady his nerves.

"Did Jacqueline send you along to protect me?" Philip asked
suddenly.

"What makes you think that?"

"She read me a long lecture about drinking." Philip smiled.
"That is quite a woman, Thomas."

The smile and the narrowed eyes were offensive, but Thomas
refused to rise to the bait. After a moment Philip went on,

"Yes. A shrewd and sexy woman. She makes Liz look like a
scrappy schoolgirl."

"Well, I wouldn't—"

"Not that I give a damn about the wench."

"You have been rather—"

"Oh, well, one has to keep one's hand in. Give the girl a thrill.
That poor stick she's engaged to—can't imagine what she sees in
him."

Thomas smiled to himself. The stock phase almost constituted
a declaration of love. Then the smile faded as he contemplated
Philip's classic profile. The pose was probably unconscious, but
the words . . . you couldn't believe a thing the man said.

"No," he snapped, as Philip reached for the bottle. "Leave
that alone, you've had enough. Frank's a pleasant-enough lad.
Why don't you lay off him?"

"Oh, he won't last," Philip said. "Not with Sir Richard the
Third in the running. Liz would never have accepted Honest
Frank if Mum hadn't been so dead set against him."

"Why should Mrs. Ponsonby-Jones be against it? I should think
Frank would be considered a good match."

"Ho," Philip said derisively. "He's as poor as the proverbial
church mouse, old boy. And not well thought of by his firm.
There was some talk of a forged check while he was at Oxford. . . ."

"Where did you pick up garbage like that?"

Philip smiled. "I can tell you equally jolly tidbits about the
others. Isobel is a lush, of course. She'll end up in a Haven for
Alcoholics one day. And she'll continue writing her ghastly
books; her readers will never know the difference. You know
about Sir General 'Bloody' Kent, I suppose; they let him retire, to

save the good name of the service, but if he hadn't done so he'd have ended up in the dock. One of his junior officers is still rather badly scarred. . . ."

Thomas exclaimed in horror. Philip went on, with growing relish. "Dear old Mum is a gambler. She's heavily in debt. Her son is peculiar, to say the least. Rawdon has killed half a dozen patients since he got on this natural-food-kick, by prescribing wheat germ instead of penicillin—"

"And you?" Thomas inquired drily. Philip was baiting him, of course, and doing a good job of it. Face and voice were trained to carry conviction.

"Why should I incriminate myself? Ask Fearless Frank; I expect he has my dossier at his fingertips."

The bell rang before Thomas could think of an appropriate reply. He rose, wary of his skirts, and followed Philip out. The actor's face was as bland as butter. Thomas wondered how many of the scurrilous stories were true. He also regretted his virtuous interruption. It would have been interesting to hear what Philip had on the saintly-looking rector.

At the head of the stairs Philip stopped, catching his breath. There were no electric lights below. The hallway was dark except for the pale flare of candles. Across the polished floor a figure moved with the smooth silence of a ghost. It wore robes of apple green, trimmed with silver. The long gauzy veil lifted like a cloud from the tip of the tall cap.

Liz looked up and laughed at their startled faces. She sank to the floor in a lower curtsy as the two men descended the staircase. Thomas replied with a bow that in his opinion didn't compare too unfavorably with Philip's courtly gesture. It was easier to play the game in semidarkness. Thomas was no longer self-conscious, but he found it increasingly difficult to keep track of which century he was living in.

The drawing room was also lit by candles. Sir Richard had a certain flare for the theatrical. He was King Richard to the life as he raised a tall beaker to greet the newcomers—Richard as he might have been in the happy days when he lorded it over the north, before the deaths of brother, son, and wife. On his smooth brown head he wore a circlet of gold; and Thomas was reminded of the famous story of the crown plucked from the thornbush after the Battle of Bosworth. Richard had worn it into battle, disdaining the warnings of his friends that he would thus be marked out for the fiercest attacks of his enemies.

Thomas forgot Bosworth as the smiling host handed him a goblet—a high, carved beaker of gold flashing with fake jewels. Or were they fake? Thomas shrugged. He took a hearty swallow, and almost choked. Weldon was going all out for authenticity. The drink was not gin or Scotch or brandy, but a heady mixture of spiced wine.

Someone smacked him on the back—a misguided gesture that brought on the fit of coughing he had thus far managed to avoid. When Thomas had cleared his streaming eyes, he saw Kent grinning at him. The bronzed soldier was the only one in the group who was not wearing a wig or long hair. Thomas saw him, not as the eventually ineffectual Buckingham, but as the product of an era far removed from the fifteenth century. Kent's very features resembled those of certain hawk-nosed Roman busts.

"Take it slowly," Kent warned, as Thomas raised his cup. "It tastes like treacle gone bad, but it's powerful stuff."

Thomas ignored him and drank again. Once you got used to it, the stuff wasn't half bad.

When he lowered the goblet, Kent had gone. Thomas blinked at the vacant space. Someone moved in to fill it. A white moustached . . . O'Hagan. Thomas studied the moustache. Amazing appendage, he thought; you don't see a face at all, you just see a moustache.

"Who're you?" he asked amiably. "I mean, I know who you are. Glad to see you. Who're you s'posed to be?"

O'Hagan was wearing a nondescript garment that might have passed as a medieval robe. Thomas rather suspected it was the man's bathrobe, but that was none of his business.

"Oh, I don't have a part," O'Hagan said. He started to walk away, but Thomas grabbed his arm.

"You must be somebody," he insisted. "Everybody's somebody."

He waved his goblet. There was a soft splashing sound and Thomas glanced around to see Wilkes refilling his glass. The sight almost sobered him. Wilkes was wearing a doublet and hose in Gloucester's livery colors, white and red. Richard's badge, the white boar, was embroidered on the left breast of the doublet. In his normal attire the butler's air of dignity overcame his physical deficiencies; Thomas now observed, with pained surprise, that Wilkes was bowlegged as well as spindle-shanked. The dignity was gone too. Wilkes's narrow shoulders slumped, but his face wore an expression of grim endurance.

"Thank you, Wilkes," Thomas said sympathetically.

Wilkes bowed his head.

"Thank *you,* your Grace."

Thomas drank.

"Amazing stuff," he remarked to O'Hagan, who had emerged from a refreshing dip into his own goblet.

"It would be a sensation at an office Christmas party," O'Hagan agreed. He giggled.

"No, but le'ssee," Thomas insisted. "You gotta be somebody. Wanna be Lord Stanley?"

"All you've got left are the unsympathetic parts," O'Hagan complained. "Stanley was a lousy traitor. Even I—I mean, nobody thinks much of him."

This seemed reasonable to Thomas, who had emptied his glass.

"You can be Lovel," he offered generously. "Richard's bes' friend."

"He met a sticky end, too. No, I think I'll be Henry the Seventh. At least he survived Richard."

He moved away. Thomas watched him critically. The man was drunk. He was swaying.

The whole room was swaying.

Thomas shook his head at Wilkes, who was advancing upon him with a full pitcher and a look of concentrated malevolence. He went to Weldon.

"Wonderful party," Thomas said. "But aren't you asking for it, Dick?"

"What d'you mean?"

"Darkness," Thomas said. "Intoxicating liquors. Perfect for the comedian."

"Nonsense," Weldon said shortly. "There will be no more jokes."

"How do you know?"

"It was Percy, of course. Who else could it be? I gave the boy a lecture. He won't dare go on."

"But Percy couldn't—"

"Use your head, Thomas. None of the tricks required any particular physical strength—except perhaps the one played on you. But with a pulley arrangement of some sort, using the hooks in the ceiling of the wine cellar, a child could have managed that as well. No, it was Percy. The boy isn't . . . we've had trouble with him before this."

"I'm sorry," Thomas said.

"Don't be sorry. Don't let regret spoil this." Weldon faced him squarely. He said softly, "This is important to me, Thomas. More important than you realize."

The red glow in his eyes might have been reflected firelight. To Thomas it looked like the glow of fanaticism.

"What's important?" he asked. "A reconstruction of a medieval banquet, or—"

"Richard." The glow became a steady light. "Richard's good name. Tomorrow is important, Thomas. I won't let anything interfere with what is going to happen. Anything! If I told you—"

He broke off. Lady Isobel had arrived.

Her costume was even more elaborate than the one she had worn the previous day, a black gown that blended with the shadows and left the wearer's powdered bust and face hanging in midair. The woman looked horrible like a waxen effigy. The long flaxen hair streaming over her shoulders was as dry as an untended wig. The thin lips were set in a smirk.

"My lords and lieges," exclaimed Lady Isobel. She curtsied. There was a sharp cracking sound. Thomas was reminded of dry bones snapping.

Thomas reached for a glass—any glass, he didn't care whose. Damn it, the charades were becoming unnerving. He began to understand the old obsession about possession, the danger of opening one's mind to invasion by the dead. He had a hideous vision of the group yielding to their various alter egos and wallowing in the treachery and blood that had marked the end of the fifteenth century. Personally he didn't feel the slightest empathy with the unpleasant Duke of Clarence, but . . . he put his beaker back, scarcely tasted. Possession was as a superstition, but there was danger in identifying too strongly with another personality.

Lady Isobel made the circuit of the room, exchanging archaic greetings and allowing the men to kiss her hand. Thomas told himself he wouldn't kiss it, but when the woman greeted him he found he had to. It was right under his nose.

He got a whiff of mixed spirits that momentarily stupefied him as Lady Isobel laughed gaily up into his face.

"Dear brother Clarence," she chirped.

"Ah, yes," Thomas mumbled. "Elizabeth."

"Your Grace, if you please. Elizabeth was always on her dignity, remember? Oh, isn't this fun? Have some more malmsey, Clarence!"

"Fun," Thomas said hollowly.

The bony fingers, still clinging to his, suddenly contracted. The long nails dug in like claws. Thomas turned.

Jacqueline stood in the doorway.

Thomas's second reaction was one of amusement. Jacqueline had upstaged the other women and made the best entrance of all. His initial reaction could not have been expressed in words. It was a long, shaken breath of pure lechery.

Of course he had warned Jacqueline, in London, that they would be wearing costume. This gown had never been wrenched from a costumer's musty racks; it was a sweeping, full-sleeved garment of ivory and gold threads. In fact, it was no more medieval than any of the other "at home" outfits popular for parties, but Jacqueline wore it royally. It was cut very low in front, and the evocative light that had picked out Lady Isobel's sharp bones made warm and pleasing contrasts with Jacqueline's curves. The real glory, however, was her hair. Thomas had never seen it unbound. It rippled in a coppery stream over her shoulders almost to her waist.

He watched while Jacqueline advanced on the group consisting of the rector, the doctor, and O'Hagan. She cut the latter neatly out the the group, removed him to a cozy sofa near the window, and sat down beside him.

Thomas was aroused from thoughts that did not become him

by Weldon's impatient exclamation. "Where are Percy and his mother? It's late; we must begin."

Mrs. Ponsonby-Jones may have delayed her entrance in order to be the last to appear, but something had happened to distract her. She trotted into the room without pausing to strike a pose.

"Where is Percy? Liz, have you seen your brother?"

Liz turned.

"No, I came down some time ago."

"He's not in his room," said Percy's mother.

Jacqueline stood up and began to run. She crossed the room doing a solid six miles an hour, and vanished out the door.

It was a ludicrous sight, but Thomas was not amused. He was still hypnotized by history. Jacqueline's streaming hair and pale face, her golden gown conjured up visions out of England's past —visions of queens and royal ladies fleeing for their lives. Catherine Howard, Henry VIII's next-to-last wife, whose wailing ghost is still seen rushing down the corridors of Hampton Court; Anne Boleyn, Mary Queen of Scots, Lady Jane Grey. All Tudor victims. . . .

Something snapped into place in his mind with a horrible click. He leaped up and followed Jacqueline. Liz and Frank reached the door at the same time. Their faces were shaped into the same expression of pallid fear.

"Where?" Frank asked. "The cellars . . . ?"

Thomas saw Jacqueline taking the stairs two at a time. Her skirts were raised to her knees.

"Upstairs," he grunted, and shoved past the others.

Jacqueline didn't bother investigating the boy's room; she looked in the other bedrooms. Thomas had never realized the sheer size of Weldon House until that time. It was nightmarish. The doors seemed to go on forever, down one unending corridor after another.

"How the hell many doors are there in this museum?" Jacqueline wailed, opening another door.

She hardly paused; but there was a split second's hesitation before she flung herself across the threshold. Thomas reached the door in time to see what was within.

The figure sprawled on the bed was Percy; there was no

mistaking that gross shape. The face was hidden by a fat white pillow.

"Smothered in the Tower" someone behind him was babbling. Thomas could not identify the voice; it was shrill with horror. "Smothered between two feather beds!"

CHAPTER FIVE

*I*n the split-second pause between discovery and action, Thomas's ingenious imagination presented him with a series of horrific pictures. It was a wasted effort. When Jacqueline snatched the pillow away, he saw Percy's familiar pink face, open mouthed and wet-lipped; the lips vibrated perceptibly to the sound of Percy's regular breathing.

Along the corridor came the pounding of feet. Not even maternal love could drive Mrs. Ponsonby-Jones's heavy frame beyond a certain rate of speed; she was the last to arrive. The staring onlookers in the doorway staggered back as she thrust through them. Catching sight of the pillow in Jacqueline's hand and the outstretched feet of her son, she gave a heart-rendering cry. She flung herself onto the bed. The springs squealed and Percy's relaxed body bounced before she gathered it into her arms.

It took considerable time to convince the woman that Percy was alive and well. Percy's head drooped over her arm; his mouth had sagged into an idiotic grin.

"He's drunk," Thomas said.

"No. Drugged, though, I think. Mrs. Ponsonby-Jones, if you would let the doctor have a look at him . . ."

Rawdon was on the other side of the bed, trying to get at his patient. It took Jacqueline's and Thomas's combined efforts to pry the distracted mother from her son, and they had to wrestle with her again when the doctor, after peering into Percy's eye, administered a few hearty slaps. The next time he lifted the boy's lid, it stayed up. The expression of the single blue eye boded no good for the slapper.

Mrs. Ponsonby-Jones was removed; she was only a hindrance. The others set about the work of restoration, and Thomas, for one, enjoyed it. Percy's howl, when he was thrust into a cold shower, warmed the cockles of his heart. The boy emerged dripping and blue, but by then he was sufficiently restored to regain his natural curiosity.

"You mean I was doped?" he inquired, through chattering teeth. "Really doped? How marvelous!"

Thomas left the boy to the tender mercies of the doctor and Weldon and returned to the drawing room, where the others had reassembled. Joining Jacqueline, who was sitting with Liz, he said, "Percy is himself again. It must have been a mild dose."

"No harm done except to our nerves," Jacqueline agreed. That her nerves were indeed affected Thomas deduced by the presence of the purse—large, white, and bulging. She must have gone to her room to fetch it as a child reaches for a furry animal in time of stress. She lifted it to her lap and began to burrow in it with both hands.

"Do you think he took the stuff himself?" she inquired.

Shocked, Thomas silently indicated the presence of the boy's sister. Liz looked at him. She was dry-eyed and unnaturally calm.

"He might have done," she said. "He has a bottle of tranquilizers."

There was a short, uncomfortable silence. Jacqueline continued to burrow. Finally she came up with a battered pack of cigarettes.

"This is the tenth time I've failed to quit smoking," she said, as Thomas took a lighter from the table. "Liz just told me about the tranquilizers."

"Mother keeps pressing them on him," the girl said in the

same expressionless voice. "She think's he's nervy and sensitive. I know he's a little horror, but. . . ."

"It's too fashionable these days to blame everything on poor old Mum," Jacqueline said, blowing out a neatly rounded smoke ring. "That doesn't mean she isn't sometimes culpable. But you're all right."

Her tone was matter-of-fact. The girl's face lost some of its pallor. She managed a faint smile.

"I'm okay, you're okay," she said. "Sometimes I'm not altogether sure of that."

She got up and crossed the room to the fireplace, where Frank was standing. He put his arm around her and she leaned against him.

"Well?" Thomas asked.

Jacqueline blew out another smoke ring. The first one had been a fluke; this attempt resembled a mashed doughnut. Jacqueline's eyes narrowed in annoyance. She tried again, producing a gusty blob with no discernible shape.

"The boy might have drugged himself," she said. "But that isn't the most interesting thing about this last incident."

"What is?" Thomas inquired resignedly.

"You were terrified, weren't you?"

"You're damned right I was, and I'm not ashamed to admit it. Percy is an obnoxious brat, but I don't want to see him—"

He broke off, staring at Jacqueline. She looked more enigmatic than usual, thanks to the veil of smoke that obscured her features like the vapor surrounding the pythoness.

"You were scared too," Thomas said. "Like the rest of us, you expected a catastrophe. And the interesting question is—why did we?"

"Precisely. No one has been hurt or seriously injured. Percy's absence could have been explained in a number of harmless ways. Yet the moment his mother announced he was not in his room, we panicked."

"The triumph of instinct over reason," Thomas said. "God knows the atmosphere around here is thick enough. Darkness, rain, the mournful sighing of the wind, and all that sort of thing —not to mention the shades of dead kings and queens gliding through shadowy halls. We're haunted by the memories of old murders. But it's more than that, isn't it?''

"How poetic." But Jacqueline's tone was affectionate; she smiled at him in a way that made his head spin. Or possibly, Thomas told himself, it was the wine.

"I know what worries me," he said, "and it isn't the atmosphere. The joker has taken care not to injure anyone seriously, but what if something goes wrong? What if he picks on someone with a weak heart or an unusual susceptibility to a drug?"

Jacqueline nodded. There wasn't time for her to comment; they were joined by the doctor, who had completed his ministrations.

"Is Percy all right?" Thomas asked.

Rawdon nodded. His gilt crown bobbed, and he made a grab for it.

"I keep forgetting the damned thing," he complained, looking as gloomy and cadaverous as Henry VI probably had looked most of the time. "Apparently the drug was in some vile fruit drink the boy habitually consumes. Did you see his room? Stocked like a shop! Biscuits, sweets—even the fruit is deadly unless it was organically grown, which is unlikely. Insecticides—"

"It would have been easy for someone to drug him, then," Jacqueline interrupted the diatribe.

"Oh, quite. The unfortunate boy never stops eating. If I had him under my care—"

Thomas had heard enough.

"I wonder what's going to happen now. Will Dick want to go on with the banquet?"

Weldon answered the question himself. He appeared in the doorway with his arm around the shoulders of a swaggering Percy.

"Here we are," he said. "Ready to take up where we were—er —interrupted. Mrs. Ponsonby-Jones will join us later on."

For a moment Thomas didn't think Weldon was going to get away with it. The room rang with unspoken questions. But Weldon stood firm, his dark eyes challenging; and no one spoke.

Liz was the first to respond. Like someone in a trance she walked forward, and Sir Richard moved to meet her. He offered her his arm, in the old courtly gesture; she placed her hand on his. The candles flickered in a sudden gust of wind; the two slight figures, robed and crowned, seemed to flicker too, like the unsubstantial fabric of a dream.

Thomas heard a voice remark softly.

"Stands the wind in that quarter? 'Nay, do no pause; for I did kill King Henry, But 'twas thy beauty that provoked me. Nay, now dispatch; 'twas I that stabb'd young Edward, But 'twas thy heavenly face that set me on.' "

The voice was Philip's, of course. Thomas turned. "I hope your quotation does not constitute an accusation."

"Did you see Weldon's face when she took his hand?" The actor's face was covered with a faint sheen of perspiration.

"Don't be ridiculous," Thomas said shortly. "At any rate, you're in the clear. The comedian appears to have skipped you. I'm inclined to agree with Sir Richard. It was Percy."

"After this last episode?" The lines in Philip's forehead smoothed out. "Yes, I see. A typically juvenile attempt to remove suspicion from himself."

"Sir Richard lectured him—accused him of perpetrating the tricks. This would be a predictable reaction."

"I wish I believed it," Philip muttered. "I can deal with Percy."

"Come along," Thomas said. "To the feast! Begone, dull care!"

Philip laughed hollowly.

II

The Great Hall was alive with ruddy, shifting light. A fire roared in the hearth, and along the wall torches set in iron brackets sent up streams of orange flame. The long table on the dais was covered with snowy linen. The floor was strewn with rushes; they were semi-dry and rustled underfoot, giving out a sweet scent as the herbs and flowers among them were crushed by the feet of the guests. Along the walls, stiff as statues, stood rows of servants in full medieval costume. Thomas was reassured to see the snout of a portable fire extinguisher poking out from under a tapestry. It was still raining outside, but Weldon was taking no chances.

Weldon led his lady into the Hall as a blare of trumpets

assailed the ears of the guests. Waiting for them near the dais was the stoical figure of Wilkes, in the uncongenial role of the medieval marshal. With his small gilt baton he indicated the chairs each diner was to occupy. As Weldon took his place, the trumpets died. Thomas let out a breath of relief. The musicians did not lack ardor, but at least one of them had to be tone deaf as well as untrained.

The unfortunate Wilkes now reappeared in the role of the medieval butler, the mandatory white napkin draped around his neck. Thomas watched with amusement as he poured wine into the cover of Weldon's cup and raised it to his own lips. He hoped the butler didn't have to go through the rest of the taster's ritual; it would take forever, if he dipped into every dish.

Weldon had tactfully dispensed with the massive salt-cellar that separated the nobles from the nonentities at a medieval table. Thomas found himself seated between Frank and Rawdon. Liz was some distance away, between the rector and Philip. Frank's expression made it clear that he did not approve of this arrangement.

Thomas took a heady swallow of wine and slapped the younger man on the back.

"Cheer up," he said expansively. "Enjoy. Dick has gone all out on this affair."

"Yes, but that damned actor—"

"He hasn't got a chance," Thomas said. He finished his wine. Frank's dark hair brushed the back of his collar and waved over his ears. His expression was lugubrious and he was sweating. The Hall was already uncomfortably hot, and the fire was roaring like a blast furnace.

"You know something?" he asked.

"Where's your crown?" Thomas demanded. "You oughta have—"

"It kept falling off."

"So does mine. But you're a prince. You oughta have—"

"You know something?"

"No, what?"

"You're drunk," Frank said seriously. "And I'm getting drunk. And I mean to get a lot more. . . ." He stopped, his eyes widening. "Good Lord," he said.

Thomas read his lips. He couldn't hear a thing except the off-key bray of trumpets. The door of the Hall opened. Through it came the vision that had astounded Frank.

It might be described as a bevy of serving wenches. Thomas assumed they were village girls; surely the house didn't have a staff of this size. Kirtled and laced and buskined to a dizzying degree, they were having a hard time controlling their laughter, as their red faces and popping eyes showed. They carried platters and bowls and flagons. As the procession entered, it divided, and down the center marched two stalwart village lads wearing baggy tights and long wigs. Between them they supported a mammoth platter on which sat a swan in full feather.

Thomas knew the swan was safely dead and roasted, its feathers restored to present a replica of life. The idea repelled him, although he knew such frivolities had been common at medieval banquets. He reached for the goblet, which one of the servants had just refilled.

Medieval diet suggests a group of lowly peasants munching stale black bread, or Henry VIII chomping on a leg of lamb while the fat drips down his front. In fact, the *haute cuisine* of the fifteenth century was extremely elaborate. Thomas let out a low whistle of approval after he tasted the soup that constituted the first course. Wilkes was dissecting the swan at a serving table—"plucking" might be a more accurate word—and his fleshy nose indicated what he thought of the task. Thomas did not watch.

Frank was not so appreciative. "What in God's name . . ." he began, indicating the thick liquid in his bowl.

"Blandissory," Thomas said, dipping into the brew again. "Made of beef broth, almonds, and sweet wine boiled together as a base and strained; then you add capon, ground in a mortar—I suppose they would use a blender today—tempered with milk of almonds and sugar. Add blanched almonds. . . ." He lifted his spoon and studied the nut peeping coyly out of the soup before putting the spoon in his mouth. It was impossible to sip blandissory genteelly from the spoon; the almonds got caught in your teeth.

"Too sweet," said Frank grumpily. "Give me a nice clear consommé."

Nobody did. By the end of the first course, even Thomas's stomach was beginning to feel the strain.

The everyday fare for a lordly household usually involved two separate courses, each consisting of three or four dishes. Picking jadedly at swan, Thomas thought with consternation of one famous medieval banquet that had included sixty separate dishes. Surely Weldon wouldn't try to outdo that feast.

The subtlety that ended the first course—which had included three other dishes of meat and fish in addition to soup and swan—was a masterpiece. It was borne in by the same grinning footmen who had opened the ball with the swan. A concoction of spun sugar and egg white, it had been formed by some Michelangelo of a chef into a representation of Sampson pulling down the pillars of the Temple.

The second course came in with a frumenty of venison. The meat, cut in strips, floated in a stewy soup made of wheat boiled in milk, egg yolks, sugar, and salt. Thomas started to describe the ingredients to Frank, but was stopped by a long, agonized expletive.

"I can't stand this," Frank muttered. "I'd sell my soul for a chunk of rare beef."

"They used spices a lot," said Thomas, who was getting his second wind, gastronomically speaking. "This next dish is ground meat—pork, probably—mixed with about a dozen spices and then baked in a pastry shell—called a coffin, if that interests you."

Frank groaned.

Thomas added, "I hope Weldon doesn't go berserk and offer us a cockatrice. They cooked a capon and a suckling pig and cut them in half; then they sewed the front part of the chicken onto the back part of the pig and the front part of the—"

"Good God," said Frank.

The entertainment—jugglers, dancers, music—which ordinarily accompanied a banquet did not appear. Apparently Weldon had anticipated that his guests would be too fascinated by the exotic food to concentrate on anything else, except possibly Ricardian gossip. Thomas found plenty of entertainment in watching his colleagues' reactions to the food.

The doctor, on Thomas's left, was having fits. He dined mainly on bread, and kept up a running commentary about what the food was doing to the collective stomachs of the group. Thomas had to admit he had a point. Everything was spiced and seasoned and sauced, and the heavy sweet wine—malmsey, by any chance? —made digestion even more perilous. He barely touched his junket of rosewater and cream and sighed with relief when the subtlety signalizing the end of the second course was borne in. The spun-sugar replica of Middleham Castle wobbled dangerously on the sturdy shoulders of the serving men. Thomas deduced that the kitchen staff had been indulging in malmsey too.

He waited apprehensively for a possible third course, but Weldon had the proper respect for effete modern appetites. The servitors passed around with basins of scented rosewater and napkins. Then the guests all settled back expectantly as Weldon rose.

Somewhere between the soup and the last subtlety, Mrs. Ponsonby-Jones had taken her place beside Weldon. No one less resembled the pale, consumptive Queen Anne; the woman's square face was ruddy with gratified pride and her bulk overflowed the chair. Apparently her *crise de nerves* had passed. Looking at Percy, Thomas agreed that there was no cause for concern —except for the dangers of gluttony. Percy shone like a greased pink pig from his hair to his third chin.

For security reasons, Weldon explained, he had decided to dispense with hired entertainment. The villagers who had assisted with the serving all were known to Weldon and the servants. Unfortunately none of them were adept in the skills of music and dance—with the exception of Tom Belden and his son, young Tom, whose performances on the trumpet had added so much to the spirit of the evening.

Therefore, Weldon continued, he had decided it would be safer, and more intimate, if they entertained themselves. He regretted the necessity of a phonograph for certain parts of the evening, but they would just have to pretend the music came from a group of live minstrels in the musicians' gallery. So, let the joy begin! They would start—he glanced at Lady Isobel, who was holding a sheaf of papers like a club—with the literary treat postponed from an earlier session.

Lady Isobel rose. Her expression was one of intense piety. Under the shield of the long damask tablecloth Thomas slid his feet out of his shoes and prepared, if possible, to sleep with his eyes open. It was clever of Weldon to bring on Lady Isobel now; their critical sense drugged with food and wine, the listeners would not suffer quite so intensely.

> *"The sun shone bright, the sky was fair,*
> *The birds did sweetly sing,*
> *Across the green of Bosworth Field,*
> *There rode the brave young king."*

The verses would have been barely endurable if they had come from a sentimental nine-year-old girl. From the gaunt old woman they were absolutely embarrassing. Liz might have been joking when she claimed to have a crush on Richard of Gloucester (was she joking, though?), but Lady Isobel really did. Her voice was low and charged with passion; it quivered as her emotion mounted. Thomas focused his attention on Jacqueline. Her expression of outraged disbelief was almost funny enough to make up for the poem. Despite all his efforts an occasional stanza got through to his brain.

> *"Boldly he mounted his great white steed,*
> *He gazed upon the sky,*
> *His slender hands took up the reins*
> *And a tear stood in his eye.*
>
> *He brushed it back with a mailed hand,*
> *'We ride to battle,' he said.*
> *'I'll live a king or die a king,*
> *And I'll have the Tudor's head."*

Thomas slid further down in his chair. A kindly man, he never enjoyed watching people make fools of themselves. This was worse than the piano recitals of his friends' untalented children. Slender hands and tear-filled eyes . . . "I doubt if he cried much," said Jacqueline's caustic voice in his inner ear.

Fortunately the last verses were more or less inaudible. Richard's gallant death—the word "gallant" appeared pretty often in the work—moved Lady Isobel to gulps and unintelligibility.

Even Weldon looked shaken when the distraught poet

dropped into her chair, resembling not so much a drooping lily as a wilted stalk of crabgrass.

"No applause, please," he said, as the other guests eyed one another with varying emotions. "It would be quite inappropriate after that . . . that . . . er. My dear Isobel, take some wine."

Lady Isobel had taken too much wine already, Thomas thought. She complied, however, and smiled wanly as Weldon patted her on the shoulder.

"The muse," she murmured. "Such a hard taskmistress. . . . It takes such a lot out of one, Richard."

"I know," said Weldon. "It does indeed. . . ."

The next performer was Liz, who sang several medieval ballads in a pleasant, if undistinguished, voice. The only ones Thomas recognized were Dufay's *"Adieu, m'amour,"* and a religious song by Dunstable. Liz then announced that she would scream if anyone asked for "Summer Is Icumen in" or "Greensleeves." The rector, who had been about to request the latter, closed his mouth and looked confused.

After the doctor had given a demonstration of how to put on a suit of armor—from which he had to be removed by two of the burlier servants—Philip took the center of the stage. It was an unfortunate choice of entertainment; the mood of the gathering was uncertain to begin with, and the two soliloquies from *Richard III* did not lighten it. The first, the opening "Now is the winter of our discontent" was a bit of sparkling black humor; but then Philip went on to Richard's agonized speech on the eve of Bosworth. All of them knew the setting: Richard, snatching a few hours' sleep before the morrow's battle, is visited by the specters of his victims, all mouthing the same curse, "Despair, and die!"

Philip became the twisted, tormented villain of Shakespeare's play. His voice rang all the changes of human passion—defiance, terror, remorse. It dropped to a ringing whisper on the final lines:

> *"I shall despair. There is no creature loves me;*
> *And if I die, no soul will pity me:*
> *Nay, wherefore should they, since that I myself*
> *Find in myself no pity to myself?"*

The spellbound audience paid the performer the supreme tribute of silence even after he had straightened up and shed his player's skin. He strolled nonchalantly back to his place at the table; and Thomas saw Liz shrink back as he seated himself beside her. He didn't blame the girl. It had been too good a performance to be wholly comfortable.

Weldon gestured; and from the darkness of the gallery, pipes and drums burst forth in a dance tune. The diners rose; all of them had practiced medieval dancing. Thomas heaved himself out of his chair, although he was dubious about his ability to move, much less tread an airy measure. As he moved gingerly away from the table, Kent plucked at his sleeve.

"Feeling queasy?"

"Well. . . ."

"Me too. Come along. I know what we need."

Thomas followed him out into the corridor. The candles were burning low. He wondered what time it was. The party could go on till dawn if the participants held out.

Kent led him to the dining room and a row of decanters on the sideboard. He poured a stiff jolt of brandy and offered it to Thomas.

Thomas drank. There was a moment in which matters hung in the balance. Then the upheaval settled, and he sighed deeply.

"Thanks. I needed that."

"Brandy will cure anything," Kent said, following his own advice. "I don't like doctors. Never need 'em."

Thomas was inclined to agree. His head felt absolutely clear as they went back to the Hall; but for some odd reason the rest of the evening became kaleidoscopic. He would be conversing with someone in a coherent manner; then the room would spin around and he would be elsewhere, with other people. At the time this situation seemed perfectly normal.

During one of these episodes he found himself with O'Hagan, who was singing "The Maple Leaf Forever." Thomas expressed mild surprise at the choice of song; O'Hagan explained that he was singing the Canadian anthem because he couldn't manage the high notes of "The Star-Spangled Banner." Thomas found this logical, but was moved to demonstrate his own patriotism and tenor voice. He sang all three verses of "The Star-Spangled

Banner." O'Hagan continued to sing "The Maple Leaf Forever." He only knew one verse, so he sang that one over and over, while he and Thomas nodded at one another in mutual approbation.

A shift in scene found Thomas discussing Buckingham's rebellion with Philip and Kent. After enthusiastically supporting Richard's takeover of the throne, Buckingham had retired to his castle in Wales, and then had returned at the head of a hostile army. Some Ricardians believed Buckingham was responsible for the death of the young princes, as the first step in his own climb to the throne.

Thomas doubted the theory and said so. Kent, who was playing Buckingham, took the criticism personally. He left, snorting with rage. Unperturbed, Thomas turned to Philip. "Man's drunk," he said seriously. " 'Magine getting so excited about a rational dishcushion. You see my point, don't you?"

"I'm sick of the whole business," Philip said. His face was flushed.

Thomas peered at him.

"Ah," he said. "Ah. Still nervous, my friend? Don't be. Got it all figured out. See, Richard didn't exactly murder Hastings, exactly. It was an exic—an extic—a legal killing. Treasons. Not like the l'il princes. Not that Richard killed the princes, mind you, but if somebody is picking on Richard's victims, then the fellows who were sexecu—I mean, they had their head chopped off . . . those fellow don't count. You see my point, don't you? I mean. . . ."

"For God's sake," said Philip, between his splendid white teeth, "I am getting so bloody sick and tired of all you bloody fools holding my hand. I am not nervous!"

The room turned upside down. Thomas next found himself dancing with Lady Isobel. This seemed such an unlikely activity for him to have chosen that he stumbled over the rushes, which had gotten trampled into heaps. Lady Isobel held him up with an unexpectedly strong arm, and giggled at him. She said something about butts of malmsey. Thomas glowered at her and then realized she was indicating the brimming bowl on the dining table.

"Oh, no," said Thomas vigorously. "Not me. Not that stuff. Gotta keep a clear head. Not get drunk."

The next scene was the dining room. Thomas put down an empty glass and wandered back to the Hall. The music was still going full blast, and Sir Richard was performing a country dance with Mrs. Ponsonby-Jones. The big woman was surprisingly light on her feet; her crimson skirts swirled as she moved. Sir Richard's crown had slipped over one eye.

Thomas looked for a partner and found none. He felt like dancing, so he did—an energetic solo, with high jumps and vigorous arm gestures. He considered another trip to the dining room and decided against it. He was feeling splendid. Arms clasped behind him, he began to stroll around the room. The hangings and potted plants placed at strategic intervals made convenient nooks that contained benches and chairs on which tired dancers might rest. Several of the alcoves were inhabited, not by dallying lovers, but by contentious Ricardians. The rector, perched on a high stool with his slippered feet dangling, was discussing the precontract of Edward IV.

"A precontract was as legally binding as marriage," he said, shaking his finger at the doctor. Rawdon looked bored, as well he might; this topic was almost as familiar as the murder of the princes.

"I know," he said testily. "That is not the question. The question is, did such a precontract really exist? It was officially recognized by Parliament, and Henry Tudor's determined efforts to suppress that decree indicates. . . ."

Thomas moved on. In the next niche, Philip and Liz were sitting side by side. For a moment Thomas thought he was getting confused. The topic of conversation was the same, although the people were different.

"Why would Henry want to suppress *Titulus Regius* unless it was true?" Philip demanded.

Liz nodded. Her eyes were shining. Thomas wondered how Philip could go on talking with a face like that six inches from his. Like the others, Philip was crackers on the subject of Richard the Third.

"Then there is the question of the Bishop of Bath and Wells," Philip continued. "Edward the Fourth imprisoned him and so did Henry the Seventh, after he took the throne. That suggests the old boy had knowledge dangerous to both men, and what could it have been but the truth—that Edward was never legally married to his queen."

"Clarence probably knew about it too," Thomas said. "He had his eye on the throne, and. . . ."

Nobody seemed to be listening to him, so he moved on. In a corner behind a rubber plant he found Frank, alone. Thomas put his head around the rubber plant.

"Clarence probably knew about it too," he said. "He had his eye on the throne. . . ."

"Oh, it's you," Frank said unenthusiastically. "What the hell are you talking about?"

"The precontract," said Thomas, surprised. "Isn't that what we've been talking about?"

"We haven't been talking. And if you are planning to discuss Richard the Third or any of his kin, don't."

"If that's the way you feel, I'm leaving," said Thomas.

"Do."

Thomas moved on. He wasn't angry with Frank; the poor guy was probably brooding about his fiancée's tête à tête with Phil. Not that there was anything to brood about; the conversation could hardly have been less romantic.

By an oblique train of reasoning this reminded Thomas that he hadn't seen anything of Jacqueline for some time. He began to look for her. The torches were burning low, and he was feeling drowsy; it was only by chance that he saw the shimmer of a golden skirt in a shadowy corner. He wandered over.

Jacqueline was not alone. She was not aware of his approach, not even when Thomas leaned forward, squinting, to make sure of his quarry. The red-gold hair flowed down over Jacqueline's shoulder and over the arm of the man who. . . .

"Hey!" said Thomas indignantly. It was bad enough to find Jacqueline in a dark corner with a man. That the man was identifiable by his snowy hair as O'Hagan made matters worse. The white rabbit had been snared by the fox, and Thomas wondered why the fox had bothered. There was something very funny going on. . . .

"Hey!" he repeated. The first exclamation had apparently gone unheard. This one had the desired effect. Jacqueline pulled away. Thomas stared in consternation. The alcove was dark, but there was no mistake; the rabbit's face stared back at him, pale and moustacheless. The moustache . . . the moustache was . . .

Jacqueline raised a hand and peeled the luxuriant appendage from her cheek.

"Oh, Thomas," she said casually. "Would you mind . . . ?"

Drunk or sober, Thomas told himself, he had a mind that worked like a steel trap. The pieces of the puzzle fell together with a resounding click; growling joyfully, Thomas leaped at O'Hagan and got a punch on the nose that sent him sprawling on his back. He wallowed among the rushes.

"That's enough of that," Jacqueline said icily. "Both of you stop it this instant."

The lights went on in a blinding flash. Whether by design or accident—Thomas suspected the former—the romantic pair had met in the area where the main switches were located.

Her hand still on the switch, Jacqueline studied Thomas with twitching lips.

"Have some hay," she quoted, rather freely. "It's especially good when you feel faint."

Thomas began to pluck dried rushes from his wig. His eyes were glued to O'Hagan; he was finding the truth hard to believe. From other parts of the hall people converged on the trio.

"Strangways," said Thomas. "I'll be *eternally* damned if it isn't James Strangways."

There could be no doubt; the face now bared to the world by the removal of the moustache was unquestionably that of the man whose photograph Thomas had seen on the back of his biography of Edward IV. The dark hair was now pure white, and there were a few more wrinkles around the eyes and the wide, mobile mouth, but the features were the same. The moustache had not been the only disguise; there was no trace of the blinking rodent in Strangways's look now. He even looked taller. Jacqueline's hand rested on his arm, and Thomas sensed that if it had not been for this mild restraint, Strangways would have vaulted his fallen form and fled.

If he had meditated flight, it was now too late. They were surrounded by a circle of staring faces, on some of which comprehension and outrage had begun to replace bewilderment.

Frank was the first to speak.

"My God," he said.

Lady Isobel plucked at his arm.

"What is it? What is happening?"

"Mr. O'Hagan has lost his moustache," said Mrs. Ponsonby-Jones. "That is very strange." She glared at Jacqueline, as if blaming her for the shaving of O'Hagan.

Percy burst into a high-pitched giggle. "Mum, you are stupid. This isn't Mr. O'Hagan. Don't you recognize him? I do! I suspected all along—"

"Be quiet," Weldon said. The tone quieted Percy; he glanced at Weldon in shocked surprise. Sir Richard's self-control was more impressive than ever. Even the tipsy crown didn't mar his dignity, and Strangways, who had been smiling, lowered his eyes under Weldon's gaze.

"I also recognize you, Mr. Strangways," Weldon said. "Your behavior surprises me, I confess. I had considered you mistaken, but not unprincipled."

"I owe you an apology," Strangways admitted. "Very bad form —isn't that the correct phrase? But I assure you, deceiving you about my identity was the only way in which I have abused your hospitality."

His voice was several shades deeper than O'Hagan's had been.

"But how did you manage it?" Thomas demanded. "What have you done with the real O'Hagan? Is there a real O'Hagan?"

"Oh, yes, he's real. He's the jackass who took over the American society after they threw me out for heresy." Strangways smiled. His front teeth were a trifle prominent, but the effect was now rather canine than rodent. "I still have a few friends in the society; they keep me informed, so I knew when O'Hagan was due to arrive. It was easy to cut him out of the crowd at the airport; I knew what he looked like, and young Frank didn't. I pointed him out to a friend of mine—he wouldn't have gone quietly with me—and my pal smuggled him away to London, where he is now hiding. The man's a bundle of neuroses; he thinks the meeting has been postponed, and that every reporter in England is in pursuit of him. Meanwhile, I stuck on my moustache and my name tag—I thought that was a particularly good touch—and caught Frank's wandering eye. Simple."

Although he demonstrated some embarrassment at being caught, Thomas thought this emotion was subordinate. He was having a hard time keeping his mouth straight, and he was standing very close to Jacqueline.

Thomas transferred his accusing stare to that lady.

"How long have you known about this?"

"I suspected it some time ago," Jacqueline said. "There is an aura, is there not?—a subtle outflow of masculine energies—no true woman could ignore its emanations. I felt it . . . here. . . ." She clasped her hands over her heaving bosom and grinned at Lady Isobel. Then her voice changed. "I thought it peculiar that Mr. O'Hagan denied knowing Strangways, when both of them had been associated with the American society. That wasn't necessarily damning evidence; but surely it was obvious that if you were harboring a cuckoo in the nest, it had to be Mr. O'Hagan. He is the only person who is not known by sight to any of you. The moustache was too good to be true; his other features are unmistakably those of the man in the photograph. If you are trying to identify someone, you look at the facial bones— nose, jaw and cheekbones, the setting of the eyes."

"Most people don't, though," Strangways said coolly.

"His hair . . ." Thomas began.

"Turned white overnight when I learned the terrible truth about Richard the Third," said Strangways.

He ducked, suddenly, as a fist brushed his jaw. Thomas, now completely sober, grabbed Kent just in time to prevent a second attack. The general's face was purple with rage. His arm felt like a steel bar, and he did not subside until Frank had added his weight to Thomas's. Kent began to swear. He was panting so hard that most of the words were obscured, but a few of the riper military adjectives came through intact; Lady Isobel squealed and put her hands over her shell-like ears.

"Let me at the bastard," Kent said, still wheezing. "Just let me knock that superior smile off his treacherous face. After all he's done to you . . . and you. . . ." His head bobbed from one side to the other, indicating Thomas and Frank, who were still holding him.

Frank looked at Thomas. The younger man's cheeks were flushed and his eyes shone with amusement.

"Now then," he said soothingly. "No harm's been done. Actually, I'm rather relieved to find that Mr. Strangways is our mysterious comedian. It makes the whole thing less disturbing."

Again his eyes met those of Thomas, and the latter nodded vigorously. "Quite right, Frank. If you and I don't choose to chastise Mr. Strangways, I don't see why anyone else should be vindictive. Let's all cool off and talk rationally."

Strangways was no longer smiling. "Just a minute," he said. "There's no reason why you should take my word for it, but for your own sakes you had better do so. I didn't play those damned jokes."

Against his will Thomas found the avowal convincing. He was still trying to adjust to the transformation. He found Mr. Hyde much more attractive than the former personality. Strangways looked younger and tougher than the false O'Hagan; his eyes were direct and honest.

Then Strangways spoiled the effect by adding, "I don't need to make fools of you. You're about to do it with no help from me."

Another roar from Kent alerted Thomas; he wound both arms about the general's writhing body.

Then Weldon's voice cut through the uproar like the lash of a whip.

"Stop it! We've had enough of this, Kent," he said. "Let him go, Thomas. Let go, I say."

Thomas did so. Kent stood still, his color fading.

"Now," Weldon went on, "let us disprove Mr. Strangway's opinion of us by acting rationally. I don't mean to hold an inquest into the jokes—if you want to call them that. Unless Mr. Strangways can prove an alibi. . . ."

Strangways was more cowed by his icy courtesy than he had been by Kent's attempted assault. He shook his head. "How can I? Everyone was coming and going."

"Precisely. The same thing applies to the rest of us," Weldon continued with scrupulous fairness. "Since, as Frank says, no harm was done, I propose to forget what has happened. A more pertinent question is—what do we do with Mr. Strangways?"

"Throw him out," Kent growled. "Kick him out the doors."

"It is one thirty in the morning," Weldon said. "There is not a room to be had in the village, and it is beginning to rain again.

Because Mr. Strangways has behaved badly is no reason why I should emulate him."

"Imprison the miscreant," said Mrs. Ponsonby-Jones angrily. "Fling him into a dungeon!"

"Don't be absurd," Liz said sharply. She moved forward, her green skirts swaying, and eyed Strangways with cool appraisal. "Perhaps you'd like us to load him with rusty chains, Mother. After that banquet, dry bread and water would be superfluous."

The rector coughed. "We can hardly imprison the gentleman," he said. His mild voice was shocked. "That would be violating the law. The police—"

There was an immediate, unanimous murmur of negation. Strangways smiled. "I'm perfectly willing to face the police," he said.

"You would be." Philip pushed forward. "Padre, think again. I'm the last man to object to publicity, but if we want to make thorough asses of ourselves for the benefit of the newspaper-reading public of the world, the surest way is to call the police in."

"Quite right, quite right," the doctor said. "It must not get out. Dignity . . . reputations . . ."

Strangways looked at Philip. The two men were the same height; their eyes met like blades crossing.

"Hearing you was a privilege," Strangways said. "I may regret my lack of manners, but I don't regret having had the chance to hear your Richard."

Philip made an impatient gesture.

"These exchanges of courtesy bore me," he said curtly. "Sir Richard, I agree that we can't convict Mr. Strangways without proof; but surely you aren't going to allow him to be present tomorrow?"

"No, no. Mr. Strangways will leave in the morning. For the present, I fear he will have to endure my company."

"But . . ." Kent began.

"I've been anxious to talk with him," Weldon went on; and Thomas was amazed to see the familiar gentle glow of Ricardian passion warm the little peer's face. "I feel sure I can convince him of his errors."

Strangways laughed. He turned to Jacqueline, who had been

oddly silent. "If I can't have your company, my dear, Sir Richard's is next best. A duel of wits, eh? We'll see who convinces whom."

He stepped forward. Weldon took him by the arm, as he might have done with any of his friends. As they walked away, Weldon was already talking.

"There'll always be an England," said Jacqueline, staring after them.

III

Instead of breaking up after the Great Discovery, the party revived. The event had sobered most of the guests; they took immediate steps to remedy this distressing development. Frank made a beeline for the punch bowl. Kent stood gnawing his lower lip.

"What about a drink?" Thomas asked him.

Kent looked up. He was playing with the jeweled dagger at his belt, and the look on his face chilled Thomas.

"Look here, General," he began.

"Oh, it's all right," Kent cut in. "If Dick wants to play the gallant fool, that's up to him. Richard forgave *his* enemies, didn't he? Yes, I'll have a drink—but not that foul brew in the bowl. I need some brandy to take the bad taste out of my mouth. Coming, Rawdon?"

He stamped off, followed by the doctor and Mr. Ellis. Lady Isobel and Mrs. Ponsonby-Jones had struck up a temporary alliance, to express their ladylike disapproval of the whole transaction. Arm in arm, they advanced on the punchbowl. Jacqueline stood like a statue, her eyes slightly crossed, communing with something invisible.

Thomas turned to Philip.

" 'Oh, what a rogue and peasant slave am I,' " he said, smiling. "Kent thinks I ought to challenge Strangways, or something."

"Wrong play, right interpretation," Philip said. "There's nothing wrong with the general except that he's out of place in a civilized society. He'd have been first rate in the fifteenth century."

The actor looked more cheerful than he had for hours.

Thomas didn't have to search far for the reason. Deny it though he might, Strangways was the obvious candidate for the part of the comedian, and he wouldn't be fool enough to try another trick now that he had been unmasked. Philip was relieved of his worst fear—humiliation.

"Let's all have a drink," he said. "Come along, Liz . . . Jacqueline. . . ."

The four of them went toward the dais. As they approached the table, Frank lifted his cup in a mock toast.

"This is a slight improvement over the last batch," he said cheerfully.

"It could hardly be worse," Philip said. He filled a cup and offered it to Jacqueline, who refused, and then served the others.

Across the room Thomas saw Weldon and Strangways seated on a bench in one of the alcoves. Their heads were together; Weldon gestured animatedly as he talked. Something stirred the branches of the plant next to them.

"Look at that," Thomas said, nudging Jacqueline. "It's Percy, eavesdropping on the debate."

"What does he expect to overhear?" Frank asked, perplexed.

"It isn't what you hear, it's how," Philip said. "When you're young you think adult conversation is loaded with forbidden secrets. Didn't you ever eavesdrop, Frank, my lad?"

"No," Frank said.

"The little paragon," Philip murmured. He reached for the dipper, jostling Frank.

"Let's dance," Liz said quickly.

Frank gave the other man a black look, but went with her. Philip drained his second cup with the air of a man who drinks for a set purpose, and filled it again.

"Thomas," said Jacqueline. "You haven't danced with me yet."

Thomas was delighted to oblige. Neither of them tried to follow the rhythm of the jigging, bouncing medieval dance. They moved languidly about the floor; after a while Thomas began to hum "Stardust." It was a delicious, relaxing interval, except for one small irritation. . . .

A hard, lumpy object banged rhythmically against his hip.

"Do you have to carry that purse even when you . . . ?"

A thought struck him and he stopped in his tracks. "What did you do with it when you were hugging Strangways?" he asked, with genuine curiosity.

"Hugging?" Jacqueline repeated. She laughed softly.

"Never mind," Thomas mumbled against her hair.

"Now, Thomas, don't do . . . we're right out in the middle of the floor; everybody can see us."

"I don't care," Thomas repeated. "Unless you want to go someplace more private?"

"Not now," Jacqueline said, with another soft laugh. "I adore you, Thomas, but you are not completely sober, and I want a man's complete attention when I—'hug' was the word, wasn't it?"

"Like this," Thomas said, demonstrating. "Perfectly good word—so far as it goes." He began to hum "Stardust" again.

IV

When he next became aware of his surroundings, it was dark. It was cold. It was wet. Something kept falling on his head. Raindrops? Someone's lawn sprinkler? Niagara Falls?

Where the hell was he?

"Stand still," said a voice, as he struggled blindly. "Please, Thomas, for God's sake, don't fall down! I'll never get you up. . . ."

She slapped him. The outrage of the act woke Thomas more effectively than the pain. He reached out, snarling. Jacqueline got in several more hard smacks before he located her wrists. He was awake by then, and fighting mad. He shook her.

"What the hell are you doing?"

Jacqueline, always an excellent tactician, collapsed like a folding umbrella, and Thomas caught her in his arms.

He was standing on the terrace outside the Hall, with rain streaming down his face and—no doubt—ruining his rented wig. The light from the nearest window stretched out across the flagstones like a fiery pathway to Hell. Biblical and Miltonian images swam through Thomas's brain, assisted by the demoralizing warmth of the body he clasped.

The body turned rigid and shoved at his chest with both hands. "Are you awake now, or shall I slug you again?" Jacqueline inquired.

"I'm awake . . . I think." Thomas shook his head. "What happened? How did we get out here?"

"We came out for some fresh air—the phrase was yours. There are some garden chairs, if you recall, under a roofed section of the terrace. We sat there for a while. I remember thinking," said Jacqueline remotely, "that you were not at your best. I admit to becoming mildly vexed when you started snoring. But then, when I tried to wake you, and couldn't. . . ."

"So you dragged me out into the deluge. 'Greater love than this . . .' I hope your dress isn't ruined."

"It's drip-dry. Thomas, you aren't concentrating. I don't think you were drunk."

"Oh, oh," said Thomas.

"Yes. Are you okay now?"

"Let's go."

When they reentered the Hall, Thomas understood why the beam of light had been ruddily red. Someone had turned out the electric lights. The torches were burning low. In the soft, hellish glow they searched the darkening Hall.

Thomas stumbled over the first body. It lay on its back in the middle of the dance floor, and even in that position it presented a formidable obstacle. Mrs. Ponsonby-Jones snored. Her expression was as affable as Thomas had ever seen it.

"She's all right." Jacqueline tugged at him as he bent over for a closer look. "She wouldn't be snoring like that if she were. . . . Where are the others?"

In the great chair of state that Weldon had occupied they found Liz, curled up like a sleepy child. Her head was pillowed on her arms and her brown hair tumbled over the curved armrest.

Percy was still behind the rubber plant. He snored even louder than his mother.

The Hall had no other occupants. They searched all the alcoves before heading for the door. Jacqueline paused for a moment to switch on the lights. In the bright glare the place looked ghastly. Thomas squinted at the heap of crimson velvet in the middle of the floor, the trampled rushes, the smoldering torches.

"The last act of *Hamlet,*" he muttered. " 'Give me the cup— there's yet some poison left. . . .' "

"Good old Shakespeare," said Jacqueline. "A *bon mot* for every occasion."

She led the way to the dining room, where they found the doctor taking his forty winks. He stirred and mumbled when Jacqueline poked him.

"Brandy," she said. "I suppose that was drugged too. Come on, let's see how many of them made it upstairs."

Kent was the only one of the crowd who had gone to bed in the conventional fashion. His clothes were piled neatly on a chair, and Thomas was pained to observe that he wore bright-striped pajamas. He did not stir, even when Jacqueline callously switched on the overhead lights. After sniffing the air, she nodded.

"Brandy again."

Lady Isobel was lying in the corridor in front of Sir Richard's bedroom door. She reeked of wine, and her fingers were crooked, as if she had clawed at the door as she fell.

"Good God," Thomas said devoutly.

Weldon's room was unoccupied. The lights shone softly on pure white sheets, unwrinkled, and on Weldon's navy-blue pajamas laid out on the pillow.

Frank and the rector were sprawled on their respective beds, fully clothed. The rector's crown remained defiantly in place, although his head drooped over the edge of the bed.

Philip's bed was turned down. Neither he nor his pajamas were in evidence. Thomas considered the alternatives and decided that Philip probably didn't wear pajamas. Jacqueline leaped to the same conclusion.

"Where can he be?" she muttered.

"Weldon is missing too," Thomas pointed out. "And what about O'Hagan—I mean Strangways? You haven't looked in his—"

"Weldon," Jacqueline said in a strange voice. "He's already skipped one. Or has he?"

She trotted off down the corridor, her purse swinging.

Strangways's room was empty too.

Thomas turned to face Jacqueline.

"Now what?"

"Downstairs."

In the drawing room they found two of the missing persons.

"Not *Hamlet,*" said Thomas. "The Sleeping Beauty. Is everybody asleep, for God's sake?"

"Considering the hour and the activities of the evening, that's not surprising. We're the ones who are abnormal."

Reasonable as this was, it did not dispel Thomas's superstitious uneasiness. The house was like the legendary castle in which all the inhabitants had been cast into a spell, dropping where they stood. Weldon and Strangways faced one another. Both were more or less upright in their chairs; Weldon's crowned head had fallen against the back of the chair. Strangways was sitting up. His eyes were closed.

Jacqueline pressed the switch that turned on the overhead lights. Strangways flung up a hand to shield his eyes; his reflexes were as quick as a cat's.

"Who is it?" he asked. "What . . . oh. Fell asleep. What's the time?"

"Three A.M.," Jacqueline answered. "Have you and Sir Richard been together all this time?"

"Together in body but not in spirit." Strangways lowered his hand.

"When did you fall asleep?"

"How should I know? He dropped off first; poor fellow has had a busy day. I was drowsy myself, so I just continued to sit." The searching dark eyes narrowed. "What's wrong?"

Jacqueline didn't answer him.

"Thomas, see if you can wake Sir Richard."

Sir Richard's slumber was sound; it took Thomas some time to rouse him, and several minutes more to explain their present errand. Strangways was on his feet by that time, and when Thomas had finished the American exploded angrily.

"Damn, I might have known. Weldon, you're a hell of a jailer. Or are you setting me up as a patsy?"

"You are jumping to conclusions," Weldon said. His voice was blurred with sleep. "We all drank too much. No doubt Philip has fallen asleep somewhere."

"Then let's find him," Jacqueline said.

In the hall they encountered an unexpected note of comedy. A procession winding its slow way across the marble floor. It was led by Mrs. Ponsonby-Jones, supported by Wilkes and one of the menservants. Her arms hung over the men's shoulders and her feet dragged. She was crooning quietly to herself, interrupting the monologue from time to time with a hoarse chuckle.

When he saw his employer, Wilkes stopped. Mrs. Ponsonby-Jones, suspended, hung like a massive red effigy. The butler's face flushed with chagrin. "Sir Richard, I am sorry to have—"

"You seem to be doing splendidly under the circumstances," Weldon said with a flash of sour amusement. "Carry on, Wilkes."

"Yes, Sir Richard."

The intertwined trio gallantly tackled the stairs. Following behind, one of the huskier servants carried Percy. The boy was upside down over the man's shoulder; the view presented to the onlookers was appalling. The servant touched his forehead to Sir Richard, who nodded formally. Bringing up the rear was Liz, stumbling and hazy-eyed. Sir Richard moved like a boy, putting his arm around her waist. She leaned against him and yawned.

"So sleepy," she murmured. "Carry me."

Sir Richard looked as if the idea appealed to him. Before he could carry out the suggestion, Jacqueline spoke.

"If she can't walk, prop her up against the wall and leave her," she said sharply. "We must find Philip."

"Phil?" The girl blinked. "What's wrong with Phil? Has something happened?"

"That's what we're trying to find out," said Jacqueline.

"I'll help her upstairs first," Weldon said.

"No," Liz was waking up. "No, I won't go up, I want to know what's happening."

"Come on, then."

From the head of the stairs the butler's voice floated down to them.

"I beg your pardon, Sir Richard, but if you are looking for Mr. Philip—"

"Have you seen him?"

"Perhaps half an hour ago I encountered the gentleman going

in the direction of the library. He spoke to me; something—"
The butler's voice broke in a grunt and a gasp of pain. A deep
feminine chuckle reverberated; Wilkes could be heard savagely
admonishing his assistant.

"Wilkes!" shouted Weldon.

"I beg your pardon, Sir Richard. Lady Isobel is at your—"

"Never mind Lady Isobel. What did Mr. Philip say to you?"

"It was not entirely clear, Sir Richard. Something to do with
the date of the death of Queen Elizabeth."

"Thank you, Wilkes. Carry on."

"Thank you, Sir Richard," said the butler faintly. The sound of
elephantine progress resumed along the hall above.

"Queen Elizabeth Woodville, of course," Weldon explained,
turning to the others. "It is interesting that Henry the Seventh
did not put out the story of Tyrrell's confession until after the
boys' mother—"

"Now that's a good example of how you people try to find
hidden meanings in meaningless events," Strangways interrupted.

"Are you going to stand here all night arguing?" Jacqueline
demanded. "Or shall we resume the search?"

"Surely there is no need for concern," Weldon said. "We will
no doubt find Philip napping over a volume of fifteenth-century
history."

Jacqueline didn't wait; she had already turned and was marching down the corridor, her purse swinging in a rhythm that
threatened nameless things. The others followed more leisurely,
so that when Jacqueline threw open the door to the library she
was the first to see what was within.

The sight struck her like a physical blow. Thomas saw her body
stiffen and sway. The purse fell from her arm and hit the floor
with a squashy thud.

Thomas ran. Jacqueline moved jerkily to one side so that he
could see too.

The room was lit by a single lamp, on the table at the far end
near the windows, and by the glow of a dying fire. Straight ahead,
Sir Richard's massive desk filled one corner of the room. In front
of it was a good-sized log, similar to others in a wood box next to

the fireplace. Philip's body lay on the floor beside the block of wood. Trunk, arms, and legs were visible. The head stood on Sir Richard's desk, staring straight at the onlookers with wide, glassy eyes.

CHAPTER SIX

*T*homas put a supporting arm around Jacqueline. She was shaking. They crossed the room together. Jacqueline put out her hand and lifted the head by its long flaxen hair.

It was a shocking gesture, even though Thomas had realized by that time that the head was plaster. The eyes had a glassy stare because they *were* glass—or some kind of plastic. The features didn't even resemble Philip's; only the hair and the bizarre setting had lent the object enough verisimilitude to give them a brief but effective shock.

Thomas dropped to one knee beside the actor and lifted the cloth that covered his head.

It was a plain square of cotton the same color as the crimson rug. Crude as the substitute head, it had nevertheless served the same function—to lend illusion, for the necessary moment of horror. Thomas threw it to one side and passed his hands over Philip's head and body.

There was blood on his hand when he looked up. Weldon and Strangways were still in the doorway. Weldon had gone limp; only the white-knuckled clasp of his hands on the doorframe kept him erect. Strangways was kneeling beside Liz, who had collapsed into a moaning heap.

"He's alive," Thomas said.

"Thank God." Weldon's voice was barely audible.

"He's had a bad knock on the head, though, and I don't like the way he's breathing. See if you can arouse the doctor. Last time I saw him, he was passed out in the dining room."

Strangways rose and ran out. He was back in less time than Thomas would have believed possible, pushing Rawdon ahead of him. The doctor was only half awake and mumbling querulously, but the scene in the library woke him with a vengeance. Without realizing it, Thomas had taken up a position that once again concealed the fallen man's head and shoulders; and Jacqueline, leaning against the desk, was still holding the plaster head by its hair.

"Dear God," said Rawdon, coming to a stop.

He was reassured and put to work; and after examining the actor he was able to reassure the others. Between them the men got Philip upstairs to his bed. Sir Richard insisted that the servants should not be brought into it, so they used the upper stairs that led to the bedroom wing by way of Sir Richard's sitting room.

Rawdon stayed with his patient. The others returned to the library. Thomas looked at Jacqueline, who was still contemplating the plaster head. He was reminded of Margaret of Navarre admiring the macabre mementos of her dead lovers. Liz lay in a chair like a stuffed dummy; she had not spoken since she came out of her faint, nor taken her eyes from the horrible head.

"It's the sort of thing they use on department-store dummies," Jacqueline announced, looking up. "The wig was probably purchased elsewhere. It's been glued on, somewhat amateurishly."

In order to demonstrate, she suspended the head by its hair and bobbed it up and down like a yo-yo.

Liz gasped. "Please don't. . . ."

Strangways seated himself behind the desk. "It wasn't meant to convince anyone for long," he agreed. "But it certainly did the trick for a few seconds. God! . . . He must have been sitting here when he was struck. Here's a copy of my book, open to page four hundred fifty-seven."

"But how did the assailant reach him unobserved?" Weldon was beginning to recover his control. "He was wary and nervous—"

"Not after Mr. Strangways was unmasked," Thomas said. "He felt safe then."

"Damn it," Strangways began.

"No one is accusing you," Weldon said. "Thomas is merely stating an observed fact. Philip was put off his guard, not only by the discovery of your true identity, but by the fact that Percy was attacked before he was."

"All right, all right." Strangway's eyes were as hard as those of the plaster head. It crossed Thomas's mind, not irrelevantly, that the American scholar would be a good man in a fight. "Thanks to Weldon's incompetence I can't prove my innocence in this case. If we are to believe Wilkes, this happened within the past half hour. Does anyone have an alibi?"

"I do," Thomas said. "Jacqueline was with me the whole time."

"No one has ever suspected you, Thomas," Weldon said.

"Thanks." Thomas was gratified. After thinking it over, he wasn't sure he should be gratified. After all, the joker had displayed ruthlessness, bravado,and cleverness.

"The others were all asleep when we found them," he said. "At least they appeared to be asleep. Maybe we should have looked at them more closely, although I don't know how the hell you can tell—"

"Will you stick to the point?" Strangways shouted. He exchanged a glance with Jacqueline that seemed to encourage him. "This is serious, Weldon. You've got to call the police. You should have done it last night."

"If Philip insists, I shall of course comply with his wishes," Weldon said calmly. "But I rather imagine he would prefer not to have his weakness exposed."

"Weakness!" Strangways literally threw up his hands. "Don't any of you have an ounce of common sense? Where is all this going to end? Do you think if you ignore it it will just go away?"

"Well put," Jacqueline said approvingly. She was still absently juggling the head. Thomas resented her nonchalance. She had been no more immune to the shock than the rest of them. He also resented the admiring way she was looking at Strangways.

"Look here, Strangways," he said belligerently. "Who appointed you judge and jury and public prosecutor? So far as I'm concerned, you're still chief suspect. You have the best reason of anyone for making fools of us."

"Oh, God." Strangways ran a hand through his white hair. "Let's try it another way. I've been here, on the ground floor, the whole time. Isn't it obvious that the assailant used the upper stairs here? Philip would have had his back to them if he was sitting at the desk. He was facing the door. He'd have seen anyone who came that way."

"Not necessarily," Jacqueline said. "He was drugged—probably unconscious before he was hit on the head. The blow was merely an additional precaution, to prevent him from waking and catching a glimpse of the joker while he was being arranged in that charming little tableau."

Again Strangways was quick to understand. A little too quick? Thomas wondered.

"The wine," he exclaimed. "Weldon and I had a cup before we left the Hall. I should have suspected—"

"No, why should you?" Jacqueline said. "It was late, and everyone had had a good deal to drink. Most of us would have been asleep by then anyhow. The drugged wine was meant for Philip."

"And to prevent a hardheaded drinker from poking his nose in where it wasn't supposed to be," Thomas added. "Our friend thinks of everything, doesn't he? Was there anyone who didn't drink from the punch bowl after . . . after. . . ."

"After what?" Jacqueline asked. "That line of inquiry won't get you anywhere, Thomas. We don't know when the drug was added to the wine. The brandy decanter in the dining room must have been doctored too. And if I were the villain, I'd make a point of drinking the fatal brew myself—or pretending to do so."

She threw the head lightly into the air and caught it.

Liz sat up straight. "Will you please stop playing with that ghastly thing?"

Her voice was high and strained. Jacqueline looked at her thoughtfully and then put the head down on the desk. "Sorry. There is nothing to be learned from this prop."

"Except," Thomas said, "that it proves premeditation."

"I would have thought that was obvious," said Strangways dryly.

"Premeditation?" Weldon repeated. "How is that possible?"

"Don't be dense, Dick," Liz said impatiently. She looked better; Jacqueline had considerately placed herself in front of the head so that it was hidden from the girl. "We must try to think. We planned this meeting in July, didn't we? After you learned of the letter. I don't remember when we assigned the various parts, or how it was determined—"

"That's important," Jacqueline interrupted. "The head was meant to represent Philip and no other. Look at the hair."

She reached for the head and Liz said quickly, "Quite right. The—the person must have known Phil would take the role of Hastings, who was decapitated. It's been settled for . . . at least two weeks, isn't that right? We needed time to prepare our costumes and so on."

"Each of you knew what part the others would be playing?" Jacqueline asked.

"Yes, of course. We had to agree so there would be no duplications."

"Then let's go back to the question of motive," Jacqueline said. "Sir Richard . . . the letter. How much is it worth?"

"Its worth is incalculable. It is proof that Richard—"

"Never mind Richard the Third," Jacqueline groaned. "Is the letter worth money? Cash? Filthy lucre?"

"Why, I've no idea. A few hundred pounds, perhaps, a few thousand . . . not enough to justify such a complex plot, if that is what you are suggesting. Why do you believe that the letter and these tricks are connected?"

"I don't know that they are. I'm grasping at straws. But none of your friends seem to have broken out before this, and the letter is the only new addition to the proceedings. Don't you think it's time I saw it, Sir Richard?"

"No. I'm sorry."

"But that's why Jacqueline came," Thomas exclaimed. "To look at the letter."

"I know why she is here," Weldon said. He smiled at Jacqueline. It was his old smile, gentle and apologetic. "Forgive me,

Jacqueline, I did not intend to sound so brusque. I'm delighted to have had the opportunity of meeting you, and we have all enjoyed your company. But you are not an expert on medieval manuscripts, any more than I am a naive fool. When Thomas mentioned you, I took the liberty of investigating your antecedents. Don't you see—I couldn't take the risk of introducing a stranger into the household unless I was sure of her. You asked about the value of the letter. When I said it was incalculable, I meant it. It is worth an infinite amount of money—to me."

"Ah," said Strangways. "I wondered when someone was going to bring that up."

Tipped back in the chair, he was totally relaxed, hands clasped on his chest and a faint mocking smile on his lips. After a moment he went on in a cool voice.

"The value of the letter on the open market is irrelevant. It is worthless to an ordinary thief because it is unique. How could he possibly sell it? But he could hold it for ransom."

Liz's mouth dropped open in a look of astonishment. Jacqueline's face remained impassive.

Weldon nodded. "You are clever, Mr. Strangways." He turned to Liz. Thomas couldn't see his face, but the change in his voice, from calm appraisal to impassioned pleading, made Thomas wince. "I know most people would think me mad to care so much about a cause that has been dead for hundreds of years. But I do care. That letter must be published. You haven't seen it. You don't know. I tell you, that single document will clear Richard's name of all the charges the Tudors invented. It will restore him to his rightful place as one of England's greatest kings—a martyr, not a murderer. I would do anything—pay any amount—to make sure it is not suppressed."

He paused. For a moment the room was silent except for the hiss of the dying flames and Weldon's heavy breathing. Liz stared as if she were hypnotized. Her eyes were dilated.

"And that is why," Weldon said, "I will not take the letter from my safe until I produce it for the public announcement. I would let the house burn down before I would open that safe. It is flameproof and the letter would survive."

He turned to face the others, who were grouped around the desk. His face was transformed.

"You must be a Sherlock Holmes fan," Jacqueline said. Her matter-of-fact voice broke the spell.

Weldon smiled faintly. "Yes, Holmes pretended to set a house on fire to persuade a certain lady to open her safe. It may sound farfetched, but recent events have been even more bizarre."

"I gather the warning is meant for me," Strangways said. "Thanks, Weldon. Once again I strongly advise you to call the police."

"No."

"Then I'm going to bed." Strangways rose. His lean face was taut with anger. "I admire you in a way, Weldon, but you're the biggest fool in this pack of fanatics."

He walked toward the door, but he walked slowly; and when Liz spoke he stopped, as if he had been expecting her question.

"The letter clears Richard? How, Dick? Can't you tell us what is in it, even if you won't show us?"

"I'm sorry," Weldon said regretfully. "I've said too much already."

Strangways turned. His eyes had a wild glow that reminded Thomas of Weldon. "Can't you guess? There's only one significant charge, and only one way of clearing Richard of it. The letter is from the boys' sister. She says she has seen them or heard from them. Is that right, Weldon? The princes were still alive in the early months of 1485?"

Weldon didn't answer. He didn't have to; Strangways' deduction was the only possible answer.

"But damn it all," Strangways exclaimed. "Don't you see, Weldon? That proves the letter is a fake."

"Typical anti-Ricardian reasoning," Weldon said bitterly. "Richard killed the princes, therefore anything that proves his innocence must be false."

"But Buck saw the letter." Strangways' voice shook with suppressed fury. He was trying so hard to control himself that his face turned bright red. "He was Richard's first defender; don't you suppose he would have mentioned that in his book if it had been in the letter?"

"Ah!" Weldon whirled to face him, his slight figure braced as if for physical combat. "So you admit the letter did exist!"

Strangways was speechless. Odd strangled noises issued from his open mouth.

"That doesn't necessarily follow," Jacqueline said.

"But Sir Richard has a point. There would be no reason for Buck to invent or fake such a letter; if he wanted to invent evidence, it would have been something more conclusive—" She caught Thomas's eye and turned pink.

"My God, Jacqueline," Thomas said plaintively. *"Et tu?"*

"Well, I'll tell you one thing," said Strangways, who had recovered his powers of speech, though he was still flushed. "I'm not leaving. You'll have to carry me out of here bodily if you want to get rid of me. I wouldn't miss that meeting tomorrow for a million dollars."

"I shouldn't allow you to leave if you wanted to," Weldon said between tight lips. "You will stay and see, and admit your error before the world."

"That will be the day," said Strangways.

Liz stood up. The folds of her skirt rippled as she walked across the room and stood next to Weldon. She took his arm. "Don't waste time arguing with him."

Weldon put his hand over hers. Thomas felt a strange pang; it was as if some premonition warned him, for although he did not know it, this was the last time he would see them standing side by side in the magnificence of golden crowns and shining robes, the shadowy survival of a past that had never lived except in the legend it bred.

Arms locked, the pair moved toward the door, and Strangways stepped back to let them pass, with a deliberate inclination of his head. When they had gone, Thomas sighed. Strangways looked at him.

"Yes," he said. "I know. . . . And I'm sorry, in a way, for what is going to happen."

II

Thomas felt as if he had been wearing his costume for a week, but before he took it off he couldn't resist one last look in the mirror. He doubted that he would ever again appear in coronet and fur-trimmed robes.

The image that confronted him was something of a shock. The debonair duke of the preceding night was a nightmarish figure— a specter out of Clarence's premonitory dream in the Tower, dead and drowned and dragged out to dry. The wig had gone stringy, as cheap wigs are wont to do when wet; the robe was wrinkled and stained; and in the cold light of dawn the crown was obviously paste.

Thomas was about to lower himself thankfully onto his bed when there was a knock at the door.

"Come in," he said, in a resigned voice. He recognized the knock. Jacqueline's style was unmistakable, even in such normally impersonal actions.

"Are you decent?" inquired Jacqueline, through a modest crack.

"No."

The door opened. "You aren't going to bed, are you?" Jacqueline asked. She was fully dressed in battle costume—hair pinned back, glasses firmly on the bridge of her nose, purse over her arm.

"Who, me? Why would I think of doing a crazy thing like that?"

"There's no point in going to sleep now. It's morning already."

Jacqueline sat down on the bed next to Thomas. A vagrant fancy slipped through the latter's mind, but it did not find a lodging place; Helen of Troy couldn't have stimulated Thomas just then.

He yawned. "I noticed it is morning," he said. "Nothing is going to happen until three this afternoon. I have had no sleep at all, and the hours of the night have not been uneventful. I am exhausted in body, mind, and spirit."

"I figured you would be," said Jacqueline. She opened her purse.

Thomas shied back. "No," he said vigorously. "No. Not some noxious remedy from that bottomless purse. I will not sniff ammonia or drink—"

"What are you raving about?"

The only thing to emerge from the purse was a slip of paper covered with writing in Jacqueline's sprawling hand.

"Here," said Jacqueline, "is the list of Richard's supposed victims. I copied it from Markham's biography."

The list read:

1. Edward of Lancaster.
2. Henry the Sixth
3. Clarence
4. Hastings
5. Rivers, Vaughan, Grey, and Haute
6. His wife, Anne
7. The princes

"So what else is new?" Thomas asked. "They aren't in chronological order," he added.

"They are except for the princes. Markham puts that one last because it is the main charge. Now look at the list from Walpole's *Historic Doubts.*"

1st.   Edward Prince of Wales, son of Henry the Sixth
2nd.   Henry the Sixth
3rd.   George, Duke of Clarence
4th.   Rivers, Grey, and Vaughan
5th.   Lord Hastings
6th.   Edward the Fifth and his brother
7th.   His own queen

"Yes, indeed," said Thomas. He collapsed backward onto the bed and lay staring at the ceiling with his hands clasped protectively over his stomach. "So what does it all mean?"

"Not a damned thing," said Jacqueline.

"Your tone is one of poorly repressed exasperation. I deduce that you are baffled."

"But it has to mean something," Jacqueline insisted. "I hoped you could tell me what."

"Don't give me that humble bit," said Thomas, still prone. The ceiling was singularly dull. No cracks, no stains, not even a cobweb in a corner. Not in a well-staffed house like this. . . .

He came to with a start as Jacqueline's finger traced a path along the sensitive area on the bottom of his foot. He sat up.

"All right," he said resignedly. "Let me get dressed and I'll go out and detect with you. Only don't insult my intelligence by intimating that you are leaning on my superior brain. You just want somebody to listen to you and say 'yes' now and then."

"Go ahead and dress." Jacqueline turned her back. As Thomas assumed daytime attire, she continued to talk.

"He isn't following the lists, Thomas. Nobody puts the princes ahead of Hastings. Why did he break the succession there? He followed it up to that point."

"Dunno," said Thomas.

"Both lists include the queen's relatives—Rivers, Grey, and the rest. Those were executions—legal, I suppose, according to the usage of the times, but—"

"Nobody is playing those parts."

"All right, but then why not include the Duke of Buckingham? Richard had him beheaded, like Hastings. The general is playing that part."

"Buckingham rebelled against a crowned king," Thomas said. "Richard hadn't been crowned when he arrested Hastings and the Woodville crowd; and some historians doubt that they were really guilty. Buckingham was running around the countryside with an army; you can't quibble about his being a traitor. . . ."

His voice trailed off. He was standing on one foot with a sock halfway on the other.

"This character is not following the lists," he said, thinking aloud. "Poisoning Rawdon—Henry the Sixth—was out of line too. So he has some weird list of his own—obviously anti-Richard. Buckingham rebelled against a tyrant and a usurper, not an anointed monarch. You don't think. . . ."

"Oh, yes, I do," Jacqueline said coyly.

Still on one foot, his shirt tail hanging out, Thomas cursed with a fluency Kent might have envied.

"Okay," he said, when he had exhausted his repertoire. "Let's go see."

It was almost an anticlimax to see the head stuck jauntily on top of one of the high carved posts of Kent's bed. The cranium was covered with a fuzzy grayish coating meant to suggest gray hair.

From where he stood in the doorway, Thomas could see Kent's

entire body, or at least that part of it which was not covered by sheet and blanket. Kent had not stirred or shifted position since they had checked on him earlier, and he was still snoring.

"This isn't particularly picturesque," Thomas said critically. "Maybe I'm getting used to it. I feel cheated."

"He just tiptoed in and stuck the head on the bedpost," Jacqueline said thoughtfully. "There was a hole at the base of the other neck too."

"He might at least have covered Kent's head."

"I'm so sorry he disappointed you, Thomas darling. But I don't blame our anonymous friend for being cautious. Why should he risk waking General Kent? He got his grand effect with Philip."

"Shall we wake him up?" Thomas asked.

"Do you really want to?"

They looked at each another conspiratorially. Thomas felt a momentary pang of compunction, but it did not endure. Kent might be a bit startled to wake and see the head grinning at him, but knowing that his own skull was firmly attached to his neck bones, he would not be frightened. The man was a bore anyway.

"No," he said. "Let's just steal away."

As he closed the door softly behind them, another thought struck him. "We can wipe one suspect off the list," he said. "Philip couldn't—"

Just then, a neighboring door opened and Philip stepped out into the corridor.

He was as white as the bandage around his head, and his eyes were uncertain. After a surprised start he advanced on the staring pair with a stealthy, theatrical stalk.

"You do me wrong, being so majestical," he declaimed inaccurately, but with great feeling, "to offer up the show of force—"

"The show is not of force," Thomas said. "What are you doing out of bed? Where have you been?"

"Where do you think I've been?" Philip asked poignantly. "I'm not a ghost, actually. I've a body. 'Gin a body meet a body. . . ."

He swayed alarmingly. Thomas stepped forward to support him.

"Good Lord," he exclaimed, as an unmistakable smell

reached his nostrils. "Don't you know how dangerous it is to drink after a head injury? Rawdon shouldn't have left you alone."

"Back to bed," Jacqueline said. "Come on, Thomas, here we go. . . ."

They dragged the protesting actor to his room. When they had him safely in his bed, Jacqueline went straight to the bureau drawer and removed a bottle of whiskey. Philip was still singing "Comin' Through the Rye" as they left.

"Put him back on the list, Thomas," Jacqueline said, tightening the cap on the bottle before putting it into her purse. "He can walk."

"Not very well. Damn it, Jacqueline, I know the guy's an actor, but nobody could counterfeit injury that effectively. I felt that crack on his cranium with my own two hands. If it weren't for that. . . ."

"Yes?" Jacqueline said encouragingly.

"He's malicious enough. He was spouting the most God-awful slanders about the others before we went down for the banquet."

"Such as?"

"It would take too long to repeat them. Can I go to bed now?"

"No. Can't you rise above the demands of your vile body?"

"It feels vile at the moment, I must admit. What do you want to do now?"

"I want to pay a call on Mrs. Ponsonby-Jones."

Thomas's head was fogged by fatigue, malmsey, and chronic sinus trouble. It took him several seconds to understand.

"Mrs. Ponsonby-Jones—Queen Anne. You think she—"

"Richard poisoned her, didn't he?"

"No, he did not. She died of consumption, or something equally lingering."

"Something with boiling oil in it."

"Your quotations are getting less and less appropriate. Mrs. Ponsonby-Jones is probably okay. The old witch was drunk as a skunk last night and drugged to boot. It would be gilding the lily to make her any sicker than she was."

Jacqueline didn't answer. She stopped before Mrs. Ponsonby-Jones's door and tried the knob.

The door was locked.

"I expect she locked herself in," Jacqueline said. "Thus demonstrating more intelligence than any of the others. However, we had better make sure."

She pounded on the door.

The noise sounded hellishly loud to Thomas, but at first it had no effect on the occupant of the room. He was beginning to feel apprehensive when there were sounds from within. The door was flung open.

Presumably Wilkes had summoned one of the female servants to help Mrs. Ponsonby-Jones into her nightclothes. She wore a voluminous gown of pale blue. Her face was a bilious yellow. The colors clashed hideously. Her puffy features were set in an expression that would have made Shakespeare's villainous Richard look like a saint. With an effort that made her quiver from head to foot, Mrs. Ponsonby-Jones focused her eyes.

"How dare you?" she moaned. "How dare you, how—"

The door started to close. Jacqueline threw herself against it. "Wait a minute. Are you all right?"

"No," said Mrs. Ponsonby-Jones emphatically.

"Have you been sick?" Thomas inquired anxiously.

The question was not well phrased. Mrs. Ponsonby-Jones's eyes looked like currants sunk in a doughy slab of pudding. She slammed the door. Jacqueline removed her arm just in time.

She and Thomas stood staring at the door until it stopped vibrating. Thomas expected an irate delegation to emerge from the other rooms, but apparently the guests were still comatose.

"Was she or wasn't she?" he asked.

"Sick? Definitely. As to whether she has been visited by the comedian, I think not. He likes to have his efforts noted and appreciated. A hung-over female tossing her cookies in private wouldn't do the trick."

"How vulgar you are."

"I haven't begun to be vulgar yet. Let's get out of here."

"Can I go to—"

"No, you cannot go to bed. I need fresh air. Let's go for a walk."

"It's raining."

"So it is. How unusual."

Thomas sighed. To walk in the rain with the lady you love is romantic when you are eighteen. When you are fifty it is merely conducive to sniffles and rheumatism.

"How about the conservatory?"

The conservatory was an acceptable compromise, but it was not the happiest locale for a conversation in that house of confusion. The electric lights did not wholly dispel the gray gloom of a rainy morning, and the rain drummed on the glass panes overhead, setting up quivering echoes in the greenery. Epiphytes hung like fleshy miniature monsters. The fronds of palm trees brushed the glass roof; they had squat, spiny trunks, like deformed pineapples. Green branches reached out at them as they walked along the graveled paths. Such was Thomas's mood that he would not have been surprised if a swollen, fecund bud had opened, fringed with fangs, and snapped at his sleeve.

"What do you want to do now?" he asked.

The damp air made Jacqueline's hair curl. Little tendrils, like copper shavings, coiled distractingly over her ears and at her temples.

"What I should do is call the police," she said, in a voice that did not match the charming curls.

"And what is your complaint?"

"Half a dozen people have been physically attacked. What do you want before you call the police? A couple of murders, or . . ." Jacqueline's mouth remained open, shaping the word she had not said.

Thomas peered at her. When she did not continue, he said, "The people who have been attacked are the ones who ought to complain. If they won't, and Sir Richard won't, there is nothing much you can do. Nothing has happened to you."

"Aha," said Jacqueline, turning on him. "So that's what's bugging you. You'd like to see me upside down in a barrel, I suppose."

"No thrill in that. I've seen your legs. They are good legs; one might even call them excellent legs; but—" Thomas looked closely at her. "For God's sake," he said, in a different voice, "of course I don't want you to be attacked. You drive me crazy with your arrogance and your sarcasm and your know-it-all airs, but I don't want anything to happen to you. I adore you."

He kissed her. She came into his arms willingly enough, but

after a brief interval he realized that she was not responding. If an embrace could be called preoccupied, this one was.

He raised his head. Jacqueline's lips were parted, receptive; her face had the same expression of severe cogitation it had worn before the embrace.

Thomas sat down on the edge of one of the raised, brick-lined flower beds. "Sorry to have interrupted your train of thought," he said.

"You didn't interrupt it." Jacqueline sat down beside him.

"No, you wouldn't let a little thing like that interfere with your thinking. Who do you think is going to be murdered?"

"Why do you think I think—"

"Oh, come now. I don't mind being Watson, but I refuse to emulate Watson's superb stupidity. Murder was the operative word. You said it and then you went into a—if I may say so— theatrical double-take. If this were a comic strip, you'd have a light bulb over your head. I think you're bananas, but if I am to have your complete undivided attention in matters of more importance, I see I must let you exorcise this weird idea first. Who do you think is going to be—"

"Whom," said Jacqueline. "Wouldn't it be 'whom'?"

"No. Subjective pronoun. 'Do you think *he* is going to be murdered?' Not 'do you think *him* is . . . ?' " Thomas hit himself on the forehead with the palm of his hand. "Grammar lessons," he exclaimed wildly. "No, no, no, not grammar lessons. Who, where, when, and why? Especially why?"

Jacqueline followed this incoherent statement without difficulty.

"Why depends on who," she explained. "If I knew for sure who was going to be murdered, then I would know—"

"Whether," Thomas interrupted. "Now there's a relevant adverb. What makes you suppose somebody's going to be murdered? Go ahead, I'm listening. Ratiocinate."

"What?"

"Ratiocinate. Reason. Think."

"Someone has said that only Americans could put up signs ordering the reader to think," Jacqueline said coldly. "All right, I will."

"Be the great detective," Thomas went on. His head felt

better. Perhaps the damp air had cleared his sinuses. "I'm no male chauvinist; I don't mind your showing off. Throw out mysterious hints. Ask meaningless questions. I'll say I don't know the answers. I'll make admiring noises from time to time, and look as stupid as I can."

"Just be yourself," said Jacqueline, breathing through her nose.

They glared at one another. After a moment the corners of Thomas's mouth lifted, and Jacqueline's snarl relaxed. Thomas put his arm around her and she leaned comfortably against him.

"There are some advantages to being my age, even if it does make walking in the rain hazardous," Thomas said after a peaceful moment. "If we were stronger we'd have had a loud screaming fight. Then I wouldn't have learned the solution until the last chapter, after three or four murders. Why murders, for God's sake?"

"The murders of Richard the Third," said Jacqueline.

"What?"

"That's what we've seen, in the not-so-funny jokes. Richard's reputed murders."

"Well, obviously," Thomas said impatiently. "You pointed that out yourself after I. . . ." He thought for a moment. "Oh. I see what you mean."

"I don't see what I mean myself. I'm on the verge of an idea and I can't quite grasp it. But . . . murders. Why reproduce ancient deaths? Carefully, painstakingly, and harmlessly? When is a murder not a murder? *Why* is a murder not—"

"There you go again."

"I'm letting my stream of consciousness trickle on. When, why, who? Mrs. Ponsonby-Jones has to be the next victim. . . ."

"There is a more crucial who," Thomas said. "Who is the comedian? If we knew that—"

"I do know."

Thomas stood up so he could see her face more clearly. He had been getting a trifle farsighted the last few years.

"You know?"

"Oh, let's not have another one of those conversations. It's so obvious, Thomas. So obvious I can't believe it," she added in a rare burst of candor.

"So you aren't going to tell me."

Jacqueline smiled at him. Her eyes were glinting with humor; they looked like clear green water.

"Thomas, do you know why the detective doesn't tell until the last chapter? So he won't make a fool of himself in case he's wrong. It's much easier to deduce the identity of the murderer when you catch him in the act of murdering, or when all the other suspects are dead. Ellery Queen made that mistake in one of his books, I forget which one, but it was funny; he kept presenting complicated solutions that were promptly exploded. So after a while he decided—"

"Damn Ellery Queen!" Thomas thought of something. "You can't eliminate the people who have been victims of the joker, you know. In the form of literature to which you refer the victims were dead. They couldn't commit murders after they were—"

"Darling Thomas, aren't you belaboring the obvious? As a matter of fact, that one has been done. By Agatha Christie. The murderer was one of the supposed victims. He was supposed to have been shot through the head, but he—"

"I am not going to say anything rude about Agatha Christie," Thomas told himself aloud. "I am going to continue with my ratiocinations. You can't eliminate our victims just because they were victimized. But maybe you can eliminate some of them. In my case—"

"I never suspected you, Thomas," said Jacqueline earnestly.

"I wish people would stop saying that. I couldn't have rigged myself up in that uncomfortable position."

"You could have had an accomplice. There may be two jokers."

"Maybe everybody is guilty," said Thomas wildly. "And don't tell me that's been done. I know, I read that book. Okay. For the sake of argument let's say I had an accomplice. I suppose Frank could have staged his accident and Percy could have drugged himself and the doctor could have poisoned his own mush—"

"Or just pretended to be sick. Rawdon is the only doctor in the group. No one questioned his diagnosis."

"Okay, so he could have done it himself. But Philip got a nasty knock on the head. Or are you going to tell me that his hypothetical accomplice miscalculated?"

"I don't have to say it, you did. But Philip didn't need an accomplice. Head injuries are tricky things. There are medically documented cases of people getting a blow on the head and walking around for hours, even days, before collapsing. Philip could have produced the wound by banging his head up against a firedog or something equally hard. He wouldn't realize the extent of the damage. He might have had time to arrange himself artistically on the floor before he passed out." Jacqueline paused.

"Aren't you being rather fantastical?" Thomas said.

"I'm not the one who is fantastical. Even I couldn't have thought up these tricks."

"That's been suggested," said Thomas.

"Naturally. But we know better."

"Do we? Okay, I'll eliminate you. And you will eliminate me? Thank you . . . I think. Anybody else?"

"Oh, Thomas, this is a waste of time. You're on the wrong track."

Thomas began to pace. Gravel crunched under his feet. He brushed at a trailing vine that seemed to be eyeing him hungrily.

"So what's your solution, Holmes?"

"You really can't see it? Maybe I'm wrong. . . ." Jacqueline sounded uncharacteristically meek. Thomas turned and looked at her.

"So it is going to be one of those conversations. That's one of the reasons why I hate mystery stories. The detective, or some vital witness, is always being interrupted in the middle of a clue, and the damned fool never gets around to finishing what he was about to say."

"Sometimes he gets killed," Jacqueline said cheerfully. " 'The murderer is. . . .' Wham! Bang! Crash!"

"That's enough of that. Is there any reason why you can't tell me what you're thinking?"

"Several reasons. My inflated ego, for one."

"That's an accurate description, but it is not a valid reason."

"All right," Jacqueline said unexpectedly. She was sitting bolt upright, with her hands folded on her knees. Her head was cocked as if she were listening to an inner voice. "The comedian is. . . ."

She stopped. Thomas stiffened. His nerves were in worse shape than he had realized; for a moment he half expected to hear a shot ring out and see Jacqueline collapse in a pool of blood. Then he heard the sound her keener ears had already picked up, over the drum of the rain. Someone was coming.

He scowled at Jacqueline, who smiled back at him. Around a palm tree came James Strangways.

"There you are," he announced triumphantly. "Wilkes said he thought he saw you heading for the conservatory. Though why the hell anyone would pick this place on a day like this. . . ."

He glanced distastefully at the lush greenery. Thomas found himself warming to the man, in spite of the fact that he was looking far too bright and healthy. His sleek white head and erect body, clad in neatly pressed slacks and a blue shirt, made Thomas feel grubby.

"Jacqueline's idea," he said. "She was about to tell me—"

"Hm," said Jacqueline loudly.

Strangways looked from one of them to the other. His wide-lipped, attractive smile warmed his lean face. "The identity of the criminal? Don't let me interrupt. I've a few ideas of my own." He sat down beside Jacqueline.

"So you think of him as a criminal," Jacqueline said.

"I consider assault a criminal act," Strangways said dryly. "That puts me in a minority in this madhouse, I know. I thought you two had a little more sense. That's why I wanted to talk to you."

"What about?" Thomas asked suspiciously. He sat down on Jacqueline's left. There was barely room for the three of them.

"What about? A plan of action, naturally. We three are the only ones in the crowd who have our wits about us. Or don't you agree with me that the situation is dangerous?"

"Yes," Jacqueline said slowly. "I do."

"Do you know the identity of the comedian?" Thomas asked.

Strangways looked at him without moving his head. The rolling eyes gave him a crafty expression. "It has to be one of two people," he said finally. "I'm not sure which. And even if I were sure, I couldn't prove it."

"Who?" Thomas demanded.

"Uh-uh." Strangways' smile was not so attractive. "I'm not sticking my neck out. I'm in enough trouble as it is."

"Then what do you propose we do?" Thomas asked. "My God, I'm tired of egotists," he added.

"It's very simple," Strangways said. "The point of all these unpleasant activities is the letter. I didn't believe in the letter to begin with, and I don't now, especially after Weldon's disclosure last night."

"How biased can you get?" Thomas said angrily. "Dick is right, you are so hung up—"

Jacqueline regarded Thomas without affection over the tops of her glasses. "Who was it who was complaining about distractions and interruptions and extraneous comments?" she inquired.

"Oh, hell," said Thomas.

"Let me finish," Strangways said loudly. The last word echoed uncannily through the muggy air. "The letter is a fake. It was concocted by the character who planned the series of jokes. He is going to steal it and hold it for ransom. The jokes are merely a distraction. They focus our attention on the victims of the moment; while we stand around yelling at each other, the criminal will have his chance to steal the letter."

"From Sir Richard's safe?" Thomas demanded. "How?"

"You don't suppose the letter is in the safe, do you?"

"But Dick said . . ." Thomas stopped. "Oh."

"I can read Weldon like a book," Strangways said arrogantly. "He thinks he's Machiavellian, poor devil. He mentioned the safe to put us off the track. I'll give you ten to one that he's got his precious letter tucked away in some hiding place he innocently considers clever. I'll also bet he keeps sneaking in and gloating over it. The criminal now has everybody so frantic, they don't know what's going on. He'll play his last joke and snatch the letter. Well?" He turned to Jacqueline. "What do you think?"

"I think," said Jacqueline calmly, "that your theory has so many holes, it leaks like a colander."

Strangways's face darkened. Thomas watched with interest. He had never seen the man so angry, even when his identity had been disclosed.

"Oh," said Strangways in a stifled voice. "So you're one of those."

"One of what?"

"Liberated women. You have to degrade men to make your-selves feel superior. I came to England to get away from them," Strangways cried. "But they're here too. What's biting you? You'd be quite a woman if you'd only accept the role you were meant for."

Thomas could have hugged himself. He watched Jacqueline's face solidify into something that could have been enlarged and carved on Mount Rushmore. Only her eyes were alive. They shot out green sparks.

"Oh, what a shame," she said in a voice of saccharine sweet-ness. "I've hurt your feelings. I've dared to imply you might be wrong about something. Forgive me. I will accept your admoni-tion. I will not offend you by presenting my weak, female at-tempts at reason."

"Wait a minute," Thomas said, no longer amused.

Jacqueline turned on him.

"You're one too," she cried, accurately but unjustly. "You're all alike! This whole weekend, all you were after . . . you didn't think I knew that, did you? You can go to hell, Thomas, and take him with you."

She stalked off down the path, emitting sparks that were almost visible.

The two men stared at one another across the vacant space her departure had left. Strangways was still red in the face. Thomas smiled at him.

"Thanks," he said, and followed Jacqueline out.

He found her, finally, in Philip's room. The actor, fully dressed, was stretched out on the bed. He and Jacqueline were talking in low tones. They both looked up when Thomas stopped in the doorway. Jacqueline looked straight through him at the opposite wall. Thomas went away.

Bed was out of the question now. He was too keyed up to sleep. He wandered downstairs in search of coffee and found Wilkes replenishing the serving dishes. The butler greeted Thomas with his usual smooth imperturbability, but his shadowed eyes held a horrible memory.

Thomas accepted coffee and refused food. He had just seated

himself when Frank came in. He greeted Thomas curtly, poured himself a cup of tea, and sat down at the far end of the table.

"No breakfast?" Thomas inquired.

"Gawd, no," Frank said feelingly. "What was in that last posset of punch?"

"More than you know." Thomas realized the other man didn't know what had happened. He rather fancied himself as a raconteur, and the tale lost nothing in his telling of it. By the time he finished, Frank was wide awake and staring.

"I can't believe it. This fellow must be insane. You mean we were all drugged?"

"Most of us, anyhow."

"Jacqueline wasn't drinking," Frank muttered. He looked up, caught Thomas's eye, and said quickly, "No, old chap, I'm not accusing her, I simply meant . . . you say Sir Richard still refuses to call in the authorities?"

"That's right. I disagree, but I understand his feelings. Ridicule would mar the grand effect he hopes to make today."

"That isn't the only reason." Frank hesitated. "I may be betraying a confidence, but in my opinion matters have gone too far for normal reticence. Sir Richard has family reasons for wanting to keep this affair quiet."

"Percy?"

"The Ponsonby-Joneses are Sir Richard's only relatives," Frank said. "If the boy did plan these tricks, he should be in an institution. He's not legally responsible for his actions."

"Then you're against calling the police too?"

"I'm about to marry the boy's sister, after all. And there are humanitarian considerations. He will end up in a nursing home in any case. Why not do it quietly, without scandal?"

"But in the meantime he's potentially dangerous."

"I'll see to it that he's not dangerous," Frank said grimly. "I plan to watch him from now on."

"It might be more useful to watch his mother. She's next on the list—"

He broke off with a start. Mrs. Ponsonby-Jones had entered the breakfast room.

Her night of dissipation had left her looking as haggard as a person one of her fleshy girth could look, but it was not her ghastly face that made Thomas's eyes bulge. Arm in arm with Mrs. Ponsonby-Jones was Jacqueline. She guided the older woman to a chair at the table—a tug boat steering a liner—and helped her into it.

Mrs. Ponsonby-Jones obviously knew of her new status as the next victim. The woman was not only queasy and ill; she was terrified. Only the stiff upper lip required of her class kept her from howling, but she clung to Jacqueline with pathetic desperation.

In what could only be called a misguided attempt at distraction, Frank greeted his future mother-in-law.

"Good morrow, madam. How does your Grace?"

"Aoow!" The sound might have come from Shaw's Eliza Doolittle. Thomas contemplated Mrs. Ponsonby-Jones with new interest. Had Sir Richard's cousin married beneath him? If so, the guttersnipe had learned her lesson well. Mrs. Ponsonby-Jones recovered herself; with one hand on her palpitating bosom, she glowered at Frank. "How can you continue this jest?" she boomed. "Must you remind me—"

"I'm frightfully sorry. But there's nothing to worry about, honestly. Forewarned is forearmed. We'll not let anything happen to you."

Thomas noticed that Frank did not address Mrs. Ponsonby-Jones directly, avoiding the use of any terms of affection or even familiarity.

"Frank is right," he said. "We'll all look after you."

The offer did not soften Jacqueline, who was still looking at him as she might have looked at a squashy beetle.

"Where is Sir Richard?" she asked coolly.

"He'll be down before long," Frank said. "I passed him in the hall."

However, the next to come was not Sir Richard, but Kent. Alcohol couldn't hurt him much, Thomas thought; he was probably pickled in the stuff. Bright-eyed and beaming, he headed for the sideboard and loaded his plate with a heap of food that induced a unanimous shudder among the others.

"How are you all this morning?" he asked genially.

"Apparently you don't know," Thomas began, hoping to tell the tale again.

"Apparently *you* don't know," Kent said coolly, "that when I awoke a short time ago, the first thing I saw was a severed head."

He took a huge bite of coddled egg and was silenced, briefly. Then he went on, "Rather inadequate job, that one. More annoying than frightening. I understand the other joke of the evening was more effective. Met Weldon upstairs and he told me about it. Sorry I missed the excitement."

Mrs. Ponsonby-Jones muttered something in which only the words "cold-blooded monster" could be distinguished. Kent raised his head.

"Yes, I am cold-blooded," he said, sounding pleased. "Rather that than soggy emotionalism. None of this would have happened if you hadn't been such bloody sentimentalists."

"What do you mean by that?" Frank demanded.

"Good morning, good morning." The appearance of the rector saved Kent from answering, if he had intended to; he smiled enigmatically and returned to his breakfast.

Rawdon and the rector had come down together. They had met Sir Richard and heard the latest news. Beneath their formal expressions of shock and regret, Thomas observed a certain morbid enjoyment of the new sensation. He had to remind himself that neither of them—nor Kent, for that matter—had actually seen the appalling tableau in the library. Second-hand sensations were hard to take seriously.

The newcomers were immensely interested, however, and Rawdon was about to plunge into an animated discussion of the latest atrocities when Ellis, glancing at the quivering bulk of Mrs. Ponsonby-Jones, tactfully intervened. Conversation became casual. Jacqueline succeeded in distracting Mrs. Ponsonby-Jones by discussing dressmaking. It was the last subject Thomas would have supposed either lady to be interested in; if he had thought about the subject at all, he would have expected that Mrs. Ponsonby-Jones patronized professional dressmakers. But she discussed patterns and pinking shears and other technical matters with growing enthusiasm, as Jacqueline's skillful questions drew her out.

"Do you mean," Jacqueline asked respectfully, "that you made those lovely costumes Liz has been wearing?"

"Yes, indeed. After all, dressmaking was once my—" Mrs. Ponsonby-Jones stopped in the nick of time. "My hobby," she went on, with an artificial cough. "As a young girl. Costume design, I mean to say."

"Where is Liz?" Thomas asked.

"Still asleep." It was Frank who answered. Mrs. Ponsonby-Jones glared at him.

"And how do you happen to know that?"

"I looked in on her before I came down." The young lawyer looked her squarely in the eye. "And on Percy. I intend to continue looking in on them, all day."

"An excellent idea," said a voice from the doorway. "But it won't be necessary, Frank."

Weldon was wearing the standard uniform of the weekending old-fashioned Englishman—shabby, well-cut tweeds. Only his shoulder-length hair reminded them of the Plantagenet monarch—the hair and the grim expression. Weldon had changed. He was no longer the lighthearted host, but a man deeply involved in a cause.

He had collected his two young relatives and stood between them. Percy looked sulky and reluctant, but his face brightened at the sight of food. Pulling himself free of Weldon's grasp, he shambled toward the chafing dishes and began heaping his plate.

Liz wore a pants suit of a shade of ash rose that set off her exquisite complexion. The knit fabric fit like a glove from shoulder to hips. Thomas noted that although Sir Richard had had an arm around Percy's shoulders, he did not touch Liz.

Liz drifted toward the table. Her eyes had a blank, unfocused look, as if she were still feeling the effects of the drug. Frank got quickly to his feet and guided her to a chair.

Sir Richard remained standing. Even without the help of crown and royal robes, he was an imposing figure. "I hope you all enjoyed the banquet," he asked genially.

There was an unconvincing murmur of agreement.

"Splendid. We'll have an even better meeting this afternoon."

Thomas happened to be looking at the rector. He saw that ingenuous gentleman's face fall. Had Ellis hoped Weldon would cancel the meeting? If so, he didn't know his host. Thomas did. He had little hope of success, but felt he had to make the attempt.

"Dick," he said, "I really think you ought to call off the

meeting today. Or if you insist on going ahead with it—do the whole thing yourself. Get everyone out of here—the lot of us.''

"An excellent suggestion.'' Lady Ponsonby-Jones nodded her head. "Of course your family will not desert you at such a time, Richard, never fear. But the others—''

"I resent the implication,'' said the doctor angrily. "Good Lord, you can't suspect me, Dick? We've known one another for—''

His was not the only dissenting voice. Thomas caught Jacqueline's eye and was encouraged by its expression. She had decided to forgive him for the dastardly sin of being male.

"Just a moment,'' she said, her voice cutting through the rising chorus of complaints. "Thomas is right, and you are acting like a group of spoiled children. Do you enjoy being knocked around, humiliated, frightened? If Sir Richard has any sense, he'll throw us all out.''

Weldon's smile only touched one side of his mouth.

He's getting to look more and more like that damned portrait, Thomas thought in alarm. It's not a hobby any longer, it's an obsession. Was it possible that Sir Richard had come to believe . . . ?

The sudden suspicion was obscene; yet Thomas couldn't get it out of his mind, even when Weldon spoke in the familiar, gentle voice. The timbre of the voice had not changed, but its tone had. Where had he acquired that unmistakable voice of command?

"My dear Jacqueline, I appreciate your concern, but I cannot accept your suggestion. In any case, it is too late for the course of action you suggest. The television people have arrived.''

In the silence Thomas heard vague sounds outside. Loud voices muffled by distance, the rumble of vehicles. . . .

"They are now beginning to set up their equipment,'' Weldon said. He was still smiling that disturbing, distorted half-smile. "But believe me, all reasonable precautions have been taken. Two of my stoutest young servants are guarding the doors of the Hall; no outsider can penetrate into the rest of the house.'' His steady eyes swept the assembled group. "I have taken another precaution. Mr. Strangways is locked in his room. No''—he was addressing Kent, who had started to rise, his ugly little face set— "no, General, you are not to go near Mr. Strangways. I am not sure he is guilty; I am merely eliminating a possible source of danger. I intend to take the same precaution with Percy, as soon as he finishes feeding himself.''

Percy dropped his fork. Bits of scrambled egg flew like snow-flakes.

''What did you say?'' he demanded shrilly.

''I am about to lock you in your room,'' said Weldon. ''Have you finished? Take along some toast, if you like; you will be incarcerated for some time, and I know you are not accustomed to going without food for more than a quarter of an hour.''

''But Richard . . .'' said Mrs. Ponsonby-Jones.

''No, my dear, my mind is made up. It is for Percy's own good,'' he added gently.

Mrs. Ponsonby-Jones subsided, with an agonized glance at Percy. Her meekness maddened her son. He burst into a furious speech whose epithets were more or less equally divided between his mother and his cousin. He backed slowly away from the table as he shouted. Thomas had never doubted Percy's emotional instability; now he was ready to believe it might be more than a mild neurosis.

''Percy,'' said Weldon quietly.

Percy stopped shouting. He was drooling with rage and excitement. ''You can lock me up,'' he said, licking his lips. ''But you can't keep me there.''

''I can but try,'' said Weldon equably. He gestured. One of the footmen stepped into the room. He was the same husky young man who had carried Percy the night before. Apparently Percy recognized him; his damp chins quivered.

''Go along with Charles,'' said Weldon.

''Oh, very well.'' Percy made a lunge at the table. Lady Isobel, who was closest to him, shrieked and shied away, but Percy's designs were on the food. Snatching a handful of bread, he sauntered toward the door. Thomas did not find his change of mood reassuring. The boy's furious frown did not wholly conceal the glint in his eyes. Percy enjoyed being the center of attention—the suspect—and he was already planning his next move.

He swaggered out, with the embarrassed footman in close attendance. There was a long, universal sigh. Mrs. Ponsonby-Jones, huddled in her chair, did not speak.

"And those are the precautions you mean to take?" Jacqueline inquired.

"You think them inadequate?"

"I do."

"What do you suggest?"

"Disperse the house party."

"I can't do that," said Weldon good-humoredly. "This is a supreme moment for all of us. Nor will I insult old friends by seeming to suspect them."

Jacqueline's glasses were slipping. She stared over them at Sir Richard, who smiled affably at her.

"You wouldn't believe me if I told you—"

Weldon laughed. It was a pleasant, low-pitched laugh, but Thomas didn't like the sound of it.

"My dear—no, I wouldn't. I know some of the surmises that have been flying about. Fantastic theories! They do more credit to the imaginations of my friends than to their intelligence. I feel quite sure of the identity of the person who has been playing these nasty little tricks on us. That is all they are; nothing harmful was ever intended. If any of you wish to leave, of course I shan't stop you. But I do most sincerely hope you will all stay and share this day of triumph."

Thomas was hypnotized by Jacqueline's glasses, which continued to slide slowly down her nose. At the last possible moment she put her finger on them and pushed them back into place.

"Oh, I'll stay," she said. "Either everyone goes, or we all remain. But may I suggest that we gather in groups from now on? That particularly applies to you, Sir Richard."

Weldon continued to smile. Thomas thought he heard Jacqueline's teeth grind together before she spoke again.

"I presume the famous letter is safe?"

"Oh, yes. I have just looked to be sure."

"Damn it," Thomas burst out. "You said you wouldn't go near it until—"

"So I did." The smile seemed to be stamped on Weldon's face. "You must allow me my little subterfuges, Thomas. And now, shall we all retire to the drawing room to await the great moment?"

He walked out, moving as if in time to the strains of a slow,

majestic march. Jacqueline jumped to her feet and followed. The
others moved like a herd of animals after a leader.

Thomas remained in his chair. The more he thought about his
new theory, the more disturbed he became.

All of them had been affected by the bizarre atmosphere of the
past few days. Thomas had felt his own grip on reality slip once or
twice. Could an innocent avocation such as historical research
fan the spark of incipient schizophrenia? That story of Jacqueline's about the scholar who worshiped at the shrine of Mary,
Queen of Scots. . . . That was not an extreme case, but the asy-
lums, he had heard, were full of people who thought they were
Julius Caesar or Napoleon. Abnormality sends out invisible waves
that touch the people within its range. One seriously disturbed
personality could sensitize others and make them behave abnormally too.

Weldon was an authority on medievel manuscripts. He had
called the meeting; naturally he knew the roles the others had
assumed. He himself was King Richard, and the victims of the
jokes were Richard's victims. Had Weldon's sense of identification with his Plantagenet prototype passed the bounds of sanity?
Was some sly, submerged segment of Weldon's personality, beset
by doubts as to Richard's innocence, denied by Weldon's conscious mind, seeking an outlet? An outwardly dutiful son, subcon-
sciously rejecting and resenting his father's belief. . . .

Thomas knew he was weltering in a morass of absurd Freudian
contradictions, but he couldn't get the idea out of his head. He
felt an urgent need to talk with Jacqueline.

A windblown spatter of rain against the windows made him
start. The room was horribly quiet. All at once he was afraid to be
alone.

CHAPTER SEVEN

When Thomas reached the drawing room he was out of breath, in part from distress of mind, in part from the speed with which he had traversed the long, empty corridor. He tried to catch Jacqueline's eye, but did not succeed; she was chatting with Mrs. Ponsonby-Jones and Lady Isobel. From the shape of the latter's smirk, Thomas deduced that Lady Isobel had taken a nip or two to brace herself for the day's activities.

All the guests were present except the two who were incarcerated upstairs. Even Philip had come down. His eyes closed and his bandaged head resting against the back of the chair, he was expressing courageous suffering. Liz and Frank were seated side by side on a sofa. The rector and Rawdon were discussing music. Kent stood by the window, his back to the room, looking out at the rain; the set of his shoulders expressed anger and frustration. He probably wants to drag Strangways down and torture him into a confession, Thomas thought.

Weldon wandered around the room, rearranging a pillow here and an ornament there. No one seemed anxious to engage him in conversation; Thomas wondered how many of the others had had the same idea he had. As Weldon passed the sofa on which

Liz and Frank were sitting, Thomas thought he saw the girl shrink back. Weldon saw it too. A touch of color came into his face and he walked away.

Finding that his performance was not getting the proper attention, Philip got up and joined Liz and Frank. He said something to Liz. She looked at him with an expression of such fury that Thomas hastened toward them. Her comment reassured him as to the nature of the offense; it was Richard the Third again.

"But that is the crux of the matter," she exclaimed. "Don't you see—all the other accusations fall to the ground! No one believes in them today. Nothing tarnishes his reputation except the disappearance of the boys. Everything else hangs on that, even the so-called usurpation. Historians admit that the story of the precontract is probably true, and yet they continue to refer to usurpation. Why? Because afterward the princes disappeared. Yet Richard's seizure of the throne was not only justified legally, it was a moral imperative, given the attitude of the period. The kingship was a divinely sanctioned gift of God. For Richard to stand aside and see the throne go to a bastard would have been to commit an act of impiety, blasphemy! It is true that bastards could be legitimized by royal decree, but a person so legitimized could hardly hope to inherit the throne. And ironically, the only person who could legitimize the children of Edward the Fourth was Richard himself, as king. He may have planned to do just that, if he had lived longer. Everything indicates that he was a man of integrity, courage, and kindness; and yet he has been accused of one of the most dastardly murders of history, on grounds that wouldn't convict a dog. No wonder we harp on it! And we'll clear him of it, too!"

In spite of the fact that he recognized the speech as a quotation from one of Weldon's more pompous articles, Thomas couldn't help cheering.

"Hurray!" he shouted, and began to clap.

The applause was echoed from behind him. Weldon brushed past, his shining eyes intent on the girl. Kent also joined the group. Thomas heard him urging the claims of the Duke of Buckingham as murderer. He went to Jacqueline, who had left the other women and was standing by the window.

"Why don't you put Weldon up as Pretender to the throne?"

she suggested, before Thomas could speak. "After all, if Henry the Seventh succeeded, as the descendant of an illegitimate son, then Sir Richard—"

Thomas was not amused. "I've just had a horrible thought," he said. He went on to explain his suspicions of Weldon. Jacqueline listened without a visible change of expression.

"Hmmm," she said, when he had finished.

"What do you think?"

"I think you're very ingenious."

"What the hell does that mean?"

Jacqueline sat down on a hassock and reached into her purse.

"Not the tatting," Thomas begged. "My dear old grandmother used to do it. She did it beautifully. I can't stand watching your fingers turn blue. Why don't you take up whittling?"

Jacqueline produced her cigarettes.

"I hate myself," she said sadly. "If people would just leave me alone and not strain my nerves, maybe I could—"

"What about Weldon?" Thomas insisted.

"Watch him. Like a hawk."

"Then you agree—"

"I will say no more, *mon ami,*" said Jacqueline. Her French accent was execrable. "The walls have ears."

Her eyes rolled meaningfully, and Thomas saw Kent bearing down on them. He held a half-filled glass; the amber liquid sloshed with every step.

"Where are you going?" Jacqueline asked.

"Out," Kent said.

"You mustn't go alone. I'll go with you, to protect you." Jacqueline batted her lashes and pouted. Thomas thought it a disgusting display, but Kent was not so fastidious.

"I can hardly reject an offer like that," he said, leering.

Jacqueline took the arm he extended and they went toward the door. Over her shoulder Jacqueline looked at Thomas and winked strenuously.

Thomas wondered what the hell she was trying to tell him. To watch Weldon? That was the only positive suggestion she had made, but it was not as easy as it sounded. The room was large, and the Ricardians paced like restless lions. Sir Richard was the worst of the lot. Thomas kept losing sight of him—first behind the draperies, where he stood for a while peering out into the rain-drenched garden; then momentarily hidden behind Mrs. Ponsonby-Jones's considerable form. Then he darted for the door, ostensibly to check on the preparations going on in the Great Hall, which were reaching a peak of activity audible even in the drawing room. Thomas headed him off and guided him toward the table where sandwiches and coffee had been laid out.

He was sweating with nervousness by the time Jacqueline and Kent returned; the smug look on the general's face did not quiet his irritation.

"Have a sandwich," he snarled, shoving a ham-and-cheese concoction into Kent's hand.

The general looked startled. "I don't want a sandwich."

"Have one anyway. You too, Dick."

"I don't want—"

"Have a sandwich!" Thomas shouted.

"Now don't get excited, Thomas," Jacqueline said soothingly. "We'll all have a sandwich. We'll eat sandwiches all day if that will make you happy. And Sir Richard will tell me about the entries in the royal household account books that indicate the princes were still alive in 1485."

Weldon's puzzled frown smoothed out.

"The payment to the footman of the Lord Bastard—is that the one? Yes, I'm certain it must refer to young Edward. In an earlier entry he is called Lord Edward, and on another occasion, Edward bastard. The 1485 entry—"

"Balderdash," Kent interrupted. "The boys were dead by then. Buckingham killed 'em. The Lord Bastard must be Richard's illegitimate son John."

"Who was not a lord," Weldon snapped.

"As a king's son he may have been given a courtesy title—"

Thomas took Jacqueline's arm and removed her. "What were you doing out there with the general?" he asked. It was not what he had meant to say.

"Distracting him," Jacqueline said coolly. "He was heading for Mr. Strangways' room. He's quite drunk, and spoiling for a fight."

"But Strangways is locked in, isn't he?"

"So far." Jacqueline was clearly worried. "Thomas, Sir Richard doesn't have anyone guarding his prisoners. The locks are clumsy old things; I'm sure they could be picked."

"My dear, don't you think you had better tell me what is worrying you?"

"I may be wrong," Jacqueline said rapidly. "But I don't think so. Thomas, surely you must see it too; it's so obvious! I'd be much more confident if you arrived at the same conclusion."

Thomas shook his head. "I told you my idea. You haven't told me a damned thing that makes any sense."

"Oh, dear. Well, then, there are three people whose movements during the next couple of hours are of crucial importance. If we can keep them under observation, we should be all right."

"Who?"

"Percy, Sir Richard, and Frank."

"Frank?" Thomas repeated, in surprise. He turned.

The others had gathered in a group around the refreshment table. Ricardian debate raged, scarcely interrupted by sandwiches and coffee. Weldon stood a little apart, watching. . . . It was Frank he was watching.

Thomas had suspected that Weldon was in love with his young cousin, but the corollary had not struck his essentially law-abiding mind until that moment. The look on Weldon's face . . . Thomas saw a possible motive for murder, as well as explanations for the other mystifying events of the past few days.

"I can't believe it," he whispered. But unwilling conviction showed in his eyes, and Jacqueline let out a little breath of satisfaction.

"At least you see the possibility. That's a relief."

"But it doesn't make sense. Frank was the first victim—"

"Forget the Ricardian lists. Forget the whole Ricardian mess, it doesn't have anything to do with the problem. Or rather," Jacqueline amended, "it does in a way, but not in the way you mean."

"Wait a minute," Thomas said, his head spinning. "I'm not sure I do see what you're aiming at. Where does Percy come into it?"

"Oh, for goodness' sakes," said Jacqueline in ladylike exasperation. "I'll have to spell it out. As soon as Percy gets out of that room—which he will do, you can count on that—then—"

"Here comes the rector," said Thomas huskily. "Let's—"

It was too late. Mr. Ellis, smiling and refreshed, was upon them.

"The moment approaches," he said cheerfully. "I confess my agitation is mounting."

"If my agitation mounts any higher I'll have a stroke," Thomas muttered. "Oh, my God—there goes Frank. Jacqueline. . . ."

"Go with him." Jacqueline was just as disturbed. "Don't let him go alone, Thomas."

Thomas darted off, leaving Jacqueline to make excuses to Mr. Ellis, who was staring at them in understandable confusion. He collided with Frank in the doorway and caught his arm in a steely grip.

"Ouch," Frank said. "Thomas, what are you—"

Thomas could think of nothing to say except the simple truth. "Jacqueline thinks we shouldn't wander around alone."

"Oh? Perhaps she's right."

Thomas sagged with relief. It was a pleasure to deal with someone reasonable. "I was going upstairs to have a look at the prisoners," Frank said. "Come along if you like."

They went to Strangways' room first, since it was nearest. The upper halls were strangely deserted. Thomas glanced uneasily over his shoulder.

"Where are the servants?"

"Gawking at the telly," Frank said briefly. "The place is in an uproar."

Thomas knocked on the door. After a moment Strangways answered.

"Who is it?"

"Thomas. Are you all right?"

There was a rich chuckle from within.

"I'm fine and I intend to stay that way. You haven't come to let me out, have you?"

"No."

"Good. Because I wouldn't come. Anyone who enters this room for any reason whatsoever is going to get crowned with a poker."

"Are you planning to remain there indefinitely?" Thomas inquired.

"Only until time for the meeting. All hell will have broken loose by then, but I'll have my alibi. How is Jacqueline?"

"Fine," said Thomas stupidly.

Another chuckle. "She'll be feeling humble and depressed when my predictions are confirmed. But I'll console the little darling."

Thomas's eyes opened wide. It seemed incredible to him that anyone could think of Jacqueline in those terms.

"Oh, come along," Frank said impatiently. "We haven't time for games. Percy is the lad I'm concerned about."

Percy's incarceration was audible some distance away. Apparently he was kicking the door. The rhythmic thuds reverberated along the hall, and for some reason the noise maddened Thomas. He pounded on the door with his fist.

The thuds stopped. Percy's voice inquired ominously, "Are you going to let me out?"

"No."

The kicking began again.

"Listen to him," Frank said angrily. "The way things are going he could ram the door down with a battering ram and no one would notice. There are a dozen ways of getting out of that room. The windows lock only from the inside. . . ."

He had to raise his voice to be heard over the kicking. Thomas shouted back, "Luckily he's too angry to be rational. Let him wear himself out kicking."

They went back down the hall with the thuds following like drumbeats. Thomas resisted the temptation to comment on restless natives.

The restlessness extended into the drawing room. Only Weldon and Kent, the two diehards, were still arguing. The others prowled around the room. Jacqueline was pacing up and down. The rector chugged along beside her; he had to take two steps to each of Jacqueline's strides. The purse, a shoulder bag with a long strap, swung back and forth in rhythm.

Thomas caught her eye and nodded, but her face did not lose its worried frown. She slowed her step as Thomas joined them.

"Splendid exercise," said Ellis guilelessly. "Since we cannot be out of doors."

Jacqueline continued to walk. She was humming drearily to

herself; again, Thomas wondered why her sub-vocal perfor-mances sounded so lugubrious. It took him some time to identify the music as Gilbert and Sullivan.

". . . I'd an appetite fresh and hearty," crooned Jacqueline.

She caught the rector's astonished eye and lowered her voice, but the look she gave Thomas was not at all abashed.

"Very appropriate," Thomas said approvingly.

"How nice to find that others appreciate Gilbert and Sulli-van," said the rector. "They are rather underrated these days, I believe. Personally I find Mr. Gilbert's lyrics extremely witty. Do you know that charming song," and at the top of his voice he caroled,

> *"Spurn not the nobly born*
> *With love affected,*
> *Nor treat with virtuous scorn*
> *The well connected. . . ."*

Thomas choked. Jacqueline had met her match. Characteristi-cally, she was delighted to find a kindred spirit. She joined in.

> *"High rank involves no shame,*
> *We boast an equal claim*
> *With him of humble name*
> *To be respected."*

The rector was equally delighted. The singing turned into a contest, with each of them dragging out the most obscure songs they could think of in order to stump the other. Jacqueline caught the rector on the second verse of the sentry's song from *Iolanthe*; Thomas, who was accustomed to the trivia with which her brain was clogged, was not surprised that she should know all the words to a bass solo. Then it was the rector's point, with an obscure ditty from *The Sorcerer,* which Jacqueline did not recog-nize.

As a divertissement the exercise was highly successful. Even Weldon stopped arguing about Richard, and listened with a smile. Thomas was torn between amusement and embarrass-ment; W. S. Gilbert had a shaft for everyone. He had carefully avoided looking at Weldon when the rector chirped out his plea for the romantic rights of the rich, but that wasn't the only appropriate verse; Gilbert had much to say about overweight elderly ladies, cowardly generals, and inept practitioners of various professions. He even satirized the Women's Lib of his day, and when the rector quoted from *Princess Ida,* Jacqueline stopped singing.

As the time for the broadcast approached, a rising hubbub proclaimed the arrival and raucous discontent of members of the press. According to Weldon, they were to be shepherded straight into the Hall, but on at least two occasions Thomas thought he saw a vague form pass swiftly through the mist and drizzle without.

The nursery-school image occurred to him again; he felt like a helpless teacher taking a group on an outing. As he rushed to head one stray back into the flock, another slipped away. He thought he had kept track of them fairly well. Weldon and Frank, at least, were present and hearty when the fun began.

Although Thomas had been watching the windows off and on, he was not looking in that direction at the crucial moment. It was Frank who saw the face. His shout alerted the others. Lady Isobel screamed. The countenance pressed against the streaming glass was dreadful enough to justify her cry. Wet, dank hair was plastered against the rounded skull, nose and lips were flattened and whitened. The eyes shone with a steady glare.

"Damn that wretched brat! I knew he'd get out!"

Frank ran toward the window. He was thrust aside by Kent, who wrestled with the fastenings. Pandemonium ensued. Lady Isobel hid under the table. After a moment of indecision Mrs. Ponsonby-Jones decided to faint. She did so, falling heavily against Philip as she collapsed. They fell to the floor, Philip swearing in a loud voice as he tried to untangle himself. Kent finally got the window up and vaulted over the low sill. He was followed, more slowly, by the doctor. The rector vibrated uncertainly on the hearthrug, like a modern dancer expressing Doubt and Insecurity; then he bolted for the door, possibly with the idea of heading the fugitive off from the front of the house. The lights went out.

Thomas knew that the moment was upon them. Something was about to happen. He had no intention of pursuing Percy;

there were enough people engaged in that futile exercise already. But he didn't know what to do. The room was a gloomy cavern through which shadowy forms moved and shouted. He could not identify any of them.

Someone grabbed his arm. Thomas recognized the perfume, the grip, and the faint gleam of coppery hair.

"Quick," said Jacqueline. "Quick, for God's sake."

She crossed the room like a cannonball, towing him with her and ruthlessly brushing aside interference. Someone reeled back from her outthrust arm. A voice rose in a banshee wail as they ran past the long table. Thomas deduced that Jacqueline had trodden on Lady Isobel's hand.

There were lights in the hall. Jacqueline began to run faster, the purse swinging wildly. Thomas ran after her. She passed the doors to dining room and breakfast room and flung herself at the oak panels of the library door. It was locked.

Thomas didn't offer to break it down. "Upstairs," he said. "Through Weldon's sitting room and down the library stairs."

Jacqueline shot him a glance of approval and took off. As they reached the central vestibule and the stairs, they saw Wilkes struggling with a determined mob. Actually, there were only a dozen people present, but they conveyed the impression of a mob. The press had broken in.

Jacqueline put her head down and went through like a fullback. Thomas was on her heels. Several of the more alert reporters followed them, but Jacqueline lost them in the maze of corridors above. Thomas could hear them bellowing for a guide as he and Jacqueline entered Sir Richard's room. He was puffing like a grampus. Speed and apprehension had winded him. Jacqueline beat him to the library stairs. He had to follow her down; the stairs were too narrow for more than one person.

He had had no time to think ahead, to imagine what he might see; but his wildest imaginings could not have prepared him for the scene that met his eyes.

The heavy draperies were drawn, but the room was well lit by the chandelier overhead and by the lamp on Weldon's desk. Flames flickered on the hearth—not the blaze of a well-laid fire, but the isolated, smaller flame of something burning—something like a piece of paper. In the center of the room Sir Richard lay on his back, his arms outstretched. His shirt had been ripped open; his chest streamed with blood from at least two wounds. Standing over him, a naked blade in his hands, was Frank.

Thomas closed his eyes. When he opened them again, the tableau had not changed. He had hoped he was having a hallucination.

Jacqueline ran forward, emitting cries of distress. Thomas thought she was wringing her hands, although he didn't see how she could, with her purse in the way; she was certainly doing everything else a frightened woman is supposed to do. She flung herself down beside Weldon's bleeding body, under the lifted blade.

Frank fell back a step before her impetuous rush. The weapon wavered. It was the huge two-handed sword that had hung on the wall, and he needed both hands to hold it. The blade was no longer clean and shining. As Thomas watched, petrified, a drop fell from its tip and made a small red stain on the back of Jacqueline's white blouse.

"Thank God you got here in time," she exclaimed, glancing up at Frank. "Did you see him?"

"Who?" Frank looked as if he were in a state of shock—which, Thomas thought, was not surprising.

"Percy," Jacqueline answered. She was still on her knees; her hands, horribly stained, were moving over the unconscious man's breast. "It was Percy, wasn't it?"

"I don't know," Frank said slowly. "I didn't see anyone. The— the damned sword was lying on the floor. I picked it up. I never really believed people did idiotic things like that."

"Shock," Thomas said. "Put it down, Frank."

He spoke gently; he didn't like the young man's looks. Frank was abnormally flushed; his body shook with his quick breathing. Instead of lowering the blade, he turned it, studying it with bemused interest. Another drop fell. Jacqueline had straightened; the crimson drop struck her forearm and trickled slowly down toward her wrist.

"He burned the letter," Frank said, indicating the fireplace.

"That doesn't matter now," Thomas said. "Sir Richard—is he still alive?"

Jacqueline didn't answer. She didn't look at him; her eyes were glued to Frank's face. Thomas realized that the young man was perfectly dry. He had not been out in the rain. He had come directly to the library. . . . And the library door had been locked when Jacqueline tried it.

Thomas knew then. In spite of his habit of self-control, a gasp escaped him. It was as if an invisible tendril of thought crossed the room, from his mind to Frank's. The younger man turned his head and looked directly at Thomas. Sir Richard stirred, moaning.

"Yes," Frank said gently. "He's alive. You had better fetch Rawdon, Thomas."

Thomas didn't know what to do. It was too late for pretense; Frank had read his cursed open face. He couldn't leave anyway, not with Jacqueline and the helpless man under the sword. He couldn't jump Frank; he was too far away, and the dripping blade hovered over Weldon's lifted face. The huge sword was as heavy as a sledgehammer; Frank didn't have to thrust, all he had to do was let go. Shock and nervous strain might excuse the failure of his grip. A sudden move from Thomas certainly would.

As his overtaxed brain struggled with split-second alternatives —all of them impractical—Jacqueline broke out again, wringing her hands and keening like an old lady at a wake. Trivialities assault the mind at such moments; Thomas was disproportionately vexed by the purse, whose strap kept slipping and getting entwined with Jacqueline's hands.

Then he caught a gleam of emerald as Jacqueline turned her head slightly; and he found that the expression "his heart sank" was not a poetic flight of fancy. Something inside him seemed to drop with a thud and press agonizingly into the pit of his stomach. She was going to move. A bare-handed, middle-aged woman against a husky young man armed with a six-foot sword. . . .

"No," he shouted. "No, don't—"

The cry helped, distracting Frank's attention for an instant. Jacqueline was already in action. Only her arm moved. Her arm —and her purse, whose strap was now wound around her fist like the cords of a sling. The massive, weighted object sailed in an accurately calculated arc, striking Frank's hands and the hilt they clasped. The impetus carried arms and sword up and back, away from Weldon's face. In a single smooth movement Jacqueline rose and took a long stride. She lifted her knee.

Thomas stood frozen, not with fear but with consternation. The brutal, effective blow and Jacqueline's white-clad elegance made a rather horrid combination.

Jacqueline herself seemed surprised. Looking down at the moaning form at her feet she remarked, in a wondering voice,

"Amazing. It really works!"

CHAPTER EIGHT

Y ou never studied karate," said Thomas. It was not a question.

"I read a book."

"You cannot learn karate from a book," said Thomas. His voice vibrated with passion. "It is impossible to learn karate from a book. No one has ever learned—"

"Well, I saw it on television, too," Jacqueline said calmly. "I'm not even sure that particular move is karate. Judo, perhaps? Or that other thing, the Chinese—"

"Where I come from, it's plain dirty fighting," said Strangways, grinning. "I wish I'd seen you in action, Jacqueline. Not that Thomas's description lacked verve. . . ."

They were barricaded in the drawing room while Wilkes and the other servants searched out and expelled lurking reporters. The meeting had been canceled; the roars of trucks and the expletives of frustrated media men reached them faintly, even through the closed and bolted windows. It had stopped raining.

"Someone will have to give them a statement," Kent said, as a particularly outraged expletive echoed along the hall.

"Inspector Whatever-his-name will handle that," Jacqueline

said. She looked apologetically at the new member of the group who stood, in formal rigidity, by the door. "I'm afraid I don't know your name either, Sergeant . . . Lieutenant. . . ."

"Constable Stewart, miss," said the young man, moving only his mouth. A wave of color ran up his thin face, from his tight collar to the roots of his sandy hair. Thomas had noticed that he blushed every time someone spoke to him. He wondered if the young fellow was really cut out for his profession.

"Thank you." Jacqueline smiled. "You don't mind if we talk, do you?"

"I have had no instructions as to that, miss."

"I'm going to talk whether it's allowed or not," said Philip decidedly. "I'm confused. What the hell has been going on?"

"Weldon will live," Thomas said. "He was stabbed three times and lost a lot of blood, but none of the wounds were fatal. The fourth—or fifth, or sixth—would have been."

"But why not dispatch him at once?" Mr. Ellis looked lost without his usual companion. Rawdon was still upstairs with the wounded man. "The unnecessary brutality . . . the cruelty. . . ."

"Richard was killed by a dozen blows," said another voice. "They hacked at his body after he had fallen."

They had forgotten about Liz, who sat quietly in a corner of the sofa. Thomas stirred uncomfortably as she turned her pale face toward them. She was pale, but composed. Weldon's survival was the only thing that really mattered to her; the mad events of the day had clarified her feelings.

His candid, sympathetic face gave his thoughts away. Liz smiled at him.

"I'm quite all right, Thomas. Mother is still having hysterics upstairs, but that's simply habit. She never liked Frank." A touch of bitterness cooled the girl's voice, but it disappeared as she went on. "Isn't it strange, how the most frightful things can have positive results? Percy has been absolutely marvelous. He's with Mother now. Perhaps all he needs is responsibility. She's coddled him too long."

"There's nothing seriously wrong with Percy," Jacqueline said. "He's pampered, frustrated, and overweight. He needs a few good hard kicks in the rear, and the chance to do his own thing."

She looked as smug as a copper-furred cat, curled up in a leather armchair and smoking like a chimney. For once Thomas didn't resent her arrogance. It occurred to him that perhaps Jacqueline sometimes sounded overconfident and autocratic because that was what people wanted from her. Certainty can be reassuring.

Liz's face relaxed visibly; and Thomas, unable to resist a small dig, remarked, "Is that how you raise your children, Jacqueline? By God! That's how you learned karate! From David."

"He lets me practice on him," admitted Jacqueline.

Thomas hadn't seen Jacqueline's son for five years. He had been a dirty, freckled urchin then; he was about eighteen now, and if he was Jacqueline's son he would be a match for her in everything but experience—neatly built and mentally agile. He had a vision of Jacqueline heaving her tall son over her shoulder in her cool pastel living room. It was a delightful thought.

The rector was still struggling with the incredible truth.

"Then it was King Richard's death the—the criminal was attempting to reproduce—as he had reproduced the deaths of the others?"

"Only this was to be a fatal accident," Jacqueline said. "Sir Richard's death was the point of the whole bag of worms. The list of the people who died violent deaths during the reign of Richard the Third is incomplete unless you add Richard himself. If you follow the pro-Richard line, Richard was not a murderer; rather, he was a victim of the treachery and self-interest that doomed the other victims. The real villains were kings like Edward the Fourth and Henry the Seventh—your favorite candidate for the murderer of the princes. Henry was also responsible for Richard's death, although he didn't strike a blow himself. 'He led his regiment from behind. . . .' "

Thomas looked sharply at her. After a moment of silence Strangways spoke.

"And that is how you deduced what was going to happen?" he inquired skeptically. "Because the logical victim of the series was Richard himself?"

Jacqueline raised cool green eyes to his face and he threw his arm up in a mock gesture of defense.

"I'm not arguing. You lucked out—I mean, you were right and apparently I was wrong. I'm just asking."

"Ah," said Jacqueline, with satisfaction. "In that case, I will explain.

"The idea that the comedian's ultimate victim might be Sir Richard wasn't deduction; it was a crazy hunch. Thomas, do you remember our discussion in the conservatory? We were both groggy with wine and lack of sleep and we talked a lot of nonsense; and yet everything we discussed, from grammar to detective fiction, had bearing on the problem of the final victim. We debated about pronouns and adverbs; but when I spoke of 'the murders of Richard the Third' I realized that two other grammatical points were pertinent—the plural and the possessive preposition. If I say 'the murder of Henry the Sixth' you understand that I am describing Henry the Sixth's violent death. But if I say 'the murders—plural—of Richard' you assume I am accusing Richard of committing the murders, not of being killed more than once. 'Of' has two different meanings. In the first case, the possessor has suffered violence; in the second, he has committed it. There is a classic detective story called *The Murder of My Aunt.* . . . Think about it.

"Of course in ordinary speech the plural word 'murders' restricts the meaning of the possessive to the active form. Ordinarily people aren't murdered several times. But here in this house, Clarence, Henry the Sixth, and the others *were* 'murdered' a second time. So, I thought to myself, what about King Richard the Third? According to the York records, he was 'piteously slain and *murdered,* to the great heaviness of this city. . . .' An unusual epitaph for a tyrant, and a better one than Henry Tudor ever got. . . .

"In the view of the pro-Richard school, Richard was a victim, not a villain; a murderee, not a murderer. What if he, like the others, was due to be 'murdered' again? Sir Richard Weldon was King Richard. I had already figured out that the comedian was Frank—"

"Wait a minute here. You're skipping. How did you know that?" Strangways demanded.

"The heads," Jacqueline said. "Frank was the only one who had a car."

There was a damp silence. Strangways was the first to catch on. He swore. "Ditto," said Thomas. Jacqueline looked from one disappointed face to the next, and lifted the corner of her lip in a silent snarl.

"I know how Holmes felt after he explained his deductions and Watson told him how obvious they were," she said.

"But it is obvious," Thomas said. "I expected—"

"A pseudopsychological mishmash of Ricardian data? Oh, I suspected Frank before that; but I could have made out a plausible case against most of the people here. When will you get it through your academic head that possibilities are not proof?"

"The plaster heads were the clincher. You yourself complained about the lack of privacy in well-staffed houses—the servants always unpacking for guests. The criminal knew this; he would have taken an awful risk trying to smuggle the heads into the house without their being seen. It might not have attracted comment or attention initially, but after the heads made their public appearance, a servant might have remembered them. Even if the criminal could count on sneaking his luggage in and unpacking it himself, where would he hide the things? A bureau drawer? A closet shelf? Under the bed?"

"What about secreting the heads somewhere in the grounds?" Thomas asked.

"Possible, but equally risky. Also inconvenient. If the heads were found, by one of the outside staff, they might not be traced to the person who brought them, but they would be unavailable thereafter, and he needed them. He had to be able to get at them in a hurry when the opportunity arose. If it would rain, he would get wet and muddy, which might arouse suspicion. . . . But there was one hiding place that was practically foolproof. The locked trunk of a car. You call it the boot, I believe," Jacqueline explained to Mr. Ellis, who nodded dumbly.

"When did you first suspect Frank?" Thomas asked.

"Let's begin at the beginning," Jacqueline said, with infuriating patience. "At first we didn't have a criminal; we had a comedian with a strange sense of humor. As soon as the pattern of the tricks became clear, I asked myself the obvious question: Were the incidents simply sick jokes, or were they camouflage, to mask a serious purpose? I really couldn't believe the first interpretation. Only a madman would perpetrate such tricks. I hope you don't mind my using that word. It isn't approved these days, but it takes too long to say 'mentally disturbed individual.' "

"Call him a Bedlamite if you like," Thomas said impatiently. "Only get on with it."

"Now madness, though its acts may seem irrational to normal people, has its own rationale. The acts become explicable when one comprehends the underlying obsession. A paranoidal schizophrenic attacks strangers because he believes they are members of a conspiracy aimed at his life. A religious fanatic may murder prostitutes. If we were dealing with a man of this type, the rationale could only be hatred of the society, or of Richard the Third—as you know, he still inspires strong emotions. Your members are all dedicated Ricardians. If any of you developed a monomania—which I could well believe—it would hardly take the form of a plot based on vicious slanders of your hero, or one that mocked the organization formed to defend him."

"Do forgive me," the rector said in his gentle voice, "but I believe there is a contradiction. You said, a few moments ago, that Sir Richard was the ultimate victim of this dreadful plot. By killing King Richard's alter ego, the criminal made him a martyr, not a murderer. Of course I cannot agree that any of us would be capable of such atrocities, under any circumstances, but in a perverse sense Sir Richard's death might suggest a pro-Ricardian bias, rather than the reverse."

"I see what you mean," Jacqueline said, smiling at him. "But I think you are being a little too subtle, Mr. Ellis. However, I had other reasons for believing that the tricks were not the work of a monomaniac. Although they imitated the deaths of Richard's purported victims, they deviated from the known facts in several ways. The accepted Tudor legend accuses Richard of stabbing Henry the Sixth with a sword or dagger. Yet the trick played on the doctor was meant to imply poison.

"Even more significant was the change in the chronological sequence. It is impossible that the young princes should have been murdered before Lord Hastings was beheaded; the younger boy did not leave sanctuary until after Hastings was dead. Now a monomaniac is usually consistent in his aberration. He will take the most appalling risks in order to stick to his self-determined rules. But our joker attacked Percy before he struck at Philip, who ought to have been the next victim. To me, these deviations suggested expediency rather than madness. It was much easier to slip some substance into the doctor's special food than to lure him away to a spot where he could be safely 'stabbed.' Philip is young and strong—a dangerous man to attack. By appearing to skip him, the comedian put him off guard.

"It was clear that the comedian was a member of the house party. The mysterious figure who lured Frank into the cellar—"

"That's when you began to suspect Frank," Thomas interrupted.

"I didn't suspect him then; I didn't suspect anyone until the pattern of the tricks made it evident that there was need for suspicion. But when I looked back on Frank's 'accident,' I found some grounds for doubt. Anyone in the house could have put on a raincoat and hat. And blows on the head often do induce mild amnesia. But it was singularly convenient for the attacker that Frank should suffer such amnesia. Remember, there were marks on his *face*. At some point he must have confronted his attacker. His injuries could have been self-inflicted; as he himself insisted, they were superficial. Any schoolboy who is lucky enough to suffer from a propensity to nosebleed soon learns how to induce that phenomenon at will. It's useful for getting out of exams and other embarrassing situations.

"The attack on Philip and the appearance of the plaster heads confirmed my suspicions of Frank, but I still didn't know what the point of the whole business could be. It was the reverse of the normal detective-novel situation, where the sleuth must deduce the identity of the criminal after he has committed a crime. I knew the criminal; but I didn't know what crime he planned to commit, or the identity of the victim, if any. So I went at the problem from another angle.

"The jokes were not the only unusual factors in this meeting of the society. There was also the famous letter. It was possible that the letter and the jokes were not connected; but I felt justified in assuming, as a working hypothesis, that one had led to the other.

"Whether the letter was false or genuine, it was valuable. We discussed that angle before." She looked at Strangways, who nodded. "The motive of the criminal joker, in that case, was profit. He meant to steal the letter and hold it for ransom.

"But surely, if that was the case, the jokes defeated the thief's aim. It would have been comparatively simple to sneak up on an unsuspecting Sir Richard while he was gloating over the letter, bang him on the head, and take the prize. The preliminary jokes made all of us, especially Sir Richard, wary and suspicious.

"The letter might have instigated the jokes in another way. If the criminal was a fanatical anti-Ricardian, he might wish to destroy evidence favorable to Richard. I know it seems incredible that anyone would go to such lengths for such a trivial purpose, but believe me, scholars are capable of insanities much more peculiar than that one. However, it was virtually certain that the joker was a member of the house party, and the only guest who opposed Richard was Mr. Strangways."

"Well?" Thomas said belligerently. "Why not Strangways?"

The maligned American grinned broadly. Jacqueline shook her head.

"Mr. Strangways is perfectly capable of playing nasty tricks," she said sweetly. "But he is not stupid. If he had wanted to steal the letter, he would not have played the tricks, for he would have seen the objection I raised in the first case. He certainly is too intelligent to continue a career of crime after being unmasked. If the letter disappeared, he would be the prime suspect.

"No; I could not believe that the tricks were perpetrated by a criminal who wanted to steal the letter, for whatever reason. They were senseless. A thief would have a better chance of success without them.

"I felt from the first that the appearance of the letter was suspiciously fortuitous. Suppose the letter was a forgery. What did it accomplish? First, it brought the members of the committee here, into a setting appropriate for the staging of the jokes. Then letter and jokes might both be elements in a complex plot.

"What plot? What was its aim, and what was its planned culmination? One answer—to discredit Richard and Ricardians. A fake letter and a series of embarrassing incidents would certainly do that. But again we return to the fact that only a confirmed anti-Ricardian would plan such strategy, and that the joker had to be a member of the house party.''

Thomas cleared his throat. Jacqueline followed his glance. This time she gave the grinning Strangways a faint smile.

"You forget, Thomas, that by this time I was reasonably certain of the criminal's identity. Moreover, Mr. Strangways is the only guest who had no control over the arrangements for the meeting. The complexity of the jokes meant that they had to be planned well in advance. It wouldn't be hard for a member of the committee to unobtrusively manipulate his fellow members into accepting the idea of costumes and role playing; other amateur historical societies do it all the time. The comedian had to know, not only what roles you were playing, but your personal idiosyncrasies. I couldn't imagine an outsider managing the business.

"So," Jacqueline continued, "I was left, finally, with a possibility that had haunted my low cynical mind from the first—that the jokes were misdirection, planned to distract witnesses from an act of violence against one of the persons here.

"I loved the idea," Jacqueline said dreamily. "It was beautiful. You are all familiar with the classic mystery-novel ploy of a series of murders designed to conceal the motive for one particular killing. But really, it is not a very practical method of committing a crime. As soon as the first murder occurs. . . ."

She indicated the constable at the door, who promptly blushed —and with reason, for he had forgotten official dignity as he got interested in her lecture, and was leaning over the back of the nearest chair.

"As soon as a murder is committed, the police are called in," Jacqueline said. "The whole sophisticated apparatus of crime detection comes into play. Not even a madman would keep on committing murders when the house is swarming with police. If our criminal planned to kill, he couldn't hope to conceal his crime among a series of killings; the first murder would be the last. But he could carry out a series of nonfatal jokes and be sure, knowing his fellow Ricardians as he did, that official interference would not be tolerated so long as no one was seriously hurt. When someone was hurt or killed, the police would be summoned and the jokes would end; but the fatality would seem to be only a joke gone wrong, one of a series of baffling incidents rather than a cold-blooded murder. I knew then that the crime would be the last of the jokes—"

"Wait a minute," Strangways said. "Your theory, if I may say so, has so many holes, it leaks like a colander. To begin with, Philip was seriously hurt. If he had insisted on calling the police. . . ."

Jacqueline inspected him coldly over the rims of her glasses. "But he wouldn't do that," she said. "Would you, Philip?"

"No," the actor said wryly. "Apparently my little foibles are no secret."

"Frank didn't mean to hit you so hard," Jacqueline said consolingly. "He got carried away. You must admit you had been irritating."

"So you decided that the murder—if there was to be a murder —would be the last of the jokes," Strangways said. "So what? You couldn't know ahead of time where the comedian meant to stop."

"It is true that that particular deduction told me very little," Jacqueline said with freezing dignity. "But I had already decided that Sir Richard might be the intended victim. For in a sense, Richard the Third was the last of this cast of characters to die a violent death. The others all survived into the next act. Shakespeare never wrote that play."

Strangways muttered something that sounded like "fanciful." But he didn't say it aloud, and Jacqueline did not take up the gauntlet.

"Now I'm going to anticipate Thomas's objection," she said briskly. "I can see it smoldering in his eagle eye. 'The best-laid plans of murderers go oft a-gley'—whatever that means. Perhaps one of the jokes was meant to be a fatal one, but it misfired. Is that what you were thinking, Thomas?"

"Forget it. I can see the counterarguments. The comedian had plenty of time to correct a mistake. He must have known I was still breathing when he put me in the barrel. Percy had a mild dose of the drug, and Rawdon's emetic couldn't possibly kill him. Furthermore, the plaster heads show that the joker had planned to continue through the 'deaths' of Hastings and Buckingham. He wouldn't have bothered with the heads if he planned to commit a murder before that. Murder would mean the police, and a thorough search of the house and grounds."

"It seems to me you are still on shaky ground," Strangways said. "You have postulated a murder—on somewhat vague evidence—and decided that none of the victims of the jokes was the potential murderee. That still leaves a number of possibilities—all the women, Mr. Ellis—and me."

"Oh, I considered you," Jacqueline murmured. "You'd be a splendid murderee."

"Hmmm. Then—"

"No one knew your identity until Saturday night," Jacqueline pointed out, in the mildest of voices. "How could anyone plan to kill you when they didn't know you would be here?"

Strangways did not reply.

"Of course the others were potential victims. But—Frank as the villain and Sir Richard as the victim—why, the motive practically hit me in the face. Not paranoia or historical mania, but two of the most comprehensible, commonplace motives for murder. Lust," said Jacqueline with relish. "Lust and greed.

"As Thomas has reiterated, Sir Richard is an extremely rich man. The Ponsonby-Joneses are his only relatives. Who else would inherit his fortune? And who would know the contents of his will better than a member of the firm of solicitors Sir Richard employs?

"True, for all I knew, Sir Richard might have left his millions to animal shelters, or to a foundation perpetuating the memory of King Richard the Third. He doesn't think much of young Percy. But his kindness and patience toward Percy's mother are manifest. He wouldn't leave her in need after his death. His feelings for Liz—"

Jacqueline paused, glancing at the girl. Liz rose.

"You'll be able to discuss it more comfortably if I'm not here," she said. "No, it's quite all right; I was about to go in any case. I'm going to Richard."

She walked slowly to the door and went out.

Thomas was struck rather painfully by the change in the girl. Even in old-fashioned robes she had been alert and alive, vibrant with health. The events of the past days might explain some of her pallor and her new air of fragility; but Thomas felt as if a ghost had passed. When the door closed, he turned to Jacqueline.

"Is she in love with Weldon, or with the reincarnation of Richard the Third? I'm not sure I like this."

"I'm sure I don't like it," Philip murmured. "But there's nothing I can do about it. Never mind, Thomas; they will always be united by their mutual passion for a dead man."

The rector made a little sound of distress.

"They'll do as well as most couples," Kent said callously. "Ridiculous business, marriage . . . at least young Frank had wits enough to fall in love with a girl who had expectations."

"Oh, he's a practical fellow," Jacqueline agreed. "He loves her —if you can call it love—but I'm sure her attractions were not lessened by Frank's discovery that Liz would inherit a sizable fortune. I don't suppose he thought of murder immediately. As Liz's husband he could expect to profit, financially and professionally, from Sir Richard's fondness for the girl.

"Then, at your last meeting, he realized that fondness was not the right word. The villagers are gossiping now about Sir Richard and Liz. Frank could hardly have missed seeing how Sir Richard felt, or the fact that Liz was beginning to reciprocate. He realized that he stood to lose, not only the girl he wanted, but the money he hoped to get with her.

"Liz and Sir Richard would have come to an understanding much earlier if it had not been for Sir Richard's modesty and the determined pushing of Liz's mother. Liz would violently resent her mother's attempts to promote a 'good' marriage. Oh, yes," she added, smiling at Thomas. "You thought Mrs. P.-J. was after Sir Richard for herself, didn't you? She's stupid, but she's not that stupid. Her hostility toward Lady Isobel—who was unfortunately naive enough to think she had a chance with Sir Richard— was on Liz's behalf. My dear man, the signs were plain to see! Do you remember our discussion about the dress Elizabeth of York wore to the Christmas party? Women know the importance of clothes. Mrs. Ponsonby-Jones supplies her daughter's wardrobe. And the costumes Liz wore were lovely, not cheap, ill-fitting things from a costumer's stock, but made for her out of expensive fabric, by her mother.

"Liz is Sir Richard's second cousin once removed, or something of the sort; the relationship is not close enough to matter. Mrs. P.-J. must have been ecstatic when she realized Sir Richard loved her daughter. Even if she had approved of Frank, she would have dumped him ruthlessly in favor of a match with a titled millionaire. What mum wouldn't? And maybe there is something to the baloney about maternal instinct. There are a few unsavory stories about young Frank's habits with money. . . .''

Thomas glanced at Philip. The actor didn't look at him; he continued to watch Jacqueline, with an amused smile on his long mobile lips.

"When Frank realized the position, he must have considered alternatives," Jacqueline continued. "He might have talked Liz into a hasty marriage. But that wouldn't solve his problem. Marriages are easily dissolved these days. Sir Richard might marry and produce children. . . . Frank saw there was only one sure way of getting the two things he wanted—Liz and a fortune. The death of Sir Richard seemed a ludicrously easy solution.

"As a lawyer, Frank knew quite well that if Sir Richard died by violence, the first people the police would investigate were Sir Richard's heirs. The murder had to be very carefully planned. As the enthusiastic Ricardian debate raged around him, Frank began to see the outlines of his plot.

"He forged the famous letter. It is not as difficult as you might suppose to produce a convincing fake. Genuine parchment can be obtained from specialty shops, and the method of aging it is described in several books. I can give you the references if you—"

"Never mind," Thomas said resignedly. "I believe you."

"As for the content of the letter, that was equally simple. Buck gives a summary of it in his book, and we have genuine letters of the period, including letters written by Richard himself. These provided Frank with models for the correct phrasing, spelling, and so on. He found everything he needed right here, in Sir Richard's library, including technical volumes of manuscript authentication, and a copy of the rare Kennett *History of England,* which includes Buck's work. As Liz's fiancé and a loyal Ricardian, Frank could work in the library whenever he liked.

"Remember that the letter was never intended to pass expert scrutiny. In this case Sir Richard was not an expert; his critical sense was dulled by his desire to believe in the letter, and the sentences Frank added exculpating Richard—probably on a second sheet of parchment, so that Weldon would believe it had been overlooked by Buck—made Weldon's acceptance virtually certain. Frank never meant an outsider to see the letter. It would be destroyed at the time of the murder, not only to eliminate any possibility of its being traced back to him, but also to confuse the motive."

"Good Lord," Thomas said, starting up. "It's a wonder Frank didn't attack you, Jacqueline. If I had realized—"

"I was never in any danger." Jacqueline sounded a little regretful. "Frank couldn't spoil the 'murders of Richard the Third' by attacking someone who wasn't on the list. Besides, Sir Richard knew from the start that I was no expert, and Lady Isobel made sure everyone else knew it. Where is she, by the way?"

"Resting," said the rector. "She was totally prostrated, poor lady, by the excitement."

"Prostrated with frustration," Kent corrected, with an unpleasant laugh. "She's lost her quarry. By this time she is probably drunk."

"Never mind her," Thomas said. "Go on, Jacqueline."

"Frank dispatched the letter," Jacqueline said. "Not to Sir Richard—that would have been too obvious—but to Mr. Ellis. I suppose he invented some tale of noble families brought down in the world, of theft and mild skullduggery, in order to explain his desire for anonymity. . . ."

Mr. Ellis looked down at his folded hands. "I was culpable. And gullible. I cannot excuse myself; I have allowed a worldly interest to assume monstrous proportions. I wanted so much to believe. . . ."

"You mustn't blame yourself," Jacqueline said, with the gentleness she always showed to the little man. "Whatever your reservations, you had to show the letter to Sir Richard; you had no choice. You tried to stop the show when it started to turn into a circus. . . .

"Of course Frank sent the letter in order to bring about an early meeting of the executive board. He didn't dare wait until October; Liz was showing signs of restlessness. He planned to commit the crime during a weekend house party, when the place was teeming with eccentric Ricardians. He did not expect that Sir Richard would fall completely for the forged letter and invite the press to the meeting, but he saw that this development could be useful. More confusion, more people wandering around, more suspects.

"The jokes were designed for the same purpose—confusion. But they served several other purposes. The whole setup suggested a joker with a mania about Richard the Third. Sir Richard's death, which horribly simulated the bloody end of his prototype, was supposed to be only a joke gone wrong. Thus it would appear to be one of a series, and the police would look for a monomaniac, not a killer who profited by Sir Richard's death. And if the worst happened and Frank was caught, the jokes gave him several choices of defense. It would be hard to prove premeditated murder. Insanity, accident—this poor young chap, troubled by his fiancée's sick passion for a dead man. . . .

"I'm sure all this was in Frank's mind, but of course he didn't mean to be caught. The bizarre nature of the jokes suggested Percy as the joker. Adolescence is an unstable period, and adolescent killers commit crimes for the most trivial reasons. That was why I was sure no attempt would be made on Sir Richard today until Percy was free. It took him longer than Frank had anticipated. He got so impatient he went upstairs and shouted directions at the boy."

"Right under my nose," Thomas said disgustedly.

"If you hadn't been with him, he might have unlocked the door," Jacqueline consoled him. "Percy would have gotten out eventually, and Frank took advantage of his appearance at the window. He knew Sir Richard would immediately rush to check on the safety of his precious letter."

"What if Percy hadn't shown himself?"

"Frank would have thought of some other method of distraction. All he had to do was point and shout, 'My God, there's Percy,' or 'I see Strangways in the garden.' The important thing was that Percy should be out, on the loose, and unable to prove an alibi. I kept Mrs. P.-J. under surveillance, just in case, but I didn't think Frank would bother with her. He had altered the correct sequence before, with Percy and Philip."

"You had it all figured out," Thomas said. "My God, yes—that Gilbert and Sullivan thing you were humming."

Jacqueline raised her voice in song.

> " 'When I, young friends, was called to the bar,
> I'd an appetite fresh and hearty,
> I was, as all young barristers are,
> An impecunious party.'

"I was trying to give you a hint, and you made a nasty remark about my perfectly normal appetite," she added severely. "You were very dim, Thomas."

"I was obsessed by my own theory," Thomas groaned. "I was sure Sir Richard had slipped a cog, and that he meant to kill Frank. I don't know about you, Jacqueline, but when we first saw Frank flat on his face in the wine cellar, I was sure he was dead. That was the one 'joke' that could have gone wrong. And Frank was Edward of Lancaster, the first husband of the girl King Richard loved, as well as the fiancé of the girl Sir Richard loved. . . ."

"That's a good example of pseudopsychological Ricardian mishmash," Jacqueline said critically. "Really, Thomas, you ought to know better. The brilliant, insane murderers are in books. In real life people kill for practical reasons."

"Why didn't you tell me?" Thomas shouted. "Just tell me! You let the thing go on—you knew Weldon was in danger—"

"I'll never criticize detective stories again," Jacqueline said. "It was impossible to tell you, Thomas, with everyone wandering around the room. I couldn't hiss, 'Frank is the comedian and he's planning to murder Sir Richard,' now could I? You would have thought I was crazy. You wanted to think I was crazy. You wouldn't have believed me without a long, detailed buildup such as the one I've just given you. And. . . ."

Her voice changed, and so did her expression. Watching the still, austere face, Thomas felt a chill. He had never seen this facet of Jacqueline's personality before.

"I had decided, by then, that it was necessary to let him proceed," she said quietly. "I chickened out, at first, and tried to talk Sir Richard into breaking up the house party. That would have eliminated the immediate danger; but if Frank meant to kill, he would have tried again. There was no proof. The only way to ensure Sir Richard's safety was to let Frank go ahead and catch him in the act.''

"So you risked Weldon's life.''

"I had to. The man who will kill for money may kill again. If I let Frank get away this time, I was risking not only Sir Richard's life, but Liz's as well—and God knows how many other lives that might one day stand between Frank and what he wanted. I hoped to stop Frank before he killed; but I was sure of convicting him whether he succeeded or failed. It was, if you like, a ruthless act. But the alternative was worse.''

The rector was the first to speak.

"It was not ruthless,'' he said. "But it was—if you will forgive me—arrogant. 'Vengeance is mine. . . .' ''

"I'm not justifying my decision,'' Jacqueline said. "I'm not such a hypocrite as that. I act as I must—and I pay for my mistakes, Mr. Ellis.''

"We all pay,'' Strangways said. "But few of us have the guts, or the naked honesty, to eschew pious rationalizations.''

Jacqueline looked at him. Thomas didn't like the look; it was almost kindly. He coughed. Jacqueline glanced at him, and then reached down into her purse. Thomas watched, fascinated. What would emerge from the unknown depths now?

A paperweight emerged. Shaped like a replica of Barnard Castle, it was made of bronze and measured approximately eight inches square.

"Goodness, that's heavy,'' Jacqueline said, putting the object back on the table where it normally stood.

"I wouldn't have thought you'd need that,'' said Thomas. "Your purse must weigh twenty pounds in its normal state.''

"It's a very effective weapon,'' Jacqueline said calmly. "I prowl the campus by night, hoping to be attacked by muggers.''

II

Monday morning is supposed to be a dismal time, but on this particular Monday, Thomas's mood was almost cloudless. The sun was shining, which in England is enough to make anyone euphoric. Sir Richard was coming along well, and his near brush with death had won him the girl he loved. Very romantic.

As for Thomas's own romantic situation. . . .

He hummed tunelessly to himself as he went buoyantly down the stairs. The house party was breaking up that morning; they had stayed the night, having their statements taken and resting up after the excitement of the day. He and Jacqueline hadn't discussed their plans, but he assumed they would travel back to London together.

She was not in the breakfast room, but Wilkes was able to inform Thomas that she had been and gone.

"She and Mr. Strangways went off together," the butler said. "I believe they said something about the library."

Wondering, Thomas went in search.

He could hear the voices through the closed door of the library, which, in view of the solidity of that structure, suggested tones of considerable passion. Opening the door a crack, he listened. He recognized the voice and he knew the subject as well as he knew his own name. It was the two in combination that stupefied him.

"Richard has been cleared of all the other charges. No one seriously believes them. As for the murder of the boys, the weight of the evidence, such as it is, is strongly in his favor. If you could consider it dispassionately. . . ."

"Now wait a minute." Strangways sounded a little desperate. "Whether Richard murdered the boys or not, he was morally guilty. By deposing young Edward the Fifth, he essentially signed the kid's death warrant. He—"

"Are you a historian or an early Church father?" Jacqueline inquired disagreeably. "You are not concerned with ethical questions, but with evidence. Maybe the word isn't familiar to you—"

"You have a tongue like an adder," Strangways shouted.

The sentiment seemed well expressed. Thomas opened the door.

Jacqueline and Strangways were standing at opposite ends of the room, Jacqueline behind Weldon's desk and Strangways near the long library table. Desk and table were covered with books, most of them open. Jacqueline's hair had been twisted back in a bun, but it was starting to disintegrate; agitated tendrils curled over her ears. Her glasses hung from the tip of her nose. Strangways, attired for travel in the proper English costume of suit, tie, and vest, had wrenched open the collar of his shirt. His navy-blue tie was under one ear.

Neither of them paid the slightest attention to Thomas.

"The hypothesis of Richard's innocence explains every anomaly in the case," Jacqueline said. "It is the only hypothesis that does so."

"The fact that the boys weren't seen again. . . ."

"They were seen, or at least heard from. But you ignore that evidence, because it doesn't fit in with your fat theories. Oh, I understand," Jacqueline said. Her voice was as smooth as cream and as deadly as acid. "You started out being a logical observer. You believed the facts. Then the historical establishment got hold of you. It's hard to fight men like Kendall and Myers and—"

"It is not," Strangways bellowed.

"What evidence?" Thomas asked, advancing into the room.

Jacqueline didn't look at him, but she answered his question because it happened to suit her purpose.

"The household accounts. The reference to the Lord Bastard, in 1485, must refer to young Edward. That's what I mean about cheating; you say the entry refers to Richard's bastard son, who was never in any other place referred to as a lord, because you can't admit that Edward the Fifth was still alive. If you had not begun with the assumption that he was dead, you would never question the meaning of that entry. You are tailoring facts to fit a theory, not basing a theory on known facts."

Strangways' mouth opened and closed like that of a fish gasping for water. He was too furious to talk. Jacqueline proceeded.

"Another entry whose significance no one seems to have seen is the list of fancy clothes ordered by Richard for 'Lord Edward.' Edward was alive then, and getting expensive gifts from his uncle —and those gifts included equipment for horses.

"Was the boy going to practice equestrian exercises in the Tower of London? The inference is plain. Richard was planning to move the boys out of London, no doubt to one of his castles in the north, where the population was loyal to him. We know that certain children of the royal household were at Sheriff Hutton in

1485—but all you historians"—the word was an epithet—"insist that the princes were not among them because Sir Thomas More says the princes were dead by then! If that is scholarship, then give me ESP!"

Her glasses fell off the end of her nose.

"Jacqueline!" Thomas exclaimed. "Darling!"

He rushed across the room and flung his arms around her.

"Hello, Thomas," Jacqueline said. "Now, then, James, there is another point you—"

"You're converted," Thomas said. He held her at arms' length, his hands on her shoulders, and beamed at her. "You're one of us. By God, if nothing else had happened this weekend. . . ."

Jacqueline squinted at him. The effect was rather charming.

"My glasses," she said. "I don't have my glasses on."

"Here they are." Thomas bent and picked them up. "Let's go, love. There's a train at eleven. Get packed. I'll ask Wilkes to send the car around—"

"Oh," Jacqueline said. "I am packed, Thomas. But I'm afraid I can't go to London with you. James and I are going to York for a few days."

"James—and—you—"

"Purely Ricardian, old boy," said Strangways. Thomas turned to stare at him in outraged disbelief. Strangways winked.

"There's the car, Jacqueline," he said, straightening his tie. "Let's be off."

Thomas stood in silence. Strangways strolled across the room, exuding self-satisfaction. He took Jacqueline's arm and led her to the door.

Jacqueline glanced back. "I'll see you in London on Thursday, Thomas," she said, and was gone.

Thomas stood unmoving. Car doors slammed and the faint sound of voices came to him through the open windows. The soft, expensive purr of the Rolls engine moved away into the distance.

The voices had not been mellifluous.

Gradually, unpredictably, a malicious smile transformed Thomas's face.

Purely Ricardian. Strangways had spoken in jest, but Thomas

had a feeling the joke was on Strangways. Never before had he seen Jacqueline's glasses actually fall from her nose. He knew her well; she had a memory like an elephant and a passion for contrived revenge that would have suited a Borgia. He could see Strangways being whipped around York from Micklegate to the Minster, viewing the remaining memories of Richard the Third and reeling under the remorseless lash of Jacqueline's voice.

A sigh of virtuous satisfaction escaped Thomas's lips, and he went upstairs to pack.

Thursday in London, Jacqueline had said. Thomas had high hopes for Thursday.

Die
for
Love

To Louise and Jim
and their four-footed friends

CHAPTER ONE

When Blaze awoke she found herself lying on a silken soft surface amid the seductive scent of strange perfumes. A cool night breeze—the air of the desert, exotic and amorous—stroked her naked flesh. Naked? A soft cry escaped her voluptuous lips as she realized the truth. Where were her clothes? What unknown hands had stripped them from her helpless body? Where was she?

"Lamps carved of alabaster gave enough light to answer the last question. Overhead a silken canopy shielded her from the night sky, a patch of which, glittering with stars, was visible through the open flap of the tent. Scarcely had she realized this when the stars were blotted out by a dark form. Stooping, he entered the tent, and Blaze's white hands fluttered, trying in vain to conceal her softness. It was the Arab who had stared at her so boldly in the bazaar. Intense blue eyes studied her over the folds of the kaffiyeh that hid the lower part of his face. 'You are no Arab,' Blaze gasped. 'I know those eyes—you are—you are—'

" 'Your husband.' The kaffiyeh fell away; it was indeed the face of Lance, Earl of Deptford, his chiseled lips curved in a mocking smile. 'Come to claim the rights you have so long denied me, my

love. The disguise disturbs you? Off with it, then.' And he flung
the robe aside.

"Blaze's eyes moved from the bronzed chest, seamed with the
white scars of a hundred duels, to the narrow waist and flat,
muscled abdomen, down to. . . ."

Jacqueline's eyes bulged. "My God," she said aloud. "It's *The
Lustful Turk.*"

"It is?"

Jacqueline looked up from the pages of *Slave of Lust.* The stewardess stood beside her, trying to read over her shoulder. Obligingly she held the book up so the girl could see better.

The young woman's eyes lit up. "It's the new Valerie Vanderbilt! I haven't read that one yet. But I just love her books, don't
you?"

Jacqueline inspected the cover of the paperback. Blaze ("the
streak of silver in the midnight blackness of her flowing locks had
given her her name") reclined on silken coverlets, her softness
discreetly veiled by the broad bronzed body of the Earl of Deptford. The title and the name of the author were printed in brilliant scarlet letters.

"Valerie Vanderbilt," Jacqueline repeated. "I must admit this
is the first of her books I have read."

"She's divine." The stewardess sighed voluptuously. "They say
she's really a countess or something, but she doesn't use her title
because her noble family has disowned her on account of she's
had so many love affairs. This one is about a Turk?"

"You misunderstood my reference," said Jacqueline. She
glanced at the cart, with its rows of bottles and glasses, whose
progress along the aisle of the plane had been interrupted by the
stewardess's literary interests. "Are you by any chance selling
drinks? I'll have Scotch. No. I'll have a double."

It was an unseemly hour for alcohol—barely eight A.M.—but as
the airlines had learned to their profit, some passengers resorted
to liquor in an effort to dull their fear of flying. Jacqueline was
not afraid of flying. What she wanted to dull were her critical
faculties.

Her reminder of duties unfulfilled was reinforced by a chorus
of requests from nervous customers nearby. Murmuring an apology, the attendant filled Jacqueline's order. When she gave

Jacqueline the glass, a pair of miniature bottles, and a small package of petrified peanuts, Jacqueline said, "You can have this when I'm finished, if you like."

"Really? Oh, that's really nice! But you won't finish it before we get to New York."

"Oh yes, I will."

"Well, that is really nice of you. Books are so expensive. I read four or five of them a week, and that really adds up, even though my friends and I exchange when we—"

A wild-eyed businessman in the seat ahead leaned out into the aisle, waving a five-dollar bill and babbling incoherently.

"Yes, sir, right away." With a smile at Jacqueline, the girl moved on.

Jacqueline refreshed herself copiously but decided she still wasn't prepared to return to the perfumed canopied tent. I should have ordered three drinks, she thought. At least I can be sure of getting the attendant's services from now on. Four or five of these books a week? If all the examples of the genre resembled *Slave of Lust,* it was a wonder the hard-core readers could talk at all, much less frame a coherent English sentence.

She turned her gaze to the window. There was nothing to be seen except an undulating blanket of gray cloud. It had been raining when she left Nebraska. It had rained in Nebraska every day for the past two weeks. The farmers were tearing their hair and the local papers carried dire predictions of crop failures— rotting corn, mildewed hay—higher prices, and general despair. Jacqueline had lived in Nebraska for three years, and in her experience the farmers were always complaining and food prices were always going up. It was either too hot or too cold, too wet or too dry. She had no great opinion of Nebraska or the agricultural community, and in this particular spring she had had far too much rain to suit her. It was one of the factors that had prompted her passionate outcry the previous Sunday, as she stood at the window of her apartment watching raindrops pelt the puddles on the balcony.

"I've got to get out of this backwater before I lose my mind!"

"Backwater is not inappropriate," her friend replied, putting his stockinged feet on a hassock and reaching for his glass. "Where do you want to go?"

"A city." Jacqueline gestured dramatically at the window. Beyond the red brick college buildings, empty fields stretched endlessly to the horizon. "Any city. Preferably one where it isn't raining."

"Cairo would seem to be your best bet. Or Rome."

"I can't afford to go to Europe."

Her companion, Professor James Whittier, head of the English Department at Coldwater College, watched her with a faintly malicious smile. Her tall, upright figure was as slim as that of a woman half her age—not that James had ever been officially informed of that number, but since she had two adult children he knew she must be over forty. Her thick auburn hair had not a touch of gray, and James, who was well acquainted with Jacqueline's hair and with the products women use to conceal that particular sign of aging, would have sworn she employed none of them. She was wearing a hostess gown in glowing peacock colors, green shading to aquamarine, azure and cobalt, with which he was equally well acquainted, and the relative age of this garment, coupled with her last statement, roused his curiosity.

"I thought you were going abroad this summer."

"So did I."

"What happened?"

Jacqueline swung around to face him and glowered at him over the tops of her glasses. The fact that she made no effort to restore them to their proper place on the bridge of her nose was a bad sign. Jacqueline's glasses were a barometer of her feelings. Slippage indicated strong emotion, often of a negative variety.

"None of your business, James. You're the nosiest man I've ever met! Do you know what your students call you?"

"I know what the female students call me," James said, passing a complacent hand over his waving white locks and smiling his famous crooked smile.

"Don't waste that crooked smile on me," Jacqueline snapped. "Mr. Buttinsky. . . . No, I think my favorite is Granny Jimmy."

"Granny, is it? Come here and let me show you—"

"I'm not in the mood."

"Hmmm." James decided this was not the time to remind Jacqueline of the nicknames the students had invented for her. She thought of herself as a detached, ironic observer of life. The fact was that she was just as inquisitive as James and even more inclined to interfere in other people's business, when she felt her advice and assistance would improve matters—and she almost always felt they would. However, she believed wholeheartedly in her self-image and would have been outraged at any suggestion that it was inaccurate.

It would also be inadvisable, James knew, to ask any more questions about Jacqueline's change of plan for the summer. She must have had financial reverses. He wouldn't get anything out of her; she was maddeningly tight-lipped about her personal affairs. Almost unfeminine, James thought resentfully. He'd have to find out some other way.

"We could go to New Orleans for a few days," he suggested. "Or San Francisco."

"It always rains in San Francisco. I'm going to New York."

"I?"

"I."

"So it's come to this," James mourned. "The first crack in the wall of love. The first wilted flower in the bouquet. The first. . . ."

Additional metaphors failed him. He picked up his glass and drank.

Jacqueline sat down in the chair opposite his, nudged his feet off the hassock, and put her own in their place. "The first sour grape in the fruit salad of togetherness."

James knew he was not the first man in Jacqueline's life; he wasn't even sure he was the only man in her life. Their affair had been conducted with the discretion demanded by the university, whose midwestern trustees still had a pathetic faith in the traditions of a vanished era. Ostensibly he and Jacqueline were co-authoring a textbook. The briefcase James carried whenever he went to her apartment brought nudges and knowing grins from his colleagues and pointed comments from the students, who were less inhibited. But those who laughed would have been surprised to learn that the briefcase actually contained three chapters of a textbook. Sometimes he and Jacqueline even worked on it.

Yet the relationship had gotten into a rut, and James knew it. He sat in the same chair he had occupied for the past fourteen

Sundays, in stocking feet and shirt sleeves, with the Sunday papers strewn around and the breakfast dishes still on the table. Presently they would wash the dishes, and then go out to dinner at the Old Redde Barn. All the pleasures of marriage without the attendant inconveniences. James liked the arrangement. Apparently Jacqueline didn't.

She began sorting through a stack of clippings and papers. "I'm going to a writers' conference," she announced.

"Business deduction?"

"Naturally."

"But you aren't a writer."

Jacqueline indicated the briefcase. "We're writing a textbook, aren't we?"

"Slowly," James said. "Very slowly."

"Anyway, I am a librarian. Library, books, writers. . . . Even the fascists at Internal Revenue can follow that connection."

James grinned. Jacqueline's feud with the local IRS office was a campus legend. Once she had tried to deduct her new television set on the grounds that her professional duties required her to watch writers being interviewed on the *Today* show.

"What conference are you attending?" he asked diplomatically.

Jacqueline flourished a newspaper clipping. "The Historical Romance Writers of the World. It's the only one I could find. The ABA meetings were last month, and the ALA is meeting in Birmingham. I wouldn't be caught dead in Birmingham."

"The Historical Romance Writers," James repeated. "Ah. I see. . . . Have you read any historical romances lately?"

"Not lately, no. I loved them when I was young. *The Prisoner of Zenda, Gone with the Wind, Forever Amber.*"

"Ah. *Forever Amber.*"

"It's not a bad book," Jacqueline said.

"No."

"What's the matter?" Jacqueline looked at him suspiciously. "You're smirking, James. I know that smirk."

"I'm not sure the IRS will buy it, that's all. University libraries don't stock many novels. Especially romantic novels."

"Then I'll have to write one," Jacqueline said. "Actually, that's not a bad idea. Someone told me they are selling very well these days."

"Oh, they are. They certainly are. . . . Well, that sounds like an excellent idea. Let's see; two weeks in New York, back here by the Fourth of July; you should have a manuscript finished before Labor Day."

"Your classroom wit is wasted on me," Jacqueline said coldly. "I'm well aware of the fact that writing a book is not the easy job laymen believe it is. But with all due modesty. . . ."

"I'm sure you could do it." James studied her for a moment, then nodded. "Yes, you could. When are you leaving?"

He drove her to Omaha. On the way they chatted about college business and the weather, but Jacqueline was not deceived by James's amiability. He was still smarting over her refusal to let him accompany her. Just like a man, she told herself. Their egos were so fragile, they took everything personally.

James made no reference to his hurt feelings, but demonstrated them by driving so slowly Jacqueline began to fear she would miss her plane. When she remonstrated, he said cheerfully, "Oh, there's plenty of time," and indeed they reached the gate several seconds before the loudspeaker announced the last call for Flight 576. "Told you we'd make it," James said. "Have a good time. Here's a little farewell present."

Jacqueline took the wrapped parcel. "Books? How nice, James."

"You said you hadn't read any historical romances lately. These are two of the hottest sellers—or so I'm told." Chastely James shook her hand. He smiled. It was a broad, evil smile, as overpowering as that of the Cheshire cat. The lower half of his face was swallowed up by it.

And that is how Jacqueline Kirby, assistant head librarian of Coldwater College, B.A., M.A., scholar and self-confessed intellectual snob, found herself in possession of two volumes entitled *Slave of Lust* and *Crimson Bloom of Love.*

II

Contrary to popular opinion, librarians are not prim, unworldly spinsters, isolated from the modern world; nor are university librarians unacquainted with what is loosely termed popular culture. If you prick them they bleed, if you drop in on them unexpectedly you may find them engrossed in a soap opera or a copy of *Playgirl*. It was pure accident that Jacqueline was unfamiliar with the publishing industry's latest and hottest fad. "I don't buy books in supermarkets," she had been heard to say. "I buy grapefruit and toilet paper in supermarkets." In fact, she bought very few books. A librarian doesn't have to buy books, in supermarkets or elsewhere. Books are the one commodity of which librarians have more than enough.

Assisted by libations of spiritous liquids, Jacqueline read on, in growing fascination, unaware of the landscape opening up below as the clouds gradually dissipated or of the wistful glances of the flight attendant who passed from time to time, lusting after *Slave of Lust*. The girl was not far away when Jacqueline closed the cover of *Crimson Bloom of Love*. Catching the hopeful gaze fixed upon her, she smiled, and the stewardess hastened to her side.

"Can I get you anything, ma'am?"

Jacqueline considered the offer. "I guess I can survive without more Scotch. Sit down a minute, if you have the time."

"Oh, I couldn't sit down. We're landing in half an hour."

"I've finished *Slave of Lust*. And this one as well. Would you like them?"

"Oh, thank you. Are you sure you don't—"

"No, I don't," Jacqueline said decidedly.

"I haven't read this one either." The attendant gloated over *Crimson Bloom of Love*. "Valerie Fitzgerald—she's good, but not as good as Valerie Vanderbilt. Of course Valerie Valentine is my all-time favorite. Don't you love her?"

"I don't know her," Jacqueline said, dazed by a superfluity of Valeries.

"Oh, you're in for a treat. She's the greatest. She's going to be guest of honor at the conference. I want to go, so bad, but I've got to work. Maybe I can sneak into Manhattan for one session."

"I'm going," Jacqueline said.

"You are? Lucky you. Oh, but—I didn't think—are you an author? What name do you write under?"

"I haven't had anything published yet," Jacqueline said. "I'm planning to call myself Valerie von Hentzau."

"That's a good name."

"I thought so."

"You look like an author," the young woman assured her. "I mean, you look like you could be glamorous if you—I mean—"

"I write for an older readership," Jacqueline said seriously, as the girl blushed and stammered. "Some of us still remember the love affairs of bygone days; it is my aim and my ambition to recreate those moments for those who are now too decrepit to engage in them."

There was no sensible answer to this, and Jacqueline received none; with a doubtful smile the stewardess retreated, clutching her books to her breast. Jacqueline settled back and reached for her purse. From its cavernous depths she took a copy of *Love in the Ruins,* hoping its astringent style would cleanse her palate of a surfeit of lust. Yet there was an anticipatory gleam in her eye as she heard the pilot announce their imminent landing. The conference promised to be a source of utter delight. She could hardly wait.

III

As the airport bus jostled through the thickening traffic toward the city, Jacqueline looked out the window with fond nostalgia. It had been three years since she left the East Coast for the pastoral charm of America's heartland. There had been good and sufficient reasons for her decision—a chance to succeed the amiably senile head librarian at Coldwater (who was still hanging in there, in defiance of all predictions); the high cost of food and housing in the eastern United States; and the proximity of Jacqueline's children, now adult and theoretically independent, but inclined to inquire too often and too solicitously into dear old mum's habits, finances, love life and refrigerator. They visited, almost always accompanied by members of the opposite sex, and Jacqueline had begun to detect ominous portents of future grandmotherhood. When they materialized, as they surely would in time, she planned to be a thousand miles away. She had no violent objection to the state itself or to babies in general; nevertheless, distance seemed a sensible precaution, and it would have been too flagrantly insulting if she waited until the condition was actually upon her before running away. Now, however, she felt she was returning to her spiritual home.

The bus disgorged most of its passengers at Grand Central Station. Drawing a breath compounded equally of satisfaction and carbon monoxide, Jacqueline lifted her suitcase and began walking. It was almost noon, and she knew the futility of trying to get a cab at that hour. Besides, her hotel was at Fifty-third, only a fifteen-minute walk.

By the time she reached Fifth, she had fallen back into the old city-dweller's stride—weaving expertly through breaks in the crowd, darting across streets against the light whenever traffic halted. Needless to say, this skill necessitates total concentration, and is one way of distinguishing the Manhattanites from the tourists. The latter, buffeted and bewildered, gravitate toward the store fronts, where they are shielded on one side at least from the madding crowds. Jacqueline was tempted by the display windows, especially those of the bookstores; Coldwater's single shopping mall contained no comparable charms. But she resisted. She had barely time to check in and change before attending the opening event of the conference—a formal luncheon at which the "mystery guest of honor" would be introduced.

She had not been able to get a room at the Harrison Hotel, where the conference was being held, but hers was right across the street. Furthermore, it offered a "vacation special" rate at a price considerably less than was usual. The room was standard American motel in decor and arrangement: two "king-sized" beds, shabby wall-to-wall carpeting, and a bedside lamp immovably fixed in a spot that rendered reading in bed an exercise in eyestrain. The view from the thirty-fifth floor took in the greenery of Central Park and the spires of the skyscrapers bordering it. The park left Jacqueline unmoved; she was surfeited with trees; but she spared a few moments to gloat over the tall buildings and the wonders they contained—wonders of which she had been long deprived. Saks and Altman's and Lord and Taylor—not that she could afford to buy clothes at those establishments, or at any of the delightful specialty shops on Park and Lexington, but even window-shopping would be a pleasure after the cut-rate boutiques of Coldwater Mall. The museums—the Guggenheim, the Cloisters, the Metropolitan—the Met's new Egyptian galleries were open, as well as the American Wing, and there was an exhibit at the Costume Institute she wanted to see. But man cannot live on museums alone, and Jacqueline's tastes were eclectic. She would have to consult friends in the city about the new places, nightclubs and cafés and bistros, for fashions in those fields change rapidly and she knew her old hangouts would probably have disappeared. Even that charming gay bar on Seventy-ninth, where she had had so many friends. . . .

With a sigh she turned from the window and began unpacking. Halfway through *Slave of Lust* she had begun to suspect that her clothes weren't going to suit the mood of the conference. There wasn't a ruffle or a diaphanous blouse in her suitcase—nor in her closet at home, for that matter. She would have to see what she could do about the problem later; for the moment, a tailored linen suit must suffice. She left the top two buttons of her blouse unfastened, arranged her hair in romantic coils and clusters, and picked up her purse.

The last act wasn't as easy as it sounds. Though Jacqueline asserted that her purses were no bigger than the ones some women carried, they were undoubtedly bigger than the ones most women carried. They tended to bulge oddly, and no one, including Jacqueline, was ever entirely certain what was inside them. The student body at C.C. had regarded Jacqueline's purses with superstitious awe since the day of the graduation exercises, when she had produced an umbrella, a raincoat, and a pair of rainboots from her bag. This would not have been so surprising in itself, but for the fact that the weather forecast had promised clear skies with no chance of precipitation. The ceremonies were outside, and when the clouds opened up, Jacqueline was the only participant who wasn't drenched.

Aside from its other advantages, the purse could serve as a defensive weapon or a form of battering ram if circumstances required. Jacqueline used it in the latter capacity when she emerged from the hotel into a crowd that filled the sidewalk.

Traffic on Sixth Avenue was backed up for blocks, and the noise level was even higher than usual for Manhattan at midday.

The light at the corner turned green as Jacqueline reached that point, and the frustrated drivers increased the volume of their complaints. Horns blared, voices rose in passionate invective. A taxi nudged the bumper of the car ahead; the driver of the latter vehicle, an elderly woman with lovely white hair, put a distorted face out the window and commented forcibly. Her words were inaudible to Jacqueline, but apparently not to the taxi driver, who replied in kind, and in Spanish. Jacqueline made mental note of several words she had not heard before. The driver was blessed with a voice of penetrating shrillness.

The problem seemed to be the cross street. The intersection was blocked by two vehicles of distinctly unusual appearance. Both were open convertibles, of a vintage no longer commonly seen on American highways. Both were pink—bright shocking pink.

Jacqueline could see only the hood of the second car, but she had a good view of the first and its occupants. The driver was obviously a native New Yorker; unperturbed by the complaints hurled at him, he stared straight ahead, bored and detached. The passengers were not so blasé. One of the women was visible only as a mop of brassy yellow hair; she had slumped down as far as she could go without actually kneeling on the floor. The other woman was a redhead, of indeterminate age and remarkable plainness. Embarrassment, or sunburn, had turned her face a strange shade of red that clashed horribly with her pink bonnet, pink gown, and pink gloves.

The third person in the car . . . Jacqueline stood on tiptoe so she could see better. At that moment the young man rose, displaying his attire in its full glory: a white shirt open to the navel, with billowing sleeves; tight black trousers; a red satin cummerbund; and a black cape, lined in scarlet. Its sable and red folds flapped as he raised both arms and saluted the audience, which returned his greeting with a decidedly ambiguous howl. Some spectators laughed, some scowled, and all the taxi drivers swore. A voice somewhere in the area of Jacqueline's left elbow let out a gasp and a comment that included the word "hunk."

Jacqueline looked down. When she wore heels she was almost

five feet ten inches tall; the girl who had sighed was a good six inches shorter. Catching Jacqueline's eye, she giggled and shrugged.

"Who is he?" Jacqueline mouthed.

"Who knows? He's gorgeous, though. Must be one of those writers." She gestured at the hotel on the opposite corner.

"Of course," said Jacqueline, enlightened and enraptured. "Rudolph Rassendyll, Zorro, Edmond Dantes . . . romance isn't dead after all."

"Huh?"

"Definitely a hunk," Jacqueline said.

Sunlight glistened on the mat of black hair displayed by the youth's open shirt. The convertible jerked forward. He sat down, more suddenly than he had intended. He was smiling broadly.

Jacqueline decided she had better get moving too. If the occupants of the pink automobiles were the guests of honor at the luncheon, that affair would probably not start on time, but she wanted to get a good seat. She crossed Sixth Avenue without difficulty—nothing vehicular was moving—but before entering the hotel she paused for another look at the procession. It had now edged forward far enough for her to see the second car in line. It was an antique Cadillac convertible, complete with tail fins, and in impeccable condition. Its owner, who probably belonged to the austere and select group of classic car collectors, would have been appalled at its present appearance. It had been decorated like a float in a Thanksgiving parade—or rather, a Valentine's Day parade. From grille to tail fins the vehicle was draped with white cotton lace. A gilded cupid had replaced the original hood ornament. To the side door someone had affixed an insignia, like a coat of arms: paired golden hearts surmounted by a crown and flanked by more gilded cupids.

There were three people in the backseat. One was a balding middle-aged man. His face was as bland and disinterested as those of the drivers. The second was a gray-haired woman who looked like a suburban housewife. The third. . . .

Beauty is, to a great extent, in the eye of the beholder and defined by personal taste. True beauty is rarer than diamonds and more remarkable. Few of the famous lovelies of stage and screen deserve that accolade; makeup, lighting, and, above all, the hypnotic hyperbole of press agents and publicity firms, create a false image that has nothing to do with beauty itself.

The girl in the pink convertible was beautiful. Sitting between the two older people, she looked like a rose in a row of zucchini. She had it all—the bone structure, the coloring, the perfect skin and sculptured features. The hair tumbling over her shoulders and clustering in soft curls around her face was not yellow or blond or fair, but pure red-gold; its strands shone like the finest silk threads. Her face was heart-shaped, curving delicately from rounded cheeks to a small pointed chin. She was wearing a low-cut blouse or dress—Jacqueline could see only the upper part of her body—of pure white, with a soft frill that framed a slender throat, and bared arms as perfect as those of a Greek statue of Aphrodite. But her beauty was not classical; the rose-petal cheeks and rounded curves were more reminiscent of the painted beauties of Boucher and Fragonard.

The parade moved forward another foot. The cries of the onlookers rose to a decibel level ordinarily achieved only by certain punk-rock groups. A red-faced policeman hurled himself into the fray and was swallowed up by the cabdrivers, who had abandoned their vehicles and were advancing on the convertibles. Reluctantly, Jacqueline tore herself away.

A list of scheduled activities posted in the lobby of the hotel directed her to the mezzanine, where registration for the Historical Romance Writers' Conference was taking place. Here Jacqueline found a cloudburst of pink and white, lace and paper hearts, and a few gilt cupids. Across from the registration table, which was draped in pink crepe paper and manned by three hard-eyed females in pink pinafores, was a row of publishers' display booths, with such names as Wax Candle Romances, Long-Ago Love, and Moonlight Love Romance. Moonlight apparently specialized in Valeries; Jacqueline saw several copies of *Slave of Lust* and a pile of books bearing the name the stewardess had mentioned as her favorite—Valerie Valentine.

As she stood admiring the decor, Jacqueline was accosted by a mustachioed man in a three-piece suit who inquired, "You looking for an agent, honey? I represent. . . ."

Jacqueline took his card. After all, one never knew.

Another booth, some distance from those of the publishers,

had the rickety homemade look of a display at a high school craft fair. Ruffles of pink and white crepe paper framed a tottery arch with a banner on which someone had laboriously and ineptly printed the name of the organization. It appeared to read, "Walentine Lowers of America." Jacqueline wondered which of the teenage girls gathered around the booth was the calligrapher. They appeared to be a fairly representative sampling of their age group; some were slim and pretty, some were chubby and homely, and most had braces or acne or both.

Jacqueline advanced on the registration table, receipt in hand. "Fans?" she inquired, indicating the Walentine Lowers.

One of the secretaries glanced up from the checks she was sorting. Jacqueline's dignified appearance seemed to impress her, for she said apologetically, "I assure you, they aren't representative of our readers. If my advice had been followed, they wouldn't be here. They should have been made to buy tickets, like everyone else."

Her more kindly colleague said, "Most of them don't have the money. You know what Mrs. Foster said about fans: Keep them out, but keep them around. Yes, miss? Are you an author or a publisher?"

Jacqueline reflected. Presumably the alternative category was "fan" or "miscellaneous." Neither appealed to her. "Author," she said, and was presented with a blank name tag, a program, and a sheaf of tickets, one for each of the events of the conference. Taking a pen from her purse, she printed her name on the tag: J. KIRBY; and stuck the tag to the pocket of her suit. It was shaped like a heart, and was bright red.

The decorations of the automobiles and the mezzanine should have prepared her for the ballroom, where the luncheon was to be held, but Jacqueline was momentarily taken aback. Standing in the doorway, she stared appreciatively. It wasn't so much the hearts and the paper lace and the tinsel cupids; she had gotten used to them. It was the balloons—hundreds of helium-filled balloons, pink, red, white, and a few purple, clinging in clusters to every conceivable point of attachment and floating free like miniature flying saucers. Jacqueline batted a pink balloon out of her path and went in.

Most of the seats were filled—not surprising, since it was

almost twelve-thirty, and the luncheon was scheduled to begin at noon. At the far end of the room, on a platform decked in red velvet and (of course) pink paper hearts, was the table reserved for the speakers and the mystery guest. There was not an empty chair at the nearby tables, but Jacqueline spotted one chair occupied only by a mink jacket and a purse. Stopping behind it, she nudged the occupant of the neighboring chair.

"Excuse me. I believe this is my place."

As she had suspected, the implication that the seat was reserved had been a bluff. Faced by effrontery even greater than her own, the owner of the mink jacket gave in with no more than a glare and a muttered "Well, really!" Jacqueline returned the glare. The woman wore an author's red name tag pinned to a décolletage exposing shoulders that should have been concealed from public scrutiny. Her dress was chiffon, printed with huge red roses on a pink background. Her features reminded Jacqueline of a vulgar midwestern adage that refers to the back end of a horse.

Jacqueline slipped into the vacated chair, put her purse under the table and her feet on the purse, and opened her program. Her perusal of that document was interrupted by a timid voice inquiring, "Do you know if smoking is allowed?"

Jacqueline turned to contemplate the speaker, who was seated on her left. The girl looked no more than eighteen. Soft brown hair framed a round, ingenuous face. Her snub nose was liberally freckled and her horn-rimmed glasses magnified a pair of gentle blue eyes. Her dress matched her eyes; it had long sleeves and a modest boat neckline. Jacqueline, an avid collector of mail-order catalogs, had seen the same garment advertised. The text assured the prospective purchaser that she would look "every inch the lady." In this case at least the claim was correct.

"I don't see any signs forbidding it," Jacqueline said.

"But there aren't any ashtrays."

There were also no waiters within hailing distance. Jacqueline retrieved her purse from the floor. After fumbling for a while she produced a tarnished brass box and removed the lid. "You can use this."

"Oh, but—"

"It's meant to be used as an ashtray." Jacqueline sighed. "I still carry it, even though I've quit smoking."

"Oh. I was about to offer you—"

"Thanks." Jacqueline grabbed for the cigarettes. "I quit smoking once a month," she admitted.

Her new friend scrutinized her name tag. "I'm afraid I haven't read any of your books. Oh, but you probably use a pseudonym."

"No." Jacqueline inhaled blissfully. "I'm not a writer."

"But your tag—"

"I lied."

"Oh!"

"You wouldn't lie, would you?" The girl's tag was also red. Her name was Susan Moberley. "I haven't read any of your books either," Jacqueline said. "Unless you are Valerie Vanderbilt."

"I wish I were. She's a big name. I'm just a beginner. My first book is coming out this fall."

"I'll be sure to look for it. What's the title?"

"I was going to call it *This Blessed Plot*. It's set in England during the reign of Richard the Second, so I got the title from—"

"I know the speech."

"Oh. Anyhow, my editor decided it wasn't a very good title. She wants to call it *Dark Night of Loving*."

"I see."

Her noncommittal tone brought a blush to Sue's freckled cheeks. "It isn't that kind of book," she said defensively.

"How many rape scenes?"

"Two. But they aren't really—"

"Got any sodomy?" Jacqueline asked. "Incest? Sado-masochistic orgies, whips, chains, dismemberment?"

Sue's face was scarlet, matching the balloon that had dropped onto the table. Jacqueline took pity on her. "You must be very poor," she said in a kindly voice.

"I don't know why you think—"

"What do you do for a living, Susan Moberley?"

"I teach school. Sixth grade."

"It figures. Where are you from? Iowa, Kansas?"

"A little town in Nebraska. You've never heard of it."

"I wouldn't bet on that," Jacqueline said morosely.

"You Easterners always assume people from my part of the U.S. are hicks. We're just as familiar with—"

"Sodomy, incest, and whips. No doubt you are. But you seem to be possessed of a reasonable degree of taste and intelligence. Doesn't the image of woman as willing victim featured in books of this kind disturb you?"

Before Sue could reply, the lady in mink, who had been eavesdropping, exclaimed vehemently, "Now I do agree with you wholeheartedly. I never allow my heroines to be exploited. They are independent, sexually liberated women who control their own destinies."

An animated discussion followed. All the authors at the table agreed with the speaker in principle and in practice. Their heroines were all independent and sexually liberated. They admitted, however, that lesser writers sometimes fell into this trap.

Jacqueline was not sufficiently familiar with the genre to be certain that the speakers were lying, but she caught strong echoes of "methinks she doth protest too much." Becoming bored with the conversation, she stopped listening and amused herself by batting at the balloons, which were sinking slowly toward the tables as the helium leaked out of them.

"I'm starved," Sue muttered. "When do you suppose we're going to eat?"

"God knows." Jacqueline reached in her purse. "Would you like half my candy bar?"

As they munched, Jacqueline added, "I suppose the guest of honor has been held up. There was a massive traffic jam outside when I came in. The center of it appeared to be a pair of pink convertibles."

The woman in mink chuckled maliciously. "That's typical of Hattie. She probably forgot to get permission from the police to stop traffic for her stupid procession."

"She wouldn't forget," said another woman across the table from Jacqueline. "She asked, and they turned her down. Naturally. So she went right ahead without permission. Naturally."

"Hattie? Who is she?" Jacqueline asked.

"You don't know Hattie? My dear, you are really out of your milieu. She organized this conference. She's head of the Historical Romance Writers of the World."

"Good gracious me," Jacqueline said humbly. "I didn't realize. Is that all she does for a living—organize conferences?"

Her informant cackled like one of the witches in *Macbeth*.
"Hattie Foster is an agent, dearie. *The* agent. All the top writers
in the field are in her stable—Vanderbilt and Valentine and
Victor von Damm—all of them. That gives her a monopoly."

"Really?" Jacqueline's curiosity was genuine. The undercur-
rents of nonacademic publishing were unknown to her, and she
was interested in almost everything.

"Think about it, dearie. Not one of the big names—all of
them. If a publisher wants to make money in this market, he has
to deal with Hattie, and she drives a hard bargain. That means
she can pick and choose among the new writers. Most of 'em
would kill to have her handle their work. Stupid jerks."

The speaker's name tag was pink. It was not difficult to deduce
that this category included agents; the bitterness in the woman's
voice was heartfelt and personal. The lady in mink, who had
shown signs of perturbation during the agent's tirade, exclaimed,
with a nervous titter, "All the big names, Pat? All of them?"

"What? Oh—oh, no. Not all." The agent got her face under
control. "Uh—ladies, you all know the famous Rosalind Roman,
I'm sure. My client."

"Dear Pat . . . Hattie isn't the only agent who counts, ladies."

There was an uncomfortable pause. Then everyone started
talking at once. Under the noise Sue said, out of the corner of
her mouth, "Bet Rosalind is one who'd kill to get in Hattie's
stable."

An outburst of trumpets sounded, ending in a dying groan as
someone switched off the tape too soon. A velvet drapery behind
the platform lifted, and in marched the gray-haired woman Jacqueline had seen riding with the beautiful young girl. A ragged
and somewhat ironic cheer greeted her. Perhaps the guests were
cheering the imminent arrival of food as much as they were wel-
coming the head of the Historical Romance Writers.

She looked like everyone's Aunt Hattie—beaming smile, twin-
kling eyeglasses, and a massive motherly shelf of a bosom. Wisps
of hair escaped from her untidy gray bun. In a cooing Virginia
accent she welcomed the guests, hoped they weren't dyin' of

starvation, laughed merrily at her own wit, and introduced the guests of honor, who emerged one by one from behind the velvet drapery and took their places as Hattie eulogized them. The hairy-chested hero in the black cape was Victor von Damm. He was followed by Emerald Fitzroy, author of *Love Blooms at Twilight* —the redhead—and then by Valerie Vanderbilt. Jacqueline would not have expected the author of *Slave of Lust* to be shy, but evidently Valerie was; her brassy wig still hid her face as she scuttled to take the chair Victor held for her.

A breathless pause followed, broken only by the growling of empty stomachs. "And now the moment you've all been waiting for," Hattie cried. "Our mystery guest. Can you guess who she is? Can you believe our luck, girls? Here she is—the Queen of Love in person—the most popular, most beautiful, most talented writer of historical romances in the whole big world—Valerie Valentine!"

The moment Jacqueline had been waiting for was the arrival of something to eat, but not all the guests were as cynical. A storm of applause greeted the appearance of the beautiful young girl with the rosy-gold hair. Exquisite in white organdy, she glided to the platform on the arm of a tall, impossibly handsome man wearing white tie and tails. He bowed her into her throne-like chair, next to Hattie's, and took his place beside her.

Hattie reached for the microphone, but her comments were drowned out by the rush of dozens of waiters. They were already late and they wanted to get the tedious job over and done with. Food was slammed down on the tables, wine sloshed into glasses, and Hattie sank back into her chair.

The food was ladies' luncheon classic—chicken à la king, one cold roll per guest, limp lettuce with bottled French dressing. The dessert was the piéce de rèsistance—heart-shaped tarts with four glazed strawberries peering coyly out from under a coating of plastic whipped cream. Then the waiters stormed the tables with carafes of tea and coffee, and the guests, sated if not satisfied, turned their attention from food to intellectual sustenance.

"Who's the man with Valerie . . . my God," Jacqueline said piously. "How can you tell them apart?"

"Valerie Vanderbilt's fans call her VV," Sue said. "Valentine uses her last name. That's her lover, the Earl of Devonshire."

"The Earl of Devonshire is eighty-four and has been happily married for sixty years to the Queen's first cousin."

"Really?"

"I haven't the faintest idea," Jacqueline said. "But I'll bet my last buck that creature has not the slightest connection with the British aristocracy."

"Maybe he's the Earl of Devonbrook. Something like that."

"My God," Jacqueline repeated.

"I guess it is rather awful, isn't it?"

"Awful?" Jacqueline fished a limp purple balloon out of her coffee. "I haven't enjoyed anything so much in years."

IV

The post-luncheon speeches were mercifully short; as Hattie merrily admitted, they were running a wee bitty behind schedule. She had only a few tiny things to say. . . .

Cliché piled upon cliché, culled in the main from the romantic poets. "Who knows better than we that love conquers all?" cooed Hattie.

Jacqueline was very bored. Not quite sotto voce, she remarked, "Oh, what a plague is love."

"All for love," Hattie proclaimed. "And a little for the bottle," Jacqueline added. "That's from an obscure poet named Charles Dibdon. He said it all. . . ."

"Sssh," the lady in mink hissed angrily. Sue giggled.

Jacqueline needed no encouragement. Hattie's, "Love is heaven and heaven is love," inspired, "Love is like the meazles; we kent have it bad but onst and the later in life we have it the tuffer it goes with us." "All the world loves a lover," Hattie insisted, and Jacqueline shook her head as she scraped up the crumbs on her plate. "Not me. Comfort me with apples and stay me with almost anything—for I am sick of love. Sick and tired."

"You must be an English teacher," Susan said, as Hattie sat down amid a spatter of applause.

"Librarian." Jacqueline spoke absently; as the meal progressed she had been increasingly distracted by the peculiar behavior of Valerie Vanderbilt. Though the latter sat hunched over with her face practically in her plate, she occasionally glanced up when she forked food into her mouth, and the features thus displayed struck Jacqueline as familiar. She ran down a mental list of well-known personalities and half-forgotten acquaintances until suddenly the connection clicked into place. But surely it was not possible. . . . As if tickled by a tendril of ESP, VV looked in Jacqueline's direction. The expression of utter panic that distorted her face convinced Jacqueline she was right.

The waiters began grabbing plates and glasses off the tables and the guests of honor retired. VV bolted for the velvet drapery, but her hope of a quick exit was foiled by Hattie, whose stout form blocked the doorway. Jacqueline said, "See you," to Sue, and took off in pursuit.

VV saw her coming and attempted to elude her. Jacqueline cut the writer off and backed her into a corner.

"Jean. How long has it been? I'd know you anywhere, you gorgeous creature!"

"You're mistaken," VV mumbled, from under her wig. "My name isn't—"

"Jean Frascatti, class of . . . well, never mind; I'm no more eager to remember the year than you. Is it still Frascatti, or have you—"

"Sssh! Don't say my name!"

It would, in fact, have taken a keen eye to spot the familiar features, now twenty years older, under the thick mask of makeup. Jean's complexion was several shades lighter than Jacqueline remembered, and her bright-red lipstick outlined a mouth that was not the same shape as her own. But they had been friends once, and although Jean had changed her appearance she had not changed the mannerisms that define an individual more unmistakably than physical features.

"Never mind," Jacqueline said. "If that's the way you want it. . . . It was nice seeing you."

"Wait." A clawed hand clutched at her sleeve. "Oh God, of all the people to run into. . . . What are you doing here?"

"I'm apt to turn up almost anywhere," Jacqueline said, unoffended. "What are *you* doing here? Are you really—"

"Yes. Why deny it?" It was a cry of anguish.

"No reason I can think of. I gather no one knows your real name."

"No one must know it." Jean's voice broke. "You promise? You won't tell?"

"Not if you don't want me to."

"Swear. Swear by—by Van Johnson."

Jacqueline laughed spontaneously. "I'd forgotten that."

"You had a terrible crush on him."

"The snows of yesteryear. . . . Ah, well. I swear by Van Johnson. I suppose, the circumstances being what they are—though I'll be damned if I know what they are—you won't want me to approach you again."

"No. Yes. Wait a minute."

Jacqueline waited. After a moment Valerie-Jean said, "If I tell you to leave me alone, you will. Won't you?"

"Certainly."

"But I'd like to talk to you. Oh God, do I need to talk."

"Fine."

"But not here. I have to be at some horrible lecture."

"Anywhere you say."

"After the lecture. I'll meet you—Oh God!" With a shriek she turned and fled, tottering on heels too high for her.

Jacqueline turned to see what had occasioned such consternation. It wouldn't take much; Jean had been terrified of beetles, boys, bats, and a hundred other things.

Bearing down on her was a woman wearing a shabby tweed suit. She was a formidable figure—heavy-set and sturdy, with strong features and traces of a mustache—but the ballpoint pen she brandished did not seem terrifying enough to have sent Jean into precipitate retreat. Then Jacqueline reconsidered. The bag hanging from the woman's shoulder was as large as her own, and she was taking a notebook out of it. "Journalist" might have been inscribed across her forehead.

"Which Valerie are you?" the mustached lady demanded, poising the pen.

"None as yet. If I do write a novel, I intend to call myself Valerie von Hentzau."

"Not bad." The woman bared her teeth. "Then your tag—"

"I lied."

"Right."

Jacqueline studied the other's tag. For almost the first time that day she recognized a name. "D. Duberstein. Are you Dubretta? The columnist?"

"That's one of the things they call me." Dubretta's keen black eyes shifted, searching. "Wasn't that Valerie Vanderbilt you were talking to?"

"I'm a great fan of hers," Jacqueline murmured.

"Oh yeah? Funny. From the look on her face I figured you were accusing her of something criminal."

"She seems rather shy."

"She's hiding something. I can tell. I wonder. . . ."

Jacqueline moved with her, blocking her path. "I'm a fan of yours, too," she said. "I read your column."

"How often?"

"About once in a blue moon."

"That's what I figured." The other woman laughed, loudly and appreciatively. "You sound too intelligent to fall for tripe like mine."

"I remember one case you covered," Jacqueline said. "A couple of years ago. Sexual harassment in the mayor's office."

"Oh, that. Almost got me fired. My readers prefer scandal about famous people."

"It was an excellent series." Jean should be safe by now; Jacqueline's motives were almost entirely sincere when she went on, "It should have been nominated for a Pulitzer."

Dubretta's features had not been designed to display the softer emotions, and years of a notoriously cynical profession had hardened them even more, but the look she gave Jacqueline struck the latter as rather touching. Pride, gratification, and appreciation lifted the corners of her mouth in a fleeting smile before she said gruffly, "Which of the lectures are you attending?"

"The one on promotion. It promises to be the most entertaining."

"Right again." They fell into step together. After a moment Dubretta asked, "What are you doing here? Off the record; I'm just curious."

Jacqueline knew the "off the record" assurance was meaningless, but she also knew she was too obscure to rate a mention in

Dubretta's column. Unfortunately. The column was considered scandalous and lowbrow in staid Coldwater, whose academic denizens read it greedily on the sly. It would have delighted Jacqueline to appear in it.

"I'm a librarian," she explained. "I wanted to come to New York, and I needed a business deduction."

They followed the last of the luncheon guests out of the room. "I've got to powder my nose," Jacqueline said. "Perhaps we'll meet again one day, when all this is over."

Dubretta grinned. "I'll save you a seat."

"You're wasting your time, Dubretta. I will never betray Valerie Vanderbilt. Wild horses couldn't drag the truth from me."

She and Dubretta parted with expressions of mutual esteem.

Jacqueline was in fact powdering her nose when she realized that among the faces reflected with hers one seemed to be staring at her—or rather, at her mirrored image. This was not another ghost from the past; the face was young enough to be a daughter, or even a granddaughter (Jacqueline winced) of the class of . . . she tried not to think about the date.

The girl would not have made a prepossessing granddaughter. A thick coating of foundation failed to conceal past scars and present eruptions, and heavy eyeshadow, inexpertly applied, made her look as if she had been punched in the nose. The tiny eyes, plump cheeks, and blobby nose completed the resemblance to a homicidal pig Jacqueline had once known, Hammerhead Jones by name. Mr. Jones had reduced Hammerhead to chops the previous February, with the enthusiastic approval of his friends and neighbors.

Jacqueline turned from the mirror to find herself nose to nose with this apparition. She stepped to one side. The girl stepped to one side. She was a big girl, as tall as Jacqueline and considerably wider. The dress she wore did nothing to minimize her bulk, though it was beautifully made and looked expensive. Yards of pink dotted swiss swung from a ruffled yoke, with puffed sleeves as big as balloons.

"Yes?" Jacqueline inquired.

"I want to talk to you."

"Do I know you?"

"I'm Laurie Schellhammer."

"What a coincidence," Jacqueline said, thinking of Hammerhead.

"Huh?"

"Never mind." The girl's tag was white. "If you're a fan, you have the wrong person. I'm not a Valerie."

"I know that." Laurie looked scornful. "I'm Laurie Schellhammer, president of the Valentine Lovers of America. I know all the big writers."

"What do you want from me, Laurie Schellhammer?"

"Are you a new writer?"

"No."

Laurie made a grab for her as Jacqueline tried to get past her. "Listen, I don't know you, so I figure you must be new in the business. I want to warn you. Stay away from that woman. She'll try to get you to tell her things. She's trying to smear all the writers. Especially Valentine."

"What woman?"

"Duberstein." Laurie spat the word as if it tasted rancid. "She's a bitch. A cheap, dirty bitch. Didn't you read what she wrote about Valentine yesterday? God, it was such a cheap shot—"

"I get the idea," Jacqueline said. Reaching in her purse, she handed Laurie a tissue. "Here. You're drooling."

Automatically Laurie applied the tissue to the trickle of saliva running down her chin. "God, I hate that woman. You stay away from her. She'll crucify you. She's trying to crucify Valentine. Well, I won't let her get away with it. I'll stop her. I won't let her. . . ."

Jacqueline made her escape, leaving Laurie muttering and dribbling.

The lecture room was filled, but Dubretta saw Jacqueline and beckoned her to the seat she had saved.

"Isn't this fun?" she inquired sardonically.

"I'm enjoying myself."

"Then you must have a weakness for weirdos."

"I do—if you mean people with unorthodox opinions about obscure subjects. They're much more interesting than so-called normal people."

"I'll point out some of the nuttier types, if you like."

"That would be nice. I can't imagine why you're being so sweet to little old unimportant me."

"Can't you?" They exchanged smiles, then Dubretta sobered. "To tell you the truth, it's relaxing to talk to an innocent by-stander—someone who has no ax to grind, and a measurable IQ."

"Pour it on, Dubretta. I love flattery." But Jacqueline sensed that there was a degree of sincerity in the columnist's statement. Praise of a writer's favorite work is the surest way to her heart, and proof of superior intelligence.

Speakers and guests began to take their places on the platform. True to her promise, Dubretta identified the more important of them. The white-haired octogenarian who supported her wobbling steps with a cane was Rosemary Radley, author of *Sweet Sensuous Sixteen*. A shambling hulk of a man with the frontal development and long arms of a gibbon was Amber Graustark, author of the seventeen-volume De Toqueville saga, which traced that fictitious and doom-laden family from medieval England to nineteenth-century Mexico.

"Amber?" Jacqueline repeated.

"Several of the top romance writers are men." Dubretta added cynically, "This is one of the few professions in which the male sex is at a disadvantage. The readership is ninety-eight percent female, and publishers think they prefer books written by women."

"What about him?" Jacqueline indicated the hairy-chested hunk.

"Von Damm? He's one of Hattie's brighter ideas." Dubretta's voice was grudging. "She figured a handsome, sexy male would go over well, and she was right. His real name is Joe Kirby. . . . Hey—you two aren't related, are you?"

"No. Believe it or not."

"I never believe anybody without an affidavit, and sometimes not then." Dubretta made a note in her book. "Joe's an out-of-work actor Hattie set up to play the part. His so-called books are ghost-written by various bored housewives from Brooklyn."

She didn't bother to lower her voice, and several of the women in the row ahead turned to stare at her. One of them said, in a well-bred Bostonian voice, "I beg your pardon, miss, but you are mistaken. Victor knows a woman's heart as few men can; he writes every word of his wonderful books."

Dubretta's face split in a wide, froglike grin. She said to Jacqueline, "Get the picture?"

"I'm beginning to," Jacqueline said, fascinated.

Hattie bustled onto the platform and took her place behind the podium. The buzz of conversation died. Dubretta fumbled in her pocket. "What the hell did I do with my cigarettes?"

Her search dislodged a flutter of miscellaneous items—crumpled tissues, business cards, coupons for coffee and soap, and a pink, heart-shaped name tag. Jacqueline bent to help her recover the objects. As she was about to restore them to their owner, she glanced at the name tag. It was not, as she had supposed, a forgotten extra. Across its width someone had scrawled a message.

"Stop it, you dirty bitch, or you'll be sorry."

The accompanying sketch was as badly done as the lettering on the Valentine Lovers sign. It might have been meant to represent a cross. Jacqueline didn't think so.

CHAPTER TWO

*H*attie had begun her introductory remarks. Jacqueline poked Dubretta and hissed, "Is this a joke, or what?"

Dubretta glanced at the pink paper heart. An expression of mild vexation crossed her face. "Damn that kid. How did she. . . . Never mind, I'll explain later."

Jacqueline found the seminar even more entertaining than she had expected. She had supposed the speakers would be publicity agents, editors, and publishers. Instead the audience heard from a fashion photographer, a hairdresser, the representative of a famous line of cosmetics, and a dress designer. A dazzled girl from the audience was selected as guinea pig, upon whom these experts went to work. By the time they finished she was unrecognizable. Mascaraed, bewigged, and draped in gold lamé, she resembled a wax mannequin. In case there was any doubt as to the purpose of the demonstration, Hattie spelled it out: "You must look the part, my dears—romance, *toujours* romance. Now don't you-all look at me, because it's just hopeless for old Aunt Hattie, darlings; so you do what I say, not what I do. And if everything else fails, well, here's Mr. Johnson, who photographs all the famous beauties, to tell you how to make your pictures lovelier still.''

Mr. Johnson discussed lighting, makeup, and—in desperate cases—air-brushing. ''They want to see your eyes, darlings. Look straight at the camera—'I love you, camera!' ''

Except for an occasional snicker, Dubretta paid little attention to the speeches; she took copious notes but her eyes moved constantly, from the audience to the guests seated on the platform. These included the wretched Valerie Vanderbilt, whose flowing locks had been tugged down over most of her face. The moment the seminar ended, Dubretta jumped to her feet. As Valerie-Jean scuttled toward the door, Jacqueline caught Dubretta's arm. ''What about that threatening message?''

Dubretta tried to free herself. Jacqueline hung on. With a shrug and a grin, Dubretta accepted defeat. ''Oh, that. The kid is the president of Valentine's fan club. She's seventeen, and crazy as a loon; thinks I'm trying to destroy her idol. She keeps slipping me these weird notes.''

''I've met Laurie,'' Jacqueline said slowly. ''Are you out to destroy her idol?''

''Iconoclasm is my job—and,'' Dubretta added, with a malevolent smile, ''my pleasure. If I could get anything on Valentine, you're damned right I'd destroy her. Come on; I'll introduce you to Joe.''

She started for the platform, where a group of admirers had converged on Joe, AKA Victor von Damm. The author was alternately kissing hands and signing autographs.

Jacqueline was about to follow when the well-bred lady from Boston addressed her. ''Forgive me, my dear, but are you a friend of that woman?''

''Dubretta? I met her today.''

''Then I may speak candidly. You don't want to know her. She is unprincipled and unscrupulous—no fit associate for a lady.''

''Do you really think so?''

''You heard what she said about Victor.'' The soft wrinkled face twisted, suddenly and terribly, into a Medusa mask. ''That was a vicious lie. You mustn't believe her. The only thing a creature like that understands is hatred. She should be silenced—forcibly, if necessary.''

Jacqueline did not reply. After a moment the other woman's distorted face relaxed. She smiled gently at Jacqueline.

"I only speak out of concern for you, my dear."

"How nice of you. Aren't you going to meet Mr. von Damm? He seems to be signing autographs."

"Oh, dear no, I wouldn't think of such a thing." A blush tarnished the wrinkled cheeks. "I think it's frightfully rude to intrude on people to whom one has not been introduced."

"Some of them expect and enjoy that sort of intrusion."

"Possibly. But not Victor—not that shy, sensitive man. Can't you see how uncomfortable he is?"

Jacqueline couldn't. In her opinion the mechanical perfection of Victor's performance stemmed not from shyness but from boredom, and when Dubretta extracted him from the group of fans he looked relieved.

Accustomed as she was to male loveliness in all its youthful variations, Jacqueline felt a faint but localized flutter when Victor von Damm stood face to face with her. He loomed over her—not only because he was several inches taller, but because he knew how to loom. He probably practiced it daily, along with hand-kissing, smiling, and smoldering looks. Resentment rendered her more than usually acerbic; when he reached for her hand she fought his attempt to raise it to his lips. A modified variety of arm-wrestling ensued. Jacqueline won, but only because Victor was distracted by Dubretta's introduction.

"Joe Kirby, Jacqueline Kirby. Are you two related?"

"Dubretta will have her little joke," said Victor. His voice was a mellow baritone. He gave Jacqueline a smoldering look. "Would that I could claim a relationship, beautiful lady."

"Come off it, Joe, she's not a fan," Dubretta said. "She's a friend of VV's."

"A mere acquaintance," Jacqueline said. "I dote on her books. I felt I had to tell her so."

"Name one of her books," Dubretta said skeptically.

"*Slave of Lust.* I especially like the part where Blaze saves Lance from being emasculated by the order of the *Emiress* of Ballahooly. She wants him for her plaything—the *Emiress* does—and the only way she can get him into the harem is by—"

"Jesus," Dubretta said prayerfully. "That does it. I'm off in pursuit of other victims. See you later."

She trotted away, notebook in hand. "Is Dubretta a friend of yours?" Victor asked warily.

"A mere acquaintance," Jacqueline repeated. "I don't think I want to be a friend of hers. I'd rather not be in the way when someone takes a pot shot at her."

"She is not universally popular," Victor said. Absently he scratched the hair on his chest. "Sorry," he said, catching Jacqueline's eye.

"I expect it itches," Jacqueline said sympathetically. "The glue."

The affected smile left Victor's face. "How did you know?"

"The top left corner is coming unpeeled. Besides, you are singularly hairless except in that one area. I'll bet it takes you months to grow a beard."

"Damn," said Victor, covering the offending spot with his smooth brown hand.

"It's been nice meeting you, Mr. von Damm," Jacqueline said, turning away.

"Don't go."

"You must have other duties," Jacqueline said. "Hattie seems to be looking for you—"

"Why do you suppose I'm clinging to you?" Victor said, with refreshing candor. "Let's get out of here. I'll tell Hattie you wanted to interview me, or something. Are you a writer?"

His arm around her shoulders, he led her toward the door. "I'm a librarian," Jacqueline said, a trifle breathlessly.

"I was going to be a librarian once," Victor said mournfully.

"What happened?"

"My damned rotten handsome face, that's what happened. It's a curse. A visiting talent scout picked me for a small part in a film. The film bombed. And there I was in Hollywood, lost in the shuffle, without so much as bus fare home."

"So you are an actor," Jacqueline said.

Victor came to a halt. Still holding Jacqueline in the curve of his arm, he said, "What am I doing? What is it with you? Hypnotism? Does everyone tell you things they shouldn't tell anyone?"

"It's my curse," Jacqueline said irritably. "I don't encourage confidences." (She really believed this.) "In fact, I have better things to do with my time than listen to people bleat about their problems. Joe—Victor—I don't care what your real name is, and if you tell me your books are really written by a team of trained orangutans, I'll just shrug. Now, if you'll excuse me, I want a drink."

A slow and wholly engaging smile transformed Victor von Damm into Joe Kirby, unemployed actor. If he had been seductive before, he was now virtually irresistible. Unwillingly, Jacqueline returned his smile.

"You really are a beautiful lady," Joe said. His natural voice was several tones higher than Victor's.

"Don't give me that. I'm too old and cynical." But she let him take her arm.

"You are beautiful, compared to that bunch of hags I associate with. Everything about them is artificial, from their painted faces to their names."

"The theater is all artifice," Jacqueline pointed out. "If you despise that, you've chosen the wrong profession."

"I agree. Is it hard to get into library school?"

"You're joking."

Joe emitted a groan as heartfelt as any Victor von Damm might have uttered. "I wish I weren't. I'd like to chuck this whole stinking business. A nice quiet grad school, someplace in Alaska—or Utah—"

"Why don't you?"

They reached the lobby. Joe had forgotten his assumed persona. The black cloak hung limp and pathetic from his stooped shoulders. He shuffled when he walked. "I can't. I can't even tell you. . . . Hey. Did Dubretta say you were a friend of VV's?"

"She said it. I denied it."

"Yeah, but . . . tell you what," Joe said slowly. "You talk to VV. There's one unhappy lady, you know? Tell her I . . . talk to her. Come on, I'll buy you that drink."

"I'm afraid I can't." His mention of Jean reminded Jacqueline that she was supposed to meet her former schoolmate. They hadn't had time to arrange a rendezvous, and Jean didn't know where Jacqueline was staying; the most sensible course was to remain in the lobby until Jean could find her. Which Jean would probably not do unless Jacqueline was alone. She was about to dismiss Victor-Joe when she heard a voice she knew, raised in poignant protest.

"But that's way too much. I can't afford a hundred and ten dollars a night! You said it would only be—"

The desk clerk interrupted Sue's protest. He spoke in a discreet murmur, but Jacqueline caught a few words. ". . . economy rate limited . . . reservation misplaced . . . nothing I can do."

Sue's chin wobbled. A single crystalline tear materialized at the corner of her eye and slid gently down the curve of her smooth cheek.

"Look at that tear," said Joe softly. "Like a diamond. It didn't even plow a track through her makeup. Who is she?"

"Who wants to know, Joe or Victor von Damm?"

"Me," said Joe, staring. "I noticed her at the luncheon. She was sitting at a table near the platform. Stood out like a rose in a garden full of weeds. Or a kitten surrounded by stray cats. . . . What's the matter?"

"I," said Jacqueline, "was sitting next to her."

"Were you?" Joe's voice was abstracted. "Damn it, she's crying. And that bastard of a clerk—"

Weeping women were no novelty to the hotel clerk. He turned away with a shrug. Joe took an impulsive step forward.

To her horror, Jacqueline heard her own voice say, "Sue, if you need a place to stay . . ."

The transformation in the girl's face, from wistful disappointment to smiling, dimpled happiness, completed Joe's bemusement. Jacqueline did not introduce him and he made no attempt to attract Sue's attention. Silent and staring, he stood a few paces off until Sue had gone.

"Damn," Jacqueline said. "I hate myself. What makes me do these things?"

"I don't know," Joe said. "But it was a damned dirty trick. I was just about to—"

"That was probably one of the reasons," Jacqueline said drily.

"Hey, what do you mean? My intentions were strictly honorable. That girl's no swinging city type; she's . . . she looks . . .

she's probably from Utah—or Alaska. . . ." He sighed. "So why did you come to the rescue? It couldn't have been kindness."

"Certainly not. I—uh—I'm on a budget. My room rent is the same whether one or two people occupy the room; she'll pay half, save me some money."

Joe wasn't really interested. "I'd better make sure she gets across the street okay," he said.

"Even if she's from Utah or Alaska, she's smart enough to cross a street by herself."

"Yes, but—listen to that racket outside. There's some kind of a riot or something. I'll see you later, Miss—um—"

"Kirby," Jacqueline shouted. "Kirby. You ought to remember that name."

The black cape billowed dramatically as Joe ran after Sue. To Jacqueline's disappointment, it did not get caught in the revolving door.

Cursing her incurable tendency to interfere in other people's business, she took up a position next to one of the gilded pillars adorning the lobby. She didn't have to wait long. Jean had been trying to attract her attention. A blond wig bobbed up and down behind the plate-glass window of the gift shop, between a rack of paperback books and a shelf of folded T-shirts. As soon as Jacqueline acknowledged she had seen it, it disappeared.

Jean was in the farthest corner of the gift shop, crouched behind a counter of souvenirs. She started convulsively when Jacqueline tapped her shoulder.

"You need a drink," Jacqueline said. "Or something."

"Not here."

"Where then?"

"Anyplace but here." Jean wrung her hands.

"My hotel is across the street."

"Your room?"

"No. I've just acquired a roommate. She's probably there now. Oh, for heaven's sake, this is ridiculous. We'll go to the bar at my hotel. Come on."

She took Jean in a firm grip and marched her toward the door. Jean revived a trifle in Jacqueline's protective shadow; but when they emerged from the hotel, Jacqueline realized that Joe's reference to a riot had had some foundation in fact. At first she thought Hattie had instigated another parade. However, the barricade to traffic was not vehicular. Bodies blocked the sidewalk and spilled out into the street. Signs were being brandished; and as Jacqueline listened, the outcry resolved itself into a ragged chant: "We hate rape. We hate rape. We hate the Romance piglets, 'cause they love rape."

"It doesn't scan," Jacqueline said. "But the sentiment has a certain merit."

Being several inches shorter than Jacqueline and considerably more distracted, Jean was still in the dark as to the nature of the demonstration. Jacqueline helpfully read a few of the signs for her benefit. "Down with Lust." "Down with Valentine, rape and sexism." "Romance writers are traitors to women." "Ah—there's a sign that says, 'Valeries, go home.' I expect that includes you."

Jean realized what was happening. "Oh God," she cried. "I've got to get out of here. Oh God, oh God."

"They can't even see you," Jacqueline said. She stood on tiptoe. "For goodness' sake. Look—isn't that Betsy Markham?"

Torn between the terror behind, where Dubretta lurked and fellow romance writers swarmed, and the confusion ahead, Jean was paralyzed by this last catastrophe. The woman Jacqueline had indicated was indeed their old schoolmate. Tall and rangy, she had cropped graying hair and a bony, rather attractive face. Either she had heard Jacqueline's voice, which was not noted for its dulcet, ladylike quality, or she was alerted by the sixth sense developed by radicals when they are the object of intense scrutiny. Betsy looked straight at Jacqueline, grinned, waved, and brought her sign down on the head of a policeman who was attempting to escort her out of the middle of the street. Hers was the sign that read, "Valeries, go home."

Betsy and the policeman vanished in a maelstrom of struggling forms. Jacqueline led her gibbering friend away.

Jean didn't come out of her stupor until they had seated themselves in a booth in the semi-darkened bar. After the waiter had brought their drinks, Jacqueline said, "Now. What's this all about?"

Jean snatched up her gin and tonic and drank deeply. Then she said in a fading voice, "You wouldn't have to ask if you had read any of my books."

"I have. *Slave of Lust.* I read it this morning on the plane."

"*Slave of* . . ." Jean shuddered. "Oh, my God."

"It was wonderfully bad," Jacqueline said enthusiastically. "Magnificently, sensationally terrible. Aside from that, about half of it was plagiarized, especially the descriptions of male anatomy. You don't suppose I would ever forget *The Lustful Turk,* do you?"

Jean's reaction to this was a wry smile. Pushing the wig away from her face, she drank again, and then said, more calmly, "Nobody but you would know it. You and half a dozen dim specialists in Victorian pornography."

"And you assumed none of the above, including me, would read your book?"

"I didn't care if you did." Alcohol, or the relief of confession, had restored Jean's courage. "I didn't violate copyright or anything; that book's been out of print for a hundred years. Who's gonna sue me?"

"Not me, dear. That little volume enlivened my junior year. Did you ever get your master's?"

Designed to be harmless and reassuring, the question had the opposite effect. Jean's eyes took on a hunted look. "Doctorate," she whispered.

"Congratulations."

"I'm an assistant professor."

Jacqueline did not repeat her congratulations; Jean's tone seemed to demand commiseration instead.

"This year," Jean went on, like the Delphic oracle pronouncing the fall of Athens, "I am being considered for tenure."

"Oh?" Then Jacqueline understood. "Oh."

"Uh-huh." Jean nodded. "If they ever find out I'm—you know—"

Thanks to her occupation on the fringes of academe, Jacqueline was able to follow the oblique references and the even more obscure reasoning. She translated. "If your colleagues learned you were writing soft-porn novels, you wouldn't get tenure. Jean, do you really believe that? This is not 1850, or even 1950."

"Not get tenure? I'd lose my job! You know how the system works; after a certain number of years you either get promoted or you move on. I'm almost—well, you know how old I am. What do you think it's like, looking for a job at my age—competing with all those smart-aleck kids fresh out of grad school?''

Jacqueline was not wholly convinced. However, she was well acquainted with the unstable and treacherous nature of the paths that lead to security in the academic world. Competition was cutthroat; there were dozens of well-qualified candidates for every position, and a seemingly unimportant factor could tip the scales. More important, Jean believed in the danger, and nothing anyone could say would convince her she was wrong.

Jacqueline tried another argument. "So what if you lose your job? You must be making a lot of money out of your books."

"I do," Jean said sadly. "I do."

"Then cry all the way to the bank. Who cares what a lot of stodgy academics think?"

"I care."

"Oh."

"I love teaching. I love the atmosphere—the quiet, the respect. . . . Oh, you wouldn't understand. You were always a rebel."

"Me?" Jacqueline was indignant. "I'm the most conventional—"

Jean giggled. "Like the time you got all those black football players from Washington Park to sit in the front row when Professor Hoffmeyer lectured on inherited racial traits?"

Jacqueline brushed this aside. "Your problem is that you're ashamed of your books. You're projecting your contempt onto your colleagues, rightly or wrongly. If you hate writing so much, why don't you stop doing it?"

"I can't."

"Why not, for God's sake?"

"Well . . ." Jean blinked rapidly. "I make a lot of money; one becomes accustomed to a certain standard of living. . . ."

"What do you spend the money on? Clothes?"

Jean flushed, and pawed nervously at her wig. "This outfit? You know I don't dress like this unless I have to. I mean—"

"What do you spend it on?"

"Oh—things. I buy a lot of books. . . ."

"Why am I doing this?" Jacqueline demanded rhetorically. "I

must be crazy. Not half an hour ago I told Victor von Damm that confidences bore me, and here I sit—"

"Victor? What did he tell you?"

"Nothing. I managed to get him off my back before. . . . Well," Jacqueline admitted, "there was another distraction. I wonder how Sue is making out. . . . Dear me. That *was* a Freudian slip. What was I saying?"

"Victor."

"Joe."

"He told you that was his name?"

"Not exactly. Someone else told me. He told me he wants to be a librarian."

"Poor Joe," Jean murmured.

"He also said you were one unhappy lady. He intimated that you two shared some hideous secret. That I should talk to you. That shocking disclosures would follow. But—" Jacqueline raised a magisterial hand. "But I don't want to hear them. I have no wish to share in the childish yearnings of two jerks who don't seem to realize they are in the catbird seat riding the gravy train up the ladder of success. What ails you people, anyway? Don't answer that."

She slid toward the edge of the seat. Jean reached for her.

"Please, Jake—"

"Tacky," Jacqueline said with a sneer. "If you think I can be softened by antique and unsuitable nicknames . . ." but she stopped sliding.

A brief silence followed. Jean said, "I read about that case in Rome. There was an article in some magazine."

It would have been hypocritical to ask, "What case?" The affair had received considerable coverage, since the protagonists had included a scholar as well known to the lay public as he was to the academic world; and Lieutenant di Cavallo of the Carabinieri had not been averse to publicity. A reminiscent smile curved Jacqueline's lips. Capri—the tiny hotel near the ruins of Tiberius' palace, the private beach they had found. . . . Lost in fond memories, she missed Jean's next comment and had to ask her to repeat it.

"And there was another time, in England—something about the society to restore the good name of King John—"

"Richard. How did you hear about that?"

"I was at a party once, with Nigel Strangways, the historian. We were exchanging 'Do you knows' and he—"

"What did he say about me?" Jacqueline's eyes narrowed.

Jean hesitated long enough to convince Jacqueline that some editing of Strangways' comments seemed expedient. "There was a murder, or attempted murder, and you were responsible for solving it. He said you were a—a remarkable woman."

"Hmmmm," said Jacqueline.

"Did you solve the case?"

"Yes," said Jacqueline.

"Then you know about things like that."

"Things like what? Your brain is decaying, Jean; how did you ever get an academic job?"

Jean ignored this. Her face was intent. "Crime," she said. "Blackmail is a crime, isn't it?"

"Is someone blackmailing you?"

Faced with a direct question, Jean backed off. In avoiding Jacqueline's gaze, her eyes were caught and held by some person or object behind the latter. With a bleat of terror she got out of the booth and disappeared into the shadows.

Jacqueline expected to see Dubretta, and did not know whether to be relieved or not when she recognized the lanky form of her other erstwhile classmate. Seeing her, Betsy waved and came toward her.

"I thought I'd find you boozing it up," she said, taking the place Jean had left.

"Don't give me that. You weren't looking for me. Why aren't you in jail?"

Betsy ran her fingers through her graying locks. "So okay, I was looking for gin. Waiter! Jail? My dear, I haven't been in the slammer since '78. One learns certain techniques. . . . Yes, waiter, I'll have gin on the rocks. Tanqueray."

"I guess I've been in the boonies too long," Jacqueline said. "I thought if a person hit a cop on the head—"

"I didn't hit him hard." Betsy dismissed this tedious problem and gave Jacqueline an affectionate smile. "How long has it been, Jake? You look marvelous. And who was that who flashed out just now? She looked familiar."

"Nigh on twenty years," Jacqueline said. "What are you—"

"She was dressed like one of those love-story bitches. How come you're snuggling up to them?"

"How come you're so hostile toward them?"

Betsy grinned. "What is this, Questions and Answers? Okay, if you don't want to tell me, you don't have to. But anyone who's read any of their cruddy books should know why I don't like them. Have *you* read any of their books?"

"Two of them. Have *you* read any of them?"

"You can't catch me that way," Betsy said amiably. "I have read, not two, but two hundred. I may never recover my wits, such as they are. For Christ's sake, Jake, you used to be a liberal. How can you stand that stuff?"

"What makes you suppose . . ." Jacqueline broke off. She was tired of fencing; she wondered if she would ever again be able to make a simple statement. She gave it a try. Gesturing at the woman standing beside the booth, she said, "This is Dubretta Duberstein. Dubretta, this is Betsy Markham. Betsy, Dubretta. Dubretta, are you—No, scratch that. I'm not asking any more questions."

"Can't find a table," Dubretta explained. "Mind if I join you?"

She might have been telling the truth. The bar was filling up and she had been standing in the doorway for some time. How long, Jacqueline was not sure. Perhaps she had not seen Jean, AKA Valerie Vanderbilt. Betsy was a reasonable quarry for a journalist, and Dubretta's notebook was ready in her hand.

"You one of the pickets?" she asked.

"Brilliant deduction," said Jacqueline, eyeing Betsy's oversized army fatigues and chestful of slogan-imprinted buttons.

"What's your gripe, Betsy?" Dubretta asked.

Betsy told her, eyes shining; free publicity was a boon to a protester. "Romantic novelists perpetuate an image of women that is archaic, sexist, and harmful," she recited. "It's the old 'women love to be raped' myth. Men still believe it; for a woman to encourage their disgusting delusion is not only degrading, it's treacherous."

Dubretta scribbled. ". . . degrading but treacherous," she repeated.

"Men are still hung up on the old *Lustful Turk* image," Betsy said. "They . . . Jake? What's the matter?"

"Nothing," Jacqueline said.

"You remember that book, don't you? We all read it. What was the name of that girl, the English major—"

"There is certainly a great deal of *The Lustful Turk* in contemporary romance fiction," Jacqueline said hastily. "You're right, Betsy; the fact that the heroine is overpowered by a sexy, handsome hero, who eventually falls in love with her, doesn't compensate for the damaging implications."

"Right on!" Betsy cried.

Jacqueline relaxed. Her diversionary tactics had succeeded, for the moment.

Betsy went on heatedly. "A great deal of contemporary fiction specializes in the victimization of women. In the horror stories and suspense thrillers, who gets shafted? Who is terrorized and chased and brutalized? A beautiful young girl, that's who."

Dubretta tossed her pen onto the table. "Is that it?"

"Hell, no," Betsy said indignantly. "I can go on at length."

"More of the same? Oh, it's fine as far as it goes, kiddo, but I can't repeat myself for a whole column. Haven't you got anything good on these people?"

"Got anything? Like what?"

Jacqueline smothered a smile, and Dubretta snorted explosively. "That's what bugs me about you do-gooders. You're so goddammed naive! You march up and down yelling slogans about justice and fair play and equality, and hitting a cop over the head now and then—yes, honey, I saw you slug poor old Jackson Billings—and what does it accomplish? Not a damned thing. Don't you understand that if you want to nail these people you have to fight dirty—the same way they fight?"

Betsy, who would not have blushed at any four-letter word in any language, turned brilliant scarlet at the accusation of naiveté. Sensing a potential ally, she leaned forward. "Is that what you're trying to do, nail them?"

"You've got to go after the people at the top," Dubretta said. "Most of the writers are poor honest slobs like you and me; they're just trying to make a buck. They're the real victims of exploitation—forced to write crap they hate, and getting screwed out of their paltry returns by publishers and agents."

"Paltry?" Betsy exclaimed. "Do you happen to know how much money Von Damm and Valentine and Vanderbilt make?"

"So go after them," Dubretta said. "But you're missing the one behind the whole thing—the spider in the middle of her sticky web. Harriet Foster. Good old Aunt Hattie. Twenty-five-percent Hattie, she's known as. Most agents take ten, maybe fifteen. And God knows how much she rakes in on the side. What I wouldn't give to expose that sugary, smiling bitch. If I could only. . . ."

Her voice had become increasingly hoarse. Now she broke off, breathing harshly. Betsy raised her hand to administer a therapeutic slap on the back. "No," Jacqueline said quickly. "Don't. Dubretta?"

After a time the columnist relaxed. She took a small plastic bottle from her purse and swallowed one of the pills it contained. "I keep forgetting to take the damned things," she said sheepishly.

"Are you all right?" Jacqueline asked.

"Sure. Three pills a day, and the old ticker stays in tempo. Now listen, Betsy, let me give you a few tips. Forget your cutesy signs and your generalized wrath. What you've gotta do is target particular people. The strongest weapon in the world is ridicule. If you could make these jerks look silly, expose their pretensions and their lies. . . ."

"Go on," Betsy said eagerly.

The two graying heads bent toward one another, ignoring Jacqueline. She listened for a while, but since Dubretta's lecture avoided personalities and confined itself to the basic principles of muckraking, she soon lost interest.

Dubretta's antagonism toward Hattie Foster had all the passion of a personal vendetta. The antics of Hattie and her stable—particularly their taste in interior decoration—were deliciously funny, and left the history-romance group wide open to satire of the kind Dubretta specialized in. But silliness wasn't scandalous. Jacqueline wondered whether the lies Dubretta wanted to expose had any connection with the hints Joe and Jean had thrown at her. There was a distinct odor of blackmail in the air; but what hold could Hattie Foster have over a carefree, harmless ham like Joe?

She was aroused from her meditations by the realization that Dubretta and Betsy had stopped talking and were staring accusingly at her.

"Jake, we are trying to have a dialogue," Betsy said.

"So who's stopping you? I haven't said a word."

"You were singing."

"I was?"

"I hoped you had gotten over it." Betsy explained to Dubretta, "She used to do that all the time. When she was bored."

"What was I singing?" Jacqueline asked interestedly.

Betsy sighed. "You started out with 'Love in Bloom.' Then you went on to 'Love's Old Sweet Song,' and 'As Time Goes By.' "

"Well, well." Jacqueline picked up her purse and got up. "Since I seem to be interfering with the intellectual tenor of the discussion, I will take my leave. Good-bye."

Crooning under her breath, she collected her room key and headed for the elevator. "Moonlight and lovers, Never out of date; Hearts full of passion. . . ."

She was no stranger to hearts full of passion, jealousy and hate. There is no more fertile breeding ground for those emotions than the damp and shady groves of academe. Yet, though she had been an unwilling participant in several cases of violent death, she had never encountered an ambience so fraught with potential violence as this one. Everybody hated everybody else, for one reason or another.

Which only went to prove, she supposed, that writers of love stories were no better and no worse than any other cross section of humanity. It was the contrast, between lace-paper valentines on the one hand and verbal mayhem on the other, that made this situation so bizarre.

The occupants of the elevator were relieved when she got out, still singing.

Her room was unoccupied, but Sue had been there; her shabby suitcase was tucked humbly away in a corner and her clothes occupied a bare one quarter of the closet. There was a note on the table between the beds. Jacqueline picked it up.

"Have gone out with Victor! Thank you so much—I'll see you soon—can't tell you how much I appreciate your kindness! Sue."

"Bah," said Jacqueline.

Also on the bedside table was a stack of paperback books. The cover of the topmost showed an exquisitely beautiful young girl crushed in the arms of a tall handsome Indian (American variety). Her off-the-shoulder blouse was about to give way and she was bent back at an angle impossible to a human spine. Jacqueline's dour expression lightened a trifle. She kicked off her shoes, settled down on the bed, and reached for *Winds of Passion.*

CHAPTER THREE

*L*ong Arrow shrugged the quiver and bow from his brawny shoulders. The muscles in his bronzed chest rippled. 'I will call you Windflower,' he said in his guttural English. 'It is the flower of love in my tribe, for it bends to the winds of passion.'

" 'No,' Flame whispered. She shrank back, her hands fluttering as she attempted to draw the rags of her blouse across the swelling whiteness of her breasts. The young warrior's eyes kindled.

" 'Come to me, Windflower.' He cast aside his breechclout of tanned leather. Hypnotized, Flame stared at. . . ."

"Jacqueline?"

"Damn," Jacqueline said. She had not heard the sound of the key in the lock. Sue smiled uncertainly.

"I didn't mean to disturb you."

"That's all right." Jacqueline marked her place and closed the book. After all, she had a pretty good idea of what had hypnotized Flame. No reader of *The Lustful Turk* could entertain any doubts on that subject.

"I thought you were having dinner with Victor," she said.

"I changed my mind." Jacqueline was treated to the spectacle of a kitten trying to look like a lion. The result was so intriguing she forgot her resolutions about detachment. "What happened?" she asked greedily.

Sue crossed to the window and stood in contemplation of Central Park. "Nothing, really," she said, with an artificial laugh. "I mean—I knew the kind of man he was. That corny way he dresses, and he just adores being fawned on by those silly women. . . . Well, I mean, I knew he was a conceited ham, I only went out with him because I thought he was so funny. . . ." Her voice broke.

Jacqueline's maternal instincts were further developed than she liked to admit, but patting and cooing and getting her blouse soaked with tears was not her idea of therapy. She studied Sue's shaking shoulders and said briskly, "While you're on your feet, could you get me a glass of water?"

Sue shuffled sideways to the bathroom, her face averted. When she emerged with the water the curls framing her forehead were damp, but she was smiling doggedly.

Jacqueline accepted the water. "Thanks. I hope you don't mind—I borrowed one of your books."

"Oh, please—I only wish I could do more. I can't tell you how much I appreciate—"

"Not at all. I'm grateful for the chance to broaden my reading. Paperbacks are so expensive these days."

Sue flung herself across the bed. "I appreciate your tact. But you needn't avoid the subject. I'm not upset. I don't mind talking about it."

Seeing that she was about to become a confidante whether she wanted to or not, Jacqueline leaned back against the pillows and resigned herself. "Did he make a pass?" she asked. "Excuse the old-fashioned terminology; I haven't read enough romance novels to learn the in phrases."

"Oh, goodness, that wouldn't have bothered me." Sue produced another forced laugh. "I can handle that sort of thing."

"I'm sure you can," Jacqueline murmured. So Joe had not made a pass, and Sue had been disappointed.

After a moment the girl burst out, "He was so nice at first. We had a drink, at a little place he knows, and we talked. . . . He's only twenty-nine, did you know that? I said it was wonderful that he was so successful, but he said he didn't care about the money; he's tired of the adulation and the artificiality; he wants to give it up and return to a simpler, more genuine way of life. I told him about Finn's Crossing, and he said it sounded wonderful. . . ."

Her chin showed signs of instability, and Jacqueline said, "So what happened to shatter this romantic aura?"

Her voice was like a dash of icy water. The chin froze, and Sue gave her a rather resentful look before proceeding. "What happened was that he didn't mean a word he said. We were sitting there when that woman—Hattie—showed up. She'd been looking for him. 'Ah jes' knew Ah'd find you-all in your favorite little pub, Victor,' she said. 'Did you-all forget that appointment with Barton and Reed?' "

"Publishers?" Jacqueline asked.

"Yes. Victor glared at her in the rudest way. Then she looked at me and said—very nicely—'Ah do hope you-all will excuse me, honey; Ah can see why Victor forgot his boring old business appointment. Why don't you-all come along? I see you're a writer from that cute little red heart of yours, and it sure enough wouldn't do your career any harm to meet Mr. Barton.' "

"It sure enough wouldn't," Jacqueline said. "Frankly, I'm surprised Hattie offered. She isn't known for philanthropy."

"And that was when Mr. Victor von Damm showed his true colors! He jumped up like he'd sat on a pin, grabbed Hattie's arm, and left. He didn't even apologize, just muttered something like, 'See you around.' Hattie was embarrassed. He dragged her out before she could say anything, but I could see she was."

"Extraordinary," Jacqueline murmured.

"No, it isn't. He's just a conceited, selfish jerk, that's all. I mean, what the woman said is true—Hattie is the biggest agent in the business, and there was my chance to get her interested in me. But precious Victor can't stand even my kind of competition."

"That's one interpretation," Jacqueline said.

"Well, I've learned my lesson. I won't fall for that again. . . . Have you had dinner, Jacqueline? If not, perhaps you'd let me take you."

"Thanks, but I'm supposed to dine with friends this evening. Good heavens, what's the time? I'm going to be late."

As she was leaving the room a little later, the telephone rang. "It's probably for you," Sue said.

"I can't stop, I haven't the time. Maybe," Jacqueline added, "it's Victor, wanting to apologize."

"Ha," said Sue. But before Jacqueline closed the door she saw the girl reach eagerly for the phone.

As Jacqueline hastened through the lobby she heard someone call her name, but did not pause or look around. She believed in being on time when a friend proposed to cook a meal, and she was sick unto death of the love writers and their problems. She had looked forward to enjoying the absurdity of the proceedings and, if possible, adding to it; conducting a group-therapy program was not her idea of fun.

II

It was late when she got back, but Sue was still awake. Jacqueline glanced at the cover of the book the girl was reading. *"Anne of Green Gables?* Don't tell me; it's a new version, where the sexy young doctor, Gilbert, seduces Anne in a field of violets."

"I found it in a bookstore this evening when I went out for a hamburger," Sue said. "I needed something to steady my stomach after all this romance. Have you been shopping?"

Jacqueline put the suitbox on her bed and stretched aching arms. "It isn't heavy, it's just bulky. I haven't been shopping. I borrowed a few things from my friend. My wardrobe wasn't quite the thing for this event."

She removed the cover of the box and lifted out a dress. Folds of lavender voile flapped and fluttered. Sue gasped. "It's gorgeous. Is that real Brussels lace?"

"I guess so." Jacqueline frowned. "The dress is a little out of date. Joan wore it to the Queen's garden party two years ago. But the matching hat is rather divine."

"It's pretty large," Sue said doubtfully, eyeing the flower-be-decked cartwheel.

"We added a few more bows and flowers." Jacqueline put the

hat on her head. Sue let out a gasp of laughter, and then clapped her hand over her mouth. "I'm sorry—I didn't mean—"

Jacqueline looked pleased. "That's just the effect I'm aiming for, my dear. Wait till you see the whole ensemble. There's a frilly little parasol, and long white gloves, among other things."

"What else did you borrow?" Sue asked.

"My gown for the ball day after tomorrow." Jacqueline put the top back on the box and simpered coquettishly. "I think I'll save it for a surprise. Joan has the most money, and the most appalling taste, of anyone I know. Lucky me, to have such friends."

"You're crazy," Sue said admiringly.

"Thank you. I'm going to hit the sack now. I want to be bright and shining for the breakfast tomorrow."

She hung the dresses tenderly in the closet and started for the bathroom. "That telephone call was for you," Sue said.

"Who was it?" Jacqueline didn't pause.

"He wouldn't leave a name. He called again about an hour ago. . . ." Jacqueline vanished into the bathroom. Sue raised her voice. "When I said you weren't back, he growled at me."

Jacqueline's head appeared. She was wearing a white plastic shower cap with "Coldwater College Swim Team" printed on it. "Growled?"

"Literally. I asked if he wanted to leave a message, and he yelled, 'Tell her she can't avoid me forever,' and hung up."

The white plastic shower cap tilted. "Tenor or baritone?"

"Rather deep."

"Ah." Jacqueline's head vanished. "Damn," said Jacqueline's voice.

"Do you know who it was?"

Water gurgled and splashed. Sue returned to *Anne of Green Gables*.

III

Jacqueline turned from the mirror. "Well?"

"It's marvelous," Sue said. "The parasol is the final touch. But I thought you'd save it for the cocktail party tonight."

"I expect there will be a few equally tacky garments at the

cocktail party. They will lessen the effect. I should stand out like a sore thumb at the breakfast. Hurry up; I want to sit close to the head table.''

She rammed two hatpins as long as sabers through the crown of the cartwheel, picked up her purse, and beckoned to Sue, who followed with a bemused grin.

Heads turned as they marched through the lobby, and a taxi driver on Sixth Avenue yelled, ''Hey, lady, where'd you get that hat?'' Jacqueline waved at him.

They were very early, but a few guests had already taken their places. Jacqueline pre-empted two chairs at a table in the first rank below the platform and arranged herself. A gaping young woman sidled up and asked for her autograph. Jacqueline signed with a flourish: Valerie von Hentzau.

''That's awful,'' Sue exclaimed, as the autograph seeker backed away, her eyes fixed on the hat. ''You aren't—''

''As of this moment, I am.'' Jacqueline opened her purse. From it she took a stenographer's notebook, a ballpoint pen, and a small thermos bottle. Taking the cap off the thermos, she filled her cup and Sue's. ''I'm going to write a historical romance novel. Had I but known what riches lie buried in the fields of schlock, I'd have done it long ago. Excuse me for a while. I may as well get my first chapter finished during this lull.''

She began scribbling furiously. Sue tried to see what she was writing, but was foiled by the hat.

Jacqueline had filled half a dozen pages with her big, sprawling script before her literary aspirations were interrupted by a gasp from Sue. It was not her first gasp; as the flame of inspiration waxed hot, Jacqueline had shoved the hat back from her brow, thus enabling Sue to read what she was writing. But this gasp had a more poignant quality. Jacqueline looked up from her work to find Victor von Damm looming, and doing it very well.

His costume helped—high polished boots, trousers that clung to the muscles of his thighs, gold braid, gold stripes, gold buttons, and a ''slung'' pelisse trimmed with fur. Jacqueline considered him in silence for a moment before remarking to Sue, ''Tacky is not the word for that outfit, is it? My generation would call it corny, but I'm sure yours has more forceful terms.''

Victor stopped looming. "I have to talk to you," he said to Sue. "I have to explain—"

"No explanations are necessary. I quite understand. I wouldn't want you to put yourself out for me. I can't do your career any good, can I? Excuse me, Jacqueline, I'm going to the ladies' room. All that coffee . . ."

She was out of her seat and away with a celerity that left Victor gaping. He turned. Jacqueline said, "You can't follow her into the ladies' room."

"Then you explain. Tell her I. . . ." His voice died away. The other seats at the table were now occupied, except for the one on Jacqueline's right; the purse and the outer extremities of the hat filled that space, and no one had had the courage to suggest Jacqueline remove either. However, Victor's presence had been noted, and the other guests were staring. One elderly woman, her eyes soft with passion, extended a quivering hand.

"Excuse me—Victor—"

Without taking his eyes off Jacqueline, Victor grabbed the hand and planted an emphatic kiss on the air above it.

"Your technique is slipping," said Jacqueline. "And so is your pelisse. That strap is supposed to go—"

"Oh, hell." Victor hoisted the dangling jacket back into place. "I better split before . . . tell Sue. She doesn't understand. I couldn't let her . . . oh, hell."

He gave the palpitating matrons a hunted look. Several had risen and were edging toward him, right hands raised. "VV gave me a message for you," he said rapidly. "Call her—room 1215— after the breakfast. Oh God, here they come!" He bolted, his pelisse again at half-mast.

"Humph," said Jacqueline. She poured herself another cup of coffee and returned to her writing.

Before long she was interrupted again. A hand removed the purse from the empty seat and a voice said, "Thanks for saving me a place."

Jacqueline scowled. "Hello, Betsy. I was—"

"Don't tell me you were saving it for someone else. I know that purse, and that trick."

Jacqueline closed her notebook. "What's this, infiltration of the enemy camp?"

"Dubretta suggested it. Should have thought of it myself."

"Spies," Jacqueline suggested, "pass undiscovered longer when they assume the enemy uniform."

Betsy was wearing the same khaki shirt and pants she had worn the day before. With her broad shoulders, muscular forearms, and short hair she looked like a boy—or, more accurately, a middle-aged man in excellent physical condition, for her skin showed the wear and tear of innumerable sit-ins and marches.

"I took off my buttons," Betsy said. She inspected Jacqueline, from her hat to her voluminous skirt, and shook her head. "You have a lot of gall criticizing me. That's the tackiest dress I ever saw."

"Thanks. Why don't you go protest something?"

"That's what I'm doing." Betsy leaned back and folded her arms. "Oh, don't worry, I'm not going to say a word. I'm just going to *look*. Where'd you get the coffee?"

"I brought it with me." Betsy reached for the purse. Jacqueline said, "There isn't any left. We should be starting soon; there's Hattie."

"Ah." Betsy sat up.

Sue slid into her chair. She looked curiously at Betsy, and Jacqueline introduced them. "So you're one of the piglets," Betsy said, seeing Sue's red name tag. "How'd you get into this racket, Sue? You look reasonably intelligent."

Jacqueline sighed. "I love the way you infiltrate," she said. "Like a bulldozer."

"Were you in the protest march yesterday?" Sue asked.

"I organized it," Betsy said proudly. "Here—have a button." She produced one from the pocket of her shirt. Bright-green letters on a daffodil-yellow background proclaimed, STOP RAPE.

"Go on, take it," Betsy urged. "Or are you in favor of rape?"

"Of course not!"

"I'll take it." Jacqueline affixed the button to the bosom of the lavender gown and studied the effect approvingly. The button was the perfect touch. "I should have brought my ERA NOW button," she remarked. "One on one side and one on the other. . . ."

Sue and Betsy ignored her. Sue had decided that the radical was just another of Jacqueline's eccentric friends, and Betsy had decided that Sue was a potential convert. "I'll bet you just started writing this slime," she said winningly. "Think what you're doing. It's not too late to quit."

"And find salvation in the arms of the movement," Jacqueline chanted. "Glory, glory, hallejujah—"

"Shut up," Betsy said. "We'll talk later, Sue. The old bag is about to open the proceedings, and I want to take notes."

Hattie breathed into the microphone. "One, two, testing. . . ." The head table was less flamboyantly furnished with authors that morning; only Victor von Damm and Emerald Fitzroy were present. As Hattie prepared to address the room, Victor leaned across the empty seat that separated him from Hattie. Her hand quickly covered the open mike, but not before the assembled throng heard, "I'm getting the hell out of here. I won't—"

Hattie's fixed smile tightened. Her reply was inaudible. After a moment Victor subsided and Hattie began speaking.

Betsy earnestly wrote down every word Hattie said in her obviously brand-new stenographer's notebook. Jacqueline was reminded of the old academic joke that describes note-taking as the transfer of words from the notes of the professor to the books of the students, without passing through the brain of either. The speech consisted solely of reiterated greetings plus a run-down of the day's activities. Hattie then picked up her fork and the waiters served breakfast.

Jacqueline, whose appetite was hearty, devoured her leathery scrambled eggs and chilly sausage and toast before polishing off the cheese Danish she had had the foresight to bring with her.

"Where are the rest of them?" Betsy asked.

"I only brought one."

"Not the Danish, damn it; the authors. The ones I particularly wanted to observe aren't here—the Valeries."

"Valentine wasn't supposed to be here," Sue informed her. "She's the big star; I understand she only agreed to make one appearance a day. She'll probably be at the cocktail party."

"What about the other one?"

"Maybe she's sick."

Jacqueline suspected this suggestion was correct, though not in the sense Sue meant. Jean's nerve had finally broken under the strain. Or—more interesting idea—was a rebellion brewing?

Jacqueline was sure Jean had been forced to attend the conference, probably by Hattie. Jean would do anything to avoid exposure; she was the perfect blackmail victim.

That didn't necessarily mean that the other writers had been subjected to the same duress. Most of them positively cried out to be exploited. However, the change in Victor's attitude suggested another recruit to the ranks of the rebellion. The day before he had reveled in the absurd pageant. Now, after his protest, he had relapsed into sullen silence, never raising his eyes from his plate.

Jacqueline considered raising this intriguing point with Betsy, but decided against it. Why should she do Betsy's work for her?

Speeches by two of the guests—a reviewer of romance novels, and an editor who praised his writers for helping to make him a lot of money—wound up the breakfast. Victor started for Jacqueline's table, but Hattie collared him and marched him away.

"Do you know him?" asked Betsy, who had not missed the byplay.

"Who?"

"The gorgeous hunk in the Merry Widow costume. I don't know why it is," Betsy went on mournfully, "but the most gorgeous men are all chauvinist pigs."

"Thank God for Alan Alda," Jacqueline said.

Betsy brightened. "Right."

Jacqueline made her escape. Sue trailed after her. "Which of the workshops are you going to?" she asked.

Jacqueline consulted her program, which was, of course, printed on pink paper. "I can't decide between 'How to Write the Erotic Romantic Historical Novel,' and 'The Leading Men of Love.' Victor will be at that one, I suppose."

"Then I'm going to the other one." Sue's lips set tightly.

"They aren't the only choices. How about 'Romantic Costumes for Heroines and Authors'? Or 'Setting the Mood: Moonlight, Powdered Wigs, and Swordplay.' Swordplay?"

"Your friend is right," Sue snapped. "It's disgusting. Exploitive, leering, prurient. . . . I'm going for a walk. I need fresh air."

She walked off before Jacqueline could point out that fresh air was not a commodity easily obtained in Manhattan. Jacqueline returned to her program. "Setting the Mood" sounded like the most imbecile, i.e., entertaining, of the workshops, but, on the other hand, writing an erotic romantic historical novel was her new goal. Though she had every confidence in her ability to produce a best-seller without any assistance whatever, the workshop might give her some useful ideas.

She wafted her lavender way along the hall, picking up promotional literature from the publishers' booths as she went. Before long she was accosted by Dubretta. "I couldn't believe it was you," the columnist said. "Do you mind if I get a picture?"

"Not at all."

Jacqueline posed obligingly for the photographer Hattie waved to the fore. Parasol over her shoulder, hat shading her face, she simpered and twirled and looked sentimental until Dubretta said, "That should do it. The satire will be wasted on most of my readers, but a few of them might catch it. 'One of the writers at the—' "

"I refuse to be anonymous," Jacqueline protested. "My pen name is Valerie von Hentzau."

"Right." Dubretta scribbled. Jacqueline looked shamelessly over her shoulder, and Dubretta said maliciously, "You'll have to wait till it comes out in print. Nobody can read my private shorthand but me. Did you see my column this morning?"

"Yes, I did. How do you keep your pens from melting in all that vitriol?"

"Just wait. I think I'm on the trail of something big. It ought to blow this whole . . . what is it with you, hypnotism? Am I the only sucker who pours out her soul to you?"

"No. Are you feeling better this morning?"

"I feel fine. Why do you—Oh, that. No problem. It's a congenital condition, but it's under control."

Jacqueline wondered. In her gray linen suit, with her iron-gray hair, Dubretta was all gray that morning, including her face.

"Don't confide in me," she said lightly. "I'm not interested."

"I think I should warn you," Dubretta said slowly, "that I'm on to that friend of yours. Oh, don't look so bland. I'm talking about Valerie Vanderbilt, whose noble family has disowned her because of her wild and woolly sex life. And who is in reality Jean Frascatti, mild-mannered English prof, who probably hasn't even kissed a man in thirty years."

"How did you find out?"

"It was damned ingenious, as a matter of fact." Dubretta smiled smugly. "You two are about the same age. I had a hunch you might have gone to school together. Your friend Betsy told me where; I tracked down an old grad who has all her college yearbooks, and—*voilà.*"

"Not bad," Jacqueline admitted.

"That makes two," Dubretta gloated. "Jean and Joe—both frauds set up by dear old Hattie. But they're small-fry. Hattie's the big fish, and I think . . . damn it, there I go again. I'd better leave before I spill my guts."

Jacqueline did not detain her. She started toward Suite C, having decided to attend the seminar that promised training in the writing of erotica; but before she had gone far, a hand caught her arm and spun her around.

"I told you to stay away from that bitch! What are you, one of her stooges?"

Laurie's pustulant countenance was only inches from hers, and Laurie's voice held the high, whining note that betokened incipient hysteria.

Jacqueline replied instantly. "Why, Laurie, what a gorgeous dress. It's even prettier than the one you wore yesterday. Where did you get it?"

Laurie's mouth remained open, but instead of continuing her tirade she swallowed and stuttered before muttering, "I made it."

Jacqueline's unexpected response had caught the girl off guard and calmed her—for the moment. However, Jacqueline's compliment had been sincere. The dress, a frothy concoction of lace-edged frills and ruffled petticoats, was unsuited to Laurie's large frame, but it was beautifully made, even though the dainty rosebud print was sweat-stained and soiled, and smears of chocolate marked the bodice.

"Did you really?" Jacqueline exclaimed. "You are clever. Where did you get the pattern?"

"I copied it from a picture in the museum," Laurie mumbled.

"Without a pattern? That's really impressive."

The look of gratified pride on Laurie's face roused an unwilling pity in Jacqueline, though the girl's heavy hand still held her hostage. She knew her advantage might be only temporary; she had seen the signs of drug addiction often enough to know that the user's changes of mood could be violent and unpredictable. The hallway had emptied. The seminars must have started.

"I make all my clothes," Laurie boasted. "I made a gown for Valentine, too. . . ."

Her idol's name brought on the change Jacqueline had feared. Rage darkened her face. Her hand tightened its grip.

"Oh, the hell with it," Jacqueline said. She swung her purse, heavily laden as usual, into the pit of Laurie's stomach.

Laurie howled like a banshee. Clutching her middle, she leaned forward, squashing Jacqueline against the wall. Tears streamed down her face.

Jacqueline could have escaped then, but it was impossible to abandon someone in such voluble distress. Squeezing out from under Laurie's weight, she patted the girl's heaving shoulders. "Control yourself. I didn't hit you that hard."

Laurie's uninhibited wails had attracted attention. Curious faces appeared in open doorways, and people sidled cautiously toward the scene. Among them was Hattie herself. She took over the job of shoulder-patting, and glared at Jacqueline.

"What have you done to this pore chile? There, there, honey, just quiet down."

"What have I done to her? If you have any influence over this perturbed person, try to persuade her to see a doctor. The girl's goofy."

"She hit me," Laurie wailed. "All I was doing was talking to her, and she hit me!" She clutched Hattie in a feverish grip.

"There, there." Pat, pat. "There, there. You just go and wash your face, honey, and calm yourself. Aunt Hattie will take care of the mean woman."

Laurie departed, snuffling and wiping her nose on the back of her hand.

Jacqueline's lip curled. "The girl is goofy," she repeated. "She's rowing with only one oar. There ain't no top rung on her ladder. She is, to put it another way, in need of help."

"I know," Hattie murmured. "You must have done something to upset her—"

"Don't try those tactics on me," Jacqueline said sharply. "The girl virtually attacked me. I feel sorry for her, but I'm not taking any guilt trips.''

"I'm not her guardian," Hattie said. "If you've got any complaints . . . wait a minute. I've seen you before. Talking to Dubretta Duberstein.''

"I know her slightly," Jacqueline said warily.

A broad, remarkably unconvincing smile stretched Hattie's jaws. "Honey, I am so sorry about all this. You just must forgive me for bein' so sharp, I was a teeny bit upset. I expect you're all shook up too. Why don't you come to my suite and let me give you a nice cup of tea?''

Jacqueline needed no urging. This promised to be even more entertaining than the workshop on moonlight and swordplay.

Hattie chatted non-stop, in her phony southern accent. "My, what a pretty gown. I noticed you at the breakfast, and thought, my, what a gorgeous gown that is. I just can't tell you how sorry I am you were upset. That pore chile has so many problems. I try to help her, but what can I do? She's from quite a nice family, you know. Pots and pots of money. But it's one of those nasty modern situations—drinking, neglect—you know what I mean. Well, here we are. You sit down over there, in that nice comfy chair, and I'll put the kettle on.''

She trotted out.

If Jacqueline had doubted Dubretta's statement that Hattie was making a good living out of love, the luxurious surroundings would have supported the columnist's claim. Living room with balcony, bedroom and bath, kitchen—If single rooms commanded a price of over one hundred dollars a day, this suite must be setting Hattie back a pretty penny.

Hattie bustled in with a tray.

"I shouldn't be keeping you from your workshops," Jacqueline said, figuring she had better speak first or she might not get a chance to speak at all.

"Oh, honey, don't you-all worry about that. I'm not responsible for Laurie—not in the least—but she's turned to me as a sort of mother substitute. I feel people ought to help others when they can.''

The image was so incongruous, Jacqueline almost laughed aloud. Hattie cultivated the kindly-old-aunt technique rather badly; her eyes were as empty as the windows of an abandoned house, and her motherly instincts, if any, resembled those of the black widow spider. Or did spiders eat their offspring? While Jacqueline was considering this point of natural history, Hattie rambled on.

"She does seem more disturbed lately. Of course, seeing Valentine has shaken the pore thing. She absolutely idolizes Valentine. I'll talk to her and tell her to behave herself."

This was not the solution Jacqueline had had in mind, but she knew it would be a waste of time to suggest that Hattie take any decisive action. She wondered when Hattie would get to the point. Subtle she was not.

"Have you known Dubretta long?" Hattie asked casually.

Jacqueline smiled. "Not long."

"Such an intellectual woman. Almost too intelligent, don't you think? Really almost masculine. I suppose I should resent all the cruel things she says about me and my friends, but I just can't hate her, honey; she's too pathetic. It's envy, that's what it is. She's never known the rapture of love, and she resents those who have."

"Have you known her long?" Jacqueline asked.

It was a random shot, designed to cut off the nauseating flow of hypocrisy, but she struck a nerve. The sandy, graying lashes flickered, and Hattie said brusquely, "No."

"Something she said made me think you were old acquaintances," Jacqueline murmured. She sipped her tea. It was terrible —teabag-cheap, and very weak. Hattie had probably used only one teabag for the whole pot.

"What else did she say?" Hattie replaced her cup in the saucer with a decisive thump and abandoned her fake accent. "What's she up to? Look here, Miss—Mrs.—what's your name, anyhow?"

Jacqueline indicated her tag with a fingertip. She had painted her nails to match her dress; her hands looked like those of a corpse in the first stage of decomposition.

"Kirby," Hattie said. "Should I know you?"

"Not yet. I," said Jacqueline modestly, "am writing my first romantic historical novel. If you'd like me to send you the manuscript when I've finished—"

"Oh, I get it." Hattie smiled cynically. "Well, you might make it at that. You've got the feeling for the—the—"

"Hype," Jacqueline supplied.

"Background," Hattie corrected. "Okay, I'll read your manuscript—if you'll do me a teeny tiny favor in return."

"I can't tell you anything about Dubretta. She dislikes you—but I don't suppose that's news to you."

"It sure isn't."

"And she would like to—I believe she used the phrase 'get something on you.' But that isn't news to you either. And," Jacqueline said, "it can't worry you, since you have nothing to hide."

"Good gracious no." Hattie laughed heartily. "I suppose she's been saying all sorts of mean, slanderous things about me and my writers?"

"Oh, yes." Jacqueline laughed heartily.

Silence followed. Seeing that her not-too-covert hints had failed, Hattie abandoned subterfuge. "What?"

"I beg your pardon?"

"What did she say? I'm entitled to know."

"But you aren't entitled to hear it from me. I am only a bystander," Jacqueline explained. "An onlooker, if you will. I do not interfere in other people's business."

She had, of course, already taken sides. Hattie was a predatory, nosy old crook. The woman couldn't even make a decent cup of tea.

"Laurie claims Dubretta is after Valentine," Hattie said. "Of course the girl is crazy, but. . . ."

"I must be going," Jacqueline said. "Thank you for the lovely tea."

Hattie stared at her from under her heavy brows and said slowly, "I'd like to look at your manuscript, honey, but I'm pretty busy. I may find I don't have time to read it."

"I see."

"I knew you'd understand."

It would have been difficult to misunderstand. Hattie could hardly have stated the proposition more crudely: Find out what Dubretta is doing and I'll push your book. Jacqueline wasn't surprised at Hattie's blatant attempt at bribery; what surprised her was that Hattie should be desperate enough to proposition a stranger. Perhaps Hattie hadn't believed her when she said her acquaintance with Dubretta was of the slightest. From Hattie's point of view it was worth a try; she wouldn't keep her side of the bargain even if she got the information she wanted.

Jacqueline smiled her sweetest smile. "Perhaps I'll see you again before long," she said meaningfully.

"I do hope so." Hattie's smile was equally saccharine and equally significant. She rose ponderously to her feet. The audience was over.

But before she could escort her visitor to the door, another door burst open and an agitated voice cried, "I tell you, I won't stand for it any more. I've got to talk to Hattie. . . . Hattie?"

Valerie Valentine—for it was indeed (Jacqueline assured herself) the Queen of Love—came to a halt. She looked like the heroine of one of her books, her tumbled red-gold hair held back by a white satin ribbon and her slender body wrapped in an opulent negligee that contained enough yards of white chiffon to drape a king-sized bed. Seeing Jacqueline, the girl's violet eyes opened wide.

"Valentine, my dear. . . ." A man appeared behind her and put his hands on her shoulders. He was not as ugly as Valentine was beautiful, but there was a distinct suggestion of the classic fairy tale in the juxtaposition of the two faces.

The newcomer, whom Jacqueline had last seen in the car with Valentine and Hattie, was the first to speak. "I'm sorry, Hattie. You have a guest?"

"As you see," Hattie snapped. "It was nice of you to come, Mrs. Kirk."

"Kirby," Jacqueline said. She braced herself against Hattie's nudges, and stood like a rock. "I know you all have things to discuss, but I just can't tear myself away till I tell Valentine how much I admire her. This is such a thrill—you can't imagine!"

Valentine started, as if she had been poked from behind. "And it's a pleasure for me to meet my readers," she said, in a breathless monotone. "You inspire me to do better. I always feel . . . did you say Kirby?" Shaking off the hands that tried to hold her back, she started toward Jacqueline.

Grudgingly Hattie introduced them. The chubby little man was

Max Hollenstein, Valentine's business manager. He took Jacqueline's hand, and as their eyes met, Jacqueline realized that here was an adversary as dangerous in his way as Hattie was in hers. His luminous, weary brown eyes were frighteningly intelligent, and there was humor as well as self-deprecation in the curve of his thin lips. Or was he an adversary? At any rate, he knew she was not simply one of Valentine's fans. Fans were not invited to take tea with the great Hattie.

"Which of Valentine's books is your favorite, Mrs. Kirby?" he asked, with a skeptical smile.

"I love them all," Jacqueline said.

The little man's smile broadened. Before he could continue his delicate inquisition, Hattie explained, "Mrs. Kirky has had a little encounter with pore Laurie. I really am worried about that chile."

"Worried? Encounter?" Max's lips twisted. "Your euphemisms enchant me, Hattie. I hope, Mrs. Kirby, that you aren't in need of more than casual first aid."

"No damage done, Mr. Hollenstein."

"I can't stand that girl," Valentine said vehemently. "She's disgusting. She makes me nauseous. I told you before, Hattie, you've got to keep her away from me."

"And I told you . . ." Hattie's teeth snapped together. "Well, honey, I'll see what I can do. Now I must run. An appointment with a publisher."

"It's been a pleasure meeting you, Mrs. Kirby," Max added.

Jacqueline had no choice but to take her departure. She turned to Valentine. "It's been such a thrill."

". . . pleasure . . ." Valentine murmured. She gave Jacqueline a look that, on a face less virginally innocent, might have been considered sly. "Let me give you one of my books."

"Oh, how wonderful," Jacqueline cried.

"It's just a paperback, but . . . wait here." Valentine flowed out the door through which she had entered. The suite was obviously more extensive than Jacqueline had imagined; beyond the door she saw, not another room, but a hallway leading to unknown regions. Hattie had her top writer and the latter's manager literally in her stable.

Before long Valentine came back, carrying a book. The cover

painting was similar in style and content to most of the others Jacqueline had seen. In this case the brawny hero was wearing part of a uniform—boots and tight blue trousers with a stripe down the side. As Valentine held it out to Jacqueline, Max reached for it.

"Have you written something charming, my dear?"

Valentine's face froze. Before Max could take the book, Jacqueline grabbed it. Opening it, she glanced at the inscription.

"Oh, Valentine, how sweet! I'll always treasure it and never allow anyone else to see it—my own private, personal message. And now I must let you busy people get back to work."

Hattie escorted her to the door. Jacqueline glanced back. Valentine had dropped into a chair, but Max stood watching, a faint enigmatic smile on his lips.

Jacqueline tucked the book carefully into her purse. The message had indeed been private and personal. It read, "Help me—please help me." And then, incongruously and rather pathetically—"With best wishes, Valerie Valentine."

CHAPTER FOUR

Jacqueline wandered into the erotic-novel seminar in time to catch the last lecture—"The Act of Love: Be Original." She paid scant attention to the speaker's examples. None was original, at least not to a reader of *The Lustful Turk*.

She had called Jean's room before going to the seminar, but there had been no answer. Perhaps Jean had grown tired of waiting and had gone out—or else she was hiding in the closet, biting her nails and muttering, "Oh God," at regular intervals. Jacqueline shook her head disgustedly. Jean was as limp and wet as a soggy mop. She had walked straight into the web in whose center Hattie squatted like a cannibalistic spider. . . .

Surely it was their mates black widow spiders devoured, not their children? No matter; the figure of speech still applied. " 'Come into my parlor,' said the spider to the fly. . . ." Jean had walked right in, and had handed Hattie the weapon with which to blackmail her. Jacqueline only hoped fear of exposure to the university was the only weapon Hattie had. Most people wouldn't have cared about that, but Jean had always been timid as a rabbit.

Jacqueline's eyes crinkled with amusement as she remembered

the night their dormitory head had almost caught Jean with *The Lustful Turk*—or was it one of the other masterpieces of Victorian pornography they had smuggled from room to room, swathed in brown paper? It had taken two hours, and half a bottle of the cheap red wine they kept hidden in the bookcase, to restore Jean. They had shared a lot of things—long solemn conversations about Life and Men and Sex, orgies of eating followed by fanatical diets. . . .

"Strawberry jam and whipped cream," said the lecturer. The phrase caught Jacqueline's attention, but after listening to the rest of the sentence she decided the procedure was messy, not sexy. She returned to her meditations.

She had better take steps to extract Jean from Hattie's clutches without delay. There was something rotten in the History-Romance business, or at least that part of it under Hattie's influence. Everything pointed to that conclusion—Victor's dire hints, Hattie's clumsy attempt at bribery, Valentine's plea for help, Laurie's strange behavior. The girl was obviously suffering from some variety of mental illness, possibly exacerbated by drugs, but the particular form her delusion had taken might be affected by the underlying malaise. Even if she didn't know the secret, the uncanny perception of the slightly goofy made her aware of her idol's fear. Valentine must be a little goofy herself to resort to such a hackneyed device as scribbling a message in a book. Presumably she had learned of Jacqueline's reputed detective talents from Jean. Were all Hattie's top writers involved in the plot? And what was the role of the smiling, enigmatic little man named Max Hollenstein?

Jacqueline was happy. Old loyalties and old friendship demanded action on her part, but she would have been the first to admit that her predominant motive was resentment. Hattie had not only served her weak tea, she had had the effrontery to offer her, Jacqueline Kirby, a bribe. It would be a pleasure to step on Hattie and squash her flat. A dark and evil miasma followed the woman, like the slime of a snail's track. . . . Not bad, Jacqueline thought, reaching for her notebook. I can use that to describe Sir Wilfred Blackthorn, the villain.

II

Sue slammed the door. "You didn't go to the awards ceremony."

Jacqueline did not look up from her book. "Was I supposed to?"

"You want to know who won?"

"Not particularly."

"Valerie Valentine!" Sue kicked the foot of the bed. "Valerie Valentine, Valerie Valentine. Three awards in three different categories. And you—you're reading one of her books!"

"Had I but known, I would not have transgressed," Jacqueline said sarcastically. "Actually, I was writing my book, but the font of inspiration dried up. I'm priming the pump."

"Disgusting," Sue muttered.

Reaching the end of a chapter, Jacqueline closed *A Willow in Her hand.*

"No," she said. "It isn't. It's good. It's better than good. In terms of characterization, style, pace, all other literary criteria, it is far above every other romance I've read. It shouldn't even be put in that category. And this sleazy cover is a complete misrepresentation of the action, the setting, and the mood."

"I know," Sue admitted, in a small voice. "It was her books that inspired me to write. Damn, damn! It just isn't fair. She's got everything—looks, talent, fame, wealth. . . ."

"But not love," Jacqueline said. "The Earl of Whatever is obviously a publicity stunt; the only man in poor Valentine's life seems to be that middle-aged manager of hers."

"If she hasn't got it, it's because she doesn't want it." Sue kicked the table. "She could have any man she wanted. They're all crazy about her."

Enlightenment dawned on Jacqueline. "Victor is not in love with Valentine," she said.

"You wouldn't say that if you had seen them today." Jean kicked the bureau. "He was all over her, bowing and kissing her hand, and . . . Hattie kept throwing out hints about a royal love affair—the King and Queen of Romance. . . ."

"So that's Hattie's latest scheme," Jacqueline mused. "The Earl must have turned out to be a dud."

Her suggestion did not convince Sue. "I hate that girl," she muttered. "Valentine, Valentine . . . everything just falls into her lap. I could kill her."

"Don't say that," Jacqueline said sharply.

Sue's shoulders sagged. She sat down on the edge of the bed. "I didn't mean it."

"I know. But don't say it. How did the other awards go?"

"Valerie won the top three—Historical Romance, Historical Novel, and Classic Historical Romance."

"The categories seem to overlap somewhat," Jacqueline said. "Didn't anyone else win anything?"

"Victor won the Love's Leading Man award." Sue laughed cynically. "And Valerie Vanderbilt took Historical Saga. All Hattie's writers, by a strange coincidence."

"That reminds me." Jacqueline reached for the phone. "Excuse me a minute. . . . Jean? Where the hell have you been? I've been calling all day. . . . Well, most of the day. I lost track of . . . what? I thought you wanted . . . I know it's late. I tried to. . . . Yes, I'll be there. I want to talk to you too. Afterwards? . . . Fine. See you then."

She hung up. "We'd better get ready for the cocktail party. I didn't realize how late it is."

"I'm not going."

"Oh yes, you are. Sulking is childish."

"I am not sulking!"

"Besides, I need a foil—someone who looks normal. Don't desert me; I'll buy you a drink or two, and then we'll have dinner and talk about everybody."

A faint gleam of interest showed on Sue's face. "Big deal," she murmured. "The drinks are free."

"You poor innocent." Jacqueline swung her feet off the bed and stood up. "I've attended similar affairs; your exorbitantly priced ticket entitles you to one cocktail. After that you're on your own, with Hattie getting her cut of every drop you imbibe."

"Well . . . what are you going to wear?"

"The same thing I wore this morning. But I've added a few touches."

The hat now boasted a ruffle of lace five inches wide. It hung down over Jacqueline's eyebrows in front. Amid the flowers and bows on the crown perched a stuffed cockatoo, its molting wings spread. It had one red glass eye. The other was missing. A cascade of glaringly fake amethysts dribbled from Jacqueline's ears to her shoulders. Her sheer gray stockings had clocks of tiny hearts running halfway up the calf.

She applied makeup with a lavish hand. Her cheekbones were not inconspicuous even when unadorned; following the advice of the expert at the lecture she had attended, she "sculptured" them so enthusiastically that they stood out like snow-covered islands in a muddy sea. Heavy black false lashes dragged her eyelids down to half-mast.

Squinting between the lace fringe and the eyelashes, Jacqueline outlined her mouth with frosty plum lipstick and then turned from the mirror. "How's that?"

"You aren't going like that!"

"Am I not? Hurry up and get dressed. Or are you going in your petticoat? You know," Jacqueline said musingly, "that might not be a bad idea."

Sue snatched her dress off the hanger and backed away, as if she feared Jacqueline might bustle her out the door in her underwear. "You're kidding. Aren't you?"

"On second thought, it would be more effective at the ball tomorrow night. It is a costume ball, you know; the others will be dripping with ruffles and encased in crinolines. We'll slash that lacy camisole and rip the petticoat in a few strategic places, and you can go as Blaze, heroine of *Slave of Lust,* trying to veil her snowy charms from the lascivious eyes of the Sultan. We could bleach a lock of your hair, too. Blaze had a silver streak rippling through the midnight glory of—"

"Stop that!" Sue put on her dress and attacked the zipper so forcefully that it jammed.

"Turn around," Jacqueline said. As she dealt efficiently with the zipper she said, "The trouble with you is, you have no sense of humor."

"I do, too!"

"Now let's have a look at you."

Sue tugged her skirt straight and posed, looking self-conscious.

"Humph," Jacqueline said.

"You don't like my dress?"

Jacqueline shook her head. "Sexy doesn't suit you. Black is not

your color. The neckline is too high. The skirt is too long. Other
than that. . . ."

Sue glared at her and Jacqueline said approvingly, "Good.
When someone is rude to you, don't cry—swear. All I'm saying is
that you are one of the few writers present who should wear what
Hattie seems to think of as romantic clothes. Ruffles and lace and
organdy look ridiculous on elderly ingenues like Valerie Vanderbilt and Emerald What's-Her-Name. You could get away with that
image. And take off your glasses."

"I can't see without them."

"Obviously you did not attend the lecture on how to promote
yourself. Don't you want to be a successful romance writer?"

"I'm beginning to think I don't."

"Indeed? Well, we'll discuss it later. It's time to go."

III

As Jacqueline had predicted, some of the ensembles worn by the
guests at the cocktail party were almost as remarkable as hers.
Emerald Fitzroy exposed her brittle collarbones in an off-the-
shoulder gown of crimson taffeta whose vivid color wrought
havoc with her sallow complexion. Another writer, whom Jacqueline did not know, had obviously made her dress. It was pink
muslin with pink, red, and purple hearts appliquéd at random.
She had forgotten to remove the basting threads. However, Jacqueline's cockatoo rescued her from anonymity; it rose over the
heads of the crowd, squinting malevolently out of its single red
glass eye.

At the door Jacqueline and Sue exchanged their tickets of admission for other tickets entitling them to one cocktail apiece.
"Told you so," Jacqueline remarked, as they got in line at a table
where bartenders were sloshing various liquids into small pink
plastic cups.

Having settled this first and most important matter, Jacqueline
inspected the gathering. A string quartet was sawing away at one
end of the room; the results of its labors were inaudible except at
close range, since all the people in the crowded room were talking to one another, or in a few cases to themselves. The latter

appeared to be fans, nervously rehearsing the graceful speeches they hoped to address to their favorite writers as soon as they got up the courage to approach them. The classification of colored name tags was unnecessary; it was possible to distinguish editors from authors, fans from publicists by the clothes they were wearing. The older fans had donned the standard "afternoon" or "cocktail" dresses of their youth—linen, silk, and linen- or silk-look polyester. A few perspired gently in fur jackets.

For the most part, the writers doggedly tried to live up to the romantic image. There were even a few picture hats—though none, Jacqueline observed complacently, was of the dimensions of her own. The editors, publicists, and agents had made token concessions to the mood, in the form of pink shirts and dresses, but most wore the usual New York business attire, which is one of the drabbest in the universe.

It was on these individuals that Jacqueline's mercenary attention focused. She had not yet decided which publishing house to favor with her completed manuscript—when she completed it. In the course of the past few days she had identified the big names. The pretty blonde, who resembled the heroines of the contemporary romances she peddled so successfully, was an assistant editor of one of the big lines—Lost Love Romances. The tall, broadshouldered woman in the pinstripe suit was Margo Barrister, editor-in-chief of Windblown Romances; her companion, a graceful young man with shoulder-length blond curls, was Robin Bernstein, who represented the rival Wax Candle line. It was rumored that Wax Candle had lost its shirt on Regencies and was now focusing on earlier historic periods, specifically the Late Stone Age.

From the fixed smiles on the faces of the two editors Jacqueline deduced that they were being poisonously polite to one another, and she wondered if their antagonism had anything to do with the fact that Windblown's most recent hit had featured a Neanderthal hero and a Cro-Magnon heroine. ("From our joining, Fleet Gazelle, will come a new people.") Maybe, Jacqueline mused, I can change my setting from fifteenth-century France to the Middle Paleolithic. It shouldn't be too difficult. Stone axes instead of swords, a lake village on stilts instead of a castle. The villain could be a wicked medicine man. . . .

"I want another drink," Sue announced, jogging Jacqueline's elbow. "How do I get it?"

Annoyed at having her literary plotting interrupted, Jacqueline was brusque. "You buy a ticket. Get one for me if you will." She took a twenty-dollar bill from the mauve satin envelope with which she had reluctantly replaced her usual huge purse. She felt undressed and incapable without the purse. But Art must be served, and the purse had not matched her ensemble.

"Thanks." Sue took the money and vanished into the mob. Under the lace fringe Jacqueline's brow furrowed. Then she dismissed Sue with a shrug. She was tired of dewy-eyed innocents who had to be protected from themselves and everyone else.

Along one side of the room was a row of tables draped in white with the usual decorations, where the promotional gimcracks of the publisher sponsoring the cocktail party were prominently displayed. Among the litter was an enormous reproduction of the cover of Valentine's latest book—the one Jacqueline was reading. Not far away was Valentine herself, and as she studied the arrangement, Jacqueline's painted lips cracked in an appreciative grin.

It was a masterpiece of romantic kitsch, but it had the practical purpose of isolating the Queen of Love from the admirers who—Hattie hoped—might otherwise have trampled her. White picket fences twined with artificial vines and roses enclosed a space that was meant to suggest a lovely garden. The floor was covered with imitation grass of the variety used in football stadiums. Wrought-iron patio furniture and potted plants were scattered about. In this enclosure Hattie and her stable had taken their picturesque places. A wobbly arch of plastic greenery framed the baroque bench where Valentine sat, with the "Earl of Devonbrook" beside her, stiff as a wax dummy. Victor von Damm, once again wearing his Prisoner of Zenda garb of black trousers and flowing white shirt, leaned over the back of the bench. Hattie, in gray satin with a huge corsage of sweetheart roses dangling from the shelf of her bosom, was seated at a nearby table. Her eyes never left Valentine. At first Jacqueline thought VV had found an excuse not to attend. Then she made out a rigid form trying to hide behind a skimpy screen of fake roses and a potted rubber plant.

Having located the stars of the evening, Jacqueline turned her eagle eye (critics were inclined to substitute the name of another, less socially acceptable bird) upon the assemblage at large, and was gratified to see many familiar faces. The genteel lady from Boston, heading purposefully in the direction of the bower, and Victor von Damm; Emerald, scowling in the direction of the bower—she had not been asked to join the elite; the haggard woman agent, looking for clients; the bald head and cherubic countenance of Max Hollenstein, buttering up the editor-in-chief of Moonlight Love Romances. And surely that was Betsy, almost unrecognizable in flowered silk, gold sandals, and a brassy wig that was the identical twin of Jean's. It must be the most popular model this year.

Betsy's eyes moved shiftily around the room. She saw Jacqueline, and twisted her face in a violent grimace before she disappeared behind a large publisher.

Another familiar face made Jacqueline wish she had a portly publisher to use as a screen. Laurie was wearing a flowing pink caftan, ornately embroidered in gold thread. When her black-rimmed eyes found Jacqueline, the latter conquered a cowardly impulse to retreat. But Laurie's greeting was more than amiable, it was positively friendly.

"Hi, Mrs. Kirsky. Listen, I'm really sorry about what happened. I didn't feel too good. I was sick at my stomach. Afterwards I threw up."

"I'm sorry to hear that," Jacqueline said sincerely.

"Oh, I'm okay now. I get sick at my stomach a lot, but it doesn't last. As soon as I throw up—"

"Maybe you shouldn't be drinking," Jacqueline said, glancing at Laurie's pink plastic glass. (Anything to change the subject.)

"It's just diet ginger ale. I'm on a diet. I haven't had anything to eat all day except a candy bar and some cottage cheese."

"Good for you."

"So Hattie said I should apologize. She says you're a friend of Valentine's. I guess you were just sucking up to that woman to find out what she wants so you can tell Valentine."

Curiosity overcame the repugnance Laurie's proximity inevitably induced. Jacqueline said, "Can I ask you a question, Laurie?"

"Sure."

"What is Dubretta Duberstein trying to do to Valentine?"

"She writes lies about her," Laurie said. "You know that note-book she carries, the one she's always writing in? It's full of lies about Valentine. Like, she's a Lesbian, or she's frigid, or she's an ex-hooker. Like that."

"But what possible difference . . . would it bother you to learn that one or all of those things were true?"

"They aren't true!"

"Of course not. So why worry about lies people tell?"

Laurie's eyes turned toward the enclosure where Valentine sat enthroned. "She's the most beautiful thing in the world," the girl murmured. "Like an angel. Throwing mud on somebody like that is like—is like. . . ."

"Blasphemy?"

"Yeah. Yeah, that's it." Laurie nodded emphatically. "You do understand."

"Yes, I understand."

Laurie smiled at her. "Valentine was right. You are a nice per-son. So I'm glad I talked to you. I've got to get back to Valentine now. Good-bye, Mrs. Kirky."

Jacqueline's face was very sober as she watched the girl billow off in a cloud of pink. The peculiar combination of loathing and pity Laurie inspired was not a comfortable feeling.

"You sure know how to stand out in a crowd," said a voice at her elbow. "Where did you get the dead pigeon?"

"It's a cockatoo," Jacqueline said, turning to find Dubretta beside her. "You're in costume too, I see."

Dubretta tugged at the enormous corsage of sweetheart roses that covered one entire side of her suit jacket. "It's just like Hat-tie's, but twice the size. I don't know why I try to be funny; you're only the second person who's caught the joke."

She began to rummage in her shoulder bag, which was almost as big as the one Jacqueline usually carried. The liquid in her glass sloshed wildly, and Jacqueline said, "What are you looking for? Maybe I can—"

"Oh no." Dubretta pressed the purse tightly against her side. "Nobody, but nobody, puts a hand in this. It's full of goodies tonight. You can hold my drink, if you will."

Jacqueline obliged. Dubretta dug into the purse with both hands and finally extracted a cigarette. She lit it and then retrieved her drink. Jacqueline looked hungrily at the cigarette. There had not been room in the mauve envelope for the pack she had guiltily purchased, and she had decided it was time to quit smoking again. Her nostrils flared as she tried to inhale the smoke Dubretta blew out.

"You seem very merry this evening," she said.

"I'm not drunk, if that's what you mean. This is only my third. I may tie one on, though. I've got things to celebrate, and my mama taught me never to pass up a free drink."

"Free, my eye."

"Never having to buy a drink is one of the perks of my profession," Dubretta said with a grin. "My victims have been trying to get me liquored up in the hope of loosening my tongue."

"Did it work?"

"What do you think?" Dubretta gestured at the inadequately hidden form of Valerie Vanderbilt. "Have you said hi to your friend yet?"

"Why don't you leave her alone?" Jacqueline demanded.

"She's a pusher," Dubretta said. "The crap she peddles stupefies the brain just as dope rots the body. In a way she's the worst of the lot. They're doing the best they can. Their best is pretty cruddy, but they don't know the difference. She knows."

The brutal accuracy of the analysis silenced Jacqueline. She found it hard to believe that Dubretta was as noble and disinterested as she pretended, but the columnist had unerringly pinpointed the cause of Jean's present agony. She did know better. She suffered from the painful self-loathing of a patriot who has betrayed the Cause.

"Bah," said Jacqueline.

"Bah? I thought you'd agree with me. Whose side are you on?"

"I'm not on anybody's side. I dislike the quality of these books as much as I dislike anything that smacks of censorship. Who are you to tell people what they should or shouldn't read? Besides, not all of it is bad. Have you read Valentine's books?"

"Valentine." Dubretta's eyes rested on the slender, gold-crowned figure. "She's really something, isn't she? Beautiful, successful, brilliant. . . . Oh yes, I've read everything she ever wrote. She's good. If Hattie hadn't lassoed her and labeled her as the Queen of Love, she could have made a name as a serious writer."

There was a curious, almost gloating note in her voice. She lifted her purse to her breast and closed her arms over it, as if she were holding a baby. "Just look at her," she said softly. "Beauty like that is unreal. She's like a woman of legend—Guinevere and fair Rosamund, Helen of Troy. . . ."

Jacqueline shivered. Was it only a coincidence that all the fabled women Dubretta had mentioned were doomed by their own loveliness to death or disgrace? The columnist might not have had too much to drink, but she was behaving very oddly.

Sue joined them. She handed Jacqueline a glass and sipped at her own with such primness that Jacqueline suspected she had had an extra on the side.

"Who're you?" Dubretta asked. "One of Hattie's stable?"

"No such luck," Sue said bitterly.

"I wouldn't be so sure, dear. Before this night is over, you'll be thanking God you aren't mixed up with that bunch."

Victor bent down to speak to Valentine, who looked up at him with a smile. Sue snorted. "What a ham," she said distinctly.

"Victor? He sure is," Dubretta agreed. "Better not fall for him, honey; he's all sham, including that pretty face of his. Too pretty, if you ask me. . . . Now there—there is a good-looking guy. And he's been staring at you."

"He's too old," said Sue, looking at the man Dubretta indicated.

"His white hair is premature," Jacqueline said. "But he is definitely too old for you."

"Friend of yours?" Dubretta asked curiously.

"Not any more." Jacqueline raised her glass in an ironic salute. From across the room, Professor James Whittier saluted her with even greater irony. Jacqueline beckoned. James shook his head. Jacqueline shrugged. James started toward them.

Amused at the exchange, Dubretta watched his approach. "Just my type," she announced. "What a gorgeous head of hair! A few wrinkles add character to a man's face. He looks intelligent, too."

"I am," said James, who had heard most of the speech. "And I have a terrific sense of humor. Who are you, you perceptive woman?"

"This is Dubretta Duberstein," said Jacqueline. "Don't pretend you don't know who she is; you read her column every day. Dubretta, may I present Professor James Whittier, chairman of the English Department at Coldwater College, Nebraska. He is a distinguished scholar and a rotten sneak."

Dubretta shifted her shoulder bag so she could shake hands. The strap caught on her corsage and pulled it from its moorings. James bent to pick it up. Their hands met among the blossoms, poetically but confusingly; James pricked his thumb on a loose bit of wire, and Dubretta gave the battered flowers a rueful look before dropping them into her bag.

"You her boyfriend?" she asked.

"No," Jacqueline and James said in chorus.

"He just happens to be in New York at the same time I'm here," Jacqueline added. "It was a spur-of-the-moment decision, no doubt."

"Since when am I obliged to tell you of my intentions?"

"I told *you.*"

"And you made it plain that my company was not welcome. I can take a hint," James said loftily. "You wanted to be alone; I have left you alone. It is indeed pure coincidence that we happen to be—"

"You didn't try to catch my attention in the lobby yesterday?" Jacqueline demanded. "You didn't telephone two—no, three—times?"

James's face took on a look of righteous indignation. "I meant from the first to attend this debacle. It promised to be an event worth the attention of a connoisseur in schlock. So far it has lived up to my expectations, and I hope . . . where the hell did you get that hat?"

"I hurt your feelings," Jacqueline said gently. "I wasn't deliberately ignoring you, James."

"You weren't?"

The two gazed soulfully at one another. "Shall we leave you two alone?" Dubretta asked.

"No," Jacqueline said. James's face fell. Jacqueline added,

"But perhaps he deserves some compensation for my inadvertent rudeness. Let's introduce him to Hattie and the gang."

"Good idea. I have a few things I want to say to Hattie."

As they passed the podium, the ensemble began "Some Enchanted Evening." James nudged Jacqueline. "Don't do it. Don't sing."

" 'When you have found him, Never let him go. . . .' Oh, all right. What a killjoy you are, James."

"How did you like the books I gave you?"

"You have opened vast new vistas of enjoyment, James," Jacqueline said fervently.

The audience outside the picket fence had diminished as the professionals, having paid their respects, turned to the real purposes of the evening—drinking and dealing. Only a few shy matrons stood by, ogling Victor von Damm, and a woman with the desperate look of a competing agent sought to attract Valentine's attention. Hattie, ever alert, moved to block the attempt.

As they approached, James let out a profane exclamation. "What in God's name is that?" he demanded, indicating the lumpy object squatting on the floor outside the gate.

Laurie was sitting cross-legged, the folds of her pink caftan spread around her like a puddle of melted strawberry ice cream. Her head turned toward them with the alert suspicion of a sentry's. Then she smiled. "Hi, Mrs. Kirsky."

"Hi," Jacqueline said.

"Friend of yours?" James inquired.

Hattie saw the procession bearing down on her. Dismissing her defeated rival, she squared her shoulders and prepared to deal with this new threat.

"Well, just look who's here. Dubretta darling, how nice of you to mingle with us despicable characters! And Victor's cute little friend! And Mrs. Kirk!"

"Her name is Kirby," Dubretta said. "Same as Joe."

Hattie ignored this. "Who is Joe?" James demanded of Sue. She shrugged helplessly. "I never know what's going on," she admitted.

"And who's this ha-a-andsome man?" Hattie asked coquettishly. "I'll just bet he's a big important publisher or investor."

"He's a teacher," Dubretta said, as James self-consciously

fingered his tie. "An English teacher, Hattie. If he has any money to invest, I'd advise him to look elsewhere."

"Dubretta just doesn't like us, Professor." Hattie showed all her teeth. "Ours is the fastest-growing segment of the publishing industry; we control over forty percent of the paperback market, and I myself—"

"That's today, Hattie," Dubretta interrupted, cradling her purse. "Today. Better wait till tomorrow before you invest, Professor."

"You're planning to write some more mean things about us." Hattie's fixed smile did not change. "You just go right ahead, Dubretta honey. You know the old rule of publicity—"

" 'Mention my name, I don't care how.' But you may not like the way your name will be mentioned in my next column, Hattie. I told you," Dubretta said, unsmiling, "that one day I'd get even. It was a long time ago; but I haven't forgotten."

For a moment Hattie's features reflected the deadly malice of Dubretta's. Before she could reply to the columnist's threat, a soft voice called, "Mrs. Kirby. Hello, Mrs. Kirby."

Valentine rose, with such ineffable grace that all eyes were drawn to her slender white figure. James gulped audibly. Jacqueline scowled at him.

"Come in, won't you?" Valentine said. "Join us."

Hattie looked as if she were choking, but got a grip on herself. "What a charmin' idea. We'll all have a friendly little chat."

Dubretta was the first to pass through the gate Hattie opened. James followed, stepping heavily on Jacqueline's foot as he stared bemusedly at the smiling Queen of Love. The fans let out a sigh of envy and admiration as Victor bent over Jacqueline's hand.

"Where've you been?" he muttered. "VV was looking for you."

"She can't have looked very hard," Jacqueline retorted. The stuffed cockatoo wobbled, as if nodding agreement.

Victor did not reply, but turned hopefully to Sue. The girl ignored his outstretched hand and walked past him, her nose in the air. She followed James, who had homed in on Valentine; Victor followed Sue, leaving Jacqueline alone with the cockatoo.

Her lip curled as she watched James go into his act. It was a performance with which she was only too familiar, consisting of an intense, burning stare, a deep reverberant voice, and quotations from the Elizabethan poets. "Was this the face that launched a thousand ships?" he inquired, taking Valentine's hand in his. "And burnt the topless towers of Ilium?"

Valentine stared—as well she might, Jacqueline thought sourly. Sue continued to ignore Victor with an ostentation that verged on caricature. No one paid the slightest attention to the "Earl," nor did he seem to be aware of their presence. One could not help but wonder what thoughts, if any, were passing through his handsome head.

Jacqueline had not been unmoved by Valentine's plea for help; she simply couldn't figure out how to respond to it. Valentine was a virtual prisoner in Hattie's suite. There was no way Jacqueline could reach her without endangering the secrecy Valentine obviously wanted. Even if Val answered the telephone herself, she couldn't speak freely without the risk of being overheard. Jacqueline had decided she would have to wait for the girl to get in touch with her. If this was the best Valentine could do, it wasn't very good. There were too many people standing around. Though Hattie was deep in conversation with Dubretta—not a cordial conversation, to judge by their grim faces—she kept a close watch on Valentine.

Jacqueline decided she might as well take advantage of the concentration of the others on the Queen of Love to have the long-delayed conversation with Jean. But when she turned to the corner where her friend was trying to imitate a potted plant, she met the quizzical gaze of Max Hollenstein.

"How nice to see you again, Mrs. Kirby. Perhaps you can persuade VV to come out and face her admirers."

The rubber plant shook violently and a thin voice squeaked, "He knows me! I met him at the MLA meetings two years ago."

"James? He couldn't possibly recognize you, Jean. He has a terrible memory for faces anyhow, and you look—"

With an agile bound Jean cleared the fence and melted into the crowd. Max let out a low whistle of amused admiration, and Jacqueline said, "She used to be standing-jump champion of our dorm."

"Ah, so that's where you two met. You know the hideous truth about our VV."

"I don't know anything," Jacqueline said. "Presumably you do. Would you care to enlighten me as to the cause of the air of imminent eclipse that shadows this bright assembly? What the hell is the matter with everyone?"

Max's eyes widened in simulated horror. " 'Clouds and eclipses stain both moon and sun. . . .' "

" 'And loathsome canker lives in sweetest bud.' But you wouldn't call Hattie a sweet bud, would you?"

The expression on Hattie's face as she spoke to Dubretta was anything but sweet. Max chuckled. "She does look angry. Perhaps she's caught on to Dubretta's little joke. I don't know why she lets Dubretta get under her skin."

"You don't resent Dubretta's attacks?" Jacqueline asked.

"I shouldn't admit it," Max murmured, pretending to glance guiltily at Hattie, "but I enjoy Dubretta's pungent comments. She has a pretty wit and a forceful personality. Her attacks, as you call them, aren't damaging; they are merely entertaining."

"Then why are Hattie and Jean so uptight?"

"Dear Mrs. Kirby," Max said earnestly, "you've been infected by VV's peculiar moods. I've tried to convince her that she's worrying needlessly; even if the academic world does learn of her second profession, the worst she has to fear is a little ridicule."

"That's threat enough to Jean."

Max's eyebrows rose. "Has she always been so—er—" He paused delicately.

"Neurotic? No. Shy, self-conscious, conventional, yes. But I've never seen her as bad as this."

"But this is her first public appearance," Max argued. "Even experienced actors suffer from stage fright. And, of course, there is Laurie. Valentine isn't the only one whose nerves are affected by the poor creature. 'Fandom,' as I believe it is called, attracts some unbalanced persons—not as commonly in our profession as in certain others, notably films and television, but. . . ."

"But Hattie has added a show-business element to her profession," Jacqueline said. "That's one of the reasons for her success as an agent."

"True. It has contributed to her success, but, as is so often the case, it has certain drawbacks. Laurie is one of the drawbacks."

"I see. Everything is A-OK except for a few loonies."

"How well you put it." Max laughed. "But I'm forgetting my manners, and dear Hattie, of course, has never had any. Let me get you a glass of wine." He indicated a table behind him, where bottles and glasses had been set out.

Hattie had not forgotten her manners, or perhaps she had decided the best way of dealing with Dubretta was to get her drunk. She and Max collided on their way to the refreshment table, to Max's disadvantage. Recovering himself, the little man said breathlessly, "I was about to offer Mrs. Kirby a glass of wine."

"We'll all have a glass," Hattie said. She and Max exchanged glances. Then Hattie reached for a bottle, and Max said casually, "I'll do it, Hattie."

Afterwards, when it became critically important to recall the exact train of events, Jacqueline could not decide how much of the confusion was planned and how much was accidental. The others wandered toward the table, except for Valentine, who remained in her seat. Even the "Earl" got up, to Jacqueline's relief; she had begun to wonder if he was dead.

The pink lump on the floor beyond the fence made a slow heaving motion, like lava lifting over the rim of a volcano. "You said I could give her the wine."

"Now, Laurie," Hattie began.

"You said I could."

"Oh, very well. But you must be careful."

"I'll be careful." Laurie fumbled at the fastening of the gate.

"I don't want any wine," Valentine said quickly. "Really I don't."

"I'll be careful," Laurie crooned, with a look of canine adoration. She lumbered toward the table.

James skipped out of her path as she bore down on him and sought refuge at Jacqueline's side. "The kid is bombed out of her skull," he said under his breath. "What kind of witches' Sabbat is this?"

Trust James to pronounce the word correctly, even when he was perturbed. Jacqueline said, "She was all right—for her—when I talked to her half an hour ago."

"I'm sorry we haven't anything to offer except wine," said Max, trying to preserve the social amenities, while Laurie hovered over him, breathing heavily. "This is Valentine's favorite. It's a rather pleasant Bordeaux, and of course red wine suits the theme of the conference."

"I'd have expected a rosé," Jacqueline said. Max smiled; Hattie explained seriously, "That's what I wanted, but Val doesn't like any of the pink wines, and Max backed her up. He's got no feeling for setting the right mood."

The bottle Max had selected contained just enough wine to fill one glass. He set it aside. "There seems to be some sediment in this one. I'll open another bottle. No, Laurie, don't take that. Valentine doesn't want that one."

Laurie stared, uncomprehending. Again she reached for the glass Max had placed on the table. He started to open a new bottle, repeating patiently, "Not that one, Laurie. Here's another glass. Take this one. It's better."

Laurie didn't seem to hear him. Her hand remained poised over the first glass he had filled. Max poured wine into several other glasses. They were not the cheap plastic throwaways the bartenders had been using, but crystal goblets, which set off the ruby-red glow of the wine.

"Take this one," Max said, in the same slow, patient voice. He selected a glass he had filled only half full, perhaps because he had no great confidence in Laurie's steadiness of hand.

Laurie was obsessed by the first glass. She made no move to take the one Max was offering her. Before she could decide, Valentine glided toward the table. "I'll take this one," she said, selecting a glass at random. "I don't want anyone to wait on me. I'll get it myself."

Laurie's face puckered, and tears made havoc of her makeup. "You said I could give it to her! You promised!"

"Oh, for God's sake!" Hattie snatched the glass from Valentine's hand and put it back on the table. "Give it to her, then. Take one—any one—that one, Laurie. Go on, give it to her."

The transfer was made, though Valentine's lovely face was rigid with disgust, and she was so reluctant to touch Laurie's hand that she almost dropped the goblet. At a gesture from Hattie, Laurie trundled back to her post, and the others, who had been prey to various uncomfortable emotions, took their wine.

Jacqueline was never certain what happened in the next critical seconds. James and Max had their heads together, discussing wine; Sue and Victor-Joe withdrew to a corner where they could speak privately. Valentine stared at her untouched goblet as if it bore the visible marks of Laurie's hand. Dubretta and Hattie stood side by side, unspeaking, sipping their wine. The "Earl"— she had not the faintest recollection of what he was doing, or where he was.

The goblet fell from Dubretta's hand. It bounced undamaged on the rubbery artificial floor surface. Dubretta doubled over, clutching her middle. Hattie, who was closest to her, instantly backed away. Dubretta crumpled to the floor.

Her falling body, or the rush of the others to assist her, over-turned the table, which was one of the small tottery variety. Wine poured out in a bloody stream, staining the artificial turf. Glasses bounded and rebounded in macabre playfulness.

Jacqueline was the first to reach the recumbent woman. Dubretta's breath came in ragged gasps. She tried to speak. "Forgot . . . pills. . . ."

Jacqueline disentangled the straps of Dubretta's purse from her arm and turned the bag upside down. An assortment of coins and other small, loose objects bounced down and up. One was the plastic bottle of pills. Jacqueline caught it in midair and wrestled with the cap, cursing the well-intentioned regulations of the pharmaceutical industry. Removing the cap at last, she took out one of the pills and got it into Dubretta's distorted mouth. Someone handed her a glass. Wine. Probably not advisable, but it was the only liquid immediately available. She held Dubretta's head and helped her swallow.

"Get a doctor, quick," she ordered.

"I'll make an announcement." The speaker—Max Hollenstein —started for the gate. Hattie got in his way. "Like hell you will. People are staring already. Pick her up, take her away from here."

"Hurry," Jacqueline said, her hand on Dubretta's wrist. The pulse was faint and irregular. Dubretta's eyes stared blankly. Then an expression of surprise spread over her face. "Blue," she gasped. "It's . . . blue."

The erratic beat under Jacqueline's fingers flickered and faded out.

CHAPTER FIVE

Jacqueline snatched up Dubretta's compact, wiped the mirror on her sleeve, and held it before Dubretta's lips. "Where's that damned doctor?" she exclaimed.

"Victor's gone to find one." Pale but composed, Sue knelt on the columnist's other side. "Anything?"

"No." Jacqueline threw the mirror aside and ripped Dubretta's suit jacket open. Placing the flat of one hand over the motionless breast, she struck it with her clenched fist, waited a moment, and repeated the gesture.

"No good," she muttered. "Sue—do you know CPR?"

The girl nodded mutely. Jacqueline cupped one hand over the other in the center of Dubretta's chest. Sue turned Dubretta's head to the side and bent over, her lips covering those of the fallen woman, her hand pinching her nostrils shut. Jacqueline began pumping. ". . . four—five—now, Sue. . . ."

It seemed to both of them that they repeated the movements a thousand times before Victor returned, towing a tall man wearing glasses and a bright-red tartan waistcoat. They had to force their way through a whispering, staring crowd, and when the doctor took in the scene he scratched his head and asked,

"Which is the patient?" His confusion was understandable. Valentine had fainted, and was being supported by Max and the Earl. Laurie was struggling to reach her fallen idol, and was being forcibly restrained by Hattie and James.

"Here." Jacqueline stood up. "I think it's her heart."

"It usually is," was the dry response. The doctor fussily adjusted his trousers and knelt. After a brief examination he said, "Well, you seem to be correct, madam. Did she have a heart condition?"

"Never mind that now." Abandoning James to struggle with Laurie, Hattie bent over the doctor. "Is she dead or isn't she?"

"She is," the doctor said brusquely. He rose and dusted off the knees of his trousers. He patted Sue on the arm and his voice softened as he went on, "It's no use, child. I'm sorry."

"She didn't even know the woman," Hattie said. "I don't know what she's bawling about. Look, Doc, I have to get this—this thing out of here. It's ruining the party."

Realizing that he was the focus of myriad curious stares, the doctor stepped back. "I'm not a cardiac specialist," he said quickly. "I'm a dermatologist, and I don't . . . there's nothing I can do. I didn't actually *do* anything—you saw I didn't. . . . You had better call the—er—the authorities. Excuse me, please."

He removed himself with more speed than dignity. He was replaced by one of the hotel staff, whose chief concern, like Hattie's, was to clear away the mess as quickly as possible. The body, discreetly draped in a sheet, was removed via a service door. Then Hattie took a deep breath and considered what to do next.

Valentine, conscious but pale and shaken, leaned against Max's arm. James and Laurie were locked in motionless combat, reminding Jacqueline of two equally matched wrestlers. Sue, weeping beautifully, had taken refuge in the embrace of Joe-Victor, on whose face gratification struggled with a seemly sobriety. Through a gap in the screen of roses Jacqueline saw the gleam of a brassy blond wig. She began edging toward it, but when Hattie cleared her throat, the wig eclipsed itself.

"First things first," Hattie announced. "Professor—what the hell are you doing? I told you to get that girl out of here."

James rolled his eyes, but was too hard-pressed to reply. Hattie went on, "Victor, stop whatever you're doing with that girl and help Max take Val to her room. You. . . ." She eyed Jacqueline, but before she could express her feelings, Jacqueline said, "I'm going to call the police. Unless someone has already done so?"

She turned an ironically inquiring gaze upon the hotel official. He nodded glumly. "Yes, madam, I'll attend to that."

"But—" Hattie began.

"It must be done, madam. The regulations are clear. In cases of sudden death—"

"She died of a heart attack," Hattie insisted. "The doc said so."

"A mere formality . . . unpleasant but necessary . . . follow the proper procedure. . . ."

"Son of a—" Hattie began. She caught herself in the nick of time and, after a struggle, recaptured her misplaced image. "Ah just don't know what Ah'm sayin', Ah'm so upset," she explained to the audience outside the fence. "Valentine, honey, you go lie down. Aunt Hattie will be with you as soon as she explains to the nice people."

She climbed nimbly over the fence and headed for the platform, where the musicians, with admirable dedication to duty, were rendering a spirited version of "It's Love, Love, Love." Max led Valentine away. Joe, in flagrant disregard of the general's orders, tenderly escorted Sue through the mob. Laurie released her stranglehold on James and set off in pursuit of Valentine. James reeled backwards into a chair, where he sat breathing raggedly. And Jacqueline was appalled to find herself crooning the obscure lyrics of the song the quartet was playing. "When your heart goes bumpity-bump. . . ."

She stopped singing. Once again a gleam of gold nylon hair showed behind the lattice of roses, and this time it did not disappear when she approached. Peering through the screen she asked, "How long have you been there?"

"I saw the whole thing." Jean's teeth chattered. "Oh God, oh God. What will happen now?"

"How should I know? If I were you, I'd get out of here."

"Come with me." A quivering hand reached for her through a gap in the lattice.

"Not now. I'll talk to you later."

The sound of the strings was replaced by Hattie's voice, her accent firmly in place. "Deah friends, Ah hate to cast a shadow over this happy gatherin'. . . ."

Jean disappeared and Jacqueline turned to see that a squad of waiters had begun restoring order. The table had been set back on its legs, the unopened bottles of wine had been replaced on its top, and the used wineglasses had been removed. A waiter knelt, blotting up puddles of wine, while another brushed shards of broken glass into a dustpan. Someone must have stepped on one or more of the goblets; Jacqueline had a vivid memory of the way they had bounced, undamaged, when they fell.

Speed was of the essence. Swooping, she snatched a gleaming fragment from the path of the whisk broom, holding it carefully to prevent the few drops of liquid cupped in its curve from spilling. Then she pounced on the man who was wiping the floor. "I'll take that," she announced. Too surprised to protest, he let her whisk the stained cloth from his fingers.

With both hands occupied and her elbow holding her lavender bag against her side, she looked around for help. She might have known she would need her usual purse.

Everyone had left except for James. Jacqueline advanced on him and he looked up from his gloomy inspection of a ripped seam in the shoulder of his jacket.

"Take this," she ordered. "No, not that. This. No, not that! How dull you are, James. What's the matter with you?"

His tie under his left ear, his snowy mane in wild disorder, James was too enraged to speak even if Jacqueline had given him the chance. "Take my purse," she said. "Slide it out from under my arm. Open it. Take out my handkerchief. Hold it out. . . . That's right. Splendid work, James."

A powerful stench of eau des violettes wafting from the handkerchief made James's nose twitch like a rabbit's. "I'm not going to ask what you think you're doing," he mumbled. "I'm not going to ask."

Jacqueline laid the fragment of glass on the handkerchief, which was lace-trimmed and embroidered with purple violets. The wine-stained cloth went into a plastic trash bag commandeered from the supplies on the cleaning cart. Then Jacqueline wrapped the handkerchief carefully around the piece of glass and the small spot of scarlet surrounding it.

"Thank you, James."

"I am not going to ask what you think you're doing," James repeated.

"You shouldn't have to ask. A man of your superior intelligence—"

"Are you ready to leave now, or do you want some more garbage?"

"James, we can't leave. The police should be here soon."

"The police? Good Lord, that's all I need. Let's go."

"It is every citizen's duty to assist the police, James."

One of the waiters approached. "Excuse me, ma'am, does this belong to you?"

Jacqueline murmured an abstracted thanks, slung the purse over her shoulder, and went on with her lecture. "We shouldn't leave the scene. The police will want to question the witnesses."

"Everyone else has gone," James pointed out.

"All the more reason why we should do our duty."

"God, you're revolting when you're being self-righteous. Are you coming with me or not?"

"Not."

James stalked away. Jacqueline shifted her shoulder bag into a more comfortable position. Then the truth hit her. She had not carried her shoulder bag. This one must belong to Dubretta.

Jacqueline made a quick and—she hoped—unobtrusive exit, mingling with the departing guests. Finding an unoccupied couch in a corner of the lobby, she sat down and emptied the purse onto the seat beside her.

Whether the waiter had found all the scattered contents she did not know, but she assumed he had; the cleaning process had appeared to be quick and thorough. Dubretta's purse contained almost as much junk as her own. The untidy heap was copiously sprinkled with tobacco. Fastidiously, Jacqueline brushed each article before returning it to the bag. Tissues, comb, lipstick, compact, keys, cigarettes, matches, wallet, coin purse, letters and bills, checkbook, the corsage, crushed and wilting, a tube of toothpaste. . . .

"Hmm," Jacqueline said.

She put most of the things back in the purse, leaving aside a few that required more detailed examination. The wallet contained some bills, which she didn't bother to count, and several credit cards, plus a black-and-white snapshot of a pretty young girl. It was an old photograph; the girl's dark hair was arranged in the long page-boy coiffure popular in Jacqueline's youth. She wondered if it could be a picture of Dubretta, for the setting of the eyes and the shape of the nose resembled the columnist. Remembering her last view of Dubretta's dead, time-scored face, she shivered, and closed the wallet.

The vial of pills was half full of small yellow tablets. The label bore a brand name, followed by the generic designation and the dosage. Jacqueline borrowed Dubretta's pen and a scrap of paper —the register tape from a grocery store—and carefully copied the information before she restored the bottle to Dubretta's bag.

There was only one personal letter. It was addressed to "Dubretta," in care of the newspaper in which her column appeared, and began, "You muckraking old bitch."

One of Dubretta's fans, evidently. Jacqueline put the letter in the purse.

One item remained. Jacqueline riffled through the pages of the stenographer's notebook. It was the same one in which she had seen the columnist writing over the past few days. About eighteen or twenty pages were filled with Dubretta's peculiar and, to Jacqueline, unintelligible shorthand.

With some difficulty Jacqueline squeezed the notebook into her lavender satin evening bag. It made a noticeable bulge, but that could not be helped. She stood up, shaking the tobacco crumbs from her skirt.

"Disgusting," said a woman sitting nearby.

Jacqueline looked at the mess on the carpet. "I couldn't agree more," she said, and caught her glasses as they were about to fall off the tip of her nose. Restoring them to their place, she set off in search of someone who could be bullied into giving her the information she wanted.

His directions led her to an office in the service area of the hotel. Assuming that if she knocked she would be told to go away, she turned the knob and walked in.

Four pairs of eyes stared at her. Dubretta's head had fallen to one side. The transparent film of secretion had not yet dried on her eyeballs; they glistened in the light, as if she were about to welcome the newcomer.

One of the three men said, "Hey!" Another began, "Who the hell—"

Jacqueline put out her hand and pressed Dubretta's eyelids shut.

"Which of you is in charge?" she asked briskly.

The man who had said, "Hey," scowled and pulled the sheet back over the dead woman's face. The second speaker had started to his feet when Jacqueline entered. He was scowling too. The third man remained seated. From the cigarette he held between his fingers a thin stream of smoke rose smoothly toward the ceiling.

He was neatly, almost foppishly dressed, though to Jacqueline it was obvious that his suit had come off a rack in a discount men's store. The deep wine of his tie matched the stripe on the handkerchief in his breast pocket and the socks exposed by his extended legs. A fringe of piebald hair—part gray, part black, liberally sprinkled with white—framed his high forehead. His heavy eyebrows were straight and black; they formed an emphatic parallel to the lines creasing his brow. Only two incongruous notes marred the elegance of his appearance: a seamed white scar bisecting his left cheek from jawline to eyelid, and a pink plastic rose in his buttonhole.

"I'm O'Brien," he said. "And who might you be, lady?"

Jacqueline frowned critically. "The rose jars with your ensemble, Mr. O'Brien."

"Not in the best of taste, in any sense," O'Brien agreed. "Found it stuck to Dubretta's sleeve. Where'd you get her purse?" He added, with a grimace that produced a slash in his right cheek, balancing the scar, "It jars with your ensemble."

Jacqueline sat down in the chair the other man had vacated. His eyes widened indignantly, but before he could protest O'Brien said, "On your way, Kelly. Nothing more to do here."

"I'm leaving too," the third man grunted. "Waste of time, of which I have not enough as it is. Nobody but you would have had the gall to drag me down here to tell you Dubretta's ticker finally gave out on her."

When the others had left, O'Brien turned cool gray eyes to

Jacqueline, who had settled back with the air of one who plans a long stay. He held out his hand. Jacqueline gave him the purse. "Thanks. Where'd you get it?"

"The waiter thought it was mine."

"You a relative?"

"No. I felt I ought to bring the purse to you at once."

"So you have. I really can't see," said O'Brien meditatively, "why you are still here."

"Don't you want to ask me any questions?"

The deeply creased cheeks were evidently O'Brien's version of a smile, and the only visible indications thereof. Jacqueline smiled back at him. "There are pills in her purse. A variety of digitalis."

"Everybody knew about Dubretta's wonky heart."

"So you believe it was a natural death?"

"I don't believe in anything," O'Brien said plaintively. "Not Santa Claus or Tinker Bell or justice or truth. When I have received the official medical report, I will have an informed opinion as to how she died. At the present time I know nothing to contradict my uninformed opinion that she had a heart attack. Can you give me one good reason why I should sit here discussing it with you?"

"No," Jacqueline admitted.

"Oh, come on. Think of a reason. Compared to what lies in store for me the rest of the night, this is a restful interlude. I'd like to prolong it."

Jacqueline muttered under her breath. O'Brien cocked his head. "What did you say?"

"Nothing."

"It sounded like 'smart. . . .' "

"Just your vulgar imagination," Jacqueline said primly. She took her wallet out of the bulging satin evening bag, taking care to keep O'Brien from seeing what else it contained. Extracting a card from the wallet, she handed it to O'Brien. "How's that for a reason?"

The card was a trifle frayed around the edges, but the look of age only added to its baroque elegance. Hand-engraved in an ornate antique script and bordered in gilt, it was one of

Jacqueline's favorite souvenirs. O'Brien held it at arm's length and translated effortlessly.

" 'The bearer, Mrs. Jacqueline Kirby, is an honorary member of the Carabinieri of Rome, with the rank of sub-lieutenant.' All stamped and sealed and signed, by Guido di Cavallo.''

"Do you know him?"

"He spoke at a police conference I attended. Quite the rising star."

"So I understand."

"An honorary carabiniere," O'Brien mused. "And are you also a writer of historical romances?"

He was looking, not at her name tag, but at her hat. Jacqueline straightened it. "I'm a librarian. From Coldwater College in Nebraska."

"Holy shit!" O'Brien let out a roar of laughter, which he cut off as abruptly as it had begun. "Sorry, Mrs. Kirby."

"I've heard the word before," Jacqueline said gently.

Unaware of the implications of that deceptive mildness, O'Brien went on, "You're an entertaining woman and I have enjoyed this little encounter, but I fear I must move on. You know, of course, that this card entitles you to a polite 'Hello' from the NYPD—but nothing else." He handed it back to her.

"I am well aware of that," Jacqueline said. "I thought it might get your attention."

"You already had my attention," O'Brien assured her. "I regret the necessity that forces me to turn it in another direction."

Jacqueline bowed her head meekly and rose, the green plastic trash bag tucked under her arm. The meekness was also an ominous sign; perhaps O'Brien suspected as much, for he reached the door before Jacqueline and took hold of the knob.

"Was there anything else you wanted to tell me, Mrs. Kirby?"

Jacqueline blinked at him from under the lace fringe. "Not a thing, O'Brien. Not a blessed little old thing."

"I figured you for one of these writer types, looking for publicity," O'Brien explained, resisting her attempt to turn the knob. "I don't need a self-appointed private eye to tell me Dubretta wasn't popular. But if you have any solid evidence, I'll listen."

"If I discover anything of that sort I'll be sure to tell you," Jacqueline said earnestly.

O'Brien opened the door and Jacqueline went out, clutching her trash bag. She turned and wriggled her fingers coyly at him in farewell. O'Brien took the rose from his lapel and flourished it in response.

II

Jacqueline was not at all surprised to find James lying in wait for her when she walked into the lobby of her hotel.

"I've decided to overlook your outrageous behavior," he announced.

"Your magnanimity overwhelms me. Excuse me, James. I want to change. This dress is making me bilious."

"I'll come up with you."

"No, you won't."

"I'll wait for you down here," James said, less enthusiastically.

"Don't bother."

"I made a reservation at Le Perigord."

Jacqueline hesitated. James played his trump card. "I'll pay."

"Well. . . ."

James had to admit that only Jacqueline could have walked into an elegant French restaurant carrying a green plastic trash bag and wearing a lavender picture hat two and a half feet in diameter. She was persuaded to check the hat, but refused to part with the trash bag. James bided his time until after she had selected the most expensive items on the menu. Then he indicated the trash bag, upon which one of Jacqueline's elegant purple shoes was firmly planted.

"What do you think you're doing?"

"You said you weren't going to ask me that."

"And you said, correctly, that it should be self-evident. I know what you're doing, as a matter of fact. Playing detective."

Jacqueline's eyes shone like green garnets, in a look of delicate mockery James found enchanting—when it was directed at someone else. "Dear James. You want to play too."

"I intended to offer you the benefit of my considerable experience. . . ." It sounded so pompous, even James couldn't keep a straight face. He gave Jacqueline his famous crooked smile.

"Right. I want to play too. But I'll be damned if I'll play Watson to your Sherlock Holmes, if that's what you had in mind."

"I fully intended to ask your advice, James."

"That would be a first. . . . Never mind. Ask. I'm all ears."

While she prodded snails out of their retreats, Jacqueline gave James a synopsis of the situation up to the death of Dubretta. "The atmosphere was positively poisonous with passion, James," she finished. "I had no idea writers were so greedy and selfish. They're as bad as academicians."

"No doubt. But we don't often murder one another."

"I don't suppose writers do either," Jacqueline admitted. "And of course I'm discounting the usual verbal exaggeration— you know what I mean—'I'd like to kill that woman,' 'I wish she were dead,' and so on. We all say things like that. But in this case several people had good reason to wish Dubretta would drop dead. She'd been after Hattie Foster for years; she said so, to-night. She also said she had found evidence that would destroy Hattie or damage her badly. The hints she dropped were as broad as Hattie's hips, and she kept hugging her purse like a bag of gold. I'm convinced the evidence is in this book."

She extracted the notebook from her evening bag and gave it to James. When he realized what it was, the timid, law-abiding professor replaced the amateur detective. He stuttered, "Did you steal this from Dubretta? Holy God, Jacqueline, you can't do that!"

"I didn't steal it. It was in her purse. The waiter gave it to me by mistake."

"But—but—You've got to give it to the police!"

Jacqueline's teeth snapped viciously on the last of the unfortunate gastropods. "O'Brien believes Dubretta died from natural causes. He patronized me, James. He practically patted me on the fanny and told me to go home and tend to my knitting."

"Did he? That explains a lot. . . . Well, but look here, Jacqueline, maybe he's right. All you've talked about so far is motive. As we both know, that's the weakest part of a case. What about means and—uh—opportunity?"

He looked so pleased with himself, Jacqueline didn't have the heart to sneer. "What about them, James?"

"I was so busy wrestling with that monstrous young woman, I

didn't follow all the action," James said. "But if Dubretta was murdered, the method has to be poison, administered in her glass of wine. The wine—Why are you looking at me like that?"

"I agree with your first conclusion, but isn't your second a bit sweeping? We don't know what else she had to eat or drink that evening. Some poisons don't take effect immediately."

James didn't appreciate her interruption or her logic. "If you don't believe the wine was poisoned, why did you take samples of it?"

"I didn't say it wasn't poisoned. I only said it wasn't the only possibility. Certainly any proper investigation of Dubretta's death would include testing the remains of the wine. Unfortunately, I wasn't able to collect the used glasses. The waiter had removed them by the time I got my wits together, and I couldn't quite see myself chasing him down the corridor and grabbing the tray out of his hands. However," Jacqueline went on more cheerfully, "the broken wineglass is the important one. The rest of us were holding our glasses when the table fell over, so the broken glass must have been Dubretta's. The others that fell with the table had no wine in them. What's more, Dubretta's glass didn't break when she dropped it. I remember seeing it bounce."

"Someone must have smashed it deliberately," James exclaimed.

"It is certainly possible. The wine the waiter was mopping up came from the bottle. We should have that tested too."

"I know a chemist at Columbia," James offered eagerly.

Jacqueline was about to say, "So do I," when she had second thoughts. It might be a trifle awkward, in view of certain events in her past, if her chemist and James's turned out to be the same person. Besides, James would be flattered if she left this job to him. He might even be deluded into believing they were equal partners in what Jacqueline had come to think of as her investigation.

She took her foot off the trash bag and nudged it toward James. "Try to talk him into doing it first thing tomorrow," she urged.

"I will. Jacqueline, I don't see why we have to consider other means of administering the poison; the party began at five, so she

couldn't have had dinner before she came. Anything she in-
gested at lunch would have taken effect before then.''

Jacqueline realized he had fallen in love with his theory, and
with the macabre thrill of having actually witnessed a murder, so
she didn't raise any further objections. To consider other hypotheses was nonproductive anyway; for all she and James knew, half
the population of New York might have wanted to exterminate
Dubretta Duberstein, and half of that select group might have
had a chance to do so during the afternoon. Actually, it wasn't
particularly productive to speculate at all until they had received
the results of the chemist's tests, but that consideration had no
effect on either of them.

"The big problem is not means but opportunity," Jacqueline
said. "How did the poison get in Dubretta's glass?"

After a somewhat acrimonious discussion they managed to
agree on a few facts. There had been a single glassful of wine left
in the first bottle. The second bottle had been corked and sealed;
they had both watched Max open it. That a foreign substance
could have been added to the bottle thereafter was unlikely, verg-
ing on impossible. Also impractical—why poison a whole bottle
unless the killer's goal was a general massacre?

Where they disagreed was on the disposal of the glasses of wine
Max had poured. James insisted that someone—he couldn't remember who—had taken the glass Max had set aside, claiming it
was full of sediment. Jacqueline felt sure that glass had not been
touched. They couldn't even agree on their own glasses. James
claimed he had passed the glass Max gave him to Jacqueline. She
distinctly remembered taking hers from Max himself. Valentine
had selected a glass, apparently at random, had had it snatched
away by Hattie, and had received a second glass from Laurie, via
Hattie. Laurie had touched not only the first, sediment-filled
glass, but several of the others. The glasses filled by Max had
stood on the table during Laurie's tantrum, during which time
someone could have added poison to a particular glass without
being observed. The only other thing the two amateur sleuths
agreed on was that neither had the faintest idea where and how
Dubretta had obtained her glass.

"I've always been suspicious of those detective stories where
every person at the party knows exactly where his or her drink

was at any given moment," James grumbled. "Anyhow, we agree it could have been done. Now let's make a list of the suspects."

Hattie obviously headed the list. There was no question about that. She was the one threatened by Dubretta's discoveries—whatever they may have been—and she had fussed over the glasses of wine. By forcing the issue between Valentine and Laurie, she had created a distraction that might have provided her with an opportunity to tamper with Dubretta's glass.

"Besides, she makes a rotten cup of tea," Jacqueline said.

James was not deceived by her flippancy, but he wasn't sure what she meant. Out of loyalty to Jean, Jacqueline had glossed over the peculiarities of Hattie's relationships with her authors, mentioning only the agent's reputation for squeezing them financially. He gave her a questioning look, shrugged, and went on to the next suspect.

His favorite candidate for chief suspect was Laurie. Jacqueline agreed that she was unstable and antagonistic to Dubretta, whom she had actually threatened. She did not voice aloud her feeling that James's partiality for Laurie was prompted in part by personal vindictiveness, and in part by his literary tendency to dismiss the most obvious suspect—Hattie.

They agreed that Max had had the best opportunity to poison one of the glasses. He had acted as host and had handed glasses to several people. If Dubretta had unearthed some scandal involving Valentine, the latter's business manager might have had solid mercenary reasons for silencing the columnist.

Valentine's name was the next to be mentioned, by Jacqueline. James summarily dismissed her from consideration. "She has the same motive as Max," Jacqueline argued. "Ridiculous," said James.

Victor and Sue were the last to be considered. James thought Victor might be a dark horse, for reasons he refused to specify, but insisted Sue was obviously innocent. Jacqueline callously added both to her list.

"That's all the suspects, then," James said, summoning the waiter to refill his coffee cup. "Let's talk about the motive."

There was another suspect, though Jacqueline didn't feel obliged to tell James that. Jean was not a very likely suspect. As she had demonstrated, the gaps in the lattice were wide enough to admit an arm, and the table had been within her reach; but although Jean could have poisoned the open bottle, or even one of the glasses, she couldn't have made sure the deadly liquid reached the right person. Nevertheless, Jacqueline added Jean to her private list. Something was rotten in the romance-book biz, and until she knew what secrets lurked in the hearts of VV and Victor von Damm, she couldn't be certain Jean was in the clear. It was imperative that she talk to her friend at once.

"Check, please," she said to the waiter, and to James, "The motive is in this notebook, somewhere. I'll get to work on it right away."

James looked sulky. He picked up the check, which had been placed discreetly on the table, and his expression changed to one of abject consternation. Swallowing, he handed over a credit card and then returned to his grievance. "Since when are you a cryptographer? I want—"

"The word, I believe, is cryptanalyst. And since when are you?"

But she agreed to James's suggestion that they walk instead of taking a cab. It was a fine night, for Manhattan. Now and then a genuine breeze struggled into the canyoned streets, and a full moon hung low over Rockefeller Center. Jacqueline had every intention of calling Jean as soon as she got in; conscience as well as detective fever demanded that she do so. However, when the desk clerk handed her her key he also gave her a message slip, and Jacqueline realized her obligation to Jean would have to be postponed again.

Frustrated by the hat, James rested his chin on her shoulder, trying to read the note. Jacqueline held it up. "Valentine wants to see me."

"Are you going?"

"It's rather late. . . ."

"Not really. A lot has happened since five o'clock, that's why it seems later than it is. Besides, she says, 'As soon as you get in, no matter what time.' "

"I can read." Jacqueline shrugged her shoulders, dislodging James's chin.

"I think we ought to go."

"We?"

James dodged the hat brim as she turned to face him. "This is an equal partnership, isn't it?"

Jacqueline neglected to answer the question. "That's not why you want to go with me. Valentine is not for you, James. She's a remote, glimmering star, far beyond the grasp of mortal men."

Recognizing Jacqueline's peculiar version of agreement, James took her arm as she walked toward the revolving doors. "Swinburne? Keats—in his corny youth?"

"Kirby. I'm practicing romantic clichés." She didn't say why, and James wisely didn't ask.

III

Jacqueline had scarcely touched the bell before the door of Hattie's suite was flung open. When he saw her, Max's tired brown eyes lit up. "It was good of you to come, Mrs. Kirby. Valentine is very distressed. She has some notion—"

"Is it her? Max, is it Mrs. Kirby?" Valentine ran toward them. Her flying draperies fell like dying moths as he stopped her and put a protective arm around her. "Val, my dear, let Mrs. Kirby catch her breath. Shall we go in and sit down?"

As she entered the living room of the suite, Jacqueline had an uncomfortable sensation of déjà vu. The fat cabbage roses printed on the draperies and slipcovers irresistibly recalled the dreadful plastic flowers of the bower, and the same faces confronted her. Valentine and Max, Hattie and Victor von Damm, the Earl, looking more than ever like a waxwork escaped from Madame Tussaud's, Jean, hunched miserably in a chair. Only Sue was missing. Apparently Hattie had tightened the lasso and dragged Victor back to the stable.

Hattie was the first to speak. The sugary sweetness of her voice aroused Jacqueline's darkest forebodings.

"Honey, I sure do appreciate you helping us. Why didn't you tell me you were a famous detective?"

Jacqueline cleared her throat. "Who told you that?" she inquired gently.

The huddled form of Valerie Vanderbilt quivered. Hattie glanced betrayingly at her and said, "Why, sure 'nuff, everybody

knows that. Now, Mrs. Kirby, you've just got to help. That policeman is on his way here right this minute—"

"O'Brien?"

"I think that's his name. He'll be here any second, and Valentine has this idea—"

"It's not an idea, it's the truth." Like a cloud bathed in the
rosy hues of dawn, Valentine pulled away from Max and approached Jacqueline. "You've got to help me, Mrs. Kirby. Someone is trying to kill me!"

IV

Jacqueline took the girl's fluttering hands in hers. "Sit down,"
she said quietly. "Here, on the sofa. You're confused, Valentine.
It was Dubretta who died."

"It was a mistake." Clinging to Jacqueline's hands, Val drew a
long shuddering breath. "The poison was meant for me."

"Poison?" Jacqueline's eyebrows disappeared under the lace
fringe of the hat. "Dubretta died of a heart attack, Valentine. At
least that's what the police believe. Why would anyone want to
harm you?"

Before the girl could answer, Hattie exclaimed stridently,
"Why, honey, that's a stupid question, if you'll pardon me. A girl
like Valentine attracts enemies just by being what she is. Every
other writer in the business is green with envy, and there must be
hundreds of men who—"

"Every other writer?" Jacqueline repeated.

"Oh, I didn't mean you, VV." With a deliberation that verged
on insult, Hattie glanced at Jean, who had risen shakily to her
feet. "You're a good writer, but you aren't in Val's class, and
you're smart enough to know it."

"I beg your pardon." James had been feeling left out. He
looked at Jean. "Haven't we met? Of course—you're Dr. Jean
Frascatti. We met at the MLA meeting in LA two years ago. I
thought your paper on Richard the Second was . . . Dr. Frascatti?"

He hastened to support Jean as she swayed, one hand pressed
to her brow. "It's too late," she muttered hysterically. "The die is

cast, the battle lost. . . . Where's the cup? There's yet some poison left. . . ."

James shook his head sympathetically as he helped her into a chair. "You mustn't be morbid. This has been a trying day for everyone, but . . . VV? Did I hear Mrs. Foster call you VV? Are you the author of *Slave of Lust?*"

Jean shuddered violently. Her eyes, glazed with despair, remained fixed on James.

"How marvelous," the latter exclaimed. "Clever woman! I'll wager you're the only member of our underpaid profession who is solvent these days."

"Marvelous," Jean repeated dully. "Marvelous? Clever?"

"How many of us have the intelligence to augment our paltry incomes by making use of the neglected masterpieces of literature?" James perched on the arm of Jean's chair and smiled his crooked smile. Jean's pale cheeks regained their color, and she looked at James with dawning adoration.

Seeing that that particular situation was under control, Jacqueline turned back to Valentine. "I'm sure a lot of people envy your beauty and your success, Valentine; but people don't kill other people because of envy."

"Normal people don't," Valentine said. Her voice had a harsh, grating quality.

"Laurie!" Hattie clapped a theatrical hand to her forehead. "What about Laurie?"

"What about her?" Jacqueline asked.

"I sure do pity the creature, but we all know she isn't right in the head. I blame myself," Hattie said nobly. "Yes, I really do. I should have seen it coming."

"Don't be silly, Hattie," Valentine snapped. "I can't stand the girl—she gives me the creeps—but she wouldn't hurt me. She adores me."

"Love turned to hate," Hattie murmured vaguely. "I'm not sayin' it had to be Laurie. What about that girl—the little schoolteacher—"

"That's a crock of crap, and you know it!" Victor's black cloak flared as he strode toward Hattie. She didn't flinch, even when he shook his fist at her.

"Oh, I'd hate to think it was little Sue. But you haven't been nice to her, Victor—now, have you? Leading her on and then dropping her. . . . She knows how you feel about Val, of course."

Victor's look of horrified bewilderment transformed him back into Joe Kirby. "Me—Val—since when have we—I don't—she never. . . ."

"In heaven's name, Hattie, control yourself," Max exclaimed. "What you say is nonsense. We are all talking foolishly tonight— and small wonder, after what has happened. I'm sure we will find that by morning things will look quite different."

"But that policeman is on his way here now," Hattie said. "Mrs. Kirby, I want you—"

The doorbell rang. Jacqueline said, "You don't want me. I don't know what the devil you do want. A lawyer?"

"Good gracious, no." Hattie's nostrils flared and she drew a deep, sensuous breath. "Why would I want a lawyer? I'm going to appeal to the police to protect pore little Valentine."

She went to answer the door.

It wasn't difficult for Jacqueline to understand Hattie's sudden change of attitude toward Dubretta's death in general and Jacqueline in particular. The great god publicity beckoned, and Hattie was sharp enough to sense the delicious possibilities. Jacqueline pictured the headlines: "Queen of Love threatened. Who tried to kill Valerie Valentine? Famed private detective on the case. . . ." And her picture, smirking under the brim of the lavender hat.

Jacqueline had no objection to appearing in the newspapers, but she was damned if she was going to be manipulated by Hattie. It is one thing to make a fool of oneself, deliberately and cheerfully; quite another to be made a fool of by someone else.

Before she could decide what to do about it, O'Brien was among them.

His eyes went straight to Jacqueline. "Well, if it isn't Mrs. Kirby. Nice to see you again, ma'am. And Miss Valentine—Mr. von Damm—Miss Vanderbilt—your Grace. . . ." The barely concealed amusement in his voice as he pronounced the names rose to the surface when he addressed the Earl, who looked as blank as he always did. O'Brien glanced at James. "And Mr.——?"

James drew himself to his full height. "Professor James B. Whittier. I am chairman of the English Department at Coldwater College."

"Right." O'Brien's gaze lingered on the trash bag James was holding under his arm, but he didn't comment on it. He went on, "I'm sorry to bother you at this hour, Mrs. Foster. I have a little problem I hoped you could help me with."

"Thank God you are here, Inspector." Hattie grabbed his hand.

"Lieutenant," O'Brien corrected gravely.

"What does it matter? You're a police officer, and it's your duty to protect us innocent citizens. Look at that pore chile—" The pore chile was Valentine, who started nervously as Hattie jabbed a finger at her. "Inspector, you must protect her from the assassin who tried to kill her. He will certainly try again, and—"

"Just a minute, ma'am," O'Brien interrupted. "This is the first I've heard of an attempt on Miss Valentine's life. When did it happen?"

"Why, tonight, of course. Dubretta's death was a mistake. The poison was meant for Valentine."

O'Brien looked at Jacqueline. She shook her head. "I'm not taking the rap for this, O'Brien. Did I ever mention the word 'poison'?"

"It was implicit in—"

"All I did," said Jacqueline, in the high, penetrating voice she adopted when she wished to control a conversation, "was ask whether you were satisfied that Dubretta died a natural death. This was Valentine's idea."

O'Brien's gaze shifted to Valentine. Though his countenance was as impenetrable as a boulder, the girl's beauty had its effect; when he addressed her his voice was unusually gentle. "Tell me about it, Miss Valentine."

Like many writers, Valentine was not a fluent speaker. "Well— uh—there was a mix-up about the glasses of wine. I was supposed to have a certain one, then I took another one, and the one I finally got wasn't either of them. Dubretta took the one I was supposed to have."

O'Brien blinked. "You want to go over that again, miss?"

Valentine looked frightened. She had explained the situation as well as she could, and was apparently incapable of clarifying it. Max came to her rescue. "The fact is, Lieutenant, no one can be certain who got a particular glass of wine."

"I didn't notice you," O'Brien said, in chagrin. "Who are you?"

Max smiled. "Most people overlook my presence, Lieutenant. I am not a conspicuous person. I am Max Hollenstein, Miss Valentine's business manager. I was pouring the wine, and I think I know as much about it as anyone—which isn't much." He went on to tell O'Brien what had happened, glossing tactfully over Hattie's insistence that Laurie be allowed to hand Valentine her glass, and ended, "Honestly, I don't see how anyone could have tampered with a specific glass, if that is what you are wondering. They were being passed back and forth like damp babies."

"But she took my glass," Valentine insisted. "The one Hattie grabbed away from me. Hattie put it on the table and Dubretta took it. She only drank about half of it and then she just crumpled up."

The implications of this passionate and ingenuous declaration escaped Hattie; she returned O'Brien's inquiring look with a puzzled frown.

"Well, Miss Valentine," O'Brien said, "I haven't received the coroner's report yet, but it looks as if Dubretta had a heart attack. That should reassure you. Unless you have an enemy."

"Not one but a hundred," Hattie cried. She expanded on the theme, in more or less the same terms she had used before, but when O'Brien invited her to be specific, she rolled her eyes and looked coy. "Dubretta was one of the ones who hated Valentine," she suggested.

"Hoisted by her own petard?" O'Brien's lip curled. "Not Dubretta. She was too smart to make a dumb mistake like that. The fact is, Miss Valentine—and the rest of you—there's no indication that murder was intended or committed. Do any of you know anything that would contradict that conclusion?"

No one spoke. "Oh, come on," O'Brien said. "No threatening letters, no. . . . Yes, Mrs. Kirby?"

"It's probably irrelevant," Jacqueline began.

Instead of following up this tantalizing remark, O'Brien agreed. "Probably. Well, ladies and gentlemen, I'll leave you in peace. Oh—I almost forgot the reason I came. One of Dubretta's possessions has been misplaced. Did any of you see her notebook this evening?"

The faces of the listeners did not change. O'Brien elaborated. "She always carried a stenographer's notebook. With a red cover. She said the bright color made it easier for her to keep track of it."

"That's right," Jacqueline said. "She was taking notes yesterday, at the lecture."

Silence followed this disingenuous comment. No one seemed anxious to add anything until Joe said tentatively, "Maybe it was in her purse. I remember her hugging it in both arms like she was afraid somebody was going to steal it."

"That's right," Max agreed. "Didn't you find her handbag, Lieutenant?"

"We have it," O'Brien said. "The notebook wasn't in it."

"But that's—" Hattie stopped.

"Yes, Mrs. Foster?"

"That's strange. Maybe she didn't bring it with her today. The notebook, I mean."

"Dubretta's notebook was part of her," O'Brien said. "She'd no more leave it behind than she'd go out without her clothes."

"Oh, who cares about a silly notebook?" Hattie snapped. "Lieutenant, I demand police protection for pore little Valentine."

"If I thought she needed protection, she'd get it," O'Brien replied shortly. "No one has anything more to tell me about Dubretta's notebook? All right, then. Mrs. Kirby, I'd like a word with you. In private."

All eyes turned toward Jacqueline. James took a step forward. "What are you implying, Lieutenant? If you have anything to say to Mrs. Kirby, I insist on being present."

"Don't be silly, James." Jacqueline rose, tucking her evening bag firmly under her arm. "The lieutenant and I spoke earlier today; no doubt he wishes me to elaborate on certain points I raised at that time."

She fixed James with an icy stare. Jean put a timid hand on his arm. "Please don't go, Professor Whittier."

Bookended between two women, one who plainly didn't want

his company and the other pleading for him to remain, James did not find the decision difficult.

"But, Mrs. Kirby . . ." Valentine began.

"Don't worry about a thing, my dear," Jacqueline said. "You're perfectly safe. I have decided to take the case."

O'Brien opened the door for her and she swept superbly out. "What case?" he inquired, the creases in his thin cheeks deepening.

"If there is no case, why are you so determined to find Dubretta's notebook?"

"You believe in taking the war into the enemy's camp, don't you? Why don't you give me the notebook, Mrs. Kirby?"

They stepped into the elevator. "What makes you think I have it? This is an absurd conversation," Jacqueline went on acrimoniously. "Five questions in a row and not one answer."

"You asked two of the five. All right, I'll give you an answer. That suitcase of Dubretta's had been searched. She was a smoker and she never used a cigarette case; the bottom of her bag and every object in it should have been covered with tobacco. It was too clean."

"Very good," Jacqueline said admiringly. "There are a few flaws in your reasoning, however."

"Don't try to pin it on the waiter," O'Brien warned. "She had over a hundred in cash. A thief wouldn't have left that much."

"She might have cleaned it herself," Jacqueline said. "Before she came to the party. Is that all you had on your mind, O'Brien?"

"As a matter of fact, I have a favor to ask. If you aren't too tired, there's someone I'd like you to meet."

"All right."

"It isn't far from here and it shouldn't take . . . did you say, all right?"

"Yes."

"No questions, no hedging, no cries of alarm?"

"I'm not at all alarmed. And I presume you'll tell me who it is in your own good time."

"You are a damned annoying woman," O'Brien said.

"So I've been told."

O'Brien's car was unmarked, but its position, in a clearly

defined "No Parking" zone, gave away its official status. Once they were under way O'Brien said, "I'm taking you to see Dubretta's sister. She wants to talk to the person who last saw her sister alive."

"You have a literal mind, I must say. And a lot of information I didn't expect you to have."

"I spoke with a number of the witnesses earlier. It's just routine, Mrs. Kirby; just routine." O'Brien turned right onto Fifty-fourth. This move resulted in a screech of brakes and a scream from the driver of the car that had barely missed him, and he said, with visible restraint, "Would you mind taking off your hat, Mrs. Kirby? I can't see a damned thing on my right."

"Sorry." Jacqueline reached up. O'Brien glanced apprehensively at the pair of long steel hatpins she removed from the crown of the cartwheel.

"Put those away, will you?"

Jacqueline stuck them through the hat and tossed it onto the backseat. O'Brien ducked reflexively. It may have been embarrassment that made him rude. "You sure you didn't run one of those lethal weapons into Dubretta's windpipe?"

Jacqueline did not reply.

The late night joggers and dog-walkers were out in full force, the latter armed with the implements required by the city's most recent and most stringent "Curb Your Dog" regulations. It had always been a source of wonder to Jacqueline that New Yorkers, whose living space probably cost them more per square foot than anyone in the world, favored large dogs—retrievers, Dobermans, Saint Bernards. An elderly couple passed, towing, or being towed by, matched Irish wolfhounds.

Before long O'Brien pulled up in front of a block of apartments that dated from the period when architects could afford to dabble in whimsy. Turreted towers and crenellated battlements topped a facade of timber and brick in the Tudor manner. The defenses were feudal; O'Brien's ring at the outer door was answered by a doorman who peered suspiciously at him until he produced his identification.

The woman who admitted them to Dubretta's apartment was stout and white-haired. She tried to smile at them, though her lips trembled and her eyes showed signs of recent tears.

"I'm sorry to be so late, Anne," O'Brien said.

"Night and day are the same to us, Patrick. You ought to know that."

"How is she?" O'Brien asked in a low voice.

The woman shrugged fatalistically. "For once I thank God she's the way she is. Mercifully she doesn't . . . sssh."

"Who is it, Anne?" The light, youthful voice came from a room at the end of the hallway. Then the speaker appeared in the open doorway. The face was that of the girl in the photo in Dubretta's wallet, but if Jacqueline had not been expecting to see those features she would never have recognized them, distorted as they were by rolls and lumps of fat. Dubretta's sister was only five feet tall, and enormously overweight. Yet her skin was fresh and unlined, and the smile with which she welcomed them was radiant with goodwill.

O'Brien bent to kiss her cheek. "This is the lady I was telling you about," he said. "Mrs. Kirby, I'd like you to meet Dubretta's sister, Prudence."

"Come into the living room, Mrs. Kirby. Would you like a cup of coffee, or something else to drink?"

"No, thank you." Jacqueline followed her into a pleasant though shabby room. It served as a study as well as a living room; bookcases lined the walls, and two desks stood side by side.

"Please sit down, Mrs. Kirby," Prudence said.

"Call me Jacqueline. I only met your sister a few days ago, but I liked and admired her very much. I'm so very, very sorry."

Prudence sat down on a sofa whose sagging cushions marked it as her favorite seat. Tears overflowed her eyes. "You tried to help her. I wanted to thank you, and ask you if—if she—"

"It was very sudden," Jacqueline said gently. "She felt no pain; there was only a moment of . . . surprise."

"She would be surprised," Prudence murmured. "She never believed anything could happen to her. Did she say anything? I hoped she might ask for me."

"She did say something—one word, actually, repeated twice. It meant nothing to me at the time, but . . . it must have been your name—your nickname. Prue."

Prudence nodded. After the hints the housekeeper had dropped, Jacqueline had expected to find Dubretta's sister handicapped in one way or another; but except for her weight problem she appeared to have no disabilities, mental or physical.

A stifled sob burst from the housekeeper. "What are you crying about, Anne?" Prudence asked.

"I'm sorry, Prue. . . ."

"I can't imagine why you should be crying." Prudence's voice rose in pitch. She began to talk in a rapid, breathless monotone. "Here's one of my fans come to visit and you stand there crying. Would you like to see where I work, Mrs. Kirby? That's my desk there, beside Dubretta's. I'm working on a book right now. My latest. My publisher keeps nagging me, he wants it on the fall list. It will be his big book. He's budgeted half a million for promotion."

Through the horrified paralysis that gripped her Jacqueline was aware of O'Brien, eyes intent, body poised like a tiger's. Prudence's long speech gave her time to recover her wits. When Prudence rose, with surprising lightness and quickness, and beckoned her to the desk, Jacqueline followed without delay or comment.

"These are all my books," Prudence said, with a sweeping gesture. The bookcase she indicated was filled with paperbacks. Jacqueline recognized several of the authors' names. "I write under several different noms de plume, of course," Prudence went on quickly. "The demand for my work is so great. It takes up a great deal of my time. Not just the writing, but the public appearances and autographings, dining with publishers, and so on. And fan mail! I feel obliged to answer each and every letter. Dubretta helps me with that. She is a great help to me. That's her desk, next to mine. She should be here soon. She's late. It's really most inconsiderate of her to be late. I have a lot of letters to answer. Anne, have you made coffee? You know Dubretta always wants her coffee when she comes in. We'll have to work late tonight. I have a lot of fan mail to answer."

"Then I mustn't keep you any longer," Jacqueline said. "Thank you so much. I'm so grateful to you for letting me come."

"I'm always happy to see one of my fans." An uncertain smile flickered across Prudence's face. "I wish Dubretta would come. She's late. She knows I worry. And I have so many things to do. . . ." Turning her back on Jacqueline, she began shifting the papers on her desk.

The housekeeper accompanied them into the hall. "Will you be all right?" O'Brien asked softly.

"Oh yes. This is. . . ." The housekeeper smiled wryly. "This is normal. She's like this whenever Dubretta is late. Don't worry, Patrick. I'm used to dealing with her."

"Call me if you need anything."

Neither of them spoke until they were in the car and O'Brien had started the engine.

"How long have you known Dubretta?" Jacqueline asked.

"Almost twenty years. She was a cub reporter on the old New York *Post* when I was a rookie cop. She drove me crazy. Whenever there was a brawl or a murder or a drug bust, Dubretta was in the thick of it, waving that damned notebook and asking questions in that strident voice of hers." O'Brien was silent for a moment. "Quite a woman," he said.

"You became friends."

"Yeah," said O'Brien.

"And Prudence?"

"She was the prettiest thing you ever saw. Little and light on her feet, and always laughing. An honor student at CCNY. She had a lot of boyfriends, but Dubretta guarded her like a dragon."

"You might have warned me. For her sake, if not for mine."

"I wouldn't have let you say anything to upset her." The whites of his eyes glinted as he glanced at her.

"Brrr," said Jacqueline, shuddering affectedly.

"You handled it well," O'Brien admitted with a grudging air.

They glided to a stop at Forty-fourth, as the light turned red. Park Avenue lay quiet and at peace under the streetlights, in a deceptive serenity.

The light changed. O'Brien put his foot down on the gas. "It happened during the sixties—the height of the drug culture, if you remember. I was on the desk the night the call came in—some kid overdosed on a combination of heroin and PCP. Only one of hundreds. . . . But I knew the name.

"It could have been an accident—a mistake in the dosage. But she never touched the stuff. 'I'm too chicken,' she used to say. A little pot, maybe, for recreational purposes, but never the hard stuff. What made her do it? She couldn't or wouldn't say. But she had been trying to get a book published. You saw, tonight, the form her delusion has taken."

"I also see what you're getting at," Jacqueline said. "But even if she had suffered a cruel disappointment, or had been victimized by—let's say some anonymous member of the publishing profession—that would be insufficient cause for suicide."

"You know better than that, Mrs. Kirby. Christ, they slash their wrists over rock stars, and starve themselves into anorexia for some sick dream of beauty. And Prue had—call them emotional problems—before. There's a background—Dubretta hinted at it once, when she got tight—neglect, child abuse, God knows what. The overdose may have set off an illness that would have appeared sooner or later anyway."

"That seems likely." Neither of them voiced the corollary: whatever the real cause of Prudence's illness, Dubretta had fixed on Hattie as the scapegoat. She needed to blame someone, and perhaps the real villain was beyond her reach.

O'Brien stopped in front of the hotel. He left the engine running. "What about the threatening letters, Mrs. Kirby?"

Jacqueline had been expecting the question. Her acquaintance with Patrick O'Brien had been brief, but she had already learned to respect his abilities and his brains. She turned to retrieve her hat from the backseat. "Dubretta got several of them. They were just notes, incoherent and scrawled. She said they came from the girl who is the president of Valentine's fan club."

"Name?"

"Laurie Schellhammer," Jacqueline said, rather reluctantly. "But the notes don't mean anything, O'Brien. Laurie is seventeen, and not quite—er—"

"I get the picture."

"She couldn't have poisoned Dubretta's wine."

"Are you still harping on poison, Mrs. Kirby?"

"Good night, O'Brien."

"Good night, Mrs. Kirby."

Jacqueline got herself, her billowing skirts, and her hat out of the car unaided. After one quick identifying look, the doorman had left them strictly alone. She was so preoccupied that she gave short shrift to the man who tried to accost her as soon as she entered the lobby. Jacqueline looked through him and darted past before he could speak.

He caught up with her at the desk, where they were joined by two women. A single glance told Jacqueline what she should have realized immediately, even before they all spoke at once. "Mrs. Kirby, I represent the *Daily Bugle*—" "Mrs. Kirby, I wonder if I might—" And from the third, obviously a neophyte, "Are you Mrs. Jacqueline Kirby?"

"No," Jacqueline said.

She snatched her key from the clerk and headed for the elevators. The trio of reporters followed, spouting questions. Jacqueline broke into a run. With all three in pursuit, she pounded across the lobby and squeezed herself into an elevator whose doors had begun to close.

She knew they would be hot on the trail, via the next elevator, so she bolted down the hall, her key in her hand. She was mentally braced for a tussle at the door of her room, but none of them had thought to stake it out—or else none of them had had enough money for a respectable bribe. She opened the door and slammed it shut behind her. The room was pitch-dark. Cursing Sue's midwest awareness of economy, she fumbled for the light switch.

For several seconds she stood perfectly still.

The room was a shambles. Every article of clothing had been torn from the hangers and thrown onto the floor. Her suitcase and Sue's had been upended. The mattresses of both beds were askew, sheets and blankets trailing; every drawer in every piece of furniture stood open.

Jacqueline shifted her lavender evening bag from one hand to the other. Until that moment she had actually forgotten Dubretta's notebook.

CHAPTER SIX

Rigid with horror, Blaze gazed upon the rape of her chamber. That was how she felt it—as a violation, a ravishment. Rough, cruel hands fumbling among her treasures, touching her silken. . . ."

Jacqueline shook her head. She had been reading too many romantic novels.

Her first act was to pick up the gown she meant to wear to the ball. Murmuring maledictions, she restored it to a hanger and smoothed the crumpled flounces. Turning to the next most pressing matter, she made a quick search of the room. She did not find the burglar. She had not expected she would; but she was half afraid she might find Sue, unconscious or worse. Sue wasn't under the bed or in the bathtub, and Jacqueline felt sure she would have noticed if there had been a body in the closet.

After exchanging the loathsome lavender gown for a robe and restoring the room to relative order, Jacqueline propped herself up in bed with all four pillows and (after a guilty look around the empty room) lit a cigarette.

None of her belongings was missing except for a few pieces of costume jewelry. She hoped Sue had not been foolish enough to leave cash or expensive jewelry in her suitcase. They would probably be gone as well.

Taking the costume jewelry had been an error though. No professional thief, even a beginner, could have mistaken her *faux perles* earrings and vermeil chain for the real thing, despite the misleading terms the jewelry industry had invented for those frauds. And only a professional thief could have gotten into the room without leaving any trace of his entry or exit.

Blissfully inhaling, Jacqueline glanced at the door, which was now bolted and chained. The thief had to have come in that way. There were no balconies or fire escapes within reach of her window. The lock had not been broken, nor was there any sign of tampering. The old credit-card technique, known to all readers of thrillers and all viewers of TV detective series, would not have worked on this lock. Probably there was no such thing as a burglar-proof lock, but in this case the most likely explanation . . . Jacqueline reached for the telephone.

The assistant night manager's first reaction was alarm, but when Jacqueline assured him she was not reporting a robbery, he became indignant. It was impossible that her key could have been given to the wrong person. The hotel personnel were trained to observe. . . .

Jacqueline thanked him and hung up. If any of the desk clerks had given a stranger her key, he wouldn't admit it. She had always had her doubts about the system. No clerk had ever asked her for identification, he had simply handed over the key she requested. With guests checking in and out daily, it was impossible for anyone to remember which face went with which room.

She reached for Dubretta's notebook. It was lucky she hadn't had time to change clothes that evening, for she would probably have decided to leave the notebook in her room. Lucky, too, that she had spent the evening in the company of a police officer. If she had gone window-shopping or walking alone. . . .

The notebook would have to go to O'Brien in the morning. Jacqueline had never had any sympathy with heroines of thrillers who clung doggedly and feeble-mindedly to the clue that (*a*) would have solved the case on page 50 if the police had had it, and (*b*) rendered said heroine vulnerable to kidnapping, assault, and mayhem. However, the hour was late; O'Brien (poor man) had had a long hard day; it would be cruel to disturb him now.

Conscience thus speciously assuaged, Jacqueline lit another cigarette and went to work.

Her knowledge of codes and ciphers came from such standard works as Dorothy Sayers' *Have His Carcase* and the Friedmans' pleasant book about the reputed Shakespeare ciphers. That, she considered, should be sufficient.

And indeed, a quick survey of the contents of the notebook confirmed what she had assumed from the beginning. Dubretta's was not a conventional code, but, as she herself had described it, an arbitrary and personal form of shorthand. Having been educated in the era when women were advised to learn secretarial skills as the best means of breaking into one of the professions, Jacqueline had wrestled briefly with shorthand before deciding she would rather scrub floors. She recognized some of the conventional symbols in Dubretta's book, but no longer remembered what any of them meant, except for the slash and comma that signified "Dear Sir" in the Gregg system. Instead of cheering her, this discovery cast her into deeper gloom. Not only was it unlikely that Dubretta would write rough drafts of letters in her scandal book, but the symbol appeared in the middle of a page, surrounded by others. Obviously it did not mean "Dear Sir." If Dubretta had used this common symbol for something other than its original meaning, she had probably done the same thing with other symbols. An expert knowledge of shorthand would not be of much help in decipherment.

Modesty was not one of Jacqueline's more conspicuous attributes, but she knew when she was licked. She felt sure she could decode the book if she had enough time. One simply listed groups of symbols and compared the frequency, and . . . something along those lines. But if she could do it, an expert, assisted by a computer, could do it much more quickly.

Was that why O'Brien wanted the notebook, or was he just tidying up loose ends? Everything he had said gave the impression that the police were satisfied that Dubretta had died from natural causes. Jacqueline felt sure that O'Brien himself was not satisfied. He could deny it all he wanted to, but he had his suspicions. Not that he would ever admit she was right. Shaking her head in sorrow over the unaccountable egotism of the male sex in general, and O'Brien in particular, Jacqueline put the notebook under her pillow and reached for *A Willow in Her Hand*.

It was after two when she turned out the light. Sue had not returned. Jacqueline hoped she was enjoying whatever she was doing. She slept the sweet sleep of the innocent, and dreamed she had been carried off into the desert by Patrick O'Brien, riding an ostrich and dressed in a flowing burnoose, uniform trousers with a stripe down the side, and the lavender hat, complete with cockatoo.

II

"Have you seen the papers?"

"How can you speak of newspapers at a time like this?" Jacqueline murmured, twining her arms around O'Brien's bronzed shoulders. "And would you mind taking off that hat?"

"Oh, I'm sorry. Were you asleep?"

Jacqueline opened one eye. Sunlight assaulted her naked eyeball. She closed the eye.

"Brilliant deduction," she muttered.

"Your picture is on page three," Sue exclaimed. She rattled the paper under Jacqueline's nose.

Jacqueline sat up. She had neglected to braid her hair the night before, and the tumbled bronze mass fell over her face, tickling her nose and getting in her mouth. She pawed irritably at it. Sue laughed.

"You look like one of Valentine's heroines," she said. "Beautifully disheveled, and drowsy with loving."

"Drowsy with five hours' sleep, you mean. How dare you speak to me at this hour in that cheerful tone of voice?"

"I brought you some coffee." Sue sat down on the other bed and proffered a plastic container. "My mother's like that in the morning too. I figured—"

Too outraged to speak, Jacqueline seized the coffee and drank.

"I've been with Joe," Sue said. Flushed and dewy-eyed, she stared dreamily at the ceiling. "He's wonderful, Jacqueline. Do you know what his real ambition is? To find a nice little town, somewhere in the Midwest, and settle down. He wants me—"

"I know what he wants," Jacqueline growled. "And I don't want to hear about it."

"Oh no, you're wrong! Joe isn't like that. We didn't—we were talking."

"All night?"

"In an all-night coffee bar. That's where I got your coffee."

"It was a kindly thought," Jacqueline admitted, the caffeine finally having reached her brain. "Let me see that newspaper."

There were two newspapers, the *Times* and the less reputable periodical in which Dubretta's column appeared. The *Times* had treated *l'affaire des* romance writers with the contempt it deserved; but the *Daily Blank*, never known for reticence, had pulled out all the stops. Hattie must be rolling on the floor in fits of rapture, Jacqueline thought. Never had so much publicity been attained for so little expenditure.

They hadn't made the headlines, but a box on page 1 referred readers to the story. It used the precise phrases Jacqueline had imagined. "Who tried to kill Valerie Valentine? Queen of Love threatened. Famous detective on the case."

Turning to page 3, Jacqueline was about to remark, "Who is that blowsy-looking frump in the . . ." when she recognized herself. The picture was the one Dubretta's cameraman had taken the day before. Parasol over her shoulder, hat over her brow, Jacqueline leered at the reader. The caption read, "Famous private detective?" She could not blame the editor for adding the question mark.

There were also photographs of Valentine and Victor von Damm. The story was a masterpiece of innuendos and non sequiturs; its style leaned heavily upon the meaningful question: "Who handed Dubretta the fatal glass?" "Was the wine poisoned?" "Is there in the past of this exquisite and talented young writer a man driven mad by jealousy and tormented passion?"

"And why, and wherefore, and if not, why not?" Jacqueline murmured.

"What did you say?"

"Nothing."

The story went on to misspell Jacqueline's name and describe her as a professor of astrophysics at a well-known eastern university, and a writer whose "best-selling novels have appeared under a pseudonym. She shuns publicity, preferring to allow the local police to take credit for the cases she solves." Picturing O'Brien's reaction to that, Jacqueline grinned broadly.

The reporter had made the most of his non-interview. "When questioned by this reporter, Ms. Kirky replied in her low, throaty voice that she was unable to discuss the case at the present time. It is rumored that she is working closely with the New York Police Department. When asked about Ms. Kirsky's relationship with the department, Lieutenant Patrick O'Brien refused to comment."

Jacqueline laughed aloud.

"What's so funny?"

"Everything. There isn't a sentence in this story that isn't mirth-provoking."

"Are you a professor of astrophysics?" Sue asked, wide-eyed.

For once Jacqueline was not tempted to embellish a handsome lie. "My dear girl, you know who and what I am. I told you the day we met."

"I thought you might have been under cover," Sue explained.

"Under . . . you don't believe that guff about my being a detective, do you? Didn't they teach you in college that the printed word is not sacrosanct? In other words, don't believe everything you read in the paper."

"Joe said you were a detective. He said Valerie Vanderbilt said—"

"Never mind that. What else did Joe say?"

"About what?"

"He told you his real name was Joe Kirby."

"Yes. Are you sure you two aren't—"

"I'm sure. He also told you that Victor von Damm's books are ghost-written, by a couple of Brooklyn housewives?"

"Well. . . ."

"Does that bother you?"

"Joe explained how it happened," Sue said, avoiding Jacqueline's eyes. "It was Hattie Foster's idea, all of it. A lot of books are ghost-written. You know, the ones by famous Hollywood stars, and politicians, and . . . the real author's name doesn't appear, but everyone knows. . . . It's done all the time. There's nothing wrong with—"

"It's a form of fraud, though," Jacqueline said soberly. "Not in the legal sense, perhaps, but morally and ethically. Besides, the examples you mentioned aren't comparable. People don't buy a memoir because it is written by Famous Actress, they buy it because it is about Famous Actress. There's no actual misrepresentation. But Victor von Damm's fame and reputation rest on his writing. And Victor von Damm is nobody. He doesn't exist."

"He hates it," Sue said in a low voice. "He wants to quit."

"Why doesn't he?"

"He's going to quit. But it will take a little time to set things straight. He can't just walk out."

"Why not? Oh, forget it," Jacqueline said, as Sue looked at her tearfully. "I gather he didn't tell you anything that—"

The telephone rang. Jacqueline stared at it in consternation. "Who the hell could be calling at this hour?"

"It's eight-thirty," Sue said.

"My God." The instrument buzzed again. Jacqueline snatched it up. "Yes?"

Sue retreated tactfully into the bathroom, leaving Jacqueline free to express her emotions. "No, James, you didn't wake me up. Sorry to disappoint you. That does not mean I am in any mood to talk to you at the crack of dawn."

"What do you mean, crack of dawn," James demanded. "It's eight-thirty."

"When I am on vacation, eight-thirty is the crack of dawn."

"When did you go to bed?"

"None of your business."

"I was not inquiring into your social activities, Jacqueline. I was exercising my prerogative as duly appointed co-sleuth, to ask what information you elicited from O'Brien."

"I don't feel like discussing it at the crack of—"

"Meet me for breakfast, then."

"What an obscene suggestion."

"Lunch, then."

"Where?"

"The Algonquin. Noon."

"Well. . . ."

"I thought that would get you, you greedy snob."

Jacqueline hung up. Scarcely had she done so when the telephone rang again. Jacqueline snatched it up. "What do you want now?" she shouted.

"Sue," said a meek, surprised voice. "Is she—"

"You just left her half an hour ago."

"So? Is that any reason why I can't—"

"Why didn't you tell her the truth?"

Silence followed. Then the voice of Victor von Damm, stiff with aristocratic hauteur, said, "I don't know what you're referring to."

"Neither do I," Jacqueline admitted. She rubbed her forehead. "Sue is busy now. Call later." She hung up.

She expected Joe to protest this brusque dismissal, and was not surprised when the telephone shrieked an immediate summons. Before she could pronounce the devastating comment she had prepared, a voice cooed, "Good morning, Mrs. Kirby. I do hope I didn't waken you."

"You damned well—" Jacqueline began.

"Oh, good," Hattie said. "I figured you'd be up and busy with your detecting. Did you see our publicity this morning?"

"Yes, I did, and I thought it was the most—"

"Those boys and girls on the New York papers are really efficient, aren't they? The reason I'm telephoning, Mrs. Kirby, is to tell you I've called a press conference for eleven A.M. I think that's the easiest way of dealing with this sort of thing; I mean, reporters can just drive you crazy if you don't cooperate. They're just doin' their job, after all. Room 415 at my hotel—eleven sharp. Don't be late."

"No."

"What did you say?" Hattie asked doubtfully.

"No. Meaning, I won't be there."

"But—but—you have to come. I told the man from the *Times*—"

"Aunt Hattie—if I may call you that—get one thing straight. I don't know what you're holding over the heads of your terrorized authors, but you've got no hold over me. They may jump when you crack your whip. I don't."

From the other end of the line came sounds of struggle and alarm. Then another voice said breathlessly, "Mrs. Kirby."

"Mr. Hollenstein?"

"Max—please. I couldn't help overhearing Hattie's side of your conversation, and I don't blame you for refusing her invitation—"

"You usually have a keener ear for the appropriate word, Mr. —Max."

The manager chuckled. "Don't take it personally. She talks that way to everyone. But I wish you would join us, for your own sake, if not for Valentine's. Heaven only knows what Hattie will say if you aren't there to defend yourself."

Jacqueline heard Hattie's indignant rebuttal: "Why, Max, you ought to be ashamed!"—and Max's reply. "Be quiet, Hattie. Mrs. Kirby?"

"I have a lot to do this morning," Jacqueline said.

"I think you should come."

"Has something happened?"

"I'd rather not discuss it over the telephone."

"All right. I'll be there. Do tell Hattie 'Go to hell' for me, won't you?"

She slammed the telephone into its cradle. The bathroom door opened and Sue's head appeared. "Is anything wrong?"

"Why do you ask?"

"You were yelling."

"So I was." Jacqueline smiled and stretched. "My, that felt good. Is there any more coffee?"

"I'm sorry—"

"That's all right. Hurry up in there, will you?"

Sue's head vanished. Jacqueline swallowed the dregs of her coffee and studied the empty cup regretfully. This was beginning to look like a three-, or even four-cup morning. She transferred her gaze to the telephone, but it remained silent. Throwing the covers back, she got out of bed and cautiously opened the door.

The hallway was empty. So much for Hattie's belief that the press was hot on the trail of the Big Story. In a world reeling with war and corruption and famine and imminent nuclear holocaust, the death of one columnist was an extremely minor story. It would probably be forgotten in a day if Hattie left it alone. Which Hattie had no intention of doing.

Jacqueline reached the telephone just as it rang for the fourth time. "Now what?" she asked resignedly.

"Is that you, Jake?"

"Who else? That's all I do, answer telephones."

"It's me. Betsy."

"I know."

This response constituted a conversational dead end. There was no reply from Betsy. After a moment Jacqueline said, "Well?"

"Have you seen the newspapers?"

"I have."

"Is it true?"

"Is what . . . Betsy, what the hell do you want?"

"I was there," Betsy said.

"I know. I saw you. For God's sake, get to the point."

"Was it really . . . did somebody try to . . . ?"

"So far as I know, the official view is that nobody tried to do anything to anybody. Dubretta died of a heart attack."

"But the paper says—"

"Another example of our inadequate educational system."

"What?"

"I thought you were a rough, tough radical. Do I detect a yellow streak?"

Unlike Sue, Betsy was well acquainted with Jacqueline's peculiar conversational style. She replied irritably, "I wish to God you could talk like a normal person. I know perfectly well that all this crap about somebody trying to kill Valentine is probably just another publicity stunt. But if it isn't . . . I was there, Jake—slinking around in that ghastly wig and revolting dress, as if I had something to hide. That was your idea, you know! An evil-minded cop might interpret the things I've been saying about the Queen of Schlock as threats."

"That's pretty farfetched, Betsy."

"Oh yeah? Have you read Dubretta's column this morning?"

"I haven't had time. I've been on the phone for hours," Jacqueline added pointedly.

"She quoted a couple of the things I said. Taken out of

context. . . . Call me a coward if you like, but I prefer to anticipate trouble instead of being ambushed. Can I count on you,
Jake?''

"I'll be happy to testify as a character witness," Jacqueline said.
"I'll say you're all talk and no do. That you're basically chicken.
That—"

"God damn it, Jake!''

"All right, calm yourself. You're making a mountain out of a
molehill and brewing a tempest in a teapot and also crossing
your bridges before you come to them. I'll keep an eye on the
situation and let you know if anything interesting develops.''

Betsy thanked her effusively and Jacqueline hung up, reflecting on the unaccountable tendency of people to be reassured by
a series of meaningless aphorisms.

Betsy had gone off half-cocked (she had forgotten that one).
Yet Betsy had a point. An evil-minded investigator might consider
that she had a motive. Jacqueline whipped out her notebook and
added Betsy's name to the list she and James had compiled. Not
that she really believed Betsy had poisoned the wine. But a detective had to be impartial.

She heard the sound of rushing water from the shower in the
bathroom, and decided Sue would be out of the way for a few
more minutes. From under her pillow she took Dubretta's notebook, and opened it. She had had a couple of ideas during the
night.

One was a promising lead. She was so deeply engrossed that
she failed to respond quickly enough when the bathroom door
opened and Sue, fetchingly draped in a towel, darted into the
bedroom.

"Son of a gun," said Jacqueline, trying to sit on the notebook.

"Why, that's—isn't that the book the detective was looking for
last night?''

"No.''

"Joe told me about it. He said it had a red cover—''

"I picked it up by mistake," Jacqueline said.

This explanation was so weak even Sue refused to buy it. Head
on one side, she looked quizzically at Jacqueline, who said sul-
lenly, "I'm going to give it to the police this morning. As soon as
you get out of the bathroom and give me a chance to shower.''

"I forgot my toothpaste," Sue said, retreating with the tube.

"Humph."

When Jacqueline went back to her research the promising lead had evaporated. Sue had broken her train of thought—and had made it necessary for her to carry out her promise of returning the notebook. She had intended to do that anyhow, but now prompt action was imperative. Sue would probably mention the notebook to Joe; she was in that state of imbecile infatuation where not even a promise of silence would keep her from confiding in the beloved. She might tell other people, and Joe certainly would, and before long the omnipotent O'Brien would know for certain what he already suspected.

Jacqueline had considered various methods of handing over Dubretta's property. The easiest way out was to put it in an envelope with no return address and drop it in the mail. However, she had no great confidence in the United States Postal Service; the book might take two days or two weeks to reach the police, or it might disappear altogether. Besides, that was a coward's way out. She was not intimidated by Lieutenant O'Brien.

The safest and surest method was to deliver it herself. She reached for the phone. The operator gave her the number of the local precinct station, and a telephone call elicited the information that Lieutenant O'Brien was indeed at that location. "Do you want to talk to him, ma'am?" the sergeant inquired.

"No," Jacqueline said hastily.

She hadn't expected O'Brien would be on the job so bright and early. He had implied he was on night duty. Apparently the visit to Prudence Duberstein had been made on his own time.

Sue was still in the bathroom, so Jacqueline returned to the newspaper. Dubretta's column appeared in its usual place. It contained no revelations. Jacqueline had not expected any; Dubretta hadn't had time to write up the new information she had collected. Instead the column featured a sardonic review of the previous day's proceedings, including a description of the protest march and an interview with Betsy, "Chairperson of the Women's United Front Against Sexism."

Jacqueline, who had a penchant for acronyms, performed a mental operation on the initial letters of this organization, and decided Betsy should have chosen a different name.

Her eyebrows lifted as she read. Betsy and Dubretta must have gotten smashed after she left them. But smashed or sober, Betsy had a habit of shooting her mouth off. Statements like "Verminous leeches who ought to be exterminated," and "Mindless creeps who belong on the list of people who never would be missed" could indeed be taken the wrong way.

She was about to bang on the bathroom door when Sue finally emerged, wearing a lacy nightgown. She fixed wide, nearsighted blue eyes on Jacqueline and said humbly, "I'm sorry."

"Stop apologizing for everything," Jacqueline grumbled. "Are you going to bed now?"

"Just for a few hours. Then I'm meeting Joe. Do you know if Hattie has canceled today's workshops?"

"I can't imagine that she would. And in all fairness to her, I don't see why she should."

"Are you going to the conference this morning?"

The red notebook lay on the bed in plain sight. Sue carefully avoided looking at it. Jacqueline picked it up and brandished it. "I am returning this—*taking* this—to the police station. Then I am having lunch with a friend—at the Algonquin, if anybody wants to know. But first I am going to have two, possibly three, cups of coffee, downstairs, in the coffee shop of this hotel. I'll call later and let you know what I plan to do this afternoon."

"I wasn't trying to pry. I just wondered."

"Okay, okay."

After Jacqueline had closed the bathroom door she heard the telephone ring. Shamelessly she eased the door open and listened. She couldn't make out the words—Sue must have retreated under the bedcovers with the phone—but the soft, intimate murmur of the girl's voice brought a reluctant smile to Jacqueline's lips. It had been so long since she felt that way that the memory was as remote as ancient history, but it had been marvelous while it lasted. She hoped this affair would be longer-lived. Joe might or might not be serious about Sue. He was so soured by romance writers that anyone outside the trade would look good to him, and Sue was so credulous she'd believe anything he told her. He had not been honest with her. Hattie was unquestionably blackmailing him, as she was Jean, but unless she had evidence of something more serious than the Von Damm masquerade, there was nothing to stop Joe from thumbing his nose and walking away clean. He wasn't a timid rabbit like Jean, and there was nothing illegal about what he had done. Unless. . . .

Jacqueline closed the door and began brushing her teeth. She felt sure she could get the truth out of Joe. She had successfully intimidated stronger characters than he. If she only had more time! Things were happening so fast she couldn't keep up with them, and in the meantime her own book was suffering.

So much to do—and she loved every bit of it. The face that looked back at her from the mirror wore an expression of bright anticipation. She thought complacently, Not bad, considering that I only had five hours' sleep. I think I'll make my heroine a little older—mid-forties, perhaps. Those fans at the conference—a lot of them are middle-aged, I'll bet they would really identify with a heroine closer to their own age, instead of some nubile chit in her twenties. The wise woman of the tribe, priestess of the Goddess. . . . (Which Goddess? Never mind, I'll figure that out later.) Desired by all men, but sacred. "Her lissome figure in its scanty covering of deerskins moved gracefully along the path to the shrine. Watching from behind the bushes, Lurgh the hunter wet his lips. To possess this woman he would risk the wrath of the Goddess. . . ."

III

As she drank her coffee Jacqueline wrote busily in not one but two notebooks. First Oona the priestess dealt with Lurgh the hunter, eluding his sweating hands and striking him down with the sacred staff of the Goddess before he had done more than remove the deerskin from strategic portions of her anatomy. "She pointed a quivering finger at the gasping, panting hulk sprawled across the path. 'The wrath of the Goddess be upon you, profaner of the sacred virgin,' she cried."

The second notebook contained Jacqueline's thoughts on the case. She was grateful to Max Hollenstein for wrestling the telephone from Hattie, for she had been dying to attend the press conference. It was a matter of principle not to yield to Hattie, and if Max hadn't apologized and cajoled, she would have had to think of an excuse. However, that appointment meant that she would have to postpone some of the other plans she had made for the morning. Thoughtfully she considered the list she had made earlier.

It was a pity she couldn't wait until after the press conference before running her other errands. She was meeting James at twelve. The Algonquin was on West Forty-fourth, only three blocks from the library and four blocks from the police station. If she delivered the notebook first, she would have to go to Forty-first, then back to Fifty-third, then back to Forty-fourth. However, it couldn't be helped. To carry Dubretta's notebook with her to the press conference would be asking for trouble. The person who had searched her room must have been looking for the notebook. Not only had O'Brien stressed its importance, but he had practically accused her, Jacqueline, of having it. The group of people who had been informed of those facts at ten P.M. the night before would be at the press conference, or at the hotel, and she had no reason to suppose that interest in the notebook had diminished in the meantime. The notebook must go to the police at once, there was no question about that.

Well . . . almost at once. Jacqueline's eyes glinted as she considered what she meant to do.

Avoiding the temptations of the shops on Fifth Avenue, she walked along Sixth to Forty-second and then went to Fifth and climbed the stairs between the noble stone lions. The copying machines on the third floor were all in use; she had to wait. When a machine became available she methodically reproduced the pages upon which Dubretta had written. Tucking the sheaf of papers into her purse, she yielded the machine to the impatient Indian student, turbaned and bearded, who was next in line.

Forty-second Street is one of the main cross-streets in midtown Manhattan, with traffic going in both directions. Even hardened New Yorkers are wary of running the lights on Forty-second, though they do it all the time on other, one-way streets. However, they jostle and jockey for position at the curb, so as not to lose even a second when the vehicular traffic stops. Jacqueline wormed her way to the brink and stood poised. It was after ten-thirty, and she had to drop off the envelope containing Dubretta's notebook and get back to Fifty-third before eleven.

The shove that sent her tumbling forward did not come until after the light had changed. It was hard enough to mash her midriff against the fender of a taxi that had screeched to a stop, and knock the breath out of her. She fell, ungracefully and emphatically, and was stepped on by a dozen feet.

New Yorkers are not, however, the callous robots they are reputed to be. A dozen other feet avoided her, by agile quicksteps, and several hands reached out to help her up. "Don't do that," several voices objected. "Hey, lady, are you okay? She might have a concussion or a broken leg. Hey, lady, don't move till you're sure you're okay."

Dazed though she was, Jacqueline had no trouble deciding it was safer to move out of the street rather than stay where she was, under the fender of one taxi and in the path of a number of others. Supported by a pair of Good Samaritans, she limped back to the curb and propped herself against a lamppost to survey the damage.

Most of it was cosmetic—a broad smear of dust and oil across the middle of her pale-green dress, scraped and bleeding knees, and the total destruction of a pair of panty hose.

One of the Samaritans, a heavy-set black woman, tried to dust off her dress. "You okay, dearie? Maybe you better sit down."

"My purse," Jacqueline said. "About two feet square, white, shoulder strap. . . ." Traffic was in motion again. There was no handbag visible between the rolling wheels. She had not expected to see it.

The other woman shook her head. "Honest to God, what some people will do. Practically kill a person just so's they can grab her purse. You want me to—"

"No, thanks. I really appreciate your help." Jacqueline gave her an abstracted smile. As soon as the light changed, she dashed across the street.

The open, parklike area surrounding the library offered few places for concealment. It was more likely that the thief had scooped up her purse as she fell, and proceeded on across Forty-second, mingling with the majority of the pedestrians who had not stopped to assist her. Office buildings and stores lined the opposite side of the street. If she was quick enough. . . .

She found the purse in the third doorway she investigated, that of an office building. She had expected the thief would discard it as soon as possible—it was large enough to be conspicuous and therefore dangerous—but she was both relieved and surprised that she had found it before a second, more mercenary thief had picked it up. Nothing had been taken except the notebook and the bundle of copies.

Jacqueline glanced uneasily over her shoulder. The thief must have been on her trail from the time she left the hotel. Unless he had actually watched her reproduce the pages he wouldn't have recognized them, for they had been folded so that only the blank side showed.

Limping and ruminating, and glancing nervously from side to side, she made her way back to her hotel. Unaccustomed as she was to self-recrimination, she wasn't particularly proud of her performance that morning. Not only had she lost what might have proved to be a valuable clue, but she was going to have a hard time explaining to O'Brien how she had lost it. If Sue hadn't seen the damned notebook that morning—and, in all probability, broadcast the news to the world, via Joe—she could simply deny that she had ever had it. Maybe, she thought cravenly, I can buy another notebook, scribble some nonsense in it, and pretend that was the one Sue saw.

She might or might not have yielded to this ignoble impulse, but she was not given the chance to decide. By the time she reached her hotel her scraped knees were aching, and the look on the doorman's face, as he leaped to perform his duty, told her that she looked even worse than she felt. She went as rapidly as she could toward the elevator, but somehow she was not surprised to see a familiar figure waiting there.

O'Brien was wearing a light-gray suit. His tie, his socks, and the stripe on the handkerchief in his breast pocket were of deep forest green. The controlled facade of his face cracked for an instant when he saw Jacqueline, but he said only, "Don't tell me. The bad guys got it."

"No comment," Jacqueline said.

O'Brien followed her into the elevator. He remained discreetly silent, in the presence of the other occupants, but got off with Jacqueline at her floor.

"Get lost, O'Brien," Jacqueline said.

"You've always wanted to say that, haven't you?"

"Don't you have any other business?"

"My business is with you."

"Later. As you can see, I have to change."

"I'm coming in with you." O'Brien whipped the key from her fingers. Before Jacqueline could object, he added, "I think it would be better if I went in first."

Jacqueline shrugged. "It's not necessary. The room was searched last night. And this morning. . . ."

"Yes?"

"Later."

O'Brien opened the door. Sue had drawn the draperies, and the room was dusky with shadows. Jacqueline reached past O'Brien and switched on the light. "See? All quiet. That's Sue. She's asleep."

O'Brien looked at the motionless hump in the bed. "Sure she isn't dead?"

"Get lost, O'Brien," Jacqueline said, out of the corner of her mouth. It sounded even better that way.

O'Brien's face creased in his sinister smile. He leaned against the wall and folded his arms. "I'll wait out here, Mrs. Kirby. Just scream if somebody jumps out of the closet with an ax."

Jacqueline slammed the door in his face. Sue stirred. "What?" she asked sleepily.

"Go back to sleep," Jacqueline snarled.

Ten minutes later she emerged from her room wearing a navy-blue suit, a row of Band-Aids across her knees, and a sour expression.

"That was quick," O'Brien said. "May I offer you my arm?"

"You may not." Tucking her purse close to her side, Jacqueline walked away. O'Brien fell in step with her.

"On your way to the press conference?"

"I'm late. So if you'll excuse me—"

"Those things never start on time. Don't you want to know why I was waiting for you at the critical and dramatic moment?"

"You wanted to see me," Jacqueline said. "I wasn't in my

room. You knew I would be at the press conference at eleven—
you seem to know everything—so you hung around, hoping I'd
come here to change before attending. Don't you have any other
responsibilities?''

''You're a smooth-talking lady, Mrs. Kirby, but you can't get me
off the track that easily. Your deductions are correct, as far as
they go, but you've omitted one major item. The notebook. Now
please don't waste my time by denying you had it. I know you did,
and so do a lot of other people.''

''Thanks to you,'' Jacqueline said venomously. The elevator
reached the lobby. She stepped out, with O'Brien close on her
heels.

''I owe you one for that,'' he said seriously. Jacqueline glanced
at him in surprise. ''It's your own fault, in a way,'' O'Brien insisted. ''I figured you for one of those romance crackpots, playing out some private fantasy. I didn't think the notebook was
important, but it irked the hell out of me that you would have the
gall to make off with it the way you did. Later I got to thinking. . . .''

''That Dubretta's death might have been murder?''

O'Brien grabbed Jacqueline's arm and spun her around to
face him. ''Wait a minute. Just one minute.''

''Oooh.'' Jacqueline shivered. ''Golly-gee-whiz, Lieutenant,
you really scare me. I do believe this is police brutality. Hey,
everybody, look at the—''

''Mrs. Kirby.'' O'Brien's grip relaxed. It took another twenty
seconds or so for him to get his voice under control. ''Give me a
break, will you? Just let me say what I came here to say, and you
can go.''

''Okay.''

''All I want is . . . okay?''

''Okay.''

The encounter had not gone unobserved. People were looking
at them, and one very large man had begun walking slowly in
their direction. O'Brien smiled. Jacqueline smiled. Neither smile
was convincing, but the big man stopped, gave O'Brien a
thoughtful look, and allowed himself to be removed by a woman
who appeared to be his wife.

O'Brien fingered his tie. ''One of these days,'' he said under his breath, still doggedly smiling, "somebody is going to wring your neck, Mrs. Kirby."

"Spit it out, Lieutenant. I'm late."

"Where was I? Oh. I got to thinking. Not that Dubretta's death was murder; no, ma'am. But that notebook of hers could be dangerous, for reasons that have nothing to do with murder. She collected dirt, and she was looking for scandal about the romance writers. It occurred to me in the dark reaches of the night that maybe I had put you on the spot when I fingered you as the one who stole Dubretta's notebook. I stopped by this morning because I thought maybe . . . and," O'Brien concluded, staring at Jacqueline's bandaged knees, "I was right. Wasn't I?"

Jacqueline glanced ostentatiously at her watch. "Much as I enjoy these verbal sparring matches, I must be on my way. So I will be brief. I did find, to my utter astonishment, that somehow Dubretta's notebook had found its way into my purse."

"You didn't notice it until you got back to the hotel last night," O'Brien suggested politely.

"How did you know? Someone had entered my room while I was absent and had turned the place upside down. I assumed it was a casual thief—"

"Like hell you did."

"—and, since nothing of value was missing, I decided to forget the whole thing. It was late when I realized I had the notebook. I didn't want to disturb you at such an hour, but as my roommate will tell you—if she hasn't already told you—I had every intention of giving it to you this morning. In fact, I was on my way to the station house—"

"The check is in the mail," O'Brien murmured.

With an effort Jacqueline kept her face straight. "Precisely. I was about to cross Forty-second Street when someone shoved me. Luckily for me, traffic had stopped, but I careened off a taxicab and fell flat on my . . . knees. By the time I got my wits together, my purse had disappeared. I found it shortly afterwards, in a doorway where the thief had left it. The notebook was gone."

She saw no reason whatever to mention the loss of the pages she had reproduced. They were gone, along with the notebook, so why bring them up?

"Traffic had stopped," O'Brien repeated.

"You do have a logical mind, Lieutenant. That thought occurred to me too. One can never be certain, of course, but unless there was an error in timing I might suppose that the miscreant didn't intend to do me serious harm. Just dent me a little, so he could make off with the evidence in the confusion."

Somewhat to Jacqueline's annoyance O'Brien waved this consideration aside. He might not care whether she was demolished or merely dented, but the distinction was of some concern to her.

"Did you read . . . of course you did. What was in the notebook?"

"I couldn't read it. Believe it or not, O'Brien."

"I believe it. Dubretta's private shorthand was one of her trademarks. You realize, Mrs. Kirby, that if we had had that notebook we might have deciphered her code?"

"But why would you bother?" Jacqueline asked innocently. "This isn't a murder case. Is it?"

O'Brien stepped back a pace. "Get lost, Mrs. Kirby."

"Right." Jacqueline started for the door, then paused. "Lieutenant."

"Yes, Mrs. Kirby?"

"I want to report an assault. Forty-second and Fifth Avenue. Someone pushed me in front of a taxi and stole my—"

"Get lost, Mrs. Kirby," O'Brien said out of the corner of his mouth.

It sounded even better that way.

IV

The press conference was a fiasco. There were only three reporters present, and not a single photographer. Jacqueline was no help. In her prim navy-blue suit, with her glasses perched insecurely midway down her nose and an expression of bovine perplexity on her face, she was ignored by the reporters, including one of the young women who had tried to interview her the night before. When Hattie pointed her out as the famous detective who was investigating the attempt on Valentine's life, she looked so horrified that the same reporter burst out laughing, and the others smothered skeptical smiles. A few pointed questions made it clear that Hattie had no evidence whatever of murder or attempted murder, and the reporters closed their notebooks and wandered off in search of new sensations. This one hadn't been worth much to begin with.

Hattie fastened a malignant look on Jacqueline. "You let me down, Mrs. Kirsky."

At least one was never in doubt as to how one stood in Hattie's estimation. Unlike some of the other characters with whom Jacqueline was involved, enigmatic she was not. One of the more engaging demonstrations of her animosity was her inability to remember Jacqueline's name. When they were on good terms, it flowed trippingly from her tongue.

"I couldn't let you down," Jacqueline replied crisply. "You're already down so far, there's no place lower to go. What did you hope to accomplish by this inane performance? And where is your stable? You'd have made a stronger impression if you had produced Valentine, sighing and wringing her lily-white hands."

"She's too upset," Hattie said. "If you think this is just a publicity stunt—"

"I know it's just a publicity stunt. Where is Max?"

"With Val. She can't be left alone. She—"

"You didn't get here until a quarter past eleven. Where were you?"

"Shopping. I ran out of—"

"Anyone see you?"

Hattie's bosom swelled to alarming proportions. "What the hell is this, a third degree?"

"Where's Laurie?"

"How should I know? She hangs around the lobby near the registration table, until Val—"

"I want to talk to her."

"So who's stopping you?"

Jacqueline started for the door. Hattie said, "Max wants to see you."

"I haven't time now. I have a lunch date."

If Hattie had expostulated, Jacqueline would have walked out. Hattie's silence worried her. "Has something happened?" she asked.

Hattie's square jaw sagged. "Oh hell," she muttered. "What's the use? You try to help these kids, you give 'em everything you've got, and what do they do? They stab you in the back. You can't depend on 'em for a damned thing."

Her tone invited commiseration, from one aging P. to another, and was as phony as her southern-lady act; but Jacqueline sensed a genuine grievance.

"Don't tell me, let me guess," she said. "Valentine has decided no one wanted to kill her after all. That's what Max wanted to tell me."

"When I think what I could have done with that," Hattie muttered, a far-off look in her eyes. "Sometimes I'd like to strangle that little jerk."

"Really."

"Just a figure of speech," Hattie said quickly. "Ah love that little girl like my own chile."

"Cheer up," Jacqueline said. "Your publicity ploy has fallen flat for the moment, but I'm sure you'll be tickled to know that I'm on your side. Dubretta was murdered. You know it and I know it, and I'm going to find out who did it."

It was a good exit line, and Jacqueline decided she had better take advantage of it before Hattie could voice her reaction. She was very much afraid Hattie didn't appreciate her offer of alliance.

V

The food at the Algonquin was excellent, but that wasn't why Jacqueline liked the place. As James had implied, she was a literary snob; the old hotel might be a little shabby around the edges now, but it retained the glamour of the old *New Yorker* days, when Dorothy Parker and Thurber and Ross met over lunch and scandal. Another cat had replaced the famous Hamlet, but he had the same conscious look of superiority as he sat in front of the newsstand with his paws tucked under his snowy breast.

The lobby cocktail lounge was a favorite meeting place for literary and theatrical celebrities, and those who considered themself to be celebrities. Jacqueline was pleased to see that

James had secured a table. He was not alone. At first she didn't recognize the woman with him. Her graying hair hung lank and limp around her face, which was innocent of makeup except for a touch of pale pink lipstick. She wore a severely cut dark suit and a white shirtwaist blouse, buttoned up to the neck.

James seemed engrossed by the conversation of this drab female, and Jacqueline frowned as she made her way toward them. It was not until the woman looked up and smiled that she recognized Jean.

After somewhat stilted greetings had been exchanged, James said, "I'm trying to persuade Jean to join us for lunch."

"I wouldn't dream of intruding," Jean said. "But this seemed like a good opportunity to explain. . . . Why are you looking at me like that, Jake?"

"Is that the way you normally dress?" Jacqueline asked.

"Why yes. What's wrong with it?"

"I think I prefer Valerie Vanderbilt. At least she has some pizzazz."

Jean flushed angrily, and James said, "For God's sake, Jacqueline, control that trivial mind of yours. I persuaded Jean to come out of the closet, so to speak. She's agreed to tell us about her deal with Hattie."

"It's high time," Jacqueline said. "Excuse me a minute." Extending a long arm, she intercepted a passing waiter and ordered a martini. Then she leaned back and looked expectantly at Jean. "Go ahead."

"I've been behaving very stupidly," Jean began. "James has helped straighten me out. As he says, it's really a trivial problem. I followed his advice; I talked to Hattie, and—just as he predicted —everything is all right now."

She turned an adoring smile on James, who cleared his throat and tried without conspicuous success to look modest. Jacqueline was sorely tempted to point out that James's advice was not only self-evident to anyone with an ounce of sense, but it was precisely what she had told Jean herself. Jean was apparently one of those dim females who only heeded advice when it came from a man. Fearing, however, that criticism would halt the flow of information, Jacqueline simply coughed pointedly and said nothing.

"Tell her about your talk with Hattie," James prompted.

"Oh. Well, I just told Hattie I was tired of writing. I didn't want to be Valerie Vanderbilt any more. And do you know what? She said fine, if that was what I wanted. She was sorry to lose me, but the most important thing was that I should be happy. And she won't tell anybody that I was Valerie Vanderbilt!"

From the delight in her voice Jean might have been announcing that she had won the Irish Sweepstakes. The waiter brought Jacqueline's drink, and just in time; she felt the need of a restorative.

"Wait a minute," she said. "Let me get this straight. Hattie is releasing you. In exchange for what?"

"Why, nothing." Jean blinked. "Oh well, I told her she could use the Vanderbilt name. She'll get someone else to write under that pseudonym. It's done all the time in the book business. Like Alexandre Dumas, and the Nancy Drew books."

Jacqueline reflected that Hattie had a miraculous talent for making questionable deals sound reasonable. She ought to have been a politician.

Jean rambled on, in an orgy of self-congratulation, until Jacqueline interrupted her again. "How big a percentage is she giving you?"

"Percentage?"

"For the use of the Vanderbilt name. You created it."

"Not really. Hattie—"

"And I thought the academic world was a bog of hypocrisy," Jacqueline muttered, half to herself. "Start at the beginning, Jean. How did you get into the romance business?"

It was a long, rambling story, made even more discursive by Jean's reluctance to discuss Hattie's questionable tactics and her own stupidity at being taken in by them. Jean had been reading historical romances on the sly for some time before she decided to try her hand at one. She insisted she had done it as a joke, but when pressed by Jacqueline, she admitted that money had been a consideration. There was also the implicit challenge, to which most students of literature are susceptible: this stuff is so bad, surely I can do better.

After completing the manuscript, with the help of several obscure Victorian masterpieces of pornography, Jean had decided to send the book to Hattie. Hattie had responded promptly and flatteringly. She adored the book. It was sensational. She would be honored to handle it and was sure she could sell it.

She had no trouble persuading Jean to use a pen name. Somewhat appalled at the accomplishment of what had been only an idle daydream, but seduced by the opportunity to make money, Jean had signed a contract with Hattie.

Since she was afraid to risk her anonymity by getting in touch with other writers, Jean didn't realize for some time that the contract she had signed was a disaster. When a dim inkling began to dawn, she fought the realization. It was a normal reaction; people will submit to almost anything rather than admit they have committed a stupid blunder. Even now Jean tried to deny Jacqueline's criticisms. Written contracts between authors and agents were not the rule in the publishing business, but some agents insisted on them; twenty-five percent was admittedly a little higher than the average commission. . . . All right, it was more than twice the average. No, Hattie never forwarded royalty statements from the publisher, but the checks were larger every time, and there was no reason to suspect. . . .

Jacqueline dropped the subject. Hattie had taken Jean to the cleaners, and there was very little Jean could do about it. The twenty-five percent commission was outrageous, but Jean had agreed to it, in writing. Hattie's additional rake-offs from the royalties were probably covered by creative accounting. (Office expenses had gone up, and everyone knew postage was sky-high these days.) By comparing the publishers' copies of the royalty reports with the checks she had received, Jean might be able to prove fraud, but it would involve a long, costly, acrimonious court battle—the last thing a wimp like Jean would want to engage in, especially if it meant admitting she was Valerie Vanderbilt.

Jacqueline didn't doubt that Hattie owned the name Valerie Vanderbilt, and God only knew what else. She would have given a good deal to read the contract Jean had signed; there might be a clause, in very small print, committing Jean to a year in a brothel of Hattie's choice if she reneged on her agreement to write sixteen more books on Hattie's terms. Jean had obviously never even read the damned thing. This did not surprise Jacqueline; intellectuals were no smarter about business than the average high school graduate, and their touching assumption that they were smarter made them even more vulnerable.

Jean hadn't found her situation too unpleasant until Hattie had decided it was necessary for her to attend the Historical Romance Conference. Jean had been aghast when Hattie first made the suggestion. When she refused, Hattie turned her reason for refusing into a weapon against her. She'd lose her job if the truth were known? Nonsense. Her colleagues would think more highly of her if they knew of her success as a writer. She was too modest, that was her trouble. What a pity she didn't have a friend who would tell the world how wonderful she was!

"That sounds like Hattie, all right," Jacqueline said. "You really are hopeless, Jean. Why didn't you tell her to take her contract and stick it in her ear?"

"Jean doesn't resort to vulgarity," said James, who was tired of being excluded from the conversation. He patted Jean's hand. A gentle ripple of rapture ran across her plain face.

"Anyway, it's all right now," she murmured. "Thanks to James —and," she added hastily, glancing at Jacqueline's darkening brow, "and you, Jake. I let myself get all worked up about nothing. It's always been one of my weaknesses. Once I faced the problem, it solved itself, and Hattie couldn't have been nicer."

Jacqueline grunted. She felt sure she knew the reason for the change in Hattie; it had nothing to do with nice. When Jean had first joined the stable, Hattie had just begun her nefarious career; it had taken her several years to develop her ingenious approach to the promotion of romance writers. The new and lucrative angle was glamour, and of that commodity Jean had none. She was a liability instead of an asset; the new VV would undoubtedly be a breathtakingly gorgeous actress or model, who could posture and perform in public.

"I really must run now," Jean said. "I've taken too much of your time."

"Wait a minute. What about the other writers, particularly Valentine and Von Damm. Does Hattie have similar contracts with them?"

"Honestly, Jake, I don't know anything about their arrangements with Hattie—aside from what everyone knows, like Joe pretending to be Victor. He says he wants to break off with Hattie; he's very bitter about her. But he never went into detail.''

"And Valentine?"

Jean's face twisted unpleasantly. "Nobody talks to Valentine, Jake. Hattie watches her every second."

"You must have spoken with her at least once," Jacqueline said pointedly.

Jean blushed. "Oh—the detective thing . . . I'm sorry about that. I was so upset I didn't know what I was saying. It happened a couple of days ago. Hattie was talking to some publisher, and Valentine got away from her. She saw I was—well, upset—and asked me what was wrong. Not that she cared," Jean added vindictively. "She was just bored and inquisitive. I don't remember exactly what I said, I was too distraught; but I may have used the word 'blackmail,' and explained that I intended to consult you, and . . . that was the only time I've ever talked to her. Honestly.''

The headwaiter informed James that their table was ready. Jean left, visibly relieved to escape Jacqueline's inquisitorial questions.

Scarcely had James and Jacqueline seated themselves, however, when they were approached by a waiter. "Excuse me, but I believe you were sitting with the lady in the gray suit—at the second table from the door? I'm afraid there has been an accident.''

James struggled to rise from the banquette, endangering the glassware on the table. The waiter said quickly, "She doesn't appear to be injured, sir, only shaken up. I thought you might wish—''

"Yes, yes, of course." James extricated himself. "Where is she?"

Jacqueline followed at a more leisurely pace. "Save our table," she instructed the headwaiter. "We'll be right back.''

Jean was sprawled in a chair. She did not lack for attention; the doorman was patting her, a waiter offered her a glass of water, and James stood by wringing his hands. Jacqueline arrived in time to hear him demand a doctor, the manager, the police, and a drink, in that order.

"I don't want a drink," Jean stammered, fumbling with her disheveled hair.

"I do," James said. "Are you all right? What happened? Why doesn't someone fetch a doctor?"

Jacqueline saw at a glance that the waiter's diagnosis appeared to be correct. Jean was rumpled and scratched, and her skirt bore traces of contact with the filthy sidewalk, but there was nothing else wrong with her. Jacqueline sent James back to hold their table—never losing sight of the essentials—and removed her friend to the ladies' lounge.

"My stockings are ruined," Jean wailed.

"And your purse is gone," Jacqueline said.

"Oh my God." Jean stared wildly around the room. "It is. It is! It had all my credit cards and my makeup. . . ."

"Any family jewels? Wads of cash?"

"I never carry much cash in New York. I—"

"Then it's more of a nuisance than a disaster. Did you see the person who took it?"

"See her? Of course I saw her. She's hard to miss. It was that awful girl, Laurie."

CHAPTER SEVEN

Jacqueline returned to the Oak Room and picked up the menu. "I'm starved. Let's order as soon as he brings our drinks. I wonder if they have snails?"

"How can you talk about food at a time like this?" James demanded. "Where's Jean? Where are the police? What have you done about—"

"I put Jean in a cab. She's gone back to her hotel; she'd rather be robbed of every penny she possesses than appear in public with torn hose. She'll call the police and report the incident. . . . Oh, good, *escargots à l'arlésienne.*"

"You had snails last night."

"I plan to have them again tonight. I can't get snails in Coldwater."

"And a damned good thing, if you ask me." James raised a hand to his brow. "Why am I talking about snails? What happened to Jean? Why don't you tell me what the hell is going on?"

"I will, I will. Just a minute." Having given her order and nagged James into doing the same, Jacqueline settled back against the padded leather banquette and gave James a brief, well organized account of recent events. It was an ill wind that blew no one good, she thought piously; Jean's misadventure allowed her to gloss over her own, and cut short James's sarcastic comments about her loss of the notebook.

"That is so typical of you," he remarked. "If you had given O'Brien the notebook last night, or let me take charge of it—"

"You're missing the point, James. As of ten-thirty this morning, the thief had Dubretta's notebook. Why attack Jean?"

This proved an effective distraction. James ate pâté and pondered. "Two possibilities," he said finally. "Either two, or more, people are after the notebook, or no one is after the notebook."

"It was the only thing stolen from my purse," Jacqueline argued. "It and the copies I had made of it. I had two stenographer's notebooks of my own, and they weren't taken."

"The thief thought the notebook might contain what he wanted. He found it did not contain what he wanted. He's still looking for what—"

"She, not he. Jean was certain the person who knocked her down and grabbed her purse was Laurie."

"How about you? You didn't see your assailant?"

"No. And I think I would have spotted Laurie if she had been following me this morning. As Jean said, she's hard to miss."

"So you incline toward my first theory."

Jacqueline prodded the last snail out of its shell. "I incline toward it, but I'm not certain. What if the notebook is a red herring? Granted, there are a number of people who might want to suppress Dubretta's notes, but suppose there's some other object someone wants even more?"

"Such as?"

"The possibilities are endless. Maybe she had microfilm concealed in her tube of toothpaste. Maybe—"

"Toothpaste? Why would Dubretta have a tube of toothpaste in her purse?"

"I don't know. But she did. She may have been fanatical about brushing after meals. James, you're getting off the subject."

"I don't even know what the subject is," James said.

"Murder," Jacqueline said, as the waiter removed her plate. He didn't give her a second look. The Algonquin is a favorite haunt of mystery writers.

"Murder in the plural," Jacqueline went on. She put her notebook on the table and took out a pen.

"But there's only been one murder. If it was murder."

"What I mean is that Dubretta may not have been the intended victim. Valentine thought the poison—"

"What poison?"

"James, you seem determined to be disagreeable today. 'What poison' is your department. Did you see your chemist friend?"

"Yes, I did. And a damned humiliating interview it was," James added resentfully. "First I had to listen to a lot of stupid jokes about my love life."

"What does your love life have to do with . . . oh, I see."

"I put up with it." James looked martyred. "I thought it was better to have him assume one of my ladies was trying to do me in rather than explain the true facts."

"That was very wise, James."

"Yes, it was. He also pointed out, at some length and with considerable sarcasm, that there are several hundred poisonous substances known to man—and woman—and that without some idea of what to look for—"

"James, please don't go on and on about things I already know. Be brief. Is he going to do the job?"

"Yes."

"And don't sulk. When?"

"It will take a little time," James recited.

"Well, keep after him. Where was I? Oh, yes. Valentine seems to have changed her mind about being murdered, but the point is worth considering. If there was an error, several people are potential victims. Hattie is a logical murderee if ever I met one, and there have been moments when I myself have contemplated removing Laurie to a higher sphere."

"Really, Jacqueline!"

"So what we'll do is this." Jacqueline shifted the notepad to one side so that the waiter could put her *rognons de veau* in front of her. She continued to write while using her fork with her left hand. "We'll write down the suspects and consider their motives for all the potential victims."

"That is the most illogical—"

"Hattie. Dubretta was threatening her. We agree Hattie had a motive for killing Dubretta? Good. She might also have wanted to get rid of Laurie. She may use the girl for various illicit purposes —stealing people's purses, for instance, or poisoning drinks. Laurie has been increasingly unstable and may constitute a danger if she tells what she knows. Now Valentine. Actually, I can't see why Hattie would want her dead. She's Hattie's biggest moneymaker. But one never knows. Valentine is afraid of something. Maybe she knows about Hattie's scam and was threatening to go to the police."

"What scam?"

"Never mind that now. Dubretta. She hated Hattie's guts. But I agree with O'Brien—for once—that Dubretta wouldn't make a stupid mistake like drinking the poison she had prepared for Hattie. Besides, she had her weapon of revenge in her hand. Exposure, ridicule, criminal prosecution perhaps—far more satisfying than a quick death."

Seeing that James's mouth was full, she paused to swallow, and resumed before he could speak. "The same basic objection applies to the possibility of Dubretta trying to murder anyone else. She wouldn't drink her own lethal brew.

"Valentine. She was one of Dubretta's targets. She—"

"That's outrageous," James exclaimed. "That girl is as innocent as a lamb."

"I'm sure Laurie would be delighted to enroll you in Valentine's fan club," Jacqueline said. "As I was saying—Valentine had an excellent opportunity to poison the wine."

"How? I can't see how anyone could have poisoned the wine."

"Never mind that now. Valentine is repelled by Laurie. Laurie is the type that's faithful unto death; the only way Val could get the girl off her back was to kill her. Laurie was only drinking ginger ale that night, but she'd toss down a glass of green slime if Valentine told her to. And by claiming she was the one in danger, Valentine disarms suspicion."

James shook his head in dumb disbelief. Jacqueline turned a page.

"Max. Same motive as Valentine's for poisoning Dubretta. If Dubretta threatened his client, who is probably his chief source of income . . . neither he nor Valentine had reason to kill Hattie—unless they figure they can do without her now that Val is established. I wonder how much commission Hattie collects from Valentine? Twenty-five percent can amount to a lot.

"Joe, AKA Victor von Damm. Dubretta knew his real identity, and it didn't worry him. But I suspect Hattie has some other hold over him. Maybe Indiana wants him. Maybe he's an escaped ax murderer. He'd kill to keep Dubretta from sending him back to the Big House. Or he'd kill Hattie to get out from under her thumb. He's been increasingly restive, and she's been pushing even harder lately. No particular motive for killing Laurie, outside of her general loathsomeness. Poor kid. . . ."

"Poor kid?" James roused himself from the stupor of disbelief into which Jacqueline's wild theories had sent him. "She's the hottest suspect of all. She had her pudgy paws all over those wineglasses, and she hated Dubretta."

"Oh, she's on the list," Jacqueline agreed. "But only if Dubretta was the intended victim. I don't believe Laurie would want to kill Hattie or Valentine. Now Sue . . . were you about to speak, James?"

"What's the use?" James said mournfully.

"She's an unlikely suspect, but I don't know her well; she may have a few buttons undone in her brain. She's jealous of Valentine for professional and personal reasons. Then there's Jean. Even a soggy rabbit will bite if it's cornered. Dubretta knew of Jean's true identity. Hattie was blackmailing her. Valentine is Hattie's top author, overshadowing Jean—"

"But those are contradictory motives," James groaned. "Either Jean wants out of the romance business or she wants to be number one—you can't have it both ways."

"It all depends on the identity of the victim," Jacqueline said, in the tone of a parent admonishing a dull child. "Jean could be putting on an act, pretending she wants out, when she really wants to be the Queen of Love. Mere theorizing, of course. . . ."

Her thoughtful gaze rested on James. He squirmed. "If you put me on that list," he began.

"A sudden passion for Valentine. A noble desire to defend her against all traducers." Jacqueline's face was rapt. "I love it, James."

"We are not amused," James said.

"There's one person we've forgotten."

"The mayor of New York? Frank Sinatra? Bella Abzug?"

"The Earl of Devonbrook."

"You're out of your mind, my girl. The man is an android. Hattie probably winds him up every morning."

"He's a dark horse," Jacqueline murmured.

"Very dark."

"I must talk to him. Tell you what we'll do, James. We'll divide up the suspects. You take the women, I'll take the men."

James's face brightened, then as quickly fell. "Not if I have to include Laurie."

"If you want Valentine, you'll have to take Laurie."

"I don't think she likes me," James said.

"Coward."

"Right. I'm not going to play any more."

"I'm not playing, James."

Her eyes were downcast and her lashes shadowed her elegantly modeled cheekbones. The hollows under those structures seemed more pronounced than usual, and her mouth had taken on a soft, pensive curve. She didn't often look like that, for her green eyes held a hint of mockery even in her tenderest moments. James found himself short of breath. But he was a man of iron control—he told himself—and this did not seem an appropriate time to express the proposition that had entered his mind.

Instead he said, "You really believe it was murder."

"Don't you?"

"It's awfully tenuous, Jacqueline—surmises and hypotheses and ifs and maybes. . . . As an intellectual game it is entertaining, if somewhat tasteless, but. . . ." He shrugged.

"It was murder, James."

"How was it done?"

"I have a couple of ideas, but they're so far-out, I'll have to do some research before I can be sure." She looked up at him, and her green eyes gleamed with the familiar amusement. "The real reason Holmes never told Watson what he was thinking is because he didn't have the solution figured out yet."

II

Before James departed he had grudgingly agreed to meet Jacqueline later at the romance conference. "The Love Lottery is at four," she explained. "The winner gets a date with Victor von Damm. You wouldn't want to miss that, would you?"

James's response was repetitively profane. However, when Jacqueline reminded him that most of Victor's fans were old enough to be his mother, and so infatuated that the few brains they possessed turned to mush in the presence of their idol, he agreed that it might be amusing to watch Victor cope with an elderly, inarticulate admirer. They parted on reasonably amicable terms, and Jacqueline hastened back to Fifty-third Street. The Romance Editors' Forum was due to begin at two-thirty, and she wanted to look them over before selecting a publisher for her book.

All the major publishers were represented. A dozen or more chairs had been arranged behind a long table. Hattie was on the platform, heckling the attendants who were setting out glasses and carafes of water, notepads, pencils, and microphones. She pretended not to notice Jacqueline until the latter tapped her on the shoulder.

"Oh, hello, Mrs. Kirsky. Are you attending the forum? You'd better find a seat, dear, this will be one of our most popular events."

"I thought you'd like my report on Dubretta's murder," Jacqueline said.

"Ssssh." Hattie drew her to one side. "I don't want talk like that disrupting the meeting. This is a professional association, you know. We can't allow a tragedy, however sad, to interfere with our work."

"Oh dear." Jacqueline's mouth drooped. "You mean I can't be the famous detective any more?"

Hattie looked at her suspiciously, and then decided she was making a joke. She tittered in a genteel fashion. "Now you know I pushed you into that. It wasn't nice of me, was it? But it wasn't all my fault. Valentine really was in a state. Pore chile, she's such a sensitive, high-strung creature—the artistic temperament, you know. She's all over that now."

"Everything is fine? No more worries?"

"Not a one." Hattie tugged her drooping corsage of white orchids back into place.

"You must have neglected to mention your new peace of mind to Laurie."

"What on earth do you mean, honey?"

"A little while ago she knocked Jean down and stole her purse."

"What?" Hattie's surprise was genuine. The hairs on her upper lip quivered. "That stupid little . . . are you sure?"

"Jean recognized her. What was she after, Hattie?"

"How the hell should I know what's in that chile's vacant mind?" Hattie shook her head. "I can't imagine what's wrong with her."

"How about drugs?"

"They all take 'em," Hattie said, with chilling indifference. "Well, it's only a couple more days. The conference ends tomorrow night, and that will be the end of Laurie. You'll excuse me, Mrs. Kirk, I must open the forum."

Jacqueline found a chair. Keeping up with Hattie's changes of mood was a full-time activity, but just now it was Valentine, not Hattie, she wondered about. Hattie was a pragmatic soul; the publicity stunt had backfired, so it had been abandoned. But why had Valentine changed her mind? Or had she?

Jacqueline dismissed the problem and concentrated on the discussion. This particular forum had been designed for authors and would-be authors rather than readers. There were over a hundred people present. Apparently everybody thought she could write a romantic novel. (Or perhaps everybody already had.) The editors were refreshingly candid about their requirements, and so specific Jacqueline wondered why they didn't feed the plot into a computer and program it to change the names next time around.

Heroines had to be beautiful, voluptuous, and "feisty." Sweet Sixteen wanted them unawakened but capable of sensual passion. Last Love wanted them capable of sensual passion, period. Heroes could have dark, auburn, or fair hair, so long as they had hair. Gray hair was okay for Last Love, but the editor warned it was risky; a streak of white at each temple went over better. Some

lines accepted chubby heroines, so long as the baby fat was voluptuous fat, and providing the heroine sweated off the excess before the end of the book.

Jacqueline took copious notes. She was particularly struck by
the fluffy-haired young editor who warned, "Your heroine must
not be promiscuous. She can tumble into bed with someone every forty pages or so, but she has to be in love with him. Or
raped, of course."

Jacqueline raised her hand. "What about *Forever Amber?*" she
asked seriously.

Half the audience laughed, the other half looked blank. The
editor looked blank. "There are always exceptions to every rule,
but only if you really know what you're doing," she said. Jacqueline did not write down this piece of advice.

By the time the forum ended, her brain was teeming with ideas
and with an uneasy feeling that Betsy and the Woofasses might be
right after all. Several editors had warned that their heroines
must be "liberated," independent women, proud of their own
sensuality. So far, so good; Jacqueline had no quarrel with that.
But the same editors had warned against promiscuity. Was it
more liberated to be overpowered against one's will than to seek
amorous adventures (the phrase had been used by one of the
more old-fashioned editors) for the sheer fun of it? The word
"love" kept cropping up. The heroines were all monogamous, in
intent if not in actuality, and the happy ending consisted of cap-
turing the hero and making him monogamous too. The books
were anti-feminist, and anti-female, not only because of their prurient interest in rape but because they voiced the tired old moral
view (invented and enthusiastically supported by most men) that
a woman's only legitimate goal in life was to devote all her time,
energy, and sexual abilities to one man. So far as Jacqueline
could see, the only difference between the new romances and the
old love stories was that "love" had replaced marriage as a pre-
requisite for sex.

In a mildly disgruntled mood she made her way toward the
Washington Room, where Victor von Damm was to be handed
over to the winner of the Love Lottery. But this was a spectacle
she was destined never to enjoy.

James was waiting for her. His famous crooked smile was no

longer crooked, it was lopsided. His lower lip was swollen to twice its normal size. A reddening bruise on his temple matched a scraped patch on his jaw. As Jacqueline approached, slowly and delicately, he held out his arms. Both wrists were ringed in red.

"Oh, James," Jacqueline breathed.

"Is that all you can say?"

"When did it happen?"

"Just now."

"Don't tell me it was—"

"It was."

"James, darling, you're hyperventilating." Jacqueline took a paper bag from her purse, shook out the contents, and offered it to her afflicted friend. "Breathe into this."

James snatched the paper bag and crushed it in his fists.

"This is serious, James," Jacqueline exclaimed. "Tell me—"

"You're damned right it's serious! That girl ought to be locked up. She was waiting for me when I came out of my room, on my way over here. She shoved me back into the room and—and—"

"Hit you on the head?"

"No, that happened when I fell," James admitted, more calmly. "She caught me off balance, damn it. The fall stunned me for a minute. Then she—she—she sat on me. If you laugh, I'll kill you."

"I'm not laughing." And indeed, after a momentary spasm, Jacqueline's face remained grave. "She actually tied you up?"

James nodded. "With my own necktie. Half choked me getting it off. While I was lying there trying to catch my breath, she tore the room apart. Threw everything onto the floor, pulled out all the drawers—"

"Did she look under the mattress?"

"What difference does it make? The damned notebook wasn't there anyway."

"I just wondered. Go on, James."

"No, she did not look under the mattress. It wasn't what you would call a carefully organized search." James sounded more relaxed now that he had confessed the worst. "It only took her a couple of minutes. She looked in my jacket pockets too. Then she bolted out, leaving the door open."

"Someone saw you and came to the rescue?"

"No, I got loose without any help. I tell you, Jacqueline, the girl has flipped her lid. I'm going to call the police."

"Yes, you had better do that." Jacqueline's expression changed from serious to grim. "Try to get O'Brien if you can. I'll meet you here—in the bar—in an hour or so."

"I'll be plastered in an hour or so. Where are you going?"

"I'll be back as soon as I can."

Jacqueline found Hattie behind the makeshift stage applying more glue to the false hair on Victor's chest. "You again?" the agent demanded. "Are you trying to drive me crazy?"

"I'm looking for Laurie."

"I don't know where she is, and I don't care. Stand still, Victor."

"It itches," Victor complained. "Hey, Mrs. Kirby. When you see Sue, will you tell her—"

"Shut up, Joe. Hattie, this is serious. Laurie just attacked a friend of mine and ransacked his room. I've got to find her."

"Wow." Victor whistled softly. "I told you that kid was flaky, Hattie."

"I'm not responsible for what she does," Hattie said. "Don't try to involve me, Mrs. Kirsky. She's crazy as a loon. You can't believe anything she says."

"I don't give a good goddamn about you," Jacqueline snapped. "I want that girl. I've got to find her before she hurts someone—or herself. Where does she hang out? What's her address? Phone number? Who are her friends?"

"I don't know her address. Her last name is Schellhammer, and she lives on Park or Fifth, in the upper eighties. Joe—I mean, Victor—will you stop squirming?"

"Her friends," Jacqueline insisted. "She's president of Valentine's fan club, isn't she? Where are the rest of them?"

"Probably hanging around outside," Hattie said disinterestedly. "They usually are."

Realizing she had obtained all she could from Hattie, Jacqueline left. A group of fans were waiting outside the door. Among them were several of the girls who had been clustered around the Valentine Lovers booth on the opening day. Jacqueline pounced on the nearest, a vacant-faced child with protuberant blue eyes. "I'm looking for Laurie."

The girl's eyes bulged till they looked as if they were about to pop out of her head. "I don't know. . . ."

"You're choking her," said another girl, bespectacled and plain.

"Sorry." Jacqueline released her grip. The pop-eyed child scuttled behind a friend. "Does your club have a vice-president?"

"That's me," said the plain one. She stood her ground as Jacqueline turned to her. "Are you a friend of Laurie's?"

"I guess you could say that," was the cautious reply. "What's she done now?"

Jacqueline nodded, satisfied. "You're the one I want to talk to." She drew the girl aside. "What's your name?"

"Meredith. Meredith Katz. Who are you?"

"My name is Jacqueline Kirby."

Meredith's lips parted in a sardonic smile. Light flashed blindingly from her braces. "The famous sleuth?"

Jacqueline grinned back at her. "What are you doing in this bunch of—er—fans?"

Meredith gave further proof of the intelligence Jacqueline had acknowledged by recognizing this as a compliment. "They're okay. I happen to admire Valentine's writing."

"So do I. Listen, Meredith . . . I don't suppose anyone calls you Merry."

"You're damned right they don't."

"Laurie is in deep trouble, Meredith. I want to help her."

"What kind of trouble?"

"Assault."

"Wow." Meredith pondered for a moment; but Jacqueline noticed she did not appear to be surprised. Finally the girl said slowly, "I guess you could call Laurie a friend of mine, mainly on account of she hasn't got any other friends, just the fan club. She's always been pretty weird, but lately she's gotten a lot worse. I mean, really weird. I wouldn't mind giving her a hand, but . . . how do I know you want to help her?"

"You'll have to take my word for it," Jacqueline said flatly. "It's a gamble. Like everything else in life."

"Let me think about it."

Meredith duly thought about it. While she was thinking, Jacqueline glanced at the door of the Washington Room, where an usher was taking tickets. The group of teenage fans stood to one side.

"Why don't they go in?" Jacqueline asked. "Are they waiting for you?"

"Are you kidding?" Meredith laughed scornfully. "Tickets for this conference cost three hundred bucks. Most of us don't have that kind of bread. We pooled our dues so Laurie could get in."

"Laurie had to buy a ticket?" Jacqueline repeated.

"There's a free reception for fans tomorrow afternoon," Meredith said in an expressionless voice. "Tea and cookies and a talk from Aunt Hattie."

"Don't tell me, let me guess," Jacqueline said. "Part of your dues goes to Hattie."

"Half. They go to the national organization, to be precise. You can also guess who's executive secretary."

"I might have known," Jacqueline muttered. "That old bat doesn't miss a trick."

Meredith said abruptly, "If I see Laurie I'll tell her you want to talk to her. She stays at my house sometimes. I don't know where she is right now. Usually she's hanging around waiting for Valentine to make an appearance, if she isn't running errands for Aunt Hattie."

The word "aunt" was obviously meant to be ironic, and Jacqueline acknowledged it with a wry smile. "Errands," she repeated. "What kind of errands, Meredith?"

"Oh, you know—going for coffee, taking Hattie's clothes to the cleaners. I wouldn't be surprised if she polishes her shoes and washes her undies."

"Neither would I." Intriguing as the conversation was, Jacqueline knew time was running out. "Could Laurie be at home, do you think?"

Meredith's thin lips curled. "There's nobody home but the maid. Her folks are in Europe. They usually are in Europe. She could be there, but I doubt it."

"I get the picture." Jacqueline tore a page from her notebook and wrote quickly. "Here's my room number and the telephone number of the hotel. Meredith, this is serious. Try to convince her I'm on her side."

"Okay." Meredith took the slip of paper. Jacqueline delved in her purse again. "I won't be using my ticket for this affair. Do you want it?"

"You mean it?"

Jacqueline gave her the ticket. Meredith gloated over it for a moment and then said nobly, "We'll draw straws. Thanks."

"Have fun," Jacqueline said.

Laurie was not in any of the public rooms of the hotel. Jacqueline used a house phone to call Hattie's suite. Max answered. When Jacqueline explained why she was calling, his voice mirrored her concern.

"I was afraid something like this would happen. I tried to persuade Hattie only yesterday that she ought to warn the girl's parents she was unwell, but. . . ."

"You know Hattie," Jacqueline finished the sentence for him. "I understand her parents are out of town anyway, so it wouldn't have done any good. You haven't seen her today?"

"No. Wait, I'll ask Valentine."

Jacqueline heard Valentine's emphatic negative, but Max duly repeated it. "Not since last night, she says. What can I do?"

"Nothing, at the moment. Just hang on to her if she comes to you, and call me immediately."

After she had hung up, Jacqueline moved to a public telephone and looked in the book. There was only one Schellhammer on Fifth Avenue in the upper eighties. Jacqueline dialed the number.

The phone rang for several minutes before she gave up. She stood for a moment in a rare state of indecision before making up her mind. It was essential that she cover all the places to which Laurie might go, especially since there were so few known to her. Much as she hated to take the time, she would have to go to the girl's home.

She accomplished the remarkable feat of finding a taxi by going to the head of the line waiting outside the hotel and announcing, "Official business," as she flashed her Rome police card at the couple who had been about to get into the cab. Whenever the taxi stopped for a traffic light she wrote in her notebook. She didn't expect to find Laurie at home, but at least she could leave a message. And that message had to be as persuasive and reassuring as she could make it.

The building facing Central Park confirmed Hattie's claim that Laurie's parents were wealthy. Some of the apartments in the beautiful old structure had been handed down in the same family for generations. Rented or owned, they cost astronomical sums per month. The security arrangements were correspondingly stringent, but Jacqueline's respectable appearance and glib lies got her past the guard and into the elevator before he remembered to ask the name of the school at which she claimed to be a teacher.

The maid was at home. She simply hadn't bothered to answer the telephone. Despite the guard in the lobby, the apartment had the usual multiple locks and bars. Again Jacqueline's announcement that she was one of Laurie's teachers won her admission.

The maid was a woman in her forties. Her coarse black hair was wound around her head in a heavy braid and she wore a neat print housedress, but she had taken advantage of her employers' absence to replace her shoes with loose slippers. "Laurie ees not 'ere," she announced. "Meester an' Mees' Schellhammer ees not 'ere. They come back soon."

This was obviously a memorized speech, including the precautionary refusal to admit the owners were out of town. As soon as Jacqueline began questioning the woman, her supply of English dried up. She shook her head and repeated her prepared statement.

Jacqueline switched to fluent if ungrammatical Spanish. "Where is the Laurie? I have the need to speak at her. It is of an important much urgent."

"You are a teacher of Spanish, señora?" the maid asked doubtfully.

"I am the teacher of the English," Jacqueline replied. "The young woman is not in the school for today and the week. At what hour is it the possibility that she returning to the house is?"

The maid replied with an expressive gesture, eyes rolling, shoulders raised. "Who can say? It is very strange, here in America. There is no respect for the father and the mother, no discipline for the child. It is very different in my country."

On the grand piano in the living room Jacqueline saw a large studio portrait of a man and woman in formal evening dress.

Their faces might have been stamped out of the same mold, not because they really resembled one another, but because they had been groomed and exercised and dressed by the same fashionable firms.

She gave the maid the note, impressing on her the urgency of giving it to Laurie immediately if the fugitive turned up.

The visit had been useful, if only to give her a clearer insight into Laurie's problems. It appeared to be a classic case of an Ugly Duckling despised and ignored by her beautiful parents. The more they nagged her about her weight and her looks, the more Laurie would eat.

Knowing the futility of looking for a cab at rush hour, Jacqueline started walking. It was after six when she entered the cocktail lounge where James was waiting for her.

"I can't stay," she announced. "Did you reach O'Brien?"

"He wasn't there."

"Damn it, James—"

"What message was I supposed to leave? You didn't tell me where you were going or when you'd be back."

"You didn't report the attack, did you?"

James's eyes fell. "I don't want to get the kid in trouble."

"Like hell. You were embarrassed. You didn't want to admit you were mugged by a seventeen-year-old girl. Of all the curses with which I have been afflicted in the course of a long hard life, male ego is the worst. Get up from there."

She hauled him out of his chair and led him out of the hotel, lecturing all the way. "Get over to the precinct house right away. It's on West Forty-first, just off Broadway. You'd better walk, it will be faster. If O'Brien isn't there, leave a message asking him to call me. But whether he is there or not, report the assault and swear out a complaint."

"I thought you felt sorry for the kid. This will mean a criminal record for her. Isn't there a less drastic method of locating her?"

"Not in a hurry, no. Even if I reported her as missing, which I haven't the authority to do, it would be several days before the police would take action—and they don't take much action in cases of missing juveniles. They'll be forced to act on a complaint of assault and battery."

"Why is it so important to—"

"James, will you go? If you don't understand the urgency of the matter I'll explain it to you later."

"Where and when?"

Jacqueline rolled her eyes heavenward. "Come to my room after you've been to the police, then."

"That's better," James said. "What are we going to do in your room?"

"I will be waiting. I don't care what you do, so long as you don't expect me to do it with you."

A cunning expression spread over James's countenance. "I'll go if you promise to buy me dinner afterwards. It's your turn."

"I'm not planning to go out for dinner."

"That's okay with me," James said.

"All right, I'll buy you dinner. Get going."

"See you later." With a jaunty flip of the hand, he started off. Jacqueline watched him for a moment, with a faint ambiguous smile on her lips. Then she plunged into the traffic and made her way across the street.

III

She was relieved to see Sue unbruised, unmarked, and unmolested. The girl was getting dressed to go out; slim and dainty in a white petticoat and lacy bra, she turned from the mirror to greet Jacqueline.

"Are you feeling better?"

"Better than what?" Jacqueline realized she was referring to her pre-coffee morning grumpiness. "No," she said, after thinking it over.

"What's the matter?"

Jacqueline almost hated to tell her. She made a charming picture of Young Love—radiant face, shining eyes, that indefinable glow that comes from the heart to illumine the body. . . . Jacqueline pulled out her notebook and wrote the sentence down.

Sue put on her dress and pirouetted. "How do you like it?"

"You just bought it, didn't you?"

"How did you know?"

Jacqueline took a pair of shears from her purse and cut off the tags dangling from the wisp of eyelet framing the neckline of the dress. It was a copy of one of the "antique dresses" in vogue that year. The skimpy, low-cut bodice was modeled after a Victorian chemise. The skirt had three layers of ruffles, tucks, and lace inserts with narrow blue ribbons running hither and yon. "Is this what you had in mind?" Sue asked with a smile.

"It's perfect—for you." Jacqueline sighed. "I always wanted to be cute," she said wistfully.

"But I'm sure you were—I mean, you still are—"

"I was never cute. Gorgeous, yes. Cute, no. Ah, well." Jacqueline sighed a second time and then became practical. "Whom are you going out with?"

"Joe, of course." Sue turned for an anxious inspection of an already flawless face.

"I thought he had a date this evening."

"Oh, he's just buying the winner of the Love Lottery a drink," Sue said callously. "He'll dump her as soon as he can."

"Hmph. Do me a favor before you go?"

"Of course."

Jacqueline handed her the plastic bucket from the bureau. "Get me some ice. I'm expecting a call, and I don't want to leave the room."

Sue lingered, bucket in hand, watching Jacqueline as the latter took a bottle of Scotch from her suitcase and attacked the seal. "Are you going to drink all that?" Sue asked, laughing.

"No such luck."

When Sue returned, Jacqueline had assumed the peacock-blue robe. Her skirt and blouse were on a hanger, ready to be put on at a moment's notice. Her shoes were on the floor under her clothes. The top of the bureau was littered with packets of food—chips, peanuts, crackers, cheese straws. Jacqueline extracted a jar of mixed munchies and another bag of nuts from her purse and added them to the collection.

"Thanks," she said, taking the ice bucket.

"You're having a party," Sue deduced, seeing that the glasses from the bathroom had been added to the display.

"In a way. Before you go, I must warn you about something. Have you seen Laurie today?"

"Laurie? Oh—that girl."

"That girl. Have you seen her?"

"No. Should I have?"

"It's probably lucky for you you haven't." Jacqueline told Sue what had happened, and was pleased to see that Sue's reaction was proof of kindliness of heart, if not of quick perception. "Poor girl. I hope you find her."

"You may find her before I do," Jacqueline said grimly. "Both the people she has—er—contacted are friends of mine. I'm not sure there is any pattern in her behavior, so I can't be certain what she'll do next, but you might be a target. Be careful."

"Oh my goodness." Sue's eyes widened. "Do you really think—"

"I don't know. Where are you meeting Joe?"

"Downstairs in the lobby."

"Good. Don't leave the hotel. I don't believe she'd venture inside, but on the street you're fair game. Warn Joe. Tell him— and this is very important, Sue—tell him that if he spots Laurie he is to hold on to her. Sock her in the jaw, do whatever he has to do, but don't let her get away. Is that clear?"

After Sue had gone, Jacqueline settled down with the Scotch on one side and the telephone on the other. She suspected her vigil would probably prove fruitless, but she was afraid to take any chances. Her sense of uneasiness increased with each passing minute. There was some logical cause for concern, considering Laurie's behavior, but the real cause was harder to define. Danger, danger. . . . The word kept echoing in Jacqueline's brain.

By the time James arrived she had eaten half the nuts and a packet of potato chips. She admitted him and returned to her chair.

"Well?" she said.

James took off his jacket and loosened his tie before turning to the impromptu bar. "Cutty Sark? I thought you were economizing."

"There are basic standards below which I refuse to sink. Help yourself," she added sarcastically, as James filled his glass.

He pulled up a chair next to hers and sank into it. "This is nice. Much better than going out to dinner."

"Did you see O'Brien?" Jacqueline removed his hand from her shoulder and returned it to him.

"He wasn't there."

"James—"

"I left a message," James said quickly. "And I filled out a complaint. They said they'd get right on it."

"Hah."

"What more could I do?"

"You could keep your hands to yourself. I am in no mood for dalliance, James. You still don't get the picture."

"No, I don't. What are you so uptight about? I'm the one who should be shaken to the core." James touched the lump on his intellectual brow. "I need sympathy and TLC," he said sulkily.

"That bump on the head must have scrambled your brains," Jacqueline said. "But then you haven't seen as much of Laurie as I have. Over the past few days she has exhibited violent changes of mood, from aggressive to amiable to lachrymose. She's taking a drug of some kind—"

"Maybe she's just psychotic," James said, putting his feet up on the foot of the bed.

"Just? The point is that she's getting worse. The violence is becoming more violent. She's after something and she'll go to any length to get it. If you had been a fragile old man with a bad heart; if your head had hit the corner of the dresser instead of the floor. . . ."

"I see what you mean." James looked pained. "What's she after, do you suppose?"

"Maybe nothing. A figment of her own disturbed imagination. What really worries me is the possibility that someone put the idea into her head."

"Hattie?"

"She's the most likely person, certainly. But anyone could manipulate Laurie by telling her Valentine was in danger. Suppose, for instance, that the unknown killer got Laurie on the trail of Dubretta's notebook. Mr. or Mrs. X has it now, but he's been unable to reach Laurie to tell her to quit looking. Or else she is so far gone she can't be stopped. Not only is she a danger to others, she may be in danger herself, from the person who is using her. If we can find her, she may tell us who put her on the trail of the notebook."

"You haven't the slightest evidence to support that theory," James said.

"No."

"But your other point is well taken," James admitted magnanimously. "Have you warned the other people she's likely to attack?"

"I hope so. Since I've no idea what criterion she is using to select her victims, I can't be sure I've covered everyone; but I did warn Sue, who will warn Victor. Hattie and Max know what has happened. I also called Betsy. She wasn't at home, but I left a message telling her it was vitally important that she get in touch with me."

"Betsy?"

"I forgot, you haven't met her." Jacqueline explained Betsy. "Her involvement is only peripheral, but to a mind obsessed she might seem the logical person to have Dubretta's notebook. She knew Dubretta, she doesn't like Valentine, and she's a friend of mine."

"You've done all you can, then," James said reassuringly. "Relax, why don't you?"

A scuffle ensued. It was interrupted by a knock on the door, which distracted James and allowed Jacqueline to extract herself without the necessity of the physical violence she had been contemplating. Smoothing her hair, she went to the door and admitted O'Brien.

"Why, Lieutenant, how very dedicated of you to come by. Won't you join us?"

"Thank you." O'Brien nodded politely to James, who had regained his chair and was trying to look as if he had never left it. "I hear you were looking for me, Professor."

"I wasn't looking for you," James said. "I went to the station to file a report."

"I know. Sorry to hear about that. Sure you're okay?"

There was not the slightest trace of amusement in his voice or in his face, but James flushed angrily. "Certainly I'm sure. She caught me off balance."

"Crazy people can have astonishing strength," O'Brien said gravely. James did not reply. With the air of a man who has extracted all the entertainment he decently can from a situation, O'Brien turned to Jacqueline.

"You wanted to see me, Mrs. Kirby?"

"Sit down," Jacqueline said. "Have a drink."

"Thanks." O'Brien poured a discreet amount of Scotch into a glass and added ice cubes.

James said, "I thought you weren't supposed to drink on duty."

"I'm not on duty," O'Brien said calmly. He sat down on the foot of the bed. "Was there anything special you wanted to talk to me about, Mrs. Kirby?"

"That depends. Need I explain to you why it is imperative that we locate Laurie without delay?"

"No. At least," O'Brien added, "I have my own reasons for wanting to find her. I don't know that they are the same as yours. You have a free-wheeling imagination, Mrs. K."

"What are your reasons?"

"They're pretty obvious, aren't they? The girl has physically attacked two people in the last twelve hours. Or should I say three people?"

His eyebrows rose fractionally. Jacqueline was learning to read O'Brien's eyebrows. The degree of interrogation implied by this movement was minimal.

"No, I don't think it was Laurie who took my purse," she said.

"I figured you'd have mentioned it if you had thought so," said O'Brien. "In your expert opinion, is she liable to go after anybody else?"

"Possibly."

"That's a big help. If you could give me a name, I might be able to arrange protection."

"With your manpower shortage?" Jacqueline asked sarcastically. "I've warned, or tried to warn, the potential victims."

"Then what did you want to see me about?"

Jacqueline looked exasperated. "A number of things. For example, the autopsy on Dubretta."

O'Brien sipped daintily. "There won't be an autopsy."

"But—"

"Her symptoms were consistent with death from congestive heart failure. She's been under treatment for that complaint for years. According to her doctors she was stabilized, but it was a serious condition, and . . . one never knows. Sometimes she'd forget her medication, and she didn't take good care of herself." O'Brien studied Jacqueline's outthrust lip and contemptuous eyes and said defensively, "Mrs. Kirby, to say we have a manpower shortage is a laughable understatement. The coroner's office is piled high with stiffs. We aren't about to go digging up work when there's no reason for it."

James stared ostentatiously at his watch. "Well, that's that. Right, Jacqueline? It was nice of you to stop by, Lieutenant."

"No trouble at all," O'Brien said. "I haven't got anything else to do tonight. This is excellent Scotch, Mrs. Kirby."

"Have another."

"I don't mind if I do."

In a voice thick with annoyance James growled, "Hadn't we better order, Jacqueline? Room service always takes forever at this hour."

"Good heavens, James, can't you ever think of anything except your stomach?" Jacqueline demanded. The barefaced injustice of the charge left James speechless. Jacqueline went on, "There's a deli across the street. I'll have a pastrami on rye and one of those big kosher pickles. And coffee. How about you, Lieutenant?"

"Sammy makes a good shrimp-salad sandwich," O'Brien said. "Coffee for me, too."

"But you—" James sputtered. "You said you were taking me to dinner."

"I am." Jacqueline took money from her purse. "Get whatever you want, James."

After James had gone, O'Brien took the chair he had vacated, and crossed his ankles. "You're a vicious woman, Mrs. Kirby," he remarked.

"I assumed you wouldn't talk freely while he was here."

"You assumed right. But I'm not sure I'm anxious to talk freely now that he's gone."

"Let's not waste time. He'll be back soon. You also believe Dubretta was murdered."

O'Brien met her intent gaze with a face as blank as a stone wall. "Ah," Jacqueline said, in a satisfied voice, "you do believe it. Have you anything to go on, or is it your detective's sixth sense?''

The creases in O'Brien's cheeks deepened, in his version of a smile. "There ain't no such animal, Mrs. Kirby, except in the type of fiction you obviously read too much of. My suspicion—and it's even less solid than that—stems from something Dubretta said to me four or five days ago—the last time I saw her alive.''

"Well?" Jacqueline leaned forward.

"I had stopped by to see Prudence. Dubretta came in as I was leaving. We talked for a couple of minutes and I asked her what she was working on. It was one of our standard conversational exchanges; sometimes she'd give me a hint, sometimes she'd just laugh and tell me to read her next column. This time she laughed. But she said . . ." O'Brien's eyes grew remote. " 'It's no big deal, O'Brien. No government scandal or corruption. This is a grudge case. If I can pull it off it'll give me the greatest satisfaction I've had since I started in this business.' Then she laughed again. 'If I drop dead in the next week or so, O'Brien, it won't be heart failure.' ''

"Aha!"

"Aha, hell. It's not evidence, Mrs. Kirby.''

"Maybe not. But it fits my theories about the case.''

"I figured you were going to tell me your theories sooner or later, whether I wanted to hear them or not." O'Brien's voice hardened. "Get this straight, Mrs. Kirby. I'm not playing Sherlock Holmes with you. So far as the department is concerned, the case is not only closed, there never was a case to start with. I'm screwing around in my spare time because—well, just for the hell of it. I'm talking to you because you have an in with that bunch of fruitcakes across the street. I am not going to confer with you or exchange information with you or defer to your opinion. If you want to give me what you've got, I'll think about it. And that's as far as I'll go.''

"Why, of course, Lieutenant. I have better things to do with my time than play Sherlock Holmes. And," Jacqueline added, outrage getting the better of her, "if I did play, it wouldn't be with you.''

"Spit it out, then. Your boyfriend will be back soon.''

Jacqueline's eyes narrowed to malachite slits, but she kept her temper. "Hattie Foster is the agent for the three top-selling authors in historical-romance fiction, plus several of the lesser lights. As one of her jealous rivals said to me, she has a corner on the market. And that market means a lot of money. Romance editors claim to control forty percent of—"

"I know the stats."

"Good for you. Hattie is making an excellent living out of the writers she handles, not only because they command top prices, but because she is skimming off more than her share of their royalties. Her commission is more than twice the normal rate, and although I can't prove it, I'm pretty sure she is also chiseling money on the side. It's easy to cheat writers; they are very naive.

"I'm not familiar with Hattie's arrangements with Valerie Valentine. The girl was her first important client; handling Valentine gave Hattie her start. Valentine is as important to her as she is to Val, and Max, Valentine's business manager, is a shrewd man, so I rather doubt that Hattie is getting away with much there. The others are in a different category. Victor von Damm is Hattie's Frankenstein monster. She created him, out of two bored housewife-writers and an unemployed actor. She could legitimately claim she's entitled to more than the usual agent's fees because, without that combination, Victor von Damm wouldn't be making the money he does. It was a rather original idea, actually. The romance business is dominated by women authors. The few men who write use women's names. Victor von Damm is a unique phenomenon—a kind of literary glamour boy."

"Victor is played—literally—by Joe Kirby. He's getting fed up. He wants to quit and Hattie won't let him. What hold she has over him I don't know. If I had access to police files," Jacqueline said pointedly, "I'd check up on Joe."

"Checking on all the writers' backgrounds would certainly be a reasonable starting point," O'Brien agreed blandly. "Including that of Valerie Vanderbilt."

"Valerie Vanderbilt is Jean Frascatti, an English professor," Jacqueline said. "Hattie was blackmailing her too, but in a different way." She went on to explain Jean's dilemma.

O'Brien's eyebrows soared. "That's crazy," he said. "Your friend sounds like a nut."

"The threat was real to her."

"Real enough to kill for? No, it won't work, Mrs. Kirby. Motive is the least important consideration in a murder investigation, for the simple reason that some people kill for reasons you and I would consider absurdly inadequate. But in this case there isn't a motive. So Dubretta found out Victor von Damm was an actor and Valerie Vanderbilt was an embarrassed English prof. So what? She could broadcast those facts to the world and the world wouldn't so much as blink. Even the readers of this romance tripe don't care. The disclosure wouldn't lop five bucks off Hattie's income, and her hide is so thick she's incapable of shame. She didn't like Dubretta's jeers, but she'd shrug them off the way you'd shrug off a mosquito."

"What about Dubretta's grudge against Hattie? She told you it was a grudge case—"

"Hattie was the one who turned down Prudence's first book, years ago," O'Brien said, his face taking on the shuttered, defensive look it assumed whenever Dubretta's sister was mentioned. "She was an editor at one of the publishing houses then, and she was notorious for her vicious rejection letters. She's done nothing since to lessen Dubretta's contempt for her. But again, so what? I'm telling you, Mrs. K., there's no motive."

Jacqueline started to speak. O'Brien waved her to silence. "I need to know two things. First, Dubretta's symptoms. Was there anything—anything she said or did, anything in the way she looked—that was inconsistent with death from heart failure?"

"That's a stupid question, O'Brien. Heart failure isn't a medical term. There are different kinds of heart disease, and they can exhibit an infinite variety of symptoms."

"That's what I thought you'd say. What about opportunity? Did you see anyone drop anything into one of those glasses? Did anyone hand Dubretta her glass? Was it possible for anyone to ensure that she got a particular glass?"

"Well. . . ."

"Right. You can amuse yourself with motive from now till doomsday, Mrs. Kirby, but unless you can tell me how it could have been done, you're talking to yourself."

"I have an idea," Jacqueline said haughtily. "Unfortunately I have been so busy with other matters I haven't had time to check it out." A frown replaced her lofty look; she struck her hands together. "Damn. Why doesn't that girl call?"

Realizing that genuine worry underlay her attempt to change the subject, O'Brien did not pursue it. "What makes you think she'd call you?" he asked.

"It's a far-out chance." Jacqueline ran a distracted hand through her hair. "But we had a kind of rapport going yesterday. I left messages with her best friend, the maid at her apartment, and with Max and Hattie. The only reason she might turn to me is that she hasn't got anybody else. Now that she's in trouble, Hattie will dump her, and Valentine has always loathed her." Jacqueline paused. Then she said again, "She hasn't got anybody else."

"I see."

The silence was broken by a peremptory pounding on the door. "Damn," Jacqueline said. "I didn't think he'd be back so soon."

"Sammy's Deli closes at five. As you probably know."

"Certainly I knew. I also knew that James wouldn't quit until he spent the money I gave him. He's a petty man in some ways. I figured it would take him at least half an hour to find a place that was still. . . ." A second, more emphatic thud sounded on the door. "I guess I'd better let him in," Jacqueline said resignedly.

But when she opened the door she found herself confronting Betsy Markham. Jacqueline's eyes opened wide. Before she could speak, Betsy pushed her out of the way and slammed the door.

"I think the fuzz is after me," she gasped. "You took your time about. . . ." Seeing O'Brien, she came to an abrupt halt, physically and verbally. "Oh, damnation."

"Good evening, Ms. Markham," said O'Brien, rising.

"Hi, O'Brien." Betsy collapsed onto the bed, propping her shaggy gray head on one hand. "Sit down, sit down. I can't stand you when you're polite."

"I take it you two know each other," said Jacqueline from the doorway.

"Yeah," said Betsy.

"Ms. Markham is a frequent performer in my precinct," O'Brien said. "By the way, Ms. Markham, Jack Billings says next time don't hit so hard. He's got a lump the size of Plymouth Rock.''

"I'm sorry. The damned sign slipped,'' Betsy explained.

As the eyes of the other two focused on her, a harsh flood of color moved up her weather-beaten throat till it blended unprettily with the purple-and-green bruise under her left eye. After a moment her sense of humor triumphed over her embarrassment. "Your message came too late,'' she said throatily, indicating the eye. "At least I presume your call referred to the large young person who clobbered me this afternoon.''

"When?'' Jacqueline demanded.

"Three, four hours ago. I was on my way to a meeting of the executive committee of WUFAS. No sooner did I walk out of the house than the kid jumped me. She was trying to get my knapsack.'' Betsy indicated the lumpy khaki pack beside her on the bed. "So I gave her a karate move—you know—'' She came up off the bed with an ear-splitting shriek, hands lifted. Jacqueline and O'Brien jumped. "Like that,'' Betsy said, subsiding. "I hit her on the shoulder and then she hauled back her fist and socked me in the eye.''

"Don't do that,'' Jacqueline protested.

"Just demonstrating.'' Betsy grinned. "How about pouring me a drink? In view of the fact that your message came too late.''

Jacqueline complied. "She didn't get your knapsack, I see.''

"Apparently she changed her mind,'' Betsy said equably. "She dumped the contents out while I was squirming around on the pavement with her on top of me. I was yelling my head off, too. You can't ever get a cop in this town when you need one.''

"So that makes three,'' Jacqueline said to O'Brien, who had taken no notice of Betsy's criticism.

"Your arithmetic is faultless,'' was the courteous reply.

"I found your message on my answering machine when I got back from the meeting,'' Betsy rattled on. "So I thought I'd come on over and tell you what I think of your friends. What's Hattie Foster doing, using the girl as a hit person?''

Jacqueline and O'Brien exchanged glances. "It was her idea,'' Jacqueline said cryptically.

"Hmmm,'' said O'Brien, even more cryptically.

The arrival of James ended the discussion. "I had to go clear down to Broadway and Forty-second," he complained, placing a leaking brown paper bag on the bureau.

"I don't suppose it occurred to you to get another bottle of Scotch," Jacqueline said, looking sadly at the depleted remains of that beverage.

"Luckily I got an extra sandwich." James stared at Betsy.

"Oh, I couldn't intrude," said Betsy. The contrast between her New England boarding-school accent and her sixties protest costume made James stare even more.

Jacqueline introduced them. "How do you do," James said. He looked at Betsy's shiner, she studied his lumps and bruises, then they said in chorus, "Laurie?"

A bond having been established, James formalized his invitation and Betsy was persuaded to accept an egg-salad sandwich. He and Betsy exchanged lies about their encounters with Laurie, both claiming she had caught them off guard. Betsy demonstrated her karate move, and James explained what he would have done if he hadn't slipped and hit his head.

"Of course I had an additional handicap," he explained, having thought up this excuse during his search for sandwiches. "My mother drilled it into me from childhood—don't hit a girl."

"That's sexist," said Betsy.

"You're damned right," said James. "Most of the girls in my grade school were bigger than I was."

Jacqueline and O'Brien ate in silence. Jacqueline's eyes kept turning to the telephone.

It was not quite eight o'clock when the first call came. Jacqueline's hand shot out like a rattlesnake striking, but her expression changed when she heard the voice on the other end of the line. "Max?" she repeated, glancing at O'Brien. "You did? When? What did she say?"

She listened for a few minutes, then said, "Thanks," and hung up. Again it was to O'Brien that she spoke. "Laurie just called. Max said she was pretty incoherent. She kept saying someone was trying to kidnap her, and asking if Valentine was all right. He tried to find out where she was, but couldn't make much sense out of her. He thought she said something about the Village."

Betsy jumped up. "Let's go look for her."

"A lot of people are already looking for her," said O'Brien, not moving. "That's not much of a lead."

"Anyway, this is a job for the police," James said, looking alarmed. "You can't go wandering around the alleys of Manhattan at this hour. If Laurie doesn't clobber you, someone else will."

They were still arguing when the telephone rang again. This time Jacqueline did not address the caller by name. After a brief and obviously unsatisfactory conversation she hung up and pushed her glasses back up to the bridge of her nose. They immediately began slipping again.

"Well?" said James.

"That was Meredith, Laurie's best friend. Laurie must have called her right after she talked to Max. She kept giggling and saying she was like Midas; everything she touched turned to gold."

"My God," Betsy muttered.

"Did she say where she was?" O'Brien asked.

Before Jacqueline could answer, James said pedantically, "None of you seems to have thought of the most obvious place. Maybe the girl has gone home."

O'Brien did not move or speak, but Jacqueline turned on him. "You staked out the apartment, didn't you? I thought you had a manpower shortage. I don't suppose it occurred to you that the sight of a police car would keep her away?"

A shade of vexation crossed O'Brien's face. "If she spotted us it was a blunder on someone's part. She hasn't gone home. I'd have heard."

"She told Meredith she was at the museum," Jacqueline said.

"Is there a museum in the Village?" Betsy asked, with the normal ignorance of a native of New York.

"There are a hundred museums in Manhattan." O'Brien eyed Jacqueline's glasses, which hovered on the brink of catastrophe. "But they're all closed now."

"She might be lurking outside one of them," Betsy insisted. "Check the museums, O'Brien. She shouldn't be hard to spot—big as she is, and wearing what looks like an antique nightgown. Even in Manhattan that getup—"

"What?" Jacqueline whirled, just as O'Brien, unable to control himself any longer, reached for her glasses. "What was she wearing?"

"You know, dirty white with lace and ruffles. Like an old-fashioned costume."

O'Brien made another stab at the glasses, missing by a foot as Jacqueline turned and began scrabbling among the objects on the top of the bureau. Finally she found what she was looking for —a booklet describing sights and shops (especially shops) for visitors to the city. She thumbed through the pages; stopped; stared; threw the booklet on the floor; ripped off her robe and threw it on top of the booklet.

James let out a wordless bleat of disapproval, and O'Brien's eyes popped. Jacqueline grabbed her skirt and blouse and got into them.

O'Brien rose slowly to his feet and brushed a crumb off his lapel. "Where?"

"The Metropolitan Museum. I should have known. . . . The Costume Institute is having a Romantic Images show. That must be where she got the idea for the dress she wore the other day. She said she made it herself. We talked about clothes . . . sewing. . . . She's making a dress for Valentine. A copy of an antique gown."

"But the museum is closed," James objected.

"Not tonight. It's open till nine."

Betsy grabbed her knapsack. "Let's go," she cried.

"No." Jacqueline paused. "You stay here. I don't think she'll call—Meredith said she mouthed obscenities when my name was mentioned, so apparently I'm back on her hate list. But we can't all go barreling into the place, we'll scare her off."

"I can get you there in ten minutes," O'Brien said coolly. "It's eight-fifteen."

"I'll stay," James said.

Jacqueline wasted no more time. She headed for the door, with Betsy and O'Brien close behind her. James reached for the bottle. Not until the door had closed after the hunters did he see Jacqueline's neat blue pumps on the floor. She had gone out in her bedroom slippers.

IV

O'Brien brought the car to a strictly illegal stop in front of the museum. Jacqueline was out before the wheels stopped turning. She went up the monumental staircase at a pace that left the others far behind.

By the time O'Brien and Betsy reached the door, Jacqueline was out of sight. They were further delayed by a guard who informed them that the museum was about to close, and by another guard who wanted Betsy to check her knapsack. Having peremptorily disposed of these persons, O'Brien gazed helplessly at the huge hall, with galleries leading off in all directions.

"Where's the costume place?"

"You're asking me?" Betsy indicated her droopy army fatigues. O'Brien turned to one of the guards.

They made their way through the Egyptian halls against the stream of exiting visitors and took an escalator going down. Here they were again informed that the museum was closing, and O'Brien identified himself. After a bewildered glance at the artistically shadowed exhibit hall beyond, where life-sized mannequins postured and posed in a variety of extravagant costumes, he looked at the girl behind the desk where souvenirs and postcards were sold. "Did a woman just come in here?"

At any other time of day this question would have been received with amusement. Instead the young woman replied, "Tall, red-haired? She ran down the escalator and went past me before I could stop her. Is she a policewoman? What's going on?"

Instead of answering, O'Brien beckoned to Betsy. "Stay here. Stop her if she tries to go out this way."

"Right." Betsy assumed her kung-fu stance.

O'Brien plunged into the gloom. Guards tactfully shepherded visitors toward the exit. O'Brien waved them away when they attempted to intercept him, but as he penetrated farther and farther into the shadowy hall he began to exhibit signs of nervousness. The life-sized mannequins stood or sat in various poses, separated from the spectator only by inconspicuous rope barriers. Their elaborate and extravagant costumes had the unnerving authenticity that derives only from actual use; all the garments had been worn, by the beauties and worthies of other times. The contrast between the realistic clothing and the blank, eyeless faces, which were covered with coarse fabric in shades of beige and brown, had an uncanny effect that was increased by the lighting—soft but sharp spotlights on the figures themselves, shadowy spaces between the exhibits. The insistent beat of a Viennese waltz in the background, pouring from concealed speakers, lost its gaiety in that ambience and took on the macabre suggestion of a dance of the dead.

Rounding a corner, O'Brien shied back as he found himself confronted by a figure clothed entirely in black, from the sable plumes atop its bonnet to the tip of the black parasol lifted in a menacing gesture. A transparent black veil hung from the bonnet; behind it, the featureless head, swathed in black fabric, seemed to stare inquiringly at him from empty eyesockets.

Jacqueline's face peered round the figure. "She isn't here."

O'Brien took the handkerchief from his breast pocket and mopped his brow. "How can you tell? This is worse than the chamber of horrors at a wax museum."

Jacqueline glanced at the grisly figure looming over them. "This is how widows were supposed to dress a hundred years ago. Cute, isn't it? Laurie couldn't disguise herself as one of the mannequins, if that's what you're thinking, not even if she put a stocking over her head. She's too big. These clothes were made for women wearing corsets so tight they couldn't take a deep breath. It's no wonder they swooned all the time."

"I didn't come here for a lecture on fashions," O'Brien said between his teeth. "I don't know why I came here, period. This was a far-out idea, Mrs. Kirby. If the girl was here, she's long gone."

"She was here. One of the guards remembered her. I'm going back to the main door. Maybe I can catch her on the way out."

She was gone before O'Brien could stop her. Avoiding the embrace of an elaborately ruffled blue tea gown, and the flirtatious gesture of a white, pin-tucked morning dress, O'Brien retreated to the desk, where Betsy was waiting. She had abandoned her karate stance and was studying the nearby exhibits with somewhat sheepish interest.

Interrogation of the guards persuaded O'Brien that the costume galleries had been swept clean of visitors, but when one of them asked if he wanted to speak with the director, O'Brien caved in. He had no reason to suggest, much less insist upon, a thorough search of the museum—a laborious process that would have necessitated the approval of various high officials. Several of the guards remembered seeing Laurie. No one had seen her leave, but as they all pointed out, there were several possible exits.

O'Brien climbed the stairs, swearing under his breath. "This is ridiculous," he informed Betsy. "I don't know why I let that woman talk me into coming here."

"It was rather interesting," Betsy said. "Did you notice that pleated coral silk evening dress with crystal beads? Of course clothes like that are symbols of the oppression of women, but they are rather—"

With a wordless snarl O'Brien broke into a trot and pulled away.

Jacqueline was not in the lobby. The last of the visitors were being urged out the great front doors; she was not among them. O'Brien and Betsy went out. Standing at the top of the staircase, O'Brien scanned the area, which was brightly lighted by street-lamps and by the lights on the facade of the museum itself. He caught a glimpse of a distinctive mop of auburn hair behind the balustrade on the left, at the bottom of the stairs, and started toward it.

When Jacqueline saw him she made a violent and peremptory gesture. O'Brien understood its meaning but went on anyway. Looking over the balustrade, he demanded, "What are you doing?"

"Will you get away from here?" Jacqueline hissed. "I thought I saw her—at least I saw something large and white in those bushes. If she thinks I'm alone she might—"

"Throw a rock at you," O'Brien said. "Where was she—it— whatever you saw?"

"There." Jacqueline pointed.

"Stay here." O'Brien added, "Both of you," and glared at Betsy, who had joined them. He sauntered toward the path that led alongside the museum.

"Arrogant bastard," Jacqueline said.

"He's not so bad," Betsy said cheerfully. "In fact, he's rather attractive—if you like the strong, sardonic type. Maybe I'd better go with him, in case he gets into trouble.''

"Yes, why don't you?''

No sooner had Betsy set out in pursuit of O'Brien than Jacqueline headed in the opposite direction. She went as fast as she could without actually running, but the facade of the Metropolitan covers two city blocks. After an extremely cursory investigation of the area she had indicated, O'Brien returned in time to see her turn into the path that led into the park on the south side of the museum.

"Damn it, I told her to stay here,'' he exclaimed.

"I guess she was trying to get rid of us,'' Betsy said. "That's Jake for you. She never lets—''

O'Brien began to run. Betsy kept pace with him, talking as she went. "She never lets anybody interfere with her. She can drive you crazy, but she's efficient, in her own peculiar way. Maybe she really did see the girl.''

The pedestrian path on the south side of the museum parallels Seventy-ninth Street for a short distance and then divides. Without hesitating, O'Brien took the right-hand path. It was not entirely deserted; a few joggers and dog-walkers had braved the fringes of the park, but as O'Brien and Betsy went deeper into the night-darkened regions, the lights shone on empty paths and benches. Finally they spotted their quarry ahead. Jacqueline was walking slowly, swinging her purse. Her disheveled hair shone ruddy in the lamplight.

"Mrs. Kirby!'' O'Brien's shout shattered the silence.

Jacqueline looked back. The concentrated venom of her expression could almost be felt. She turned and plunged into the darkness beside the path.

O'Brien put on a burst of speed. By the time Betsy caught up he had found and retrieved Jacqueline. She was rigid with fury, but she did not resist, and when O'Brien demanded, "If I let go of you, will you stand still?'' she nodded curtly.

"It's too late now. She's gotten away.''

O'Brien released his grip. Jacqueline rubbed her arm and then began tucking up loosened strands of hair. Her hands were unsteady.

"Did you really see her?'' Betsy asked.

"I think so. There was someone following me, in the shadows."

"Probably a mugger," O'Brien growled. "Mrs. Kirby, are you out of your mind? Haven't you heard about the park at night?"

"I am well aware—"

"You wouldn't last ten minutes in some parts of this place," O'Brien went on heatedly. "Come out of here."

Without replying Jacqueline turned back toward Fifth Avenue. The others followed. After an interval O'Brien said, "I'll call in and report she was seen. Though God knows I didn't see her. . . . Maybe someone will spot her when she comes out of the park."

But it was not until dawn the following morning that Laurie was found. The jogger who saw her thought at first she was sleeping, for she lay neatly disposed, with her skirt pulled down over her knees and her arms folded. It was not until he bent over for a closer look that he realized the back of her head had been smashed in.

CHAPTER EIGHT

O'Brien was at Jacqueline's door at eight-thirty, shortly after the report reached him. The promptness with which she responded to his knock, and the lines of strain on her face, told him she had not slept. He was not inclined to be sympathetic; he hadn't been to bed either. One look told her the truth before he could speak. Every muscle in her face gave way, and for a moment she looked her full age.

"I'm sorry," O'Brien said. "We tried."

"B.S.," Jacqueline said clearly. She tightened the sash of the peacock-blue robe and stepped back. "You'd better come in."

O'Brien glanced at the huddled lump in one of the beds. "I wouldn't want to disturb . . . her?"

"Your humor is particularly out of place this morning," Jacqueline remarked. "That, as you know, is Sue Moberley, and I don't give a damn whether we disturb her or not. Sit down and tell me."

"I'll stand, thank you. I shouldn't even be here. Her death is being put down as a mugging. Her skull was fractured and her purse was taken."

"Where was she found?"

"Not far north of the museum." O'Brien made this admission without visible signs of chagrin or guilt. "You know the playground, around Eighty-sixth? She was near there, under some bushes. She was found around seven this morning. The coroner thinks she'd been dead six or seven hours."

"Anything unusual? Oh, don't be cute, O'Brien; you wouldn't be here if you were satisfied she had been mugged."

"There was nothing to indicate that was not the case. Only . . ." O'Brien hesitated. "She'd been laid out. Stretched out with her hands folded and her clothing arranged. Her eyes were closed. She looked . . . peaceful."

"There is that," Jacqueline said. "Well. Anything else?"

"Your hypothetical murderer did not leave a scrap of his tie in her clenched fist, if that's what you mean."

"The murder weapon?"

"A rock. Picked up from the ground. It had blood and hair on it. Yes," O'Brien went on, anticipating Jacqueline's next question, "it's being tested for fingerprints. But a rough surface like that won't have taken prints."

"What are you going to do now?"

"I'm going back to work. There's plenty of it. Two burglaries, six assaults, a couple of rapes, three drunk and disorderlies. And the day is young. Good-bye, Mrs. Kirby."

"O'Brien."

"Yes?" O'Brien was already at the door.

"This is the last day of the conference. Tonight is the Grand Ball."

O'Brien turned and looked at her. Her unbound hair streamed down her back in a torrent of molten bronze. She was still wearing the shabby bedroom slippers in which she had led the hunt for Laurie.

The corners of his mouth lifted briefly. "Are you inviting me to be your escort, Mrs. Kirby?"

The evil expression on Jacqueline's face made O'Brien sorry he'd made the suggestion. "Never mind," he said quickly.

"It's a costume ball," Jacqueline murmured. "James won't like it, but . . . I'd be honored, Lieutenant, if you would agree to go with me. I'll even find you a costume."

"I'll bet you'd enjoy that. I'll find my own costume, thanks. What time?"

"Nine. Unless you'd like me to take you to dinner first."

"No, thanks. I'm not in the mood for pastrami on rye tonight. See you at nine."

After he had gone the blanketed lump on the bed reared up, and a pair of sleepy blue eyes blinked at Jacqueline. "I had the most peculiar dream," Sue mumbled. "I dreamed that policeman came in and said he was going to take you to the ball."

"It wasn't a dream." Index finger on the bridge of her glasses, Jacqueline stood deep in thought. "He meant to attend all along," she said, as much to herself as to Sue. "By tomorrow morning the suspects will be scattered to the four corners of the globe. This is his last chance to catch the killer. He has no authority to hold them. Laurie's death hasn't changed the official view of the case. So he—"

"Laurie?" Caught in the middle of a yawn, Sue choked. "Dead?"

Jacqueline explained as she got dressed.

II

James didn't like it.

"You said I could go with you. Are you planning to seduce O'Brien, or employ him as a bodyguard?"

"I might point out that I did not say you could go with me; that I never invited you to come to New York in the first place; and that your references to O'Brien are childish, libelous, and un-called-for. Instead I will simply remark that in view of the recent tragedy your reaction is tasteless in the extreme."

James added another spoonful of sugar to his coffee and sought a change of subject.

They were having breakfast in a coffee shop down the street from his hotel. Jacqueline had arrived first; the book she had been reading lay on the table. "I see," James said, "that you're reading Valentine's latest."

The distraction worked better than he had hoped, for reasons he had not anticipated. "Just getting an idea of what is selling," Jacqueline explained. "For my book, you know."

"I didn't know. At least—I thought you were joking. Are you joking?"

"Certainly not."

"Interesting title. What's it about?" His nod indicated Valentine's book, and his casual dismissal of Jacqueline's big news about her own venture into literature didn't please her. Her eyes narrowed.

"The heroine loses her lover to another woman, so she turns to satanism and black magic in the hope of getting him back."

"Sounds corny."

"It isn't corny. Valentine has researched Aleister Crowley and his crowd—a particularly nasty bunch of sickies, if you recall— and has created a similar cult. Poor Magdalen doesn't realize what she's getting into until it's almost too late. There are some very powerful descriptions of her struggle with evil, in the cult and in her own soul. Of course," Jacqueline said smoothly, "you recognize the source of the title."

James said promptly, " 'In such a night stood Dido with a willow in her hand upon the wild sea-banks, and waft her love to come again to Carthage.' *Merchant of Venice,* Act V, Scene—er."

Jacqueline waited. James smiled, smugly pleased. Jacqueline smiled back at him. "If you've finished your literary commentary," she said, with suspicious mildness, "perhaps we could return to the reason why I woke you from your slumbers. The death of a seventeen-year-old girl."

"I'm sorry about the girl," James said sulkily. "But I hardly knew her. If you expect me to go into mourning over every victim of our current crime wave, I'd have to wear a black armband for the rest of my life."

"She was murdered." Jacqueline's eyes were cold and opaque as jade.

"Of course she was. Anybody who wanders around Central Park at midnight—"

"James, don't be obtuse. She was killed by the same person who murdered Dubretta."

James would have objected if she had given him time. She didn't. "The ball tonight is our last chance to catch the killer before the delegates to the conference leave New York. Are you going to help me or aren't you?"

"Since when have you needed my help?" But two of the four lines on James's forehead smoothed out, and Jacqueline fanned the feeble flame of interest with the wind of flattery.

"Why do you think I asked you to be Jean's escort tonight?"

"To get me out of your hair so you can work on O'Brien," was the prompt reply.

"I need O'Brien to make the arrest once I've exposed the killer. I've read about citizen's arrests, but I'm not sure I could get away with—"

"You're serious." James stared at her. "You really think. . . . Who is it?"

Jacqueline met his look with one of crystalline candor. "It's one of three people, James. I'm certain of that. If you'll help me, we can eliminate two of the suspects before tonight."

"Oh no." James shook his head vigorously. "I'm tired of sitting around listening to you utter veiled hints like the classic detectives of fiction. That's your idea of helping, but it isn't mine. Tell me whom you suspect and why—especially why—and I might cooperate. Might."

"You force my hand, James." Jacqueline looked pensively at her egg-stained plate, giving James a breathtaking view of her long curling lashes. "I didn't want to put my cards on the table in case I was wrong. But I need you. If that's the only way I can get your help. . . ."

"You're damned right it is." James squared his shoulders and spoke in a gruff voice.

"All right. The three suspects are Hattie, Max—and Jean."

The last name broke James's calm. "Jean? Of all the unlikely people . . . do you really think . . . is that why you want me to be her escort?"

"Yes." Jacqueline put both elbows on the table and leaned forward, holding James's eyes with her own. "So far two people have been killed. I think a third person is in danger. The killer must dispose of that person tonight, before the delegates disperse. If we can't eliminate the other suspects we must watch all three, and watch them closely. It won't be easy. Our aim will be to prevent another murder—but not prevent an attempt at murder."

"In other words, you propose to set some poor innocent up as a decoy," James said slowly. "That's pretty cold-blooded, Jacqueline."

"It's the only way I can think of. The third victim will be in danger anyhow."

"You could at least warn. . . . Who is it?"

Jacqueline's breath caught in a tremulous gasp. "Me," she murmured modestly.

III

They separated at the corner of Fifth and Forty-third. James headed purposefully toward Sixth Avenue, where he could catch an uptown bus. "Sit on that chemist buddy of yours until he gets results," Jacqueline had instructed. "I don't care what you tell him, just make sure he knows every minute counts."

As soon as James was out of sight, Jacqueline headed for the library. She felt bad about deceiving James, but she comforted herself with the assurance that she had told him part of the truth. Only one statement had been a flat-out lie. It wasn't her fault if he had leaped to erroneous conclusions.

She spent an hour in the main reading room, but when she emerged her brow was furrowed. She was sure she was on the right track, yet she had failed to find substantiating evidence. Weaving a path around the students and tourists and derelicts sunning themselves on the stairs between the stone lions, she pondered alternatives, and decided it was unlikely that the experts she might consult would have anything useful to add. Most of them derived their expertise from the books she had been reading.

With a fatalistic shrug she took out her notebook and considered her next move. Maybe something would occur to her during the course of the day.

Since the demise of the late lamented Brentano's there are only five major bookstores on Fifth Avenue between Forty-second and Fifty-ninth. Jacqueline visited all of them. She did not buy a single book, but by the time she finished she had a good idea of what was selling in the romance trade. Valerie Valentine's position as Queen of Love was unchallenged. No fewer than six of her books were in print, and they occupied the choicest places on the racks. Heaps of them filled the heavy cardboard display boxes known (appropriately, in Jacqueline's opinion) as dumps. VV ran a distant second—three books in print, one dump to every five of Valentine's—with Victor von Damm not far behind VV. Together the three took almost half the shelf space allotted to historical-romance fiction. If Hattie had not cornered the market, she controlled a sizable share of it.

One of the bookstores had a window display keyed to the conference (paper hearts and cupids) and featuring Valentine's latest book. It had appeared in two formats—a hardcover edition and a trade paperback, larger than the usual softcover, and printed on better paper. As Jacqueline had learned from her assiduous study of the trade, this was a departure, and a testimonial to Valentine's selling power. Only the top few romance writers had achieved the status symbol of hardcover publication, and that only in recent years. Most of the books were produced as cheap, original paperbacks. Apparently Valentine's publishers believed her readers would shell out four times the paperback price for a longer-lasting format. And apparently they were correct.

By the time Jacqueline finished her survey it was almost time for lunch, so she consumed fettuccine Alfredo and strawberry pie smothered in whipped cream, assuring herself that food was essential if one lacked sleep. An afternoon nap would have been nice, but she knew she wouldn't have time for that luxury.

The inner woman having been satisfied, she started on the next stage of her investigation. The first stop found her on the mezzanine of the hotel where the romance conference was in progress. Workshops and lectures were in full swing, and it was evident that the news of Laurie's death had not affected the participants. The only exception was the little group that huddled around the booth, with its ill-made sign.

Jacqueline approached them reluctantly. Her feeling that she was in some way responsible for the tragedy was unreasonable, but apparently it was shared by some of the Valentine Lovers.

Most of the girls turned or stepped back without looking at her. Meredith stepped forward instead and faced her. The girl's square, unattractive face was expressionless but her brown eyes, magnified by her thick glasses, were hard and accusing.

"I tried," Jacqueline said. It wasn't what she had meant to say. The words came out of some deep inner pool of guilt.

"Swell," said Meredith. Jacqueline reflected wryly that it was a less pejorative response than the one she had given O'Brien when he made the same disclaimer.

"How did you find out?" she asked.

"That cop told us," Meredith said. "O'Brien?"

"Right. Meredith, can I talk to you for a minute?"

Meredith shrugged and allowed Jacqueline to draw her away from the others. Jacqueline chose her words carefully. It was essential that she find out whether Laurie had confided in Meredith, but the last thing she wanted was to involve the girl in a matter that had already snuffed out two lives.

"Did Laurie say anything to you about what she was doing yesterday?"

"You mean that business about a notebook? No. O'Brien told us about it. Laurie never said a word."

"But you knew she was angry at Dubretta Duberstein."

"A lot of them were." Meredith glanced at the group of whispering, sober-faced girls. "Dubretta wrote some nasty things about the conference and about us fans. She said she'd think we had been brainwashed by pink goo except that none of us had any brains to start with."

"She can't have talked to you if she said that."

This time flattery had no effect. Meredith said coolly, "I'm smart enough to wonder what you and O'Brien have on your tiny minds. Why all the questions?"

"I can't tell you."

"At least you're honest," Meredith said grudgingly.

"I can't even ask pertinent questions," Jacqueline mumbled, half to herself. "Just one more, Meredith. Was Laurie the only one of the group who had close associations with Valentine and Hattie and the other writers?"

"She was. We were allowed to worship from a distance. And pay our dues, of course."

"None of you ran errands for Aunt Hattie or Val?"

"No. That's two questions." But instead of turning away, Meredith hesitated. Finally she said, "You've got some pull with that crowd."

"Not much. What is it you want me to do?"

"Make them—make them . . ." Meredith groped for words. Then she burst out, "It's like Laurie was just a—a thing. She was here and now she's not here, and nobody gives a damn either way."

"I think I understand what you mean. You want Hattie to acknowledge the fact of her existence."

"Well—yes."

"I'll buy that. What did you have in mind? Some sort of tribute?"

"Laurie would've liked that," Meredith said. "She was making a dress for Valentine, you know. I saw it. It's gorgeous. She worked her tail off on that dress. If Valentine wore it tonight and Hattie said something. . . ." Her voice broke. One huge, magnified tear formed in the corner of her eye.

"I'll see what I can do," Jacqueline said.

"Okay." Meredith pressed her lips tightly together. "Thanks," she added.

"Don't thank me." After a moment Jacqueline turned away, leaving Meredith in command of the field.

IV

Either the newspapers had not yet made the connection between Laurie's death and the romance writers, or—which Jacqueline considered more likely—they didn't care. The hallway outside Hattie's suite was deserted. From Hattie's behavior, however, one would have supposed that the place was under siege. She took her time about answering the door, and then peered warily out through a crack, leaving the chain in place. The sight of Jacqueline did not relieve her anxieties. "What do you want?" she demanded. "I'm busy."

"So am I," Jacqueline said. "I won't take much of your time, but I'd rather not yell my questions through the door."

The not-so-veiled threat had the desired effect. Hattie opened the door and switched on the southern accent. "I'm sorry if I sounded rude, honey. We are in such a state you can't imagine. That pore chile—"

"I know. How did you find out?"

"That nice policeman—Kelly, or whatever his name is—came by a few hours ago to tell us. Well, you can just imagine, honey. Valentine is so upset. . . ."

The cries coming from Valentine's room certainly bore out this claim, but after listening to them Jacqueline began to doubt that Laurie's death was the cause of Valentine's woe. She kept repeating, "No, I won't. I tell you, I won't do it!"

"Won't do what?" Jacqueline asked.

Hattie's smile grew fixed. "Don't you worry your head about that, dear. It's none of your business, is it?"

Jacqueline slid neatly through the other woman's attempt at a block and sat down. "I want to talk to Valentine and Max anyway. Maybe I can help. I always think we should help others when we can, don't you?"

Hattie didn't miss the reference, but before she could reply, Max appeared in the doorway. "Did I hear—ah, it is you, Jacqueline. I'm glad to see you. Perhaps you can help me talk some sense into Val."

"I'll be glad to." With a smug smile at Hattie, Jacqueline settled back in the chair. "What seems to be the trouble?"

Max ran his hand over his scanty hair. "She's a very high-strung, sensitive creature. The news about that unfortunate child hit her hard. She—but if you wouldn't mind, you had better come and see for yourself."

"I don't mind." Jacqueline rose with alacrity.

"Max," Hattie began ominously.

"Something has to be done, Hattie. She can't go on like this. And she does admire Jacqueline. . . . If you'll just wait a minute, Jacqueline, I'll tell her you're here."

He disappeared. Jacqueline and Hattie stood smiling fixedly at one another like matching gargoyles until he returned and reported that Valentine would be happy to see Mrs. Kirby.

The other part of the suite consisted of a second, smaller apartment that could be rented separately or made part of a larger ensemble by unlocking a door. It had its own entrance. There were three other doors, two of which were closed. The third led to Valentine's bedroom.

It was a pleasant but not particularly luxurious room, with wide windows giving a view of the park. It did not share the balcony outside Hattie's sitting room. Not, Jacqueline thought, an appropriate setting for the Queen of Love and her manager. Hattie had the lion's share of the living quarters.

Jacqueline turned her attention to the girl who lay across one of the twin beds. Valentine's chin was propped on her hands and her mouth was mutinous, but she looked almost as enchanting in anger and disarray as when she was dressed in her formal smile. Her pouting lips might have inspired a poet to babble about rosebuds, and the hair tumbling over her slim shoulders foamed like molten gold.

On the other bed lay an evening dress of pink damask patterned with chrysanthemum petals, its tiered skirt festooned with a triple garland of pearls and beads. Hand-embroidered lace trimmed the flounces and the wide band of fabric atop the bodice, which was caught by glittering pins at either side to form tiny cap sleeves. The long smooth waistline and draped skirt belonged to another time, and Jacqueline thought she could even name the designer. The dress was an exact copy of a gown by the great Worth, which she had seen at the Costume Institute the night before.

"I'm not going to wear it," Valentine said. "So don't try to talk me into it. Hattie and Max have been nagging me all morning and I'm sick of being lectured. I won't wear it, and that's final."

"Is that the dress Laurie made for you?" Jacqueline asked. She knew it must be, but found it hard to believe, even though she had noted Laurie's skill as a needlewoman. The dress was a masterpiece.

"That is correct," Max said. "The girl had been working on it for weeks—"

"Months," Jacqueline corrected, contemplating the delicate hand embroidery and the painstaking perfection of the beaded garlands. "She must have started it as soon as the exhibit opened in April."

"Naturally, Valentine was flattered and pleased," Max went

on, glancing at Valentine, who looked nothing of the kind. "Hattie had given the girl Val's measurements, and we had a fitting last week when we arrived in New York. Val had planned to wear it to the ball tonight. It suits the theme of her last book, which as you know is set in late Victorian times. There is even a scene in which Magdalen goes to a ball wearing a Worth creation."

"I remember the scene," Jacqueline said. "It's a magnificent gown, Valentine. Why don't you want to wear it?"

Valentine dropped her head onto the bed and covered it with her arms. From the tangle of red-gold came a muffled voice. "She's dead, that's why. It's sick. Like—like grave clothes."

Hattie burst out, "Now that's just silly, Val. It's all the more important that you wear the dress. It's like a tribute, don't you see? That fan club can drive you crazy, but you don't want to alienate them. You can't afford—"

Jacqueline was about to administer an admonitory kick in the shins when Valentine interrupted the tirade. Lifting herself with both hands, she screamed. It was an exquisitely musical scream, like a fanfare from a golden trumpet, and just as piercing. Having caught Hattie's attention, Valentine went on, "You've said all that a dozen times, Hattie, and I'm sick of hearing it. I'm not going to wear that damned dress! I swear to God, when I put it on I can feel her hands all over me, touching me—cold, dead hands, like lumps of frozen lard."

The simile lacked the elegance of Valentine's written prose, but it had a certain power. Max winced, and Jacqueline fought a sudden desire to slap the lovely, petulant face. She decided that, come hell or high water, Valentine was going to wear the dress.

"I understand perfectly," she said, sitting down on the bed beside the distraught Queen of Love. "And I admire your sensitivity. You think it would be tasteless and unfeeling to wear a dress that will undoubtedly be the most beautiful gown at the ball. Everyone will be envying you. There's only one other gown like that in the world, and it's in a museum. Yes, you're quite right to refuse to flaunt it."

Valentine's face went absolutely blank. Jacqueline patted one of her small, pink-nailed hands. "Yes, my dear, I agree. Someone ought to wear it, though. Hattie has a point. Laurie's friends would be pleased by such a tribute. Especially if Hattie made a graceful little speech about it. I was talking to the girls about that very thing just before I came here. And the publicity value . . . I wonder if it would fit Sue. She's about your size.''

"Sue," Valentine repeated. "That girl Victor has taken up with? The dumpy little schoolteacher?"

"Oh, I wouldn't call her dumpy," Jacqueline said seriously. "She has a nice little figure. Not as nice as yours, of course. We may have to pad the bodice; that gown requires a beautifully shaped bosom and shoulders to set it off. But I think I could fix it. Shall I take it with me now?"

"No!" Valentine got up. "I don't know. . . ." Crossing to the other bed, she touched the lacy flounce with a tentative finger.

"All hand-embroidered," Jacqueline crooned. "You can't find work like that these days. Oh, I suppose a French designer could reproduce it, but the cost! Thousands and thousands of dollars.''

Valentine's five fingers and palm pressed against the damask of the dress. Jacqueline wondered why she had never noticed before what a predatory little hand it was—like a delicate ivory crab.

"I'll think about it," Valentine said. "Maybe. . . ."

"Well, let me know." Jacqueline got to her feet. "I'd like to have it by five at the latest. It will take a while to alter it to fit Sue.''

Valentine didn't reply. Max was smiling; as his eyes met Jacqueline's his eyelid dropped in a wink.

Jacqueline had hoped to talk to Valentine alone, but she realized there was no hope of that. "Maybe you can help me with something," she said. "I'd be so grateful for your advice."

"What?" Valentine looked up. "Me?"

"Yes. You see, I'm writing a book, and I need a title. I think titles are awfully important. And yours are particularly good."

"Thank you," Valentine said abstractedly. Her eyes returned to the dress.

"I came up with one I rather like, but I want to ask your opinion.''

"Valentine," Max said sharply.

"What? Oh—I'm sorry, Mrs. Kirby. Were you—"

" 'Come Again to Carthage,' " Jacqueline said rapidly. "That's my title. It's a quotation, of course—"

"It won't sell." Hattie shook her head. "You need something with more—"

"Lust?" Jacqueline inquired. "Thanks, Hattie. Valentine, what do you think?"

"I agree with Hattie. It's kind of a boring title, Mrs. Kirby. If you'll excuse my saying so."

"No, you mustn't apologize. I appreciate your opinion. Turning to another, more important matter, I wonder if I might ask a few questions."

Max and Hattie converged on her, each taking one of her arms. "Val has to rest now," Hattie said.

Max added, "We'll be more comfortable in the sitting room, Jacqueline."

They left the Queen of Love contemplating the ball gown with a pensive frown.

"I assume you want to talk about—about the girl," Max said, closing the door. "I didn't want to destroy the good work you did by reminding Val. That was very clever, Jacqueline."

"Yes," Hattie admitted. "Thanks."

"I wasn't exaggerating," Jacqueline said. "If Valentine refuses to wear the dress, I'd like to have it. I wouldn't want it thrown in the trash."

"Oh, we'd never do that," Hattie said.

Jacqueline was willing to bet she wouldn't—not now that she had been made aware of the gown's monetary value. "I wanted to ask you about Laurie's telephone call last night," she said.

"I didn't talk to her," Hattie said. "I was out all evening."

"What time did you get back?"

"Around one, I guess. I was . . . hey. What are you getting at?"

"Laurie was killed between midnight and one o'clock. Whom were you with last night?"

"God damn it to—" Hattie's voice rose in a roar. Max clapped his hand over her mouth. "You fool," he said softly and evenly. "Do you want Valentine to hear you?"

Hattie subsided, glowering. Jacqueline deduced that once again she had fallen from the heights of approval to the pits of Hattie's regard. It did not distress her unduly.

"The girl was a victim of the random violence that marks our society," Max said. "That is what Lieutenant O'Brien indicated to us."

"Did he? How interesting. Did he ask where you were last night, Max?"

"I went to bed early, as did Valentine. I didn't even hear Hattie come in."

"I see." Her opinion of the little man's intelligence rose another notch when he made no attempt to protest the implication. Instead he said soberly, "As for the telephone call, I think I told you the essentials. I called you immediately, Jacqueline."

"I appreciate that. Tell me exactly what she said."

But Max had little to add to what he had already told her. Laurie had asked for Hattie, and, on learning that her mentor was not available, for Valentine. "Val didn't want to talk to her," Max explained. "And I saw no point in persuading her to do so; the girl was literally babbling. I told her you had been trying to get in touch with her. Her response was—er—profane. Then she went off into a mumbled monologue about the dress she had made for Valentine; it would have been Greek to an ignorant male like myself even if she had been sensible—words like darts and tucks, and so on. I kept asking where she was. I thought she said the Village, but I may have been wrong."

Hattie stared pointedly at her watch. "I'm late for the workshop. You'll have to excuse me, Mrs. Kirsky."

"I was just leaving." Jacqueline sauntered toward the door while Max repeated his thanks. Her hand on the knob, she stopped as if struck by a sudden idea. (She had picked up the trick from a favorite TV detective, and had always wanted to try it.)

"By the way—what has become of the Earl of Devonbrook?"

Hattie looked blank. "Who?"

V

"You're going as what?"

"An Arab princess," Jean said. "That was the setting of my latest—"

"Oh, yes—*Slave of Lust.*"

The costume laid out on Jean's bed was fashioned chiefly of pink chiffon, or a cheap imitation of that fabric. Dubiously Jacqueline studied the voluminous transparent trousers and the exiguous sequined wisp of the bodice and the yards and yards of pink veiling. She transferred her skeptical gaze to her friend's meager body.

Jean blushed. "Of course I'll wear a body stocking under it. And—do you think?—long tights, the kind with built-in panties."

Jacqueline tried to visualize this ensemble, perhaps with an added blouse, if Jean's feet got colder, and her imagination reeled.

"Oh, you're always criticizing my clothes," Jean said, reading her expression correctly. "What are you going to wear?"

"I haven't decided."

Jean turned to the bed and pretended to fluff up the veil. She glanced slyly at Jacqueline over her shoulder. "Do you have an escort, darling, or are you going alone?"

Jacqueline leaned against the wall and crossed her arms. (She had not been invited to sit down.) "James has been here?"

"Oh yes, some time ago. You don't mind, do you, Jake? I wouldn't want to steal your boyfriend."

The obvious response to this was a sarcastic "Oh, yeah?" but Jacqueline didn't make it. Remembering their college years, she decided that Jean owed her a few. Besides she certainly was not catty enough to tell Jean she had practically had to threaten James to force him to take her. Not unless Jean got off a few more digs like the last one. . . .

"I'm going with O'Brien," she said.

"The policeman?" Jean's eyes opened wide. "Oh, well . . . he's rather attractive, in his way."

"He's about as attractive as a rattlesnake," said O'Brien's date. "And I doubt if he attends social functions of this sort for their own sake."

She expected this ominous hint would bring squeaks and twitches from the white rabbit, but something had stiffened Jean's spine. "Are you still harping on that murder theory? Really, Jake, you ought to grow up and stop playing games. O'Brien said the police were satisfied Dubretta died of a heart attack and Laurie was killed by a criminal—"

"O'Brien was here? This morning?"

"Yes. I thought it was most considerate of him to take the time to reassure me."

Jacqueline gritted her teeth. So far O'Brien had been ahead of her every step of the way. She wondered whether he was asking the same questions she was, or whether he was on another, parallel track. Both led to the same goal, and she had never doubted that O'Brien was as single-minded, and as tight-lipped, as she was.

"The police may be satisfied, but O'Brien isn't," she said. "He's tricky, Jean. Watch out for him."

"I've nothing to worry about." Jean lifted the veil and draped it across her nose, studying the effect in the mirror. "I need. . . ." She spat out a fold of veiling and went on, "I need lots of eye makeup. Don't you think so?"

"Yes," Jacqueline said truthfully. Jean's lashes were even grayer than her hair, and the faded blue of her pupils blended into the whites of her eyes. She added, with a certain malice, "Is that why you chose that costume—to hide your face from inquisitive reporters?"

"Oh, no." Jean continued to admire her reflection, adjusting the veil in different positions. "I don't care about that any more."

"You don't?"

"Oh, no. Not any more." Jean's voice was soft and dreamy. "It's all settled. There's nothing to worry about any more."

VI

Before she left, Jacqueline ascertained that Jean also claimed to have retired early the night before. Her hotel was one of the mammoth chains; if she had taken her key with her, she could have come in at any hour without being observed.

Jacqueline's next stop was the shabby brownstone where Betsy had lived all her life. Tall office buildings now towered over the house, which gave the impression of huddling earthward for fear of being squashed. The neighborhood was no longer what it had once been, but the property, Jacqueline surmised, was worth a tidy sum of money.

Her hope that for once she had anticipated O'Brien was dashed by Betsy as soon as she opened the door. "Well, well, the third musketeer. You just missed O'Brien."

"The three horsemen of the Apocalypse would be more like it."

"I thought there were four."

"Need I remind you who, or what, the fourth horseman was?" Jacqueline followed Betsy into the hall. Dust lay thick on lovely old furniture and a single bulb shone from one of the Limoges sconces. All the other bulbs were burned out.

"You want a beer or something?" Betsy asked hospitably.

"No, thanks. Just a brief chat."

"Come on upstairs then. I want to show you something."

"I'm surprised you still live here," Jacqueline said, removing her hand from the stair rail. It felt sticky. "Why don't you get yourself a pad in the Village or someplace equally chic?"

"Believe it or not, this is cheaper. The trust pays all the expenses. That means I can give most of my income to WUFAS and the other organizations I belong to. If I moved, I'd have to pay rent. Do you have any idea what apartments in Manhattan cost?"

"Then you don't own the house?" Jacqueline asked curiously.

"Oh yes, I own it. I just can't sell it." Betsy chuckled. "Mother and Dad didn't have a very high opinion of my good sense, let alone my political views. Everything's tied up in trusts. Just as well, I guess. Handling money is a bore, don't you think?"

"I wouldn't know," Jacqueline said glumly.

Betsy threw open a door and ushered Jacqueline into her bedroom. It represented her austerity stage, and the furniture had probably been taken from one of the little attic cubbyholes that had been occupied by a maid in long-gone days. An iron bedstead and a cheap pine bureau, two straight chairs and a table, bookcases made of boards and bricks, filled with paperbacks, made up the furnishings. The floor was bare. Jacqueline didn't know whether to feel pity or exasperation; Betsy's emotional development seemed to have gone into deep freeze during the sixties. It was time she grew up.

Then Betsy took something out of the closet and Jacqueline's mouth dropped open. For once she was taken completely by surprise.

Betsy held the garment up high so its skirt wouldn't touch the dusty floor.

In comparison to the elaborately embroidered and beaded gown Laurie had made for Valentine this dress was almost austere. Yet the infinitesimal pleats covering every inch of the silk tunic and straight skirt shouted the name of the designer as loudly as Worth's tailoring had proclaimed his work.

"Fortuny," Jacqueline breathed. "There's one like it at the Costume Institute—it's coral instead of turquoise, but. . . ."

"I know. I saw it last night. Then I remembered Mother had one like it. I dug it out of a trunk in the attic when I got home. It had been rolled up in a wad for forty years, but you'd think it had just been cleaned and pressed."

"Those magic pleats were one of Fortuny's trademarks."

Jacqueline's admiration for the Worth copy had been simple artistic appreciation. The emotion she felt now could only be described as hunger—no, lust would be closer to the mark. The dress would look absolutely divine on her. She remembered Betsy's mother—a handsome woman of impeccable taste, whose daughter's slovenly clothes had driven her wild. Mrs. Markham had been about Jacqueline's height. And the color would be sensational with auburn hair. . . .

Jacqueline swallowed. "How much do you want for it?"

"I wouldn't sell Mother's clothes," Betsy said in a shocked voice. "I thought I'd wear it tonight. What do you think?"

She held the dress against her.

Jacqueline glanced at the heavy bronze bookend supporting a stack of historical romances, and wondered if anyone had ever committed murder over a dress. The Fortuny was three inches too long for Betsy; it trailed on the floor. Her spare boyish figure would suit the straight lines well enough, but that cropped gray hair and those bony, freckled arms. . . .

With an effort she got her mind off frivolities and back onto the serious business for which she had come. "I didn't know you were planning to attend the ball."

"I thought I might as well. I haven't got a date, though. I asked O'Brien, but he said he was busy. How about that boyfriend of yours—the professor?"

"He's taking Jean." Jacqueline sat down on the bed. Both

chairs were occupied, one by a pair of grubby jeans, the other by stacks of mimeographed literature announcing a march on Washington for purposes unspecified.

"Damn. Oh, well. How about if I go with you? We've done it before."

Jacqueline considered the advantages and disadvantages of this plan. Both involved O'Brien's reaction to having Betsy with them. After some deliberation she decided it would serve him right. "Fine," she said. "Come to the hotel about seven-thirty and we'll get dressed there. And, Betsy. . . ."

"Huh?" Betsy was trying to get a look at herself in the small mirror over the bureau.

"Don't do anything to the dress till I see it on you," Jacqueline said desperately. "I'll take care of any necessary alterations. Don't even cut off a loose thread. Promise?"

"Okay."

Jacqueline breathed a sigh of relief. Betsy was a woman of her word. She was also capable of taking a pair of shears and whacking the priceless garment off at the knees if it got in her way. A shudder ran through Jacqueline's body at the thought.

Watching Betsy squat and bend in a vain attempt to see her entire figure in a mirror six inches square she said, "Never in all the years I knew you were you interested in clothes. In fact, I don't think I've ever seen you in a dress—except for that ghastly disguise at the cocktail party. Are you in love, or are you abandoning feminism?"

"Clothes don't have anything to do with feminism," Betsy said scornfully. "There's no conflict between women's rights and looking nice."

Since this obvious fact was one Jacqueline had known for twenty years, she could not disagree. Still, there had to be some reason for Betsy's volte-face. "So what brought it on at this particular moment? Romantic balls aren't your scene."

"It's my last chance to get some dirt on Aunt Hattie and the piglets." The answer was so glib Jacqueline suspected Betsy felt the need to rationalize her decision. "After all," Betsy went on, "Dubretta never found what she was looking for, did she? There's been nothing in the papers."

"If she found anything, it's gone for good." Jacqueline saw no reason to go into detail. It was typical of Betsy that she had never inquired into the reason for Laurie's attack on her. Crazy people do crazy things; that was enough for Betsy.

There was another reason for her lack of curiosity. Jacqueline wondered whether it had occurred to O'Brien. She felt sure it had; O'Brien didn't miss much. But she refused to take it seriously. Betsy was on her list of suspects, but only for the sake of detectival completeness. Betsy had no reason to purloin Dubretta's notebook. Betsy couldn't have been the unknown assailant who had pushed her into the street and escaped unseen. Her chief talent was hitting people over the head with signs.

Betsy continued to stare at her reflection. In a different, more serious voice she said, "I'd like to find out what she was after. Not only for the reasons you might think. I liked Dubretta."

"So did I," said Jacqueline.

VII

Her last call of the day was on Victor von Damm. That harassed celebrity had just emerged from the final symposium, one in which the leading publishers of historical romances boasted about their past successes and described their future plans. Jacqueline cut him out from the herd and announced her intention of talking with him.

"Come up to my room," Victor said, running a hand through his waving black hair and giving the hovering ladies a malignant look. "It's the only place where I can get a minute's peace."

Jacqueline waved at the well-bred lady from Boston, who was still in devoted attendance, before following Victor. "They seem very well behaved," she remarked. "I don't see anybody trying to tear the buttons off your shirt or whack off a piece of your ambrosial locks. What are you complaining about, anyway? I thought adoring fans were part of the deal."

"They look at me all the time," Victor said hysterically. "They hover and they stare at me. If I go to the bar for a drink, there are always three or four of them at the next table. Looking."

"You have to expect people to stare if you walk around dressed like that." Victor's billowing white shirt was showing signs of wear. "Is that the only shirt you've got?" Jacqueline asked critically.

"Hattie's too cheap to supply unnecessary changes of costume," Victor said. "Here we are. Come in."

His room was an example of Hattie's penny-pinching habits; since he wasn't expected to entertain fans or publishers, it was an ordinary hotel bedroom, without sitting room or bar. Victor went straight to his suitcase and took out a bottle. "Want a drink?"

Jacqueline shook her head. Victor uncapped the bottle and raised it to his lips.

"Great," Jacqueline said. "Go on, turn yourself into an alcoholic. You are already a fraud and a hypocrite and a chiseler and—"

"You don't understand." Victor put the cap on the bottle and put the bottle down. "This is it. Tonight is the last public appearance of Victor von Damm. I'm through."

"Oh, yeah?"

"I mean it." Victor dropped into a chair. His saturnine features relaxed, and Joe Kirby made a tentative appearance. "It's funny," he said, in Joe's lighter, more diffident tones, "the closer I get to breaking out, the harder it is to hang on. You'd think that after two years of this crap I could handle a few more hours."

"Maybe," Jacqueline suggested, "you're suffering from a sense of impending doom."

Joe gazed sadly at her. "You don't like me, do you, Mrs. Kirby?"

"I don't trust you. You're weak, Victor-Joe; weak, vacillating, and undependable. You've got Sue on a string and you treat her like a yo-yo—up one minute, down the next. You don't have the guts to act on your resolution. Why should I assume you mean it this time?"

"Things have changed. Hattie's agreed to let me go."

"I see." Jacqueline's voice dripped sarcasm. "You've been struggling to free yourself from the web. You're the helpless fly and Hattie is the spider."

"Hattie has a contract," Joe said. "You ought to see that contract, Mrs. Kirby. It commits me for the rest of my life to anything Hattie wants."

"Why did you sign it?"

"I was broke." After a moment Joe added morosely, "I was also stupid."

"Contracts have that effect on some people," Jacqueline said. The slight softening of her voice made Joe look up hopefully.

"Mrs. Kirby, I really mean it, about getting out. Hattie owns the Von Damm name. I've never had anything to do with the writing end of it, I was just a hired front man. She can get somebody else before Victor's next public appearance."

"A look-alike?" Jacqueline appeared dubious. Then her eyes narrowed thoughtfully and her glasses began to slip. James would have recognized the look; Jacqueline's outrageous imagination was going into action.

"You know what might work," she said. "Victor von Damm could die. Heroically. Saving a girl from being raped or a child from being run over—"

Joe recoiled. "Hey," he protested.

"Oh, you wouldn't really die. It would be a fake. Then Hattie could discover a whole trunk of Victor von Damm manuscripts and publish one or two a year—in black covers with a tasteful 'In Memoriam' notice. Victor von Damm could become the idol of a cult. Look what happened to Valentino and James Dean and Elvis Presley. Grieving women swathed in mourning would visit your grave on the anniversary of your death. . . . Souvenir stands selling books and locks of hair—you could send a fresh supply of hair now and then—make sure she pays you for it—little bottles of the water in which your broken, bleeding body was bathed. . . ."

"Jesus Christ," Joe gasped. "Mrs. Kirby, you're worse than Hattie. That's the sickest, most ghoulish thing I ever . . . I wonder if it would work."

"Work?" Jacqueline glowed with creative enthusiasm. "It would be the greatest publicity stunt of the century. I'm going to sell it to Hattie. And I'll make her pay through the nose."

"You'd have to have a body," Joe said uneasily. "You can't have a heroic death without a body."

Jacqueline waved this minor detail aside. "That's no problem. I can think of three or four ways around it already, and I haven't really put my mind to work on it yet. Maybe Victor could be kidnapped while rescuing a girl or a child. The body would never be found. Instead of a grave we'd build a cenotaph. Or he could fall overboard on a cruise or disappear while visiting some trouble spot—Hattie could identify a body. . . . Good heavens, Joe, the possibilities are endless."

"You terrify me," Joe said sincerely.

"Hattie would be a fool not to jump at the idea," Jacqueline assured him. "And that would get you off the hook—if you really want to get off it."

"I do. Sue and I are going to get married."

Jacqueline wrenched her mind away from the dazzling vision of Victor von Damm's heroic death. "I'll talk to Hattie then. On one condition. I can understand how you got into Hattie's clutches—though I think you're a wimp to have submitted so long. I can also understand why you didn't want Sue mixed up with her. What I don't understand is your vacillation. One minute you appear to defy the old witch, then she reels you back in. Was it only the contract that kept you subservient? And why has she changed her mind about releasing you?"

"You never know what Hattie is thinking," Joe said gloomily. "But I think her major concern was this conference. It turned out to be the breaking point for me. I'd made publicity appearances, on talk shows, autographings, book and author luncheons, that sort of thing. I didn't mind them. It was like putting on a performance—acting a part for a couple of hours and then taking off the makeup and going home. This was different. Hattie was on my back every damned minute. Then I met Sue. She's so honest, so innocent—there isn't an ounce of sham in her. She made the whole thing look so shabby and cheap. . . ."

Jacqueline could see why Joe had never been involved in the writing end of Victor von Damm. Even by the dubious standards of historical romance, his style was insipid. "All right, I'll see what I can do," she promised. "I came to ask you about something, Joe. Have you seen Lieutenant O'Brien today?"

"Yes, he was here a couple of hours ago. Is something wrong, Mrs. Kirby?"

Jacqueline unlocked her clenched teeth. "No, nothing. He told you about Laurie?"

Joe nodded. "I'm sorry. Poor kid must have been nuts to

wander around the park late at night. But maybe she's better off. She never had much of a chance."

"Hmph," said Jacqueline. "Did O'Brien inquire into your whereabouts last night?"

"I was with Sue. You probably know better than I do what time she got in. We weren't watching clocks." Seeing the gravity of Jacqueline's expression, Joe's reminiscent smile faded. "O'Brien said it was just routine. Was it?"

"No. Laurie was killed by the same person who murdered Dubretta Duberstein."

Joe's face turned a sickly shade of gray. "You're kidding."

"I don't kid about things like murder."

"Yes, but . . . oh my God." Joe buried his face in his hands. "You've just thrown me back to the spider," he muttered.

"What do you mean?"

"That was the other hold Hattie had over me." Joe raised his head. "You know how she tried to get publicity out of Dubretta's death. It backfired; the press wouldn't go for the idea that Valentine was the intended victim. So Hattie gave up the murder stunt. That's all I thought it was—a publicity stunt. But before that she told me Dubretta's dying words accused Sue."

"What?"

"She accused Sue," Joe insisted. "You heard her too. 'It's Sue.' That's what she said. Hattie threatened to tell the police if I didn't knuckle under."

"Oh, for. . . ." Jacqueline saw the shadow of Victor von Damm, nobly risking worse than death to save the woman he loved. She didn't know whether to shriek with laughter or sneer. "That's the most idiotic thing I've ever heard, Joe. Even if Dubretta did mention Sue's name—and I, who was closest, am not certain what she said—Sue had no reason to harm her. No one with an ounce of sense would pay any attention to such an accusation."

"I guess you're right," said Joe, banishing the ghost of Victor von Damm. "But Sue did have a motive for wanting to kill Valentine—at least, some people would consider it a motive. I tell you, Mrs. Kirby, you don't know what it's like dealing with Hattie Foster. She kind of hypnotizes a person, you know? You get so you believe everything she says."

"Strange," Jacqueline said. "My reaction to Hattie is precisely the reverse. I get so I don't believe anything she says."

"I guess I was a jerk."

"I guess you were."

"Now you tell me Dubretta was murdered." Joe shook his head. "I don't know what to do."

"For starters, stop believing everything you hear." Jacqueline rose. "I must be going."

Joe stared at her. "You mean I shouldn't believe you?"

"Believe this." Jacqueline pointed a stern finger. "All sorts of things are going to happen tonight. Be on your guard. Watch Sue. And be ready to do exactly what I tell you to do."

She left Joe staring bemusedly at the spot where her index finger had pointed. He was certainly a good hypnotic subject. No wonder Hattie had found him so easy to push around. It augured well for his relationship with Sue, if the girl could learn she would have to wear the pants in that branch of the Kirby family. Joe was an outstanding example of the fact that people's personalities didn't match their looks. The macho face and figure of Victor von Damm clothed a malleable, naive man who only needed someone to lead him firmly and gently into the right path.

Jacqueline was pleased with her scheme for killing Victor. In fact, she thought it was nothing short of brilliant. If only she could get an equally brilliant inspiration about the murders! There was still one vital piece of the puzzle missing, and the most aggravating part of it was that she almost had the answer. Something tickled her subconscious, like a word well known but momentarily misplaced. Something she had heard or read. The harder she tried to capture it, the farther it retreated.

VIII

When she got back to her room she heard the shower running behind the closed bathroom door. Surmising that Sue would be primping for a good long time, Jacqueline made her own arrangements. After assuming the peacock-blue robe she arranged her pillows—and Sue's—against the headboard of her bed and then lined up on the table two cardboard cartons of coffee, a hamburger wrapped in greasy paper, mustard and catsup, two chocolate bars, an apple, a pack of cigarettes, and a lighter. From her purse she took her notebook and pen. She had fallen behind with her novel. Now that the other business was settled. . . . A shadow of uneasiness crossed Jacqueline's brow. She had it worked out—well, almost worked out. What worried her was not what she was going to do with the information but whether O'Brien would cooperate with her plan.

There was nothing more she could do at the moment. She took a bite of the hamburger, wiped mustard off her chin, and began writing.

When Sue emerged from the bathroom Jacqueline was eating a chocolate bar and scribbling industriously. "Oh," Sue said brightly. "You're back."

Jacqueline glanced up. Sue was wearing a robe and a coiffure of huge pink curlers. Her eyes peered out of a mask of thick brown glop. She looked like an aboriginal witch doctor.

Jacqueline returned to her writing without bothering to reply. Sue sidled toward her and read over her shoulder. After a while she said timidly, "I don't think mammoths and copper weapons existed at the same time."

"Oona has just discovered copper," Jacqueline said, without looking up.

"Oh, yes." Sue read aloud. " 'Oona discovers copper.' "

"I'll fill that in later," Jacqueline explained abstractedly. "Do you mind not talking? I want to finish this chapter."

She filled two more pages before planting an emphatic exclamation point at the end of the last sentence. Closing the notebook, she reached for a cigarette.

"You're looking very bright and cheerful," she said.

This was an accurate description of Sue's emotional state, though how Jacqueline reached it was anybody's guess. Sue's face was completely encased in brown plaster. She sat down on the other bed and squinted at Jacqueline through the mud.

"I haven't had a chance to tell you—you were out all day. Guess what?"

"You and Joe are getting married," Jacqueline said thoughtlessly.

"Oh. Did you see Joe today?"

"About an hour ago. I think we've figured out a way to detach Hattie's claws from his gizzard."

"Oh? But he said Hattie had agreed—"

"Hattie's word is not her bond. This should make it a sure thing. Sue, do you know what you're doing? You only met the man a few days ago."

"You sound like my mother," said Sue, smiling.

"Damn."

"Oh, I like it," Sue assured her.

"You mistake my meaning," said Jacqueline.

"I couldn't be more certain. Joe is wonderful. He's flying back with me, to meet my folks and find out about applying to grad school." Sue sighed ecstatically. "To think that only day before yesterday I was wishing I'd never come to the conference."

"What are you going to do about your book?"

"I'm glad you asked me that, because I'd like to get your opinion." The solemn voice and the intent blue eyes peering through the muddy mask were almost too much for Jacqueline's sobriety, but she politely refrained from laughing. Sue went on, "I'm going to use my own title. And I'm going to take out all the parts the editor made me put in. You know, the parts—"

"The dirty bits?" Jacqueline suggested.

"Yes. That was never part of my book. If I can't sell it on its own merits, then I won't pander to people's depraved tastes."

"That's very nice," Jacqueline said. Betsy would be pleased; she had made one convert.

"I'm glad you agree." Sue's glance strayed to the notebook in which Jacqueline had been writing, but she did not point out that Jacqueline was not living up to her own standards. The manuscript had a good many dirty bits.

On her part, Jacqueline refrained from telling Sue of the dire events she expected would occur that evening. Why spoil the girl's pleasure? It would be as bad as kicking a baby chick. Sue had never been a serious suspect in Jacqueline's estimation. Sue was the heroine, and Jacqueline had always resented mystery writers who pinned the crime on the heroine, thus depriving the reader of the happy ending he or she had every right to expect.

She crammed the rest of the candy bar into her mouth just as the telephone rang. "Hello," she mumbled into it.

"Who's this?"

Jacqueline swallowed. "Me, of course. James?"

"Of course."

"Well?"

"The tests were all negative."

"What?"

"The tests were all—"

"I heard you. What did he look for?"

"The usual. Strychnine, arsenic, prussic acid—"

"James, you silly man, it couldn't have been any of those. Didn't you observe Dubretta's symptoms?"

"No, I did not, as you are well aware. If you knew what poison wasn't used, why didn't you tell me? This is the most inept excuse for a criminal investigation I've ever seen."

Jacqueline had to admit there was some justice in his complaint. Nor did this seem the moment to tell him that everything he had done that day had been a waste of time.

"It was essential that we tidy up the loose ends," she said vaguely, and then, before James could ask what the devil she meant, she went on, "Did you interview the suspects?"

"Nobody has an alibi."

"Is that all you can say?"

"That's what it comes down to. It took me the whole damned afternoon to learn that much. Nobody was home the first time I went round. I don't know why I couldn't simply telephone them."

"I told you why. It's very important to watch faces and judge the subtle nuances of voices when they answer significant questions."

"The nuances were too subtle for me," James grumbled. "I didn't track down that weird libber friend of yours till almost five. I asked her where she was last night between midnight and one A.M. and she laughed and suggested I dump Jean and escort her to the ball tonight."

"I guess you just can't help being irresistible, James. What did Betsy say?"

"She said she couldn't see any reason why I couldn't take her."

"No, no. Where was she last night?" Jacqueline wasn't really interested, but poor James needed to feel useful.

"She said she was at home, watching 'Kojak.' It's her favorite program."

"Did you ask her about the plot?"

"I did, as a matter of fact," James said smugly. "And what's more, I checked it in the television guide. Of course she could have done the same thing. Or seen it the first time around. It was a rerun."

"That's very clever, James. You did good. I'm proud of you. Good-bye."

"Wait a minute. You haven't told me—"

"I have to make another call, James. I'll see you later."

James's mention of Betsy had reminded her that she had forgotten something, and for reasons she would have hated to admit. Vanity, vanity, saith the sage, and he had saith right. She had been so fascinated by Betsy's fabulous gown she had neglected to pursue the purpose for which she had visited her friend. It would probably turn out to be another dead end, but she couldn't afford to overlook any possibilities. Reaching for the telephone, she dialed Betsy's number.

The phone rang for some time without result. Jacqueline was about to give up when she heard the receiver being picked up.

"Where the hell were you?" she demanded.

"In the attic. You know, there are lots of things in that trunk of Mother's. I found a fan and a pair of satin slippers—they're too small for me, but—"

"Never mind that," said Jacqueline, with a catch in her voice. Her feet were several sizes smaller than Betsy's. Vanity, vanity, all is vanity, she reminded herself. "I forgot to ask you, Betsy. When Laurie jumped you yesterday, you said she kept mumbling to herself while she was searching your knapsack. What did she say?"

"How do you expect me to remember?" Betsy said indignantly. "I tell you, Jake, your hearing doesn't function too well when you've just been socked in the eye and you've got three hundred pounds sitting on your backside."

"Try," Jacqueline urged.

"Well . . . she talked about Valentine—how sweet and angelic and beautiful she was, that sort of slosh. She said that right after she hit me. I started to get up, and she sat on me and started calling me names. One of them was yellow-bellied sapsucker."

"Good heavens."

"It's amazing how insulting some ornithological terms can be," Betsy mused. "You break that name down, and apply it to a human being. . . . I guess she had yellow on the brain. Yellow-bellied coward was another of her charming epithets."

"Yellow," Jacqueline repeated.

"Is that all? I've got a lot to do if I want to get to your place by seven-thirty. See you then, Jake."

Betsy hung up. Jacqueline sat holding the telephone until a mechanical voice began to drone, "Please hang up. You have left the instrument off the hook. Please hang up."

Sue took the telephone from her paralyzed hand and replaced it. "What's wrong?" she asked anxiously. "Was it bad news?"

"News," Jacqueline mumbled. "News . . . by God, that's it!" She leaped up and tore off her robe. She was dressed and halfway to the door before Sue recovered. "Where are you going? What's the matter? Can I do anything?"

Jacqueline stopped. "Time. What's the time?" She looked at her watch, as did Sue; they chanted in chorus, "Five twenty-five." "The library will probably be closed," Jacqueline went on. "Pray God some of the bookstores stay open later."

She stormed out the door, leaving Sue staring.

IX

Forty-five minutes later she returned, transformed. Her smile could only be described as smug, and her eyes glowed.

"Is everything all right?" Sue asked.

Jacqueline looked surprised. "Yes, of course. Why do you ask?" She tossed her purse onto the bed and stretched like a contented cat. "I'd better get ready. It will soon be time for the ball! La da da da da da dadadada, la da da da. . . ." To the strains of "Tales from the Vienna Woods" she waltzed into the bathroom and closed the door.

At precisely seven-thirty Betsy appeared with the Fortuny gown slung carelessly over her arm. The dress and the brown paper bag she carried made her look like an unusually healthy specimen of bag lady after a successful raid on a trash bin.

Jacqueline rescued the dress and hung it carefully on a hanger. From her shopping bag Betsy extracted her latest discoveries—a pair of beautifully cut satin slippers that had been dyed to match the dress, long white gloves (cracked and faded to a sickly tan), and an ostrich-feather fan, with half the feathers reduced to bare sticks. Jacqueline got rid of the fan and the gloves, over Betsy's vehement protests. Then she picked up one of the shoes.

"You weren't planning to wear these, were you?"

"I thought I could cut out the toes," Betsy explained, removing a pair of wire-cutting shears from her knapsack.

"You touch those shoes and I'll stab you to the heart," Jacqueline said sincerely. "Haven't you got anything else?"

Betsy extended a foot. She was wearing sneakers. Jacqueline groaned. "Sue!"

Sue emerged from the bathroom. She had removed the mask. One eye was made up, complete with liner, lid color, crease color, highlighter, false eyelashes and a partridge in a pear tree. "Hello," she said uncertainly.

"Hi," Betsy replied. "Do you know you've only got one set of eyelashes?"

"What size shoe do you wear?" Jacqueline demanded.

It was a forlorn hope. Sue's feet were as small as the rest of her, and Betsy's had spread, from miles of marching.

"Go buy some," Jacqueline ordered.

"The stores are closed." Betsy reclined ungracefully on the bed. "I'll just wear my sneakers."

The intensity of Jacqueline's response got her off the bed in a hurry. "I have a pair of white sandals someplace," she offered. "If I can find them."

"Find them." Jacqueline shoved her toward the door.

Betsy left. "I don't know why I bother," Jacqueline exclaimed dramatically.

"You're a very kind, sweet person," Sue said. The look Jacqueline directed at her sent her trotting back into the bathroom.

The next time she came out she had the second set of eyelashes in place. Scissors in hand, Jacqueline was working on her borrowed ball gown. Bows and artificial flowers went flying as she snipped them off and tossed them away. By the time she finished, the dress had been reduced to its essentials—a white satin-and-silk net creation with a bouffant skirt and narrow shoulder straps.

"It's very pretty," Sue said. "But now that you've taken all those extra things off, it isn't funny any more."

"Funny is not what I'm after," Jacqueline said.

X

Dainty and delectable in a Watteau-style shepherdess gown, complete with crook and stuffed lamb, Sue left to meet Joe while Jacqueline was still trying to make Betsy look like something other than a transvestite who had robbed a museum. Makeup only made her look worse and the best that could be said for the white plastic sandals was that they were a slight improvement over the sneakers. By lifting the skirt at the waist, where the resultant bulge was hidden by the tunic, Jacqueline managed to conceal the sandals while shortening the dress enough so Betsy wouldn't trip over it. She contemplated the result without enthusiasm.

"It's your hair," she grumbled. "Who cut it, the local barber?"

"I have that wig," Betsy said, entering into the spirit of the thing. "You know, the one I wore to the cocktail party."

"Don't be vulgar." Jacqueline pondered. "Wait a minute. I saw something of Sue's that might help."

Betsy submitted to the curling iron with unexpected docility, even though Jacqueline singed her neck twice. A couple of feathers plucked from the defunct fan were pinned onto a black velvet ribbon (also purloined from Sue), which was tied filletwise over the mass of short curls. Jacqueline's dour expression relaxed. "It's not bad," she said, in a congratulatory tone.

The congratulations were for herself, but Betsy didn't know that. She beamed at her reflection. "I look pretty good, don't I?"

"Go stand over there in the corner and keep quiet," Jacqueline ordered. "I've only got ten minutes to get dressed. If I know O'Brien, he'll be here on the dot."

"O'Brien? You're going with him? Why, that rat fink! Why didn't he say so?"

"We're both going with him." Jacqueline dropped her gown over her head.

"I wonder what he's going to wear."

"Can't you guess?" Jacqueline's hands moved quickly, braiding her hair into a thick club at the back of her head. Gleaming coils and flirtatious curls framed her face in a coiffure reminiscent of some past era Betsy could not immediately identify. Jacqueline fastened a wide blue ribbon across the bodice of the dress from one shoulder to the opposite hip and completed the ensemble by putting atop her head a rhinestone tiara she had bought at the dime store that morning. *"Voilà,"* she said.

"Empress Eugénie," Betsy exclaimed. "No—wait a minute—I think I've got it. . . . Alexandra! The queen of Edward the Seventh."

"Very good."

"Well, I was a history major, after all. It's the hair that does it. Alexandra had red hair too."

"Auburn," Jacqueline said firmly. "That's the best I can do at short notice. And," she added, as there was a knock at the door, "just in time. That must be O'Brien."

She went to answer it. Betsy trotted after her, chuckling and speculating. "Charles the Second? He's got the face for it— swarthy, cynical. . . . Or George Washington? I'd love to see him in a white wig."

"You're on the wrong track," Jacqueline said. She threw the door open and stood back.

O'Brien took the pipe out of his mouth, removed his hat, and bowed. The pipe was a meerschaum; the hat was a deerstalker; his heavy coat was caped and reached to mid-calf.

"What else?" Jacqueline asked rhetorically. She extended her hand in a gesture whose regality was not one whit lessened by the horn-rimmed glasses riding low on her nose. "Good evening, Mr. Holmes."

CHAPTER NINE

O'Brien voiced no objection to Betsy's joining them, even when she repeated her inane reference to the Three Musketeers. Jacqueline had an explanation ready in case he did object: this was not a social occasion, as both of them were well aware. She was vexed at having no opportunity to explain this.

Their costumes won a few amused glances as they crossed the lobby, but as soon as they entered the other hotel they became part of an equally unusual throng. It was rumored that some genuine notables would be present, including fans of the genre who had hitherto concealed their deplorable addiction, and Jacqueline heard snatches of speculation mixed with the now familiar shoptalk.

"I thought you were contemporary," said one young woman to another, whose ancient Egyptian costume certainly justified her companion's doubts.

"I'm changing lines," was the response. "Contemp doesn't pay as well."

". . . the First Lady?" cried a stately matron, her rhinestone parure glittering with the rapid rise and fall of her agitated bosom.

". . . great fan of Victor's," said her friend breathlessly.

Other guesses were bandied back and forth. The star of the latest nighttime soap hit, *Schenectady?* Visiting royalty? A Du Pont, a Kennedy, a Rockefeller?

The decorations of the ballroom represented the culminating triumph of bad taste. Everything that was not pink to begin with had been painted that color, including the grand piano. The dinner jackets of the orchestra flashed with pink sequins. Bowers of plastic greenery and artificial roses bulged out from the walls. There were pink bulbs in the chandeliers. They shed a flattering light over the ladies' complexions, but when O'Brien stood under one of them he looked as if he were about to have an apoplectic attack.

Happily unaware of this effect, he looked at Jacqueline. "Well, Mrs. K., here we are. Would you care to let me in on your plans?"

"First of all, I think you should call me Jacqueline. We're trying to create the impression that this is an ordinary date."

"Oh, is that what we're trying to create? Don't you think this rather spoils the effect?" He glanced at Betsy, who was clinging to his arm.

"It spoils something," Jacqueline agreed. "Betsy, get lost for a while."

"Where?"

"I don't care. Go sit in a bower and be a rosebud. Cruise. There's a nice-looking man over there who appears to be unattached—the one who's dressed as Julius Caesar."

"He's bald," said Betsy.

"So was Julius Caesar. So is Kojak. Go."

Betsy wandered off. "She looks different tonight," O'Brien said, mildly puzzled.

"I should hope so," said Jacqueline, with a vivid recollection of her labors. "Now. What has happened since I last talked to you?"

"Another rape, two murders, five breaking and entering—"

"You know what I mean."

"Ask me questions, Mrs.—Jacqueline."

"The autopsy on Laurie?"

"We have a very astute coroner. He deduced almost at once that her skull had been fractured."

"I don't suppose he bothered to test for drugs," said Jacqueline, with visible self-control.

"Oddly enough, he did. Negative. No hash, no pot, no heroin, no coke, no PCP—"

"Good."

"Good?"

"Did you find her purse?"

"Purses are annoyingly prominent in this affair," O'Brien complained. "By the way, that suitcase you're toting doesn't go with your costume."

"I need it. Well?"

"We found it. In a trash can several hundred yards away."

"What was in it?"

"No money, no drugs."

"No medication of any kind?"

"A small tin of aspirin and a roll of antacids," O'Brien said gravely. "Also two candy bars and a bag of peanuts."

"Hmm."

"Okay, I've done my part. Now it's your turn."

"Hmm?"

"What are your plans?"

"Oh, that. I'm going to identify the murderer of Dubretta and Laurie. You'll have to handle the arrest."

"Well, well. You know who it is?"

"Yes."

"Can you prove it, Mrs. Kirby—Jacqueline?"

"I know how it was done," Jacqueline said. "I can prove that part of it. Pinning it on the murderer could be just a wee bit tricky."

"Please," O'Brien said prayerfully. "Please don't tell me you're depending on the murderer's confession. All the suspects sitting around while you sum up the case and suddenly turn, pointing: 'It was you, Dangerous Dan. Confess!' Please don't tell me that."

"It won't be like that."

"Oh yes, it will. Why do you think I'm here, Jacqueline?"

"Because you think Dubretta was murdered."

"Because I had a hunch you were going to pull some dumb stunt. Despite the fact that you are the most exasperating female I've ever met, I don't want you to become corpse number three."

"Ah," Jacqueline crowed. "You do think Dubretta—"

"What I think doesn't matter. There is the little matter of evidence. It's only in detective stories that the murderer admits his guilt and politely takes poison, saving the cop in charge the trouble of gathering proof that will convince a grand jury he's got a case—much less a case that will result in a conviction. Your brilliant deductions don't include that little item, do they? And if you think you're going to needle the murderer into attacking you so I can catch him or her in the act, forget it. I'm going to stick to you like the paper on the wall."

"That's just what I had in mind," said Jacqueline, batting her eyelashes. "Sssh. The ball is about to begin."

A fanfare of trumpets (two) hushed the babble of conversation. The leader of the orchestra advanced to the microphone in a pink glimmer; not only the lapels of his jacket but its entire surface was covered with sequins. "Ladies and gentlemen," he began, glancing at the paper he held. "Uh—pray make way for the (What the hell is this word? Oh.) for the appearance of the Queen of Love, who will open the ball."

Turning, he lifted his baton. The orchestra burst into a march.

Heads turned and people milled about uncertainly as they tried to locate the doorway whence the Queen of Love would emerge. Hattie had planned a Grand March but, as was typical of her arrangments, she had neglected to make sure the floor would be cleared. The head of the procession was immediately swallowed up by confused spectators, until eventually people moved back, leaving the center of the room free. From the melee emerged Hattie, flushed and scowling, on the arm of Victor von Damm.

Living up to her self-proclaimed image of "For me it's too late," Hattie was a miracle of frumpiness, from her disheveled gray hair to her limp satin gown in a dismal shade of ashes of roses. What the costume, if any, was meant to represent, Jacqueline could not imagine.

The gorgeousness of Victor compensated for Hattie's dowdiness. His high black boots and white pants were so tight, it seemed impossible he could bend his knees, and indeed his stride suggested that of a military funeral. His tunic was a more gilded version of the one he had worn the day before. Fur trimmed the jacket slung from one shoulder.

Behind them, at a discreet distance dictated by the sword that was part of Victor's costume, came Valentine and the Earl. White tie and tails, fake diamond studs, and the ribbon of some undoubtedly apocryphal order distinguished the latter. At the sight of him Jacqueline swore under her breath. When O'Brien glanced curiously at her she shook her head.

Valentine was wearing Laurie's dress. Her beauty would have shone through rags and dirt, but the gown set it off as a jeweler's creation sets off a fabulous gem. Among the other costumes, which were all hired or homemade, Laurie's loving creation stood supreme.

Across the room in the front row of spectators Jacqueline recognized Meredith. She was not in costume, unless her faded jeans and man's shirt could be considered an attempt at something of the sort. Jacqueline suspected it was a demonstration of Meredith's contempt for the whole affair. But there was a look of grudging satisfaction on the girl's face as she watched the shining loveliness glide past. Jacqueline nudged O'Brien. She had to nudge twice; like that of every other man in the room, his expression was one of unconscious hunger as he looked at Valentine.

"There's Meredith," she whispered. "Laurie's—"

"I see her."

"I wonder how she got the money for the ticket."

O'Brien made no reply. "Did you by any chance find Laurie's ticket in her purse?" Jacqueline asked.

"I thought one of the kids might as well use it," O'Brien said. "They paid enough for it."

Hattie climbed laboriously onto the stage and grabbed the mike. Her audience lost interest after she had introduced the evening's mystery guests—the wife of a congressman no one had ever heard of ("a vote is a vote, honey, and at least these people can read") and a minor actor in a daytime soap opera. The restiveness of her listeners finally warned Hattie to bring her speech to a close. "The Queen of Love will open the ball," she cried.

The orchestra began "The Blue Danube," and Valentine and the Earl took the floor. Jacqueline shook her head. "Trite. And it's damned hard to dance to."

It was, especially at the funereal tempo set by the orchestra. However, here the Earl came into his own, and Jacqueline understood why he had been picked for the role. A pink spotlight wavered and finally found the pair; and as the shining figures circled and glided, there was a moment of sheer romance. Valentine's skirts swung out; her hair was like a nimbus. Then Hattie shouted, "Everybody dance," and the spell was broken.

Few people accepted the invitation. Women outnumbered men by at least ten to one. Jacqueline, who loved to waltz, looked hopefully at O'Brien. He shook his head, the slashes in his cheeks deepening.

"Sorry, your majesty. I'm afraid I can't oblige."

"So few men know how to waltz."

"I waltz divinely," said O'Brien. "But not in this outfit."

"Why don't you take off your coat?"

"It's part of the costume."

Jacqueline's frustration was increased when she caught sight of Jean rapturously circling in James's arms. James was in the full regalia of a Scottish chief. He was deplorably vain about his legs, and his dips and whirls were designed to make his kilt flare out. The maneuver also had the unfortunate effect of winding Jean's voluminous pantaloons and veils around both of them, and finally James had to stop to unwind them from his body. It was no accident that he guided his partner toward the spot where Jacqueline was standing with O'Brien. He pretended not to see her but Jean, flushed with pleasure and pink light, looked straight into her friend's eyes and smirked.

"Would you like to sit down?" O'Brien asked courteously.

"If you won't dance, you could at least buy me a drink."

"Perhaps a ladylike glass of punch?"

"A ladylike glass of booze would be more like it. There's probably a cash bar. Hattie wouldn't pass up a chance to make a buck."

"The Blue Danube" was succeeded by one of the *Fledermaus* waltzes. A few more dancers ventured onto the floor. Jacqueline caught sight of Betsy in the reluctant grasp of Julius Caesar, and

Sue, drifting dreamily in Victor's arms. Valentine was dancing with her manager. They made a surprisingly congruous couple, despite Max's bald head and paunch, and the fact that the two were almost the same height. On the dance floor Max was transformed. He lacked the Earl's professional correctness, but his waltzing had panache. He was not in costume, but in regulation evening dress.

Jean and James swung by again, both ostentatiously ignoring their wallflower friend. O'Brien asked again if Jacqueline wanted to sit down. She repeated her earlier suggestion. O'Brien conceded that it might not be a bad idea.

They found the bar without difficulty. Signs inappropriately adorned with pink paper hearts pointed the way. Business was brisk, and all the tables were occupied. At one, Jacqueline saw Emerald Fitzroy in a Marie Antoinette wig and panniered gown. With her was the woman agent Jacqueline had met at the luncheon. Their heads were close together.

O'Brien joined the line waiting to be served and Jacqueline stood aside. Before long she saw another familiar face. The Earl looked as if he were glued to the bar. He was drinking champagne, and by bribery or some other means he had captured the undivided attention of one of the bartenders. His glass was filled as soon as he drained it, which he did as soon as it was filled. Jacqueline couldn't decide what fascinated her more, the rapidity of his arm movements or the utter blankness of his face. Except for the opening and closing of his mouth, not a muscle moved, and it remained equally impassive when he fell forward, with the slow, inexorable movement of a felled tree, into the arms of Emerald Fitzroy. The table fell over. The agent jumped to her feet. Emerald sat gaping with the Earl draped peacefully across her lap. Someone screamed, "My God! He's dead!"

II

O'Brien reached the fallen man an instant before Jacqueline. Kicking the table out of the way, he lowered the Earl to the floor. Emerald began to shriek. Jacqueline shook her. "Stop that. He isn't dead."

"Drunk as a skunk," O'Brien agreed. "Boiled as a lobster. Come on, Pierre, open your baby blues." He slapped the Earl's cheeks. There was no response, except that the man's lips curved into a smile.

"You know him?" Jacqueline asked.

"Sure. He dances at one of those topless-bottomless bars on the East Side. The boys run him in every couple of months. Wake up, baby. That's it."

The Earl opened one eye, saw O'Brien bending over him, shuddered, and closed it again. "Go 'way," he mumbled. "I didn't do nothin'."

"Drunk and disorderly," said O'Brien amiably.

Both the Earl's eyes opened. They were wide and indignant. "Wasn't disorderly. See. . . ." His hands moved feebly, presumably indicating that he was fully clothed.

Someone had notified Hattie of her protégé's collapse. She pushed through the ring of spectators, her lips set and her eyes black with fury. She made one game attempt to save the situation. "He's been taken ill. One of those hereditary weaknesses like you find in old families. . . . Let me help you to your room, your Grace."

The Earl giggled. "I'd rather have Victor. How 'bout it, you ugly old bag? Little extra bonus. You got me cheap enough."

"Get him out of here," Hattie snarled.

Two waiters moved in and removed the Earl. He wrapped an affectionate arm around the younger of the two and went unprotesting.

Hattie pushed wisps of hair from her perspiring face and glared at Jacqueline. "If one word of this reaches the press—"

"Act your age," Jacqueline said impatiently. "There are thirty witnesses here; you can't shut them all up. Really, Hattie, nobody gives a damn. However, I have a proposition to put to you that could be worth. . . ." She glanced around. "Not here. When can I talk to you in private?"

Hattie hesitated. Her dislike of Jacqueline warred with curiosity and a certain respect. Finally she said, "The band takes a break about ten-thirty. I'll see you then."

She moved away, straightening her corsage. "That's one

suspect off the list," Jacqueline said. "Why didn't you tell me you knew the Earl?"

"Why should I?"

"I never seriously considered him."

"You should have. He's undoubtedly the most unlikely suspect."

O'Brien righted the table and gestured at an empty chair. Emerald had tottered out as soon as she had been relieved of the Earl; a good many other patrons had also escaped, following the tried-and-true rule of avoiding involvement. "Sit down and I'll get you some champagne," O'Brien said. "By the way—I intend to join you when you have your meeting with Hattie."

"Of course," Jacqueline said.

After O'Brien returned with their wine they were joined by James and Jean. Seeing Jean at close range, Jacqueline realized that she was indeed wearing a long-sleeved high-necked white blouse under her bejeweled bra. The effect was indescribable, but Jean appeared to be unaware of this; excitement and gratification flushed her face.

"Is it true?" she asked, gathering armfuls of pink veiling into her lap as she sat down. "Is he dead?"

"Just drunk," O'Brien said.

"Really? Well, if that isn't just like Hattie. She's so cheap! You get what you pay for, I always say."

"You knew he was a hired actor?" Jacqueline asked.

"Well, of course I knew he wasn't an earl. I'm not stupid. James, darling, I'd adore a glass of champagne."

"Have mine," said Jacqueline, who had not requested that beverage in the first place. "I haven't touched it."

There was a dreadful pause. Jean's eyes opened so wide, the whites showed all around the dim blue pupils. O'Brien grinned.

"On the other hand," Jacqueline said deliberately, "perhaps you've had too much to drink already." She picked up the glass and drained it. "James, will you dance with me?"

"Uh—yes, of course."

As they walked toward the ballroom James took her arm. "What's going on? Did she really think—"

"I guess she was settling some old scores," Jacqueline said. So much for friendship and loyalty; perhaps Jean herself hadn't realized the depth of her long-buried resentment. She added, in a lighter voice, "Or else you plied her with liquor earlier."

"I took her to dinner. You told me to take her to dinner, so I did. And a damned boring dinner it was, too. She's no murderer. She's a dull, boring woman. And a terrible dancer."

The orchestra was playing "The Merry Widow Waltz." Jacqueline went into James's arms. "Poor James," she murmured.

They circled the room once in silence, except for Jacqueline's humming. For once James made no objection, even when she began crooning one of the more banal translations of the undistinguished lyrics. " 'Though I've heard no single word of lo-o-ove from you. . . .' "

James's arm tightened. "You're a weird woman," he said fondly.

"We do dance well together, don't we?"

"We would, except for that purse." His arm pinned the straps to her body, but it kept thumping Jacqueline on the derriere. "Can't you check it or something?"

"No."

James twirled her in a flamboyant pirouette that made the purse bounce. "Still on the trail, eh?" he said.

"I have an appointment with Hattie at ten-thirty." Jacqueline grunted as the purse whacked her again. "I want everyone there, James. Especially you."

"Where?"

"Her suite. As soon as you see me leave with her, follow us. Bring Jean, and make sure Victor and Sue come too. I'll speak to them myself, but it's vital that they be there."

The music came to a languorous close. "I lo-o-ove you," Jacqueline sang.

"That's nice. Another time around?"

"Not now. I want you to—" Jacqueline broke off with a gasp, partly because she hadn't known what she was going to say next, and partly because she had seen something that demanded quick action. She started across the floor, towing James with her. "Dance with Valentine," she said rapidly. "Keep her away from the bar. It's important, James."

James's brow furrowed. "I thought you were—"

"Sssh. Please, James."

They intercepted Valentine and Max outside the bar. Jacqueline greeted them effusively. "I'm so glad you decided to wear the dress," she gushed. "It wouldn't look right on anyone else. You remember my friend, Professor Whittier, don't you? He's been admiring you from afar all evening. Would you give him a dance, Valentine?"

James glared, but could not think of any way of objecting to this high-handed act without sounding like a petulant schoolboy. "I'll dream of it through the long, cold Nebraska winter," he said, holding out his hand.

"That's a plea that would move a heart of stone," Max said, chuckling. "Go on, my dear. I know what Nebraska winters are like."

He handed Valentine over to James and turned to Jacqueline. "We were about to stop for refreshment, Jacqueline. Will you join me instead?"

"I'd rather dance," said Jacqueline. "You waltz magnificently, Max."

"I would be honored." They moved onto the floor, Max apparently unconcerned by the fact that Jacqueline towered over him. "Very good," he said approvingly. "You also dance well, my dear. But I hope Hattie has arranged for something other than waltzes to be played. Fond as I am of them, I suspect they may pall before the end of the evening."

His eyes shifted from Jacqueline's face as Valentine drifted by, a rosy glimmer in James's hold. "She is lovely," Jacqueline said. "Have you known her long?"

His smooth step faltered as Jacqueline's purse thudded into his side. "I'm so sorry," Jacqueline said.

"My fault," Max said gallantly. "I can't help wondering, however, why a woman of your obvious taste would carry an object that is so incongruous with your charming dress."

"Oh dear," Jacqueline said, as the purse pounded him a second time. "Perhaps we had better not dance. Let's sit the rest of this one out."

"If you like." Max led her toward one of the bowers along the wall. " 'Here will we sit and let the sounds of music creep in our ears.' "

Jacqueline gave him a long steady look. "You're fond of Shakespeare?"

"I sometimes think Europeans appreciate him more than his own countrymen do. May I get you something to drink?"

"The bar is awfully crowded."

"Not surprising. There's nothing else for most of the guests to do. The disparity between the sexes limits dancing. Hattie has grandiose ideas, but she is weak in tactical application."

"I have an idea I want to talk over with her. She's agreed to meet me during the intermission. I'd appreciate your joining us, Max. I know she values your advice."

"Only when Valentine is involved. I don't interfere in Hattie's other affairs."

The music ended. Max turned to watch James and Valentine. It seemed to Jacqueline that there was an increased intensity in his regard that evening. Concern, affection, fear? It was impossible to tell from Max's well-schooled face.

Hattie bustled up, fanning herself with her program. "I declare, everything is going wrong. The air-conditioning isn't working right and I can't get the manager to do anything about it. Where is Valentine? She has no business wandering off. . . . Oh, there she is. Now where is Victor? He's got to take over as her escort. He hasn't danced with anybody except that little schoolteacher."

She gave an annoyed grunt as someone touched her on the shoulder. "What do you want? I'm busy."

Meredith stood with her feet apart and her fists on her hips. "When are you going to make the announcement?" she demanded.

"What announcement? Who the . . . who are you?"

"Meredith is the vice-president of Valentine's fan club," Jacqueline said. "I told her you would say a few words about Laurie and the dress she made."

Meredith's quick, oblique glance at Jacqueline held little favor. She hated every adult in the world just then, with no exceptions. "Well?" she said.

"Announcement." Hattie looked thoughtful. "I suppose I could, dear. At the end of the ball. We don't want to spoil the festivities, do we?"

"There won't be anybody left by then," Meredith said. "A lot of people have left already. This is a damned boring party."

Max intervened to stop Hattie's hot retort. "You're right, Meredith. We'll be taking a break shortly to give the musicians a rest. Perhaps, Hattie, you could make the announcement at the beginning of the second half."

The compromise didn't please either combatant. Meredith shrugged and turned away, her lip curled. "Boring party," Hattie sputtered. "Of all the insolence!"

The group was joined by Jean, in pursuit of James, and O'Brien, whose motives were anybody's guess. The sight of him brought another martyred sigh from Hattie. "And you're the last straw," she informed him. "Hanging around like a skeleton at the feast."

"No one will recognize me," O'Brien said. "My disguise is impenetrable." He took his meerschaum from his pocket and clamped his teeth on the stem.

"I'm going to make this the last dance of the first half," Hattie grumbled. "Maybe by the time intermission is over, the damned air-conditioning will be fixed. Here, Valentine"—as James led the lady toward them—"I want you to dance with Victor. Where the hell is he?"

"I'm tired," Valentine protested. Her pearly skin shone with perspiration. "And I'm thirsty. I want to sit down and have something to drink."

"There aren't enough men," Hattie exclaimed, as if she had just observed this obvious fact. "You've all got to dance. All you men. Professor—"

"I'm bushed," James said, ducking behind Jacqueline to avoid Jean's outstretched hand. With an adept flick of the wrist, Jacqueline diverted the hand onto Max's arm. "Max is a wonderful dancer. And he doesn't seem a bit tired. We've been sitting down."

"I promised Valentine," Max began.

"I'll get her something to drink," said O'Brien. "I'm not dancing. What would you like, Miss Valentine?"

"Now for Victor," Hattie said briskly.

"I'll find him," Jacqueline said. "He owes me a dance."

As she had expected, she found Joe and Sue in the most

remote and shadowy of the bowers, happily entwined. She had to clear her throat twice before they broke apart.

"I told Hattie I'd force you to dance with me," she said.

"You go ahead, Joe," Sue murmured, as her beloved gave her an anguished glance.

"Never mind. Just stay out of her way. I'll leave you in peace if you promise me something. This is the last dance of the first half. As soon as the musicians leave the podium, come up to Hattie's suite. Both of you."

"What for?" Joe asked.

"Don't ask questions, just do as I tell you. If you forget, I'll blow your cover to the University of Nebraska admissions office."

Departing, she heard Joe's incredulous question. "She wouldn't do that, would she?" Sue's answer was inaudible.

From one end of the room she made a final check of her suspects. Max, flickering in and out of a pink haze as Jean's veils swirled around him; Jean, blissfully unaware of his martyred look; O'Brien, bending over Valentine; Hattie on the prowl, looking for Victor; Betsy . . . Betsy wasn't dancing. Jacqueline went into the bar. Yes, Betsy was there. The gray curls had gone limp with heat and the feathered diadem had slipped over one ear.

After she had spoken to Betsy, Jacqueline took up a position near the door and waited for the music to stop. Her heart was beating a little faster than usual, and as she waited she shifted her purse into her arms, pressing it to her breast in the same gesture Dubretta had used the night she died.

III

Hattie gave O'Brien a hard stare when he joined the group, but did not protest until they had reached her suite and Jacqueline began to explain her scheme for disposing of Victor von Damm. Hattie stopped her with a yelp of anguish. "Are you crazy? Not here—not in front of him!"

O'Brien closed his mouth. "She's putting you on," he said weakly. "Aren't you, Mrs.—Jacqueline?"

"Of course."

"It's not a very nice joke," Hattie said. Her face quivered with greedy speculation as the idea took hold. "Just suppose . . . just suppose something did happen to Victor. One of those strange coincidences. The lieutenant would wonder. . . ."

"I might wonder, but there wouldn't be anything I could do about it." O'Brien recovered his equanimity. "Especially if it happened out of my jurisdiction."

"Hmmm," said Hattie.

So entranced was she by her own thoughts, she didn't respond when the doorbell rang. "I'll get it," Max said.

Hattie drew Jacqueline into a corner. "I hope you'll keep in touch, dear," she murmured.

"Oh, I will—dear. I wouldn't want any of those strange coincidences happening—without me."

There was no need to say more. They understood one another perfectly.

The new arrivals were Sue and Joe. "I thought we'd drop in," Joe said unconvincingly. He looked at Jacqueline.

"Well, you can drop right out again," Hattie said. "I wasn't planning to entertain the whole damned crowd."

Still under Hattie's spell, Joe turned obediently. "No," Jacqueline said. "Sit down. Everyone sit down. This may take a while."

"What's going on?" Hattie demanded.

"Wait till the others arrive," Jacqueline said.

The doorbell rang again. O'Brien waved Max away and went to answer it. When he returned he was accompanied by Betsy, whose feathers now protruded at right angles from her left ear, and by a bewildered Roman. "Do we want Julius Caesar?" O'Brien asked.

"I don't. Do you?" Jacqueline inquired.

Caesar went willingly, once Betsy's fingers had been pried off his toga. "It's not fair," Betsy grumbled. "All the rest of you brought your friends. I don't see why I can't—"

"You're drunk," Jacqueline said critically.

"I am not. And I don't see why I can't—"

"Sit down, Betsy."

The last to arrive were Jean and James. The latter began, "I couldn't find—oh, there they are. Hello, Mrs. Foster. I hope you'll pardon the intrusion—"

"Do sit down and shut up, James," Jacqueline said sharply. "This is not a tea party."

James thrust his lady into a chair. She bounced up again. "What is this?" she demanded, her eyes darting suspiciously around the room. "James, you said Hattie asked us to come. I'm leaving."

"You're staying," Jacqueline corrected. Jean blinked and settled back.

Jacqueline took up her position beside a table near the French doors. She put her purse on the table. "The party is over," she said. "One of you won't be returning to the ball. I know who you are, and I know why you killed Dubretta and Laurie. If you would care to confess now, you'll save all of us a lot of time and trouble."

Max's chuckle broke the shocked silence. "What is that popular television game? 'Will the real killer please stand up?' "

No one else appeared to be amused. O'Brien, the only person other than Jacqueline who was still standing, looked off into space as if deep in thought. The others stared fixedly at Jacqueline.

"Oh, all right," she said. "I didn't expect you would, but I can never resist a dramatic gesture. From the beginning, then. . . .

"On my first encounter with the historical-romance writers I was struck by the vast amount of ill will in the group. Jealousy, greed, revenge—the overabundance of motive was one of the big stumbling blocks in the case. Half the people I had met had excellent reasons for wanting to exterminate the other half.

"Dubretta was the one who died. If her hints had a basis in fact, many of the people present that evening might have wanted to silence her. Yet there were at least two other potential victims, and Valentine's hysterical claim that she was the one who was supposed to die wasn't as wild as it sounded.

"Too many motives. So the question became: How? It seemed apparent that Dubretta was poisoned. It was equally apparent that the murderer had not employed any of the conventional poisons. Arsenic, prussic acid, strychnine, morphine—none induces symptoms that could be mistaken, by a trained medical man, for those of heart failure. I therefore concluded that Dubretta *was* the intended victim. If Valentine, young and healthy, had died of what appeared to be a heart attack, an autopsy would have been performed. Only the fact that Dubretta's heart condition was common knowledge made it unlikely that there would be any questions raised about how she died. The murderer counted on this. He had to select a poison that would produce that effect.

"The answer was so evident," Jacqueline said slowly, "that in retrospect it seems incredible no one thought of it. Especially those of you who stood by and watched me help Dubretta swallow a little yellow pill. None of you seems to have realized that that tablet contained one of the deadliest of all poisonous substances."

IV

Though she had stationed herself in a place that gave her a good overall view of the audience, Jacqueline couldn't gauge the immediate effect of her announcement on all of them simultaneously. The one face she was watching showed the reaction she had expected: a flash of comprehension and alarm, quickly masked. Most of the others gaped or gasped or started. Jean shivered. James half rose, his hands gripping the arms of his chair.

"You didn't think of that, did you?" Jacqueline asked him. "When we were making our list of suspects. You'll never be a good detective, James. Sentiment must not enter into an investigation. No one can be eliminated from suspicion."

James collapsed with a thud. "You didn't," he said, without conviction. "Did you?"

"No, of course I didn't. But that was one method you overlooked—substituting a poisoned tablet for one of Dubretta's pills."

O'Brien cleared his throat. "It wouldn't have been so easy, you know."

"Perhaps not. Dubretta guarded her purse carefully. 'Nobody puts a hand in here but me,' she told me. Still, someone might have managed it, when Dubretta was a little drunk and off her guard. . . ." Jacqueline glanced at Betsy, who stared back at her

in tipsy bewilderment. "Or when she was off guard because she
was with people she trusted." Jacqueline's gaze shifted to
O'Brien. He knew what she was thinking; he had been fighting
the same far-out but horrifying suspicion for days. She shook her
head. "Dubretta's medication was in the form of pills, not cap-
sules, which could have been emptied and refilled. Only a professional chemist could have reproduced the exact form of the pills.
There was nothing in her medication except what should have
been there.

"One of the problems a poisoner faces is getting hold of the
stuff. You can't pop into a drugstore and pick up a pound of
arsenic. It isn't in the pharmacopoeia. In fact, you need a doctor's prescription for any potentially dangerous drug, and phar-
macists are wary about filling such prescriptions. I understand it's
possible to buy morphine and cocaine and the like on every
street corner, but in addition to the fact I've already mentioned
—that these substances produce symptoms incompatible with a
diagnosis of heart failure—I doubted that my killer would risk
using such a source. Drug pushers are suspicious of strangers,
and they aren't reliable confederates. For a conventional middle-
aged citizen—a category that included most of my suspects—it
isn't easy to obtain illicit drugs.

"But there was one suspect who might well have access to such
sources. Laurie belonged to an age group and a social class inclined to dabble in drugs. I did not believe that Laurie was the
killer. But suppose the killer had obtained the poison from her?
She was obviously taking something; her increasing disorienta-
tion and personality problems made that painfully clear. I
thought of the obvious popular drugs—PCP, heroin, uppers and
downers of all kinds. . . . And that," Jacqueline said expression-
lessly, "that stupidity was partially responsible for Laurie's death.
If I had realized sooner what was wrong with her, I might have
been able to save her.

"I did realize that she could be in danger from the killer, not
only because she was becoming unreliable but because she might
actually have in her possession the poison that had killed
Dubretta. This assumption was confirmed when her body was
found. There was nothing on her or in her purse except aspirin.
I felt sure her murderer had removed the poison, but it wasn't

until this afternoon, when the truth finally dawned on me, that I knew what it was. Laurie wasn't on any of the standard drugs. She had been suffering from digitalis intoxication."

This time there was no betraying change of expression on the face Jacqueline watched, only the same look of disbelief that marked most of the others.

"Digitalis," Jacqueline said, "is the name given to a group of substances derived from *Digitalis purpurea,* the foxglove plant. They are used in the treatment of certain varieties of heart trouble, particularly atrial fibrillation and congestive heart failure. That was Dubretta's complaint. She was taking a form of digitalis whose generic name is digitoxin—the most poisonous of the digitalis group. Many medications are deadly poisons if the dosage isn't carefully controlled. In cases of congestive heart failure, the digitalis medication is given in two stages. The first stage is called digitalization; carefully monitored doses of the drug are given over a short period of time to get the heart functioning normally. Once this is achieved, the patient goes on a maintenance dosage. Dubretta was taking tablets three times a day, in doses of 0.15 milligrams per tablet. Tolerance for the drug varies widely. Death has been known to occur from one sixtieth of a grain, which is equivalent to—er—well, I won't bore you with arithmetic. Suffice it to say that in order to kill someone with Dubretta's pills, one would have to dump a handful of them into a glass. Not exactly inconspicuous.

"However, Dubretta was already taking almost .05 milligrams of digitalis a day. In the pharmacy manual I consulted"—Jacqueline took it from her purse and brandished it like a club—"there is a warning. 'Patients already taking digitalis preparations must not be given the rapidly digitalizing dose of digitoxin.' That dose is only .06 milligrams. The reason is obvious. On top of what she was already taking, three or four pills of a normally harmless size could kill Dubretta. As it did.

"The murderer did not get the tablets from Dubretta. He got them from Laurie—who was taking them for obesity."

"You're out of your mind," Hattie exclaimed. "I never heard—"

"It's in the book too. Digitalis is an effective diuretic, which leads to weight loss. Several people have died from taking it for that reason. And the symptoms of digitalis intoxication—a potentially dangerous overdose—are just the symptoms Laurie exhibited. Nausea and vomiting, apathy, mental confusion, delirium—and the definitive symptom, a condition of blurred vision in which everything looks yellow." Jacqueline looked at Betsy. "You said she had yellow on the brain when she was insulting you. It was literally true. And her reference to Midas, turning everything to gold. . . . She even told me she was trying to diet. I should have put the pieces together long before I did."

"I don't think he tested for digitalis," said James, to the mystification of most of his listeners. "But I still don't understand how it could have been added to the wine. Three or four pills—"

"It wasn't in the wine."

"What? I thought we agreed—"

"Not at all, James. In addition to the other objections, there wasn't time for the poison to work. Dubretta collapsed within minutes of drinking her wine. Even in her condition, it wouldn't have taken effect so quickly. The tablet I gave her didn't affect her either; digitalis takes some time to be absorbed, unlike nitroglycerin and other preparations which are put under the victim's tongue and which act almost immediately.

"The business of the sediment in the first glass of wine distracted me," Jacqueline went on. "It was so delightfully suggestive. But that's all it was—a suggestion, a distraction. Dubretta got the poison earlier in the evening, from a drink someone had bought for her. She had a glass in her hand when I met her, and she said it was her third. She also said she never had to buy her own drinks, implying that someone else had given her the one she had. You all know how the system worked. There were long lines at each of the temporary bar tables. If someone was buying Dubretta a drink, there would be no reason for her to stand in the line with the donor. Sue performed the same service for me; after she had bought the drinks she found me and gave me mine. She had plenty of time to tamper with it."

"Hey," Joe began.

"Just an example," Jacqueline said soothingly. "To show how easy it would have been for the buyer of the drink to add something to it before he or she handed it to Dubretta. Tip the pills in, mix with one of those plastic stirrers, and the job was done. Digitalis is not soluble in water, but it is soluble in alcohol.''

"But that means anyone in the room could have done it," James said, still clinging doggedly to his pet theory.

"Not quite everyone. Valentine and Hattie didn't mingle with the guests. Victor was with them, in that ridiculous artificial garden, and so was the Earl. Jean was there too—but she was hiding, and it is conceivable that she could have left the garden and returned without her absence being noted. She demonstrated her ability to get over the fence.''

Jean's face went pasty white. "I didn't," she squeaked. "I didn't do it. I never saw her till she . . . . Oh my God!''

Jacqueline let her stew in her own terror for a few agonized seconds before relenting. "No, you didn't. Some people discount motive as unimportant in a case of this kind, but it can't be dismissed. You had no reason to kill Dubretta. She wasn't the only person who knew your true identity. And even though you act like a first-class twit at times, you aren't insane enough to kill to protect your anonymity.''

"I was wearing a wig like Jean's," Betsy said. "And I was hanging around that corner of the garden. You saw me.''

"Don't try to get in the spotlight," Jacqueline said rudely. "Haven't you been listening? The poison was not in the wine. You might have bought Dubretta a drink, but your motive was even less compelling than Jean's. You had none.''

"How do you know?" Betsy tried to look sinister.

"Oh, shut up, Betsy." Jacqueline's eyes moved on. "Sue? She had the opportunity, but she had no reason to kill Dubretta. Victor? His motive was stronger than Jean's. Like hers, his true identity was no secret, but unlike her, he should not have been so easily intimidated by Hattie's threats. I speculated about a criminal past, but. . . .''

"He's clean," said O'Brien. He had been silent so long that the brief announcement had the effect of a shout. The listeners' heads turned as if on a single pivot; and on the one face Jacqueline was watching another flash of uneasiness came and went.

O'Brien went on, "A couple of drug busts. Possession, not dealing. One drunk and disorderly, a DWI—five years ago, in Wisconsin. The usual.''

"My God," Joe gasped. "Sue, that was a long time ago. I never—"

"It's all right, darling." Sue patted his hand. She glared at Jacqueline, a mother tiger protecting her cub. "You said Joe was in the clear. He never left the garden."

"Just bringing out a couple of other points that needed to be mentioned," Jacqueline said. "Hattie's hold over Joe was only a contract, plus a meaningless threat no one but an idiot would have taken seriously. Joe didn't commit this crime. It was carefully planned and brilliantly executed. He hasn't the brains."

Sue looked even more outraged. "What's all this about threats?" Hattie exclaimed. "I never threatened anybody."

"Hattie. Dear old Aunt Hattie." Jacqueline's voice was a throaty purr. She owed Hattie a few minutes of terror, and it wouldn't do any harm to establish, at the outset of the lucrative partnership she was contemplating, that she could play rough too. She went on, "Dubretta did not accuse Sue. She didn't mention a name. What she said was, 'Blue.' I don't blame myself for failing to spot that, because it is a rare and seldom-mentioned side effect of digitalis poisoning. The drug often affects the vision, but most people see everything as yellow. Occasionally they see blue instead.

"You had the most compelling motive of all to kill Dubretta. She hated you, not only for your low-down tricks, but for a more personal reason. You know what it is, and I know what it is." Jacqueline hesitated. O'Brien had returned to his rapt contemplation of the ceiling. Jacqueline said, "And there's no reason for anyone else to know what it is. She was out to get you, Hattie, and by God, she did."

"I didn't kill her," Hattie stammered. "You know damned well I didn't. I never left the garden."

"I know." Jacqueline sounded regretful. "And that only leaves one person." Her gaze moved to the chubby little man who sat watching her with a faint smile on his lips. "Everybody overlooks you, don't they, Max? As you yourself once said, you are not a conspicuous person. It's a useful characteristic for a murderer."

Max's face did not change. "Is this the moment? Do I now rise and admit my guilt, before swallowing the cyanide pill I have in

my pocket? I'm sorry, Mrs. Kirby. You have a first-rate imagination. I'm looking forward to reading your book."

"You were mingling," Jacqueline said. "I saw you among the
other guests earlier in the evening. You could have bought
Dubretta a drink, and she'd have taken it from you. She might
have been suspicious of anything Hattie offered her."

"Might, could," Max repeated. "I and a hundred other people. If I had encountered Dubretta during my mingling, I might
well have offered her something to drink. However, I didn't happen to see her until she joined us in the garden."

"You shouldn't have said that, Max. It's one of the few damaging admissions you've made. You did see Dubretta earlier that
evening. Remember her corsage—the one that was a deliberate
take-off on Hattie's? She told me I was only the second person
who had caught the joke. You were the first. You'd not miss the
humor of it. Dubretta lost the corsage before we went to the
garden. It was knocked off and stepped on, so she put it in her
purse. She wasn't wearing it when we joined you, but she was
holding her purse against her chest, so you didn't realize it was
gone. During our conversation just before the wine was poured
you mentioned it. So you must have seen it earlier."

Max's smile broadened. "I must have, mustn't I?"

He had spotted the weakness in the argument, as Jacqueline
had feared he would; and having made one verbal slip, he was
not about to make another by talking too much.

Jacqueline tried again. "I fixed on you as the killer early in my
investigation, Max. Not only were you the only suspect who had
both motive and opportunity, but you're the only one with the
intelligence to have planned a crime with so many built-in safeguards. You hoped Dubretta's death would be written off as heart
failure, which in fact it was. But if someone had suspected the
truth and looked for traces of the drug, your second line of defense would have come into play—an accidental overdose. It was
her own medication, after all, and she was notoriously careless
about taking it. If that failed, you had a third line of defense in
Laurie. She had given you the pills you used. She trusted you; in
her eyes you were an extension of Valentine, and I think you
were moved by genuine concern when you first saw her take the
tablets and asked her what they were. You may even have warned

her of the danger and advised her not to take them. Did you persuade her to give them to you, or did you just steal a few? It wouldn't have been difficult; she was in a fog a good deal of the time."

"Poor girl." Max shook his head sadly.

"Poor girl indeed. I don't know how she got the digitalis; she was a city girl born and bred and she knew all the tricks. But if the medication could be traced, it would be traced to her, and she had a strong, if irrational, motive for killing Dubretta. She had become so mentally confused, she may even have believed she did commit the crime.

"You didn't plan to kill Laurie," Jacqueline said; but there was no sympathy in her voice, only remorseless condemnation. "The original scheme went wrong on two counts. First, I became involved, and you knew I would not be easily dissuaded from my suspicions. Second, and more important, you and Hattie got your wires crossed over the problem of Dubretta's missing notebook. You both wanted it. You both realized it could be dangerous. But it was Hattie's idea to send Laurie out looking for it. Why not? She'd had the girl running her other errands. You wouldn't have done anything so foolish. You knew Laurie was unreliable and might run amok. She did; and the police were called in. If Laurie were found alive she'd receive medical attention, and it wouldn't be difficult for a doctor to diagnose what was wrong with her— especially if she had a digitalis preparation on her person. Once cured, she might talk. With me—and," Jacqueline added, nodding graciously at O'Brien, "the police on the trail, you couldn't take that chance."

Hattie jumped up. "You can't pin that on me. I never told that girl to attack people."

Jacqueline's self-control slipped. She rounded on Hattie. "You're responsible for Laurie's death too. You used her, without concern for her condition or her illness. Why did you want the notebook, Hattie? What did Dubretta find out?"

"I don't know." Hattie's eyes shifted. She sank back into her seat. "I never had the damned notebook."

"But I know." Jacqueline paused, not only for effect, but to take a deep, steadying breath. She was approaching a crucial point, the confrontation on which her hope of solving the case depended.

"Motive," she said. "Always motive, and always it seemed inadequate. Unless Dubretta had uncovered evidence of criminal activities, her discoveries didn't constitute a serious threat. It wouldn't hurt you, Hattie, if the word got out that two of your top writers were frauds—that Victor von Damm was a pretty paper doll and Valerie Vanderbilt a timid schoolteacher instead of a decadent aristocrat. A few people might laugh; some would refuse to believe it; most would shrug and go right on buying books. But suppose Dubretta learned that everything you did was a sham? That not a single one of your top writers was what you had represented them to be? That Valerie Valentine, Queen of Love, was an even bigger fake than the others? Not only would her readers resent it, but her publishers would be extremely upset. Publishers are very sensitive to ridicule. And this particular scam was more than ridiculous—it was the funniest joke of the year."

Hattie's face turned an alarming shade of purple. Max got up, quickly and quietly, and crossed to Valentine, who was slumped half asleep in her chair. "Don't worry, Val," he said. "It's all right."

"She's not Valerie Valentine," Jacqueline said. "You are. You, Max. You wrote those books. And that's what makes the joke so poisonously funny. If Hattie hadn't set up a figurehead who was so spectacularly beautiful—if the novels weren't so sensitive and so brilliantly written. . . . The contrast is just too much. Dubretta was a superb satirist; she could have had the whole world holding its sides."

"Sensitive and brilliant," Max murmured. "You give me too much credit, Mrs. Kirby."

"Anyone who talked to either of you for five minutes would know," Jacqueline said. "You and Hattie controlled Valentine's public appearances. She could memorize brief speeches and conventional responses. People always ask writers the same inane questions: 'How did you become a writer, Miss Valentine?' 'Where do you get your ideas, Miss Valentine?' Many authors write more fluently than they speak; many are inarticulate and retiring. But no writer could produce a book like *A Willow in Her*

Hand, and fail to recognize a quotation from *the same speech in the same play.* I asked Valentine what she thought of 'Come Again to Carthage' as a title. She said it wouldn't sell."

"It wouldn't," Max said, still faintly smiling.

"Maybe not. But *A Willow in Her Hand* isn't your average romance title either. It wasn't selected by Valentine's publisher. As Jean and Sue and other unfortunate writers know, publishers want juicy references to love and lust, not literary quotations. *A Willow in Her Hand* is a perfect title for that book. It comes from a speech in *The Merchant of Venice,* which describes Dido trying to charm her wayward lover back again to Carthage. If Valentine had recognized my quote, she would have made some comment, some reference to her own book. She didn't. But you know the play well, Max. Were you challenging me when you quoted the passage about sitting on a bank and listening to sweet music?"

"You are very clever, Mrs. Kirby," Max said tranquilly. "But you cannot prove it."

"I don't have to prove it. Once you're arrested for murder, the literary fraud won't matter. Your motive was as strong as Hattie's —stronger, because your feelings for Valentine are as violent and perverse as Laurie's were. You've fallen in love with your Galatea, the image you and Hattie created to assume the role of Valerie Valentine, and if the truth came out you'd lose her. She's in it for the money. She's not going to stick her neck out for you. You're in trouble, Max, and when your little friend gets that fact through her beautiful thick skull, she'll walk out on you."

Max's smile didn't change. He stroked Valentine's hand. "Would you leave me, Val? You wouldn't desert old Max, would you?"

"No," Valentine said. "I don't understand, Max. She can't prove any of that stuff, can she?"

"Of course not, darling."

Valentine yawned. "This is boring. Even more boring than that stupid ball. I don't want to go back down there. I want to go to bed."

Jacqueline glanced uneasily at O'Brien. He shook his head. There was no way in which Max could have drugged the girl, at least not after the ball began. When O'Brien had moved to prevent Max from getting her something to drink, Jacqueline had known he shared her foreboding—that Valentine might be Max's third victim. They had both been carried away by the general aura of romantic balderdash. Val was in no danger. Jacqueline's heart sank. She had counted on Valentine to turn on Max once she realized their secret was known; but the girl had been under Max's influence for so long that it was almost impossible for an outsider to override his authority. And Valentine's consummate stupidity rendered her incapable of understanding how her position could be threatened.

Seeing the derisive gleam in O'Brien's eyes, Jacqueline rallied and returned gamely to the attack. "You won't have to be Valerie Valentine any longer . . . what is your name?"

Max laughed aloud. "My dear Mrs. Kirby, you don't suppose anyone was really christened Valerie Valentine, do you? We've never tried to conceal Val's real name. But I think I'll let you track it down for yourself, since you're so determined to play detective."

The others sat watching like spectators at a Pinter play, half fascinated, half uncomprehending. Jacqueline glanced again at O'Brien. She expected to see that he was enjoying her discomfiture. Instead O'Brien nodded, almost imperceptibly, and said, "Her name is Marilyn Hicks. She was born in Monmouth, Oregon. Left home when she was fifteen. Was on the road for a few years; turned up in Jersey five years ago."

He paused, and Jacqueline took up the story. "Where Hattie found her when she was looking for someone to play Valerie Valentine. Hattie had received Max's manuscript and recognized its potential, but when she met Max she realized he'd never go over as a romance writer. It was the same technique she's always used; we should have suspected that Valentine was her first and most effective use of the glamour angle.

"The partnership worked well. Since it was necessary to keep Valentine in relative seclusion, for fear she'd open her mouth and betray the fact that she never could have written the books, she and Max kept pretty much to themselves. Val couldn't be trusted to be out on her own, and she didn't object to the arrangement. For the first time in her life she had enough money to buy beautiful clothes and all the luxuries she wanted. That was all she wanted. She isn't . . ." Jacqueline hesitated, not out of prudery, but because it wasn't easy to explain Valentine's problem. "She isn't . . . capable of feeling. It's not only sexual frigidity, it's an absence of any kind of warmth. I've noticed several times during this case the disparity between people's true natures and the false impressions created by their physical appearances. Joe looks like Victor von Damm, but their personalities aren't at all alike. Valentine is so beautiful people think of her as warm and loving and sensual. Yet over and over again she demonstrated her essential coldness. I have never heard her express interest in, or concern for, anyone but herself. For Max, however, she became everything he had ever dreamed of in a woman. Max is a romantic; his books prove that. He saw in Valentine only what he wanted to see, as foolish men have done through the ages.

"Valentine was content with the status quo until the conference began. Then the adulation and adoration went to her head. She decided to ask for a bigger cut of the profits. That is the explanation behind her seemingly inexplicable about-face after she claimed someone had tried to kill her. It was not a very intelligent plan; but Valentine isn't very intelligent. She put the screws on Max and Hattie, and Hattie blew up. Hattie doesn't like being blackmailed; she prefers to be on the other end of the process. Then Dubretta died. I think," Jacqueline said, watching Valentine's lovely vacuous face, "Valentine was genuinely frightened that night. She's not that good an actress. She was afraid she had pushed Hattie too far. Having heard from Jean of my reputed detective talents, she demanded my help. She didn't want the police; she only wanted an impartial outsider to think she had been threatened."

"That's nonsense," Max said. "Isn't it, Val?"

"Yes, Max."

"So you came to terms," Jacqueline said. "You convinced Valentine her fears were groundless and you increased her wages. She retracted her accusations. How much of a raise did you get, Valentine?"

"I don't know what you mean," Valentine said.

It wasn't working. Jacqueline could have shouted with frustration. There was only one card left to play. She took it from her purse—a worn stenographer's notepad with a red cover.

The look on Max's face confirmed her last lingering doubt—

for in spite of her pronouncements she had begun to wonder whether, after all, she had been mistaken. But before Max could speak, James blurted out, "I thought it was stolen from you."

Jacqueline froze him with a look as devastating as Medusa's glare. Max relaxed. "I thought so too."

"Did you?" Jacqueline pointed an accusing finger. "How did you get that idea? I never told you."

"Why . . . Laurie mentioned it. When she called last night."

"Laurie never had it," O'Brien said.

Again his audience jumped nervously. Jacqueline took up the dialogue without a pause. "The one I was carrying the other day was a dummy. You don't suppose I would be stupid enough to risk the real notebook?"

Max's smile faded. Jacqueline's flagging hopes began to rise. But before she or O'Brien could continue the inquisition, Betsy said, "That can't be Dubretta's."

"Shut up, Betsy," Jacqueline said between her teeth.

"No, but it can't," Betsy insisted. "Was that what the poor crazy kid was after—Dubretta's notebook? You never told me."

"You never asked. Betsy, would you mind—"

"It's a good thing I didn't have it in my knapsack that day," Betsy went on obliviously. "It was upstairs in my desk drawer. Imagine that. I was going to tell Dubretta at the cocktail party that she'd forgotten it, but I never had the chance to talk to her, and after that I forgot about it, since I assumed nobody—"

For once in her life Jacqueline was incapable of speech. It was O'Brien who interrupted Betsy with a muffled roar. "Ms. Markham!"

"You don't have to yell," Betsy said, hurt.

"Where," said O'Brien in a slow tight voice, "where did you get Dubretta's notebook?"

"It was the night of the protest march. We were having a few drinks—you remember, Jake, you introduced us. You saw her taking notes."

"Urk," said Jacqueline feebly. She had just remembered something else and was mentally kicking herself.

"The notebook was almost filled," Betsy went on. "After you left, we talked some more and had a few more drinks and she took a few more notes—and filled the remaining blank pages.

She had another notebook in her purse, so she took that out and wrote in it. And when she left she forgot the first one. It was on the seat between us, and you know how dark it was in there. And she was a little—well, you know.''

"I know," Jacqueline muttered. The second notebook—the one she had found after Dubretta's death—had had only a few used pages. She ought to know, she had copied them, at twenty cents a page. Why hadn't she realized that eighteen pages of notes might represent only one day's work for Dubretta? When the columnist realized the first book had been misplaced she had not been able to remember where she had left it.

"Where," said O'Brien, in the same measured voice, "where is the notebook now, Ms. Markham?"

"In my desk, I guess." The focus of two pairs of malevolent eyes, Betsy belatedly realized she was not popular. "Well, I didn't know," she exclaimed. "Why didn't you tell me?"

Jacqueline's rage was not mitigated by the realization that the prolonged nature of the disclosure had given Max time to recover from his initial dismay. Her only hope had been to get him rattled enough to make a damaging disclosure. It had been a forlorn hope, for he was not the man to lose his wits. And one of the weapons she had hoped to employ had failed—Valentine. Or had it? She glanced at O'Brien and got another small but meaningful nod. Taking a deep breath, she returned to the attack.

"The notebook contains the proof Dubretta had found that Valerie Valentine is a fraud. The game is over, Val. You'd better get out while you can."

"I don't know what you're talking about," Valentine repeated.

"She's talking about a criminal charge," O'Brien said. "As accessory to murder."

"What?" The charge, and its source, finally penetrated Valentine's stupor. "He said . . . he didn't kill that woman. And if he did, I don't know anything about—"

It was the first crack in her armored ignorance, and Jacqueline pounded at it. "Not Dubretta's murder, Valentine. Laurie's."

"The girl told you where she was, Mr. Hollenstein," O'Brien said. "You set up a date with her, for later that night."

"That's a lie." Max didn't look at him. He was watching Valentine.

"Your call to me gave an impression of candor and helpfulness," Jacqueline continued. "But you didn't tell me what Laurie really said to you. Did Valentine overhear your end of that conversation? Perhaps she remembers your telling Laurie when and where to meet you."

"I don't—" Valentine began.

"Under interrogation your memory may improve," O'Brien said with a sinister sneer.

"You may also remember that Max went out later that night," Jacqueline said.

"Your failure to tell me that leaves you open to a charge of accessory after the fact," O'Brien said, his eyes on Valentine.

"But I didn't think it was important!" She spun up and away, eluding Max's grasp with the flowing elfin grace that marked her movements. She hesitated for only an instant before throwing herself at Jacqueline. "Don't let him touch me!"

"He's got a gun," Jacqueline yelled, reeling from the impact of Valentine's body. The purse she had been about to throw at Max fell from her hand.

"Thanks a lot," said O'Brien. Max's automatic was pointed at him. The little man stepped back so that he could also cover Valentine, who had gotten behind Jacqueline.

"It's nothing to do with me," she gasped. "I didn't know anything about it. He said he had to meet a friend. . . ."

"Get away from her, Mrs. Kirby," Max said. "I don't want to hurt you, even though you are responsible for bringing this about."

The significance of his formality had not escaped Jacqueline. She made an attempt to reestablish the rapport they had shared. "Don't do it, Max. There are ways of escape for you, and God knows you're intelligent enough and wealthy enough to take advantage of them. But if you shoot someone in plain sight of all these witnesses—"

"I thought you would understand," Max said reproachfully. "How can I betray the classic demands of romantic tragedy? 'For each man kills the thing he loves. . . .' I have to kill her now. If you don't get out of the way, I'll put a bullet through both of you."

Jacqueline felt the full weight of the girl's slight body pressing

against hers. Valentine was whimpering. "Don't, don't let him—
please—"

"Oh hell," she said. "Max, you know I can't do that. She's a
worthless little tramp, but I have a reputation to maintain too.
Besides, she's stuck to me like a tick on a dog."

"I'm sorry," Max said simply. His finger tightened on the trig-
ger.

Jacqueline's eyes narrowed angrily. "Do something, somebody!
Why are you all sitting there like a gaggle of geese?"

Joe shook off Sue's clinging hands and rose. "I don't know
what to do," he said uncertainly, fingering the hilt of his ceremo-
nial sword.

James removed Jean's clutching hands and rose. "We'll all advance on him simultaneously," he suggested.

Max seemed more amused than alarmed by these manifestations of uneasy bravado, but the movements of the men distracted him enough to enable O'Brien to reach the gun concealed in the folds of the coat in which he had been sweltering all
evening.

"Now it's a standoff," he said coolly. "Suppose you just drop
it, Hollenstein. I can fire before you can."

"I'm not sure about that," Max said. "I wonder if Mrs. Kirby
wants to take the chance."

"Shoot him!" Jean shrieked suddenly. "Shoot him, shoot him,
shoot—" James clapped his hand over her mouth. Then Betsy,
who had been brooding in resentful silence, decided to take a
hand. She arose with her ear-splitting kung-fu yell. Max's gun
went off. Jacqueline dropped to the floor, pulling Valentine with
her. O'Brien's first shot hit Max in the thigh and dropped him,
but he did not lose his grasp of the gun. A rattling barrage went
off as he emptied the magazine.

The silence thereafter was deafening. Betsy was the first to
raise a cautious head from behind the overstuffed chair where
she had taken refuge. Victor lay flat, his body shielding Sue. Jean
had tugged James down on top of her; he was sitting on her lap,
pinned by her arms. For the first time in her life Hattie had
behaved like a southern lady. She had fainted.

O'Brien pounced on Max's gun, checked to make sure it was
empty, and threw it across the room. One of the random shots

had plowed a path through his hair, and blood streamed down his cheek. He flung aside the table under whose inadequate shelter Jacqueline and Valentine were huddled in a confusing tangle of arms and legs. O'Brien had to pry the girl's hands from Jacqueline before he could lift the latter from the floor. Her eyes were closed and her knees buckled when he tried to set her on her feet. He shook her till her loosened hair flew out in a wild tangle.

"Are you all right? Why didn't you tell me he had a gun? Where did he hit you? God damn it, say something!"

Jacqueline's eyes opened. They were as soft and green as spring grass. "I will—if you stop—shaking me."

Mutely, O'Brien complied with her request. Jacqueline surveyed the scene and nodded. She reached for her purse. "Patrick, you're bleeding all over your costume. Here. Have a tissue."

CHAPTER TEN

James sprawled across the bed watching Jacqueline pack. "I don't see why you have to go to Connecticut," he said sulkily. "Now that the other business is settled, we could have a good time."

"I couldn't enjoy myself when a sick friend needs me." Jacqueline's voice dripped with sanctimonious virtue, but there was a not-so-virtuous gleam in her green eyes as she folded a roll of pleated turquoise silk into her suitcase. It aroused in James a vague, faintly unpleasant sense of familiarity, which he decided not to pursue.

He picked up one of the newspapers that lay scattered on the bed. "I wonder if the story will make the Coldwater *Chronicle,*" he said uneasily.

"I hope—I mean, I imagine it will. What are you worried about? Your name is barely mentioned."

"The same can't be said about yours. And your picture is plastered all over the place. 'Mrs. Kirby with Hattie Foster—Mrs. Kirby with Valentine, AKA Marilyn Hicks; Mrs. Kirby with Joe Kirby, AKA Victor von Damm. . . .' And with O'Brien." James's frown deepened. "That's a disgusting picture, Jacqueline. Why did you let him hug you?"

"Hug? Hug?" Jacqueline glared at him. "If you can't tell a hug from a supporting arm, you ought to be ashamed of yourself."

"You didn't need support."

"O'Brien did. That was a nasty wound."

"A mere scratch."

"You're just jealous because you didn't get to play hero."

"Well, I would have if I'd been given the chance. You lied to me, Jacqueline. If I had known what you were planning—"

"You had all the necessary information, James. Good heavens, I practically spoon-fed you the facts about Valentine's impersonation of a writer. An English professor should have spotted that after two minutes' conversation with the little nitwit. But that's just like a man. You all go goofy over a pretty face."

"I'm not referring to that aspect of the case," James growled. "What about the digitalis?"

"I didn't figure that out myself until after your chemist friend had tested for other substances."

"Oh. Well, but damn it, Jacqueline, if you didn't actually lie, you misled me about practically everything else. All that nonsense about Jean being a suspect and you being the third victim—"

"I almost was, wasn't I? I couldn't be completely honest, James. It was touch and go up to the final seconds. I had no proof. Even when Betsy popped up with her news about the notebook (really, I wonder about Betsy sometimes), we were no better off. There was nothing in Dubretta's notes except information we already knew."

"We?" James's voice was sarcastic.

"O'Brien got it from the same sources Dubretta had used—a former secretary of Hattie's who resented her ex-boss, the firm Valentine had worked for as a—er—model, and so on. I deduced the same facts by literary means."

"But you didn't bother informing me."

"James, the information was useless. It did suggest a possible motive, but as those of us who specialize in criminal investigation know, motive is the least important part of a case. And in this case the motive was extremely complex, involving the subtleties of Max's relationship with Valentine. I was sure Max had committed the murder, once I realized the poison could not have been in the wine. He did everything he could to strengthen that false assumption, and to confuse the issue. In fact, he was almost the only one of our suspects who could have poisoned Dubretta. But without proof I had to bludgeon him into confessing, and the only weapon I had was his fear that he would lose Valentine."

"What will become of her, I wonder," James mused.

"James, you sentimental idiot, Valerie Valentine is a millionaire. Max will probably go on managing her money from Sing Sing, or wherever he ends up. He may even get off with assault or attempted murder. A clever lawyer can make hash of O'Brien's case unless it is properly presented."

"And Hattie Foster is getting off scot-free," James said. "The way she used that girl was criminal, but she'll never be charged for it. She's lost Valentine, but she still has Valerie Vanderbilt, or a reasonable substitute, and Victor von Damm."

"I have a few ideas in mind for her." If Hattie had seen Jacqueline's expression, she would have felt a cold shudder run up her spine.

Jacqueline straightened. "I think that's everything."

"You forgot your robe."

"Oh, that." Jacqueline rolled it into a ball and slam-dunked it into the wastebasket.

"What are you doing? I'm very fond of that robe."

"I'm not. I bought a new one." She lifted it from the suitcase and held it up.

After an unsuccessful marriage and a series of more or less successful love affairs James knew enough about women's clothes to estimate the price of the gleaming amber satin. "I thought you were broke," he said.

"I'm expecting to come into a large sum of money very soon," Jacqueline said. Tenderly she folded the robe back into her suitcase.

"Oh, that reminds me." James's voice took on its Granny Jimmy tone. "Tom Blackstone has registered for classes this fall. Last May he told me he'd have to quit school now that student aid has been so drastically reduced."

"Oh, really."

"He's rather a pet of yours, isn't he?"

"He shelves books at the library."

"He's a bright kid. I'm glad he managed to find the money. I wonder where?"

Jacqueline did not reply. Satisfied that his deductions were correct, James attacked from another angle. "Has the sick friend made you her heir?"

"Really, James, you have a mind like a sink," Jacqueline said disapprovingly. "I do not expect to inherit money, I expect to earn it. Hattie Foster is going to handle my book. And," she added, with a snap of even white teeth, "there won't be any twenty-five percent commissions in that deal, either."

"You weren't kidding about the book!"

"There it is, doubting Thomas." Jacqueline indicated the notebook on the bedside table. "I've only finished six chapters, but I expect to receive a sizable advance."

"Mind if I look at it?"

"You know I always welcome constructive criticism, James."

James reflected that this was probably the biggest lie she had told yet. He reached for *Lust Among the Savages* (working title).

Jacqueline scanned the room. Closet, bathroom, under the bed. . . . A stifled sound from James made her turn sharply. His chuckle developed into a hearty guffaw.

"James!" she cried indignantly.

Her colleague looked up from the pages of the notebook. He was smiling. "I hate to admit it, but this is great," he said. "Funniest damned thing I've read all year."

"Funniest?"

"A devastating satire," James said admiringly. "I knew you had a vicious tongue, but this—this is literature. The part where Oona catches Lurgh sneaking up on her while she's bathing in the stream. . . ." His eyes returned to the book. He let out another chuckle.

Jacqueline stood staring at him, her eyes shooting out green sparks, her body rigid with fury. The telephone rang. She reached for it. James paid no attention.

"Yes?" Jacqueline said. James chuckled. "Come on up," Jacqueline said. James chortled. "I know I did, but I've changed my mind. Come up." James shook with laughter.

"I'll leave my manuscript with you, since you seem to be relishing it," she said gently. "You won't forget to bring it back to Coldwater, will you?"

"No, no," James said abstractedly. He let out a gurgle of mirth.

There was a knock at the door. Jacqueline went to answer it. James went on reading and chuckling.

"You ready, Jackie?"

"Yes, I'm ready. My suitcase was heavier than I expected. If you don't mind. . . ."

"I don't mind." What followed was not silence, only a cessation of speech. Certain sounds could be heard.

James's grin froze. He looked up from *Lust Among the Savages*. "Jackie?" he said incredulously.

O'Brien came in. He wore a charcoal-gray suit with a scarlet tie. His socks were black. Passing his handkerchief over his mouth, he said, "Hi, Professor."

"Hi," James said. "Jackie?"

"Yes, James?" Jacqueline smiled at him.

"I wasn't talking to you," James said.

O'Brien picked up Jacqueline's suitcase. "So long, Professor. It's been nice knowing you."

"Good-bye, James. Thanks for all your help."

The door closed, but not before James heard a soft murmur of laughter from Jacqueline—intimate, tender, mocking laughter.

He hurled *Lust Among the Savages* across the room. It hit the wall and fell fluttering to the floor like a wounded bird.

Jacqueline had never allowed him to call her Jackie. She hated nicknames.

"That two-faced, double-crossing, cheating . . ." James cried aloud.

He sat brooding for a time. Gradually his face cleared. His comments on Jacqueline's manuscript had apparently annoyed his beloved—and his beloved she still was, despite the fact that she was two-faced, double-crossing, and cheating. She was certainly the best Coldwater, Nebraska, had to offer. The book promised considerable scope for harassment over the months to come, and the new mystery of Jacqueline's sudden affluence was yet to be explored.

James smiled his famous crooked smile. He'd lost this round, but the war wasn't over. Rising, he retrieved *Lust Among the Savages*.

"The last thing Oona remembered was the great wave crashing down on her frail canoe. Luga the sea god had taken his revenge upon the puny mortal who had dared end his cruel and sadistic worship. But the Goddess must have intervened to save her priestess. Instead of the icy waters of Luga's cold domain, warm air stroked her voluptuous unclothed body. She heard the soft sound of waves lapping gently on a sandy shore. Her long, curling lashes were sticky with saltwater. Lifting a languid hand, she rubbed them and opened her eyes.

"Standing over her was a man—if he was a mere mortal, and not a god. Luga himself, come to complete his revenge upon her helpless nakedness? Water dripped from his shoulder-length golden hair and formed a shining film over his broad, muscled chest, tanned to a glowing bronze. His eyes were the deep gray-blue of the stormy sea. They moved slowly and deliberately over her, from her rounded white shoulders to the blue-veined globes of her heaving breasts, down to. . . ."

James giggled.